THE

MARY ROBERTS RINEHART

CRIME BOOK

THE MARY ROBERTS RINEHART CRIME BOOK

The Door

The Confession

The Red Lamp

RINEHART & COMPANY, INC.

NEW YORK TORONTO

Published simultaneously in Canada by
Clarke, Irwin & Company, Ltd., Toronto

Printed in the United States of America

FOREWORD

I AM constantly being asked why I have chosen to write so many books about crime. The answer is, quite frankly, that I do not know. The only editorial suggestion I had, when asked to write my first serial, was that I keep the lovers apart until the final page!

Yet that story was about a crime. Murder fiction was not as popular then as it is now. Romance was in the saddle, and it was years later when an editor told me there were only two publishing successes, sex and murder. Yet that first book of mine is still selling after fifty years, and I still prefer crime to sex.

But when I say that I do not know just how my mind turned toward crime, I must also say that I have never written what is known as a detective story. The organized police play very small part in any of my books, and indeed I know very little about them. I do not recall ever using a private detective at all, although I may have done so once or twice in the long series of my mysteries.

As a matter of fact, my crime books are actually novels and are written as such. One might even say that each one is really two novels, one of which is the story I tell the reader, and the other the buried story I know and let slip now and then into a clue to whet the reader's interest. Some of them have an actual basis in fact, such as *The After House,* which was the record of a real crime, and which resulted in long study of the case, and the subsequent release of a man who had been in the penitentiary for seventeen years.

The Confession, in this present book, was based on the discovery of a hidden piece of paper, which was given me by the district attorney at the time it was found, and which I still have in my files. For many years, I could have called up the woman who had signed her own name and told her I had her confession, that its hiding place had been discovered, and that only the absence of a body saved her from a charge of murder.

However, these situations are few. In *The Door,* also in this book, there was a slight basis of fact on which to start, when my being in the hospital at the time made me realize the possibilities. But I believe *The Red Lamp* was the most difficult of all my crime stories. As a matter of fact, I wrote forty thousand words of it, went down to the basement and burned them, and started all over again. It has a certain interest, too, in that it is related by a man. Otherwise, I seem to have stuck very firmly to my own sex as narrators, in some cases having them assist in the solution of the mystery.

It was a great thrill to me when my first book, *The Circular Staircase*, was hailed as something new in its particular field, in that it was a mystery, plus humor. As I have said, it has sold now for almost fifty years. Yet on the day of publication I took my children and went to a remote farm in the country, so I would not have to read what I expected to be most unpleasant reviews. They were not; they were wonderful. Which may be, after all, the reason I have done so many crime books since. They have been a minor part of my work, but I shall probably always be known as a writer of detective books, which I emphatically am not.

Of the three stories in this book, *The Door* has a personal interest for me. My sons had gone into publishing for themselves and they needed something from me. As a result, I wrote *The Door*, which was on their first year's list and had one of the largest sales of any mystery ever published up to that time.

As for *The Red Lamp*, I had been seriously investigating certain types of psychic material, and the book grew out of this. For one thing emerged after twenty years or so. Fraud was evident in approximately ninety-seven per cent of the seances, slate writings and ectoplasmic phenomena, but there was always three or so per cent which appeared genuine. It was on this three per cent I based *The Red Lamp*.

One thing has always surprised me, and that is the fact that men in important positions like to relax with this type of book. I myself have been read by every recent President with the exception of Calvin Coolidge, and even he may have had his off moments. I have been scolded by Theodore Roosevelt, praised by Woodrow Wilson, and had a book made overnight for Herbert Hoover, using the galleys to cut and bind.

I think it is rather a nice record. So I hope my readers will like this book and have some pleasure solving the problems I have set them.

MARY ROBERTS RINEHART

The Door

CHAPTER I

I HAVE wrenched my knee, and for the past two weeks my days have consisted of three trays, two of them here in the library, a nurse at ten o'clock each morning with a device of infernal origin which is supposed to bake the pain out of my leg, and my thoughts for company.

But my thinking is cloudy and chaotic. The house is too quiet. I miss Judy, busy now with affairs of her own, and perhaps I miss the excitement of the past few months. It is difficult to take an interest in beef croquettes for luncheon out of last night's roast when one's mind is definitely turned on crime. For that is what I am thinking about, crime; and major crime at that.

I am thinking about murder. What is the ultimate impulse which drives the murderer to his kill? Not the motives. One can understand motives. It is at least conceivable that a man may kill out of violent passion, or out of fear, or jealousy or revenge. Then too there are the murders by abnormals, drug addicts or mental deficients; they have their motives too, of course, although they may lie hidden in distorted minds. And as in our case, a series of crimes where the motive was hidden but perfectly real, and where extraordinary precautions had been taken against discovery.

But I am thinking of something more fundamental than motivation.

What is it that lies behind the final gesture of the killer?

Until then he has been of the race of men. In an instant he will have forfeited his brotherhood, become one of a group apart, a group of those who have destroyed human life.

Is there a profound contempt for life itself, for its value or its importance? Or is the instinct to kill stronger than thought, an atavistic memory from long past ages when laws had not induced suppressions? Is the murder impulse a natural one and are all of us potential killers, so that to save extinction men have devised the theory of the sanctity of human life? And at that last moment does this hereditary buried instinct surge triumphantly to the surface, steel the hand which holds the knife, steady the revolver, put the smile on the face of the poisoner?

There must be a something of the sort. One thing we do know; once a man has killed, his inhibitions are destroyed. He has joined the alien clan, of which no member knows the other, and has set his face against the world.

Thereafter he is alone.

But I have found no answer. In our case I have looked back, searching for some variation from the normal, or some instinct of weakening or remorse. But I have found none. We know now that there were moments of terrific danger, when the whole murderous structure was about to collapse. But if there was panic then we have no evidence of it. Each such emergency was met with diabolical ingenuity and cunning, and that cunning went even further. It provided in advance against every possible contingency of discovery.

What long hours went into that planning, that covering of every possible clue, we can only surmise; the meticulous surveying of this and that, the searching for any looseness in the whole criminal plan, the deliberate attempts to throw suspicion elsewhere.

There must have been a real satisfaction toward the end, however, a false feeling of security, a rubbing of the hands and a certain complacency.

And then suddenly the whole carefully woven fabric was destroyed. Strange and mysterious and bitter that must have been. Everything provided against, and then at the last to be destroyed by a door, a thing of wood and paint with an ordinary tarnished brass knob. Months had passed. Hundreds of hands had touched that knob in the interval; the door itself had been painted. And yet it solved our mystery and brought destruction to as diabolical and cunning a murderer as the records of crime will show.

As I have already intimated, I live alone, in the usual sense of the word. That is, I am more or less without family. A secretary, usually a young woman, and the customary servants form my household. And as the first crime occurred in this household it will be as well to outline it at once.

Outside of my secretary, Mary Martin, a young and very pretty girl, the establishment at the time of the disappearance of Sarah Gittings consisted of four servants: my butler, Joseph Holmes, who had been in my employ for many years, a respectable looking man of uncertain age, very quiet; my chauffeur, Robert White, who was not white, but a Negro; the cook, Norah Moriarity, and Clara Jenkins, the housemaid. A laundress, a white woman, came in by the day, and from spring until fall a gardener named Abner Jones took care of the lawns and shrubbery.

And as my property, both houses and grounds, plays an important part in this narrative, I would better describe them also.

The house, then, sits some hundred feet back from the street. Two stone gate posts, from which the gates have been removed, mark the entrance, and the drive circles around a grass oval before the front door. Heavy old shrubbery, which I have not had the heart to thin out, shields me from the street and is spread in clumps over the grounds.

Thus the garage at the rear is partly screened from sight, although as was shown later, there is a clear view from it of the pantry window.

At the rear behind the garage, lies a deep ravine which has been recently incorporated into the city park system; and at one side of me lies an acre or two of undeveloped property known as the Larimer lot.

Through this, from the street and extending sharply down the hill into the park, runs a foot-path, an unpaved cut-off. In winter when the leaves are off the trees I can see a portion of this path. Not all, for both the lot and the path are heavily bordered with old cedars.

Our first crime took place on the Larimer lot, not far from this path.

I have no near neighbors. This part of the city was country when the house was built, and the property on the other side is very large, ten acres or so. It was recently bought by a retired bootlegger and has no part in this narrative.

The house itself—my house—is old-fashioned but very comfortable. But as I sit here in the library, one leg out before me and my pad on the other while I endeavor to think on paper, I realize that the house requires more description than that. Like the path, it too played its part.

I am writing in the library. Beside me on a table is the small bell which I ring to attract attention, since I cannot get to the speaking tube—I have said we are old-fashioned—and a row of soft pencils like the one which later on we found on the skylight over the lavatory. There is a desk, an old Queen Anne walnut one, an open fire, chairs and books. From the side windows one commands the Larimer lot, from the front the entrance drive.

So the library has not only comfort, but a certain strategic place in the house. I can not only see my callers in advance; I can sit there and survey a large portion of my lower floor domain. It lies to the right of the front door and the hall.

Across the long center hall with its white staircase and its rear door to the service portion of the house, lies the drawing room. I can see now the forward end of it, with its ormolu cabinet, its French sofa done in old rose damask, and that painting of my father which does the Bell nose so grave an injustice.

And although I cannot see it, I know that at the end of that drawing room, opening onto a blank brick wall which I have screened with arbor vitæ and rhododendrons, there is a French door with steps leading out onto the grass. Also I know, by actual measurement, that it is precisely fifty feet and around a corner to the kitchen porch.

From the rear of the library double doors open into a music room, not often used nowadays, and behind that is the dining room.

This is my domain, and today in the winter sun it is very peaceful. There has been a little snow, and the cedars at the top of the path down the hill are quite beautiful. I have a wood fire, and the dogs, Jock and Isabel—named by Judy because she had never heard of a dog called Isabel—are asleep before it.

Jock is a terrier, Isabel a corpulent and defeminized French bull. As they too played a small and not too meritorious part in our *débâcle*, it is necessary to name them.

I have listed my household as it was on the eighteenth of April of this year. Usually my secretaries do not live in the house, but come in daily for such notes, checks, bills and what not as clutter the desk of a woman who, because she has no family of her own, is supposed to expend her maternal instinct in charity.

But Mary Martin was living in the house, and due to a reason directly connected with this narrative.

During the housecleaning the previous autumn Norah had unearthed an old cane belonging to my grandfather, that Captain Bell who played so brave if unsung a part in the Mexican War.

She brought it downstairs to me, and I told her to have Joseph polish the handle. When Joseph came back with it he was smiling, an unusual thing for Joseph.

"That's a very interesting old cane, madam," he said. "It has a knife in it."

"A knife? What for?"

But Joseph did not know. It appeared that he had been polishing the knob when a blade suddenly shot out of the end. He had been greatly startled and had almost dropped the thing.

Later on I showed it to Jim Blake, my cousin, and he made the suggestion which brought Mary Martin into the house.

"Why not write the old boy's life?" he suggested. "You must have a trunkful of letters, and this sword-stick, or sword-cane or whatever it is, is a good starting point. And by the way, if ever you want to give it away, give it to me."

"I may do that," I said. "I don't like deadly weapons around the place."

In March I gave it to him. "The Life," as Judy called it, was going on well, and Mary Martin efficient enough, although I was never fond of her.

CHAPTER II

THIS THEN was my household and my house on the day Sarah Gittings disappeared. The servants lived on the third floor at the rear, their portion of the floor cut off from the front by a door. A back staircase reached this upper rear hall, allowing them to come and go as they required.

Mary had the third floor front room above the library, and Sarah the one behind it and over the blue spare room. Mary's door stood open most of the time, Sarah's closed and often locked. For all her good qualities there was a suspicious streak in Sarah.

"I don't like people meddling with my things," she would say.

But Sarah was not a permanent member of the household. She was a middle-aged, rather heavy and silent woman, a graduate nurse of the old régime who had been in the family for years. In serious illness we sometimes brought in brisk young women, starchy and efficient, but in trouble we turned to Sarah.

We passed her around. My sister Laura would wire from Kansas City, "Children have measles. Please send Sarah if possible." And Sarah would pack her bag, cash one of her neat small checks and slip off. A good bit of her time was spent with my cousin Katherine Somers in New York. Katherine was devoted to her, although just why it is difficult to say. She was a taciturn woman, giving no confidences but probably receiving a great many.

Poor Sarah! I can still see her in her starched white uniform, with its skirts which just cleared the ground, moving among our various households, with us but not entirely of us; watching nervously over the stair rail while Judy, Katherine's daughter, made her début; slapping Laura's newest baby between the shoulders to make it breathe, or bending over me to give me a daily massage, her heavy body clumsy enough but her hands light and gentle.

She was not a clever woman. Or maybe I am wrong. Perhaps in a family which prides itself on a sort of superficial cleverness, she was merely silenced.

It was Wallie Somers, Katherine's stepson, who claimed that when he told her Hoover was nominated, she said:

"Really! That ought to be good business for the vacuum cleaner."

Not a romantic figure, Sarah, or a mysterious one. All of us thought of her as a fixture, growing older but more or less always to be with us. I remember Howard Somers, Katherine's husband, telling her one day that he had remembered her in his will.

"Not a lot, Sarah," he said. "But you'll never have to go to the Old Ladies' Home!"

I don't know why we were so astonished to see her burst into tears. I daresay she had been worried about the future; about getting old, and the children growing up and forgetting her. Anyhow she cried, and Howard was greatly embarrassed.

She had her peculiarities, of course. In Katherine's house, what with guests in and out all the time, she had developed the habit of taking her meals in her room on a tray, and this habit persisted.

"I like to read while I eat," she said. "And I'm up early, and I don't like late dinners."

She had some sort of stomach trouble, poor thing.

But in my simpler household she ate with me unless there was some one there. Then, to Joseph's secret fury, she retired to her room and had her tray there.

She had come down from Katherine's a month or so before, not so much because I needed her as that Katherine thought she needed a change. Howard had had a bad heart for some time, and Sarah had been nursing him.

"Just let her putter around," Katherine wrote. "She'll want to work, being Sarah, so if you can stand a daily massage–"

And of course I could, and did.

I have drawn Sarah as well as I can, and the family rather sketchily; Howard and Katherine in their handsome duplex apartment in New York on Park Avenue, bringing out Judy at nineteen; Laura in Kansas City, raising a noisy young family; and myself in my old-fashioned house with its grounds and shrubbery, its loneliness and its memories. Dependent on a few friends, a small dinner party now and then, a little bridge; and on my servants, on Joseph and Norah and Clara and Robert, and on the Mary Martins who came and went, intelligent young women who used me as a stop-gap in their progress toward marriage or a career. A staid household, dependent for its youth on Judy's occasional visits, on secretaries whose minds were elsewhere, and on Wallie Somers, Howard's son by his first wife, whose ostensible business was bonds and whose relaxation, when he could not find some one to play with, was old furniture. Than which, as Judy once said, I have nothing else but.

As it happened, Judy was with me when Sarah disappeared that night in April of last year. She was staging her annual revolt.

"I get a trifle fed up with Katherine now and then," she would say, arriving without notice. "She's too intense. Now you are restful. You're really a frivolous person, you know, Elizabeth Jane, for all your clothes and airs."

"Frivolity is all I have left," I would say meekly. Judy has a habit of first names. Katherine had carefully taught her to call me Cousin Elizabeth, but Judy had discarded that with her stockings, which now she wore as seldom as possible and under protest. Although I doubt if she ever called her mother Katherine to her face.

Katherine was a good mother but a repressed one. Also she was still passionately in love with Howard; one of those profound absorbing loves which one finds sometimes in women who are apparently cold, and which makes them better wives than mothers. I rather think that she was even a little jealous of Judy, and that Judy knew it.

Judy would arrive, and as if by a miracle the telephone would commence to ring and shining sports cars would be parked for hours in front of the house. Joseph would assume a resigned expression, empty cigarette trays by the dozen, and report to me in his melancholy voice.

"Some one has burned a hole on the top of your Queen Anne desk, madam."

I was never anything to him but "madam." It got on my nerves sometimes.

"Never mind, Joseph. We have to pay a price for youth."

He would go out again, depressed but dignified. In his own way he was as unsocial as Sarah, as mysterious and self-obliterating as are all good servants.

So on that last night of Sarah, Judy was with me. She had just arrived, looking a trifle defiant, and at dinner she stated her grievance. Mary Martin was out for the evening, and the two of us were alone at the table.

"Really, Katherine is *too* outrageous," she said.

"She's probably saying the same thing about you."

"But it is silly. Truly. She wants me not to see Wallie. I don't think Wallie is anything to lie awake at night about, but after all he's my half-brother."

I said nothing. It was an old difficulty in the family, Katherine's dislike of Howard's son by his first marriage. It was a part of her jealousy of Howard, her resentment of that early unfortunate marriage of his. She loathed Wallie and all he stood for; not that he stood for a great deal. He was the usual rich man's son, rather charming in his own way but neurotic since the war. But he looked like Margaret, the first wife, and Katherine could not forgive him that.

"You like Wallie," Judy accused me.

"Of course I do."

"And he had a wonderful war record."

"Certainly he had. What are you trying to do, Judy? Justify yourself?"

"I think he's had a rotten deal," she said. "From all of us. A bit of allowance from father, and now I'm not to see him!"

"But you are going to see him," I told her. "You're going to see him tonight. He wants to look over an old ormolu cabinet Laura has sent me."

She forgot her irritation in her delight.

"Lovely! Has it got any secret drawers? I adore looking for secret drawers," she said, and went on eating a substantial meal. These young things, with their slender waists and healthy appetites!

She had already rushed up to the third floor to greet Sarah, and while we were eating I heard Sarah on the way down. This was nothing unusual. She would go out sometimes at night, either to the movies or to take Jock and Isabel for a walk, and I could sit at my place at the table and watch her coming down the stairs. The fireplace in the music room is set at an angle, and in the mirror over it I would see Sarah; first her soft-soled low-heeled shoes, then the bottom of her white skirt, and then her gray coat, until finally all of Sarah emerged into view.

This evening however I saw that she had taken off her uniform, and I called to her.

"Going to the movies, Sarah?"

"No." She had no small amenities of speech.

"Don't you want the dogs? They haven't been out today."

She seemed to hesitate. I could see her in the mirror, and I surprised an odd expression on her face. Then the dogs themselves discovered her and began to leap about her.

"Do take them, Sarah," Judy called.

"I suppose I can," she agreed rather grudgingly. "What time is it?"

Judy looked at her wrist watch and told her.

"And do behave yourself, Sarah!" she called.

But Sarah did not answer. She snapped the leashes on the dogs and went out. That was at five minutes after seven. She went out and never came back.

Judy and I loitered over the meal, or rather I loitered; Judy ate and answered the telephone. One call was from a youth named Dick, and there was a subtle change in Judy's voice which made me suspicious. Another, however, she answered coldly.

"I don't see why," she said. "She knew quite well where I was going . . . Well, I'm all right. If I want to go wrong I don't need to come here to do it . . . No, she's gone out."

I have recorded this conversation because it became highly important later on. To the best of my knowledge it came soon after Sarah left; at seven-fifteen or thereabouts.

Judy came back to the table with her head in the air.

"Uncle Jim," she said. "Wouldn't you know mother would sic him on me? The old goose!"

By which she referred not to Katherine, but to Katherine's brother, Jim Blake. Judy had chosen to affect a dislike for him, not because of any inherent qualities in Jim himself, but because Katherine was apt to make him her agent when Judy visited me.

Personally I was fond of Jim, perhaps because he paid me the small attentions a woman of my age finds gratifying, and certainly Katherine adored him.

"He asked for Sarah, but I told him she had gone out. What in the world does he want with Sarah?"

"He may have had some message from your mother for her."

"Probably to keep an eye on me," said Judy, drily.

I think all this is accurate. So many things happened that evening that I find it difficult to go back to that quiet meal. Quiet, that is, up to the time when Joseph brought in our coffee.

I know we discussed Jim, Judy and I, and Judy with the contempt of her youth for the man in his late forties who takes no active part in the world. Yet Jim had organized his life as best he could. He was a bachelor, who went everywhere for a reason which I surmised but Judy could not understand; the fear of the lonely of being alone.

"Uncle Jim and his parties!" said Judy. "How in the world does he pay for them?"

"He has a little from his mother."

"And more probably from my mother!"

Well, that might have been, so I said nothing, and as money meant nothing in Judy's lavish young life she was immediately cheerful again.

It is hard to remember Jim as he was in those days; as he must have been when he left his house that night. A tall man, still very erect, and with graying hair carefully brushed to hide its thinness, he was always urbane and well dressed. He was popular too. He had never let business, which in his case was a dilettante interest in real estate, interfere with a golf game or bridge, and by way of keeping up his social end he gave innumerable little tea parties and dinners. He had a colored servant named Amos who was a quick change artist, and so people dined with Jim on food cooked by Amos, to be served by Amos in a dinner jacket, and then went outside to find Amos in a uniform and puttees, standing by the car with the rug neatly folded over his arm.

There are some people to whom all colored men look alike, and to these no doubt Jim Blake appeared to be served by a retinue of servants.

"The Deb's delight!" was Judy's closing and scathing comment, and then Joseph brought in the coffee.

That was, according to Joseph's statement to the police and later before the Grand Jury, at seven-thirty or seven-thirty-five.

Judy had lighted a cigarette. I remember thinking how pretty she looked in the candle light, and how the house brightened when she was there. Joseph was moving about the pantry, and in the silence I could hear distant voices from the servants' hall beyond the kitchen.

Judy had lapsed into silence. The initial excitement of her arrival was over, and I thought now that she looked dispirited and rather tired. Then I happened to raise my eyes, and they fell on the mirror.

There was a man on the staircase.

CHAPTER III

He seemed to be crouching there. I could see only his legs, in darkish trousers, and he had no idea that I could see him at all. He was apparently listening, listening and calculating. Should he make a dash to get out, or retreat? The door from the dining room to the hall was wide open. I would surely see him; was it worth the trying?

Evidently he decided that it was not, for without turning he backed soundlessly up the stairs.

"Judy," I said quietly. "Don't move or raise your voice. There's a burglar upstairs. I've just seen him."

"What shall I do? I can close the library door and call the police."

"Do that, then, and I'll tell Joseph. He can't get out by the back stairs without going through the kitchen, and the servants would see him."

I rang for Joseph, feeling calm and rather pleased at my calmness. Such few jewels as I keep out of the bank were on me, and if he wanted my gold toilet set he was welcome. It was insured. But while I waited for Joseph I took off my rings and dropped them into the flower vase on the table.

Joseph took the news quietly. He said that Robert was still in the garage, and that he would station him at the foot of the back stairs, but that to wait for the police was nonsense.

"He'd jump out a window, madam. But if I go up, as though I didn't know he was about, I might surprise him."

"You're not armed."

"I have a revolver in the pantry, madam."

That did not surprise me. There had been some burglaries in the neighborhood recently—I believe the bootlegger had had the tables turned on him, a matter which I considered a sort of poetic justice—and I stood in the doorway watching the stairs until Joseph reappeared.

"If he gets past me," he said, "stand out of his way, madam. These cat burglars are dangerous."

He went up the front staircase, leaving me in the lower hall. I could hear Judy at the telephone, patiently explaining in a low voice, and I could hear Joseph overhead, moving about systematically: the second floor, the third, opening room doors and closet doors, moving with his dignified unhurried tread, but doing the thing thoroughly.

He was still moving majestically along the third floor hall when I heard a slight noise near at hand. I could neither describe it nor locate it. Something fairly near me had made a sound, a small sharp report. It appeared to have come from the back hallway, where there is a small lavatory. When Judy emerged I told her, and against my protests she marched back and threw open the door.

It was quite empty and soon after Joseph came down to say that he had found nobody, but that some one might be hiding on the roof, and as by that time a policeman had arrived on a motorcycle, I sent him out to look.

The officer inside and Joseph out, it seemed scarcely credible that we found nobody. But our burglar had gone; without booty too, as it turned out, for my toilet things were undisturbed.

I think the officer was rather amused than otherwise. Judy saw him out.

"If you're ever in trouble again, Miss, just send for me," he said gallantly.

"I'm always in trouble," said Judy.

"Now is that so? What sort of trouble?"

"Policemen," said Judy pleasantly, and closed the door on him.

Looking back, it seems strange how light-hearted we were that night. That loneliness which is my usual lot had gone with Judy's arrival, and when Wallie arrived at eight-thirty he found Judy insisting on my smoking a cigarette.

"You're shaken, Elizabeth Jane," she was saying. "You know darn well you're shaken."

"Shaken? About what?" said Wallie from the hall.

"She's had a burglar, poor dear," Judy explained. "A burglar in dark trousers, crouched on the staircase."

"On the stairs? Do you mean you saw him?"

"She saw his legs."

"And that's all?"

"That's enough, isn't it? The rest of him was sure to be around somewhere. The said legs then ceased crouching and went upstairs. After that they vanished."

He said nothing more, but walked back into the dining room and surveyed the mirror.

"That's a tricky arrangement you have there, Elizabeth Jane," he called. He had adopted Judy's habit. "Go up the stairs, Judy, and let me see your legs."

"Don't be shameless!" she said. "How's this?"

"All right. Yes, I see them, and very nice ones they are at that."

When he came forward again Judy insisted on examining the stair rail for fingerprints, although Wallie said that it was nonsense; that all criminals wore gloves nowadays, and that with the increasing crime wave the glove factories were running night shifts. But she departed for a candle nevertheless, and Wallie glanced up the staircase.

"Rather a blow for the divine Sarah, eh what?" he said.

"Sarah is out, fortunately. She took the dogs."

It struck me, as he stood there in the full light over his head, that he was looking even thinner than usual, and very worn. He had much of his mother's beauty, if one dare speak of beauty in a man, but he had also inherited her high-strung nervous temperament. The war must have been hell for him, for he never spoke of it. I have noticed that the men who really fought and really suffered have very little to say about it; whether because they cannot bear to recall it or because most of them are inarticulate, I do not know.

While we stood there I told him about the sound I had heard, and he went back to the lavatory and looked up.

This lavatory is merely a small washroom opening from the rear portion of the hall, and lighted by an opaque glass ceiling, in the center of which a glass transom opens by a cord for ventilation. The shaft above is rather like an elevator well, and light enters through a skylight in the roof.

Onto this well there is only one opening and this the window to the housemaid's closet on the third floor. As during the tornado of 1893 the entire skylight frame and all had been lifted and dropped end-on into the shaft, crashing through the glass roof below, my father had had placed across it some iron bars. These, four in number, were firmly embedded in the walls about six feet below the window sill.

"I suppose nobody has examined the shaft?"

"I really don't know. Probably not."

He continued to gaze upward.

"He might have swung into the shaft, and stood on the bars."

"Provided he knew there were bars there," I said drily.

Suddenly he turned and shot up the stairs, and a moment later he was calling from the third floor.

"Get a ladder, somebody. There's something on top of that skylight down there."

"You mean—the man himself?"

He laughed at that.

"He'd have gone through the glass like a load of coal! No. Something small. I can see it against the light beneath."

He ran down, rushed into the library for matches, and when Robert had brought a ladder from the garage and placed it in the lavatory he was on it and halfway through the transom in an instant.

We stood huddled in the door, Judy still holding the candle, and I—for some unknown reason—with a lighted cigarette in my hand which some one had thrust on me, and Robert and Joseph behind.

I don't know what I had expected, but I know that I felt a shock of disappointment when Wallie said:

"Hello! Here it is. A pencil!"

He found nothing else, and came down in a moment, looking dirty and rather the worse for wear, but extremely pleased with himself.

"A pencil!" he said exultantly. "Now how about it? Will Scotland Yard send for me or will it not? That's what you heard, you see."

But Judy only took one glance at it.

"Possibly," she said. "Still, as it's the sort Elizabeth Jane uses herself, with the point looking as though she'd sharpened it with her teeth, I see nothing to write home about."

That annoyed him.

"All right," he told her. "We'll see. It may have fingerprints."

"I thought you'd decided he wore gloves! Why don't you try to find how he got in? That's more to the point. And also how he got out?"

It seems strange to be writing all this; the amiable bickering between Wallie and Judy; the light-hearted experiment to find if a pencil dropped from the third floor made the sound I had heard, and my own feeling that it did not; and the final discovery of the shattered pane in the rear French door of the drawing room, and our failure to see, lying on the step outside, that broken point of a penknife which Inspector Harrison was to find the next morning.

Strange, almost frivolous.

It was Judy who found the broken pane, hidden as it was behind the casement curtains on the door, and who pointed out the ease with which our intruder had reached in and turned the key. There is another door at the back of the drawing room, a sort of service entrance which opens into the rear hall beside the servants' staircase, and it was evident that he had used this to gain access to the upper floors.

"Easy enough," said Judy. "But he couldn't get out that way. Clara was coming down to her dinner, so he hid on the front stairs."

"And I suppose he was not in the light shaft at all?" Wallie demanded.

"I don't say he wasn't," said my surprising Judy. "I only say that the pencil is not proved. I think it very likely he did hide in the shaft. He'd retreated before Joseph as far as he could go."

"But what did he want?" I demanded. "I don't suppose he broke in here to drop a pencil. If he was coming down when I saw him—"

"Well, he might have been going up," said Judy practically. "A good burglar might start at the top and work down. Like housecleaning."

Wallie had sealed the pencil in an envelope for the police, and I daresay all of this had not taken much more than half an hour. It must have been at nine o'clock or thereabouts, then, that I sent the maids to their beds and watched them as they made a nervous half-hysterical start, and nine-thirty before Joseph and Wallie had placed a padlock on the broken door in the drawing room. Then I ordered Joseph to bed, but he objected.

"Miss Sarah has not come in."

"She has a key, Joseph."

But I was uneasy. In the excitement I had forgotten Sarah.

Wallie looked up sharply from the door.

"Sarah!" he said. "Is she still out?"

"Yes. And she has the dogs. Where could she stay until this hour with two dogs? She has no friends."

I left Wallie and Judy in the drawing room, and wandered out and down the steps. It was a cool night, without a moon but with plenty of starlight, and I walked down the drive. I remembered that as I walked I whistled for the dogs. Sometimes she loosened them and they preceded her home.

It seemed to me that I heard a dog barking far off somewhere, but that was all.

I was vaguely inclined to walk in that direction. The dog seemed to be at the far end of the Larimer lot or beyond it, in the park. But at the gate I met Mary Martin, hurrying home. She had been out somewhere for dinner, and she was slightly sulky; it was a continued grievance with her that Sarah had a key to the house and she had none, but I have an old-fashioned sense of responsibility to the people in my employ, and Mary was a still young and very pretty girl.

On the way to the house I told her about our burglar, and she relaxed somewhat.

"I don't think you should be out here alone," she said. "He may still be about."

"I was looking for Sarah," I explained. "She's out with the dogs, and it's getting late."

To my intense surprise she stopped perfectly still.

"When did she go out?" she said sharply.

"At seven. That's almost three hours."

She moved on again, but in silence. The front door was open, and in the light from it I thought she looked rather pale. At that moment, however, Wallie appeared in the doorway, and suddenly she brightened.

"I wouldn't worry, Miss Bell. She can take care of herself. And she has a key!"

She glanced at me rather pertly, favored Wallie with a smile as she went in, greeting Judy with considerable manner—she seemed always to be afraid that Judy might patronize her—and teetered up the stairs on the high heels she affected.

Wallie gazed after her as she went up. At the turn she paused. I saw her looking down at us intently, at Judy, at myself, at Wallie. Mostly at Wallie.

"I wouldn't worry about Miss Gittings," she said. "She's sure to be all right."

"You might see if she's in her room, Mary," Judy suggested. "She may have come in while we were in the drawing room."

We could hear her humming as she went on up the stairs, and shortly after she called down to say that Sarah was not in her room but that it was unlocked.

"That's queer," said Judy. "She always locks it, doesn't she?"

We could hear a sort of ironic amusement in Mary's voice as she replied.

"Not so queer this evening," she said. "She knew I was out! Her key's in the door, on the outside, but she forgot to take it."

I do not remember much about the hour between ten and eleven. Wallie was not willing to go until Sarah returned, and Judy and he worked over the cabinet. The house was very still. For a time, as I sat in the library, I could hear Mary moving about on the third floor, drawing a bath—she was very fastidious in everything that pertained to herself—and finally going into her room and closing her door. But by eleven Judy had given up all hope of a secret drawer in the cabinet and was yawning, and a few moments after that Wallie left and she wandered up to bed.

But I still waited in the library. I had a queer sense of apprehension, but I laid it to the events of the evening, and after a time—I am no longer young, and I tire easily—I fell into a doze.

When I roused it was one in the morning, and Sarah had not come back. She would have roused me if she had, have put out the lights. Nevertheless I went upstairs and opened her door. The room was dark. I called to her, cautiously, but there was no answer, and no stertorous breathing to show that she was asleep.

For the first time I was really alarmed about her. I went downstairs again, stopping in my room for a wrap, and in the dining room for my rings, which I had almost forgotten. Then I went out on the street.

The dog, or dogs, were still barking at intervals, and at last I started toward the sound.

CHAPTER IV

It is one of the inevitable results of tragedy that one is always harking back to it, wondering what could have been done to avert it. I find myself going over and over the events of that night, so simple in appearance, so dreadful in result. Suppose I had turned on Sarah's light that night? Would I have found her murderer in the room? Was the faint sound I heard the movement of her curtain in the wind, as I had thought, or something much more terrible?

Again, instead of sending Joseph upstairs to search, what if I had had the police called and the house surrounded?

Still, what could I have done for Sarah? Nothing. Nothing at all.

I was rather nervous as I walked along, going toward the Larimer lot and the park. But the occasional despairing yelps were growing more and more familiar as I advanced, and when at last I let out that feeble pipe which is my attempt at a whistle, the dogs recognized it in a sort of ecstasy of noise.

I could make out Jock's shrill bark and Isabel's melancholy whine, but for some reason they did not come to me.

I stood on the pavement and called, loath to leave its dryness and security for the brush and trees and dampness of the Larimer property. Frightened too, I admit. Something was holding the dogs. I am quite certain now that when I started to run toward them I expected to find Sarah there, unconscious or dead. I ran in a sort of frenzy. Once indeed I fell over some old wire, and I was dizzy when I got up.

But Sarah was not there. Far back in the lot I found the dogs, and if I wondered that they had not come to me that mystery was soon solved.

They were tied. A piece of rope had been run through the loops of their leashes and then tied to a tree. So well tied that, what with their joyous rushes and the hard knotting of the rope, I could scarcely free them.

Asked later on about that knot, I had no clear memory of it whatever.

It was very dark. Far back on the street a lamp lighted that corner where the path took off, to pitch steeply down into the park. The Larimer lot is a triangle, of which the side of my property is the vertical, the street the base, and the ravine beyond, the hypotenuse. Thus:

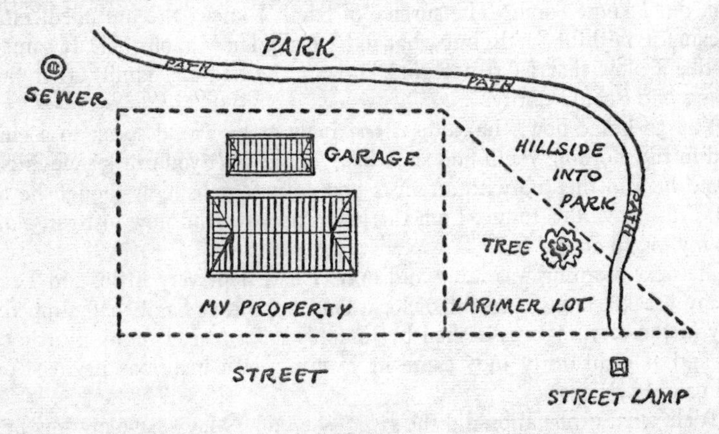

I remember calling Sarah frantically, and then telling the terrier to find her.

"Go find Sarah, Jock," I said. "Find Sarah."

He only barked, however, and an instant later both of them were racing for home.

But I still had a queer feeling that Sarah must be there. I went back to the house, to find the dogs scratching at the front door, and when I had roused Joseph I took him back with me to search the lot. He with his revolver and I with my searchlight must have been a queer clandestine sort of picture; two middle-aged folk, Joseph half clad, wandering about in the night. And so the roundsman on the beat must have believed, for when he came across to us his voice was suspicious.

"Lost anything?"

"A middle-aged woman, rather heavy set," I said half hysterically.

"Well, she oughtn't to be hard to find," he observed. "Now if it was a ring, with all this brush and stuff—"

But he was rather impressed when I told my story.

"Tied to a tree, eh? Which tree?"

"Over there; my butler's examining it. The rope's still there."

But a moment later Joseph almost stunned me.

"There is no rope here, madam," he called.

And incredible as it may sound, the rope was not there. The policeman searched, we all searched. There was no rope and no Sarah. The policeman was not so much suspicious as slightly amused.

"Better go back and get a good night's sleep, ma'am," he said soothingly. "You can come around in the morning and look all you want."

"But there *was* a rope, I could hardly untie it."

"Sure," he said indulgently. "Probably the lady you're looking for tied them up herself. She had business somewhere else and they'd be in the way. See?"

Well, it was possible, of course. I did not believe it, knowing Sarah; but then, did I know Sarah? The surface of Sarah I knew, the unruffled, rather phlegmatic faithful Sarah; but what did I really know about her? It came to me like a blow that I did not even know if she had any family, that there was no one I could notify.

"You go home now," he said, as coaxingly as he would speak to a child, "and in the morning you'll find she's back. If she isn't you can let me know."

And he said this too with an air, a certain paternalism; as though he had said: "Just leave this to me. I am the law. I'll fix it. And now just run along. I've my job to attend to."

The next morning was rainy and gray. I had slept very little, and I rang for my breakfast tray at eight o'clock. Any hope that Sarah had slipped in early in the morning was dashed by Joseph's sober face. I drank a little coffee, and at eight-thirty Judy came in yawning, in a luxurious negligee over very gaudy pyjamas.

"Well, what explanation did she give?" she said. "May I have my tray here? I hate eating alone."

"Did who give?"

"Sarah."

"She hasn't come back, Judy."

"What? I heard her. From two until three she walked about over my head until I was almost crazy."

Sarah's room was over Judy's. I sat up in bed and stared at her. Then I rang the bell again.

"Joseph," I said, "have you been into Sarah's room this morning?"

"No, madam. I overslept, and I hurried right down."

"Then how do you know she has not come back?"

"She hasn't been down for her breakfast. She's very early, always."

And just then we heard Mary Martin talking excitedly to Clara in the hall overhead, and then come running down the stairs. She burst into my room hysterically, to say that Sarah was not in her room and that it was all torn up. Judy was gone like a flash, and while I threw something about me I questioned Mary. She had, it seems, knocked at Sarah's door to borrow the morning paper. The morning paper, by the way, always reached me fourth hand; Joseph took it in and looked it over, Sarah got it from him, Mary Martin borrowed it from Sarah, and when I rang for it, usually at nine o'clock, it was apt to bear certain unmistakable scars; a bit of butter, a smudge of egg, or a squirt of grapefruit juice. Anyhow, receiving no answer, Mary had opened the door, and what she saw I saw when I had hurried upstairs.

Sarah's room was in complete confusion. Some one had jerked aside her mattress and pillows, thrown down the clothes in her neat closet, looked at her shoes, and turned out her bureau. Even her trunk had been broken open, and its contents lay scattered about. Those records of family illnesses, which she carted about with her as a veteran might carry his medals, had been thrown out onto the bed and apparently examined.

There was something ruthless and shameless about the room now. It had no secrets, no privacies. It was, in a way, as though some one had stripped Sarah, had bared her stout spinster body to the world.

Judy, rather white, was in the doorway.

"I wouldn't go in," she said. "Or at least I wouldn't touch anything. Not until you get the police."

Clara, the housemaid, was staring in over my shoulder.

"She'll have a fit over this," she said. "She's that tidy!"

But I had a dreadful feeling that poor Sarah would never again have a fit over anything in this world.

It was nine-fifteen when I telephoned to headquarters, and at a quarter to ten a policeman in uniform and the Assistant Superintendent of Police, Inspector Harrison, reached the house.

The two of them examined the room, and then leaving the uniformed man in charge of Sarah's room, Inspector Harrison listened to my story in the library. He was a short stocky man, very bald and with the bluest eyes I have ever seen in an adult human being.

As he talked he drew a wooden toothpick from his pocket and bit on the end of it. Later on I was to find that he had an apparently limitless supply of the things, and that they served a variety of purposes and moods. He had given up smoking, he said, and they gave him "something to think with."

He was disinclined to place any serious interpretation on Sarah's absence until it was necessary, but he was interested in the housebreaking episode; especially in Wallie's theory that the intruder on his first visit had swung himself into the light shaft, and he carefully examined it from above and below. There were, however, many scratches on the sill of Clara's pantry and little to be learned from any of them.

The Inspector stood for some time looking down into the shaft.

"He could get in all right," he decided, "but I'd hate to undertake to get myself out, once I was in. Still, it's possible."

After that he wandered around the house, sometimes alone, sometimes with Joseph. Wallie had arrived, and he and Judy and I sat there waiting, Judy very quiet, Wallie clearly anxious and for the first time alarmed. He moved about the room, picking things up and putting them down until Judy turned on him angrily.

"For heaven's sake, Wallie! Can't you keep still?"

"If I annoy you, why not go somewhere else?"

She lit a cigarette and looked at him.

"I don't get it," she said slowly. "What's Sarah to you? You never cared much for her."

"You'll know some day."

She cocked an eye at him.

"If eventually, why not now?"

But he merely turned on his heel and resumed his nervous pacing of the room.

Some time later he suggested that Sarah might have gone to New York, and that Judy telephone and find out. In the end, in order not to alarm Katherine, I called up Jim Blake and told him, and he agreed to invent a message for Katherine. Asked later about his manner over the telephone, I could remember very little. I know he seemed surprised, and that he said he was not well, but that he would dress and come around that afternoon.

When he called back it was to say that evidently Sarah had not gone there, and that he would be around at three o'clock.

The information had a curious effect on Wallie, however. As I watched him it seemed to me that he looked frightened; but that may be in view of what I know now. I do, however, recall that he looked as though he had slept badly, and that day for the first time since the early days after the war I saw him begin to twist his seal ring again.

When he was not lighting a cigarette or throwing it away he was twisting his ring, turning it around and around on his finger.

Once he left us and went upstairs to look at Sarah's room. The policeman opened the door but would not let him enter, and I believe he spoke a few words with Mary. Indeed, I know now that he did. But he was back in the library when the Inspector finally came in and selected a fresh toothpick, this time to make points with.

"First of all," he said, "it is best not to jump to any conclusions. The lady may not be dead; very probably is not dead. We are, however, sending to the Morgue and the hospitals. But there are many reasons why people occasionally choose to disappear, and sometimes to make that disappearance as mysterious as possible. For example, Miss Gittings had a key to the house. It is just possible that she herself came back last night and ransacked her own room."

"In a pair of dark trousers?" I demanded sharply.

He smiled at that.

"Perhaps! Stranger things have been done. But now about this key. It was outside the door last night?"

"My secretary said so."

"Well, it's inside now."

"I don't understand it, Inspector. Sarah always locked her door when she left the house. Locked the door and took the key."

"There isn't a second key to her door?"

"Not that I know of."

"Then we'll say that this key is hers. It may not be, but it looks like it and wherever it was last night it's on the inside of the door now. Suppose for the sake of argument that she had decided to go away; to say nothing and go away. She might have forgotten something and come back for it."

"Very probably," said Judy. "She might have forgotten her toothbrush."

He smiled at her.

"Precisely. Or something she had hidden, and forgotten where she had hidden it."

"I see," said Judy. "She forgot her toothbrush so she came back to get it, and as she didn't want Joseph to know she'd forgotten it she hung in the light shaft and dropped a pencil. It's perfectly clear."

"We have no proof yet that anybody was in the light shaft," he told her, without resentment. "Where is that pencil, I'd like to look at it."

I unlocked a drawer of my desk and took out the envelope.

"This been handled since?"

"I picked it up by the point," Wallie told him.

"Sure it wasn't there before?" to me.

"I think it is unlikely," I said. "The ceiling is glass and is regularly cleaned. It would have been seen."

He held it carefully by the eraser and examined it, whistling softly to himself. Then he dropped it back into the envelope and put it into his pocket.

"Well, that's that. Now, as to Miss Gittings herself. I suppose she had no lover?"

"Lover?" I was shocked. "She is nearly fifty."

He seemed to be amused at that.

"Still, stranger things—" he said. "Perhaps not a lover. Some man, probably younger, who might pretend to be interested for some ulterior purpose. Say money. There's more of that than you might think. I suppose she had saved something?"

"I don't know. A little, perhaps."

He turned to Judy.

"You accepted that it was Miss Gittings you heard moving in her room."

"Certainly."

"Why?"

"It was her room. And the dogs had not barked. They would bark at a stranger."

"Oh!" he said, and took a fresh toothpick. "That's interesting. So the dogs knew whoever it was! Very interesting." He sat for a moment or two, apparently thinking. Then:

"I gather she had few or no outside contacts?"

"None whatever."

"She never mentioned anybody named Florence?"

"Florence? Not to me."

He settled down in his chair.

"It is a curious thing," he said. "We think we know all about certain individuals, and then something happens, the regular order is disturbed, and we find we know nothing at all. Now let me tell you certain things about Sarah Gittings.

"She has been nervous for some time, two weeks or so. She has eaten very little and slept less. Sometimes she has walked the floor of her room at night for hours. At least twice in that time she was called up by a girl named Florence, and made an appointment to meet her. One of these was made yesterday morning at eleven o'clock. The cook was trying to call the grocer and overheard her. Unfortunately, the place of meeting had evidently been prearranged and was not mentioned.

"At a quarter to five yesterday afternoon Sarah Gittings left this house. She was back in half an hour, according to the butler. She asked for an early dinner and left the house again at five minutes after seven.

"But following that return of hers, Sarah Gittings did two peculiar things. She went down to the cellar, took a chair from the laundry there and carried it into the room where the firewood is stored; it is there now. And according to the laundress, she cut off from a new clothes line an undetermined amount of rope. The line had been neatly rolled and replaced, but she is a sharp woman, that laundress."

Wallie had been following this intently, and it seemed to me that he looked relieved. He had stopped twirling his ring.

"I see," he said. "She tied the dogs to the tree herself."

"It looks like it."

Judy was watching him. "Feeling better, Wallie?" she asked, looking more cheerful herself. "Weight off the old mind, and all that?"

But he did not even hear her. He drew a long breath and lighted a cigarette.

"I don't mind saying," he said to the detective, "that this thing is vitally important to me. I—you've relieved me more than you know."

But I had been thinking.

"If she took that piece of rope, it was not to tie the dogs up; I can assure you of that. She had not expected to take them. I don't think she wanted to take them. And as for this man on the stairs," I went on, rather tartly, "you tell me that that was Sarah Gittings, who had left the house only a half hour before, and who could get in at any time! I am to believe that Sarah went to that empty lot, tied up the dogs, put on a pair of dark trousers, broke her way in through the drawing room door, and deliberately let me see her on the staircase! Remember, she knew about that mirror."

"But that's where the man in the case comes in," said Judy, maliciously. "Sarah's lover. He met her at the lot and found she'd forgotten her toothbrush. Naturally, he refused to elope with her without her toothbrush. It's all perfectly simple."

Mr. Harrison smiled. "Still," he said, rising, "she *did* take the rope. And now we'll look at that broken door."

But with the peculiar irony of events which was to handicap all of us through the entire series of crimes, all traces of footprints in the ground near the steps—there is no walk there—had already been obliterated. The rain was over, and Abner Jones had commenced his spring cleaning up of the lawns and had carefully raked away any possible signs.

Nevertheless, Judy maintained that Mr. Harrison had found something on the steps.

"When he stooped over to tie his shoe," she said, "he stooped and picked up something very small and shiny. It looked like the point of a knife."

By noon there was still no news of Sarah. All reports had been negative, and I believe that the Inspector found no further clues. Judy reported once that he and the officer in uniform were going through the trash barrel in the service yard and taking out the glass from the broken window. But the rain must have washed it fairly clean. Clara had been told to put Sarah's room in order again, but when that had been done Inspector Harrison advised me to lock it and keep the key.

He left us at noon. It was raining hard, but some time later I saw him, in a dripping mackintosh, moving slowly around in the Larimer property. When I looked out again, an hour later, he was still there, but he seemed to have exchanged his soft hat for a cap.

It was not until the figure had disappeared over the hillside that I decided that it was not the Inspector, but some one else.

CHAPTER V

THE VAST MAJORITY of crimes, I believe, are never solved by any single method or any single individual. Complex crimes, I mean, without distinct clues and obvious motives.

Certainly in the case of Sarah Gittings, and in those which followed it, the final solution was a combination of luck and—curiously enough—the temporary physical disability of one individual.

And I am filled with shuddering horror when I think where we all might be but for this last.

That day, Tuesday, dragged on interminably. I could do no work on the biography, and Mary Martin was shut up in her room with a novel. The servants were uneasy and even the dogs seemed dejected; Joseph puttered about, looking aged and careworn, and the maids seemed to drink endless tea in the kitchen and to be reluctant to go upstairs.

At three o'clock, Jim not having arrived and Judy being out with the dogs, I decided to call Katherine once more. It seemed to me that she might have a clue of some sort. She knew Sarah better than any of us, and I felt that at least she should be told.

But all I obtained from her was a thorough scolding for harboring Judy.

"Well!" she said when she heard my voice. "It's about time! You tell Judy to come right home. It's outrageous, Elizabeth."

"What is outrageous?" I asked.

"Her chasing that idiotic youth. Now listen, Elizabeth; I want you to keep him out of the house. It's the very least you can do, if she won't come home."

"I haven't seen any youth yet," I explained mildly. "And I'm not worrying about Judy. I have something else to worry about."

Her voice was shrill when I told her.

"Missing?" she said. "Sarah missing! Haven't you any idea where she is?"

"None, except that I'm afraid it's serious. The police are working on it."

"Maybe I'd better come down."

I checked that at once. Katherine is an intense, repressed woman, who can be exceedingly charming, but who can also be exceedingly stubborn at times. As that stubbornness of hers was to work for us later on I must not decry it, but I did not want her then.

"You can't do anything," I said. "And Howard probably needs you. Judy says he's not so well."

"No," she said slowly. "No. He's not as well as he ought to be."

She said nothing more about coming down, but insisted that I see Jim at once.

"He was fond of Sarah," she said, "and he really has such a good mind. I know he will help you."

She had no other suggestions to make, however. Sarah had no family, she was certain of that. Her great fear seemed to be that she had been struck by an automobile, and as that was mild compared with what I was beginning to think I allowed it to rest at that.

I had made no promise as to Judy, which was as well, for when she came back she was accompanied by a cheerful looking blond youth who was evidently the one in question, and who was presented to me only as Dick.

"This is Dick," was what Judy said. "And he is a nice person, of poor but honest parents."

Dick merely grinned at that; he seemed to know Judy, and almost before I knew it he and I were standing in the lower hall, and Judy was dropping lead pencils down the air shaft.

"Does that sound like it, Elizabeth Jane?" she would call to me at the top of her voice. "Or this?"

To save my life I could not tell. They seemed to be less sharp, less distinct, but I was not certain. Indeed, when Mr. Carter, for that turned out to be the youth's family name, tapped with his penknife on the marble mantel in the drawing room, the effect seemed rather more like what I had heard.

"*That* for Wallie!" said Judy, coming down. "That pencil's probably been there for ages. I'd like to see his face when he finds six more there! And now let's have tea."

I liked the boy. Indeed, I wondered what Katherine could have against him. Poverty, perhaps; but then Judy would have enough and to spare when Howard died. And Howard had already had one attack of angina pectoris that I knew of, and others possibly which he had concealed.

Judy was clearly very much in love. Indeed, I felt that she could hardly keep her hands off the boy; that she wanted to touch his sleeve or rumple his hair; and that he, more shyly, less sure of himself, was quite desperately in love with her.

But he was businesslike enough about the case. He wanted the story, or such part of it as he might have.

"It will leak out somehow," he said. "Probably Harrison will give it out himself; they'll give out something, anyhow. Somebody may have seen her, you know. A lot of missing people are turned up that way."

We were still arguing the matter, Judy taking Dick's side of it, of course, when Jim Blake came in.

I can recall that scene now; the tap-tap of the glazier's hammer as he repaired the broken pane in the drawing room, the lowered voices of Judy and Dick from the music room, whither they had retired with alacrity after Judy had dutifully kissed her uncle, and Jim Blake himself, sitting neatly in his chair, pale gray spats, gray tie, gray bordered silk handkerchief, and hair brushed neatly over his bald spot, explaining that he had felt ill that morning or he would have come earlier.

"Just the old trouble," he said, and I noticed that he mopped his forehead. "This wet weather–"

Some years ago he had been thrown from a borrowed hunter and had sprained his back. Judy had always maintained that his frequent retirements to his bed as a result were what she called "too much food and drink." But that day he looked really ill.

"Tell me about Sarah," he said, and lighted a cigar with hands that I thought were none too steady. He did not interrupt me until I had finished.

"You've had the police, you say?"

"I have indeed. What else could I do?"

"Katherine doesn't want it to get into the newspapers."

"Why not? There's no family disgrace in it, is there? That's idiotic."

He took out his handkerchief and mopped his forehead again.

"It's queer, any way you take it. You say Wallie was here last night? What does he think?"

"He seems to think it's mighty important to find her. As of course it is."

"And she'd tied the dogs to a tree? That's curious. Just where did you say they were?"

He sat silent for some time after that. Judy was banging the piano in the next room, and the noise seemed to bother him.

"Infernal din!" he said querulously. And after a pause: "How is Howard? What does Judy think about him?"

"I don't believe she knows very much. He's a secretive person; Katherine is worried, I know that."

He seemed to ponder that, turning his cigar in his long, well-kept fingers.

"This girl who telephoned, this Florence, she hasn't been identified yet? They haven't traced the call?"

"Not so far as I know."

Asked later on to recall Jim Blake's attitude that day, if it was that of an uneasy man, I was obliged to say that it was. Yet at the time it did not occur to me. He was an orderly soul, his life tidily and comfortably arranged, and what I felt then was that this thing with its potentialities of evil had disturbed him, his small plans, possibly for that very afternoon, the cheerful routine of his days.

"I suppose they've searched the lot next door, and the park?"

"Inspector Harrison has been over it."

He sat for some time after that, apparently thoughtful. I realize now that he was carefully framing his next question.

"Elizabeth," he said, "when was Howard here last? Has he been here recently?"

"Howard? Not for months."

"You're sure of that, I suppose?"

"He hasn't been able to get about, Jim. You know that."

He looked at me with eyes that even then seemed sunken, and drew a long breath.

"I suppose that's so," he said, and lapsed again into silence.

There was, at the time, only one result to that visit of Jim Blake's. I called Dick in and told him and Judy Katherine's desire for secrecy.

"Trust mother!" said Judy. "Keep in the society columns and out of the news!"

But the story was suppressed. Not until Sarah's body was found, four days later, was there any publicity.

The discovery of the body was one of those sheer chances to which I have referred. Without any possible motive for her killing, the police still believed it possible that she had deliberately disappeared. But, as Judy pointed out, there was as little known reason for such a disappearance as for her murder.

And then on the Saturday of that week she was found, poor soul.

I have no distinct memories of those four days of nightmare, save of the increasing certainty of disaster, of Katherine's and Laura's frenzied suggestions by telephone and wire, of Judy's forced cheerfulness, and a queer sort of desperation in Wallie which I could not understand.

He had joined the police in the search, visited the Morgue, gone through her effects to find a photograph to be sent to other cities. During those days he seemed neither to eat nor sleep, and he grew perceptibly thinner. All his old nonchalance had left him, and at least once in that four-day interval he came in somewhat the worse for liquor.

It was that night—I do not remember which one—that he told me he had written me a letter and put it in his box at the bank.

"So you'll understand," he said, his tongue slightly thick. "So if anything happens to me you'll understand."

Judy looked up at him.

"You're lit," she stated coldly. "Lit and mawkish. What's going to happen to you?"

"You'll see," he said somberly. "Plenty may happen to me. If you don't believe it, look at me!"

"You're not much to look at just now," she told him. "You'd better order him some black coffee, Elizabeth Jane."

She told me later that she did not believe he had written me any letter. But he had indeed. Months later we found it where he said it would be, in his box at the bank. But by that time we needed no explanation.

The finding of Sarah's body was as extraordinary as was everything else in this strange case.

Judy had taken the dogs for their usual walk in the park, and somewhere there she met Dick, certainly not by chance. It appears that for purposes of their own they had left the main park and walked through that narrow ravine which is behind my own property, and through which a bridle path follows the wanderings of a small stream. As this ravine lies close to the lot where the dogs had been found, there had been a search of sorts. The two young people, then, were not searching. They were walking along, intent on their own affairs. In front of them a man on a gray horse was ambling quietly along.

Suddenly and without warning the horse shied violently, and the rider went off. He was not hurt, and Dick caught the horse and led it back to him.

"Not hurt, are you?" Judy asked.

"Only surprised," he told her. "Surprised and irritated! That's the second time this beast has shied at that sewer, or whatever it is. Twice this week. Yet he's seen it a hundred times."

Well, he got on again, having led the animal past the obstacle, and Judy and Dick looked at it. At some time it had evidently been intended to raise the road level there, and what they saw was a brick sewer entrance, circular, and standing about seven feet above the ground.

"Funny," said Judy. "What's happened to that thing this week?"

Dick laughed at her. Neither of them, I am sure, was thinking of poor Sarah. It was a bright cool spring day, made for lovers, and he teased her. It was a part of the game.

"I suppose that horse can see things we can't see!" he said.

"Why not? Dogs can."

And at that moment Jock, beside the base of the structure, suddenly raised his head and let out a long wail.

They were rather incoherent about what happened after that. It was Dick who finally got to the top and looked down. At first he could see nothing. Then he made out what looked like a bundle of clothing below, and Judy knew by his face.

Even then of course they were not certain it was Sarah. They did not come home; they got the park police at once, and Dick did not let Judy wait after that. He brought her back, whimpering, and I put her to bed and waited.

It was Sarah.

They never let me see her, and I was glad of that.

She had been murdered. There were indications of a heavy blow on the back of the head, not necessarily fatal; but the actual cause of death, poor creature, was two stab wounds in the chest. One had penetrated to the right ventricle of the heart, and she had died very quickly.

Only later on was I to have the full picture of that tragic discovery; the evidence that the body had been dragged along beside the bridle path for almost a quarter of a mile, a herculean task; the inexplicable fact that the shoes had been removed and thrown in after the body; the difficulty of explaining how that inert figure had been lifted seven feet in the air to the top of the sewer to be dropped as it was found, head down, into that pipe-like orifice; and strangest and most dreadful of all to me, that the very rope with which the dogs had been tied when I found them, had been fastened under her arms and used to drag the body.

The homicide squad, I believe, was early on the scene, a cordon of police thrown out, and the path closed from the Larimer lot to a point beyond the sewer. But the heavy rain and the fact that the path had been used had obliterated all traces save those broken branches down the hillside which apparently proved that Sarah had been killed on or near the Larimer property.

The body had been found at three o'clock, and the medical examination took place as soon as it could be removed. The crime detection unit, a group of specialists, had been notified before that removal, but of the seven only one found anything to do there, and that was the photographer. And a gruesome enough exhibit those pictures made; the waiting ambulance, the mounted men holding back the curious who attempted to break the line, and close-up photographs of that poor body in its incredible resting place.

Inspector Harrison, sitting gravely in my library that night, was puzzled and restless.

"It's a curious case," he said. "Apparently motiveless. She was not robbed; the purse was found with the body, although—you say she carried a key to this house?"

"Yes. Inspector, I have been wondering if she did leave her bedroom door unlocked that night when she went out. If that man on the stairs hadn't already killed her and taken both keys."

"I think not. And I'll tell you why. Now the time when you saw that figure on the stairs was at seven-thirty-five, approximately. You'd finished a seven o'clock dinner and had got to your coffee. That's near enough, anyhow. But Sarah Gittings did not die until around ten o'clock."

"I don't understand. How do you know that?"

"By the food in the stomach. It had been in the stomach for approximately four hours before she died. The autopsy showed us that. But it does not show us where Sarah Gittings was between seven o'clock and ten. Three hours between the time she left this house and the time of her death. Where was she? What was she doing during that three hours? Once we learn that, and the identity of this Florence, we will have somewhere to go."

"I have wondered if a maniac, a homicidal maniac–"

"On account of the shoes? No, I think not, although there may have been an endeavor to make us think that. No. Why did Sarah Gittings take a chair from the laundry and place it in the wood-cellar? Why did she agree to take the dogs, and at the same time take a rope with which to tie them? What was in her room that would justify breaking into this house to secure it? Those are the questions we have to ask ourselves, Miss Bell.

"About this rope," he went on thoughtfully. "You left it when you untied the dogs and went back for Joseph?"

"I left it by the tree."

"And when you got back it was not there?"

"No. We searched for it as well as we could. But a rope doesn't move itself, and it was not where I left it, or anywhere nearby."

He got up to go, and standing in the hallway stared back at the lavatory door.

"This Florence," he said, "she may try to get in touch with you. She reads the papers, and God knows they are full of it today. If she does, don't scare her off. Find out something. Coax her here if you can, and notify me."

He went back into the lavatory and stood looking up at the ceiling.

"A strong man," he said, "or a desperate one if he got himself out of that shaft, and he may have; and it took strength to put that body where we found it."

As an afterthought, on his way out, he turned and said:

"Strange thing. Both those stab wounds were exactly the same depth, four and a quarter inches."

Wallie and Jim had made the necessary identification, and the coroner's jury brought in the only verdict possible. After that and pending the funeral we had a brief respite, although hardly to be called a peace. Reporters rang the bell day and night, and the press published sensational stories, including photographs of the house. Camera men even lurked in the shrubbery, trying for snapshots of any of us. One they did get, of Judy.

They had caught her unawares with a cigarette in her hand, and to prevent the picture she had made a really shocking face at the camera. They published it, nevertheless, and Katherine was outraged.

Katherine came down to the funeral. She was shocked and incredulous over the whole affair.

"But why?" she repeated over and over, when we got back from the service. "She had no enemies. She really had nobody, but us."

"Is there anything phoney about any of us?" Judy inquired. "Some family secret, or something she knew?"

"Judy!" said Katherine indignantly.

"But I mean it, mother. If we're all she's had for twenty years–"

Fortunately for Judy, Jim Blake came in just then, and I sent upstairs for Mary Martin, who had been left to herself for several days, and ordered tea. It seemed to me that we needed it.

We were five, then, that afternoon after Sarah's funeral when we gathered around the tea table; Katherine in her handsome black, the large square emerald which was Howard's latest gift to her on one white slim hand, saddened but controlled; Judy, with her boyish head and her girlish body; Mary, red-headed, pretty, not too sure of herself and resentful of it–it was clear that Katherine rather daunted her; Jim, well valeted and showing in relaxation some slight evidence of too many dinners and too many cocktails; and myself.

Katherine inspected Jim critically as he came in.

"You look tired, Jim."

"Well, it's been an uneasy week," he said evasively.

But she could not let it rest at that. Everything attached to Sarah had grown enormous in her eyes; already she was exalting Sarah in her mind, her virtues, her grievances.

"I didn't suppose you'd bother much. You never liked her."

"My dear girl! I hardly knew her."

"You never liked her, Jim. That's all I said. Although why you should dislike the poor dear I don't know."

It seemed to me that Jim looked annoyed. More than annoyed, indeed; alarmed. Also that Mary was staring at him with a rather singular intentness, and that Judy had noticed this. There was no particular sympathy between the two girls. Judy, assured, humorous and unself-conscious, was downright and frank to the shocking point, and her small artifices were as open as herself. But there was nothing open about Mary Martin and very little that was natural, save the color of her hair.

"Her mind's always on herself," Judy had complained once. "She poses her very fingers, if you know what I mean. She's self-conscious every minute."

And if there is one crime in the bright lexicon of modern youth it is to be self-conscious.

Katherine, upset and nervous, was gnawing on her grievance like a dog on a bone.

"But you thought Howard was foolish to remember her in his will, Jim."

"Nonsense, Katherine. Howard's money is his, to leave where he likes. Anyhow, let's hope he doesn't leave it at all for a good many years."

That silenced her. She sat very still, with her eyes slightly dilated, facing the issue she had herself brought up; Howard gone and herself alone. The years going on and she alone. And into that silence Mary Martin's voice broke, quiet but very clear.

"I have always meant to ask you, Mr. Blake. Did you receive the letter Miss Gittings wrote you on Sunday, the day before the—the thing happened?"

"A letter?" said Jim. "She wrote me a letter?"

But he was shocked. A child could have seen it. His teacup shook in his hand, and he was obliged to rest it on his knee. I saw Judy's eyes narrow.

"She did indeed. I went in while she was writing it."

"A letter?" Katherine asked. "Did you get it, Jim?"

"I received no letter." He had recovered somewhat, however, and now he turned on Mary sharply. "How did you know it was to me? Did she say so?"

"No. She was addressing the envelope, and she put her arm over it so I could not see. That is how I know."

"Do speak up," Judy said irritably. "What's the sense in being mysterious? God knows we've got enough of that."

"Her uniform is still hanging in the closet, and Mr. Blake's name is quite clear on the sleeve. Of course you have to take a mirror to read it."

I do not think any one of us doubted that she had told the truth, unless it was Katherine. And Mary sat there, pleased at being the center of attention, the picture however of demureness, her eyes on her well-manicured hands, which were as Judy had said, carelessly but beautifully posed in her lap.

"I don't believe it," Katherine said suddenly. "Please bring it down, Miss Martin."

I saw the girl stiffen and glance at me. She was taking no orders, said her attitude, except from me.

"Will you, Mary? Please."

She went out then, leaving the four of us in a rather strained silence. Jim was staring into his teacup. Judy was watching Jim, and Katherine had put her head back and closed her eyes.

"I don't like that girl," she said. "She is malicious."

"There's nothing malicious in her giving us a clue if she's got one," said Judy, with determined firmness. "We don't know that she sent the letter, but if she wrote one—"

"Well?"

"It looks as if she had had something to say to Uncle Jim which she didn't care to telephone, doesn't it?"

Mary came back then, and I daresay all of us felt rather sick when we saw Sarah's white uniform once more. There is something about the clothing of those who have died which is terribly pathetic; the familiarity, the small wrinkles left by a once warm body. And in Sarah's case the uniform spelled to most of us long years of loyal service. Katherine I know was silently crying.

Judy was the first to take the garment and examine it. I noticed that Jim did not touch it. Mary had brought a mirror, and I saw that Joseph—who was gathering the teacups—was politely dissembling an interest as keen as ours. Judy however did not help him any. She looked at the ink marks on the cuff which Mary had indicated, and then silently passed both mirror and garment to me.

There was no question of what was there. Somewhat smeared but still readable was the word "Blake," and while the house number was illegible, the street, Pine Street, was quite distinct.

No one spoke until Joseph went out. Then Jim cleared his throat and said:

"I don't care what's there. I never got a letter from her."

"She put a stamp on it," said Mary.

Judy turned on her.

"That doesn't prove that she mailed it."

But Mary shrugged her shoulders. I thought then, and I still think, that at that moment at least she was sincere enough, and also that she was enjoying the situation she had forced. For once the attention was on her and not on Katherine and Judy, with their solid place in the world, their unconscious assumption of superiority.

"You knew her," she said laconically. "She wouldn't waste a two-cent stamp."

She was unwilling to give up the center of the stage, however. She said that the uniform might or might not have importance, but that she felt the police should see it. If looks could have killed her she would never have left that room, but she had put the issue up to us and what could we do?

"Certainly," said Judy shrewishly. "You might put on your things now and take it, Mary!"

And with all eyes on her Mary merely looked at her watch and said that it was too late.

When a half hour or so later Inspector Harrison came in he found us all sitting there, manufacturing talk to cover our discomfort, and Mary blandly smiling.

We had to give the uniform to him. But from that time on there was not one of us who did not believe that Mary Martin was a potential enemy, and potentially dangerous; nor one of at least four of us who did not believe that Jim had actually received a letter from Sarah and was choosing to suppress the fact.

CHAPTER VI

IT IS NOT EASY to tell of this series of crimes in entire sequence. For one thing I kept no journal. For another, I must contend with that instinct of the human mind which attempts to forget what is painful to remember.

I do know, however, that Sarah was murdered on a Monday, the eighteenth of April, and that the death of Florence Gunther did not take place until the first of May. How she had occupied herself in that interval we cannot be certain; we know that she was terrified, that at night she must have locked herself in her room and listened for stealthy footsteps on the stairs, and that in daytime her terror was of a different order, but very real.

I can find only one bit of comfort. When death did come to her it was sudden and unexpected. She may have been smiling. She must even have been feeling a sense of relief, now that her resolution was taken. She could have had no warning, no premonition.

Yet had she had only a little courage she might have lived.

It is easy to say now what she should have done. She should have gone at once to the District Attorney and told her story. But perhaps she was afraid of that, of being discovered or followed. Then too Mr. Waite was away, and she may have been waiting for his return.

We know now that she was hysterical during most of the interval, hysterical and suspicious, that she had built up the crime to fit what she knew, and that the case as she saw it was precisely the case as the police were to see it later on. But we have no details of those terrible days through which she lived from the eighteenth of April to the first of May.

On the Tuesday following Sarah's funeral Katherine went back to New York, and on the next day the District Attorney sent for me. He had some of the papers on the case before him, and he fingered them while he interrogated me.

"You had no reason to believe she had any personal enemies? Anybody who could gain by doing away with her?"

"None whatever," I said promptly, and told him of her relations to the family. "I would have said," I finished, "that she had no outside life whatever."

"She had never married?"

"Never."

"I suppose she was in possession of a good many family facts? I'll not say secrets, but facts; relationships, differences, that sort of thing?"

"Such as they are, yes. But it is a singularly united family."

"Save, I suppose, for Mr. Somers' son by his first marriage. I understand that he is not particularly *persona grata*."

"Who told you that?"

He smiled.

"He told me himself, as a matter of fact. He seems very anxious to have the mystery solved, as of course we all are. I suppose he was fond of her?"

"I never thought so. No."

He coughed.

"In this—er—family difference, I gather that your sympathies have lain with this Walter. Is that so?"

"Yes and no," I said slowly. "Walter has never amounted to much since the war, and his father has never understood him. They are opposed temperaments. Walter is sensitive and high-strung. Mr. Somers is a silent man, very successful in business—he's in Wall Street—and they haven't hit it off. Mr. Somers has financed Walter in several businesses, but he has always failed. I believe he has said that he is through, except for a trust fund in his will, a small one. But if you have any idea that Walter is concerned in Sarah's death—"

"I have no such idea. We have checked his movements that night. As a matter of fact, when he left your house he went directly to his club. He left at eleven-fifteen. He recalls your asking the time, and that your own watch was a minute or two slow. At eleven-thirty he was at his club, and joined a bridge game. That time is fixed. The man whose place he took had agreed to be at home by midnight."

He turned over the papers on his desk, and finally picked up one of them.

"Unfortunately," he said, "your own statement that Sarah Gittings had no life outside your family necessarily brings the family into this affair. Your cousin, now, Mr. Blake. How well did she know him?"

"She saw him once in a while. I don't suppose she had ever said much more than good-morning to him."

"Then you know of no reason why she should write to him?"

"None whatever."

"Yet she did write to him, Miss Bell. She wrote to him on the day before her death, and I believe that he received that letter."

He sat back in his chair and surveyed me.

"He got that letter," he repeated.

"But why would he deny it?"

"That's what I intend to find out. Actually, it appears that Sarah Gittings knew Mr. Blake much better than you believe. On at least one evening during the week before her death she went to his house. He was dining out, however, and did not see her. On Saturday night she telephoned to him, but not from your house. We have gone over your calls. Clearly this was some private matter between them. Amos, Mr. Blake's servant, says he recognized her voice; of course that's dubious, but again Mr. Blake was out. Then on Sunday she wrote, and I have every reason to believe that he got the letter on Monday."

"Why?"

"Because he went out that night to meet her."

I think, recalling that interview, that he was deliberately telling me these things in order to get my reaction to them, to watch for those reactions. Later on I believe he attempted to convey something of this system of his to the Grand Jury; that he said, in effect:

"You are to remember that guilt or innocence is not always solved or otherwise by the sworn statements of witnesses. People have perjured themselves before this. The reaction to a question is an important one; there is a subtle difference between the honest man and the most subtle liar."

So now he watched me.

"Did you know, when she left your house that night, that she was going out to meet Mr. Blake?"

"No. And I don't believe it now."

"You saw the writing on her cuff. Was that hers?"

"It looked like it. I daresay it was."

"Yet no such envelope was found in her room the next day, when the police searched it. Nor among the trash which Inspector Harrison examined. She wrote and sent that letter, Miss Bell, and he received it. Unless some one in your house found it and deliberately destroyed it."

"If you think I did that, I did not."

"No," he said. "I am sure you did not. That is why I know he got it. But why should he deny it? Remember, I am bringing no accusation against Mr. Blake, but I want him to come clean on this story. He knows something. You might suggest to him that it would be better for him to tell what he knows than to have us find it out for ourselves."

I was slightly dazed as I left, and sitting back in the car I was puzzled. How little, after all, we know of people! Sarah, moving quietly about my house, massaging me each morning with quiet efficiency; her life an open book, not too interesting. And yet Sarah had had a secret, a secret which she had withheld from me and had given or tried to give to Jim Blake.

I decided to see Jim at once and give him the District Attorney's message. But Jim had had a return of his old trouble and was in bed. And as it happened, something occurred that night which took my mind away from Jim for the time, and from everything else except Judy.

She had been in a fever of anger and resentment ever since Sarah's death. After all, Sarah had helped to bring her into the world, and she was outraged. I daresay under other conditions I might have found her determination to solve a crime amusing rather than otherwise, but there was a set to her small jaw, a feverish look in her eyes, that commanded my respect. And in the end, like Katherine, she did make her small contribution.

To Dick of course she was wonderful, no matter what she did.

So she and Dick were working on the case; she in a fury of indignation, Dick largely because of her. I know that they had gone over every inch of the lot where the dogs had been tied, but that they had found nothing. I think, however, that they were afraid I could not give their efforts sympathetic attention, for except for their lack of success they did not confide in me.

On that night, Wednesday, they had been making a sketch of the lot and the park, but Judy looked very tired, and at ten o'clock I sent Dick away. Judy started up for bed, but in the hall she must have thought of something and changed her mind. She went back through the pantry, where Joseph was reading the evening paper, and asked if he had a flashlight. Joseph had none there, and she went into the kitchen, got some matches and the garage key from its nail and proceeded to the garage.

Shortly after she came back to the kitchen door and called in to him:

"Where's the ladder, Joseph? The ladder Mr. Walter used in the lavatory that night?"

"It's in the tool room, Miss Judy. Shall I bring it in?"

"Never mind," she said, and went out again.

At half past ten I heard him making his round of the windows and doors, before going to bed. At the front door he stopped, and then came to me in the library.

"I suppose Miss Judy came in by the front door, madam?"

"Miss Judy! Has she been out?"

"She went out through the kitchen, a little after ten. She said she wanted the ladder; she didn't say why."

I was uneasy rather than alarmed, until I saw that the garage was dark.

"She's not there, Joseph!"

"Maybe she took the car and went out, madam."

"She'd have told me, I'm sure."

I was for starting out at once, but he held me back.

"I'd better get my revolver," he said. "If there's anything wrong—"

That sent a shiver of fear down my spine.

"Judy!" I called. "Judy!"

There was no answer, and together Joseph and I started out, he slightly in the lead and his revolver in his hand. It was a black night and starless; just such a night as when poor Sarah met her death, and the very silence was terrifying. Halfway along the path Joseph wheeled suddenly.

"Who's there?" he said sharply.

"What did you hear, Joseph?"

"I thought somebody moved in the bushes."

We listened, but everything was quiet, and we went on.

In the garage itself, when we switched on the lights, everything was in order, and the key Judy had used was still in the small door which gave entrance from the side. This door was closed but not locked. The first ominous thing was when we discovered that the door into the tool room was locked and that the key was missing from its nail. I rattled the knob and called Judy, but received no reply, and Joseph in the meantime was searching for the key.

"She's in here, Joseph."

"Not necessarily, madam. Robert hides the key sometimes. He says that Abner takes his tools."

But Judy was in there. Not until Joseph had broken a window and crawled in did we find her, poor child, senseless and bleeding from a cut on the head.

Joseph carried her into the house, and into the library. She was already stirring when he placed her on the couch there, and she was quite conscious, although dizzy and nauseated, in a short time. Enough indeed to protest against my calling a doctor.

"We don't want any more fuss," she said, and tried to smile. "Remember mother, Elizabeth Jane! Always in the society columns but never in the news."

But as she was violently nauseated almost immediately I got Joseph to telephone to Doctor Simonds, and he came very soon afterwards.

She had, he said, been struck on the head, and Joseph suggested that the ladder itself had fallen on her. As a matter of fact, later investigation showed the ladder lying on the floor, and as Judy said it was against the wall when she saw it, there was a possibility of truth in this. But one thing was certain; however she was hurt, she had been definitely locked in the tool room. She had used the key and left it in the door. Some one had locked her in and taken the key. It was nowhere to be found.

We got her up to bed, and the diagnosis was a mild concussion and a lucky escape. The doctor was inclined to be humorous about it.

"You have a hard head, Judy. A hard head but a soft heart, eh?"

Well, he ordered ice to what she called her bump and heat to her feet, and while Joseph was cracking the ice below she told her story. But although Joseph maintained that she had asked him about the ladder, she gave an entirely different reason herself.

"Abner has a foot rule in the tool room," was her story to me. "I wanted to measure the cabinet. Sometimes you find a secret drawer that way. So I got the key to the garage and went out. I thought I heard something in the shrubbery behind me once, but it might have been a rabbit, I don't know.

"The tool room light had burned out, so I lighted a match when I went in. The door was not locked, but the key was in it. There was nobody in the tool room, unless they were behind the door when I opened it. I lighted a fresh match, and just then the door slammed behind me and blew out the match. I said 'damn,' and—that's all I remember."

To add to our bewilderment and my own secret anxiety, Joseph brought forth something when he carried up the ice; something which was odd, to say the least. This was that just before ten o'clock, when he let the dogs out the back door, he heard them barking in the shrubbery. This barking, however, ceased abruptly.

"As though they'd recognized the party," said Joseph, who now and then lapsed into colloquial English. "Jock now, he'd never let up if it was a stranger."

But there was something horrible in that thought; that any one who knew us would attack Judy, and the situation was not improved by Norah's declaration the next day that, at two o'clock in the morning, four hours after the attack on Judy, she had seen some one with a flashlight in the shrubbery near the garage. The night had been cool and she had got out of bed to close her window. Then she saw the light, and because it was rather ghostly and the *morale* of the household none too good, she had simply got back into bed and drawn the covers over her head.

Inspector Harrison had come early at my request, and Norah repeated the story to him.

The flashlight, she said, was close to the ground, and almost as soon as she saw it, it went out.

Up to that moment I think he had been inclined to lay Judy's condition to accident, the more so as she refused to explain why she had been in the garage.

"Come now, Miss Judy. You had a reason, hadn't you?"

"I've told you. I wanted to get the foot rule."

"Did you tell Joseph you wanted to see the ladder?"

"I may have," she said airily. "Just to make conversation."

"This ladder," he persisted. "It is the one Walter Somers used in the lavatory?"

Judy yawned.

"Sorry," she said. "I lost some sleep last night. Is it the same ladder, Elizabeth Jane? You tell him."

"It is," I said flatly, "and you know it perfectly well, Judy. You're being silly."

But she had no more to say, and the Inspector stamped down the stairs in no pleasant mood and inclined to discredit her whole story. For which I did not blame him.

He did however believe Norah. She was looking pale and demoralized, and she said something about witch lights and then crossed herself. The result was that he at once commenced an investigation of the shrubbery, and that his men almost immediately discovered footprints in the soft ground to the right of the path and where Norah had seen the light.

There were four, two rights and two lefts, and when I went out to look at them the Inspector was standing near them, surveying them with his head on one side.

"Very neat," he said. "Very pretty. See anything queer about them, Simmons?"

"They're kind of small, if that's it."

"What about the heels?"

"Very good, sir. Clear as a bell."

The Inspector drew a long breath.

"And that's all you see, is it?" he demanded violently. "What the hell's the use of my trying to teach you fellows anything? Look at those heels! A kangaroo couldn't have left those prints. They've been planted."

He left the discomfited Simmons to mount guard over the prints and to keep the dogs away from them, and not unlike a terrier himself, set to work to examine the nearby ground and bushes.

"The fellow, whoever he was, stepped off the path there when Miss Judy came along. But he left footprints, and later on he remembered them. He came back, smoothed them over and planted false ones. If he's overlooked one now—"

He was carefully turning over dead leaves with a stick he carried, and now he stooped suddenly and picked up something.

"Look at this!" he said. "The key to the tool room, isn't it? I thought so. Threw it here as he ran."

He was examining the key, which is the flat key of the usual Yale lock, and now he gave an exclamation of disgust.

"Clean as a whistle," he said. "Pretty cagey, this chap. Must have been in a devil of a hurry, but he wiped it first; or he wore gloves."

He stood there for some time, staring at the key.

"Well," he said finally, "we have just two guesses, Miss Bell. Either he wanted to do away with Miss Judy, which is unlikely; or he did not like her going into that tool room."

"But he let her go in, and he locked her there."

"Not in shape to do much looking about, however," he said grimly. "Now which was it?"

He glared at me as though he expected an answer.

"I'm sure I don't know," I said meekly.

Later on I stood by while his men measured the distance between the footprints and made molds of them. They sprayed the marks with something first, and then poured in plaster of Paris which the Inspector reinforced with the inevitable toothpicks. The result was a pair of rather ghastly white shoes, which he surveyed with satisfaction.

"How do I know they were planted?" he said. "Well the stride was too long for the foot, for one thing. Here's a small foot and a long stride. Then the ground's soft; they weren't deep enough. And there's another point. When a man walks there's a back thrust to his foot, and the weight's likely to be more on the outside and back of the heel. Look at me; I walk in this earth. What happens? I break the earth at the rear as I lift my foot.

"You might try that, Simmons," he called. "Maybe the next time you won't let somebody put something over on you."

He left soon after that, greatly pleased with himself but considerably puzzled, and carrying the two molds carefully wrapped in a newspaper.

His examination of the garage and of the ladder had yielded nothing whatever.

CHAPTER VII

JUDY HAD BEEN HURT on Wednesday, the twenty-seventh of April, and Florence Gunther was not killed until the first of May, which was the Sunday following.

On either Thursday or Friday of that week, then, Wallie came in to see me.

I remember being shocked at his appearance, and still more shocked at the way he received the news that Judy had been hurt.

"Good God!" he said. "I'll stop this thing if I have to–" he hesitated. "If I have to kill somebody with my own hands."

But he would not explain that. He called Joseph and went out to the garage, leaving me to make what I could out of that speech of his, and of his conduct generally since Sarah had been killed.

He had searched far more assiduously than had the police, had shown more anxiety than any of us. His gaiety had gone, and he had a hollow-eyed and somber look during those days which I could not account for.

Nor did the discovery of the body afford him any apparent relief. To the rest of us, grieved as we were, it at least ended that tragic search. After all, it was over. We could not help Sarah, and the rest was for the police. But Wallie had not appeared to share this relief.

Yet Wallie had not liked Sarah. She was not a part of that early régime of which Joseph was the lone survival; of Margaret and the noisy, gay, extravagant days before she left Howard and a young son both of whom had passionately loved her, to run away with a man who abandoned her within six months.

I found myself thinking of those days. I had known Howard even then. Indeed, it was through me that he met Katherine. Margaret had had a brief unhappy year somewhere in Europe; then she died. And Wallie had needed a mother. But Katherine had not proved to be a mother to him.

He had resented her, and she had resented him. She had never liked him, and after Judy was born this dislike greatly increased.

It accentuated her jealousy of Margaret that Margaret had borne Howard a son, and that she had not; for Katherine was passionately in love with her husband. And she had kept nothing of Margaret's that she could avoid. Even Joseph had had to go, and so I took him. Not unusual, I daresay, this jealousy of second wives for the woman they have followed, even when that woman is dead. But it worked badly for Wallie.

Certainly Wallie was not blameless for his alienation from his father, but also certainly Katherine never raised a finger to restore the peace between them. Wallie was too reminiscent of his mother, fiery, passionate, undisciplined, handsome. When he had learned that Margaret was dying in Biarritz, abandoned by the man for whom she had left Howard, he had demanded permission to go to her. But he was refused on the score of his age—he was only fourteen at the time—and in desperation he had taken out of Howard's wallet the money for a second-class passage there.

He was too late, at that, but Howard never forgave him the theft, and he had made the mistake of telling Katherine.

After her marriage, when Wallie was in the house, she kept her purse locked away. And he knew it and hated her for it. But he was not there very often. First at school and later at college, Katherine kept him away as much as possible. And after that had come the war.

Naturally then the relationship between Judy and Wallie was almost as remote as the relationship between Wallie and Sarah. To have him grow morose and exhausted when Sarah disappeared was surprising enough, but to see him grow pale and furious over the attack on Judy was actually startling.

He was quieter, however, when he came back from the garage. He planted himself in front of me, like a man who has made a resolution.

"See here," he said. "How fond are you of Jim Blake?"

"I like him. I don't know that it's any more than that."

"What time was it when he telephoned here that night?"

"About a quarter past seven."

"And he asked for Sarah?"

"Yes."

"Why did he do that? Was he in the habit of calling Sarah? Of course he wasn't. How do you know that when she left the house that night it wasn't to see Jim Blake? To meet him somewhere?"

"I don't believe it," I said sharply. "Why would she meet him? I don't believe they've exchanged two dozen words in twenty years."

"She went out to meet him," he insisted. "I know that. I've made it my business to know it. I've been talking to that Negro of his. You know his habits; you know he dines late and dresses for dinner. Well, that night he didn't. He dined early and he put on a golf suit. And he left the house at seven o'clock."

"Good heavens, Wallie! If a man may not eat when he's hungry and dress as he likes—"

"Listen," he said doggedly. "That's not all. He carried with him that sword-stick you gave him."

"Even then—"

"Let me finish, Elizabeth Jane. That cane or stick or whatever you call it, has disappeared. It's not in the house. It stood in the hall with his other sticks until Sarah's body was found. Then it went."

He was looking at me with his tired sunken eyes, but there was no doubting his earnestness or his conviction.

"What does that look like?" he demanded. "He has an appointment with Sarah. He goes to meet her, armed. And then—"

"Wallie, I implore you not to give that to the police."

"No," he said somberly. "Not yet. But some day I may have to."

This then was our situation, during the few days which remained before the first of May. Sarah was dead; dead of two stab wounds four and a quarter inches deep, inflicted after she had been stunned by a blow on the back of the head. Judy had been attacked by the same method, a blow on the head from the rear, but no further attempt on her life had been made. Wallie suspected Jim Blake, apparently only because the sword-cane was missing, and my household was in a state of nerves so extreme that the back-firing of automobiles as they coasted down the long hill which terminates at my drive was enough to make the women turn pale.

Of clues we had none whatever.

Because of the sensational nature of the crime the press was clamoring for an arrest, and the Inspector was annoyed and irritated.

"What do they want, anyhow?" he said. "I can't make clues, can I? And if you'd listen to the District Attorney's office you'd think all I had to do was to walk out and arrest the first man I met on the street. Lot of old women, getting nervous the minute the papers begin to yap at them!"

He must have broken up hundreds of toothpicks that week. We would find small scattered bits of wood all over the place.

By Sunday, the first of May, Judy was still in bed, but fully convalescent. She had ordered a number of books on crime to read, and flanked by those on one side and her cigarettes on the other, managed to put in the days comfortably enough.

The evenings were reserved for Dick. Their first meeting after Judy's injury had defined the situation between them with entire clarity. He was on his knees beside the bed in an instant.

"My darling! My poor little darling!" he said.

She lay there, looking perfectly happy, with one hand on his head.

"Your poor little darling has made a damned fool of herself," she said sweetly. "And you'll give me hell when you hear about it. Go on out, Elizabeth Jane; he wants to kiss me."

Which, Katherine or no Katherine, I promptly did.

It was then on Sunday afternoon that there occurred another of those apparently small matters on which later such grave events were to depend. Already there were a number of them: Sarah's poor body found by the coincidence of Judy being near when a horse shied; the coolness of an April night so that Norah must go to her window to close it; Mary Martin happening to open Sarah's door while she was writing a letter, so that Sarah had made that damning record on her white sleeve; Jim Blake's deviation from his custom of dressing for dinner and its results; Judy's sudden and still mysterious desire to visit the garage at night; even my own impulsive gift to Jim Blake of my grandfather's sword-stick.

On that Sunday afternoon, at five o'clock, Florence Gunther came to see me and was turned away. I had gone upstairs to rest, and she was turned away.

Why had she not come sooner? She was frightened, of course. We know that now. Afraid of her very life. The nights must have been pure terror, locked away in there in the upper room of that shabby house on Halkett Street. But she knew she held the key to the mystery. One can figure her reading the papers, searching for some news, and all the time holding the key and wondering what she ought to do.

If she had gone to the police with her story, she might have saved her life. But if all of us behaved rationally under stress there would be no mysteries, and the dread of the police and of publicity is very strong in many people. And in addition she herself had something to hide, a small matter but vital to her. How could she tell her story and not reveal that?

She must have thought of all those things, sitting alone at night in that none too comfortable room of hers with its daybed covered with an imitation Navajo rug, its dull curtains and duller carpet, its book from the circulating library, and perhaps on the dresser when she went to bed at night, the gold bridge with its two teeth which was later to identify her.

Yet in the end she reached a decision and came to me. And Joseph, who was to identify her as my visitor later on by a photograph, answered the bell and turned her away! I was asleep, he said, and could not be disturbed. So she went off, poor creature, walking down my path to the pavement and to her doom; a thin colorless girl in a dark blue coat and a checked dress.

She had left no name, and Joseph did not tell me until I went down to dinner.

Even then it meant nothing to me.

"What was she like, Joseph? A reporter?"

"I think not, madam. A thinnish person, very quiet."

Dick was having an early Sunday night supper with me, early so that the servants might go out. That, too, is a custom of my mother's, the original purpose having been that they might go to church. Now, I believe, they go to the movies.

But I thought no more of the matter. Mary Martin had rather upset me. She had come in from a walk to tell me that she was leaving as soon as I could spare her, and had suddenly burst into tears.

"I just want to get away," she said, through her handkerchief. "I'm nervous here. I'm—I guess I'm frightened."

"That's silly, Mary. Where would you go?"

"I may go to New York. Mrs. Somers has said she may find something for me."

Judy's comment on that conversation, when I stopped in her room to tell her, was characteristic.

"Mother's idea of keeping Mary's mouth shut," she said. "And polite blackmail on the part of the lady!"

So Mary had not come down to dinner, and Dick and I were alone. He talked, I remember, about crime; that Scotland Yard seized on one dominant clue and followed it through, but that the expert American detective used the Continental method and followed every possible clue. And he stated as a corollary to this that the experts connected with the homicide squad had some clues in connection with Sarah's murder that they were not giving out.

"They've got something, and I think it puzzles them."

"You don't know what it is?"

But he only shook his head, and proceeded to eat a substantial meal. I remember wondering if that clue involved Jim, and harking back again, as I had ever since, to Wallie's suspicion of him.

Why had he telephoned to Sarah that night? Could it be that he was, in case of emergency, registering the fact that, at seven-fifteen or thereabouts, he was safely at home? But we had the word of Amos that he was not at home at that time; that, God help us, he was out somewhere, with a deadly weapon in his hand and who knew what was in his heart.

He was still shut away, in bed. What did he think about as he lay in that bed?

"Dick," I said. "You and Judy have something in your minds about this awful thing, haven't you?"

"We've been talking about it. Who hasn't?"

"But something concrete," I insisted. "Why on earth did Judy want that ladder?"

He hesitated.

"I don't know," he said slowly. "I don't think she wanted the ladder; I think she must have intended to look at it."

Upon this cryptic speech, which he refused to elaborate, I took him upstairs.

That evening is marked in my memory by two things. One was, about nine o'clock, a hysterical crying fit by Mary Martin. Clara came down to the library to tell me that Mary was locked in her room and crying; she could hear her through the door. As Mary was one of those self-contained young women who seem amply able to take care of themselves, the news was almost shocking.

To add to my bewilderment, when I had got the smelling salts and hurried up to her, she refused at first to let me in.

"Go away," she said. "Please go away."

"Let me give you the salts. I needn't come in."

A moment later, however, she threw the door wide open and faced me, half defiantly.

"It's nothing," she said. "I was low in my mind, that's all." She forced a smile. "I have a fit like this every so often. They're not serious."

"Has anything happened, Mary?"

"Nothing. I'm just silly. You know, or maybe you don't; living around in other people's houses, having nothing. It gets me sometimes."

I came nearer to liking her then than I ever had, and I wondered if the sight of Dick, intent on Judy and Judy's safety, had not precipitated the thing. After all, she was pretty and she was young. I patted her on the arm.

"Maybe I've done less than my duty, Mary," I said. "I'm a selfish woman and lately, with all this tragedy—"

And then she began to cry again. Softly, however, and rather hopelessly. When I went downstairs again I wondered if she was not frightened, too; after all, her loneliness was nothing new to her.

I can look back on Mary now, as I can look back on all the other actors in our drama. But she still remains mysterious to me, a queer arrogant creature, self-conscious and sex-conscious, yet with her own hours of weakness and despair.

The other incident was when Dick received a telephone call, rather late in the evening.

That must have been around eleven o'clock. Judy and he had spent the intervening hours together, the door open out of deference to my old-fashioned ideas, but with Dick curled up comfortably on her bed in deference to their own! He came leisurely down to the telephone when I called him, but the next moment he was galvanized into action, rushed into the hall, caught up his overcoat and hat, and shouted up the stairs to Judy.

"Got to run, honey. Something's happened, and the star reporter is required."

"Come right up here and say good-night!"

"This is business," he called back, grinning. "I can kiss you any time."

And with that he was out of the house and starting the engine of his dilapidated Ford. I could hear him rattling and bumping down the drive while Judy was still calling to him from above.

CHAPTER VIII

I WAS ASTONISHED the next morning to have Clara announce Inspector Harrison before I was dressed. I looked at the clock, and it was only half past eight. Clara plainly considered the call ill-timed.

"I can ask him to come back, ma'am."

"Not at all. You have no idea what he wants, I suppose?"

"Joseph let him in. If you'd like some coffee first."

But I wanted no coffee. I threw on some clothing—Judy was still asleep—and when I got down Mr. Harrison was standing in the lavatory doorway, thoughtfully gazing up at the skylight. He looked tired and untidy, and his eyes were bloodshot.

"I've taken the liberty of asking your butler for a cup of coffee. I've been up all night."

"Why not have breakfast?"

"I'm not hungry. I don't think I could eat anything."

But he did eat a fair meal when it appeared, talking meanwhile of unimportant matters. Not until we were in the library with the door closed did he mention the real object of his visit.

"Miss Bell, did you ever hear of a young woman named Gunther?"

"I think not. Why?"

"Florence Gunther?"

"Florence! The Florence who telephoned to Sarah?"

"I think it's possible. I'm not certain."

"Well," I said, "I'm glad you've found her. She must know something."

"Yes," he said. "Yes, I think she did know something. But she will never be able to tell it. She was shot and killed last night."

Later on I was to wonder why he did not tell me then the details of that killing. Perhaps he was still rather sick; perhaps he had reasons of his own. But what he told me then was only that the girl had been shot and that there was some evidence that her room had been gone through, like Sarah's. The body had been taken to the Morgue.

"There are certain points of resemblance," he said, "although this girl was shot, not stabbed. For instance—I don't want to harrow you—but the shoes had been removed. And although her room is not in the condition of Sarah Gittings', it had been searched. I'll take my oath to that. She seems to have been an orderly person, very quiet, and—"

But that phrase, very quiet, recalled something to me. Quiet. A quiet person. I remembered then; Joseph's description of the young woman who had tried to see me the day before.

"I wonder," I said, "if she could have been here yesterday."

"Yesterday?"

"How was she dressed? What did she look like? Joseph turned away a young woman while I was resting. It just might have been—"

He was in the hall in a moment, calling Joseph, and what I had feared turned out to be correct. Joseph not only identified a cabinet photograph of her, but recalled that she had worn a blue coat, and "a sort of plaid dress, sir; checked, it might have been."

When he had excused Joseph, who looked shaken over the whole business, the Inspector gave me such facts as he had.

Florence Gunther had been shot and killed; the bullet had gone into her brain and out again. But the murderer had also tried to burn her body, and had largely succeeded. A farmer named Hawkins, out on the Warrenville road, had gone out at ten o'clock the night before to look after a sick cow, and in a gully beside the road, not two hundred yards from his front gate, had seen a fire blazing.

Thinking that a passing motorist had ignited the brush with a lighted cigarette, he went back into the house and got an old blanket and a broom with which to beat out the flames. He had actually commenced this when he realized what lay before him. He smothered the fire with the blanket and called the police. But for the incident of the sick cow the body would have been destroyed, as the family had already retired.

As it was, identification would have been a slow matter, had it not been for the one thing which Mr. Harrison had said every criminal overlooks, and this was that where the body had been placed a small spring, a mere thread of water really—I saw it later—effectually soaked the ground at this point. Such garments as were in contact with the earth, then, were not destroyed, and they revealed the fact that the unfortunate woman had worn a checked dress and a dark blue coat.

There must have been footprints in that soft ground, the heavy marks of a man carrying a substantial burden; but a passing car with a group of curious and horrified motorists, Hawkins himself extinguishing the fire, the police and police reporters when they arrived, had thoroughly erased them. The three detectives from the homicide squad reached the spot to find the body, a crowd of curious onlookers, and not a discoverable clue to the murder.

At four in the morning Harrison went home and threw himself, fully clothed, on his bed. There was nothing then to connect this crime with Sarah, or with us; nor was there until seven-ten the following morning. The body had been taken to the Morgue, Mr. Harrison was peacefully asleep, and Dick Carter had written his story of the murder and gone to bed, a blue beaded bag in his coat pocket and forgotten. At seven-ten, however, an excited telephone message was received at a local police station from a woman named Sanderson, a boarder in a house in an unfashionable part of the city, on Halkett Street.

She reported that one of the roomers, a young woman named Florence Gunther, was not in her room, and that as she never spent the night out she was certain that something was wrong.

In view of the crime the night before, the call was turned over to the Inspector. Breakfastless and without changing his clothing, he got into his car—always kept at his door—and started for Halkett Street. The Sanderson woman, greatly excited, was waiting at the front door.

Her story was simple and direct.

She had not slept well, and some time in the night she had been annoyed by movements overhead, in Florence Gunther's room.

"She seemed to be moving the furniture about," she said, "and I made up my mind to talk to her about it in the morning. So I got up at seven and went up, but she wasn't there. She hadn't slept there. And when I found all her clothes except what she had on I got worried."

He told her nothing of the crime, but he examined the room with her. The landlady, a woman named Bassett, had been ill for some time and did not appear. It was clear to both of them that the room had been searched, although there had been an attempt to conceal the fact. But the important fact was that Florence Gunther when last seen the evening before had worn a checked dress and blue coat.

He knew then what he had found. He locked the room, put Simmons on guard at the door, sent word by a colored servant to Mrs. Bassett that the room and the officer were to be undisturbed, and with a photograph of the dead woman in his pocket had come to me.

"The point seems to be this," he said. "If this is the Florence who was in touch with Sarah, the same motive which led to the one crime has led to the other. The possession of some dangerous knowledge, possibly certain papers—it's hard to say. The one thing apparently certain is that there was something, some physical property for which in each case a search was made. Whether it was found or not—"

He broke the end from a toothpick with great violence.

"Curious thing to think of, isn't it?" he went on. "If you'd seen this girl yesterday she might be living today. She knew the answer to Sarah Gittings' murder, and so she had to go. Now, if we knew how friendly they were, how they met, what brought them together, we'd have something."

And, although we have learned many things, that association of theirs remains a mystery. By what tragic accident they were thrown together we shall never know; two lonely women in a city of over half a million, they had drifted together somehow, perhaps during their aimless evening walks, or in a moving picture theater. We have no reason to believe that there was any particular friendship between them. One thing, discovered by accident, held them together and in the end destroyed them.

The Inspector got up to go.

"I'm going down to headquarters," he said. "Then I'm going back to that room of hers. Whether the same hand killed both women or not, I imagine the same individual searched both rooms. There's a technique about such matters."

"Still, I should think that a man who has just killed—"

"Not this one. He's got no heart and he's got no nerves. But there's always a chance. If he goes on killing, he'll slip up some time, and then we'll get him."

With which optimistic words he left me!

Later on in the day I heard from him by telephone.

"Just to cheer you up," he said. "We have a clear slate for Walter Somers last night. He played bridge from eight until three this morning, and won two hundred dollars."

He hung up abruptly. It was the first time I had known that the police were watching Wallie.

From the papers, ringing with another "shoe" murder, and from various sources then and later, I gained a fair idea of the unfortunate young woman.

She was about thirty years of age, a quiet but not unfriendly woman. Shy. She seldom joined the others in the parlor of the Halkett Street house; in the evenings she took a walk or went to the movies. She had apparently no family, and received no mail of any importance.

She had been an expert stenographer in the law office of Waite and Henderson, well-known attorneys, and was highly thought of there. Recently, however, she had shown signs of nervousness, and her work had suffered somewhat.

Her life had been apparently an open book.

In the morning she was called at seven. She dressed slowly, ate her breakfast, and reported at nine at the office. She had not been interested in men, or they in her; but she had had one caller, a gentleman, about two weeks before. His identity was unknown, but he seemed to have been a well-dressed man, not young. He had arrived, according to the colored woman servant, about eight o'clock and stayed until nine-thirty. She had had only a glimpse of him and could not describe him.

On the day of her death, which was Sunday, she had spent the morning doing some small washing and mending. In the afternoon, however, she had put on the blue coat and started out. She was back in less than an hour, and had seemed low-spirited.

No one had seen her leave the house that night. It was thought that she had left the house about eight, and the police believed that she had been killed at or near that ditch on the Warrenville road where the body was found.

But on Monday afternoon we were to learn where she had been shot.

My property lies at the foot of a longish hill. As a result of this, and an annoying one it is, a certain number of cars come down in gear but with the switch off, and by and large a very considerable amount of backfiring takes place directly outside of my drive. The result is that when, quite recently, a bootlegger fired a number of shots at a policeman and finally wounded him in the leg, the poor wretch lay untended for some little time.

All of which bears directly on the killing of Florence Gunther.

Dick had telephoned me during the day, when the identity of Florence Gunther had been given out by the police, and begged me to send Judy away.

"She's not safe," he said, worried. "Until we know what's behind this nobody's safe."

I agreed to do what I could, and when he came in at six o'clock, looking rather the worse for wear, he was more cheerful. I had kept the news of the murder from Judy until then, thinking she might hear it better from him, and she greeted him with great coolness.

"Don't come near me," she said. "And don't ask him to dinner, Elizabeth Jane. He walked out on me last night."

"Listen to her! If I don't work I don't eat, my child. These millionaires' daughters!" he said to me. "They think honest toil is cutting coupons. Money's nothing to them."

Then he remembered something, and put his hand in his pocket.

"Speaking of money," he said, "hanged if I didn't forget I'd had a windfall. Look what I found!"

He drew out of his pocket a blue beaded bag, and Judy snatched it from him.

"I suppose you've advertised it?" she said severely.

"Darling, I am this moment out of my bath. Of course I shall," he added virtuously. " 'Found: bag.' Vague but honest, eh what? It's got ten dollars in it!"

"Where did you find it?"

"I just drove out from the Bell estate in my Rolls-Royce, and there it was."

"On the street?"

"On the street. Right outside your gates, oh daughter of Eve. I said to myself: 'What's that?' Then I replied: 'It's a pocketbook.' Then I shouted 'Whoa,' leaped from my trusty steed and—"

It was then that Judy found the typed slip and drew it out. "You won't have to advertise. Here's her name: Florence Gunther."

"Florence Gunther?" I said. "My God!"

It was then that Dick told her of the murder the night before. He was as careful as he could be not to horrify her, but the bare facts were dreadful enough. She went very pale, but she watched him steadily, and somehow I got the impression that he was telling her more than appeared on the surface, that between them there was some understanding, some secret theory against which they were checking these new facts.

"On the Warrenville road? Then she was taken there in a car?"

"Presumably, yes."

"Did anybody see the car?"

"The police are working on that. Apparently not."

"And you've checked up on—things?"

"They seem all right. Absolutely O. K."

Still with this mysterious bond between them they took me out to where Dick had found the bag, and standing there he pointed out where he had found it; not near the pavement, but almost in the center of the street. It had shown up plainly; at first he had thought it was a bird, and veered to avoid it. Then he saw what it was.

"You might figure it like this," he said. "She's coming again to see you. She suspects something, and she's got to tell it. Now, there are two ways for that bag to have been where I found it. Either she saw somebody and ducked out into the street; or she was in a car already, was shot while in the car, and the bag dropped out. I think she was in a car. You see there's no blood," he ended awkwardly.

Judy looked a little sick, but she spoke practically enough.

"Couldn't he have shot her there, dragged her quickly into the shrubbery, and then got a car? She must have been here at eight-thirty or so, and the body wasn't found until after ten."

Well, it was possible; but a careful search of the hedge, and the lilacs, forsythia and syringa bushes inside of it—some of them in leaf, for the spring had been early—revealed nothing whatever.

I find myself dwelling on that question of time, which Judy brought up. It puzzled the police for a long time, but now we know about it; the driving about, with that dead woman lolling on the seat; the decision to use the river, and the bridge crowded and no hope there; the purchase of oil at some remote spot, leaving the car and its grisly contents at a safe distance; and finally the Warrenville road and the sleeping farmhouse. And the sick cow.

The sick cow! Everything safe, another perfect crime. And then, of all possible mischances, a sick cow.

CHAPTER IX

THAT WAS ON Monday. Tuesday morning, Jim being still in bed and incommunicado by the doctor's orders, the District Attorney sent again for Amos, Jim's servant, and terrified him into a number of damaging statements. That early dinner of Jim's, the fact that he had left the house immediately after it, and that he had carried the sword-stick, all of these came out. And finally the frightened wretch told that the stick had disappeared.

That was enough, more than enough. After that Jim was under surveillance day and night, one of those apparently casual affairs, but sufficient to report his movements. He made no movements, however. He lay in his bed, and if he knew the significance of the men who moved back and forward along Pine Street, or that his telephone and mail were both under espionage, he made no sign.

But, although suspicion was now directed at Jim, it was only suspicion.

On Tuesday night Inspector Harrison came again to see me. I was growing to like the man. He was to oppose me and all of us for a long time, but he was at least sturdily honest with me, and he was to try later on to be helpful.

He was very grave that night. He sent Judy away, to her annoyance, closed the library door, and then turned to me.

"I came here tonight with a purpose, Miss Bell," he said at last. "I want you to think, and think hard. Is there anything at all, however remote—I don't care how absurd—which would provide a motive for the killing of Sarah Gittings? For this second crime is subsidiary to that. That I know. Think, now; some remote family trouble, some secret she knew, even some scene at which she happened to be present."

"We don't have family scenes, Inspector."

"Nonsense! Every family has them."

"There is nothing, I assure you. Walter Somers doesn't hit it off with his stepmother, but they don't quarrel. They simply keep apart."

"And Mr. Blake?"

"Why should he quarrel with them? They have been very good to him. I think Mrs. Somers even makes him a small allowance, and a man doesn't quarrel with his bread and butter."

"Tell me something about the Somers family. I know they are wealthy. What else?"

"Howard has been married twice. His first wife eloped with another man, and died in Europe many years ago. After her death he married my cousin, Katherine. They have one child, Judy, who is here. And they are very happy."

"And that's the whole story?"

"Yes, except that Howard Somers is in bad health. He has had at least one attack of angina pectoris. He had that here last year, while I was abroad with his family. He almost died, and I suppose the end is only a question of time."

"I see. How old a man is he?"

"Almost sixty. Quite a handsome man."

"Now, about this sick spell. When you say he was sick here, do you mean in this house?"

"No. The house was closed. He was at a hotel, the Imperial. Sarah Gittings came down to take care of him."

"And Mr. Blake? Was he here at that time?"

"He was in Maine. He has a small cottage there."

I believe now that certain of these interrogations were purely idle, designed to put me off my guard. For the next instant, in the same tone, he asked me a question so unexpected that it found me totally unprepared for it.

"And when did you give Mr. Blake the walking stick which belonged to your grandfather?"

I must have showed my agitation, for he smiled.

"Come, come," he said. "You're a poor witness for the defense, Miss Bell! I see Amos has told the truth. Show a Negro a police badge and he'll come clean. How long has Mr. Blake had that cane?"

"Since some time in the early spring. In March."

"You have no idea where it is now?"

"Not the faintest. He certainly didn't bring it back here."

He bent toward me, wary and intent.

"Ah," he said. "So you know it has disappeared! Now that's interesting. I call that very interesting. Who told you that it had disappeared? Not Amos. He was warned. Mr. Blake himself, perhaps?"

"No. It was Walter Somers. Amos told him."

He sat back.

"By and large," he said, "we have too many detectives on these crimes. And the family seems to be curiously interested, doesn't it? For a family with nothing to conceal. Now, I would like a description of that stick, if you don't mind."

There was nothing else to do. Much as I loathed the idea I was obliged to describe the thing, the heavy knob, the knife concealed in the shaft.

"This blade now, was it sharp?"

"Absolutely not. But I daresay Jim had it sharpened. He would have had to, if he had meant to commit a murder."

But my sarcasm was a boomerang.

"It may interest you to know that he did just that, Miss Bell. About a week after he got it."

He gave me little time to worry about that, however.

"There is something else I want to verify. On the night Sarah Gittings was murdered, Mr. Blake telephoned here, I believe; to Miss Judy. At what time was that?"

"Shortly after seven. A quarter past, possibly."

"That was a message from Miss Judy's mother, I gather?"

"Yes, but he–"

I checked myself, too late. He was bending forward again, watching me. "But what?"

"I have just remembered. He asked if Sarah was here; but that is in his favor, naturally. If he had known he need not have asked."

"Or if he did know, and wished to give the impression that he did not."

He sat there looking at me, and for the first time I realized that he was potentially dangerous to me and mine. His china blue eyes were cold and searching; under his bald head his face was determined, almost belligerent. And he was intelligent, shrewd and intelligent. Later on I was to try to circumvent him; to pit my own wits against his. Always he thwarted me, and often he frightened me. In his way, almost to the very end, he remained as mysterious as Sarah, as aloof as Florence Gunther, as implacable as fate itself.

Yet he treated me always with friendliness and often with deference, and now his voice was almost casual.

"Did he say where he was when he called up?"

"No. At home, probably."

"Don't you know better than that, Miss Bell?" he inquired pointedly. "If you don't, let me tell you. On that night Jim Blake dined early, and left the house at seven, or a few minutes after. He did no telephoning before he left. We have a list of his calls out for that night. Wherever he was when he telephoned—and we are trying to locate that—he was not at home."

And I felt again that this communicativeness of his was deliberate, that he was watching for its effect on me.

"But why? Why would Jim Blake kill Sarah?" I demanded. "What would be his motive?"

He was getting ready to go, and he stopped by the door.

"Now and then, in criminal work," he said, "we find the criminal before we learn the motive. I make no accusation against Mr. Blake. I merely say that his movements that night require explanation, and that until he makes that explanation we have to use our own interpretation. If that's unfavorable to him that's his fault."

One comfort at least we had at that time. The reporters, the camera men and the crowds of inquisitive sightseers had abandoned us, and out on the Warrenville road Hawkins had thriftily piled brush about the site of the crime, and was letting in the morbid minded at a price until the county police stopped him.

The cow had died.

But in my own household demoralization was almost complete. The women were in a state of hysteria, afraid to leave the house and almost as terrified to stay in it. On Tuesday morning the laundress had come upstairs pale and trembling, to say that the chair had been taken from the laundry again and was once more in the room where the wood was stored. And on that night, at something after twelve o'clock, Clara ran down to my room, pounding on the door and shouting that there was a man under her bed.

It required Joseph with the revolver and myself with all my courage to discover Jock there, neatly curled up and asleep.

The matter of the chair, however, puzzled me. I took Judy and went down. It was a plain wooden chair, and it had been left where it was found. Judy mounted it and examined the joists above, for this portion of the basement is not ceiled. But there was nothing there except a large black spider, at which she got down in a hurry.

I don't know what I had expected to find. The sword-stick, perhaps.

It was on Wednesday that I determined to see Jim. I had not seen him for over a week, not indeed since the day of Sarah's funeral, and if Wallie's state had bewildered me Jim's frankly shocked me.

I had been fond of Jim, but with no particular approval. The very fact that he was still idling through his late forties; that he was content to live modestly because extravagance meant work; that he could still put in weeks of preparation on the Bachelors' Ball, given each year for the débutantes; that his food and drink were important to him, and his clothes—all these things had annoyed me.

Nor had I ever quite believed in his feeble health; certainly he was a stronger man than Howard, who had always worked and who was still working in the very shadow of death. Certainly Jim was able to play golf, to sit up all night at bridge, to eat and drink what he wanted, and to dance with a young generation which liked his cocktails and the flowers he sent them.

But this was the surface of Jim Blake. Of the real man, buried under that slightly bulging waistline, that air of frivolity, those impeccable garments, I doubt if even Katherine knew anything. He went his way, apparently a cheerful idler, with his present assured, and his future undoubtedly cared for in the case of Howard's death.

There was, however, nothing cheerful about the Jim I found on Wednesday night, lying in his handsome bed and nursed and valeted by Amos. I have often wondered since just what were his thoughts as he lay there day after day, watching Amos moving deftly about the room; Amos who knew so much and yet not enough.

The two watching each other, the black man and the white, and yet all serene between them on the surface.

"I've ordered sweetbreads for luncheon, sir."

"That's right. Put them on a little ham, Amos."

And Amos going out, efficient and potentially dangerous, to prepare sweetbreads.

Jim must have had his bad hours, his own temptations. He could have escaped even then; could have slipped out the rear door to his car and gone somewhere, anywhere, for his illness was certainly not acute. But he did not. He lay there in his bed and waited for the inevitable.

He was glad to see me, I thought. He was propped up in bed in a pair of mauve silk pyjamas, and with a dressing gown of dark brocade hanging over a chair beside him. The room was masculine enough, but a trifle too carefully done, as though Jim had taken pains to place the jewel which was himself in a perfect setting. There was something incongruous in the contrast between that soft interior, shaded and carefully lighted, with Jim as the central figure, the star of its stage, and the man I had seen across the street as I walked to the house. I had walked. I felt that it was not necessary to take my household into my confidence on this particular matter.

"Well," he said, "this is a kindly and Christian act! Sit down. That's a good chair."

He was nervous. I saw for the first time, that night, the slight twitching about the mouth which was never afterwards to leave him, and as I told him my story it grew more and more marked. Yet save for that twitching he heard me through quietly enough.

"What do you want me to say?" he said. "Or to do? If the police want a scapegoat—innocent men have been arrested before this for the sake of the sensational press—what am I to do about it? Run away?"

"You can tell them the truth."

"What truth?" he said irritably.

"Tell them where you were the night Sarah was killed. Surely you can do that, Jim."

"I have already told them. I live the usual life of a bachelor. I'm neither better nor worse than others. I decline to drag a woman into this; any woman. They can all go to hell first."

I felt my heart sink. His indignation was not real. He spoke like a man who has rehearsed a speech. And from under his eyebrows he was watching me, intently, furtively. For the first time I realized how badly frightened he was.

"I see," I said, quietly. "And I daresay that's where you left the cane. Naturally you would not care to speak about it."

"The cane? What cane?"

"The one I gave you, Jim. It's missing, apparently."

He said nothing for a full minute. It must have been a terrible shock to him. Perhaps he was going back, in his mind; who knew about the cane? Amos, of course. And Amos had been talking. His distrust and anger at Amos must have been a devastating thing just then. But he rallied himself.

"What's that got to do with it? Anybody can lose a stick. I've lost dozens, hundreds."

"You carried it out with you that night, you know."

"And I suppose that proves that I killed Sarah Gittings! And that I got up out of a sick bed the other night, put a can of kerosene in my car and shot this Florence Gunther! There's no case there. I carry a stick out one night and forget it somewhere. Well, they can't hang me for that. And I wasn't out of this house last Sunday night."

What could I say? Tell him Wallie's story, that the sword-cane had not disappeared until Sarah's body was found? That he had brought it back, and that the police knew he had brought it back? He hated Wallie, and I was in no condition to face an outburst of anger from him, especially since I felt that that too might have been prepared in advance; the careful defense of a frightened man.

One thing I was certain of when I left. He was a frightened man, but not a sick man. The loose sleeve of his pyjama coat revealed a muscular and well-nourished arm, and when Amos came in reply to the summons he carried a night tray with a substantial supper and a siphon and bottle.

Jim scowled when he saw it.

"You can leave that, and I want you to drive Miss Bell home, Amos. She walked over."

"Yes, sir."

I had a flash then of the strange relationship between the two of them, shut in there together; of suspicion and anger on Jim's part, and on the Negro's of fear and something else. Not hostility. Uneasiness, perhaps.

"Can I shake up your pillows, sir?"

"No. Don't bother."

I felt baffled as I went down the stairs.

I daresay it is always difficult to face civilized human beings and to try to realize that they have joined the lost brotherhood of those who have willfully taken human lives. There appears to be no gulf; they breathe, eat, talk, even on occasion laugh. There is no mark on their foreheads. But the gulf is there, never to be bridged; less broad perhaps for those who have killed in passion, but wider than eternity itself for those who have planned, plotted, schemed, that a living being shall cease to live.

All hope that Jim Blake would clear himself, at least in my eyes, was gone. And at the foot of the stairs Amos was waiting, enigmatic, the perfect servant, to help me into my wrap.

"I'll bring the car around at once, ma'am."

"I'll go back with you, Amos. It will save time."

"The yard's pretty dark, Miss Bell."

"Haven't you a flashlight?"

He produced one at once from a drawer of the hall table, and I followed him, through his neat pantry and kitchen and out into the yard. Here in mild weather Jim sometimes served coffee after dinner, and he had planted it rather prettily. I remember the scent of the spring night as I followed Amos, and seeing the faint outlines of Jim's garden furniture, a bench, a few chairs, a table.

"I see you have your things out already, Amos."

"Yes'm. I painted them a few days ago. We'll be having warm weather soon."

I took the light while he unlocked the small door and backed the car into the alley beyond. It occurred to me that the watcher out front would hear the noise and come to investigate, but the alley was lined with garages. One car more or less would make little difference.

I have wondered about that surveillance since. Clearly it would always have been possible for Jim to come and go by the alley way if he so desired. Probably the intention was not that, but rather to see what visitors he received, and for all I know there may have been some arrangement with Amos, to warn the watcher if Jim left his bed and dressed for any purpose.

However that may be, we were not molested, and I still carried the flashlight when I got into the rear of the car. I knew the car well. I had sold it to Jim a year or so ago when I had bought a new one. It was a dark blue limousine, the driving seat covered with leather, the interior upholstered in a pale gray.

"Car doing all right, Amos?"

"Very well, ma'am."

Idly I switched on the flashlight and surveyed the interior. Undoubtedly the car had begun to show wear. There were scars on the seat cushions from cigarette burns, and one or two on the carpet. I think now that these movements of mine were a sort of automatism, or perhaps the instinct of the uneasy mind to seek refuge in the trivial. The car was of no importance to me. Let them burn it, these people who shared the "usual life of a bachelor," these men for whom Amos painted the garden furniture, these women who must be protected, not dragged in.

And then I saw something.

There was a ring-shaped stain on the carpet near my feet, well defined, dark. It was perhaps seven inches across, and I lowered the flashlight and inspected it. It looked like oil, and woman-fashion I ran my finger over it and then sniffed the finger. It was oil. It was kerosene oil.

I put out the flashlight and sat back. There were a dozen possible explanations for that stain, but only one occurred to me. Sitting there in the dark, I pondered the matter of eliminating it before Amos found it. Or had he already found it? Was he sitting there beyond the glass partition, driving as perfectly as he did everything else, and all the time aware of my movements, knowing what I had found? Did the police know, too?

Suppose I were to say to Amos:

"Amos, this carpet is dirty. I'm taking it to have it cleaned, while Mr. Blake is not using the car."

Perhaps that in itself would rouse his suspicion. He might say: "Don't bother, Miss Bell. I'll see to it." And then Amos and I would be bickering over the carpet; it would grow important to him, and if he conquered he would take it to the police.

I did the best thing I could think of at the moment. I stooped down and loosened the carpet, rolled it up carefully, and then hid it as best I could underneath my long cape.

If I looked strange to Joseph when he admitted me, he said nothing. Once Judy had said that Joseph had no capacity for astonishment, and the thought supported me that night as, certainly nervous and probably bulging, I entered my own house.

Judy called to me from the library, but I passed the door with as much expedition as I dared. She and Dick were settled there over a card table, with a sheet of paper before them. I saw that, and that Dick was apparently making a sketch of some sort. As I went up the stairs he was saying:

"Now get this. Here's the daybed. The closet door is there—"

Then I was in my room, the door bolted, and that incriminating carpet on a table under a good light. There was no question about it. A jug or can containing kerosene oil had rested on it, probably quite recently.

CHAPTER X

A LONE WOMAN who has lived in a house for many years grows to know her house. It is like a live thing to her; it has its moods, its contrary days, and it has its little eccentricities. This stair creaks, that window rattles, that door sticks.

Especially, if she is not a good sleeper, she grows to know her house at night. All houses are strange at night. It is as though, after the darkness and silence have fallen, they stir and waken to some mysterious life of their own. In my house, some of these movements I can account for. When the windows are raised the old beams creak, as though the house is cracking its knuckles, and when we have a north wind the skylight wails and whines. A metal weatherstrip that is, vibrating like a string.

Then, too, a breeze from the west will set the ivy outside my window to whispering, little sibilant voices which have roused me more than once, convinced that I was called; and an open window in the drawing room beside the speaking tube there will send on windy days a fine thin whistle through the house.

But I do not like my cellar. Perhaps this is a throwback to my childhood; I do not know. The fact remains that I go into it at night under protest, and that I have had installed in the back hall a switch by which a light below is turned on before any one need descend. A bit of precaution for which I could have shrieked with rage before that night had passed.

It was eleven o'clock when I returned, and soon afterwards I heard Dick leave the house. His paper is an afternoon one, and so he has to rise fairly early. Judy wandered in to say good-night, but I had locked the carpet in my closet, and she merely lighted a cigarette and stood inside the door.

"When is Mary going?" she asked.

"She hasn't said. Why?"

"She's been packing tonight. Dick helped Joseph to bring her trunk down from the storeroom. She doesn't seem too keen to go."

"It's her own choice," I said, rather acidly.

"Well, I hope to heaven mother doesn't wish her on us! She may. To shut her mouth about Uncle Jim."

But she did not go away at once. She stood there, smoking fast and apparently thinking.

"Don't you think Wallie's been rather queer over all this?" she said. "'So if anything happens to me you'll understand,'" she mimicked him. "If he knows anything now is the time to tell it. And if he doesn't, why don't he keep out? Where does he come in, anyhow? What's he worried about?"

"I do wish *you'd* keep out of all this, Judy."

"Why? It's the day of the young, isn't it? Everybody says so."

"It's the hour for the young to be in bed."

"All right, I'm going now. But just to show you why I'm not going back to New York, in spite of you and Dick—Wallie didn't find that pencil on top of the skylight. He took it up with him and put it there."

With which she went away, whistling softly, and left me to my thoughts, which were nothing to boast about.

I did not go to bed. I sat shut in my bedroom, with the carpet from the car rolled in my closet, waiting for the house to quiet down for the night. My mind was a welter of confusion; Jim's evasions and half truths, the possible significance of the oil stain, and Judy's strange statement as to Wallie and the pencil.

And to add to my discomfort Joseph tapped at my door after letting Dick out and locking up, and told me that the women in the house had started a tale that poor Sarah was "walking," and were scaring themselves into a fit over it. I am not a superstitious woman, but there is something of the mystic in every Christian, and I must confess that when, at something after one, the speaking tube in my room set up a thin whistle, my hair seemed to stand on end.

Ever since the night of Sarah's death Joseph had been instructed to leave a light burning in the lower hall, and it was burning then. I opened my door carefully and slipping out, leaned over the banister. Save that Jock had apparently been asleep there, and had now risen and was stretching himself drowsily, there was no sign of anything unusual. If there was a window or a door open in the drawing room I felt that it could stay open for a while. I had other business to attend to first.

Jock's attitude had given me confidence, and at something after one, wearing a dressing gown and my felt-soled bedroom slippers, I took the rug and a bottle of patent cleaner and made my way gingerly to the basement laundry, stopping in the kitchen to pick up the poker from the range. I was minded to have a weapon of some sort at hand.

I had a plan, of sorts. If the stain came out I could return the rug to Amos, and he could think what he might; lay my high-handed proceeding to the eccentricities of a middle-aged female if it pleased him. If it did not come out, I could burn the thing in the furnace.

But I was very nervous, and the basement itself daunted me; the long vistas of blackness forward, to the furnace and the coal and wood cellars, the darkness of the laundry and the drying room. The small light at the foot of the stairs, which turned on from the back hall above, made little impression on the gloom, and as I stood there it seemed to me that something crawled over the wood in the wood cellar. A rat, possibly, but it did not help my morale.

The laundry was dark, and to light it one must enter the room, and turn on the hanging globe in the center. I went in, shivering, and directly in the center of the room I struck violently against something. It was a chair, and it upset with a clatter that echoed and re-echoed in that cavernous place.

What was the chair doing there? It belonged under a window, and here it was, out of place again. What was it that moved that chair? And Joseph's somber statement came back to me, to complete my demoralization. After all, chairs did move. They moved in séances. Chairs and tables, without being touched.

I was badly frightened, I confess. A dozen stories of phantasms, discredited at the time, rose in my mind. The place seemed peopled with moving shadows, sinister and threatening, and from somewhere I seemed to hear footsteps, spectral, felt rather than heard. And when I finally found courage to try the laundry light, it had burned out.

Such efforts as I could make then to remove the stain were of no practical value, and I decided once for all to burn the rug and take the consequences.

I did one of the hardest things I have ever done in my life when I went forward to the furnace cellar, carrying the rug. Once the light there was on, however, I felt better. I built a small fire of paper and kindling, and thrust in the rug. It began to blaze, although not as rapidly as I had hoped. I stood there, watching and wondering about the dampers; like most women, I know nothing about a furnace.

I wandered about, waiting for that slow combustion to become effectual, examined the windows and the door to the area way, and was retracing my steps forward to the furnace again, when I stopped suddenly.

Some one was moving about over my head.

I pulled myself together. The dogs had not barked. It must be Joseph, Joseph who had heard the whining in the speaking tubes and come down to investigate. But to have Joseph discover me burning that rug would have been disastrous. I turned out the furnace light at once, and went back toward the foot of the stairs, where the small light still burned. To my horror, I saw that light go out, and heard the bolt slipped in the door above.

"Joseph!" I called. "*Joseph!*"

It was not Joseph. The footsteps had ceased, but there was no answering call. Somebody, something, was lurking there overhead, listening. The thought was horrible beyond words.

I was crouched on the foot of the staircase, and there I remained in that haunted darkness until daylight. At dawn I crept up the stairs, and half sat, half lay, on the narrow landing. Perhaps I slept, perhaps I fainted. I shall never forget Joseph's face when, at seven o'clock, he unlocked the door and found me there.

"Good heavens, madam!" he said.

"Help me up, Joseph. I can't move."

"You're not hurt, are you?"

"No. You locked me in, Joseph. I've had a terrible night. You—or somebody."

"I locked you in, madam? At what time?"

"About two o'clock, I think."

"I was not downstairs after midnight," he said, and helped me to my feet.

He got me into the pantry and made me some coffee. Norah was not yet down; my household slept badly those days, and therefore late. He had had a shock, however. His hands shook and his face was set. I can still see him moving about, his dignity less majestic than usual, making the coffee, laying a doily on the pantry table, fetching a cup and saucer from the dining room. While he waited for the coffee to boil he made a tour of the first floor, but reported everything in order. The drawing room door and windows were locked.

"But I would suggest, madam," he said, "that we change the lock on the front door. Since Miss Sarah's key is missing it is hardly safe."

Norah came in as I finished my coffee, and she gave me a queer look. But I did not explain. I went up and crawled into my bed, and I did not waken until Joseph came up with a tray of luncheon.

He came in, closed the door, drew a table beside the bed, opened my napkin and gave it to me. Then he straightened and looked at me.

"I have taken the liberty of destroying the rug, madam."

My heart sank, but he spoke as calmly as though he had been reporting that the butter was bad.

"The dampers were wrong," he said. "It's a peculiar furnace. You have to understand it."

He looked at me, and I looked back at him. Our relations had subtly changed, although his manner had not. We shared a secret; in effect, Joseph and I were accomplices. Between us we had compounded a felony, destroyed evidence, and Joseph knew it. Whether he had seen the stain or not, he knew that carpet.

"You should not have tried to do that, madam," he said. "In the future, if you need any help, you can always call on me."

Then he went out; strange inscrutable Joseph, living the vicarious life of all upper class servants. Somewhere he had a wife, but he never mentioned her. His room at night, the pantry and the newspapers by day, apparently comprised his life and satisfied him.

It was when he came to remove the tray that he told me, very quietly, that his revolver was missing.

"I have been keeping it in my bedroom lately, under my pillow," he said. "Now it is gone. Taken by some one who knew the habits of the house, madam."

CHAPTER XI

WHATEVER WAS the meaning of that unpleasant episode, it was impossible to go to the police with it. I was seeing rather less of the Inspector now; he and the entire homicide squad were working on the Gunther case; the crime detection unit of photographer, chemist, microscopist and gun expert were at work, but I believe their conclusions were unimportant. The bullet was missing. From the size of the wounds in the skull and the fact that it had passed entirely through the head, they believed that it had been a large caliber bullet fired at close range, and that the time of her death had been about eight or eight-thirty.

The bag, then, had lain in the street for almost three hours.

Outside of these facts the murder remained a complete and utter mystery. She appeared to have been without friends or family, one of these curious beings who from all appearances have sprung sporadically into being, without any past whatever. She had had no ability for friendship, unless that odd acquaintance of hers with Sarah could be called friendship.

Strange that two such reserved women should have found each other, have somehow broken down their repressions, have walked, talked, maybe even laughed together. For it seems now that during the month or so before the murders, they had met a number of times. One pictures them walking together, maybe sitting together in a moving picture theater, and then one day something said; a bit of confidence, and both were doomed.

The day passed without incident, save that Mary Martin took her departure. She even cried a little when she left, although she had shown no affection for any of us.

Judy seemed relieved to have her gone.

"Thank heaven," she said. "I don't have to whisper any more. She was always listening, Elizabeth Jane. I've caught her at it, leaning over the banisters. I'll bet my hat she knows something. And I'll bet two dollars, which is all I have in the world at the moment, that she took Joseph's gun."

"Why would she take Joseph's gun? That's silly."

"Is it? Well, ask Norah. She knows."

And ask Norah I did, with curious results.

It appeared that on the day before Joseph had missed his revolver, Norah had gone upstairs to her room to change her uniform before she prepared luncheon. She wears rubber-soled shoes in the kitchen, as it has a tiled floor, and so she moved quietly.

Joseph, it seems, was downstairs. The door at the top of the back stairs is a swinging one, as otherwise the maids forget to close it, and it swings noiselessly. She pushed it open, and there was Mary Martin, down the hall and just coming out of Joseph's room. She stepped back when she saw Norah, and then reconsidered and came out again.

"I was looking for some matches," she said.

According to Norah she had no matches in her hands, however, and she looked so pale that Norah was curious. When Mary had shut herself in her room Norah glanced inside Joseph's door. There were matches on his bureau, and his revolver lay on top of the bed.

But with Mary gone, and the house quiet again and with no "snooping," as Judy called it, I went into the library that night to find Dick grinning and Judy with her mouth set hard.

"Well, tell her, if you think it's so funny."

"Tell her yourself, lady of my heart. Do your own dirty work."

"Don't be such an ass. It's a perfectly simple thing I want, Elizabeth Jane. I want to get into Florence Gunther's room."

"The answer is just as simple, Judy," I said shortly. "You'll do nothing of the sort."

But she was argumentative and a trifle sulky.

"Oh well, if you must have it. I want to look for something. That's all."

"For what?"

"I don't know. But now listen to this; I don't know why poor Sarah was killed, or Florence either. But I do know why their shoes were taken off. One or the other of them had something; I don't know what, but she had. It might have been a paper—"

"Give me the papers and take the child!" said Dick.

She ignored that.

"Now Dick has struck up an acquaintance with a blonde out there at the house on Halkett Street. She's named Lily, and he's quite fond of her; he's even had her out to lunch."

Dick groaned, and she grinned maliciously.

"Her name is Sanderson, Lily Sanderson, and she's rather a mess. But she likes to talk, and she's got something she hasn't told the police. She won't even tell him, but she might tell us."

"Who are 'us'?"

"You and I, Elizabeth Jane; you to give staidness and respectability to the excursion, I to use my little wiles to wheedle her if necessary. Dick says she's afraid of the police, but once she sets eyes on you she'll open up like a flower."

I declined at once, but she has her own methods, has Judy, and so in the end I reluctantly consented to go.

The appointment was made for the next night, Friday. Evidently Miss Sanderson was uneasy, for she made it Friday because the colored woman would be off for her afternoon out. And it was she herself who admitted us when, having left the car at the corner, Judy and I presented ourselves on the following evening.

She opened the door with her fingers to her lips.

"Now how nice!" she said, in a loud clear tone. "Here I was, afraid I was to have an evening alone, and this happens!"

All the time she was urging us in with little gestures, and Judy's face was a study. Miss Sanderson was a large blonde woman with a slight limp, and she was evidently prepared for company. She was slightly overdressed, and her room when she took us up to it was very tidy. Suspiciously tidy, Judy said later, as if she had just finished with it.

When she had closed the door she lowered her voice.

"You never know who's around in a place like this. It's all ears. And since poor Miss Gunther's awful end–" She looked at me with her pale blue eyes, and they were childish and filled with terror. "I haven't slept much since. If there is a homicidal maniac loose, nobody can tell who'll be next."

"I wouldn't worry," said Judy. "There's no maniac loose. Whoever killed her knew what he was doing."

That seemed to relieve her. She was, for all her clothes, a singularly simple woman, and I am glad here to pay my bit of tribute to Lily Sanderson. She had her own small part in the solving of the mystery, and of the four major crimes which it involved.

She liked Judy at once, I think. There is something direct about Judy, for all her talk about using her wiles; and Judy, I think, felt the compassion of youth for her, for the narrow life that one room typified, for the loneliness of soul which was feeding on this one great excitement. I saw her looking about at the dreadful reach at beauty which the room revealed, the tea table at which nobody obviously ever had tea, at the silk shawl draped over the bed, at the imitation shell toilet set, the gaudily painted scrap basket, and at the screen which concealed the washstand in its corner, and behind which, I had no doubt, Miss Sanderson had dumped a clutter of odds and ends.

"You are very comfortable here, aren't you? It's quite homelike."

Miss Sanderson smiled her childlike smile.

"It's all the home I have," she said. "And Mrs. Bassett likes everything to be nice. She's very clean, really."

Before she settled to her story she opened her door, looked out, closed it again.

"I'm only talking because you were friends of poor Florence," she said. "And I don't know if what I have to tell you is important or not. I won't have to go to the police, will I?"

"Certainly not," said Judy sturdily.

"You know I told them that I'd heard her moving things about, that night? Well, I did. I didn't like to say what I really thought." She lowered her voice. "I thought she had a man up there. That's what I went up in the morning to speak to her about."

"A man?" I asked. "Could you hear him?"

"A man and a woman," she said. "I could hear them both."

Her story amounted to this:

She was a light sleeper, and she was wakened some time after midnight by movements in the room above. As Florence never stirred about in the night, this puzzled her. Especially as the movements continued.

"Somebody seemed to be moving the furniture," she said. "Very carefully, but you can't move a bureau in a house built like this without it making some noise. Even then I might have gone to sleep again, but there were two people. One walked heavier than the other."

She was curious, rather than alarmed. She got up and opened her door, and at last she crept up the stairs and—she seemed to apologize for this—put her ear to the door. There was a man talking in a low tone in the room.

That scandalized her. She went downstairs "with her head whirling," and stood there, uncertain what to do. She seems to have been in a state of shock and indignation, imagining all sorts of things. And the sounds went on, only now she could hear a woman crying. She was outraged. She thought Florence Gunther had a man in her room and that they were quarreling.

Finally she took her haircurler and rapped vigorously on the chandelier. The noises ceased at once, but although she set her door open and waited inside in the dark, nobody came down. Whoever they were, they must have escaped down the rear staircase.

But she could not sleep. A sort of virtuous fury possessed her, and half an hour later she threw something on and went up valiantly to Florence's room.

"I was going to give her a good talking to," she said. "It makes me sick now to think of it, but this is a respectable house, and—well, you know what I mean. If she was carrying on with anybody—"

The door was closed but not locked, and she spoke to Florence and got no answer. She turned on the switch inside the door, and there was the room; in chaos. She seemed unable to describe it. She made a gesture.

"Even her shoes," she said. "Her poor shoes were on the floor. But she hadn't been robbed. Her dime bank was still on her dresser, and she had an old-fashioned watch for a clock, beside the daybed on a table. It was still there."

She shot downstairs after that, trembling, and got into bed. Even then she was not certain that Florence was not concerned in it somehow. She knew that one of the two in that room had been a woman. Then too she "didn't want to be mixed up in any trouble." She might lose her position, and in addition she had a childish fear of the police.

"If they knew I'd been up there—"

She went to sleep finally, but at seven she went up the stairs again and opened the door. The room had been straightened. It looked better.

"Not just right, you know. But things were put away. The way the police found it."

"And what do you think now?" Judy inquired. She had lighted a cigarette and was offering one to "Lily."

"Oh, may I? I'd love to. We aren't supposed to smoke here, but every now and then I open a window and— It rests one, I think."

"Yes, it does rest one," said Judy politely. "And now what were those people after? Have you any idea?"

"Not really. But she was in a lawyer's office, and they get some queer things sometimes. Letters, you know, and so on. If she had something like that it might explain a lot. It had to be something small, or they'd have found it. But I'm sure I don't know where it is, if it's there."

"Oh, you've looked?" said Judy.

"Yes. The room's kept locked, but my key fits it. I suppose it's hardly the correct thing, but she was a friend of mine–"

Her eyes filled with tears, and Judy patted her heavy shoulder.

"Of course it was the correct thing. Perfectly correct. As a matter of fact I'd like to go up myself and look around. You don't mind, do you?"

Miss Sanderson not only did not mind, but looked rather gratified.

"I'll wait down here with the curler," she said with a conspiratorial air, "and if I hear anything I'll rap on the chandelier."

I was all for waiting below, but Judy took me with her, maintaining that the very sight of me would remove her from the sneak thief class if we were discovered, and at last I consented. Nevertheless, I was frankly trembling when we started up the stairs. Miss Sanderson had preceded us, creeping up with a stealth which gave the entire procedure a clandestine appearance which was disquieting, to say the least. After unlocking the door, however, she left us as noiselessly as we had come, and Judy moved the key from the outside to the inside of the door.

As we stood there in the darkness I think even Judy was uneasy, and I know that I felt like a criminal. The house was exceedingly quiet. Mrs. Bassett, Miss Sanderson had said, slept at the rear of that floor, but she was ill, had been for some time. And whatever was the mysterious life of the women behind the closed doors around us, it was conducted in silence.

Judy drew the shades before she turned on the light, and then the two of us gazed at this strange room, from which Florence Gunther had started out in a checked frock and a blue coat and with a blue bag on her arm, to a sudden and unaccountable death.

It was neat now, very orderly, the daybed covered with the imitation Indian rug, her clothing still in its closet, her shoes in a row underneath. Practical shoes, flat heeled, without coquetry, each with its wooden tree. Judy looked depressed and angry.

"She had so little," she said. "Why not have let her alone?"

But she was businesslike, too.

"No use looking in the obvious places," she announced. "They'll have seen to that. Something small. I suppose the police took it for granted that they got it, whatever it was. But if Lily is right–! If I wanted to hide a paper here, where would I put it? I hid a love letter once from mother, in my can of tooth powder."

Poor Florence's tooth powder was on her washstand, but although with much difficulty and a pair of scissors Judy finally worked the top off, she found nothing there. Then she examined the bottles on the dresser; one dark blue one interested her, but it contained an eye lotion and nothing else. The wall paper—"she might have loosened the paper and then glued it back again"—showed no signs of being tampered with, and the baseboard was close to the wall.

She reached the clothes closet, then, by elimination, and with small hope.

"They'll have done that first," she said.

Apparently she was right. No pocket, no lining, no hem of any garment, revealed so much as a hint. Save one thing, which at first looked as though our search was useless. There was an old pocketbook in the closet, and she brought it out and examined it.

"Look here!" she said. "She's carried something in this pocketbook, hidden. See where she's cut the lining and sewed it up again?"

"It's not sewed now."

"No," she said slowly. "Of course, if she transferred it to the blue bag—!"

But time was passing, and I was growing impatient. The whole excursion seemed to me to be an impertinent meddling, and so I was about to say to Judy, when there came a sharp rap from the chandelier beneath our feet.

Neither one of us moved, and I know I hardly breathed. Some one was coming up the stairs, moving very quietly. The steps halted just outside the door, and I motioned wildly to Judy to turn out the light. But in a moment they moved on again, toward the rear of the house, and I breathed again.

After that we locked the door, and Judy matter-of-factly went on with her search. She was on the floor now, carefully inspecting Florence's shoes.

"I used to hide my cigarettes in my slippers," she stated. "Mother raised hell about my smoking. I'll just look these over and then we'll go."

"And the sooner the better," I retorted testily. "If you think I'm enjoying this, I'm not. I've never spent a night I enjoyed less."

But she was paying no attention. She had found, in a pair of flat black shoes, leather insoles designed to support the arches. Glanced at casually each was a part of the shoe, but Judy's sensitive well-manicured fingers were digging at one of them diligently.

"Flat feet, poor dear," she said, and jerked out the insole.

It was, I believe, a quite common affair of its sort, although I had never seen one before. In the forward portion was a pocket, into which fitted a small pad of wool, designed to raise the forward arch.

Behind this Judy dug out a small scrap of paper, neatly folded.

I think we were both trembling when she drew it out and held it up. But without opening it she dropped it inside the neck of her frock and finding a pin, fastened it there. She wears so little underneath that this precaution was necessary.

"No time now to be curious, Elizabeth Jane," she said. "We have to get out of here, and to stall off Lily."

Everything was still quiet as we relocked the door and went down. Miss

Sanderson was peering out of her door and beckoned us in, but Judy shook her head.

"They made a pretty clean sweep," she said, "but thank you anyhow. You've been very sweet to us."

"He didn't try to get in, did he?"

"Somebody stopped outside the door and then went on. Who was it?"

"I couldn't see. It was a man though. It might have been the doctor," she added doubtfully. "I just thought I'd better warn you. Won't you come in again?"

She was clearly disappointed when we refused. She must have had many lonely evenings, poor soul, and to entertain Judy would have been a real thrill; Judy Somers, whose pictures were often in the New York evening papers and in the smarter magazines.

"I've got some sandwiches," she said.

"Thanks, no. I never eat at night."

She saw us out, rather forlornly.

"If anything turns up, I'll let you know."

"Please do. You've been wonderful."

She brightened at that, and the last we saw of her she was peering around the half-closed front door, loath to go back to her untasted sandwiches, to her loneliness and her wakeful nights.

We found the car around the corner where we had left it, but not until we were in my bedroom with the door locked did Judy produce that scrap of paper. And then it turned out to be completely unintelligible. Neatly typed, on thin copy paper was this: "Clock dial. Five o'clock right. Seven o'clock left. Press on six."

"Clock dial!" said Judy. "What clock? There's something in a clock somewhere, but that's as far as I go. It wasn't her clock. She didn't have one. As far as I can make out, we're exactly where we started!"

Which turned out to be very nearly a precise statement of the situation.

CHAPTER XII

JUST WHEN Amos discovered that his carpet was missing from the car I do not know. With Jim in bed the car was not in use, and it may have been a couple of days before he missed it, or even more. I hardly think he suspected me, although he may have.

But some time before Sunday he saw Wallie and told him. Just why he should have told him I do not know. Certainly he believed Jim Blake to be the guiltiest wretch unhung, but we also know that he had a queer affection for him. Maybe Wallie questioned him; Wallie had his own problem to solve, and he may have gone to Amos.

The result, however, was an extremely unpleasant interview between Wallie and myself a day or two after Judy had found the paper. I know now that he was frightened, terrified beyond any power of mine to imagine, and with Wallie as with other nervous persons anxiety took the form of anger.

He stalked into the house then late on Sunday afternoon, looking so strange that at first I thought he had been drinking again.

"Do you mind if I close the door?" he demanded. "I've got some things to say that you may not want overheard."

"Then I'd better leave it open. I don't care for any more secrets, or any scenes."

"Very well," he said savagely. "It's you I'm trying to protect."

But he slammed the door shut, nevertheless, and then confronted me. "I've got to know something. Of all the damnable, outrageous messes—! Did you or did you not take the rug out of Jim Blake's car the other night?"

"Why? Is it missing?"

"You know damned well it's missing."

"I don't like your tone, Wallie."

He pulled himself together then, and took another turn about the room.

"Sorry," he muttered. "I get excited. God, who wouldn't be excited? I'll ask you in a different way. Was the carpet in the car the other night when Amos drove you back here?"

"It was."

"And you left it there?"

"Why shouldn't I?"

"That's not an answer."

"Now see here, Wallie," I said. "I won't be bullied. There is no reason why I should answer any questions you put to me. Go to the police, if you like. Then if they choose to come to me—"

"The police. I'm trying my very best to keep the police out of this. But that Negro of Jim Blake's blabs everything he knows. They'll get it out of him yet. All I want to find out is why the carpet was taken. What was on it? It told something. What did it tell?"

I eyed him.

"Wallie," I said, "do you believe that Jim Blake committed these crimes? You've insinuated that, and that there was a reason."

"I could think of a reason, but this Gunther thing— No, I don't believe he's got the guts."

"If you could think of a reason, it's your business to tell it. Tell me, at least. If I'm to work in the dark—"

"Ah, so you have been working! Now look here, what was on that carpet? Oil? Blood? You took it, didn't you? Amos says you did."

"Why should he say that?"

"He says that if you got in the car and it was missing, you'd have asked about it."

I made up my mind then to make a clean breast of it.

"I did take it, Wallie. I took it out and burned it in the furnace. There was oil on it; a ring of oil. Something containing kerosene oil had been carried in it."

"My God!" he said, and seemed to sag lower in his chair.

He had aged in the past few days. That is the only way I can describe the change in him. That buoyancy and gaiety which had made him likable, with all his faults, had deserted him. But I could not feel sorry for him. He knew something; I rather thought that he knew a great deal.

"Do you think Amos knew what was on that carpet?" he asked.

"I haven't an idea. If he did, the police may know it too; but I think, if they do know it, they would have taken it away for safekeeping. No, I think you and I, and Joseph, are the only ones so far."

"Joseph? What's Joseph got to do with it?"

He listened intently while I told him of my attempt to burn the carpet, and of my being locked in the cellar. I could not gather from his face what he made of the incident. He had had time to recover, and the fact that the carpet had been actually destroyed seemed to reassure him. But when I finished he remained sunk in a silence which was more like brooding than anything else. I finally broke in on this.

"Isn't it time you told what you know, Wallie? If this thing is to go on, none of us are safe. Even Judy."

"Judy's all right," he said roughly. "And I don't know anything."

"That's not entirely true, is it?"

"You'll know all I know, when the time comes." He got up, looked at me furtively, and then began to finger the pens and pencils on my desk. "I suppose," he said, with an attempt at casualness, "that you are one of the incorruptibles, eh? A lie's a lie, and all that?"

"I will assuredly not perjure myself, if that's what you mean."

"Why put a label on everything? What's perjury anyhow? What's the difference except the label between your pretending you have a headache and making a statement that might save a life?"

"Perjury is a lie before God."

"Every lie is a lie before God, if you believe in God. All I want you to do is to say, if it becomes necessary to say anything, that that carpet was not in the car the other night. Wait a minute," he said, as I started to speak, "your own position isn't any too comfortable, is it? You've destroyed valuable evidence. And what do you do to Jim Blake if you tell the truth? I tell you, there's more behind this than you know. There are worse sins than lies, if you insist on talking about lies. I give you my word, if you tell about that carpet, Harrison will arrest Jim. Arrest him immediately."

"I'm not going to volunteer anything, Wallie."

"You've got to do more than that. You've got to stick it out. There are always thieves about, and what's to have hindered some one crawling over Jim's fence and getting in by the garage window? The car hadn't been out, according to Amos, from the day Jim took sick; or went to bed, rather. He's not sick. That carpet might have been gone for a week."

I was in a state of greater confusion than ever when he had gone. Judy and Dick were out; on the hillside of the Larimer lot, I suspected, and after Wallie's departure I sat down at my desk and made an outline of the possible case against Jim Blake. I still have it, and it is before me now.

(a) Sarah had tried to communicate with him by call and telephone.

(b) She had finally written him a letter, which he had probably received, but had denied receiving.

(c) On the night she was murdered he did not dress for dinner, but dined early and went out, carrying the sword-cane.

(d) From some place, not his house, he telephoned to Judy, offering her mother's anxiety as an excuse, and asking for Sarah.

(e) He was out that night for some time. He offered no alibi for those hours, intimating that to do so would affect a woman's reputation.

(f) When he returned he still carried the sword-cane, but on the discovery of Sarah's body it had disappeared.

(g) Also, shortly after that discovery, he had taken to his bed, although actually not ill.

From that it was not difficult to go on to the second crime.

(h) Sarah and Florence Gunther knew each other, probably shared some secret knowledge. The paper Judy had found might or might not refer to that knowledge. Certainly one or the other of them possessed some knowledge or some physical property, or both, which had been desperately sought for in each case.

(i) According to Inspector Harrison, the two rooms had been searched by the same individual.

(j) The oil stain on the carpet of Jim's car may not be suspicious in itself, but coupled with the above is highly evidential.

To this list I added certain queries:

(a) Would Jim, under any conceivable circumstances, have attacked Judy?

(b) Was he capable of such sustained cunning as had been shown throughout? The planted footprints, for example?

(c) Had Jim actually worn golf clothes on the night of Sarah's murder? If not, had he had time after his telephone message to break into my house? Fifteen minutes, or at most twenty, was all he had had.

(d) Was Sarah in Jim's house for the three hours still unaccounted for?

And under the heading "Florence Gunther":

(a) Did Jim know her?

(b) Was Jim the visitor testified to by the colored woman at the Bassett house?

(c) Why had so cunning a murderer overlooked the oil stain in the car?

I studied this last.

Surely were Jim guilty, lying there in his bed he would have gone over inch by inch the ground he had covered; have thought of every detail, have followed his every act, searched for the possible loose thread in his fabric.

He knew he was under suspicion. He had only to raise himself in his bed to see that figure across the street. Then why would he have left that stain in the car? Why not have burned the carpet? Burned the car?

There was more than that. He was definitely under suspicion, and there had been a city-wide search for the "death car," as the press called it. But either the police had not found that stain, or they had chosen deliberately to ignore it. Why? Jim Blake and a box of matches could at any time destroy that evidence.

It was too much for me. And to add to my anxieties Joseph told me that day that the maids were talking of leaving. Ever since Norah had found the kitchen poker in the laundry the haunting of the house had been an accepted matter, and it was finally getting on their nerves.

Yet the remainder of the day was quiet enough, on the surface. Since Wednesday night Judy and Dick had been working over the house clocks at intervals, and that Sunday was no exception. I have no doubt that the servants thought them slightly mad.

One by one the clocks were taken into the library, and there investigated. By and large, I had quite a collection of odd springs and wheels, and Dick would sit there over his wreckage, his hair rumpled, and try to reassort what Judy called "the innards."

"Now where the devil does that go?"

"Don't be such an ass! Right there."

"It doesn't fit. Try it yourself, since you know so much."

And with this very wrangling, which was the cloak to hide their deeper feelings—after the fashion of youth today—they would be making love to each other. They would jeer at each other, their mouths hard and their eyes soft.

"Keep quiet! How can I do anything if you jerk my arm?"

"Well, you're so damned clumsy."

The final result, even the servants' alarm clocks having been investigated, was that the establishment ran rather erratically. Meals were at queer hours, and I remember that on that very Sunday, with nobody the wiser, we found that we had breakfasted at eleven o'clock and lunched at half past three.

Then that Sunday night at eleven o'clock, or as near that as our ruined time system allowed me to judge, Katherine called up from New York.

Howard had had another attack. He was better, but she wanted Judy at home.

Judy left the next morning. Dick was working and so I took her to the station, and on the way there I gathered that she and Dick had reached an *impasse* in their love affair. She stated it quite flatly, after her fashion.

"He's crazy about me," she said, "but I'm a child of the rich! If he condescends to marry me I'm to live on his salary, and a bit he has outside! It's absurd! It's sublime! It's perfectly barbaric these days for a man to insist on supporting a wife. It's childish vanity; the great male 'I am.'"

It was quite characteristic of her that she should be crying at the moment. But she wanted no sympathy, and I gave her none.

"If you'd rather have things than have Dick—"

"Oh, to the devil with things. It's the principle of the thing. He'd deprive me to nurse his own vanity."

Well, it is a problem which is confronting a good many young people today; both of them right and both of them wrong. I had no solution, and whatever their troubles it had not affected Dick's feeling toward her, for he came in to see me that night, out of sheer habit.

"Tried to pass by," he said, "but the old bus just naturally headed in and stuck its head over the hitching post."

I was glad to see him. I had been very lonely; missing Judy, even missing —to tell the truth—the Inspector, with his blue eyes and his toothpicks and his general air of competence. He had deserted me almost completely for several days.

And in the expansiveness of that hour, then and there I told Dick about the carpet. He was incredulous.

"But see here: the first car the police would examine would be that car."

"So I think. But they may know about it, at that."

"You're sure Amos hasn't been carrying oil in it?"

That had not occurred to me. I felt rather foolish, and the net result of the talk was that Dick saw Amos the next day and learned certain things.

On the night of Florence's death, being a Sunday, he had been out and Jim was alone. But he could not have taken the car out, for Amos carried the key to the small door of the garage from the garden. The main doors to the alley were bolted on the inside.

Not that Dick asked these direct questions. He asked Amos where he was on Sunday night, and if any one could have got at the car.

But Dick was not satisfied. He watched the Negro leave the house on an errand, and then climbed the rear wall into Jim's yard. There he found two interesting facts; the side window into the garage had a broken pane, and it was possible to reach in and unlock the sash. And there were marks on one of the newly painted garden chairs.

He got into the building and examined the car. The driving seat and the one next to it were leather and could be washed, but there were no blood stains.

"Amos doesn't watch the mileage," he said, "so he doesn't know whether the car was out or not. But he does suspect that the gas is lower than it ought to be."

He did, however, discover that Amos had carried no oil in the rear of the car. He had said to him:

"What's all this about the carpet being missing? You've done away with it yourself, haven't you? Spilled something on it?"

"No, sir!" said Amos. "I never carry nothing back there. Mr. Blake's mighty particular about that car, sir."

All of which, important as it was, did not help us at all. Nothing was clearer than that Jim himself, locked out of the garage, might have placed a garden chair under the window, broken the pane, and taken his car out himself on Sunday night.

That was on Tuesday, the tenth of May. Sarah had been dead for three weeks, and Florence Gunther for ten days. Apparently the police had found nothing whatever, and we ourselves had nothing but that cryptic cipher, which was not a cipher at all but a key.

I daresay I should have shown it to the police; but already I had done a reckless thing with the carpet and I was uneasy. Then too the Inspector had ceased his almost daily visits, although I saw him once on the Larimer lot, poking about with a stick and the faithful Simmons trotting at his heels. But he did not come to the house, and soon—on Wednesday morning, to be exact—I was to receive a message which made me forget it entirely for the time.

Howard Somers was dead.

CHAPTER XIII

So FAR I am aware that I have painted a small canvas of the family; only Judy, Wallie and myself, with a bit of Katherine. As Laura was never involved, it is unnecessary to enlarge on her. She remained in Kansas City, busy with her children, mildly regretful over Sarah but not actively grieved.

The one figure I have not touched is Howard Somers. Perhaps this is because I never understood him particularly, never greatly liked him. Katherine's passion for him had always mystified me.

But Howard was to add his own contribution to our mystery, and that by the simple act of dying. It was not unexpected, although Katherine had sturdily refused to accept it, or to face its possibility. I fancy that there must have been times after that almost fatal attack the summer before when she was abroad, when he must have wanted to talk to her. There are many things in the heart and mind of a man facing death which must long for expression.

But I know from Judy that her mother never let him speak. It was as though, by admitting the fact, she would bring it closer.

"We really ought to paint the place at Southampton, before we go up next summer," she would say.

And her eyes would defy him, dare him to intimate that there might be no next summer for him.

All this I was to learn from Judy later on, trying perplexedly to understand the situation among the three of them, and that strange silence of Howard's about matters which concerned them all.

"Probably he wanted to tell her, poor darling," she said. "But how could he? She wouldn't let him. It was like Wallie, only worse. She wouldn't speak about Wallie, you know."

"Do you think he was seeing Wallie?"

She shrugged her shoulders.

"He must have been, but he never said anything. He never even told her that Wallie had been with him when he took sick last summer. I suppose he didn't want to hurt her."

And, without being aware of it, she had drawn a picture for me which was profoundly to affect my judgment later on; of the barrier Katherine had for years been erecting between Howard and his son, and of a relationship there perhaps closer than she imagined. The two driven to meetings practically clandestine, and Wallie with Margaret's charm, her eyes, much of her beauty, making his definite claim on his father's affection.

A conversation I was to have with Doctor Simonds later on was to confirm this.

"Whatever their trouble had been," he said, "they had patched it up. Wallie was there every day. For a night or two he slept there, in the suite. Later on he relieved the nurse for a daily walk. He was Johnny on the spot all through."

He had insisted on knowing his father's condition, and had gone rather pale when he learned it.

"How long?"

"A year. Two years. Nobody can say. It might even be longer."

But that was some time later.

Howard had died on Tuesday night, or rather some time early on Wednesday morning. A footman called me to the telephone, but it was, of all people in the world, Mary Martin who spoke to me.

"I am sorry to have bad news for you," she began, and went on to tell me. Mr. Somers had seemed fairly well during the evening. Miss Judy had sat with him until after eleven. At eleven Evans, his valet, had brought a whisky and soda and placed it in his bedroom, and a short time after that Judy had gone to bed.

Katherine had found him in the morning, in his dressing gown and slippers, lying across the bed as he had fallen.

I took the eleven o'clock train and was at the apartment at something after two that afternoon. Mary was in the hall when I was admitted, her red head flaming over her decorous black frock. She was talking competently and quietly with what I gathered was an undertaker's assistant, and she greeted me with considerable manner.

"Mrs. Somers is trying to get some rest," she said. "Have you lunched, or shall I order something for you?"

"I have lunched, Mary. When did it happen?"

"The doctors think between three and four this morning. It was his heart."

"Then there will be no inquest?"

"Inquest?" I thought she looked at me strangely, as though I had shocked her. "No. It was not unexpected."

She went on, as she led me to my room. The doctors had not been surprised. He had died very quietly, that was one comforting thing. And she had notified the family. She had called up Mr. Blake, and had telegraphed Laura. Also—she hoped this was all right—she had sent a wire to Mr. Walter.

"Why not?" I said rather sharply. "He is his son. And is Mr. Blake coming?"

"He will try to be here for the funeral."

Judy was shut away with Katherine, who seemed to be dazed and entirely unprepared. In my room I had time to think. Mary was there, apparently at home; and as Judy had predicted, Maude Palmer was gone. She had worked fast, I reflected, had Mary Martin. She had been out of my house less than a week, and there she was.

I know now what happened, how it came about. Katherine has told me.

On the Friday before Mary had called at the apartment and asked for Katherine. Katherine was dictating letters in that small room off the great drawing room which she likes to call her study. She went out and Mary was waiting in the hall, soft voiced and assured. Within the next half hour she had told her things we had never dreamed she knew, about the sword-cane, for example, and Jim's refusal to alibi himself the night of Sarah's murder. She knew—or guessed—that he was not ill but hiding, and then, bending forward and speaking cautiously, she told her that the carpet was missing from Jim's car.

Katherine was stunned.

"How do you know that?" she demanded sharply. "Amos, I suppose."

"Partly Amos. Partly my own eyes. Miss Bell tried to burn it, but it didn't burn. When I went down to breakfast the cook told me the poker was missing, and I found it in the cellar. So I looked about, and the carpet was there. It was in the furnace."

"You'd swear to that?"

"Not necessarily," said Mary, and sat waiting for Katherine to comprehend that.

Within an hour Katherine had dismissed poor Maude Palmer, who had been her secretary for five years, giving her two months' salary in advance, and the next morning Mary Martin was threading a new ribbon into the machine in that small neat room where Katherine attended to the various duties of a woman of wealth and position.

What were her thoughts as she sat there? Was she exultant or depressed? She may have been frightened. Indeed, I think now that she was, for some time during that day she asked Katherine not to tell me she was there.

"Why?" Katherine asked. "Miss Bell would be glad to know that you are in a good position."

"She would think I had used what I know, to my own advantage."

Katherine gave that faint cold smile of hers, and the girl flushed. But in the end she agreed to say nothing, for a time at least.

"Of course, when Miss Judy comes back—" she said.

"It may be all right then," Mary said quietly, and turned back to her machine.

Incomprehensible, that girl, now as I look back; hiding as definitely and more safely than Jim was hiding. She never gave even Katherine the address of her room downtown. She must have felt safe too for the first time, for on that night, as we know now, the night of the day she was engaged, she walked out on the Brooklyn Bridge and dropped something into the water. She had not tied a string around it, and as it fell the paper blew away.

Then she walked uptown to a branch post office, bought a stamped envelope and sent a note to Wallie. Not giving him her address; just a line or two. After that she went to her room and "slept very well."

Anyhow there she was, established, settled in that handsome Park Avenue apartment where a dozen servants moved quietly about in the early hours of the day, later on to disappear and only emerge on the ringing of bells or the ritual of the table. What she felt I have no idea. She adapted herself, I fancy. She had learned a good bit while with me. But she was there for a definite purpose. That over she moved on. Vanished. A queer girl, I think now; not entirely explicable, even by the light of what we now know.

I settled down, then, to the hushed routine of a house in mourning. Katherine did not appear. People called, spoke in low voices, went away. Flowers began to arrive, and Mary entered the names of the senders neatly in a small book. She was to stay there at night now, until after the funeral.

I thought she looked changed, not so pretty and rather worn. Once, carrying some cards into her room to be entered, I found her with her head on her desk, and I thought that she was crying. But she was not crying. Her eyes were defiant and rather hard.

I had not the faintest idea that there was any mystery about Howard's death until I talked to Judy. Then I was fairly stunned.

And as the apartment itself figures in that story of hers, I must begin by describing it.

It is of the duplex type; on the lower floor are the large drawing room, a small living room, a library, and Katherine's study. Behind these, along a corridor, lie the long dining room, the pantry, kitchen and servants' rooms, and above, connecting by a front and rear staircase, are the family rooms; Katherine's boudoir connecting with her bedroom, Howard's study opening from his. Judy's room, guest chambers, a room for Katherine's maid and a small sewing and pressing room opening from it, constitute the remainder of that floor.

On that Tuesday evening, then, Judy met Mary in the lower hall preparing to go. Judy was resentful of her presence in the house and inclined to be short with her, but Mary detained her.

"I don't think your father ought to be alone at night," she said.

Judy eyed her.

"And why?"

"Because he's a very sick man. If he—if he should take sick in the night, he mightn't be able to call for help."

"We have no intention of neglecting him," said Judy shortly, and turned away.

But she was worried nevertheless, and she spent that evening with Howard in the study off his bedroom. He had a heavy cold and was rather uncomfortable. Mostly he read, and when at eleven o'clock Evans, his valet, brought the highball and placed it beside the bed in the bedroom, she prepared to leave him.

What followed she had not yet told her mother.

The telephone rang, and Judy herself answered it. It was for Howard, apparently a long distance call, and he appeared rather surprised when he answered it.

"Tonight?" he said. "Where are you? It's pretty late. You'll be a couple of hours yet."

But in the end he agreed, and Judy said he seemed thoughtful as he hung up the receiver.

"Your Uncle Jim," he said. "He's motoring up. I thought he was ill."

"He has been," said Judy, thinking hard. "I wish you wouldn't see him, father. He'll upset you."

"Why?"

"I don't know. He's in trouble, father. Of course it's silly, but the police are trying to connect him with Sarah, and all that."

"Nonsense! Why should he want to do away with Sarah? It's an outrage."

She wanted to wait up, but he said Jim had been very urgent that his visit be kept a secret. He proposed to come in by the service entrance and up the stairs, and she was to unlock that door on the floor below. He called up the night watchman while she was still there and asked him to admit a visitor there, or better still, to open the door onto the alley and go away. He was smiling when he hung up the receiver.

"Probably thinks I'm receiving my bootlegger," he said.

"Or a lady, father!" said Judy. "I think I'll tell mother!"

"Your mother is not to know. He's very insistent about that."

She persuaded him to go to bed and see Jim there, and after he was settled she went in and herself gave him a book and fixed his light.

"Door unlocked?" he asked.

"All fixed."

He had not touched the whisky in the glass at that time. She remembered that.

She kissed him good-night and went to her own room. But she was very uneasy. How Jim had escaped surveillance did not interest her, but she was fearful for Howard; Jim bursting in on him with that whole hideous story, perhaps begging for help to escape, perhaps—she says this entered her mind—perhaps even confessing.

She heard no footsteps by two o'clock, and she dozed off. At three she wakened suddenly, sat up and finally got up. She went along the corridor to her father's door, and listened. She could hear voices, one low and quiet, her father's louder and irritated.

Shortly after that she had heard a sort of thud, "Like somebody falling," she said with a shiver. She had sat up and listened, but it was not repeated, and soon after that she heard Jim come out and close the door.

She went to sleep after that.

At nine o'clock the next morning she was wakened by a shriek and the sound of a chair being overturned. Quick as she had been to throw on a dressing gown and run out, Mary Martin was before her. She was standing staring into Howard's room, where Katherine lay in a faint on the floor, and Howard was quite peacefully dead across his bed.

He was in his dressing gown, a thing of heavy dark brocade, and his face according to Judy was very quiet and very peaceful. Whatever his last thoughts had been, if indeed he had any, they were wiped clean.

Some weeks afterward Inspector Harrison was to give me a little talk on just such things.

"There is no expression on a dead face," he said. "In two minutes it's wiped clean, like a slate. All this stuff about expressions of horror on murdered people is pure nonsense. I've seen a fellow beaten to death, and he looked as peaceful as though he'd died in his bed."

Judy called for help, and the servants flocked in. Katherine's maid, a hysterical Frenchwoman, was entirely helpless, and it was Mary Martin who threw up the windows and ran into Howard's bedroom for water.

"But she dropped the glass," said Judy, gazing at me with reddened eyes. "She took the highball glass from beside the bed and dropped it on the bathroom floor. It broke into bits. I want to know why she did that. There were glasses in the bathroom."

I tried to reassure her. After all, her father had been a dying man for some time. And any one might drop a glass. But she was not satisfied.

"How did she get there so quickly?" she demanded. "It's as though she was waiting for it."

I advised her to say nothing, especially to Katherine in her grief. But she only made a small gesture.

"She'll know soon enough that Uncle Jim was here," she said. "The night watchman saw him. And he told Evans this morning when he heard that father was–gone. All the servants know it, probably."

"He recognized your Uncle Jim?"

"I don't know. He knows somebody was here."

"And the doctors? They think everything is all right? I mean, that it was his heart?"

"Why would they think anything else?" she said drearily. "If it was poison–"

"Hush, Judy."

I got through the remainder of the day somehow; not for years had we faced an emergency without Sarah, and I missed her now.

Sarah would have taken hold; would have put Katherine to bed matter of factly and with authority, have driven out that hysterical Frenchwoman who was wringing her hands in the servants' hall, have given us all sedatives or got the doctor to order them, and then flatfootedly and as if death were as normal as living, have read a book until we were all safely asleep.

But Sarah was gone. Florence Gunther was gone. And now Howard.

CHAPTER XIV

WALLIE ARRIVED that evening. Katherine was still shut in her room. Now and then Judy would wander in, but Katherine was absorbed in her grief, alone with it. She would kiss Judy and then forget she was there.

But she made a ghastly mistake when she refused to see Wallie. One gesture from her then, one bit of recognition of their common grief, their common loss, and things would have been different.

Whatever might be his weaknesses, Wallie had cared about his father, and he looked stricken when I went in to see him. His face was blank and expressionless, and he had little to say. He sat slumped in his chair, and for the first time I saw a hint of gray in his hair. He was only in his middle thirties, but he might have been fifty as he sat there.

"It was the heart, of course?"

"Yes. It was bound to come before long, anyhow, Wallie."

He seemed to hesitate, to bring his next question out with an effort.

"Then there was no post-mortem?"

"No."

"I asked for *her*, but I suppose she won't see me."

"She's not seeing any one, Wallie. I haven't seen her myself."

"Does she know I'm here?" he insisted.

"I told her, yes. Through the door. She's quite shut away, Wallie."

But I did not tell him that I had urged her and had been refused. It had seemed to me that death ought to wipe out old angers, old jealousies. But she had been coldly stubborn, would not even unlock her door.

"I have no intention of seeing him, Elizabeth. Do go away."

"Shall I tell him you will see him later? He seems to think it is important."

"Nothing is important, and I never want to see him again."

Of course that was pure hysteria, but no man has ever understood a woman's hysteria.

Mary Martin came in just then with a number of telegrams, but he did not so much as look at her. She glanced at him, waited a moment, then put down the telegrams and went quietly away.

"Give her a little time, Wallie," I begged him.

"No," he said. "She's had her chance. I'm through."

His face had hardened. It was as though he had come with some overture of peace, and the impulse had died as I looked at him. He was standing in the big drawing room, with its tapestries, its famous paintings, its well-known collection of eighteenth century French furniture, and I saw him look around as if appraising it. Then he smiled unpleasantly.

"She has good taste," he said. "Good taste but bad judgment. I daresay I can see *him?* After all, he was my father."

I asked no one's permission for that, and he had had about five minutes alone with Howard before he left. Judy took him to the door and left him there. It must have been five minutes of pure agony, knowing what we know now, but he came out quietly enough.

When he left I thought I saw Mary waiting in the hall, but she disappeared when she saw me. She was staying for the night, working late in order to attend to all the detail, and I could still hear her at her desk when at last I went up to bed.

But I did not sleep. I had taken two cups of coffee, and my mind was racing like a mill stream. The news that Jim Blake had been with Howard, that for all his pretended illness he had driven his car the night before to New York, arriving stealthily after that long distance call, had been a profound shock.

True, that might have been explicable. He was in great trouble. He might have felt the need of Howard, of some balanced judgment. But suppose that the shock of his story had destroyed Howard? Suppose he had died before Jim left?

Suppose the thud Judy had heard had been his body as it fell? Then why had Jim slipped away like a thief in the night? His own sister in a room beyond, with only her boudoir intervening, and he had not called her.

It seemed monstrous, inhuman.

Then of course Judy's suspicions played their part. We would probably never know the truth. Unless we told Katherine the whole story she would never permit an examination of the body, and to tell her the story was to involve her own brother.

So I turned and re-turned. How long could this visit be kept under cover? Not long. The servants knew, and from the servants to Mary Martin was only a step. Then, when it was known, what? How would the police argue? That Jim had made a confession to Howard, and that the shock had killed him? Certainly they could argue that this secret visit of Jim's was not the act of a consciously innocent man.

But what did any of them know, after all? That Howard had had a visitor, but not necessarily that visitor's identity. Or did Mary suspect who that visitor had been? Moving in her mysterious way among us all, never of us but among us, unfathomable, shrewd, unscrupulous when she chose to be, she had her own methods, her own purposes.

Suppose then that she made inquiries downstairs? Suppose she had talked to the night watchman, got a description of the visitor, was proposing to give that description to Wallie?

And Wallie perhaps already suspicious, asking about a post-mortem, maybe about to demand one.

Still, she had broken the glass. Why should she do that? What picture had been in her mind? Did she suspect or did she know of something—a powder perhaps—shaken into that glass beside the bed, and Howard drinking it? Sitting there, talking maybe, and drinking it.

Where was the glass now? She had broken it, but the pieces would be somewhere about. Suppose they were, and Wallie was suspicious? Suppose he had gone to the police that night, and early morning would find the trash-can examined, and Jim's guilt proved beyond a doubt?

I thought that it would kill Katherine.

Outside it was raining, a heavy spring shower. I got out of bed and paced the floor in my bare feet, to the accompaniment of heavy thunder and the beating of the rain on neighboring roofs. Suppose I got those pieces of glass and disposed of them? Hid them and then carried them off? Dropped them in a river or out of the window of a railway carriage? Innocent or guilty, they would be gone.

Looking back, I know that I was not entirely normal that night, but I was on the verge of desperation. I was ready to pay any price for peace. It did not even seem to be important that Jim Blake might be a cold-blooded and deadly killer; what mattered was that it should not be known, that we be allowed to go back to our quiet lives once more, that no scandal break to involve us all.

So, thinking or not thinking, I put on a dressing gown and went quietly down the stairs.

As I have said, the dining room, kitchen, pantries and so on are at the rear of a long hall. One passes from the dining room through a butler's pantry into the kitchen, and beyond the kitchen, opening from a rear hallway, is a small cement-floored room in which is the dumb-waiter by which refuse cans and so on are lowered to the basement, there to be collected. This room I knew well. During the day it was there that the boxes had been taken as the flowers were unwrapped, and when last I saw it that day it had been waist deep in paper.

To this room, therefore, I went. Save the dumb-waiter, there is no access to it other than by the one door, and I felt my way along in the darkness, fearful of rousing the servants. But outside the door I stopped, almost paralyzed with amazement. Some one was in the room. There was the stealthy movement of paper, the sound of a lid being fitted cautiously onto a can.

It took all my courage to fling that door open, and for a moment, after the darkness, the blaze of light almost blinded me. Then I saw, sitting calmly on the floor, Mary Martin. She was looking at me with a half smile, and the light on her red hair was positively dazzling.

"Good heavens, how you scared me!" she said.

"What on earth are you doing here?"

"I couldn't sleep," she said, "and I got to worrying about a card. That bunch of orchids and lilies of the valley—the card's been thrown away."

She had emptied one of the trash-cans onto a paper before her. Now she ran her fingers through the debris, the flotsam and jetsam of the day; a chipped cup, bits of string, old envelopes, even sweepings from the floors. And suddenly she picked something up and waved it before me.

"Here it is," she said. "Now I can sleep in peace."

I do not know why I felt that she was acting. Perhaps the open window had something to do with it; the rain driving in and blowing over her, and that assumption of hers that this was as it should be; that she liked sitting in that chaos and allowing the rain to wet one of those alluring negligees which she affected.

"Why don't you close that window?"

She drew her kimono about her, and got up.

"I will," she said. "Not that I suppose it matters here."

And then, at the window with her back to me, I saw her release her clutch on the kimono, so that it blew out into the room, and I saw her lower the window with one hand. I knew then that she had dropped something over the sill.

And I saw another thing. There were no bits of glass among the trash on that paper. If she had thrown them out, as I suspected, the rain would wash them clean of evidence. They were gone.

But lying in bed later on I was bewildered beyond thought. Had this unfathomable girl lain awake as I had, reached the same conclusion, acted on the same impulse? Or was there something more sinister there, some knowledge I did not possess which she did? And once again I was back in my house at home, hearing that desperate weeping of hers.

"It's nothing. I was low in my mind. That's all."

I have rather a confused memory of the next two days. I recall that early the next morning I made an excursion into the courtyard of the building, but without much result. It was still raining, and although here and there I could see very small pieces of glass, there was nothing large enough to be worth salvage. Which was not surprising, considering that if I was right they had had a sheer drop of twelve stories.

Dick Carter appeared on Thursday. I did not know he had come until I saw him in the library with Judy. I happened to walk in on them, and I saw at once that things were not well between them. He was standing at a window, staring out, and Judy was huddled in a chair.

"I don't see what difference it makes," she was saying.

"Don't you? Well, I do."

Nevertheless, it was from Dick that I got the first intimation that some one besides myself was suspicious of Howard's death. Judy had disappeared, but the boy stayed around after she had gone, uncomfortable but apparently determined.

"I suppose it's all right?" he said to me. "No chance of anything queer, eh?"

"What do you think?"

"I don't know. Suppose Blake told him something and the shock killed him; that's not murder. That is, supposing it *was* Blake."

"Good heavens! Do you think it was some one else?"

"Well, figure it out for yourself. Blake's sick, or he says he is. But he comes here in the middle of the night, driving his own car for ninety-odd miles, sees Mr. Somers and gets back, presumably, at daylight or thereabouts. That's some drive for a sick man. Then all this secrecy. Why? The police couldn't have stopped him if he'd wanted to take a train and come here. They've got nothing on him yet. All he had to do was to pack a bag and come. Or hire an ambulance! He's coming for the funeral, isn't he?"

I sat down. My knees were shaking. Dick looked at his watch.

"What times does the night watchman come on duty?"

"I haven't an idea."

"Well, he's the boy to see."

I made up my mind then to tell him about Mary and the glass, and I did so. He listened attentively, but when I told him she had actually found the card, and that I was not certain she had thrown anything from the window, he made rather light of it.

"Wait a minute," he said. "Now either we've got another crime or we haven't. In the first place, who would want to kill a man who had only a few months to live anyhow? But grant that. Grant that there was poison in the glass. Something quick, like cyanide. First we have to admit that Howard Somers, drinking a highball, is talking to some one he knows, and trusts. He's not scared. He's drinking a highball. But you've got to go further; you've got to figure that Mary Martin knew he was going to be murdered, and how. Yet she warns Judy that he's not to be left alone at night. Only did she do that?"

"I haven't an idea," I said dismally.

"I suppose there's no chance of a post-mortem?"

"Not unless we told Mrs. Somers; and not then. It's her brother who is involved."

Naturally we said nothing to Judy of all this, and the day passed quietly enough, people coming and going, more flowers, and Mary keeping her neat entries and moving decorously about. Once I caught her eyes on me, a curious speculative look in them, and I thought she was depressed all of that day.

Late in the afternoon she asked to be allowed to go home for the night, and I told her to go. She remained to dinner and left at nine o'clock, and at nine-fifteen Dick called me on the telephone.

"Listen," he said, "I'm at a drugstore around the corner. I wanted to tell you; there may be something in what we discussed today."

"Yes?"

"The lady in question—do you get that?"

"Yes. All right."

"She's been interviewing the night watchman. Interesting, isn't it? Just thought I'd tell you, so you can keep an eye on things."

He hung up the receiver, and I was left to make of that what I could.

I remember that Alex Davis was there that night, Howard's attorney. He was settled comfortably in the library with a glass of old port at his elbow, and what with the port and probably an excellent dinner tucked away, he was unusually talkative. A fat man, Alex Davis, with small sharp black eyes set in a broad expanse of face.

"I suppose you know," he said, "that there will be a great deal of money. More, I fancy, than any one realizes. Poor Howard was a secretive man."

"I suppose he left a will?"

"Yes. A very fair one, I think. He's taken care of the servants and certain charities, and there is provision too for Mrs. Somers' brother."

"And Wallie?" I asked.

He cleared his throat.

"He has already done a good bit for Wallie. Certain businesses which failed, and last summer certain notes to be paid. But there is a very fair arrangement; a trust fund with a substantial income. Not large. Substantial. Of course this is in confidence. I am one of the executors."

And I saw that this last pleased him; that it was a vote of confidence, as well as providing certain emoluments; that already he saw his name in the press everywhere; the size of the estate, the inheritance tax royalty calculated. "Mr. Alexander Davis and the Guaranty Trust Company, executors."

He leaned back and patted his substantial abdomen.

"Howard was a money maker," he said. "A lot of people are going to be surprised."

I was not listening very attentively. I was thinking of Mary and of that conversation with the night watchman, and after Alex Davis had taken his complacent departure I wandered into Katherine's study and looked about me.

The desk was cleared. There was no sign of those small personal belongings which she was wont to keep by her. Nor were they in the drawers of the desk, or any place else.

It came to me with a shock of surprise that Mary Martin had gone, and gone for good.

Jim arrived at noon the next day, for the funeral. Save for a certain pallor—he had been in the house for over three weeks—he seemed much as usual; impeccably dressed, with a black tie and a black band on the left sleeve of his coat.

I had no chance whatever to talk to him. He went at once to Katherine's room, and their luncheon was served to them there.

Only during the solemn process of carrying Howard's body downstairs was he seen at all until after the services. But that seems to have been sufficient. Some time in that slow and affecting progress Jim came face to face with an individual whom I was later to know as Charles Parrott, a man of middle age, with a cap drawn low over his face. This Parrott was carrying in the chairs usually provided for such occasions, and was opening them and placing them in rows, and as Jim passed him he gave him a long steady look. Jim did not notice him, apparently.

I was not there at the time. The name Charles Parrott meant nothing to me. But in due time Charles Parrott was to play his own part in our tragedy, to make his own contribution to the tragic *dénouement* which was to follow. For Charles Parrott, introduced by Dick by methods of which I have no knowledge, was the night watchman of the building. And he identified Jim Blake as being of the same build and general appearance as that visitor to Howard whom he had admitted two nights before.

True, he stubbornly refused under oath to make a positive statement. "He's the same build. He looks like him. But that's as far as I go."

So Jim moved about, unsuspicious, changing the flowers, softening the lights, and Parrott watched him. He disappeared when Jim had gone upstairs again, to remain with Katherine and Judy during the services. Wallie was not asked to join them. He was left to sit alone, where he chose. A cruel thing, perhaps; a stupid thing certainly. Katherine had taken the strongest affection he had ever felt, the deepest grief, and flung them back in his face.

So he sat alone, rigid and cold during the services, and stood alone at his father's grave. However he had wavered before, some time then he made his decision. He went that night to call on Alex Davis, sitting complacent and smug in his library, and slammed out only a half hour later, leaving Alex in a state bordering on apoplexy.

Half an hour later Alex Davis was frenziedly ringing the bell of the apartment and demanding to see Katherine. He was admitted and taken up to her, but Judy and I knew nothing of all this until later.

Judy had determined to talk to Jim, and asked me to be present in the library.

"I can't stand it any longer," she said. "He was here. Why doesn't he speak up? He must know that watchman saw him. Even if father was–was alive when he left, why doesn't he say something?"

But Jim's reaction to her first question was a surprise to both of us. He denied, immediately, categorically, and almost violently, that he had made any visit to Howard Somers on the night of his death.

"Here?" he said. "Why, it's madness. Why should I have come like that? You've lost your good common sense, Judy."

"Some one was here and used your name. He telephoned on the way, from somewhere in the country."

When she had told her story, however, he looked ghastly. Not only was there the implication that Howard had been murdered, but there was the terrible possibility which the situation held for himself. What was he to do, where to turn? To go to Katherine and demand that the body be exhumed? And that with the police watching him, and maybe poison to be found? All that he must have thought of, sitting there so neat and dapper in his chair.

"It's terrible," he said. "It's all terrible. And this night watchman? He says he recognized me?"

"He says the man was your height and build."

Suddenly he was savagely angry. "And so this fellow, this Parrott—he's in the secret, is he? He's been brought here to look me over! Good God, Judy, do you want to send me to the chair? I wasn't here. How the hell could I get here? I've been sick for weeks. If somebody came here that night, using my name and impersonating me, he was a liar and an impostor, and before God I believe he was a murderer too. Why should I have come here in the night? I could come at any time."

Then he quieted, although he was still shaking.

"Does your mother know anything of all this?"

"Nothing."

"Then keep it from her. You can do that much. She is in great trouble."

"So am I in great trouble," said Judy bitterly. "But I suppose that doesn't matter."

He looked at her.

"You believed it, did you? Do you still believe it?"

"I don't know. No, of course not."

"Judy," he said, more gently, "what motive could I have? What possible reason? Your father was my friend. To put the thing boldly, what could I possibly gain by his death? By any of these deaths?"

And as if in answer to his question a footman knocked at the door and said that Katherine wanted to see him in her room.

I have no picture of that scene, but I can see it: Katherine frozen in her chair and Alex Davis walking the floor, and after a habit of his snapping his fingers as he walked. Into that scene Jim was projected, and in forcible language he was told what Wallie had said.

Briefly, Wallie had claimed that, during his illness the summer before, his father had made a second will. That this will was in Howard's safe deposit box at the bank in New York, and the copy in the hands of Waite and Henderson, Mr. Waite having personally drawn it, here in my own city.

By this will, Wallie received no trust fund and no annuity, but a full half of the estate, and the previous will had been revoked. The new will made no provision whatever, either for Sarah or for Jim.

"He may be lying," said Jim, still apparently confused.

But Alex Davis snapped his fingers with excitement, and said that if so it was fairly circumstantial lying.

"He's even got the names of the witnesses," he said, and drawing a slip of paper from his pocket he read them aloud. "Sarah Gittings and Florence Gunther."

I believe it was then that Jim collapsed.

Naturally I knew nothing of this at the time, nor did Judy. Both Katherine and Jim were still shut in their rooms when I left early the next morning.

But I was sufficiently dismayed and confused. If we were to believe Jim—and I did—then the possibility of a third murder was very real. And once more, sitting in the train, I endeavored to fit together the fragments of that puzzle. I saw Howard, that night, waiting in his room, settled in his bed, the highball beside him, a book in his hand. Getting up to admit his visitor, finding it was not Jim, but making no outcry. Still calm, putting on his dressing gown and slippers, talking. Judy had heard them talking.

Some one he knew, then; knew and trusted. Was it Wallie? Wallie was not unlike Jim in build, although taller and slimmer. Might not that be the answer, and no poison, no third murder. A talk between father and son, and then Wallie going and the heart attack after he had gone.

I admit that this comforted me. I sat back and tried to read.

Shortly before the train drew in to the station Dick Carter came through the car. He looked depressed, but he forced a smile when he saw me.

"Well," he said, "I'm back on the job! Even funerals can't last forever."

He sat down in the empty chair next to mine, and said that Judy had telephoned him of Jim's denial.

"She believes him," he said. "In that case—this Martin girl seems to be fairly vital. It begins to look as though she's the key, doesn't it? Take that glass, for instance. She thought fast that morning and she was still thinking that night. It's not coincidence, all that glass stuff. Get why she did that, and we've got somewhere. Where does she come in in all this, anyhow?"

"I wish I knew."

"Tell me something about her," he said, leaning forward. "Who is she? What do you know about her?"

"Nothing, really. She answered an advertisement last fall. I tried her out, and she was efficient. Very. She had no local references."

"And on that you took her into the house? To live?"

"Not at first. But she was really very capable, and sometimes I work at night. I rather drifted into it."

He was silent for some time. Then he made a circle on a piece of paper and marked it around with perhaps a dozen dots. It bore a rough relation to a clock-face, but without the hands, when he held it out to me.

"This dial thing," he said. "It may not refer to a clock, you know. It might be a safe. You haven't a safe in the house, have you?"

"No."

"A safe, or something resembling a clock, but not necessarily a clock. Something round. Would that mean anything to you? A picture, maybe? Have you any round pictures, with nails at the back?"

"One or two. I can examine them."

The train was drawing in. He helped me into my wraps, and we sat down again while we were being slowly moved into the station.

"I suppose," he said, not looking directly at me, "that you realize what all this has done to me?"

"To you!"

"About Judy. I'll be nobody's kept husband, and Judy's got a couple of millions or so. I fade, that's all."

"Judy has a right to a vote on that, hasn't she?"

"She's voted. She'll keep the money."

"I don't believe it."

"Well, the equivalent of that. She says I'm a poor mean-spirited creature to refuse to let her support me in luxury. She says it takes a strong man to marry money, and I'm weak or I'd do it."

Then the train stopped.

I was glad to get home, to find Robert at the station and Joseph at the open door. I like my servants; I have to live with them, and so when I do not like them they must go. And the house was cool and quiet, after New York. I relaxed at once under Joseph's care; the well-laid tea table, the small hot rolls, the very smoothness and greenness of the lawns outside the windows. For the first time since Sarah's death I felt secure. Surely now it was over; we had had our three tragedies, according to the old superstition.

I leaned back and looked at Joseph, and for the first time I realized that he was pale, almost waxy.

"Have you been ill, Joseph?"

"No, madam. I have had an accident."

"An accident? What sort of an accident?"

But as it turned out, Joseph had had no accident. Dragged out of him, and later corroborated by the maids, came the story of an attack in broad daylight so mysterious and so brutal that it made my blood run cold.

The story was this: on the afternoon of the day I left for New York, he had allowed the women servants to go out. He often did this in my absence, getting himself a supper of sorts, and apparently glad to have his pantry to himself.

The house was locked and Robert was washing the car in the garage. According to Robert, and this was later found to be true, the first knowledge he had of any trouble was at four o'clock that afternoon, when he heard a faint rapping on the pantry window and looking toward the house, saw a bloody head, wavering with weakness, inside.

Robert was frightened. He made no effort to get into the house alone, but summoned a white chauffeur from the garage of my bootlegger neighbor, and the two of them broke open the basement door and rushed up the stairs.

They found Joseph unconscious on the pantry floor, his head bleeding profusely from a bad cut, and as Doctor Simonds later discovered, his body a mass of bruises. It was two hours before he recovered consciousness, and then he could give no description of his assailant.

"I saw and heard nobody," he told me. "I was on the second floor. It looked like rain and I was closing the windows. I had finished that and was about to go down the back staircase when I felt that some one was behind me. But I never saw who it was. The next thing I remember, madam, I was at the foot of the stairs, trying to crawl to the pantry."

And this story of his was borne out by the fact that the maids later found blood on the stairs and a small pool at the bottom.

Doctor Simonds however did not place too much confidence in the story of the attack, when he came in that night to see me.

"Sure he was hurt," he said, with that cheerful descent into the colloquial with which the medical profession soothes its fearful patients and its nervous women. "Surest thing I ever saw. It took four stitches to sew him up! But why assault? Why didn't Joseph catch his rubber heel on something and pitch down those stairs of yours? There are twenty odd metal-edged steps there, and every one got in a bit of work."

"He says he felt that there was some one behind him."

"Exactly. He was stepping off as he turned to look; and why he didn't break that stiff neck of his I don't know. It's a marvel to me that he's up and about."

But Joseph stuck to his story. He had been attacked by some one from the rear, armed either with a club or a chair. And as we know now, he was right. Joseph had indeed been murderously assaulted, and very possibly left for dead.

As it happened, it was during that call of Doctor Simonds' that I first learned of the possibility that Howard had left a second will. He had attended Howard during his illness at the Imperial that summer before, and expressed regret over his death.

"Of course it was bound to come," he said. "He knew it. He was not a man you could deceive, and that attack he had here was a pretty bad one. By the way, did he alter his will at that time? Or do you know?"

"Alter it? I don't know, I'm sure."

"He was thinking of it. Walter had been very attentive to him, and they'd patched up a peace between them. It was rather amusing, in a way. Poor Miss Gittings hated Walter, and she would have kept him out if she could."

"I hope he did change the will," I said, thoughtfully. "After all, his only son—"

"He may, and he may not. I talked it over with Walter, and he said there would be hell to pay if it did happen. He wasn't sure, of course. But he got me to give him a letter, to the effect that his father was capable of drawing such a document; 'not under drugs, or mentally enfeebled.'" He laughed a little. "'Mentally enfeebled,'" he said. "If Howard Somers was mentally enfeebled I wish I had arteriosclerosis!"

But Joseph's injury had made me most uneasy. What was the motive? What had been gained by it? I must confess that once again I considered the possibility of a killer who killed for the sheer lust of murder.

That day I bought a new revolver for Joseph, and moved him to a guest room on the second floor. Before he retired I made the round of the house with him, and even of the garage and the cellars. Then, with my own door locked, I was able to pass a quiet if not an easy night.

But again I did not sleep. I lay in bed with a pencil and a sheet of paper, and tried that night to put together what we knew about this unknown. I wrote down that he was crafty and physically strong; that he had no scruples about taking human life; that he knew my house even to the detail of the air shaft and its window; that he was—at least probably—of the same height and build as Jim Blake; that my dogs knew him; that, although since Sarah's death the front door lock had been changed, he was still able—if Joseph's story were accurate—to enter my house at will; and that his motive, still hidden, had somehow already involved and destroyed Sarah and Florence Gunther and possibly Howard, and might in the end affect others, God only knew who.

I was badly frightened by that time, and when just as I had finished the list I heard the stealthy padding of feet in the hall, I was in a cold sweat of terror. It was only Jock, however, moving restlessly about, with the call of the spring night in his blood and a closed and double-locked front door between him and his kind.

CHAPTER XV

THE NEXT DAY I went through my house, acting on Dick's suggestion. I imagine that the servants thought that our recent tragedies had slightly unbalanced me, as I took down one circular object after another and examined it. One or two old daguerreotypes in round frames I literally ripped open, but at the end of these acts of vandalism I was no wiser than before.

It was that afternoon that I was sent for by the District Attorney; a disquieting interview, with accusation and suppressed anger on his part, and sheer dismay on my own.

"This is a curious case, Miss Bell," he said. "Two horrible crimes have been committed by the same hand, and two attacks, one of them certain; the other, on your butler, at least possible. We have either a maniac loose in the community, or we have a motive so carefully concealed that so far we have not found it. I think there is a motive. Of the two women killed, one was apparently negligible, without background. The other had no background save a certain family, to which she had been loyal and from which she had certainly received a considerable measure of confidence. These two women became friends; the secret of one became the secret of the other. Therefore, granting there was some detrimental knowledge, when one died the other must die. That's simple. But the family in question has done nothing to help the law. It has even withheld certain matters from the police."

"I deny that, absolutely."

"Do you? Is that entirely wise, Miss Bell? If this case comes to trial, and you are put under oath on the witness stand—"

"How can it come to trial? You have made no arrest."

But he ignored that.

"I want to urge you to tell what you know, Miss Bell, as a public duty. You owe that to the community. If there is a man of this description loose, a wholesale murderer, shrewd, without conscience or scruple, defeating justice to serve his own ends, then your obligation lies plain before you."

"I know nothing. If you think you are describing Jim Blake, I do not. He is as innocent as you are."

He bent forward.

"Then why did you burn the carpet from his car? You need not answer that. We know that you did. We are not guessing."

"If you are going to try to convict a man on purely circumstantial evidence—"

"What *is* circumstantial evidence? It is the evidence on which we rely every day of our lives. Your door bell rings; you have not seen anybody at the door, but you know that somebody is there, ringing that bell. That's circumstantial evidence."

He leaned back and spoke more quietly.

"This cane," he said, "the one with the hidden blade. How wide was that blade?"

"It was very narrow; perhaps a half inch at the widest part. It tapered."

"And it had a double cutting edge?"

"I don't remember."

"You haven't seen it since you gave it to Jim Blake?"

"Not since."

"And when did you give it to him?"

"I've already told you that; last March. He had admired it."

"Did he ask for it?"

"Hardly that. He said if I ever wanted to get rid of it, he would take it."

"He dropped in to see you rather often?"

"Not so often. Once a month or so."

"And where did you sit, when he called?"

"In my library, usually."

On my way out I saw Mr. Henderson, of Waite and Henderson, and bowed to him. It seemed to me that he looked worried and upset, but I laid this to the death of Florence and its continuing mystery, and thought no more of it.

That was on Saturday, May the fourteenth, and that night Inspector Harrison came in. He looked tired and rather untidy, and when he took off his overcoat a flashlight fell to the floor.

For some reason he brought it into the library with him, and sat snapping it on and off as he talked. Perhaps he was out of his customary ammunition. He began rather apologetically.

"I've got the habit of dropping in here," he said. "I suppose it's because I like to talk and you're willing to listen."

"I daresay," I observed, "although I had hoped it was due to my personal charm."

That embarrassed him. He smiled rather dubiously, gave me a quick glance, and then proceeded quite calmly to focus the flashlight on my feet.

"You see," he said. "I've been studying those molds I took. It's my belief that they were made with a woman's shoe. Not *that* sort; a big woman's shoe. Flat heeled and sensible, and considerably worn. A woman who walked on the outsides of her feet; maybe bandy legged."

"I assure you, Inspector–"

"No need of it," he said politely. "But before I go I'd like to look over the closets here. Somebody appears to have pretty free access to this house, and it's just possible we'll locate that pair of shoes."

He made no immediate move, however. He surveyed himself rather ruefully.

"I've been tramping about," he explained. "It's a curious thing, but things can be seen at night that can't be seen in daytime. Take blood on furniture. In the daylight it looks like varnish, but in a good electric light it often shows up. Then take marks in the ground. Look at what your car headlights do! I've slowed down for a rut no deeper than my finger."

"And now you have found something?"

"Well, I have," he said. "It's bad news for you, Miss Bell. It's like this; I went to the museum and looked at one of those sword-sticks they have there. They look like other sticks, but there's one difference. The ferrule is open at the bottom. When you put it down on the ground it makes a circle, not a hole. I took it out and tried it. You get the idea, don't you? A ring is what it makes. In the one in the museum the blade is loose, so it makes a ring with a dot in the center. That's the tip of the knife. In yours the blade is hung better. There's only the ring."

I could hardly speak.

"And you've found such rings?"

"A dozen of them. Maybe two dozen. I've got them marked and covered, and tomorrow we'll lift them. I thought I'd better tell you."

"Then Jim–"

"He was there, all right. There are a half dozen of the things in the bridle path between the sewer and the foot of the hill; and there are others on the side of the hill. What's more, I think I have found what stunned Sarah Gittings before she died."

It appears, then, that the examination of poor Sarah's body had shown more than we had known. The wound at the back of her head had been made with a blunt instrument, as we had been told; but the nature of that instrument was unknown. However, inspection had shown in her hair and in the wound itself numerous small fragments of bark from a tree.

"Of course the body had been dragged, and that would account for some of it. But there was bark deeply buried in the tissues. And there was another thing: the blow had been struck from above. The lower side of the wound was torn. Either she had been struck by a very tall man, or she was sitting down. I had to argue like this; we'll leave out the tall man for the minute, and say she was sitting down. Now where does a woman like that sit, if she's out in the open? She's a neat woman, very orderly, and she isn't young. She doesn't sit on the ground. She finds a tree stump, or a fallen tree or a stone, and she sits on that."

But he had been some time in coming to that, and Florence's death had interfered. There had been rain, too, and sunlight. Sunlight, it appeared, faded blood. That night, however, he had started out, and he had found what he was looking for. Near a fallen tree at the top of the hill, and perhaps forty feet from where the dogs had been tied, he had turned his flashlight on the broken branch of a tree, about four feet long, and both heavy and solid. When he turned it over, on the side protected from rain and weather, he had found stains and one or two hairs.

He had wrapped it up carefully and sent it back to headquarters.

I felt sick.

"And you found the marks of the sword-stick there, too?"

"Well, no. But that's not surprising. A man doesn't walk up to commit a murder swinging a stick. He crept up behind her. I doubt if she knew anything until it was all over."

I was thinking desperately.

"This sword-stick in the museum, would the blade of such a stick have made the other wounds?"

"They would," he said promptly. "But we have to be careful there, Miss Bell. All stab wounds look alike. You can't tell whether a blade has had two cutting edges or one. You see, every knife has two cutting edges at the point. Take this knife here." He drew a substantial one from his pocket. "It cuts both ways for half an inch. No. Taken by itself, the fact that Jim Blake carried that stick that night doesn't prove that he used it, or that it's the weapon that was used. It's the rest of the case—"

He had said what he came to say. There had been no new developments in the death of Florence Gunther. The bullet had been fired at close range, and from the left. The point of entry was a neat hole, but on the other side there had been some destruction. He was inclined to believe with Dick that she had been shot while in a car, and in front of or near my property.

"Even a head wound bleeds some," he explained, "and that sort of wound is generally pretty—well, pretty messy. Of course that may be wrong. She may have been stunned first like Sarah Gittings; and killed in the country somewhere."

He got up to go, and as he stood there with the light shining down on his bald head, I saw that like the rest of us he looked tired and depressed.

"There are times," he said, "when I don't like this job of mine. And this is one of them. Take you. Take little Miss Judy. She's got troubles enough just now, and the chances are that in a day or two we're going to add to them."

"You're going to arrest Jim Blake?"

"I'm going to do just that, Miss Bell. I don't mind telling you that we think we've got the motive. Maybe you know about it, maybe you don't. But we've got the motive now, and we know he was on that hillside that night. Only I'd like to find that sword-stick first."

He was on his way to the door when I stopped him.

"How did you know I had burned that carpet, Inspector?"

"Well, somebody had burned it, and it looked as though you might be the guilty party."

"But how did you know?"

He gave me a whimsical glance.

"Did you ever examine one of those things, Miss Bell? Well, I'll tell you something maybe you don't know. That carpet had snaps—or buttons—on it to fasten it to the floor; and those snaps are metal. They won't burn. A smart man now, going carefully through certain ash-cans, can find them without any trouble."

He turned, his hand on the doorknob.

"But I'll say this to you, Miss Bell, in confidence. I'd like to know why you burned that carpet. I'd been over that car myself with a magnifying glass the day after Florence Gunther was killed. If you found anything in it, you're smarter than I am."

I could only stare at him in silent stupefaction.

"Never mind, then," he said. "You think it over. There's no hurry." And with that he left.

It was only after he had gone that I remembered the shoes he had meant to examine.

I had two days in which to think that over, although thinking did me no good whatever. I had burned the carpet and thus put a weapon against Jim in the hands of the District Attorney, and no statement by the Inspector that he had found nothing suspicious on or about it would alter that.

They would believe, as he believed, that I had found something incriminating there which they had overlooked.

But mingled with this was a sense of relief. If they had not found the oil stains on the day after Florence's murder it was because they were not there.

Those two days, however, were all I could bear. I saw nobody, heard nothing. It was as though there had been no murder of our poor Sarah, or of Florence; as though there had been no mysterious unknown, able to enter my house at will on some equally mysterious errand. But by the third day, Tuesday, I began to relax. Nobody had been arrested. Life was once more a quiet round of breakfast tray, lunch and dinner. I even prepared to go over my notes on my grandfather's biography, as a matter of *morale*; that poor endeavor we all make in trouble to provide some sort of protective mechanism for the mind.

So I got out the material. Mary's neatly typed pages, my own illegible jottings, and those ruled notebooks in which Mary had taken down my dictation. Their queer symbols meant nothing to me; they were as unfathomable as the girl herself. And it occurred to me, sitting there, that these books were in her hand, were all that remained to any of us of Mary Martin. She had come, played her strange part, and departed. A queer girl, with her poses, her defiant beauty, and her faculty of being around where there was trouble; or of carrying it with her. Who could say which?

I turned over the pages, but although here and there I found notes in longhand—"Send to Laura for daguerreotypes" I recall was one of them, and another "Have Joseph find out about terrapin for dinner party"—there was nothing of any value until I reached what appeared to be the latest book.

Not on the pages, but inside the cover in ink, she had written: "New number, East 16."

Now I happen to have a peculiar faculty, one born of necessity, for I frequently forget my glasses. I have a flair for remembering telephone numbers. And this number ran familiarly in my mind.

It did not come at once. I sat back and closed my eyes, and at last it came. I saw Dick Carter sitting at my desk, with Judy beside him, and he was calling East 16. Then I knew. Dick had called East 16 the night he was arranging for Judy and myself to visit Lily Sanderson.

New number, East 16. That meant that there had been another number, an old one, and that Mary had known it. But it seemed to me that it meant much more; that Mary had known some one in that house, possibly Florence Gunther herself. What that would explain I did not trouble to contemplate. It seemed to me that I must see Lily Sanderson again, see if she had met Mary about the house or with Florence, and that then we must find Mary herself. Find her and make her talk.

When I called East 16, however, Miss Sanderson was at work. And then that afternoon, as though she had caught my mental message, Lily Sanderson herself came to see me.

It was fortunate that Joseph was taking his afternoon out, or he might not have admitted her. He had his own methods of discriminating between people making social calls and people who came for purposes of their own. Indeed, I have seen him; the swift glance at car or taxicab, the rapid appraisal, gloves, shoes, garments. And then the quick decision.

"Madam is not at home."

Or a widening of the door, a bow; taking the cards, rather in the grand manner, and through it all a suggestion—merely a suggestion—of welcome.

But as it is Clara's rule to admit all comers Lily Sanderson gained access without trouble, and I found her in the drawing room, rather stiff and formal.

"I hope you don't mind my coming," she said. "I just had a feeling I had to see you."

"I am glad you came. Would you like a cup of tea?"

"If it isn't too much trouble. I came from the store, and I've had a hard day. I didn't take time to go home and change."

She watched with interest while I rang for Clara and ordered tea, and the long drawing room seemed to fascinate her.

"Such a lovely place," she said. "I was looking at your bushes, as I came in. And this room! That's a lovely cabinet over there."

"It is lovely," I agreed. "It is very old."

And as I sat there looking at this big blue-eyed woman with her faint limp, her almost childlike assumption of sophistication, her queer clothes, I felt that I liked her. Liked her and trusted her.

She did not come immediately to the reason for her visit, and I did not urge her. It was after the tea had come and Clara had gone that she finally brought up the subject.

"I don't know whether it's valuable or not," she said. "But as a friend of Florence's you ought to know. She was seen getting into a car, the night she was killed. Two people saw her."

"What kind of a car?"

"A large one; a limousine."

"Did they notice the color?"

"They don't agree about that. They're the Italians who keep the fruit stand at the corner. I don't know their names. We call him Tony. They knew Florence well; she often bought apples there. Tony says it was black, but Mrs. Tony says it was blue."

The story was as follows: on the night of Florence Gunther's murder both the Italians at the fruit stand saw her coming along the street. She shook her head, to say she wanted nothing, and then waited for a street car. Both of them saw her distinctly. She seemed restless, walking a few steps each way, then back again.

Before a car arrived, however, an automobile drew up before her; a closed car with a man at the wheel. Owing to the fact that the street light was directly overhead, neither of the Italians saw him clearly, except that he wore a soft hat.

There was some conversation. The man and woman at the fruit stand were interested. They had known her for a long time, and she was always alone. She seemed to demur at something, the man appeared to insist. Finally he opened the door and she got in beside him.

But—and here was the curious part—the woman at the fruit stand maintained that this same car had been standing halfway down the block in the shadow for some time. That she had seen it there, and that the man driving it had been working at something about it; front and rear.

"She thought he was rubbing dirt over the license plates," Miss Sanderson said. "And they had been held up a month or so before, so she watched him. She says now that he got into the car the moment he saw Florence. Then he drove up rather fast, and threw on the brakes in front of her, as though he had just seen her. But Mrs. Tony was interested in the license plates, and she went out and looked at the rear one. He had blacked it. She couldn't read it, at all."

But that visit of Lily Sanderson's was disappointing in one way at least. I asked her point blank if she knew a young woman named Mary Martin, and it produced no effect whatever.

"Mary Martin?" she said thoughtfully. "No, I can't say that I do."

"I think she knew Florence Gunther. If not, she certainly knew some one at the house."

"I can ask, if you like," she said. "I've only been there since last fall, and most of the rest are new too. You know how it is, everything's fine at first. Then you're caught doing a bit of washing or having a gentleman friend more than one night a week, and there's trouble. And that reminds me. I've got something to tell you about the man who called on Florence Gunther. Clarissa saw him."

"Clarissa?"

"The colored woman at the house. And a surly creature she is, at that. I gave her a dress the other day, and she talked. He was a thin man, rather tall; she thinks about fifty. Well dressed, she says. He had a cane with him, and he wore a sport suit. Out our way that means something!"

CHAPTER XVI

It was that evening, Tuesday the seventeenth, at dinner, that I received one of Katherine's characteristic terse telegrams.

"Arriving tonight eleven o'clock train."

The telegram was not only unexpected but ominous. That Katherine, sunk in grief as she was, should leave her house and come to me at that time seemed almost incredible. I could think of only two things; either that Jim had told her of the danger in which he stood, or that something had aroused her suspicions as to Howard's death.

In any event her coming was certainly significant, and I am not ashamed to say that I took a small glass of sherry before I left for the station. Nor did the sight of Katherine in her widow's weeds, with that white cold face of hers set like a mask, improve matters. She offered me her cheek, and as I offered mine at the same moment, what resulted was rather like the nose rubbing of the Africans, or whoever it is.

Not then, nor later when I showed her her room and the Frenchwoman, Elise, began to lay out her toilet things, did she offer any explanation of her visit. Judy, she said, was all right and would come with Jim the next morning. She herself had come on business. And then very politely she put me out and left me to lie awake most of the night, wondering.

It was not until ten the next morning that I got my explanation, and then it was clear enough, and worrying enough, in all conscience. At ten o'clock the door bell rang, and it was Jim, accompanied by Judy and, to my intense surprise, Alex Davis.

Judy looked odd and uncomfortable, but she was irrepressible, as always. "It's not a convention," she said. "It's merely a delegation."

She went upstairs to Katherine and the two men waited in the library, Jim moving about restlessly, Alex Davis glancing over some notes in his hand. In five minutes or so the bell rang again, and Joseph announced Mr. Waite.

I was practically beyond speech by that time. I listened dumbly while Mr. Waite made his apologies; he had just got off the train; he had been taking the sun cure in Arizona for his arthritis and was much better, thanks. Then his eyes fell on the black band on Jim's sleeve, and he said something polite about Howard's death.

But it all seemed unreal to me, and when Joseph ushered in Doctor Simonds I was not surprised to see Alex Davis rise and clear his throat, as though he were about to address a meeting.

"I believe that completes us," he said, as though he had announced that there was a quorum present. "And now, if Joseph will notify Mrs. Somers—"

Bewildered as I was, I had to admire Katherine as she came in, in her long black gown and with her fine head high in the air. There was a superb dignity about her, a refusal to make any concessions to the expected, so unlike my own fluttering as to make me self-conscious.

She shook hands with no one, smiled at no one. She simply sat down and looked at Alex Davis.

"Very well," she said. "I believe we are all ready."

And then Alex Davis did indeed make a speech. He referred to his late dear friend, Howard Somers, and to the grieving woman who sat there, finding herself in a position which it was difficult for her to accept.

"In all their conversations together, this husband and this wife, she was led to believe that the bulk of his fortune would come to her. Now she is confronted with a new will, a will she cannot explain and does not accept." I saw Mr. Waite frown slightly. "A will in which a wastrel son receives one half of this large estate. It is to discuss, not the validity of this will—" he glanced at Mr. Waite—"but the circumstances under which it was drawn, that she has asked you to meet her here today."

He sat down, and Mr. Waite took off his glasses and polished them with his handkerchief.

"Am I to speak?" he inquired. "I presume, since the integrity of the document is not in question, that it is really up to the doctor."

Urbane as he was, I saw that he was irritated. Under Alex's fine words he must have seen, as I did, that it was the will itself which was under fire.

"I actually know nothing," the doctor said. "Walter Somers told me, during his father's illness here last summer, that he was thinking of changing his will. He asked my opinion of his father's mental condition, and I said I wished mine were as good. Later on he asked me to give him a note to that effect, and I did so."

He sat back, smoothing a small Van Dyke beard with a hand deeply stained from cigarettes. Katherine eyed him and spoke for the first time.

"You had given him no drugs, doctor?"

"Drugs?" he said rather testily. "I gave him drugs, of course. That's my profession. But I gave him nothing that could by any stretch of the imagination affect his mind."

Mr. Waite's story was given circumstantially and directly.

On the twelfth of the previous August he had received a telephone call from Walter Somers, asking him to see his father that afternoon at the Imperial Hotel and to draw up a will for him. As he knew that Mr. Somers had been very ill and was still a sick man, he took the precaution of calling up the doctor here, who was attending him, and inquiring as to his mental condition. Doctor Simonds said that he knew Mr. Somers was contemplating a new will, and that he was entirely competent to make one. The result was that he had drawn up the draft late that afternoon, and took back the finished document at something after four o'clock the next day. It was signed in duplicate.

Katherine listened with slowly rising color.

"Do you mean to say that you would draw up a will as vital as that, as—revolutionary, without question? What about undue influence being brought to bear? A man may appear to be normal, but after a severe illness, when he is weak and broken—"

"There was certainly no influence evident at the time. The manager of the hotel took me up, and Walter Somers met me at the door and took me in. Then he went out and I did not see him again, either that day or the next."

"Was Sarah Gittings present?"

"She left the room. She was there when I first went in, and she came in on the second day to witness the signatures. And I may add this. There was some discussion of the terms of the will. Mr. Somers himself knew that it was what you have called revolutionary, but he said that Walter had reached years of discretion, and that he felt that there was plenty for all."

"That is not the question," said Katherine sharply. "The money's nothing. What does money matter? What does matter is that at the end he should have repudiated me. What brought that about, Mr. Waite? What happened here last summer to change his entire attitude toward me? Why did he put that will in his box, endorsed in his own hand 'to be given to my son Walter in the event of my death'? That is very serious, Mr. Waite. Had he ceased to trust me? And that fund of fifty thousand dollars to be administered by Walter at his discretion! What did he say about that? What secret was he covering?"

"He said that Walter understood."

"And that is all he said?"

"That is all."

She leaned back in her chair, apparently exhausted, and there was a short silence broken at last by Alex Davis.

"Have you the duplicate of the will with you, Mr. Waite?"

And then some of Mr. Waite's air of offended dignity left him. He stirred in his chair.

"I was coming to that. As a matter of fact, a very strange thing has happened to that copy, Mr. Davis. It has disappeared from our files. Mr. Henderson has been searching for several days, ever since Mr. Somers' death, in fact. He has a theory as to its disappearance, but as it is not a pleasant one–"

I happened to glance at Jim and his mouth was twitching crazily.

"I think we must hear it, nevertheless."

"It's like this. On the day of Sarah Gittings' murder–that afternoon in fact–a clerk in our office opened the safe at Florence Gunther's request, and left her there to secure certain documents. Later on she returned these papers, and he closed and locked the safe. She was a trusted employee, and everything apparently was all right.

"When Mr. Somers died, however, in my absence Mr. Henderson, who knew about the will, went to the safe for the duplicate and found it was gone.

"No suspicion attached itself to Florence Gunther, who had herself gone with me on both days to the hotel and who had later witnessed the will. But during the intervening time she had been murdered, and naturally everything pertaining to her had become a matter of great interest.

"Four days ago Mr. Henderson telegraphed me that the will was missing, and to come back. When he met me at the train this morning he told me that one of our clerks, a man named Lowrie, had remembered that on the afternoon of the day Sarah Gittings was killed he had seen Florence Gunther on the street; that he saw her meet a heavy-set woman whom he believes now, from the published photographs, to have been Sarah Gittings, and there on the street pass to her a long envelope of the legal type.

"If that is true, it is at least possible that the duplicate of the will was in that envelope."

Jim spoke for the first time, trying to control his mouth.

"Why would she have done that?"

Mr. Waite considered.

"She was a reliable woman," he said. "If she did that at all, and I am only telling you the office talk, she meant to show that will to Miss Gittings and then to put it back in the safe. But things happened and–Mr. Henderson has been to the police, and it was not found among her effects. The effects of either of the two women."

"But why have shown it to Sarah?" Jim insisted. "She knew about it. She'd witnessed it."

"She had no idea of the contents."

"Florence Gunther knew the terms, I suppose?"

"Naturally. She had typed it. I have had very little time to think, but it strikes me that these two women met, and that the will came up for discussion. One of our strictest rules is that such matters are kept absolutely secret so far as our office force is concerned, and Florence Gunther was no talker. Besides, in this case there had been particular instructions that the existence of this document remain confidential, so I cannot understand—"

"Who gave you those instructions?" Katherine interrupted.

"Mr. Somers himself."

"Now about this fund, this fifty thousand dollars," Alex Davis said. "He merely said that Walter Somers would understand?"

"That is all. Naturally I wondered, but it was not my affair. He was not a man to explain why he was doing certain things. I rather thought that the family understood."

Katherine looked at him.

"Understood? With the entire proceeding to be secret and confidential!"

"I didn't think of it in that light. It might, of course, refer to charity."

"Charity! And given to Walter Somers to disburse! I'm not an idiot, Mr. Waite, and I give you credit for more intelligence than that."

"Perhaps if you talk to Walter?"

"What good would that do? He's as secretive as his father, and not so honest. I know what you think, Mr. Waite; I know what you thought when you were drawing that will. You thought Howard Somers had been leading a secret life, and that this provision was to provide for somebody. Well, I do not believe that, and I'll fight that clause, and this will in court if it ruins me."

That was all. Katherine rose, and the men scrambled to their feet. She gave to each of them a steady look, said "Thank you, you have been very good to come," and then turned and went out.

I did not see her again until dinner.

During the afternoon however, I heard Judy telephoning to Wallie, and he came at six o'clock. From six until almost seven he was closeted with Katherine in her room, and the very fact that their voices were never raised seemed to me an indication of the tenseness of that meeting.

There was no compromise in either of them. Only suspicion and jealousy on Katherine's part, and a fury of hatred and revenge in Wallie. I know now that a little gentleness, some remorse for that tragic youth of his, and he would have weakened. But poor Katherine was as she was; she made no play for sympathy. She sat perfectly still and interrogated him.

"You refuse to say what this secret fund was for? Or for whom?"

"Absolutely."

"You know what you are doing, of course. You are allowing your father's memory to be besmirched. For I warn you I shall take this will into court."

"Then it will be you who are doing the soiling," he said, and stood turning the ring around his finger.

Just before seven he went down the stairs and out the front door. I was sitting in the library, but he did not turn his head.

In the meantime other things were happening of which we had no knowledge at the time. We knew of course that Mr. Henderson had been to the District Attorney, and that the police had learned that the two murdered women had been the witnesses to the second will.

But we knew nothing of the activities of the night watchman in New York, Charles Parrott.

He was shrewd enough, this Parrott, but even a stupid man might have been suspicious. Here was Howard receiving a secret visitor at two in the morning, a man who ducked in past him, with his cap drawn down over his head, a large ulster overcoat and a muffler about the lower part of his face. And in the morning Howard was dead.

That apparently roused no suspicion in itself. But two things followed it. One was that fatal attempt of Mary Martin's to bribe him to say nothing of the night visitor. That had failed, and so she had vanished. Then there was that early morning search of mine. He was still on duty, and the sight of a woman of my age wandering in that courtyard in the rain and carefully inspecting the ground must have been unusual, to say the least.

And then came that fatal move by Dick Carter the day of the funeral.

"Which one is it?" Parrott had asked.

"Dark coat and striped trousers," said Dick.

"Well, he's the same build. I didn't see much of his face."

He read the papers, and he knew Sarah Gittings; knew about her murder too, and Florence's, the "shoe" murders.

He went to Evans, the valet, a day or so later.

"Did you see Mr. Somers when he died? I mean before he'd been moved?"

"I did," said Evans with dignity.

"How about his feet? Did he have anything on them?"

"I believe he was in his stockings," said Evans, and through the simple and fortuitous circumstance that poor Howard had dropped his slippers before he picked up his highball, Parrott went to the police!

The rest is shrouded in mystery. Some time toward the end of that week a lieutenant from the homicide squad in New York took a train and saw Inspector Harrison and the District Attorney. On Monday an order was obtained to disinter Howard's body, and a secret examination made. Nothing was given out, even Katherine did not know.

But it was discovered that Howard Somers had died, not of an acute heart attack, but of cyanide of potassium, "probably administered in whisky."

Cyanide of potassium! And Howard had had a cold, and could not detect its peculiar and unmistakable odor; and Mary Martin had opened the windows, so that no one else might notice it. Opened the windows and broken the glass.

They kept their secret well, did the authorities. After all, murder had not been proved; men with hopelessly broken health had killed themselves before this. And our own local authorities were not minded to let go of Jim, anyhow. They had Jim, and now they had the motive.

Mr. Waite saw the District Attorney that afternoon, Tuesday, the seventeenth. I think myself that he was frightened. And small wonder. Of the three who had met in that room at the Imperial Hotel only he himself was left.

He must have been worried; he must have wondered how long he had left for those little vacations to cure his arthritis, for the pleasant routine of his office, for his golf and bridge, for the little dinners with good wines and his friends about him.

So it is not extraordinary that he went to the District Attorney that morning after he left us, and asked for police protection. Or that in doing so he virtually signed Jim Blake's death warrant. The District Attorney listening absorbedly and Mr. Waite telling that story.

"And what do you make out of it, Waite? There was still a valid copy of the will among Somers' papers."

"Wills have been destroyed before this."

"You think the Gittings woman got the copy to show Blake, and then he killed her?"

"He may have, hoping to get hold of the original later."

"And later on the Gunther girl got troublesome and had to be put out of the way?"

"Something like that, perhaps. I don't know. It's damned sordid. Only I don't want to be the next to go!"

"You're all right. As for its being sordid, almost all motives for crimes are sordid; cupidity, sex, jealousy. Sordid, all of them, but actuating motives just the same. Well, you don't need a policeman; we'll get this bird now, thank God. The press has been yelling for weeks, and I've had a few letters myself."

That was on Tuesday afternoon, May the seventeenth.

That night the District Attorney sent for Jim to question him for the second time, and in Jim's absence they searched his house; issuing a search warrant on a trumped-up charge against Amos for bootlegging.

For the sake of form two Federal officers ostensibly conducted the search, but Inspector Harrison actually did so. Amos opened the door, and protested violently that he knew nothing of any liquor. But they pushed past him and went upstairs, taking him along. In Jim's room they found the golf suit and the shoes which Amos admitted Jim had worn the night of Sarah's death, and later they smuggled them out. Also they discovered that Jim had recently burned some letters, and Inspector Harrison spent some time on his knees examining the fireplace.

But they still had that pretense of bootlegged liquor to carry out, and they had not found the sword-stick. So they went over the house. Amos was calmer by that time. It was only when they got to the door of the cellar that he showed excitement.

"Nothing down there but the furnace, sir," he said to the Inspector.

That made them suspicious, so they went down and turned on the lights. At first glance it was unsatisfactory; a cement floor, a whitewashed brick wall. They went over that wall carefully for loose bricks, but there were none. They were quite sure by that time that Amos was uneasy. Indeed, one of the Federal officers drew a notebook from his pocket and pretended to write down a memorandum. When he had finished he passed the note to the Inspector.

"I guess that's correct, Inspector?"

"I believe so," said the Inspector.

But what he had read was this:

"Watch the Negro. He's scared."

They started to search again.

CHAPTER XVII

THERE IS NO RECORD of that scene in the District Attorney's office, but from what we know now, and from what was brought out at the trial, I can measurably reconstruct it. Jim, wary and uneasy, holding one of his eternal cigars in a mouth that twitched steadily, taking the opportunity they offered of lighting them, the careful bestowal of their ashes, to think; and the District Attorney, firing questions at him, endlessly, interminably.

"You knew nothing whatever of this will, then?"

"I never heard of it until Alex Davis told me, in New York."

"He told you you had been disinherited?"

"Yes. That didn't bother me. What worried me was my sister."

"Why?"

"That's evident, isn't it? She was devoted to her husband. She had to learn that without her knowledge he had done a thing which affected her child as well as herself."

"And in favor of her stepson."

"Yes."

"What were her relations to this stepson? Friendly?"

And Jim pausing, lighting a fresh cigar, or pulling on the one he had.

"Not entirely. The usual difficulty. He resented her."

"And she resented him?"

"Probably. Somewhat."

"You're fond of your sister, Mr. Blake?"

"Very. She is all I have."

"You saw this second will in New York?"

"I did."

"Do you remember how the envelope was marked?"

"Yes. Perfectly."

"It was endorsed in Mr. Somers' own writing, 'To be handed to my son Walter in the event of my death.' Is that right?"

"Yes."

"Why was that, Mr. Blake?"

"I don't know."

"Doesn't it show that Mr. Somers wanted to be certain that this will reached his son's hands? That there would be no—interference?"

"You can construe it that way if you like."

"You had no knowledge of this will when you made that night visit to Howard Somers?"

"I never made such a visit. How could I? You've had men watching me for weeks."

"Now, on the night of Sarah Gittings' death, I want you to describe your movements."

"I have said all I intend to say. I went out for a walk. After I had started I remembered that my sister, calling from New York, had given me a message for Sarah. I went to a drugstore and telephoned, but she had gone out."

"What was this message from your sister to Sarah Gittings?"

"I've told you that. She wanted her to look after my niece, Judy. There was a young man here she was fond of. My sister didn't approve."

"After you telephoned, where did you go?"

"I walked on. I went to see a woman. I don't intend to say more. Then I started back."

"That would have been when?"

"Perhaps nine o'clock. I don't know exactly."

The District Attorney bent forward.

"And you still decline to give the direction you took?"

"I do. I have done nothing wrong. I decline to be put on the offensive."

"But suppose I show you the route you took that night, Mr. Blake? Suppose I tell you that from that drugstore you went to the path through the Larimer lot, and down that path to the park? And that later you returned by the same route? I warn you, Mr. Blake, that we know a great deal, and that you are only damaging yourself by these evasions."

And still Jim obstinately silent, and the District Attorney leaning back in his chair and watching him.

"You carried the sword-stick that night?"

"I told you before that I did."

"Did you see Sarah Gittings during that walk?"

"No. Absolutely not."

"Yet you were on that path that night, Mr. Blake. We know that. You went down that path into the park, and later on you went up again. At one point you stopped for some time. You either sat or stood on that hillside, and you smoked a cigar. You were not alone at that time. A man does not pause on a dark hillside on a cool spring night to look at nature."

And then Jim made his unconscious admission.

"I was alone. Absolutely alone."

"Ah! you admit then that you were there?"

"I was there, yes."

"You met nobody? Talked to nobody?"

"I did not."

"At what time were you there?"

And again that almost infinitesimal pause, and Jim mopping his forehead.

"I went down about half past seven."

"And you came back?"

"Something after nine."

"And reached your house a little after ten? Come, come, Mr. Blake, that's childish."

"I don't know the time."

"What route did you follow, coming back?"

"I cut across the park, coming up by the bridle path near Miss Bell's house. From there I walked along the Avenue."

"That would take you past the Larimer lot where the dogs were tied at about what time?"

"Possibly a quarter past nine."

"And you carried the sword-stick?"

"Yes."

"Why?"

"There had been some hold-ups around the park. I don't own a revolver, so I carried the stick."

"You saw or heard nothing suspicious? Near the lot, I mean?"

"I heard some dogs barking."

"Where?"

"Back on the Larimer lot."

"You knew Miss Bell's dogs well, didn't you?"

"Yes."

"Well enough to recognize the noise they made? A dog's bark is as individual as a man's voice, Mr. Blake."

"I didn't recognize them, no."

"Where did you put the sword-stick, on your return?"

"In the hall, with my others."

"And it disappeared from there?"

There must have been a slight delay, a slower reaction to that question.

"It disappeared. Yes."

"Just when?"

"I don't know. I was ill at the time."

"How did you learn that it was gone?"

"I had gone into the hall to call Amos. I looked down, and it was not there."

"You didn't ask Amos about it?"

"I don't recall. I think possibly I did."

"And he said it was missing?"

"That's the way I remember it."

"Now, Mr. Blake, I am going to the night of the twenty-seventh of April. Where were you that night?"

"The twenty-seventh of April?"

"The night Judy Somers was struck down in the Bell garage."

Jim stared across the desk.

"You are not intimating that I attacked my own niece, are you?"

"I have asked you a question."

"I was at home. So far as I can recall, I have not been out of the house at night since Sarah Gittings was killed. And I certainly never struck Judy. That's —that's ridiculous."

The District Attorney glanced at the paper in front of him.

"Do you recall the night when Miss Bell went to see you, after Florence Gunther's body was found?"

"Perfectly."

"Had you sent for her?"

"No."

"Not telephoned, or sent any message?"

"None whatever."

"She walked over?"

"Yes."

"But you sent her home in your car?"

"I did."

"During the course of that visit, were the two crimes discussed?"

"Somewhat."

"Did you make any suggestion to Miss Bell about your car?"

"I don't know what you mean. It had been her car. I bought it from her."

"There was nothing said about the carpet of that car?"

"Nothing."

"Do you keep the mileage of this car, Mr. Blake?"

"No. Amos may. I don't know."

"Who carries the key to the garage?"

"Amos. I don't drive myself."

"You don't know how to drive?"

"I can drive, but I dislike it."

"Is the window of the garage kept locked?"

"Usually. Not necessarily."

"If some one entered the garage by a window, could he take the car out?"

"Yes. The doors to the alley are bolted. The key is to the small door into the garden."

"That is, some one who wished to take out the car could climb through the window, providing it was not locked, and take the car out?"

"Probably. The window is rather high."

"But if he took a chair from the garden it would be easy?"

"I imagine so. I hadn't thought of it."

"So that if Amos had the key, it would still be possible to take the car out?"

"I never crawled through a window and took that car out. If that's what you mean."

"Do you know Miss Bell's garage?"

"I've been in it once or twice."

"It overlooks the ravine in the park, doesn't it?"

"Yes."

"Do you know the tool room?"

"I've never been in it."

"But you know she keeps a ladder there?"

"I know she has a ladder. I don't know where she keeps it."

This, or something very like it, went on for hours. And some time in that long interrogation they brought in the man Parrott. He came in on some excuse or other, looked Jim over and went out again. Jim was not suspicious.

But by midnight he was showing signs of exhaustion, and even the District Attorney showed strain. It was a warm spring night. The men who came and went had taken off their coats, but Jim still sat there in his hard chair, neat and tidy, and twitching, and faced them all down.

"You still decline to account for the time between seven o'clock and ten-thirty, on the night of April eighteenth?"

"I shall do that if necessary. Not before."

"What were your relations with Sarah Gittings?"

"Relations? I knew her, of course. Had known her for years."

"In case of distress she might come to you?"

"She might, yes."

"Then this letter to you would not be unusual."

"I never received a letter from her. Why should she write me? She could have seen me at any time."

"We have absolute proof that she did write to you, Mr. Blake. And we believe that you received the letter."

"You can't prove that."

"Perhaps not, but I can damned well try. Some one made an appointment to meet Sarah Gittings on the night she was killed; to meet her and see with his own eyes this copy of Howard Somers' will which the Gunther girl had abstracted from the files. From that appointment Sarah Gittings never returned, and during that evening the copy of the will disappeared."

"Why should I destroy it? Or her? The original document was safe in New York."

"Did you know Florence Gunther?"

"No."

"Never saw her?"

"No."

"Never waited for her on Halkett Street, near a fruit stand, with a car?"

"Absolutely no."

And, if the two previous denials had lacked force, this last was impressive enough.

But the heat and tension were telling on them both. Hours had passed, putting a fine edge on Jim's nerves. He had exhausted his cigars, and no one offered him any. He asked for water, and after a long delay it came.

And then, on top of his exhaustion he was told that Howard Somers had been poisoned. He very nearly collapsed, but if they had hoped to wear him into confession they were disappointed. He was still fighting. But he said a curious thing.

"How do you know he was poisoned? How do you know he didn't take the stuff himself?"

"I'm not answering questions. I'm asking them."

Jim was angry now, however, and he braced himself for one last effort. "I never went to New York to see Howard Somers the night he died. Some one else used my name, that's all. And the more I think over this case—and God knows it's all I do think of—the more I am convinced that a definite attempt is being made to put the guilt on me.

"Why would I have killed him? I stood to lose by his death, not to gain. He was my sister's husband and my friend. If you are trying to show that I escaped the watch on my house, climbed the window of my garage and drove my car to New York that night, I swear before God that I never did it, or thought of it. As for this will, I had never heard of a second will until Alex Davis revealed its existence in New York.

"I swear before God that I have never killed any one, have never thought of killing any one. And I protest against your methods. You are wearing me out. But you can't wear me into confession. I'm innocent."

They had worn him out, however. His face was gray with exhaustion, and sweat was running down his face. Now and then he ran his finger under his collar, as though it choked him. The whirring of an electric fan, the tick of a clock on the wall, and the District Attorney never relaxing; watching him, firing at him his staccato questions, deliberately trying to torture him until confession would be sheer relief.

Some time in that last half hour a memorandum was placed on the desk, and the District Attorney nodded his head.

"Send him in when he comes."

Jim had listened, with an impassive face. But he felt—perhaps his exhaustion had sharpened his faculties—that something vital had happened. The questions began again, sharper, a little excitement in them.

"You have admitted that on the night Sarah Gittings was killed, you carried with you this sword-stick, and that later on it disappeared. You had no theories about that disappearance?"

"None whatever."

"You left it in the hall and it disappeared?"

"Yes."

"And when did you notice that it had disappeared?"

"It was several days later. I don't know exactly."

"I think you do know exactly, Mr. Blake. It disappeared on the day Sarah Gittings' body was found."

"Possibly. I'm not certain."

"What is your explanation of that disappearance?"

"I've told you that before. I think it was stolen."

"As a part of the plot against you?"

"Possibly."

"You did not conceal it yourself? I mean, you did not feel that its presence was a dangerous thing in your house?"

"I thought of that, naturally. Yes."

"But you did not hide it."

Jim made an effort, moistened his dry lips.

"Not exactly. I put it in a closet."

"What closet?"

"The liquor closet, in the hall."

"And you locked it there?"

"Yes."

"Then the story that it was missing from the hall was not true?"

"Not entirely. But it is true that it disappeared. It was taken from there."

"You had the key to that closet?"

"Yes."

"Was there more than one key?"

"No. I have wondered since if Amos took it. I was in bed. He could have taken the key."

"And why would Amos do that?"

He was utterly confused by that time, faint, sagged in his chair and gray of face.

"He may have known—he may have thought—"

"*What did Amos know?*"

And then Inspector Harrison walked into the room, and laid something on the table. Jim took one look at it, and fainted dead away.

CHAPTER XVIII

IN THE CELLAR Inspector Harrison had renewed his prowling about, the Federal officers mildly interested, and Amos watching his movements with a sort of fascinated terror.

He rapped on the cement walls again, inspected the ceiling. Now and then, furtively, he looked at the Negro, and it seemed to him that the Negro was increasingly alarmed each time he neared the coal cellar. But the coal cellar was full of coal. It had overflowed into the main cellar, and lay about. And suddenly Inspector Harrison remembered that it was spring.

"Plenty of coal, for the summer?" he said to Amos. "Cook with coal?"

"No, sir. With gas," said Amos.

"And when did you get in all this coal?"

"I don't rightly remember, sir. Seems to me it was in May some time."

Inspector Harrison stooped down, and cleared a few lumps from the margin of the heap.

"What's under here? Cement?"

"I don't rightly know, sir."

But it was not cement.

There was a shovel on the coal, and at first they put Amos to work on it. He was terrified. He made noisy protests, but there were three of them, grim and determined. They were not inhuman, however, for as the Negro began to play out they took the shovel from him. One after the other, they dug into the coal, throwing it out onto the clean cemented floor, scrutinizing it, and then falling to work again. It required more than two hours to clear the place, but at last they reached the end and they had found nothing.

There was the hard-pounded black earth, glistening with black dust under their flashlights, and no sign that it had been disturbed. One of the men laughed.

"Well, that's that," he said, "and now I want a bath and a bed. Let's go."

But the Inspector was not listening. He was watching Amos, and Amos was smiling again.

"If that's all you gentlemen want," he said, "you all can go up and I'll put out the light."

The Inspector was wiping his face, which was streaming.

"What's the hurry, Amos?" he said gently.

"There's no liquor here, sir. You've seen for yourself."

"Have I? Well, maybe that's so. Now, Amos, if you'll go wherever you have to go to get a bucket of water, and will bring it here——"

"There's a lavatory on the first floor, sir."

"Do what you're told," the Inspector said sharply. "And be quick about it."

The Federal officers were examining their hands for blisters and swearing at the dust. Amos went cheerfully up the cellar stairs, and came back in a moment with his pail. He carried soap and a towel also, and his face was a study when the Inspector passed them back to him.

The next procedure, however, astounded the Negro. With one of the officers holding a light close to the surface of the ground, the Inspector went over it carefully. He would pour a little water on the earth and watch it, then move on, repeating the performance.

Suddenly he muttered something and asked for the shovel. Amos gave it to him, his eyes fixed on the earth, his color the peculiar gray of the terrified Negro.

And there, not more than a foot beneath the surface, Inspector Harrison came across the sword-stick.

I can still see the rather smug complacence of his manner at the trial.

"I then sent Amos for a pail of water."

"Perhaps you would better explain to the jury your purpose in sending for that water."

"In case of buried objects the surface of the ground may not appear to have been disturbed. In case however that it has been recently dug up, small bubbles of air will appear when water has been poured over it."

"And were there such bubbles?"

"Plenty of them."

So there they stood in that cellar, the four of them. One of the Federal officers whistled softly. Amos was staring at the thing, popeyed with terror. It must have savored to him of witchcraft, that discovery; this detective, this policeman, muttering incantations to himself and then turning out that weapon into the cruel light.

"My Gawd Almighty!" said Amos, and turning, ran up the stairs.

They did not bother to follow him. The Inspector carefully wrapped the thing in paper, and some one telephoned to the District Attorney's office. They had been holding poor Jim for the message.

But they held him after the message also. Jim Blake was placed under arrest that night, and within three days he had been indicted by the Grand Jury for the murder of Sarah Gittings.

He was to be tried only for the murder of poor Sarah, but in the opinion of the public at that time Jim Blake was guilty of two, and in the minds of the police, of a third one.

Press comment was universally approving. That the police would not have taken this drastic step "without good and sufficient reason"; that "murder is murder, whether committed by the gangster or by the individual in high place in the community"; that "the District Attorney's office is to be congratulated in having at last taken steps to solve these crimes," these were some of the comments.

Jim had been arrested after one o'clock Tuesday night, or rather early Wednesday morning, the eighteenth. Sarah had been dead for precisely a month.

We were stunned with horror. It came as less of a surprise to me than to the others, but it was a shock for all that.

We did little or nothing that first day. Jim was in a cell in the jail and had sent for his lawyer, Godfrey Lowell. Late in the day Godfrey came in to see me, and his face was very grave. Jim's cell was damp and the food terrible, but these things he passed by with a gesture.

"He's not telling all he knows," he said. "He says he's innocent, and I believe he is. But he isn't frank. He's holding something back."

Nevertheless, Jim's story as Godfrey told it to us that afternoon in the library, was sufficiently damning. Katherine hardly spoke during that recital. Dick sat holding Judy's hand, but I doubt if Katherine noticed it.

Briefly, Jim admitted having had an appointment to meet Sarah that night, but not in the park or by letter. She had, he maintained, telephoned to him. "I have never received a letter from her, then, or at any time." In this message, evidently sent after she had met Florence Gunther on the street and received the envelope, she had asked him to meet her that night on a very urgent matter.

The address she gave was a house on Halkett Street, and he determined to walk, going by way of the park.

On the way, however, he found that he had left the house number in his other clothing—he had changed to a walking suit—and he stopped at a drugstore to call her up. She had started, however; he talked to Judy for a moment and then went on, taking the short cut through the corner of the Larimer lot.

He remembered that the house was in the seventeen hundred block on Halkett Street, and that he was to ask for a Miss Gunther. When he reached the block in question he had walked along slowly, and at one of the houses a youngish woman was waiting on the steps.

He asked if she knew of a Miss Gunther in the vicinity, and she said that that was her name, and that Sarah had not yet arrived.

They went together into the house and waited in the parlor. It was a boarding house, but although the door into the hall was open, he saw no one except a colored woman who passed by shortly before he left.

The Gunther woman had been silent and very nervous. As time went on and Sarah did not arrive she seemed almost hysterical, and at twenty minutes to ten he had gone away, still in the dark as to why he had been there at all.

"Florence Gunther apparently refused to tell him," Godfrey said. "He came home by the same route, mystified over the whole business. He reached the path up the hill at or about ten o'clock, stopped to rest halfway up and then went on. He maintains that he knew nothing about Sarah until he got your word that she was missing, and that he never saw her that night at all."

"And the sword-stick?" Judy asked. "What does he say about that?"

"That he hid it in the closet, but he did not bury it."

Katherine spoke, after a long silence.

"When they found the stick, I suppose they had searched the house?"

"I understand that they did, and that they found certain things which they believe strengthen the case."

"His letters? Everything?"

"He had burned his letters. He had felt that this was coming, and yesterday he more or less got ready. Nothing important, he says, but he didn't care to have them going through his papers."

I thought that Katherine looked relieved.

I have re-read that paragraph. I know now that she was relieved. But I do not know even now what she had thought of that frantic inquiry of his, and his warning to send the reply by hand. It was burned, anyhow. She must have found some comfort in that.

How could she know that after that scene in the District Attorney's office Inspector Harrison had gone back to Jim's house, armed with a small box and a delicate pair of tweezers, and had taken from the grate in that handsome room of Jim's certain charred and blackened fragments of paper ash.

Some time, that day or the next, he must have spent a painful hour over them. They had to be steamed and softened, and then they had to be laid out on a gummed paper and carefully pressed down. But he had his reward in the end. He had one sentence of nine words.

It must have puzzled him, however.

Late that evening the Inspector came in to see me, but he made no mention of his discovery in the fireplace. He seemed indeed to be rather apologetic, and he broke numberless toothpicks into fragments and strewed the floor with them.

He had to tell me that Howard had been poisoned, and he plainly hated doing it.

"No need of telling Mrs. Somers or Miss Judy," he said. "After all, he may have done it himself, although that would be small comfort to them." He looked at me. "Everything all right with them?" he asked. "Happy married life, and so on?"

"Absolutely. He never killed himself, Inspector."

"Maybe not. Cyanide of potassium," he said reflectively. "Quick and sure, but no imagination in it. No real imagination in any of these murders, for that matter. Now Walter has imagination; Blake hasn't."

"Walter?" I said sharply.

"He didn't commit them, of course. Why should he? Leave out his affection for his father, and still he wouldn't. The copy of the will is missing. To kill the witnesses wouldn't get him anywhere. No, Walter Somers is out. I don't have too much faith in alibis, but he didn't do it."

Before he left he told me that the Grand Jury would have the case by Friday, and that it would undoubtedly bring in a true bill. But he did not seem particularly happy over it.

"The more I study crime," he said, "the less I know about the criminal. Take this case: these three murders were cold and audacious. They were committed by a man without fear and without scruple. They were fiendishly clever.

"Yet we run into this situation; we find and arrest the criminal, because he has not been clever at all. He has buried his weapon in his house, although if he killed Somers he could have dropped it into a dozen streams on that trip of his. He has absolute nerve, a thing few men possess, and he faints when he is confronted with it. He is strong enough to get into that air shaft and to pull himself out later—a thing I couldn't do, and I'm a strong man for my age—and here's his doctor swearing he's a sick man, has been sick for several years.

"I've built this case. I've got evidence enough to convict Jim Blake and still have some left over. But I'm not satisfied. Not yet anyhow."

He broke three toothpicks in rapid succession.

"Personally, I don't believe we have scratched the surface of the thing. Go back to the night Miss Judy was hurt. And, by the way, has she ever told you why she went to the garage that night?"

"She said she wanted a foot rule."

"But she asked Joseph where the ladder was kept, didn't she?"

"Yes."

"Now what did she want with that ladder? To look at it or to use it?"

"I haven't any idea, Inspector."

"Curious," he said. "She had something in her mind. She's shrewd. Now let's go over that night.

"Joseph has heard the dogs barking in the shrubbery; they stop suddenly, as though they had recognized the intruder. You and Joseph start to the garage, and Joseph hears something. He calls 'What's that?' There is no answer, and you both go on. Some one is in the shrubbery, or has passed through it. The next day I find footprints there; not the original ones. Planted. And by the way, those prints were made by a woman's shoe. I've done some work on them! Not shoes from this house, however. Joseph and I have seen to that.

"But here's the point. Miss Judy was hurt at ten o'clock, and it was two when Norah saw this figure on the grounds.

"And here is what I want to know. Where would Jim Blake go, between ten and two o'clock at night, to get a pair of shoes belonging to a heavy woman who walked on the outsides of her feet? He has no women in his house. Even his laundry goes out.

"And why would Jim Blake cover those footprints as skillfully as he did, and then bury that cane in his cellar? The act of a fool or a lunatic, and the man who made those prints was neither."

"Have you told the District Attorney all this, Inspector?"

"He wants an indictment. That's his business." And he added: "A man who's been indicted by the Grand Jury has a pretty hard time of it. His trial may prove him innocent, but he's got the stigma anyhow."

He picked up a pencil from my desk, examined it, laid it down.

"Let's go back still farther," he said, "to when Blake first talked to you about Sarah Gittings' disappearance. When was that, and where?"

"In this room, the next day. When she did not come back I sent for him. He was uneasy, but that was all."

"You recall nothing else?"

"Nothing important. I remember now that he asked about Howard."

"What did he ask?"

"It was something about his health, and if he was able to travel; if he had been here lately."

The Inspector slid forward on his chair.

"That's an interesting point. Now why would he ask such a question? The talk, I gather, had been about Sarah Gittings?"

"Entirely."

"And he knew Mr. Somers' condition, of course. Did you understand from that that he had reasons for thinking that Somers had been in town?"

"Yes. I remember that it surprised me. He asked me if I was certain that Howard had not been in town. I thought it unlikely, myself."

"I suppose you have no reason to think that he had been here?" And when I shook my head, "Don't answer that too quickly. Think it over, Miss Bell. Sometimes we think we know all about certain individuals, only to find that we know nothing at all. Why did Howard Somers secretly alter his will last summer while he was here? What is this secret fund of fifty thousand dollars? And what made Mr. Blake ask if he had been here recently?"

"I don't believe Howard was here. He was ill, and his wife seldom left him."

"But it would be possible? Some night when his wife had retired early? Or was out to dinner? He had a fast car, of course, and a dependable chauffeur."

"Possible? Yes, I daresay. But why?"

"That's the point, exactly. If you can induce Mr. Blake to tell his attorneys why he asked you that question it might be helpful." He moved impatiently. "If people only told all they knew, there would be no miscarriages of justice. But out of fear or self-interest or the idea of protecting somebody they keep their mouths shut, and so we have these mysteries. Look at you yourself; you burn that carpet, and produce evidence against Jim Blake that to the average jury is enough to send him to the chair! Why did you burn it? What did you find that we'd overlooked? I'd been over that carpet with a fine tooth comb."

"And there was no oil on it?"

"Oil! You found oil on that carpet?"

"I did indeed. A ring of oil."

He got up and reached for his hat.

"It may interest you to know," he said, "that there was no oil on that carpet when I examined it, the morning after Florence Gunther's murder."

But whatever conclusion he drew from that, his last speech that night was a small comfort to me.

"Well, I don't see how that will help with a jury," he said, rather heavily. "On the surface it's a water-tight case, Miss Bell. He had the weapon and the motive. The only thing he didn't have—and you'll have to excuse the word—was the guts. Mind you," he added, "I'm not saying that Blake is innocent. He looks as guilty as hell. But I am saying that there are discrepancies, and I've got to have an explanation of some of them."

CHAPTER XIX

THAT WAS ON Wednesday the eighteenth, a month after Sarah's death and about six weeks before Joseph was shot.

I went upstairs that night exhausted both mentally and physically, to find Judy curled on my bed and very despondent.

"Let me stay awhile," she pleaded. "Until mother comes in, anyhow. I want to talk."

"I didn't know she had gone out," I said in surprise.

"She took Robert and the car. I think she went to Uncle Jim's. To Pine Street."

That surprised me, but Judy explained that it was to select some clothing to be sent to the jail.

"Only why would it take her all this time—" she added, almost pettishly.

"I didn't hear the car."

"You're a little deaf, you know, Elizabeth Jane. I wouldn't be surprised if a lot goes on that you don't hear. Or hear about."

"What goes on that I don't hear about?"

"You didn't hear Elise scream last night."

"I had taken a sleeping tablet," I said with dignity. "And what did Elise scream about?"

"She saw the ghost," said Judy.

And when I came to examine that story, and to talk to Elise, I had to admit that she had seen something.

The Frenchwoman was still pale when I saw her. It appears that she had wanted to tell me the story, but that Joseph had sternly ordered her to keep quiet. Also that she was under no circumstances to tell the women servants, or she might "have the cooking and the housework on her hands." That seems to have been sufficient, but she had told Judy, talking in her rapid gesticulating French.

But her story gained credibility by the fact that she spoke no English, although she had understood Joseph well enough. She could have had no knowledge of the talk in the kitchen and servants' hall, and indeed Joseph had told me later that he had warned both women to keep their mouths closed over the whole business.

Her story, punctuated by dramatic pauses where Judy saw that my French was inadequate, was as follows:

She was occupying Mary Martin's room, and the night as I have said was sultry and like midsummer. She went to bed leaving her door open, but the breeze was from the opposite side of the house. She got up and opened the door across, thinking that it belonged to a room there.

It was, however, the door to the attic staircase which she had opened, and she was surprised to find not only the steps but that a faint light was going somewhere above.

She was curious rather than alarmed. In her bare feet and nightdress she went on up quietly, but not thinking of caution. However, near the top she must have made some sound. She had only an instant to see a white figure bending over something. The next moment she was tumbling down the staircase. But she was not quick enough. The thing, and she shuddered when she said it, the thing overtook her and passed her. She felt the brushing of its spectral garments, as she put it, and it was then that she screamed.

When Joseph found her—the women would not stir out of their rooms—she was locked in her room and was still screaming. It was some time before he could induce her to open her door.

When I talked to her, which was that night, she was still sitting in Katherine's room and obstinately refusing to go to bed.

"I think you dreamed it, Elise," said Judy. "What's the use of being a fool? There is no such thing as a ghost."

"I saw it. I touched it, mademoiselle."

"Well, you can't touch a ghost. And mind you, nothing of this nonsense to mother. Go to bed and say your prayers. That ought to help."

We had to take her up ourselves finally, and wait until she was safely locked in. Then and only then did Judy look directly at me.

"Now," she said. "She saw something, or somebody. She may be an idiot, but I'll say this for her. It takes a lot to keep her out of her bed."

Together we went up to the attic, but although it was rather ghastly at that hour of the night, I could not find that anything had been disturbed. Judy it appeared had been up before, and had found nothing.

It was from Joseph, still waiting in the pantry to admit Katherine, that I secured what looked like a partial explanation.

"The sewing room window on the second floor was open," he said. "I think he got out there, madam. He could drop to the roof of the kitchen porch."

He had, it seems, instructed Elise to say that she had seen a mouse! Which as Judy said was from the sublime to the ridiculous.

Katherine came in very late, and I thought she looked rather better.

She had been going over Jim's house, she said, and she had decided to move over there.

"It looks as though I shall be here for some time, Elizabeth," she said. "At least until they have cleared Jim of this ridiculous trumped-up charge. And there are three of us. I don't like to crowd you. I can get the servants from New York, and be quite comfortable."

I made no demur. I saw that she was determined, although Judy looked rather unhappy over it.

"What will you do with Amos?"

"I shall let him go," she said with decision. "I don't like him and I don't trust him."

The net result of which was that Amos gave his damaging testimony before the Grand Jury and then disappeared.

That was on Friday, May the twentieth.

I daresay some such system must exist, but the whole proceeding drove me almost to madness. And it was sheer farce from beginning to end. The result was a foregone conclusion, with as Godfrey Lowell says, the indictment typed and ready to sign before it began.

There was no chance from the first; from that sonorous opening by the District Attorney: "Gentlemen of the Grand Jury, it becomes my duty this morning to bring to your attention a most serious case. On the night of the eighteenth of April last, when most of us were peacefully asleep in our beds, a human life was ended under circumstances so brutal that they stun the normal mind. A woman named Sarah Gittings, a nurse, devoted solely to a career of service, was atrociously murdered." There followed certain details, dramatically presented, and after that: "Through the efforts of the police department an array of facts has been discovered, which points to a certain individual as the guilty man. These facts will now be presented to you by certain witnesses, and it is for you to decide whether a true bill shall be presented against this prisoner, or not.

"Shall we proceed, Mr. Foreman?"

From that until the end the mounting testimony against Jim was appalling. The District Attorney grew more and more unctuous, and his secret satisfaction was evident. When all was over he made, I believe, a dramatic gesture with his hands, and standing by the table, ran his eyes along the half circle of chairs.

"Gentlemen," he said, in a low voice, "I have done my duty. Now must you do yours."

As he closed the door behind him and stepped into the hall, Dick says that he was still acting for the benefit of the press men and the crowd. He stood still, half leaning against the door like an exhausted man, and mopped his forehead with a fine handkerchief, faintly scented. Then he drew himself up, justice personified, and marched along the corridor.

But in between those two dramatic moments were two days of sheer horror for us.

The secrecy of the procedure, the oaths of silence, the occasional cheerful amusement of the twenty-three men who sat in that semicircle of chairs, the terrified or determined faces of the witnesses, the avid crowd of reporters outside studying these faces as they came and went, and then rushing to their typewriters: "It is reported that Miss Bell stated—"

Building a case that might send a man to the chair, out of staircase gossip, a look, a gesture, or such information as was refused by the District Attorney but managed somehow to reach them *via* his office.

Experts came and went. The heap of exhibits on the long table grew; poor

Sarah's stained and pierced clothing, the ghastly fragments of Florence Gunther's checked dress and blue coat, for although Jim was only charged with Sarah's murder, there was no legal limits, no laws of testimony, to be considered before the Grand Jury.

The sword-stick was brought in, its ancient mechanism arousing a sort of childlike interest among the jurymen; and small boxes of earth, each duly ticketed and bearing the impress of the stick as Jim had touched the ground with it. And Dick telephoned once to say that there was a story among the newspaper men that something had been carried in, carefully covered with a cloth, and that the story was that a letter Jim had burned had been restored, and had been introduced as incriminating.

We were all in the library, and I thought Katherine started when Judy repeated this. But she said nothing. She sat staring at her emerald ring, and made no comment.

The list of exhibits grew. Sarah's uniform, with a mirror so that the writing on the sleeve might be read; the plaster casts of the foot marks Inspector Harrison had made in my garden; the snaps from the carpet which had been rescued from my furnace; even the pencil which Wallie had found in the airshaft, the fragments of broken glass from my drawing room door, the rope which had once tied the dogs, and had later on been used to drag poor Sarah's body down the hill; and certain pages in Sarah's own hand of her sick-room records, designed to show that the reversed writing on Sarah's sleeve was authentic.

There were photographs, also. Showing the sewer structure, showing poor Sarah within it, showing the well-marked spot where the body had lain near the tree and that room of hers as it was discovered the next day. Florence's room was there too, and Sarah's, in the disorder in which we had found it on the morning of the nineteenth of April.

It must have been like sitting through a crime play to those jurymen, lifted out of their humdrum lives into that welter of crime and clues and blood.

And against all that, what had we? My own testimony, received with evident skepticism, that the man on my stairs the night of Sarah's murder had not worn light golf knickers, but conventional dark trousers! At no time was it brought out that the stains in Jim's car had been put there later; were not there when the police examined it the following day. It was sufficient that I had burned the carpet. And when I suggested that any juryman over forty was welcome to try to hang in the light shaft by his hands, and then to try to pull himself out of it, there was general laughter.

There was also one other development which left us in little doubt of the final outcome. This was the introduction on the second day of the colored woman, Clarissa, from the Bassett house on Halkett Street.

It was Dick too who reported this to us. He had seen her taken in, uneasy and yet somehow deadly. A big woman, powerful and determined but frightened. When she came out her relief was manifest, and Dick took advantage of that relief. He followed her, caught her at a corner, and brought us what he had learned.

Briefly this woman, Clarissa, having positively identified Jim at the jail, stated that on the night of Sarah's murder he had spent some time at the Halkett Street house with Florence Gunther. He had sat in the parlor with her for an hour or more, and she remembered that he had a stick.

That we already knew. But she had further testified that, going forward to lock the front door before leaving for the night, she had heard Jim speaking and that she remembered distinctly what he had said.

"He said: 'I'd better start, then. I may meet her on the way back.'"

Some little hope however we had on the second day. The jury sent out for copies of the two wills, and they were duly produced. It looked for a time as though they might be looking for a larger picture; that the clause referring to the fifty thousand dollars might lead elsewhere.

But to offset that the District Attorney produced those two exhibits which he had held for the psychological moment. He brought in Jim's walking suit and his golf shoes, to prove that by laboratory test there was blood in minute quantities on both. And he re-introduced the sword-stick.

The blade of the weapon had been carefully washed, but from inside the sheath, when it had been soaked in the laboratory, there had come a pine needle of the same variety as had been found on Sarah's clothing; and unmistakable traces of blood. Human blood.

It was after that that the District Attorney made his dramatic gesture.

"Gentlemen, I have done my duty. Now must you do yours."

I daresay none of us was greatly surprised at the outcome. Certainly at least twenty-two out of the twenty-three men on the Grand Jury believed Jim guilty, and the indictment was signed, late on the second day.

Katherine received the news better than I had expected.

"An indictment is not a verdict," she said, quoting Godfrey Lowell, no doubt.

Judy, however, took it very hard and as for Wallie, the effect on him seemed devastating. Newspaper extras had announced the result, and he came in while Judy and I were at dinner. Katherine had retired to her bed, and to tea and toast on a tray.

"The damned fools!" he said. "The—damned fools!"

Judy looked at him out of eyes that were red and swollen.

"Since when have you changed your mind? You were sure enough."

"Well, I was a damned fool myself. That's all. He didn't do it. And he'll never suffer for it; I promise you that, Judy. Nothing is going to happen to him."

"Even if you have to tell all you know? Why don't you do that now and save time? You might die or get run over, and then where is he?"

He said nothing. I had had a good look at him by that time and I must confess that his appearance shocked me. His clothes were unpressed; his eyes were congested, as from sleepless nights, and he had developed a curious *tic;* now and again, by some involuntary contraction of the muscles, his left shoulder lifted and his head jerked to the right. I saw that he tried to control it by keeping his left hand in his coat pocket, but in spite of him up would go the shoulder. It was pitiful.

I saw, too, that he had not wanted to come; that he had dreaded the visit, and that to reinforce his courage he had taken a drink or two before he started. Not that he showed any effect, but that the room was full of it.

Judy eyed him.

"You look terrible," she said. "And stop jerking. You'll have me doing it. Stop jerking and tell us where Mary Martin is."

He said he did not know, and sat in silence until we had finished. It was not until Judy had gone up to her mother and we had moved into the library that he spoke again.

"Look here," he said. "How soon are you going away for the summer?"

"How soon are they going to release Jim Blake?"

"That's ridiculous," he said sharply. "He's well enough where he is. He'll get some of the cocktails and food out of his system, that's all. They'll never send him to the chair. They can't send him to the chair. It's absurd."

But it seemed to me that he was listening to his own words, trying to believe them; and that when he looked at me his bloodshot eyes were pleading with me. "You believe that too, don't you?" they said. "They'll never send him to the chair. They can't send him to the chair. It's absurd."

"When I'm certain of that I shall go away. Not before, Wallie."

He jerked again, rather dreadfully.

"Not if I ask you to go?" he said.

"Why should you ask me to go?"

"Because I don't think you are safe here."

"Who could have any design against me? I have no enemies; no actively murderous ones anyhow. I mind my own business and my conscience is as clear as the ordinary run of consciences. Why should I run away?"

"I'm telling you. That's all. Get away, and get Judy away."

"Then you know something I don't know, and it is your business to tell me what it is."

He refused to be drawn, however, and with all the questions I had in mind, managed to get away before I could ask him any of them. Save one, and that had a curious effect on him.

"Can you tell me," I said, "why Mary Martin suggested to Judy that your father should not be left alone at night?"

"Because he was sick. That's enough, isn't it? Why try to read into this case something that isn't there? And why drag her in? She has nothing to do with the case. Absolutely nothing. She's as innocent as—as Judy."

I made my decision then, to tell him the facts as to his father's death. I told him as gently as I could, with my hand on his arm. But he showed no surprise and pretended none. Save that he grew a shade paler he kept himself well in hand.

I felt then that he had been certain of it from the day Howard died.

Jim was arraigned a day or so later. It was a hideous ordeal for him, and for the rest of us; the courtroom crowded, and the crowd hostile. It seemed to me that the concentrated hatred in that room was a menace in itself, that if thought is a force, as I believe that it is, there was enough malignancy there to have destroyed a man.

They had brought him from the jail in the Black Maria; very carefully dressed, he was, and holding his head high. He had not come alone. There were criminals with him, black and white and even one yellow man. He had to wait while they entered their pleas, and he fixed his eyes on Katherine. I saw her smile at him, and her whole face warmed. A queer woman, Katherine, filled with surprises.

He listened gravely to the reading of the indictment, and nodded a sort of mute thank-you to the clerk when he had finished. I saw him draw a long breath, and I fancy he had meant that his "Not guilty" was to be a full-bodied and manly thing, a ringing assertion of his innocence. But he failed. At the last moment he looked at the crowd, and its concentrated hatred struck him like a blow in the chest. I saw his spirit fall under it and lie there a broken thing, and Judy moaned a little. His "Not guilty" was not heard beyond the front benches, and he knew it.

Some hysterical woman somewhere giggled, and he heard it. I have never seen such torture in a man's face. When they took him out he stopped at the prisoners' door, as though he would come back and face them down, but Godfrey Lowell put a hand on his arm, and he went out to face again the battery of news photographers waiting outside.

I have one of those pictures now. It shows him handcuffed to another prisoner and with his head bent. The other man is smiling.

CHAPTER XX

So WE ENTERED into that period of dreadful waiting between the indictment and the trial. Not that the waiting was to be long. The prosecution was doing everything possible to get the case on the docket before court closed in June, and the press was urging haste.

On the twenty-fourth of May, Tuesday, Katherine moved into Jim's house, and took Judy with her. Apparently she paid no attention to the curious looks of the neighbors, or to the cars which halted in the street to survey the house. She was like a woman set apart, not so much hardened as isolated.

As Laura wrote: "She seems superhuman to me. I'd come on if she wanted me, but quite frankly she doesn't. And what is this mysterious fund, anyhow? Poor dear Howard leading a double life seems rather incredible, at his age and with that heart of his. As for the rest of it, I don't see why Wallie shouldn't have his share. No matter what you think about Margaret, she stood by Howard in the early days, and he was certainly crazy enough about her; although I wouldn't care to tell Katherine that."

She said she would be on for the trial, and to be sure to get the best men to defend Jim; and she ended by saying that the whole thing was preposterous, and that the Grand Jury must be insane. "Collective insanity," she put it.

Dick was rather at a loose end after the move. There could be no informal dropping in at any house of Katherine's. Amos was gone, and a part of her own staff from New York had taken his place. Just how they found houseroom I do not know, but somehow they managed. Judy reported to me daily, and so matters went on for a week or so; Jim in jail, I alone once more in my house, and Katherine moving silently and austerely about that little house, sipping her after-dinner coffee in the back garden and passing, in order to reach it, the door to the liquor closet, and the passage to the cellar stairs.

Then one day Judy told me that her mother wished to see the manager of the Imperial Hotel, and wanted me to go with her.

"But why, Judy?"

"She didn't say. She thinks something must have happened here last summer; I know that."

"The hotel wouldn't know about it."

"They might know if father had had any visitors."

She glanced at me, then looked away. I think she felt that there was something shameful in this prying into a dead man's past, and that she had herself refused to go.

I agreed, however. It seemed the least I could do, although I do not frequent hotels. I had never been inside the Imperial in my life. I daresay I belong to a generation which is absurd to the present one, but it has always seemed to me that well-bred folk should use hotels as necessities, not for pleasure.

But the hotel manager, a short ruddy man, swollen somewhat with good living, was unable to help us.

"I knew Mr. Somers well, of course," he said, "and I gave him the suite he usually occupied. I remember asking him if he wanted so much space, for he came alone. Usually he brought his valet. He said he did, and I went up with him myself.

"I thought he looked tired, and I suggested he have dinner in his sitting room. He said he would, and that his son would dine with him.

"The attack came on just after dinner. I was in the lobby when the word came, and I went up. The hotel doctor was there, and we got Doctor Simonds also. He—it looked pretty serious for a while."

"Walter Somers was there when it occurred?"

"Yes. He telephoned for help."

As to visitors, he did not know. The floor clerk might remember. From her desk near the elevator she could see the doors of the suite clearly, and of course Mr. Somers was an important guest. It was a chance, anyhow. She had known Mr. Somers for years, and naturally his grave illness had been a matter of interest and solicitude.

A pleasant enough little man, if rather unctuous. He took us to the sixth floor and left us with the floor clerk. I imagine he had wanted to remain, but Katherine's "thank you" was a dismissal. He turned and went away.

The clerk at the desk on the sixth floor turned out to be a middle-aged woman, with keen eyes and a shrewd mouth. Long ago, I daresay, she had lost any illusions as to the men and women whose comings and goings it was her business to watch. They came and went, intent on their own affairs, hardly aware of her at all. But she saw them and studied them; their tragedies, their serio-comedies. A thousand small dramas were played about her, and sometimes she was audience, and occasionally she was God.

I saw that Katherine had impressed her, even before she heard her name; her air of breeding, the heavy handsome black she wore. But Katherine was intent on herself and her problem; her eyes were on that long corridor, with its mirrors and heavy jars, its chairs and its rows of doors.

"You were here, I believe, while my husband was ill last summer?"

"Yes, Mrs. Somers. He was in six-ten, the corner suite down there."

But Katherine did not look, although I did.

"And I suppose that you know we are in trouble. Very great trouble."

"I do indeed. I am so sorry."

But the interview, at the time at least, appeared to develop very little. Miss Todd, the floor clerk, was on duty from four o'clock in the afternoon until midnight, when she turned in her keys to the main office and went home.

She knew of no visitors to Howard during those hours.

"His son came and went," she said. "At first, when Mr. Somers was critically ill he stayed all night, getting such sleep as he could, and there was a day nurse and a night nurse. When Miss Gittings came she replaced the day nurse, and after he began to gain strength she took the case herself. The night nurse was dismissed. She wanted it that way."

"The evening he was taken sick, do you remember anything unusual about that?"

"Well, I do; in a way. Mr. Walter Somers came out about ten minutes before the attack. He had his hat, and I remember thinking he had eaten his dinner in a hurry. He came along to about that third door there, then he turned right around and went back again."

"And it was after that that he telephoned for help?"

"About ten minutes. Yes."

Katherine hesitated. She was a proud woman, and only desperation could have forced the next question.

"You don't know if there had been a quarrel? Some excitement, to bring on the attack?"

It was Miss Todd's turn to look embarrassed.

"Well, I hardly like to say. The waiter, William, said there were some words while he served dinner, and that Mr. Walter looked upset. But these waiters talk a good bit."

"He had no idea what the trouble was? Did he hear anything? I am sorry," Katherine interrupted herself, "but this may be more vital than you realize. What was said? What did this William hear?"

"William's gone now, but he said Mr. Somers had accused Mr. Walter of lying about something. And he said: 'You can't put that over on me. I know. I've got the facts, and if you think you are going to hold that over me you can think again.' Those are not the exact words, but after he took sick William came here and told me."

Katherine sat very still, thinking that over. It must have satisfied that furious jealousy of hers that Howard and Wallie had quarreled. But it must have puzzled her, too, as it was certainly puzzling me. She drew off her gloves, sat smoothing them absently.

"But of course that was nothing serious," Miss Todd went on brightly. "Things were all right after that, and Mr. Walter was devotion itself. He came in every day. He was nice to everybody. We all liked him."

Katherine moved in her chair.

"Did Mr. Somers have any other visitors?"

"Well, it was summer and his friends were all away. There were the doctors, of course; Doctor Simonds had called in several. But I remember no callers."

"Were you on duty when Mr. Waite came in?"

"Yes. Both days. The manager, Mr. Hendrickson, brought him up himself. He had only the stenographer with him; she sat here until Mr. Waite opened the door and signaled to her. A quiet person. They came back again the second day, and I think they called up the notary from downstairs. Mr. Walter brought him up, I believe, but I was at my supper at the time."

"Was his son—was Walter Somers with his father at these times?"

"On the first day he met Mr. Waite in the hall and took him in. But he did not stay. He came out and rang for the elevator. I remember that, because he brought me some flowers from the sickroom. He said his father had suggested it. He had just received a large box."

I saw a quick flicker of suspicion in Katherine's eyes, and I knew that her quick jealousy had been again aroused. Flowers to her meant a woman, and with some justification, at that. Men do not ordinarily send boxes of flowers to other men. And this had been in midsummer, when practically all the few people Howard Somers knew in the city would be out of town.

"Flowers?" Katherine said. "I suppose you have no idea who sent these flowers?"

"I haven't an idea," said Miss Todd, looking slightly surprised. "Mr. Walter Somers would know, of course. He came out and got some vases for them."

Katherine's face set, as it always did when Walter was mentioned. Nevertheless, she was calm enough on the surface.

"And who brought these flowers, Miss Todd? Walter Somers?"

"No. They were delivered by the florist. At least I suppose so. An elderly man brought them. Usually such parcels are left here at the desk, but he said he had been told to get a receipt for them, and I let him take them in himself." She stopped suddenly. "That's curious," she said. "I don't remember his coming back this way, now that I think of it."

"He delivered the flowers and did not come back?"

"He may have, of course. I was pretty busy that day. I just don't remember seeing him again. But there is a service staircase near the suite. He could have walked down. I remember him," she added, "because it was a rainy day and he was soaking wet. He seemed old and feeble to be out and working."

She remembered nothing else of value. The messenger with the flowers she had seen only once; a shabby man, elderly and with longish white hair, and considerably stooped. Several times, during the illness, a squat heavy-set woman had come to give Howard a massage. She had reported at the desk the first time. After that she had merely nodded and passed by.

Visitors were forbidden. Walter came and went, getting little sleep at the beginning but later on in better spirits. It was evident that Miss Todd had liked Walter. Sarah Gittings had gone her efficient way. "Very particular about his food she was, too!" As Howard improved he had insisted that Sarah take a walk in the afternoons, and she did so. At such times Walter often stayed with his father and read to him. Sarah would wait until Walter could come, after office hours, and then dutifully go out.

There was no fuel there for Katherine's jealousy and suspicion to feed on; the record of a normal illness, with no women visitors save a muscular *masseuse*. No men, even, save Walter and the doctors, this messenger from a florist, the elderly man with the stooped shoulders and a box of flowers, and Mr. Waite himself, sole survivor now of that little group of three which had stood by a bed in that hotel suite and watched a wavering hand sign a will which was to send four people to their deaths and three others into danger and injury.

Before we left Miss Todd asked if we would care to see the suite. Katherine refused, but I agreed. It seemed to me that the secret, whatever it was, might lie there; that if the florist's messenger could depart by a rear staircase, it would be possible for others who wished to avoid scrutiny to arrive by the same method. Something had happened to Howard Somers in those rooms, I felt; something which had altered his attitude toward his family and toward Walter, and which Jim had indicated in his defense.

And—strange how things will come to one at the most unusual times!—it was while walking down that corridor, with its Chinese vases on pedestals, its gilt mirrors here and there over console tables, that I thought of Margaret Somers.

Suppose Margaret were still alive? And suppose that Walter knew this, had secured that fund of fifty thousand dollars for her? No wonder, in that case, that he had refused to explain it! He had shown a real fondness for Judy, and detest Katherine as he certainly did, he would certainly never willingly invalidate his father's second marriage at the cost of exposure of Margaret's deception.

So perfectly did this theory fit the facts that I found myself stopping in the hall and turning to look back at Katherine, secure in the dignity of her grief, handsome and immobile in her chair.

The suite was a four-roomed one. Each of the rooms opened onto the hall, and the sitting room occupied a corner. To the right was the room which Howard had occupied, and beyond it a small one for maid or valet. Opening from the sitting room on the left was another bedroom, and just beyond it lay the service staircase.

Miss Todd was explaining.

"The small bedroom was used by the nurses, as it connected with the sickroom. The one beyond was kept for Mr. Walter, and for several nights he slept there."

But whatever their secret, the rooms yielded nothing.

I was still thinking of Margaret, and I wondered then if Katherine suspected what I did; if behind her strangeness during these last weeks there had been such a suspicion; a terror in which she saw her wifehood not only stultified but destroyed, and Judy nameless. And I know now that she had suspected, had feared just that. Why had Howard come, almost stealthily, to the city, light of luggage and without his valet, prearranging to meet Walter and dining upstairs so that they might talk undisturbed, unless it was that Walter had some shocking and terrible thing to tell him? Something which Howard refused to believe, and later had believed.

When I went out into the hall again she had not moved in her chair.

Miss Todd glanced toward her.

"She looks very sad."

"She is in great grief, naturally."

She was locking the door. Now she turned to me swiftly, and lowered her voice.

"He was a fine man, Mr. Somers," she said. "No nonsense about him; you know what I mean. If you sat where I do——! So you'll understand me when I tell you this: there was a young woman who tried to see him, after he began to improve. I think myself that she had waited below in the lobby until she saw Miss Gittings go for her walk, and then came up. She didn't come to the desk. She got out of the elevator somewhere below and came up the service stairs. I happened to see her, or she'd have been inside. She had tried the bedroom door, but it was locked, and I caught her before she got to the sitting room door."

"What excuse did she give?"

"She said she must be on the wrong floor. She was looking for a Mrs. Stewart, from St. Louis. But I took the trouble to find out that there was no Mrs. Stewart from St. Louis or anywhere else, in the house." We were close to Katherine now, so she lowered her voice still further. "She was a pretty girl," she added hurriedly, "with bright red hair. And she went as white as a sheet when I spoke to her."

CHAPTER XXI

I HAD PLENTY to think of that day, and plenty of time in which to think.

It is a strange fact that death or sickness brings friends in numbers. They call, send flowers, telephone. But real trouble, a trouble like ours with its accompaniment of tragedy and shame, embarrasses them. The kindest thing apparently is to stay away.

I did not miss them, but I did miss the Inspector. I had grown fond of him, and his visits had been breaks in what were long and not too cheerful days. But he too, perhaps out of some mistaken sense of delicacy, was absenting himself, and I was much alone.

I needed him badly that day. Elise's discovery of a "ghost" in the trunk room, the possibility that Mary Martin as long ago as last summer had tried to see Howard, and that angry statement of Howard's to Wallie, "if you think you are going to hold that over me you can think again"; all these must have some bearing on our mystery.

And he was friendly to us. I knew that. Friendly and not too certain of Jim's guilt. I was resolved that from now on there would be no reservations on my part. I would show him the clock dial paper and tell him of that quarrel in the hotel. But before I did that I would go over Sarah's record of Howard's illness. She had a habit of scrawling on them odd facts, not always relating to the patient.

"Set mouse trap," I recall seeing on one of them long ago.

It was with a certain amount of hope then that I went up to Sarah's room that afternoon.

The records I had placed in the lower drawer of her wardrobe trunk, and I got them out and laid them on the bed. They were all there; Judy's diphtheria, the measles among Laura's children, the time I fell downstairs and broke my collar bone, and Katherine's periodical quinsy.

At last I found what I wanted. I sat back and went over it carefully. The early days of that sickness at the hotel had been active ones; the records showed treatments, hypodermics, careful comments on the patient's pulse, his weakness, his depression. It was clear that he had been depressed.

Then came improvement. "Patient more cheerful." "Appetite better." "Sitting up in bed today." On the eighth day came an entry at four o'clock. "Mr. Walter with patient from four to six while I took walk. Reports him more cheerful." After that, not regularly, but often, came the entry. "Out for walk. Patient comfortable."

It was not until I reached the date when Mr. Waite had made the rough draft of the will, August 12th, that I found anything of importance. The page for that date, and the one for the day following, were missing!

I could not believe it at first. I went over the record again and again; I even searched the other records, neatly clamped together and docketed. But it was not until I re-examined the page dated August 11th that I found anything, and what I found was more surprising than helpful.

At the bottom of the column marked Notes, Sarah had written in pencil "August 12th and 13th withdrawn for safekeeping." And beneath that: "Clock dial. Five o'clock right. Seven o'clock left. Press on six."

"Withdrawn for safekeeping." Then Sarah had known that she had written something on those two pages which was of grave importance; I only prayed that she had not known how grave. What visitors had she entered in that column on the 12th? Or what had happened to make Howard Somers, on that very day, decide to make a new will and leave Wallie a half of his estate plus a secret fund?

It was beyond me. I locked the room, went downstairs and telephoned for the Inspector.

He came that night, looking sheepish and uncomfortable.

"Didn't know you'd care to see me," he said.

"You know well enough that you don't believe Jim Blake is guilty, Inspector."

To my alarm he shook his head.

"I'm not so sure. He was with the Gunther girl that night, according to the colored woman. He knew about the will all right. Mind you, I'm not saying he'd planned the thing. He got excited and angry, and Sarah Gittings wouldn't give up the will. Maybe he knocked her down first. Then he went crazy, and he finished the job."

My heart sank.

"After that he'd have to do away with Florence. She knew too much."

"And Howard?"

"Murder's not proved there."

However, when I told him of what we had learned at the hotel, and about Mary Martin, he seemed less certain.

"Funny thing about that girl," he said. "We can't locate her. You'd think she'd be looking for work, but she hasn't. The District Attorney isn't interested, but I am. She knows a lot, if you ask me."

"Do you always find what you are looking for, Inspector?"

"Pretty often."

And then I laid out on the desk that page from Sarah's record, and the clock dial Judy had found in Florence's shoe. His face was a study when I explained the latter.

"So Judy found it, eh?" he said, and poked it with the end of a toothpick. "Intelligent girl, Miss Judy. And what does she think it means?"

"In view of the record, I think it indicates the place where Sarah hid the two missing pages."

He placed the two clock dial directions side by side, and fell to studying them.

"They are not ciphers," he said. "They are perfectly clear directions, if one only—— I suppose you've tried all your clocks?"

"The young people have," I said resignedly.

"The chances are that it doesn't refer to a clock at all. Something which might be described in clock fashion; that's all. And something to which one or both the women had access. Not a safe, either."

"You think I'm correct as to the records?"

"It's probably so. What happened is this: until Sarah learned the terms of the new will those records lay in her room. They had no importance, no value. But she learned the terms of the will, and then for some reason they were important. So she hid them. She may have hidden them first in the wood cellar; that would account for the chair.

"But before she went out that last night she hid them again. Now let's see. She didn't leave the house between her return at five-fifteen and seven, when she left again?"

"I don't know. I don't think so."

"Still, that means nothing. She didn't die until ten o'clock. Between seven and ten she was somewhere, and according to the colored woman she was not at the house on Halkett Street."

I was tempted then to tell him Jim's story to Godfrey Lowell of that evening. But I did not.

"She went somewhere, and she hid those records," he said. "Find where she went and we find them, and perhaps some other things I'd like to know. Why, for instance, with these two women dead, does the search for these records go on? What did Sarah Gittings record on at least one of those two days which is vital to the killer? Here's Jim Blake under indictment, and they're apparently still important."

"Still very important," I said, and then I told him about Elise and her ghost.

He asked at once to see the window, and later on he talked with Elise, while I interpreted as best I could. It was not until he was with us in the hall on the way out that he asked me if I suspected any of the servants.

"They could be bribed, you know," he said. "Are you sure all this fright is genuine?"

"I have almost to put the women to bed myself, Inspector. As to Joseph, he puts up a good front, but I notice that he draws the window shades before dark now, and I'm terrified to walk suddenly into his pantry at night, for fear he'll shoot me."

"He still maintains that he was attacked?"

"He's sure of it."

I went out to the drive with him. It was a warm spring night with plenty of stars, and he stopped and looked up at them.

"Mighty nice," he said. "I like the stars. I like nature, too. And I'm in this sort of business!" But a moment later he was advising me to get back into the house.

"Either Jim Blake's guilty, or whoever is guilty is still free. And that's not a nice thought, Miss Bell. It's somebody who can think faster than the police, and see every angle and every emergency. A dangerous mind, Miss Bell, prepared to go to any length to attain its end. Big men in business often have it, professional gamblers have it; some traders on the Exchange have it. Lombroso says there's a criminal type. There may be. But there is a criminal mind, and this fellow has it."

He waited to see that I got safely back into the house, and then went on.

That was the evening of the 27th of May, and long shall I remember it.

At half past nine Judy and Dick came in. Katherine had made it clear that Dick was not welcome at the Pine Street house, and so now and then the two of them met in my library. On such occasions I would discreetly retire, but I think even Katherine would have found these meetings harmless enough. Early and late the two were on the crime. On one never to be forgotten night, for example, Dick had lowered himself into the light shaft by his hands, and found that it was just possible to obtain a precarious foothold on the iron bar beneath.

But getting him out had been a different matter, and when at last he hung panting on the sill, both Judy and I were exhausted.

"Well," he said. "If Jim Blake did that by himself, he's a better man than I am, Rudyard Kipling."

On this particular night they came in filled with suppressed excitement. Amos had emerged from hiding long enough to see Dick that day, and had told him certain details which he had withheld before the Grand Jury.

Dick did the talking, while Judy watched him.

"In the first place," he said, "do you believe Jim Blake is guilty?"

"I do not."

"Well, neither do we. But I've got something to tell you that will make you think. Amos went into his room the next morning, and he found some blood on Jim Blake's clothes, and a handkerchief pretty well soaked with it. He showed it to Blake, and Blake said he'd cut his hand the night before. The hand was tied up, all right, and there was a cut. Amos saw it later. Of course he might have done that himself to explain the blood, but we don't believe it. Amos is hiding because he doesn't want to tell that at the trial. He cleaned the clothes as best he could, but when he sent the laundry out some time later he found that Jim had washed the handkerchief.

"But there's something else. The next day, after Sarah was missing, at noon and after you had telephoned to him, Jim Blake got out of bed, dressed in some old clothes and went out. It was raining, and when he came back he was wet and his shoes were muddy.

"Now, I'll admit that all that looks queer. I believe he was on that hillside the next day, looking for something. What? Either he'd killed Sarah and was afraid he'd dropped something incriminating, or he knew something had happened there the night before.

"He was there. He saw somebody, or something, but he isn't saying what or who. Now why?

"Why has he done the things he has done? Why leave that sword-stick around until the body is found, and then only put it in a closet? That's foolish.

"And why go to bed? Guilt? The normal thing would have been to go around as though nothing had happened. But he goes to bed, like a baby. Now what puts him to bed; if he wasn't guilty he wasn't scared. So what's the answer? He's shocked. He's had an awful jolt of some sort. He's either happened on the body, or on the murderer with the body. If he saw only the body he'd have notified the police. But if he saw the murderer—"

"I daresay I'm stupid, Dick. If he'd seen either of them, why not call the police?"

Judy turned to me.

"Dick believes," she said patiently, "that Uncle Jim recognized somebody on the hillside that night, and that he is either afraid to tell who it was, or that he has—other reasons."

"For not telling?"

"For not telling."

"Reasons so strong that he is willing to go to the chair rather than tell them? That's ridiculous."

"Not if he recognized the person he saw on that hillside, or wherever it was."

And I saw between them once more that practically wordless exchange which I found so irritating; Judy staring at Dick, and Dick making a gesture, at once protesting and protective.

"But who could that be? Not Wallie. We know that."

Judy looked at me, and I have never seen so tragic a look in a child's eyes.

"Dick thinks it might have been father."

I do not blame them, poor young things. Indeed, thinking that over later, I was not so sure that they were not right. Here was Jim, asking the day after Sarah's death about Howard, and if I was certain he had not been down recently; and burning his papers later on, as though some such inquiry might have been made by letter and answered.

And there was the whole situation; a secret will, to be kept from Howard's family, and even embodying a further secret clause. Howard might have had reason in his own mind for desperate measures to prevent Katherine learning of that will. And then, unable to bear that weight of guilt, or confronted with Jim the night of his death, he had resorted to suicide.

I was, however, profoundly shocked at the time, so much so that Judy rang for some sherry for me.

"I know," she said, "I feel like that too. But if Uncle Jim's innocent he's not going to the chair. And it will be the chair unless something is done, and done soon."

Apparently there was something to be done, simple enough on the face of it. We were to go, the three of us, to the path into the park, and there conduct an experiment as to the possibility of recognizing each other.

"It's the same sort of night," Dick said. "Stars but no moon. You two can go down to where Uncle Jim said he rested—" even then I noted the Uncle Jim—"and I'll cut across the hillside. I'll stop when you can see me enough to recognize me."

And this we did. That end of the park was deserted, and we saw no one. Dick left us at the Larimer lot, and cut across directly to the hillside. We could hear him working his way through the brush for some time, then we lost him. Judy and I followed the street to the path, and then down the hill.

Halfway down we stopped and Judy lighted a cigarette. She had not spoken at all until then. An unusual thing for her, and by the light of the match I thought she was crying.

"It's a crazy idea," she said. "We're all crazy. And why the devil doesn't he come?"

It did seem to be taking Dick a long time. Judy sat down finally, her hands clasped about her knees.

"There's more light than I thought," she said. "That street lamp up there helps. I can see you plainly, Elizabeth Jane."

But stare as we might we could not see Dick, and at last Judy got up. "I'd better go over," she said. "He may have fallen."

I had a queer feeling even then that something was not right. The silence was appalling, and I remember wishing we had brought the dogs. Judy was ahead, hard to follow in her black dress, and so we progressed for some two hundred feet along the steep hillside.

But we did not find Dick at all. Judy was frantically calling him by that time, and I remember looking up to see my own garage towering above me, and so excited was I that I hardly recognized it. And then hearing Judy's voice Joseph came on the run, and in no time at all we had the police there.

They found Dick unconscious in a deep wash beneath the Larimer lot. Whether he had fallen or had been struck we did not know, but he had a deep wound on the back of his head.

They took him to the hospital at once, and up to the operating room. There was no fracture, however, but a bad concussion of the brain, and both Judy and I spent the night in his room.

Some time during that endless night, with Judy sitting beside the bed where Dick's long figure never moved and nurses came and went in that silence which is as ominous as death, a thought came to me, who seemed not to be thinking at all. This thought was that here was a crime which could not be laid to Jim; which might even help him. Whether Dick lived or died—and I prayed God that he live—the unknown killer was still at large.

And, now that Dick was to live, something of that relief, and more, was in Judy's mind.

Toward morning she got stiffly out of her chair and coming over to me put her hand on my shoulder.

"You see, we were wrong," she said, rather childishly. "We were both wrong, Elizabeth."

At dawn Dick became conscious and reached out for Judy's hand. But it was not until evening of that day that he told his story.

He had reached the edge of the lot, and was climbing down the hillside. When he reached the gully he stopped, hesitating whether to cross or go around it, and at that moment he heard a sound above him.

There was at this point no direct light from the street lamp, but a faint reflected radiance. The crest of the hill, however, with the lamp behind it, stood out clearly silhouetted against the night. And against that outline something was moving; an indistinguishable mass, close to the ground.

It was perhaps eight feet above him, and he had thought at first that it was a dog. He decided to go up the hill and around the head of the wash, and then the thing came at him. That was all he remembered, and even now that is all we know.

It is probable that nothing more than surveillance of our movements was intended. But Dick altered his course, recognition was imminent, and the reaction was quick and violent.

CHAPTER XXII

WITH THE SURPRISING recuperative power of youth Dick was out again in a few days. But although preparations for Jim's trial were going on rapidly, that attack had not only completely undermined the *morale* of my household, it was causing Inspector Harrison some sleepless nights also.

He had examined the hillside again but without result. The weather had been dry as well as warm, and there were no footprints. He was completely baffled, and he did not hesitate to say so.

"I don't want any miscarriage of justice," he said. "I'm not like the District Attorney. I do my work and my job goes on, convictions or no convictions; and I don't give a particular damn for the press. What I want is the guilty man. And I'm not so sure we've got him."

Dick had been hurt the twenty-seventh of May, Friday. On Monday morning I came downstairs to find the Inspector having a comfortable cup of coffee in the pantry. He was not at all abashed, put down the kitchen clock which he had been examining, said briefly that it needed cleaning, and followed me into the front hall.

After his habit, he stopped at the lavatory and looked inside.

"Has it ever occurred to you," he said, "that that pencil Walter Somers produced was not what he found in that air shaft?"

"I think Judy——"

"Ha!" he said. "Trust Miss Judy. She knows. Well, it wasn't. Now, here are the facts about the pencil, Miss Bell. In the first place, I believe that it was yours; to be truthful about it, we found your fingerprints on it. Yours, and Walter Somers'. No others. In the second place, I believe it was taken from your desk that night, and deliberately placed on that skylight. I have not said that it was taken for that purpose, although it might have been. Do you recall Walter Somers using a pencil that night? Before he started the investigation?"

"I don't think he did. He may have."

"He didn't look into the skylight, get down and go on some errand into the library?"

"He went in for some matches."

"Matches, eh? Well, he's a smoker, and the average cigarette smoker carries them. I think he got that pencil, and let's see if I'm right. We have to remember, of course, that Walter Somers knows something he's not telling. Now, he looks down that air shaft, and he sees something there which he recognizes; a key, maybe; or a watch charm, or a fountain pen, or a false tooth! Anyhow, something that he knows at sight, or suspects. He comes down, goes into the library for matches and picks up a pencil and slips it in his pocket. He climbs the ladder, gets this object, shows you the pencil instead, and there you are.

"Being afraid of nothing, he seals it up for the police. Clever, wasn't it? Only it was a bit too clever."

"He fooled us all, then."

"Not quite all of us," said the Inspector cheerfully. "You're not a smoker, I take it?"

"I don't smoke. No."

"Don't carry pencils around in your pockets?"

"Women have no pockets nowadays."

"All right. And what sort of clothing did Walter Somers wear that night?"

"His dinner jacket."

"Black. Now here's what the microscope showed, Miss Bell. That pencil had been carried in the pocket of a black suit; in the side pocket, where a man often carries a package of cigarettes. There were bits of tobacco from cigarettes caught around the eraser, along with black filaments from the pocket. Now, I've watched Walter Somers. He doesn't use a cigarette case; he carries his cigarettes in a paper packet in his right hand coat pocket. And I don't mind telling you that I've had that coat, and that this pocket bears out the facts. He had that pencil there before he climbed that ladder."

"Walter!" I gasped. "But I thought you said——"

"Not so fast," he warned me. "No, he didn't kill Sarah Gittings, if your alibi for him is correct. Although alibis are tricky things. Still, three alibis are good and sufficient for anybody. But look at the case against him!

"He gets his father to change his will in his favor. The news leaks out, and he's afraid it will get to Mrs. Somers and the good work will be undone. So he kills Sarah Gittings for fear she'll talk, and Florence Gunther because she's trying to see you and tell you what she knows. Then, later on—"

"He would never have lifted a hand against his father."

"No? Well, I daresay not. Anyhow, he didn't. We have him checked for that night too. But it's a pity. It's a perfect case otherwise. But to get back to this pencil. We have only two guesses; either he had had it in his pocket for some time, and substituted it for what he found on the skylight. Or he already suspected or knew what was there, took the pencil from your desk, and used the ladder to remove something which was damaging."

"To him?"

"Not necessarily; but to some one." He sat back, thoughtfully. "I've already said that this is a family matter, Miss Bell. I've never seen a family more apparently united to frustrate justice and protect a criminal! It's disunited every other way, but when it comes to these murders it turns a solid front to the world. Now, what was the purpose of that little drama on the hillside the other night?"

"To see if poor Jim Blake could have recognized somebody there," I said defiantly.

"Precisely! And Jim Blake keeping his mouth shut and ready to take what comes! Who is he protecting? Who is Joseph protecting? He helps somebody out of that shaft, or at least to get out of the house. He finishes your job in the cellar and burns the carpet, and later on he gets knocked on the head for his trouble. How far can the police go, in a case like that?"

They had not found Mary Martin. That is strange, when I think back over it. She was not trying to hide; not then, at least. She was indeed, as the Inspector was to admit disgustedly later on, "under their noses."

Nor were any of us seeing much of Wallie. Judy suggested that he was trying, like the police, to locate Mary.

"But why?"

"Because he's crazy about her."

"I don't believe it."

"Don't you? I found her in his arms the day he came to New York, after father died. He had gone out, but he came back."

"Judy!"

"Well, I did. She was crying, and he was smoothing her hair and whispering to her. I just backed out and let them be miserable."

"She may have broken down, and he was trying to quiet her."

But she only smiled, as from the depths of some secret knowledge which she knew well enough I did not possess.

I thought over that after Judy had gone. I thought back to the night of Sarah's death, and Mary's sudden pause in the drive when she learned that

Sarah was still out. Wallie had been nervous too, I seemed to remember. At some time in the evening he had asked about Sarah.

"And where was Sarah, while all this was going on?"

"She was out."

"And she's still out?"

"Yes."

It seemed to me now that he had looked slightly surprised and rather thoughtful; but how much of this impression was due to what had followed I was not certain.

But what did Mary Martin know? What possible business could she have had with Howard? A business so furtive that she must wait until Sarah was out, and so urgent that she had gone as white as a sheet when she was stopped.

She had not gone to Walter. Her errand—providing there was an errand—was one she was apparently concealing from Walter. It was a part of that same motive which had lain behind that strange procedure of hers when she had walked into Katherine's New York apartment and by sheer audacity superseded poor Maude Palmer.

According to Katherine she had not wanted me to know that she was there.

"Why?" Katherine had asked.

"She would think I had used what I know, to my own advantage."

Frightened, beyond a doubt; pale, as she had been pale that day at the hotel. But quietly determined. Hiding herself away in a little room downtown, going out at night to throw something into the river, and then—going to bed and "sleeping well." As though some weight was off her mind, as though now at last all was well, and safe. Poor Mary!

I had had my talk with the Inspector on Monday morning, and on Tuesday he asked permission to go over the house once more. Never have I seen a more exhausting search, or less result from it, unless I except the bewildered indignation of the servants. But at the last I did a thing I shall regret to the end of my life. I locked the ormolu cabinet and put the key away.

Simmons was in charge, and he came to me about it. But I explained that it had been examined, and that my mother's Chelsea figures inside were very precious and not to be handled. He was satisfied, and so it was not opened.

Nothing else escaped them; the chair and sofa cushions, the mattresses, even the kitchen utensils and the washing machine in the laundry were closely examined; and the unfortunate Simmons spent some warm hours in the wood cellar, carefully moving the wood. But they found no papers, nor anything resembling a clock dial save on the clocks themselves.

The mere fact of the search, however, had greatly unnerved both Clara and Norah, and had a result beyond any of our expectations.

Norah asked that night to be allowed to keep Jock in her room, and Clara took Isabel. The total result of which was that I was awakened at three o'clock in the morning by a most horrible scream. It seemed to come from the back of the house, and was both prolonged and agonized.

I leaped out of bed and threw open my door. Joseph had similarly opened his, and I heard his voice.

"Who is it? What's wrong?"

There was a moan, and turning on the lights Joesph and I ran to the back stairs. Norah in her nightdress was crouched there on the landing, her hands over her eyes.

"I've seen her!" she wailed. "I've seen her!"

"Stop that noise," said Joseph sternly. "You're scaring the whole neighborhood. Who have you seen?"

"Miss Sarah. I saw her, right at the foot of those stairs. She was standing there looking at me. In her uniform, too. All white."

And to this absurd story she adhered with the dogged persistency of her type.

It appeared that Jock had wakened and had demanded to be taken out. He had whimpered and scratched at the door, and at last, none too happily, Norah had started down with him.

At the top of the back stairs, however, he had stopped and given a low growl. Norah had looked down. There is a lamp on the garage, and since our trouble I had ordered it left burning all night. Through the pantry window it sends a moderate amount of light into the pantry, and in that doorway Norah claimed to have seen her figure.

"And after that, what?" I demanded.

"I don't know. I shut my eyes."

Only one thing struck me as curious in all this. So far as I know, Elise, terrified by Judy's dire threats, had said nothing of the figure in the attic and was now at a safe and discreet distance.

The next day I went over the house again with Joseph. New locks had been placed wherever possible and bolts supplemented them at the doors, and in the basement I had had placed over the windows, gratings of stout iron well set into the bricks.

"What is it, Joseph?" I asked. "Do these women imagine these things? Or is somebody getting into the house?"

"They're very nervous, madam. And nothing has been taken."

I looked at him. It seemed to me that he stood not so erect as formerly; that he looked older and very tired. And lately I had noticed that he was less certain in his movements, slightly inco-ordinate. I put my hand on his arm.

"This is wearing on you, Joseph," I said. "Would you like a vacation? I daresay we could manage."

But he shook his head.

"Thank you, madam, but I'd prefer to stay. I've been a bit shaken since the attack; that's all."

"And you still have no idea who struck you?"

I thought that he hesitated. Certainly the arm under my hand perceptibly tightened. But although I know now that Joseph knew perfectly well who had struck him and that his very soul was seething with anger, it shows the almost incredible self-control of the man that his voice was as impassive as ever.

"Not the slightest, madam."

He must have been intensely curious. That searching of the house by the police, what did it mean? But he said nothing, asked no questions. A perfect upper servant, Joseph. A very perfect servant.

The incident did not add to my peace of mind. I would lie in my bed at night and imagine that I heard stealthy movements, faint stirrings. Nor were these limited to the lower floor; sometimes they were over my head, and once indeed in my very boudoir, next to my bedroom. When I called out sharply they ceased and were not renewed.

It was on the second day after Norah's experience, and sitting alone in my study that evening, that I decided to spy on my house; to lock myself securely in my room and listen to it. And this was less difficult than may appear.

The old speaking tubes in the house are simple of operation. To use them one opens them and drawing a long breath, expels it into the tube. The result is a wail of no mean caliber, wherever the tube may lead. But, once opened, these tubes are excellent conductors of sound, and as during a long invalidism my dear mother had managed her household from her bedroom, some four of these tubes led to the chamber which I now occupy, practically forgotten but still serviceable.

Joseph was out, but Clara was in the pantry. I shall never forget her face when I told her to go to the wood cellar and to bring me a small piece of wood to the library.

"And a knife, Clara. A very sharp knife."

"A knife, ma'am? A butcher knife?"

"The sharpest one you can find, Clara."

She was still staring at me as I turned and went out, and it shows the state of nerves in the household that after she had brought me the knife she turned and ran like a scared rabbit.

I cut my wood—and also my finger—and in the end I managed to prop open all the tubes except that in the pantry. After I had sent Clara to bed I opened that one also, and by midnight I was safely locked in my room with the lights out, and ready for my vigil.

For the first hour nothing happened. I heard Joseph come in the back door, apparently pick up the knife, mutter something and put it away. I heard the sound of the refrigerator opening and closing, and gathered that he was taking a little refreshment up to bed with him. And then, until one o'clock, there was a complete silence.

At that time I began to hear a faint sound. It came from the drawing room, and was too far away to identify, but it was unmistakable. Now and then it stopped, only to resume again. It was a stealthy scraping, rather like that of a mouse nibbling at a board. And indeed, as it went on interminably, I believed that that was what it was. The tube ran through the old walls, and we are liable to onsets of mice, as are all old houses.

I do not know how long it lasted, or when it ceased. It stopped abruptly, and although I listened intently there was nothing further. No stealthy footsteps followed it. The silence was complete.

I was up early the next morning, a trifle ashamed of the whole proceeding, to remove the strips of wood. The drawing room was undisturbed, as was the rest of the lower floor.

But Joseph was to interpret those sounds for me that very morning, and with my breakfast tray.

"I think we will not be troubled again, madam."

"Troubled?"

"At night. I have found the means by which the person entered."

And so indeed he had. According to his story he had gone into the drawing room to open it, and had set the rear door open. On the upper step he noticed some bits of putty, and on examining it he found that it was soft.

The device had apparently been a simple one. The old putty around one of the panes had been carefully dug out and fresh soft putty substituted. To gain access to the house it was only necessary to remove this, a matter of a moment, and with adhesive material fastened to the pane, to draw it carefully out.

Inspector Harrison, examining the pane, decided that adhesive tape had been used for this purpose.

As there is no path there, the steps leading directly onto the grass, there were no footprints. But as a result of this discovery the Inspector himself that day placed a heavy iron bar across the door, and personally examined the doors and windows.

He was not entirely satisfied, however.

"That bolt on the door," he said to me, "it's beyond a normal man's reach from that pane. Now it's conceivable that Joseph might forget that bolt once, and on the night that somebody had planned to get in. But twice, or a half dozen times! I don't believe it."

"He might have pushed it back with something. The man outside, I mean."

"Well, he might," he admitted grudgingly.

CHAPTER XXIII

THE IMMEDIATE RESULT of that discovery was my decision to tell Katherine all I knew. Partly to save her in her trouble and partly because I did not trust her discretion at that time, I had never told her about the missing sheets from Sarah's records.

She listened attentively while I told her of that excursion of Judy's and mine to Florence Gunther's room, and of what we had found there, and I showed her Sarah's record of the eleventh of August.

"Have you told Godfrey Lowell that?"

"Not yet. I've been trying to locate the missing pages."

She got up, rang the bell and ordered the car.

"It is hard to forgive you for this, Elizabeth," she said. "To hold that back, with Jim's very life hanging on it!"

"I don't see how it helps Jim."

"Don't you? Don't you know what was on those records? That Howard never made a will at all, or that he was drugged when he did it. One of those two things."

She had not waited for Elise. She was dragging out her outdoor garments, hurrying about—strange to see Katherine hurry—with two purplish spots of excitement high on her cheeks. Judy came in and stood by helplessly.

"It's been clear to me from the start. That man Waite has forged this will, and Walter Somers bribed him to do it."

"With what?" Judy demanded.

"On his prospects. How do you know that fifty thousand dollars wasn't the bribe?"

She was still talking when we got into the car, still feverishly excited. Judy begged her to be calm, not to say anything disastrous, but I doubt if she heard her. But when she made that flat statement to Godfrey Lowell, he sat upright in his chair, stiff and angry.

"I have the utmost confidence in Mr. Waite," he said. "An accusation of that sort necessarily involves his probity, Mrs. Somers."

"How do you know how honest he is?" she said sharply. "Men have been bought before this."

"The will was witnessed. I can have those signatures examined if you like. But——"

"What good would that do? The witnesses are dead. Maybe that's the reason why they are dead."

But Godfrey shook his head.

"No," he said. "I understand and I sympathize with you, Mrs. Somers. But that will was made by Mr. Somers, properly drawn by a man above reproach and signed and witnessed by two persons in Mr. Waite's presence before a notary. He has already sworn to that before the Grand Jury. He will so testify at the trial."

"Then why did Sarah hide the records of the two days when the will was drawn?"

"She did that?"

"She did. What was on those records, Mr. Lowell? Did she show that some pressure was brought to bear on Howard, or that he had been drugged?"

"Doctor Simonds says he was not drugged."

"What does he know? He wasn't there, was he?"

"Barring evidence to the contrary we shall have to take his word. He was there that night, and Mr. Somers was normal then."

Before we left he referred again to Katherine's statement about Mr. Waite.

"I know that you have had a great burden to bear, Mrs. Somers, and that naturally it is difficult for you to accept certain things. But some facts we must accept. During that illness all unpleasant feeling between Walter Somers and his father had been wiped out. In his conversation with Mr. Waite, Mr. Somers mentioned this. He was feeble, but quite clear as to his wishes. He felt that perhaps an injustice had been done to his son, and he wished to rectify it. That is why the will was drawn as it stands, and—as it will stand before any court, Mrs. Somers."

"Have you examined the signature?"

"I have, at Mr. Waite's own request. We have even had an expert on it. A forged signature under the microscope shows halts and jerks; the hand works slowly, and there are tremors."

"And this shows none of these?"

"Mr. Somers was not allowed to sit up. It shows the weakness of a sick man, writing in a constrained position. That's all."

She sat there, smoothing her gloves after that habit of hers, and her face looked drawn in the glare from the wide-open windows. Her anger was gone, and something disquieting had taken its place.

"Then this secret fund is beyond question?"

"Beyond question."

She said nothing more until we had got into the car. Then she spoke, looking ahead of her and with her face a white mask.

"So she is living, after all!"

"Who is living, Katherine?"

"Margaret."

Just how long she had been brooding over that possibility I do not know, but I think it explains much that had almost alienated me at the time; her refusal to accept the will, her frozen attitude even to Judy, the hours she spent locked away in her room, inaccessible even to her maid.

"I don't believe it, Katherine."

"I do," she said with stiff lips. "It would be like her, wouldn't it? To hide away for all these years, and then when she knows Howard is ill and dying, to let him know. She told Walter, and Walter told him."

Nothing I could say could shake that conviction. And here again we had grazed the cheek of truth, touched it and gone on. For Margaret was not living, as we were to learn at the end.

Certainly one of the most astounding things about our series of crimes—and perhaps about all baffling crimes—is the narrow margin by which, again and again, the solution evaded us. Despite the extraordinary precautions taken by the criminal, on at least a half dozen occasions safety was a matter of seconds only. One such incident was the sound outside Florence Gunther's room, the night Judy and I were there. Another, for example, was Clara's failure to identify the figure in the pantry door. Again, had the intruder on my staircase the night of Sarah's murder happened to have crept a few steps lower, the entire situation would have been changed. That I was resting when Florence came to see me resulted in her death before she had told her story.

There were others, also.

Had Judy turned that night in the garage she might have seen who it was who struck at her. And Dick, deciding by the merest chance to retrace his steps around the wash, confronted that crouching figure and was violently flung into the gully.

These and a dozen other instances which I was to recall later, had given me an almost superstitious attitude toward the case. Clearly it was not meant that we were to know until the deadly roster was complete, the whole sanguinary business finished. Then, when it was all over, Katherine with her deadly pertinacity was to step in, and the door was to play its part.

The next incident was a fair example of the narrow margins to which I have referred.

I have said little about reporters, but of course life had been made miserable by them for weeks; masculine and feminine, they had more or less invaded us. Dick's injury had resulted in a fresh influx, and so I had instructed the servants to inspect all callers from the library bay window before opening the doors.

A day or two after the visit to Godfrey Lowell the bell rang and Joseph tiptoed upstairs to say that a suspicious looking woman was on the doorstep. By that I knew he meant probably a reporter, but something made me ask what she looked like.

"A big woman," he said. "Rather flashy, madam."

"Humph," I said. "Big? All the ladies of the press so far have been small, Joseph. Small and young."

The bell rang again, almost fiercely, and suddenly a curious thing happened to me. I had a vision of Florence Gunther standing there, ringing the bell and being turned away. It came and went while the bell was still ringing.

"Let her in, Joseph. I'll see her."

He disapproved, I knew. It was in every line of his back. But in the end he admitted her, and it developed that my caller was Lily Sanderson.

She looked tired, I thought, too tired even to be self-conscious.

"I guess you have enough bother without my adding to it," she said. "But I had to come. I had really."

She sat down and put her hands to her hat.

"I guess I look something dreadful. I've been losing a lot of sleep, and what with being on my feet all day——"

"Would you like some tea?"

"No, thanks. I feel too mussy. I want to get home and get my shoes off. My feet swell something dreadful these days. Not getting to bed properly, you know."

"Can't you slip them off now? Your shoes?"

But the idea seemed to outrage her sense of the proprieties. She shook her head.

"I'll just give you my message and be getting on. It's about Mrs. Bassett. She's sick. She's got—" She lowered her voice, as always will women of a certain age when mentioning cancer. "She's got a cancer, and it's too late to operate. She's living on morphia. Her daughter's there now, but I relieve her at night. That is, I sleep on a sofa, and if she gets bad she calls me."

But the point of the matter was this: after Mrs. Bassett had had morphia she would grow talkative, "what with the pain stopping, and anyhow I guess morphia does loosen the tongue." And Miss Sanderson would listen.

"It's really awful," she said. "Me working all day and trying to sleep, and her talking on and on. Sometimes she'll say: 'You're not listening.' And I'll wake up and tell her I am. But what I'm coming to, she's talked a lot about Florence. She's got her on her mind. And she knows something, Miss Bell. She knows something about that murder."

"What makes you think that?"

"She's as much as said so. The other night she called me in the middle of the night and told me to get somebody from headquarters; she wanted to make a statement about something. So I got the telephone book, but I didn't know what to look for, and then I heard her calling like a crazy woman. I went in, and she was running her tongue over her lips—morphia makes them dry, you know—and looking at me with a queer sly look. 'I haven't anything to tell the police,' she said. 'It's this stuff they give me. I guess I was dreaming.' But I didn't believe her then and I don't now. She meant to tell the police something, and then she got frightened."

"It might not have been about Florence, at that."

"Listen!" She leaned forward. "I told you I heard two people in that room the night Florence was killed, didn't I? And that one of them was a woman and she was crying? Well, why wasn't that Mrs. Bassett?"

She sat back, having made her effect, and gazed at me triumphantly.

"Mind you," she said. "I'm not saying she had anything to do with the murder. She's a decent sort of woman, and she's had a hard time; roomers at the house, and going out to give body massage into the bargain. She knows something, that's all I say. And I stick to it."

"Would she talk to the police if they went there?"

"I doubt it. She's thought it over, and she's made up her mind. She's afraid; afraid of somebody."

She had, however, no more idea as to this somebody's identity than I had. She knew no more of Mrs. Bassett than the average roomer knows of her landlady. She believed that there was a husband living, but she had never seen him. The daughter had given up a good position to take care of her, she understood. She rambled on while I thought. Only one thing struck me as being significant in all this, and that was that Mrs. Bassett had given massage.

"What does she look like?" I asked. "I mean, in build? Is she tall?"

"She's medium height, and stocky. Very muscular. Even now she isn't as weak as you'd expect."

I sat up. Was it possible that Mrs. Bassett was the heavy-set woman who had given Howard Somers massage at the hotel? And if so, what would that mean? What did she know? What had she learned in those rooms, during those mysterious days of the illness, that might be valuable now? That, it seemed to me, was the important thing, and not Lily Sanderson's guess that she had been in Florence's room the night she was killed.

One could imagine her, her sleeves showing her strong arms as she bent over the bed, working mechanically. And then, something being said, some quarrel going on or some name being mentioned which had registered in her mind. Then, lying in her bed, the impulse to tell what she knew, and the second impulse, more profound, to be allowed to die in peace.

"Did she ever mention any of her patients?"

"I think not. She isn't what you would call talkative."

"I wondered. We know that a woman answering that description gave massage a few times to Mr. Howard Somers here last year. But I daresay Doctor Simonds would know."

That, however, did not interest Miss Sanderson. What she wanted, and finally brought out, was that I should myself see Mrs. Bassett and talk to her. That night if possible.

"Her heart's bad, and she may go any time like *that*." She snapped her fingers. "If you could work on her she might talk. Tell her all the trouble and sorrow that's going on. She's kind enough. I could have yelped myself when I saw that picture of Mr. Blake with the handcuffs."

Here the feeling that she had committed an indelicacy caused her to get up suddenly and prepare to go.

"That's fixed, is it? You'll come? Say about nine o'clock? I'll be watching for you. She'll have had her hypo at eight, and the daughter's going out. I've promised to relieve her early. I can smuggle you in." But she seemed loath to go. "I don't know why," she said, "but I get a funny feeling in that house at night. She thinks she hears things, and she lies and listens."

I let her out myself, and watched her go down the drive to the street. It occurred to me then that she was frightened, that she had been frightened all along; that she knew that to meddle in this matter might be deadly; that the same fear which had turned Mrs. Bassett stubbornly silent was in her. There was pathos in that. These two women, one worn with watching, one dying, and no peace for either of them. Shut in those two upper rooms, awake in the long night, and the sick woman "hearing things."

Doctor Simonds did not remember the Bassett woman. He had suggested massage, and either Sarah or Wallie had found some one. He himself had never seen her. He had two or three *masseuses* on his list, but they were all Danes or Swedes, there was no one named Bassett.

CHAPTER XXIV

I DID NOT TAKE the car that night. I had no desire to let Robert know of that visit. But I took Joseph, out of sheer panic, to see me safely down the hill and into the lighted portion of the park. There he turned back, and I went on alone.

A week of June had passed. The trees were in full leaf, and the scent of flowering shrubbery was in the air. I remember thinking that it would soon be two months since Sarah had been murdered, and that Florence had been dead for more than a month. And what did we know now, more than we knew then? Almost nothing. That Sarah had known Florence, that they had shared the knowledge of the will, and that Sarah had hidden two pages of a record which was being diligently sought by some one unknown!

Cleared of all extraneous matter, that was our case. We might suspect that Howard had been murdered, but we did not know it. We might believe Judy had been attacked, but had the ladder possibly fallen, after all? Had Joseph tumbled down the stairs? And had Dick surprised some venial malefactor who had simply pushed him out of the way?

And was the answer of the Grand Jury the correct one? Was it, after all, as simple as that, that Jim had killed Sarah to get the duplicate will, trusting to luck—and possibly Katherine—to get hold of the other?

I daresay I walked slowly, for it was after nine o'clock when I rang the door bell.

Almost at once it was opened and Lily Sanderson slid out on the step, closing the door behind her.

"Well, wouldn't you know it?" she said. "The husband's come to see her! He's up there now, and the daughter too, and there's been all sorts of a row. She'll be upset, and it's bad for her. It might even kill her."

I saw that she was crying, and I realized that her tears were not for me and my disappointment; that for a little time she had fed her starved womanhood on service, and that she had developed an affection for this unfortunate woman who had become for the time at least her child.

"You need sleep," I said. "Let the daughter stay tonight, and go to bed."

But she shook her head. She had stepped into the vestibule and drawn me in with her. "Look here," she said in a low voice, "what do you suppose the fuss is about? She's sick, and he knows it. Why is he jawing her? Is he afraid she'll tell something?"

"Who is he? What does he look like?"

"I never saw him, and I don't want to."

But she caught something in my face—we were in the vestibule, and there was a little light—and she turned swiftly and went into the house. She was back again almost immediately, her finger on her lips.

"He's coming down," she whispered. "Don't move."

She had partially closed the door behind her, and we stood there waiting, while the man slowly descended to the second floor. Still as it was on that by-street, his movements were amazingly quiet. Indeed, had I not been told that some one was descending that staircase, I would not have believed it. A creak now and then, the indescribable faint sounds of a moving body, were all I could hear.

Then, part way down the second flight he stopped. Evidently he had seen the partly opened door, and was looking at it. Lily Sanderson's face was curious in that half light. It was as though that descent, harmless enough until then, had become sinister. She stared at me, her mouth partly open, and thus we stood for an absurd time, waiting for the man on the stairs to make the first move.

Suddenly the tension became too much for her. She made an odd little sound and threw open the door. There was no man on the stairs, nobody in sight. She looked profoundly shocked, and she gave a sort of hysterical giggle.

"Can you beat that?" she whispered. "He went back!"

"Back where?"

"He went up to the second floor and down the back stairs. That is, if he's gone." Some rather awful thought evidently came into her mind at that moment, for she left me and ran up the stairs, her heavy legs and ridiculous heels moving with incredible rapidity. She went all the way to the third floor, and I could hear voices there; the daughter's, I imagined, and her own. She came down more quietly.

"It just occurred to me," she said breathlessly, "that—but she's all right. The daughter is with her."

"What in the world did you think?"

But she seemed rather ashamed.

"It was funny, his slipping out like that, wasn't it?" she asked. "Maybe Clarissa saw him."

As it turned out, however, Clarissa had already gone home. Her kitchen was dark, and I think it took some courage on Lily's part to go in and turn on the lights. But it was empty, and she turned her attention to the door. She looked around at me with a startled face.

"I forgot! He couldn't get out here. Clarissa takes the key with her. It's locked now, and the key's gone."

It was then that we both heard a sound from the pantry, and the swinging door into it opened and closed a few inches. It was an uncanny thing, and I can still see poor Lily, leaning on the kitchen table and staring at it, and admire the courage with which she raised her quavering voice.

"Who's there?"

In the silence which followed we both heard the front door softly close.

Evidently Mrs. Bassett's husband, or whoever the stealthy visitor might be, had found himself locked in the kitchen, and when we went there had taken refuge in the pantry. There were two swinging doors, and the opening of one, as we found by experiment, caused the other to move. As he escaped by the simple expedient of going forward through the dining room, this had happened.

But as Lily said, now blind to the proprieties and sitting weakly in a chair with her slippers in her hand, why escape at all?

"I don't believe it was her husband, Miss Bell," she said. "Anybody could come here and say that. That's why I went upstairs."

"To see if it was her husband?"

"To see if he had murdered her," she said, and somehow my blood ran cold.

I took a taxicab home that night, and I did not feel safe until I was in my own house once more, with Joseph double barring the door and the dogs, as usual in my absences, settled on the best library chairs.

I told the Inspector the next day of that experience in the Halkett Street house, but he pooh-poohed the idea of its having any connection with the crimes.

"Why make so much of it?" he said. "Most men tiptoe out of a sick-room. They may raise the devil inside but they tiptoe out. Watch that some time. And as for his hiding, well, maybe he did and maybe he didn't. How do you know he hadn't been crying? He'd rather be caught without his clothes than crying."

He was not so certain, however, after he had seen Mrs. Bassett that night. He had arranged with Lily Sanderson as I had, and this time the daughter was out. He stopped by on his way home.

"Not that I got anything," he said. "But there's something peculiar there."

She had absolutely refused to talk. Asked about her request for the police some time before, she denied having made it.

"I get queer ideas when I've had the dope they give me," she said, and lay there quietly, looking at something he could not see.

When he tried to discuss the murder of Florence Gunther she said nothing whatever. Nor was she much more communicative about her husband.

"My daughter's a good girl, but the least said of him the better."

Then she had said she was in pain and had called sharply for Lily, and he had come away.

"But she knows something," he told me. "Not necessarily that the husband has anything to do with it. She knows something. She had a queer look about her. I've seen it before."

"What sort of look?"

"I saw it once before in the face of a man just before he jumped out of a tenth story window."

And so, like everything else which might have helped in the defense, that too had come to nothing. I believe the Inspector made at least one other attempt to see her, but either she was frightened, or more likely she had been warned, for she told him nothing. And before our mystery was cleared up she was dead.

By the tenth of June, Jim's trial began. Public opinion and the prosecution had done everything possible to expedite the proceedings, and the defense was equally anxious. Jim was not bearing the confinement well. The jail was dark and airless, and the general feeling against him so strong and so infuriated that the authorities could do nothing to ameliorate his situation.

There had been leaks of various sorts. It was known that Jim's clothing had shown minute blood stains in spite of Amos, and that he had been on the hillside the night of Sarah's death at ten o'clock. Two persons, a man and a woman, had come forward to state that they were coming up the path that night, and that they had seen a man in light golf clothing, standing beside the path and wiping something from his hands with a handkerchief.

The man, named Francis X. Dennis, made his statement unwillingly enough.

"I didn't want to be mixed up in this," he told the reporters, "but my wife thinks we'd better speak up. We'd been taking a walk, and we came along to the foot of the hill about five minutes to ten.

"My wife's hearing is better than mine, and she stopped and said there was somebody scrambling through the bushes overhead. We listened, and it seemed like somebody was running along the hillside. We didn't start up until it got quiet again, and my wife was kind of nervous.

"Well, when we'd got about halfway up there was a man. He was about ten feet off the path on our right and I saw that he had on a light golf suit and a cap. He didn't pay any attention to us. He seemed to be busy with his hands, wiping them.

"After we'd got up the hill my wife said: 'He's cut himself. He's tying up his hand.' I said maybe he'd slipped and fallen when he was running, and—well, I guess that's about all."

It was a body blow for the defense, coming when it did and with a detail the more convincing because it was unstudied. Both these people believed that it was Jim they had heard running along the hillside below the Larimer lot toward the path, and Godfrey Lowell threw up his hands in despair.

"This case is being tried in the press," he said. "We'll have a verdict before we even get into court!"

But I have thought about Godfrey since, sitting in his office and talking to the imposing array of counsel who were to help him, and going home at night to lie awake for hours, studying the darkness for some weakness to attack, some point to be made:

"And I say to you, gentlemen of the jury——"

What? What could he say? That Jim was a good fellow who gave good dinners and played excellent bridge? That he was a decent citizen, who had spent that evening conversing harmlessly with another woman who had since been murdered? And that he was given to nosebleed, which would account for the blood on his clothes?

Jim still stubbornly silent, and Godfrey lying there and wondering. Was Jim innocent, after all?

I believe that until the day before the trial he was uncertain. Then I was able to give him a little, a very little help. Small as it was it heartened him, and on it he hung his defense, but even then he was not sure.

It was an odd conversation I had with the Inspector that second evening before Jim's trial. He marched in like a man with a purpose, and I saw that whatever that purpose might be he had dressed for it. He was always neat enough, but that night he was resplendent.

"This is a social call," he said. "I'm not a policeman now; I'll ask you to remember that."

And he added, not without embarrassment, that he felt very friendly toward all of us; that he had enjoyed his talks with me, and that he liked Judy. Then he sat still and stared at his well-polished boots.

"In that case," I suggested, "out of office hours, so to speak, and the whisky being some my father put away years ago, would you like a highball?"

Which he would, and did.

Perhaps it warmed him; perhaps he had come for the purpose. The upshot of it was that he said he did not want any miscarriage of justice the next few days, and that things were looking pretty black.

"The prosecution's going to get a conviction. It's out for one, and it'll get it. Mind you, the District Attorney thinks he's right. I've talked it over with him, and he has God with him, as he sees it. But there are one or two little points they're not likely to bring up, and I thought I'd talk them over with you."

And then and there, categorically, he outlined the defense for us. As I wrote it down for Godfrey Lowell at the time, I have it before me now.

(a) Jim was being tried for Sarah's murder, but the story of Florence Gunther's would inevitably enter the case. Why was it that there was no oil in Jim's car the morning after Florence's death, although I found it later? "Tell Lowell to bring that out. The prosecution won't."

(b) Find Amos, and get him on the stand. "He buried that sword-stick. His prints were thick on it."

(c) Ask the microscopist who examined Sarah Gittings' clothing if he found anything wrapped around a button. "I may lose my job over this, but he did. He found a longish white hair."

(d) Ask him—the miscroscopist—if that hair was living or dead? If it came from a head or a wig. "I think it came from a wig, myself. Make them produce that hair in court. They've got it."

(e) Ask the microscopist what he found on that piece of wood from the Larimer lot. "He found something besides blood and that dead woman's hair. He found some fibers from cloth on the end of it. Black cloth, or grayish black. They've got those, too."

(f) Put a lot of emphasis on that three hours from seven to ten. Where was she? "I'm not so sure myself that the whole solution doesn't lie there."

And

(g) Why were both those stab wounds the same depth?

He leaned back, like a man well satisfied with himself.

"Now here's the situation, to my mind," he explained. "And Lowell's welcome to use it if he likes. Here's a man who has worked himself into a mood to kill. He's out to kill. And he's got a sword in his hand; a rapier, rather. It's got a blade a foot and a half long, and it's as sharp as a dagger. What does he do? He drives it home with all his strength, and this man who did this had strength, plenty of it. If your grandfather ever fought a duel with that weapon, he'd have run his man through, wouldn't he? Providing he got the chance, of course!

"But here are two stab wounds, and both of them short. That's not accident, that's necessity. That's a short knife, to my mind anyhow. He might have gone short the first time, but not the second. Never the second."

I was re-reading my notes.

"What do you mean by the wig?" I asked.

"Well, that hair was peculiar. It had no root, for one thing. A hair that's torn out usually has a root; and there was no dust on it, nothing that ought to be on hair in active service! Nothing but a lot of brilliantine. Mind you, that's only a chance. Still, it has its points. A man old enough to have white hair and wear it long is too old to have put that body in the sewer."

"You mean that whoever it was was disguised?"

"I say there's a possibility of it. You see, men often disguise themselves to commit crimes. That and to make an escape are practically the only times any criminal uses disguise at all. In other words a murderer is seen at or near the scene of the crime, and identified by certain marks; hair, eyebrows, clothes or what not. But in his own proper person he has none of those marks."

"And they won't bring that out at the trial?"

"Well, why should they?" he said reasonably. "It wouldn't help Blake any. How do we know he didn't wear a wig that night?"

"Then why bring it in?"

He smiled.

"For the effect on the jury," he said. "Nobody has shown that Jim Blake wore such a wig, or even owned a wig. As a matter of fact I don't believe he did. But get Lowell to work that three hours and the unknown in a white wig, and dress clothes, and at least he's got a talking point."

CHAPTER XXV

I TOOK THOSE NOTES to Godfrey the next day, and by the eagerness with which he seized on them I realized his desperation.

"Where on earth did you get all this?"

"Never mind, Godfrey. It's our case; that's all."

And that was the situation the day before Jim's trial opened; Laura arriving in the early morning, having left her children for once, and outraged over the whole situation. But not for a moment taking the outcome seriously; coming in from the car, smartly dressed and vocative, followed by that mass of hand luggage which she requires for a twenty-four hour journey.

"Don't look at me. I'm a mess, but of course I had to come. Of all the ridiculous and pointless accusations! How are you, Joseph? How d'you do, Clara! Charles told me to see that I had an extra bolt on my door! Isn't that like him? That cabinet looks well in there."

Nor did she once consider a possible unfortunate outcome for Jim until the trial began. Then the dignity of the court, the gravity of the counsel for both sides, all the panoply of a trial in which a sovereign state with all its resources is opposed to a single individual in a prisoner's box, began to impress her.

Our faces, too, must have told her something of our doubts; Judy pale and thin, and Katherine as if she had been chiseled out of marble.

"Oh, the poor dears!" said Laura. "Somehow I didn't realize it had been like this."

But it was Jim who struck her dumb; Jim, so carefully dressed, so drawn, so isolated. She reached out and caught my hand, and for once she was silent. Silent she remained, through that ghastly impaneling of a jury which required days, and until the opening speech of the State's Attorney. During that speech, however, her color rose and her eyes flashed.

"How dare they?" she muttered. "How *dare* they?"

I have no space here for that trial, for its heartbreaks and its insufferable dragging hours and days. Witnesses came and went. The audience, those who had won the daily battle for admission, sat and fanned themselves with hats, handkerchiefs, newspapers. To such few points as told in Jim's favor they were cold; they were united against him, a seething mob of hatred, waiting and furiously hoping for revenge.

Laura said they were like the market women who knitted around the guillotine while the French aristocracy was being executed, and so I felt that they were.

In vain Godfrey Lowell fought, cross-examined, almost wept out of his exhaustion and anxiety; in vain he made the Inspector's points, from "a" to "g." The jury was hot and growing weary. Sarah's blood-stained clothing and the sword-cane were on the table. They reasoned from cause to effect.

He had had the cane, she had threatened his easy-going life, he had been seen where she was killed, he killed her.

Judy's eyes were sunk in her head by the end of the third day, but she remained throughout the trial, from that sonorous opening speech of the District Attorney, of which I reproduce only a paragraph or two:

"We will show, gentlemen of the jury, that this unfortunate woman, on the day before she was killed, wrote to this defendant and asked him to meet her, on urgent business. A reconstruction of a portion of this letter as shown on her blotter will be produced in due time. And we will show that she sent this letter. She not only wrote it but she addressed an envelope, and the imprint of this envelope, left on the cuff of that uniform of service which she wore, has been examined by experts and pronounced to be her own handwriting. It has been compared, as the law requires, with valid examples of her handwriting; samples easy to obtain, for this good and faithful friend to this family had for years kept a record of all their illnesses, day by day.

"We will show that on the night of the crime, this defendant varied from his ordinary procedure; that he dined early and without dressing, which in this case means that he did not put on a dinner jacket. That is more important than it may sound. There are certain individuals, gentlemen, to whom a dinner without a dinner jacket approaches the unthinkable. It is cataclysmic. And so revolutionary was it in the habit of this defendant that his servant made a mental note of it.

"Following this early meal, and he ate very little, he went out. He had put on a light golf suit and a pair of heavy shoes, and this suit and these shoes will be shown to you later on, stained with blood; the blood, we fully believe of this dead woman.

"But there was another and even more terrible, more sinister object in that house that next morning. The sword-stick stood once more in the hall, where it had stood before. But this sword-stick, or sword-cane, gentlemen, had become a matter of intense importance to this defendant.

"Either on his return the night before, or during that day, or even following the discovery of Sarah Gittings' body, this defendant proceeded furtively and secretly to wash the sword-cane.

"But he could not clean the interior of the sheath. That remained for the experts of our department. They have found human blood in that sheath, and also another object.

"The age of human blood, after a certain period of time, is difficult to determine. My friends of the defense may urge that this blood may be from some ancient duel long since forgotten. But of this other object discovered the age is unquestioned. Adherent to this sheath was a needle from a pine tree, and this needle was fresh, gentlemen of the jury. It came from a particular variety of evergreen to be found only on that slope of the city park down which this unfortunate woman had been dragged.

"Numbers of similar needles, from similar trees were found clinging to her clothing on the recovery of the body. And I may add that in the opinion of the experts for the state, this blood inside the sheath was similarly fresh."

Why go on? Bit by bit he built his case, and bit by bit Jim sagged in his chair. When he reached the question of motive, and named Florence Gunther, there was such a stir in the courtroom that it had to be called to order.

"Now, gentlemen of the jury, it is not our purpose here, directly or indirectly, to try this defendant for the murder of Florence Gunther; but here and there this girl's name will have to enter the record.

"On the day of this murder Florence Gunther took from the safe of her employers a certain document, sealed in a brown manila envelope and duly endorsed. This document has disappeared, but its identity has been established."

And with the description of the will which followed, the supplying of the motive, the case was indeed as Godfrey had predicted; over before it commenced.

He fought on doggedly, but what were such things as hairs and fibers to a jury which had already reached its verdict? And we had a blow or two which were unexpected, at that.

One was the proof that Sarah had indeed written the letter to Jim, as claimed by the state. A photograph had been made of her blotter and greatly enlarged, and certain words had come out clearly enough. So far as they could put the words together, allowing for certain undecipherable places, she had written somewhat as follows:

"Dear Mr. Blake: I must see you as soon as possible on a very urgent matter. When I tell you that I believe that there is a—"

The first page had ended there, or she had used less pressure, for that was all. And even in this only certain words were at all clear; "urgent" and "possible" and "believe," for example. But the "Dear Mr. Blake" was beyond dispute.

Katherine, too, had her own particular shock to face. This was the reconstruction of that charred fragment of a letter from her to Jim, which had been found in his fireplace.

"Your message alarms— What am I not to say?"

She had no warning. She had not expected to be called and I am sure she had not the slightest idea of what was to confront her on the stand.

"Can you identify this?"

"I don't even know what it is."

Putting up her lorgnette and staring down at that flat board, and then lifting her head slightly.

"Do you recognize it now?"

"I think it is something I have written."

"To the defendant?"

"Yes."

"Do you remember when you wrote that?"

"No."

"Or how you sent it? By mail?"

She was under oath, and she would not lie.

"By hand."

"By whose hand?"

"By my chauffeur. I was sending certain things to my brother by car, and the letter went with them."

We know now that that was true, that she had no idea then that Jim's mail was being watched. But on the face of it the admission was fatal, and when later on she was asked to explain that sentence and refused, there was little more to be done.

In the eyes of the jury and of the audience that day Katherine had as much as admitted that she knew something about the crime which she was "not to say." And the next question, ruled not competent by the court, was not only designed to show that, but had a sinister purpose not lost on the jury or the crowd.

"Did you see your brother the night he went to New York?"

"What night was that?"

"The night of your husband's death."

"I did not," said Katherine haughtily. "He was not in New York that night."

But the effect had been made. The introduction of Charles Parrott was likewise fought, but on the District Attorney's statement that he was important to their case he was put on the stand, and he made his semi-identification.

"He's the same height and the same build," he said, "but he was pretty well covered. It looks like him, but that's as far as I go."

The purpose of the prosecution was then revealed. Judy was unwillingly obliged to say that the telephone call had been apparently from Jim, and Howard's check-book was introduced.

It was shown that on the day, or night, of his death he had drawn a check to cash for a thousand dollars. The book was found on his desk in the morning, with the stub so marked. This check had not been presented, but evidence was introduced to show that two days before Jim had called up a local steamship agency and inquired about sailings.

And underlying all this, brought out again and again, was the sinister reference that when Jim had left the apartment in New York that night, or just before he left, Howard was dead.

Judy made a fine witness, and she got over more than the prosecution allowed to enter the record; she deliberately talked until they stopped her, and I think the jury found her a bright spot in a long day.

"Why hasn't Mr. Waite been murdered?" she asked once, out of a clear sky. "Why wasn't he the first to go?"

And again, relative to the finding of the cipher, she brought a laugh.

"Why did you search that room?"

"I thought the police needed a little help." And after the laugh, and before she could be brought to order: "Why on earth would Sarah hide whatever she did hide, if she was going to tell Uncle Jim about it? She trusted him. She wasn't hiding it from *him*. Find who she was afraid of and—"

They stopped her then, and under pretense of getting her handkerchief I saw her looking at a card in her bag. Evidently she had made some notes on it.

When they took her back to the night of Sarah's death, and the intruder in the house, she was ready for them.

"You didn't see him?"

"No, nor since. He's been breaking in ever since, while Uncle Jim has been locked up. He didn't find what he wanted on Sarah, so he—"

She was making a valiant effort, but I heard none of her testimony after Godfrey Lowell had read aloud the cipher itself. Laura suddenly caught my arm.

"For God's sake, Elizabeth!" she whispered. "Didn't Sarah tell you about the cabinet?"

"What about it?"

"Let's get out of here. We've got to get home."

It took us some time, however, to escape from that crowded courtroom. The very doorways and the halls outside them were filled, and when we finally reached the street, Robert had left his car and joined the morbid throng inside the building. Laura was exasperated and almost tearful, and I was not much better.

It was Wallie who finally found him for us, and who went with us to the house.

I had my key, for all the servants were at the courthouse, and at first glance everything appeared to be as it should be.

On the way Laura made her explanation.

"I meant to write you," she said, "but I had some buying for Sarah to do, and so I wrote her. She was to tell you. Why didn't you tell me she had hidden something? It's in the cabinet, of course."

It must have been forty minutes from the reading of the cipher to the time we turned into the drive. Save for a natural urgency to get into the house and find the key to the mystery, I think none of us except Wallie realized the necessity for any haste. And he had his own reasons for not stressing that.

He said very little during the drive. I remember now that he was very white, and that he jerked his shoulders and head even more than usual. But when I had unlocked the front door and opened it everything seemed quiet and in order. The dogs came to meet us, Isabel with corpulent dignity, Jock effusively. The servants were all at the courthouse, and the house was very still.

Laura turned at once to the drawing room on the left, and as I had restored the key to the cabinet some time before, she unlocked the center door without difficulty.

The cabinet is a fine example of Louis Fourteenth, of satinwood and kingswood. It is really a small secretary; that is, a shelf draws out and forms a writing desk, and above are three doors. The two outer doors are of glass, and behind this glass are my mother's old Chelsea figures. The center door, however, is solid, and on this is fastened a very handsome oval piece of ormolu.

It was the center door which Laura opened, and I then noticed for the first time that this ormolu was fastened to the walnut lining of the door inside by some dozen very small bronze rosettes, ostensibly covering the heads of the screws. There was one in the center also, and thus they formed what might be interpreted as a clock dial.

"Five o'clock right, seven o'clock left, press on six," said Laura, and did so. "Give me your knife, Wallie."

But Wallie's knife had a broken point. I remember that now, although it meant nothing to me at the time; I remember that, and that his hands were shaking when he tried to open it. In the end I had to get my own penknife from my desk, and Laura inserted the blade along the metal binding of the door.

It sprang open, revealing between the inner lining and the front of the door a flat space, the size of the door in area but hardly more than a half inch in depth.

But that space was empty.

We stared at each other. My disappointment was more than I could bear, and Laura was almost in tears. What Wallie felt I can only surmise. He bent over and examined it, and I saw then that there the lining was badly scratched. Laura saw it too.

"Those weren't there when you got it, were they?"

"I don't think so."

Wallie spoke then, for the first time.

"Why should anything be there?" he said. "Somebody was quicker than we were, that's all."

"You mean that this has been done recently."

"Since those directions were read out in court," he replied grimly. "You'll find a window broken somewhere, or a door left unlocked."

He was right. With all of us out of the house there had been no one to put in place the chain which now supplemented the lock of the kitchen door. The key of that door lay on the floor, as though it had been pushed out from outside and a duplicate or skeleton key had been used. And the door now stood open.

It was that night that Wallie disappeared.

I was less surprised than I should have been, perhaps, when he was not in the courtroom the next morning. On the evening before, at seven o'clock, he had telephoned Judy and told her not to worry.

"I'm going on the stand tomorrow," he said, "and everything will be all right, Judy."

"What do you mean, all right? If everything isn't as wrong as it can be, I don't know what it is."

But he said that he was going to testify, and that he had plenty to say. That she was to be ready for a shock, but not to think badly of him. He had got himself into this mess, and he would "take his medicine."

"Go to bed and get a decent sleep," he said. "Let me do the staying awake. And don't worry. Jim Blake isn't going to the chair."

She said later that he was not drunk, she was certain, but that his voice sounded queer.

"I've made up my mind," he finished, "and I feel better for it. It's a clean slate and to hell with what happens, for me."

But he did not appear.

I was bitterly disappointed, and Judy looked puzzled and anxious.

"He lost his nerve," she said. "He'll never tell now, whatever it is that he knows."

But the trial went on, although the papers commented unpleasantly on his absence, and Godfrey Lowell was upset. Still, on the surface at least, Wallie's testimony could neither damn Jim nor save him. Whatever the true story of that pencil in the shaft, the fact remained that Wallie was in my house at ten o'clock, and Jim was in the park.

Things went badly for Jim that day. Amos had not been located, but there was his damaging testimony before the Grand Jury; and now read into the record, over protest, that the cane had been in the hall until Sarah's body was found and then disappeared; and that further and damning fact that he had found a bloody handkerchief of Jim's the morning after Sarah's murder and placed it with the soiled clothes; that on listing the laundry the following Monday he had found this handkerchief, but that in the interval it had been washed clean and dried.

The accumulated mass of testimony was overwhelming. Nothing could shake the opinion of the experts that Sarah's letter to Jim was in her own hand, or that the drops of blood here and there on his clothing and inside the sword-stick were human blood.

"How do you know they are human blood?"

"By the shape and size of the corpuscles. Also by their numbers and groupings."

Indeed, so badly did things go that on the day following Godfrey Lowell at last put Jim himself on the stand. Jim had asked to testify and so he did, although how he thought it would help him nobody can say.

CHAPTER XXVI

I HAVE BEFORE ME now that statement of Jim's. Given much of it in question and answer, and broken by cross-examination and objections here and there, it takes many pages of the stenographic report.

As I have also, however, that document which Jim himself prepared later as the basis of an appeal, I shall use that instead.

I give it word for word.

"I had nothing whatever to do with the death of Sarah Gittings, or of Florence Gunther. I am willing to swear that before God. If I have kept back part of what little I know, it has been partly because I saw that things looked pretty hopeless for me, and partly because of my sister, who has been and is in deep trouble.

"I did not see Sarah Gittings on the night of the eighteenth of April. I had expected to see her. She had made two previous attempts to get in touch with me, both of which had failed. But on that day, a Monday, I received a telephone message from her, in which she mentioned a letter she had sent me. She seemed disturbed when I said that I had not received such a letter.

"I examined my desk, but there was no such letter. Then she asked me to meet her that night on a matter of vital importance.

"I agreed to do this, and I started rather early, intending to walk to the address she had given, which was at 1737 Halkett Street. I was to ask for a Miss Gunther. I wrote down the address, but on the way I found that I had left it in my other clothing, so I stopped at a drugstore and telephoned to the Bell house, hoping to catch Sarah before she started.

"She had gone, but I remembered that the address was in the seventeen hundred block, and rather than go back I decided to make inquiries in that block.

"I walked across the park and out. I walk rather slowly, and it was fully eight when I reached the block, and possibly eight-fifteen when I had located the house. Miss Gunther was waiting on the steps, and she took me into the house. I had never seen her before. She seemed very nervous, and had very little to say. When I asked her why I had been sent for, she said that Miss Gittings would tell me.

"We sat there until perhaps twenty minutes to ten. I asked her repeatedly to give me an idea of what it was all about, but she would not. It was not her affair, she said. But she asked me to keep my visit a secret. She made me promise it, as a matter of fact. She said she 'didn't want to be mixed up' in anything. And I did so promise.

"She seemed unduly uneasy about Sarah Gittings. I could not understand it, and as time went on she was more and more uneasy. She said she was sure something terrible had happened, and at last she began to cry. I tried to reassure her, but she said I didn't understand, and at nine-forty her condition was such that I advised her to go to bed, and myself started for home.

"In my statement to the District Attorney I said that I had reached the path to the Larimer lot at nine-thirty. This was not true. I saw that I was under suspicion, and so I changed the time. I was on the path, or beside it, at or about ten o'clock.

"I took the same route on my return, but when about halfway up the hill toward the Larimer lot I sat down to rest. I left the path and moved some feet to the right; that is, in the direction of the Bell house. I lighted a cigar there and rested. I may have been there five minutes, when I heard some one moving on the hillside to my left, and some distance away.

"At first I thought it was a dog. I had heard dogs barking a few minutes before. I had thrown away my cigar, and I believe that against the hillside where I sat I was practically invisible to any one at that distance. But I was not certain that it was a dog, and as that part of the park has been the scene of several hold-ups, I pressed the spring which released the knife in the cane, and then waited.

"There were two people in the park below. I could hear them talking, and it occurred to me that somebody on my left was hiding there, possibly with the idea of attacking and robbing them. But this was not the case, and I believe now that this man on my left was the one who killed Sarah Gittings, and that he was dragging her body down the hillside for later disposal.

"With the two people, Mr. and Mrs. Dennis as I now know, at the foot of the hill, and myself more or less hidden above, something alarmed this man. Possibly a park policeman. I believe that this end of the park had been watched at night for some time.

"He ran toward me. I could hear him coming, and he was breathing very hard. I had the general impression of a tall man, in evening dress or dinner clothes, and wearing a soft cap drawn down over his face. That was my impression of him. I may be wrong.

"But I swear that this man was there, that he ran toward me, and that he almost ran over me. So close was he that in passing he struck my stick with his foot and knocked it to a considerable distance. He ran past me and disappeared along the hillside beyond, taking a slanting direction down into the park.

"When I had recovered I felt around for my stick, and unfortunately it was the blade which I found. I cut my hand, and I bear a small scar from that cut to this day.

"I have not invented this. The blood on my clothing and on my handkerchief that night was my own blood. Mrs. Dennis saw me tying up my hand. I went home and went to bed.

"The next morning I was not well. My servant, Amos, brought me some coffee, and laid out my fresh clothing. He picked up the handkerchief I had used the night before, and asked me if I had hurt myself. I told him I had cut my hand but that it was nothing of any importance.

"I never thought of Sarah Gittings in connection with all this until I learned that day that she was missing.

"I began to worry then. I had had an appointment to meet her, and I was uneasy. I called up Florence Gunther at her office, but she was not there, and I had no knowledge of the house where she lived save the street number. That is, I could not call her on the telephone.

"But in view of what had happened on the hillside the night before, I felt anxious. Some time around noon of that day I went back to the Larimer lot and walked over it, I also examined the hillside. But I found nothing suspicious.

"I went to the Bell house that afternoon, but Sarah was still missing, and in addition the house had been entered the night before and Sarah's room had been searched. In leaving the Bell house I again went back to the hillside. I located the spot where I had rested, and went to the left of it along the hill for a considerable distance. I found nothing suspicious and no trace of Sarah Gittings.

"The next day I had a desperate letter from Florence Gunther. She had seen in the papers that Sarah was still missing, and she was certain that she had been killed. She begged me not to bring her name into it; that it meant the loss of her position, and maybe physical danger also. Also she asked me to destroy the letter, which I did. I should have acted anyhow; as it turned out, my silence did not save her.

"But in that interval several things had happened. While I was debating what to do Sarah's body had been found, and she had been stabbed. Not only that, but I had been on the spot, or close to it, at the very time the reports said she had been killed.

"Walter Somers and I made the identification that day together, and Walter drove me home. I let myself into the house through the garden, and I found Amos in the front hall with the sword-stick in his hands. He was trying to get the blade back when I found him.

"I knew then that he suspected me. Later on I sent him out and examined the stick. There was a little dried blood on the blade, and some bits of grass and earth. That frightened me. I took it to the lavatory downstairs and washed it, and then I hid it. I put it in my liquor closet in the lower hall, and locked it there.

"But things grew worse. Mary Martin had produced the uniform, and it was evident that Sarah Gittings had written to me, as she had claimed. I was frantic, and that night I made an attempt to see Florence Gunther. She was not at home, but I found her walking on the street, near an Italian fruit stand. But I was horrified to see her go white when she saw me.

"She refused to speak to me, and when I insisted she said that I had killed Sarah; that she knew it and knew why, and that if I didn't leave her she would call an officer. On the way home I worked that out. I remembered that on the night when I saw her, while we waited for Sarah, I had idly shown her the mechanism of the sword-stick. I am not surprised that she believed that I had killed Sarah Gittings. It is easy to see why, now. She believed that Sarah Gittings had come to me with that copy of a will which disinherited me, and that to get possession of it I had killed her.

"I made no more overtures. I was afraid I would drive her to the police.

"I went home that night a sick man, and took to my bed. Some time during that week, however, I crawled downstairs. It seemed to me that if she told the police and they found the stick hidden, it would damn me. I decided to put it back in the hall, where it had stood before.

"I unlocked the door, but the stick had disappeared. I do not yet know how it disappeared, or why it was found in the cellar. My personal belief is that my servant Amos was alarmed at the situation in which I found myself, and that he buried it himself.

"It is also my belief that Amos has been either killed or bribed to leave the city, for fear he may make this confession and thus help to clear me.

"In a similar manner, I believe that a ring of oil was planted in my car, so that I might be suspected of having killed Florence Gunther. The police know that this ring was not in the car the day after her murder.

"During this trial, much has been made of the fact that by a new will made by my brother-in-law, Howard Somers, I lost a bequest originally devised to me. In reply to that I say most solemnly that I never knew that Howard Somers had made a new will until Mr. Alexander Davis told me in New York, following Mr. Somers' death. Even had I known of it, the murder of these two unfortunate women could certainly not benefit me. The will itself was safe among Mr. Somers' papers in a New York bank vault and Mr. Waite could testify to its existence and its authenticity.

"I know nothing whatever of Florence Gunther's death. When I found that she suspected me of Sarah Gittings' murder I made no further attempt to see her, and I solemnly swear that I never did see her. Nor did I make any visit to Howard Somers on the night of his death. Whoever saw him that night deliberately used my name to gain access to him. Nor did I receive a check from him for one thousand dollars.

"As to leaving the country, I had such a thought at one time. My position was unbearable, and I was helpless. I did nothing further about the matter, nor have I attempted to escape.

"I have not invented this story since my arrest, or preceding it. I have told the absolute truth, under oath. I have never killed any human being. I am innocent of this charge. If I suffer for it I suffer for another man's crime."

Much of this was in the story he told on the stand. I believe that outside of ourselves hardly a soul in that crowded courtroom believed it. And against it was that mass of accumulated testimony, including our own unwilling appearances on the stand.

It should have helped him that on that very day the body of poor Amos was found floating down the river, but it did not. He had been drowned, poor wretch, and although we have our own suspicions we do not know to this day that he was murdered.

But I think I can reconstruct that scene: Amos confiding and amiable, flattered at being consulted. On a bridge, maybe, or on the river bank somewhere; and then a sudden thrust of a muscular arm, and the muddy swirling waters closing over his head.

Jim was found guilty after only three hours' deliberation by the jury. Guilty of murder in the first degree.

CHAPTER XXVII

JIM WAS SENTENCED to the chair on the twenty-fifth of June. One and all the newspapers were gratified by the verdict, and not a few kind words were said of the acumen of the police and the fairness of the trial.

Godfrey Lowell at once moved for an appeal, but he warned us that lacking fresh developments there was little to be hoped from a new trial, if it was granted.

We were stunned. Katherine took to her bed, not as a refuge but out of sheer necessity, and Doctor Simonds saw her daily. Judy went about, a thin and pale little ghost of herself, thinking eternally of the mystery, as convinced as ever of Jim's innocence.

"He's protecting somebody," she said. "He *saw* that man on the hillside. He was twenty feet from the path, and that precious Dennis pair saw him well enough to know he had on a golf suit and was wiping his hands. And this man he tells about; he almost ran over him. Uncle Jim saw him, and he knows who it was. He knows and he won't tell. And Wallie knows. Wallie ran away so he wouldn't have to tell."

She looked as though she had not slept for days, and I myself took a sleeping tablet every night and then lay awake until morning. I was alone once more, for Laura had had to go back to her children. She had wept noisily on the way to the train, and had promised to come back as soon as possible.

Of our small family group then only Katherine, Judy and I remained, for Wallie was still missing. That defection of his had angered me almost beyond words. He had known something which might have saved Jim, and he had gone away. Somewhere he was hiding until everything was over.

And then, on the twenty-eighth of June, the steward called up from Wallie's club. Wallie had not been seen since the night of Wednesday, the twenty-second, and this was on the following Tuesday.

"We would like to know where he can be found," he said. "We have a number of messages for him, and one that seems to be urgent."

"Urgent?"

"Yes. A lady has been telephoning every day. Today she made me go up and look at his room. She seems to think there's something queer about his absence. She asked me to call you and tell you."

"Queer?" I said, with that now familiar tightening around my chest. "What did she think? Did she give any name?"

"No. A young woman, I imagine. I don't want to alarm you, but she seemed very nervous. As a matter of fact, she said something about notifying the police."

"She gave no reason for that?"

"No, but I've just been up to his room. It doesn't look to me as though he had meant to be gone for any length of time. His clothes are all there. And his car's missing. Still, I don't think you need to be particularly alarmed; he was erratic at times, as you probably know. If this girl hadn't seemed so excited——"

"His car is gone?"

"It's out of the garage. Yes. Has been since last Wednesday night."

It was Tuesday then, and he had been gone for six days. Of course that might merely bear out Judy's theory that he had simply "beat it," as she put it, but I myself was not so certain. It was hardly conceivable that he had taken himself off for an indefinite stay without extra clothing, or even a toothbrush.

The thing worried me. Who was it who had telephoned? Was it Mary Martin, and if so why had she suggested the police? My entire experience with Mary convinced me that she regarded the police with fear, if not with horror. Yet who else? With all his faults Wallie had apparently steered clear of the type of underworld woman who might naturally think of the police.

In the end I called the club again and got the steward.

"This young woman who telephoned, Mr. Ellis—did she give any name?"

"No. She called from a pay station. I thought she was crying, as a matter of fact, but she hung up before I could find out anything."

"Why do you say she was young?"

"Well, her voice was young, if you know what I mean."

I was sure then that it was Mary, and the fact that she had been crying convinced me that something was terribly wrong. I left the telephone and went into the library and there I had as bad an attack of palpitation of the heart as I have ever had in my life.

Joseph found me there and hurried for some bicarbonate, and when I felt a little better I told him the story. It upset him greatly. The hand holding the glass shook until the spoon clattered, and he had to steady himself by a chair.

"The police, madam? Then this young person thinks he has met with real trouble?"

"She was crying, Joseph."

In the end I called up Dick Carter, and that evening he and Joseph went to Wallie's room at the club. They examined everything there, but without result, and the story they brought back was ominous, to say the least.

On that previous Wednesday night Wallie had eaten no dinner. Instead he had gone into the writing room and there had written for a long time, until eight or after. The boy on duty there "thought he was writing a book." When he finished he had asked for a long manila envelope, put into it what he had written, taken his hat and a light overcoat from the man in the hall and gone out.

He stood on the outside steps for a moment, and then he came back. He seemed nervous and irritable, and he went into the telephone booth and talked to some one for a considerable time. Then he started out again, and so far as was known he had never come back.

Dick and Joseph examined his room carefully. Joseph, who occasionally went there to go over his clothing and to put things in order for him, said that he found nothing missing.

"But you must remember, madam," he said, "that Mr. Walter has been under a great strain lately, and it is not unusual for him to start out on an evening ride in his car and then to keep on. I have known him to do that a number of times."

"For six days, Joseph? And when he was to testify at a murder trial the next day? That's ridiculous."

"That is probably the reason, madam."

"Nonsense, Joseph! Nobody believes that Mr. Walter had anything to do with it."

From the club they went to the garage. The night man remembered clearly his coming there, and that he must have meant to return, for he had ordered the car washed that night.

"I'll be in about eleven," he had said. "I want it properly washed, too. The last time it looked worse than before you started."

He had seemed to be in a bad humor. It was about a quarter after eight when he reached there, and he ordered the car filled with gas and oil. He said he was going into the country, and he stood by watching while this was done. He seemed to "be in a hurry to be off."

But after he was in the car something happened of which the mere telling made my hands cold and sent despair into my very soul.

To quote the man at the garage:

"He had an overcoat—it's still here—and at the last moment he threw it out to me. It was a warm night. Then he asked for it again and he took a revolver out of it. He tried to slip it out so I wouldn't see it. But I saw it all right. He put it in the pocket of the car."

To me that night that revolver meant only one thing. Wallie had killed himself. Somewhere he had stopped his car on a lonely road and ended a life which had ceased to be endurable.

But why? What did he know? What had he done? Was it possible after all that those three alibis of his were wrong? Had he slipped out of my house that night of the eighteenth of April and killed poor Sarah? I went over that night once more, and I was certain that he had not.

Late as it was by that time, almost midnight, I called up Inspector Harrison. I had evidently wakened him from a sound sleep, but he said he would come as soon as he could, and while I sat there waiting my mind fairly seethed.

If Wallie was innocent, then what did he know that he would rather die than tell, and for which he would let Jim suffer? And once more I harked back to Judy and that strange suspicion of hers about her father. Were we all wrong, after all? Was Howard being blackmailed, and that will with its ambiguous clause his final price for silence? Was Katherine right and was Margaret living? And were Sarah and Florence Howard's desperate last attempt to keep that secret under cover?

Wallie and Jim both silent, the one ready to go to the chair if necessary before he would speak, and the other perhaps dead by his own hand; what did that look like?

And when the Inspector came I told him all that was in my mind, my fears for Wallie, my suspicions about Howard. He listened attentively, biting hard on the end of a toothpick and silent for some time after I had finished.

"It's ingenious," he said at last. "It's even possible. Funny thing Miss Judy would think of that, isn't it, and the rest of us would miss it? Sure he might have recognized this fellow if he was there; especially if he knew him. There's more to recognition than features. There's the outline and the clothes and the way a person moves. And here's a thing that struck me at the trial. If he was inventing that man, why put him in evening clothes? It was plausible enough up to that minute. Then the jury just sat back and yawned. Now, Mr. Somers had white hair, I think, and he wore it fairly long?"

"Yes."

"Queer case, isn't it?" he said. "Unless Blake invented the evening coat to fit the black fibers on that log. Well, let's get to this other matter."

When he left it was to go to the garage and secure a description of Wallie's car, and I believe it was almost morning before he got to his bed again. He had started the entire machinery of the city and county on the search by that time, and the only reason he did not extend that search over the country was because he felt certain, as he confessed later, that Wallie was dead by his own hand, and not too far away.

That was on Tuesday, and on Wednesday morning the papers were filled with his disappearance. "Young Millionaire Missing." "Police Hunting Walter Somers."

And on Thursday afternoon, the last day of June, we had some news. Wallie's car had been found on the Warrenville road, not far from the end of the street car line, and about two miles nearer the city than the Hawkins farm. Some boy scouts, out for a hike, had selected for lunch a gully with a small stream flowing through it, and a half dozen had wandered up this ravine for a half mile or so.

The car had been driven over the hill, and was upside down and badly demolished. A local deputy constable had notified the police and kept the boys away. They had been anxious to turn it over.

When Inspector Harrison arrived on the scene with Simmons and four or five others, the ground had not been disturbed. They found no footprints, however, save the smaller and unmistakable ones of the boys, and they were forced to the conclusion either that the car had been empty when it started on its wild journey, or that Wallie had been thrown out somewhere on the hill.

But they found no Wallie, and nothing further to help them.

The Inspector, reporting the matter, had his own opinion of it.

"He deliberately got rid of that car," he said. "It might have lain there for a year, if those youngsters hadn't happened on it."

There was no sign of the revolver, and although inside it—it was a roadster, with one seat and a rumble—there were certain scratches, and a leather seat cushion torn in one place, these were probably the result of the terrific impact after it had shot down the hill.

There was however an unexpected result to the discovery and description of the car in the press. A woman named Wiggins came forward to say that she had seen such a car as she was leaving the street car at the end of the line at something before nine on the evening of Wednesday, June the twenty-second. She fixed the date absolutely, as she had gone to town to see her daughter off on a train, also she remembered the car distinctly, because it had almost run over her.

And she stated positively that there had been two men in it at the time.

The Inspector was very sober when he told me that.

"It looks now," he said, "as though somebody knew that Walter Somers meant to go on the stand that next day and tell all he knew. And that he was—prevented."

"Murdered is what you mean, isn't it?"

He cleared his throat.

"It's possible. It's very possible. And I suppose Walter could swim and Amos couldn't!"

Which was what he left me with, to make of it what I might.

Those few days had told terribly on Joseph. The maids reported that he walked the floor at night until they were almost crazy, and for the first time in my service he was forgetful and absent. I was startled one day to have him pour ice water into my soup, and his hands were so uncertain that he broke a piece of my mother's Lowestoft china, a thing he had not done in all his years of dusting and washing it. On the plea that he knew Wallie's habits I loaned him my car, and he took his afternoons and joined the search. That he went to the club I know, but I have no other knowledge of his movements save one.

Dick had taken Judy out to the road above the gully, and they were surprised to find my car there. When they got to the edge they saw Joseph below; he was sitting on a rock, his head on his breast, and when they called to him he jumped and then came toiling up the slope.

"What on earth are you doing?" Judy demanded.

He looked down sheepishly at his muddy clothes.

"I was looking for the revolver. Mr. Walter never killed himself, Miss."

"Joseph," said Judy impulsively, "why don't you tell what you know? You know something."

"What little I know is Mr. Walter's secret, Miss." And that was all he would say.

CHAPTER XXVIII

THAT NIGHT Joseph was shot. Not killed, but painfully injured. The bullet struck his collar bone and broke it, near the shoulder. But fired from only five or six feet the impact was terrific, and at first I thought that he was dead.

The two children had come in about eight-thirty, and Judy was very low. The appeal was still pending, and unless we secured a new trial Jim would go to the chair early in September. There was strong pressure being brought against a re-trial.

"James Blake has had every opportunity to prove his innocence, and has failed. A jury of thoughtful men and women found him guilty and sentenced him to death as the penalty of at least one crime. There is no question but that an acquittal would have found him at once accused of at least one other murder, and possibly two.

"There is however more at issue than this. In the past the murderer with wealth at his command has found it possible to evade punishment for almost indefinite periods, with the result that the sacredness of human life—"

It is not surprising then that our group of three was silent that night. Judy I remember had gone back to the night of Sarah's death, as though she was desperately attempting to prove something to herself.

"Why wasn't it Wallie after all?" she said. "He was in dinner clothes that night. Suppose he broke into the house here that night? Why hadn't he stunned Sarah with that piece of wood, and then come here to get whatever it was, the records or the will? She may have lain unconscious for those three hours. Then later on he could have gone back to her."

Well, that too was possible, although Dick thought the question of time entered into it.

"He'd have had to work pretty fast," he said. "It takes time to get old putty out of a window. When I was a housebreaker—"

"He didn't finish. He broke the pane."

I recall that they wrangled about it, and that finally they decided to go out and experiment a bit. Dick's idea I think was to get Judy's mind away from Jim's tragic situation, and as I needed the same thing myself rather badly, I trailed along. It was a steaming July night, for it had rained during the day. Somewhere in the grounds next door the ex-bootlegger's children were exploding a few premature firecrackers, and on the street a steady procession of cars was passing, the riders not so much seeking a breeze as producing one.

We went out by the pantry and kitchen. Joseph was reading the paper in the pantry, and I remember that as we passed through the pantry Judy asked him the time.

"Ten o'clock, Miss."

"Aren't you hot in here, Joseph?" I asked. All the windows were down and the shades drawn.

"It's safer like this, madam."

I remember too that when we went outside, Dick carrying a flashlight, the dogs went with us; and that Jock saw a rabbit or something of the sort in the shrubbery by the garage and made a dash for it. I whistled him back, and he came reluctantly.

We made our way slowly about, Dick turning the flash alternately on the trees, one or two of which grow close to the house, and onto windows and doors. At last we reached the back drawing room door and Dick turned the light full on it.

"Now for the knife," he said. "Durn you, I'll learn you, Miss Judy."

"Knife? What knife?"

"I gave you a pocket knife, oh love of my life. What the hell did you do with it? I put it on the desk for you."

Judy maintained that he had done nothing of the sort, and after a momentary squabble Dick went back by the kitchen to get it. As I have said somewhere, it is exactly fifty feet around the corner from this door to the kitchen porch, and as he was running he made it very quickly. It could not have been more than three minutes from the time he left us until he rejoined us.

Jock, I recall, was restless, and Judy was obliged to hold him. She was slightly querulous. In his excitement Dick had carried the flashlight with him, and she grumbled.

"He might have left us with the light, anyhow. I feel creepy."

And indeed she did, for when Dick unexpectedly turned the corner, having left the house by the front door and emerging from behind us, she jumped and screamed.

As I sit here, recalling that night, I am again obsessed with that peculiar fatality which seemed to attend all our actions during those months of terror. Here again was an instance of it. Dick goes into the house by the kitchen door and departs by the front door, leaving both wide open, and as a result we have not only another crime, but no clue whatever to the identity of its perpetrator. And in that night's tragedy lay the whole story. A matter of deadly reasoning; deadly inevitable, and as coldly and recklessly carried out.

Dick came back, as I say, and began working with the knife on the hard putty around one of the panes.

"It's hard," he said. "Look at this. Like cement. No, lady love, Wallie hadn't time to meet Sarah and knock her senseless, get here, dig out as much of this as he did dig, and then be seen on the stairs apparently on his way out, when he was seen. All those little things took time."

They wrangled about it, Judy sticking to her point. Wallie had taken the pencil up the ladder with him, because he had dropped something of his own down the shaft. Later on having to dispose of the body, he used the same ladder to reach the top of the sewer. That was why she had wanted to look at it. There was red clay around the sewer.

But we were not there more than fifteen minutes in all, perhaps less. And next door the firecrackers were popping, and the cars on the street were backfiring after coasting down the hill. What was one report more or less to us, as we stood there? When we started back toward the kitchen Judy and Dick lagged behind me, like the lovers they were, and as I was leading Jock by the collar, it so happened that I was still in this stooped position when I reached the pantry door.

Joseph was still there, in his chair. But he did not rise when I entered, and I released the dog and straightened up, rather surprised. I saw then that a thin stream of blood was slowly spreading over his shirt front, and as I stared at him his body relaxed and slid out of the chair and onto the floor.

His eyes were open, and he seemed to be looking at me. It was as though we gazed at each other, Joseph and I, and as though he said: "You see what happened to me. It is incredible, but here I am."

He was not conscious. Just when that look of shocked surprise left him I do not know. One moment it was there, the next it was as though a hand had been passed over his face and left it smooth. I dropped down on my knees beside him, stricken with grief. I caught his hand, which had served me for so many years. Strange, in all that time, how seldom I had touched his hand.

I felt a deep remorse, an overwhelming pity. There, under the light, still shone beneath his thin iron-gray hair the scar from that mysterious attack which might have killed him. I put my hand up and touched it, and with that I remember that I began to cry.

I realize now that some time in those shocked first seconds I heard the front door slam, but it no more than registered on my dazed brain. On the kitchen porch Dick and Judy were still talking, and the red spot on Joseph's shirt front spread a little, but very little.

I got up and went into the kitchen.

"Judy," I said, "will you go around by the front door? Joseph is—not well."

"Not well? You don't mean that he's been drinking?"

"No. Please do what I tell you."

I left them and went back to the pantry. There was no indication there of any visitor. The evening paper lay on the table, and Joseph's reading glasses beside it. Apparently he had stopped reading, and perhaps had dozed.

I had noticed lately that he dozed rather often; a sort of half-sleep, like that of a very old man. Although Joseph was not that. He was perhaps in his late fifties.

Of a weapon there was no sign whatever.

I was apparently calm enough by that time. I knew that we had probably heard the shot, but that we had laid it to customary explosions in the street. I knew that Jock had not seen a rabbit, but something infinitely more sinister, and even to an extent I was able to reconstruct the crime; Dick had left open the door to the kitchen, and Joseph had not closed it, or certainly not locked it.

There had been ten minutes after Dick had passed through the pantry, and a shot required but a second of time. I think it was then that I remembered the slamming door, and I realized that while I stared at Joseph the murderer was still in the house, working his way forward.

The sharp ringing of the door bell over my head at that moment sent a chill over me. But it was only Dick and Judy, to report that the front door had been closed, although Dick had recklessly left it open, and to stare at me with curious eyes.

"Look here," Judy said. "Something's happened to Joseph, hasn't it?"

"He's hurt."

"Who hurt him?"

"I don't know," I said, and then I broke down and began to cry again. That shocked them profoundly. I remember Judy pushing me into the library and Dick running back. Then I believe I fainted, for I recall very little until the police were in the house, and Doctor Simonds was bending over me.

They took Joseph to the hospital that night, and they extracted the bullet. He was not badly hurt, but was suffering considerable pain.

"He's strong," Doctor Simonds told me, "and he has kept himself in good condition. He's not flabby like most butlers. But he's had a shock, more of a shock than he cares to tell about."

"He won't say who did it?"

"No. He says he doesn't know. But as he was shot from in front at pretty close range, that's unlikely. Unless he was asleep."

In spite of myself I could not get Wallie out of my mind after I had learned that. Wallie with his revolver, and that odd statement of Joseph's that he did not know who shot him.

Inspector Harrison was very noncommittal. One curious thing he had found that night, ranging over that first floor while Doctor Simonds worked over Joseph in the pantry. This was that the criminal, whoever it was, had paused long enough in the library to take a glass of sherry!

A decanter had been brought in earlier in the evening with some biscuits, but none of us had touched it. Yet sherry had been poured and apparently drunk. A little had even been spilled on the top of my old desk, and as it lay for some time the desk bears the stain to this day.

"But it's incredible," I said.

"Not incredible probably if we know the answer, but it certainly argues a degree of recklessness that's unusual, to say the least. If Jock saw this person with the gun near the garage, and you heard the front door slam, it looks as though he simply walked in the back and out the front of the house."

"Stopping in the library for a little wine," I said bitterly.

"Precisely. Stopping in the library for a little wine."

There was no weapon anywhere. True, Joseph's own revolver was in the pantry drawer where he kept it, but it had not been fired and the chambers were clean and new.

Dick had gone with the ambulance, and as Robert was not about I sent Judy home in a taxicab soon after. It was not until she had gone that the Inspector ceased his ranging over the lower floor and coming into the library planted himself in front of me.

"I'm going to ask you a few plain questions, Miss Bell, and I want plain answers. First, tell me again about young Carter going back into the house."

"He ran back for a knife. I've told you——"

"Yes. Whose idea was this 'experiment,' as you call it?"

"I think it was his. I really don't think it was Judy's. He and Judy had both been talking about it."

"But Miss Judy left the knife in the house? Are you sure of that?"

"He accused her of it. Half jokingly, of course."

"That's different. Now let's go over this. He ran in by the kitchen, through the house and into the library, and then out by the front door?"

"Yes."

"Why the front door?"

"I daresay it was nearer."

He paced the floor for a moment, and the toothpick between his strong white teeth had an aggressive tilt. I began to feel uneasy, without knowing quite why.

"How well do you know young Carter? What do you know about him?" he fired at me suddenly.

"Nothing at all, really; except that he is rather a dear boy and–Judy thinks so."

"Where does he come from? Who are his people?"

"I haven't the remotest idea. I imagine he is practically alone. I know he is an orphan."

"He's poor, I take it?"

"Poor and very proud, Inspector."

"Humph," he grunted. "Doesn't it beat the devil the way a good-looking boy with nice manners can get everywhere, and no questions asked? Now understand me, Miss Bell, I'm not saying Dick Carter fired that shot tonight; but I am saying that he had an excellent chance to fire that shot. And I'm going to tell you something else. He had a revolver in that Ford of his, parked in the front drive."

I was angry and outraged, but he lifted a hand against my protest.

"Now wait a minute. I'm thinking out loud, that's all; and I have a good bit of respect for your discretion. I've got that gun here, and we have a man in the department who'll be able to tell us if it's been fired lately. Magazine's full, of course. He'd have had time to do that, and to slip it into the pocket of his car on the way back to you and Miss Judy."

"But why on earth would he shoot Joseph?" I demanded angrily. "Just because he has an automatic, and I happen to know that he has carried one in his car ever since this trouble began, it is ridiculous to suspect him."

"I told you I was only thinking out loud," he said, blandly, and soon after that he went away.

It was the next day that Dick was sent for and interrogated, and Judy came around to see me with black shadows under her eyes and a look of despair in them.

"They suspect him," she said. "They've got something against him now, and they may get more. Listen. What became of that knife Dick had last night?"

"I haven't seen it since. It may be on my desk downstairs."

"It isn't," she wailed. "They've got it, and it was Wallie's. Dick found it in his room the night he and Joseph searched it, and brought it away. It had the point missing from one blade."

"Do be rational, Judy. What has that got to do with it?"

"I'm as rational as you are. That knife had the point broken off a blade, and if that point fits the piece the Inspector has, the piece he found on the step after Sarah was killed, what will they think?"

"Did Joseph see him take the knife?"

"No. He just slid it into his pocket. You see we have always been sure that it was Wallie on the stairs that night, and Dick thought the knife might prove it. He showed it to me, and I thought so too."

"You can tell them that, Judy."

"And would they believe me? They would not. How do they know I'm not mixed up in the whole rotten mess? How do they know Sarah didn't write me about the will? I came down that day, didn't I? And I telephoned Dick that night. How do they know I didn't tell him Sarah was out with that copy of the will in her pocketbook? I stood to lose a lot by that will, and so did Dick if he married me."

"You're crazy, Judy!"

"Am I? Uncle Jim saw that man on the hillside, didn't he? Saw him and recognized him. Who's he protecting? Can't they easily think he's being noble and protecting Dick for me?"

"And—Joseph?"

"They'd find a reason for Joseph, if they wanted one."

"Still I daresay that even in their wildest moments, Judy, they would not accuse Dick of knocking himself unconscious on the hill, or of trying to brain you in the garage."

She laughed a little, in spite of herself, and she went away somewhat comforted. But I myself was not so sure.

They released Dick, however, after that interrogation, and things seem to go on much as before. But I have reason to think that he was more or less under observation from that time on.

CHAPTER XXIX

YET THINGS WERE MOVING rapidly to the *dénouement*, although none of us suspected it. It was the next day that Inspector Harrison found, on the hillside below the garage and leading up to it, those footprints of which he was to say nothing until his case was completed. I saw him from a rear upper window, tramping about with Simmons at his heels, and every now and then he would stoop and plant a stick in the ground. Toothpicks, maybe, although they would be a trifle small.

But this was the next day. That night he left a policeman on guard in the house, and the next morning one appeared to patrol the grounds. That continued to the end.

I think it was the next day, or the day following, that Lily Sanderson called up to say that Mrs. Bassett was dead.

"She simply slept away," she said. "One of the boarders here thinks she got hold of the morphia and took an overdose, but if she did who can blame her?"

She seemed very sad and desolate. I told her to come in some time, and then what with one thing and another I am afraid I forgot them both; Lily getting her sleep now, in that meretricious bedroom of hers, and Mrs. Bassett resting at last after more trouble than most human beings are called upon to bear.

I was not well during that day or two following the shooting of Joseph. I had been profoundly shocked, and what with worry about Wallie and the long strain I almost collapsed. Doctor Simonds ordered me to bed on, I think, the second day, and Judy stayed with me as much as possible.

She was still anxious about Dick, still fearful for him. She seemed to think that because everything was quiet that that very quiet was ominous, and in her desperation she was casting about for some one, any one, on whom to throw the guilt.

Thus, I think it was on Wednesday, she said to me suddenly, after the doctor had gone:

"I don't like that man."

"Why not, Judy?"

"He's oily, and he's always around!"

"Only when he's sent for."

"Is he?" She looked at me queerly. "Do you suppose he just happened to be passing the house the night Joseph was shot?"

"Was he? I didn't know that."

"Well, he was. I picked him off the street. Dick was at the telephone, and I ran down to the gate to see if I could find a policeman. He was passing by in his car then."

"Well, that was fortunate, wasn't it?"

"That depends," she said slowly. "Look back a little, Elizabeth Jane. He takes care of father when he is sick here; and he knows about the will; he knows us all, and all about us. And when you think about it, he's always around, isn't he? Somebody throws Joseph down the back stairs, and where is Doctor Simonds? He's apparently waiting in his office to be called. I get hurt in the garage, and he's at home sitting by the telephone! Joseph gets shot and he's passing by the house."

"Really, Judy!"

"I'm going to get rid of this if it kills me. Uncle Jim gets sick, and who is in and out of his house day and night? Simonds. It's like that nursery rhyme about the warm cot, only the answer isn't mother. It's Doctor Simonds. He could get into the garage and put that oil on the carpet of the car, and so bring Uncle Jim into it. And he's got a car of his own and drives like the devil.

"How do we know he didn't go to New York that night and see father? And he's tall and rather thin, and he's got evening clothes and wears them. What I'd like to know," she went on, her voice raised and her color high, "is where Doctor Simonds comes in in all this. We've been taking his word right along, but how do we know he isn't lying?"

"A reputable doctor——" I began.

"Oh, I'm sick of reputable doctors and reputable lawyers. I don't trust any one any more. How do we know those two didn't get together, Mr. Waite and Doctor Simonds, and cook this thing up with Wallie? Doctor Simonds dopes father, and Mr. Waite draws the will. And Sarah's suspicious. She puts on the record that father was queer that day."

"And so your Uncle Jim saw him that night on the hillside after he had killed poor Sarah, and is willing to be tried for his life to protect him? Don't be silly. Are you intimating also that Doctor Simonds did away with Wallie and shot Joseph?"

"Why not?" she said more calmly. "Wallie was coming out with the whole story on the stand, so he had to be got out of the way. And Joseph knew something, or suspected somebody, so he was shot. And don't forget this. He meant to kill Joseph. That was the big idea."

"I don't believe it. Doctor Simonds has attended me for years and–"

She made an impatient gesture.

"Why is it," she demanded, "that all women over a certain age have a soft spot for their doctors? Doctors are human. I'm asking you to think, not to be sentimental. Wallie knows the question will come up of undue influence, or of father not being capable of making a will. So what do they do? Doctor Simonds writes him a note, that father is perfectly capable of making a will. And whose word have we that the two were as reconciled during that sickness as Wallie pretends? Doctor Simonds again! You never heard Sarah say so, did you?"

"She never talked. And she didn't like Wallie."

"Then again, come down to the night Joseph was shot. Who could walk into this house without suspicion? Suppose we'd happened in before he got Joseph? Would we have suspected him of anything? No! He'd have said he saw the door open and dropped in, or that he wanted to use the telephone, and you'd have given him a glass of the sherry he likes so much and thought nothing of it."

"Why would he have come in the back door?"

"How do we know he came in the back door? Why didn't he come in the front, take a glass of wine, and then wander back. Maybe he hadn't planned to kill Joseph just then, but there was the chance, and he took it."

I think that was on Wednesday, and Joseph had been shot on Sunday night.

It is hardly surprising that I could not sleep that night, although everything was safe enough now that crime had at last entered my very house. From the night of the shooting an officer had patrolled the grounds in the daytime, keeping out the curious crowds which would otherwise have overrun us, and another one had stayed downstairs in the house at night.

The maids left him a night supper in the pantry, and a coffee pot on the range. About two in the morning there would steal through the house the aroma of boiling coffee, and although I had begun to suffer from a chronic insomnia, that homely and domestic odor acted on me like a narcotic. Downstairs was the law, armed and substantial, and awake. I would go to sleep then.

But that night I did not. I lay in my hot bed and listened to the far-off movements below, and that theory of Judy's grew until it became a nightmare. At last I got up, put on a dressing gown and slippers, and went down the stairs.

The pantry looked very comfortable, bright with lights and with that solid square blue figure drawn up to the table before the cold roast beef, the salad, the bread and cheese and coffee which were to stay it until morning.

But the officer was taking no chances in that pantry. The shades were closely drawn, and a chair was placed against the swinging door into the kitchen.

I must have moved very silently, for when I spoke he leaped to his feet and whirled on me; none the less impressive because the only weapon in his hand was a silver fork.

"I've come for some coffee," I said.

"Come in, ma'am. Come in," he said heartily. And I gathered from the zeal with which he served me that he too had found the night long and not a little dreary.

So we sat there, the two of us, companionably supping. He recommended mustard for the cold beef and so I took mustard, which I happen to despise.

All the time he carried on a running fire of conversation, like a man who is relieved to hear the sound of any voice, even his own. And when my complaisance regarding the mustard brought tears to my eyes, he even leaned over and patted my arm.

"You get that coffee down, ma'am," he said, "and you'll feel better. I guess you've been through plenty."

Here, however, he delicately decided to change the subject.

"What's happened to the red-haired girl who was here the night of the—the night you sent for us? I haven't seen her since."

"That was my niece, Judy Somers. She does not live here. But she is not red-haired."

"I don't mean Miss Somers. This girl was red-headed, all right. She was running up the drive just ahead of me. When she heard me, she stopped."

I sat perfectly still. Fortunately he was busy with his coffee, into which he was putting lump after lump of sugar. I managed to steady my voice.

"A red-haired girl?" I said slowly. "Did she speak to you?"

"I'll say she did. Caught me by the arm and wanted to know what was wrong in the house. I said: 'What business is that of yours?' and she said she worked here. She had a right to know. The rest had gone on, and I was in a hurry myself, but she hung onto me, and I saw that she looked sort of sick. 'Somebody been hurt,' I said, and with that she let me go."

"You didn't see her again?"

He looked at me and smiled.

"I've been watching for her here. She was a right good-looking girl. But I haven't seen her. You know who it is, I suppose?"

"Yes. But she is not in my employ any longer."

I thought he looked disappointed, but certainly not suspicious. He had however little more to tell. The precinct men had arrived before. He had come from headquarters in the side car of a motorcycle which had dropped him at the street, so that he was afoot when he overtook her.

I slept not at all that night. I was remembering a conversation I had had with the Inspector the morning after Joseph was shot, and following that examination he had made of the hillside.

"Just what do you know about Joseph, Miss Bell? His private life, I mean."

"I don't believe he had any."

"He'd never seemed in any fear, had he? For himself, I mean?"

"Not that I know of."

"Never took any precautions, I suppose? Didn't act like a man with anything hanging over him?"

"Not at all. He had looked very tired lately, and I had asked him if he wanted to go away. I have never seen him show any fear, except that last night as we went through the pantry he had the windows all closed. I spoke about it, and he said it was 'safer.' Or he felt safer."

"What about women? I suppose you wouldn't know about that?"

"I am sure there was nothing of the sort."

"Well, I'm not. I'll come to that later. But there are some things about this shooting that make it just a little different from the others. In the first place, the method's different. There's no attempt to camouflage the crime, and no attempt at even ordinary care against detection. In the others care was taken. I'll go further and say that I've never seen a case where such steps were taken, during and later, to cover every possible trail.

"But look at this. You're around the corner, only fifty feet away. You've got a dog, two dogs. Except for the fact that you held the terrier that night he'd have made a row that would have awakened the neighborhood. The house is fully lighted. Joseph is awake, or was until a moment or so before the shot. If he was asleep the criminal can't know it. The shades are drawn.

"Then again, why shoot him in the house? He must have been in and out. He goes to the garage sometimes, he is not always shut up at night. Since Walter's disappearance he's been out at all hours and in all sorts of places.

"But he's shot right here, in a bright light. The psychology's different, that's all. Look at this: I've just shot Joseph back there. I've got the revolver in my pocket, and so far I've got away with it. I've been watching the place, so I know you three are outside and may come in at any moment. The front door is open; the hall is brightly lighted. You may come in that way, walk right in on me. What's my normal procedure?"

"I should think you'd get out as fast as possible."

"Absolutely. But I don't. I saunter into that library, in a full light, pour myself a glass of sherry, put down the glass and then take my departure. And if you didn't use cut glass sherry glasses I'd leave a decent fingerprint instead of what we have. It's too reckless to be normal! Unless it's a woman."

At four o'clock that morning, unwilling to disturb the Inspector until later, I called Dick and asked him what he thought of it. He was drowsy and only half awake.

"She was running up the drive, toward the house," I said. "And she didn't know what had happened. She asked the officer."

But I could hear him yawning over the telephone.

"Sorry," he said. "The old bean isn't working very well. Probably she knew a lot more than she was admitting. Maybe she was running out, and when she heard your policeman she reversed the process. It's an old dodge, you know."

I sat on the side of my bed, the telephone on my knee, and tried to think. If that casual hypothesis of Dick's was correct, then Mary Martin had shot Joseph. It would have been easy enough. She knew the house and the habits of all of us; that the two maids retired early, that Joseph sat reading until late in the pantry; if she had seen Judy and Dick and myself go out into the grounds, she knew that the lower floor outside of the pantry was unoccupied. She had only to enter by the kitchen, fire her shot, and go forward, in order to escape.

But she had not escaped. In the ten, perhaps fifteen minutes between my finding Joseph and the arrival of the police, she had had plenty of time, but she had not gone.

Had she been upstairs during that interval, on some mysterious errand of her own? In Sarah's room, perhaps, or Joseph's, and then later on in the upper hall, peering over the banister and watching that influx of blue coats and muscular bodies; still later on stealing down the stairs, step by step. Sounds from the pantry, men talking, and Mary looking over her shoulder. Then the still open front door, a run for freedom, and the sound of a motorcycle stopping and escape cut off.

Had she turned in a panic, and started back toward the house? Or had she already planned the maneuver in case of necessity? To believe that last was to believe her old in crime, infinitely cunning and desperate.

I had worked myself into a condition bordering on hysteria by seven in the morning, when I called up Inspector Harrison, but his very voice quieted me. He was angry enough, however, when I had told him the story.

"The damned blockhead!" he exploded, referring to the policeman. "I'll break him for this."

"He didn't know. She said she worked here."

"She did, did she? She's a quick thinker. But what *was* she doing there?"

"You don't think she shot Joseph?"

"Well, I don't think she's the temperament to shoot Joseph and then go in and take a glass of wine. No."

I felt relieved. I was not fond of Mary, but the picture I had drawn for myself during the night had revolted me.

"Then I'm glad I talked to you. And by the way, Mrs. Bassett is dead."

I told him of Lily Sanderson's message, and he was silent for so long when I had finished that I thought we might have been disconnected.

"Hello," I said. "Central, I've—"

"I'm still here, Miss Bell. I'm sitting on a chair thinking what a damned fool I've been. I don't belong on the force. I ought to be a paperhanger!"

And with that he hung up the receiver.

CHAPTER XXX

WE KNOW NOW of that frantic rush he made, within ten minutes of my calling, to the Halkett Street house, and of that frenzied search he made later on that day, along the highways and particularly the byways of the Warrenville road. Some time after midnight he found what he was after, and not too late.

That had been in his mind all that day; the fear that he would be too late. And in the meantime he had set his guards. There was to be no escape this time, not even by death.

Even then he did not know the story, of course. But he knew the criminal and his incredible cunning. Let all go on as usual. Confide in no one. Disarm him, throw him off the track, and then into that fancied security of his thrust the long arm of the law. That was his method, he has said since, and that it answered is shown by the fact that for ten days apparently nothing happened.

Ten hot July days, with Godfrey working on the appeal; with Jim growing weak from heat and strain; with Joseph in the hospital, receiving our visits with great dignity, but refusing to alter his original story that he had been asleep and had not seen his assailant; with no word whatever of Wallie, or of Mary Martin; with the flowers on Mrs. Bassett's grave shriveled in the sun, and the policemen still on duty in my house and grounds, and with Katherine still in the house on Pine Street, stubbornly refusing to accept that repudiation of her which she considered Howard's second will to be.

Some time in that ten days I made a list of possible and impossible suspects, with a notation following, and as it is before me now I reproduce it. It shows better than I can tell it the utter confusion of my mind.

This is my list:

Godfrey Lowell	(*Unlikely*)
Inspector Harrison	(*Why?*)
Doctor Simonds	(*Possible*)
Mr. Waite	(*Possible but unlikely*)
Wallie	(*Improbable, and why?*)
Dick Carter	(*Possible but incredible*)
Jim	(*Possible but unlikely*)
Abner	(*No*)
Amos	(*Dead*)
Joseph	(*Himself shot*)
Robert	(*Unlikely. No reason*)

In such fashion did I fill in those ten interminable days. There were apparently no new developments, and the Inspector obstinately absented himself. Judy had grown thin to the point of emaciation, and still by night our guard ranged the lower floor and by day patrolled the grounds.

And then, on the seventeenth day of July, Katherine made her resolution and precipitated the crisis. It came that night.

Joseph had come home from the hospital that day, I remember. He took hold of the household much as usual, tottering from the silver drawer to the kitchen closets; but he was much shattered, and with that bandaged arm of his he could do very little. I arranged to send him to the country for a few weeks, and he agreed gratefully.

She was an intelligent woman, Katherine. Perhaps I have done her less than justice in this narrative. She was strange during that time, more frightened than she wanted us to know, and the result was that she withdrew herself.

I think from the time Jim took the stand at the trial, maybe even before it, she knew that he was protecting somebody.

"You say that you saw his white shirt front? What do you mean by that?"

"Just what I say. A white shirt front."

"He wore no vest?"

"I can't say. I had only an impression of evening clothes. He might have worn a dinner jacket."

"But you are sure of the cap?"

"No. I think it was a cap."

"Yet he came, according to your story, so close to you that he knocked this stick out of your hand. You could see a cap and a white shirt front, but you could not see anything more?"

And it was then that Jim hesitated. He was under oath, and an oath is a solemn matter. Then he glanced toward Katherine, and sat up a little in his chair.

"That is all I saw. I was on the ground. His face was turned down the hill."

Whom would he protect with his life but Howard? Howard with his heavy white hair, his invariable dinner dress in the evenings, and something to be kept hidden at any cost. Small wonder that Katherine thought of Margaret, or that she reverted to the will as the key to the mystery.

And so, very close to the end now, I go to the scene that afternoon, when at Katherine's request I accompanied her to Mr. Waite's office.

She had made the appointment and we were admitted at once. I was rather shocked by the change in Mr. Waite. He looked worn and not too well, and I thought there was a certain apprehension in his eyes when he greeted us.

He rose, but did not come forward.

"I am lame again," he explained, indicating a cane which stood beside him. "The old trouble. Well, I can only say that I am shocked and grieved, Mrs. Somers. Of course the appeal——"

"An appeal will do no good," said Katherine somberly.

"Still, new facts may come up. The case is of course not closed until——"

"Until they have killed an innocent man," Katherine finished for him. "And that is what they will do, Mr. Waite, unless the truth can be brought out."

He stirred uneasily in his chair.

"The truth? What is the truth? I am as much in the dark as you are." And seeing her face, he bent toward her across the desk. "I know what you mean, Mrs. Somers, and–I can understand. Nevertheless, I tell you that as surely as I sit here in this chair, Mr. Somers outlined the provisions of that will and signed it when I had prepared it. He was as rational as I am now. He discussed his family and his affairs. He even recognized that the will would be a blow to you, and said that he meant to leave an explanatory letter with it. Just why he did not do so I don't understand."

He was not acting. He was telling us facts, and I think Katherine saw it as well as I did. She sat stiffly upright, but the antagonism was gone from her voice.

"He did not explain the fund of fifty thousand dollars?"

"He did, and he did not. The son was to administer it for some purpose. He simply said that Walter would understand. He was of course still very weak, and he was not a talkative man, I understand. To be frank, I was in pain that first day, and not much better the second. I don't recall many details, although of course I have tried to since. A will is a routine matter."

"He did not appear to have been drugged?"

"Absolutely not."

"And Sarah was there? Sarah Gittings?"

"She left the room, but she came in once and gave him some medicine."

But Katherine was stubborn. Here were the facts, and she still refused to accept them. Mr. Waite saw that, and stiffened in his chair.

"The will was genuine, Mrs. Somers," he said. "If you have any doubt of it, I will go to the hotel with you, and we will repeat my own actions of those two days. I will show you that on the first day I was taken to Mr. Somers' room by the hotel manager himself, and that the floor clerk saw us and remembers this. I will show you that Walter Somers received me at the door and took me in, and that on both days Florence Gunther was with me. The floor clerk saw her there also."

"That is what she says. I know that, Mr. Waite."

He made an angry gesture.

"But she may be lying? I wonder if you realize what you are saying? If I had forged that will—and it seems to me that this is what you imply—why should I have gone there at all? Good God, madam, what had I to gain by such a criminal proceeding? It's nonsense, insane outrageous nonsense."

Katherine, however, seemed hardly to hear him. Certainly his words had no effect on her. She looked up from that careful inspection of her gloves.

"You would be willing to go to the hotel?"

"Of course I'll go to the hotel. Do you think I am afraid to go?"

She stood up, and for the first time it apparently occurred to her that he was angry; white with anger. She looked at him with that faint childlike expression which so altered her face.

"I'm sorry. It's only that I don't understand. You see, there was no reason, no reason at all. Not if Margaret Somers was dead."

He was polite but still somewhat ruffled when we started out. None of us, I am sure, had any idea that any *dénouement* was imminent. I remember that Mr. Waite delayed a moment or two to sign some letters, and that he grunted as he got up and reached for his stick.

"I've lost four teeth and two tonsils to cure this thing," he grumbled, "and I'm just where I started."

And so we reached the hotel, Katherine silent and absorbed, Mr. Waite limping, and I trailing along and feeling absurd and in the way.

We were fortunate in one thing: the rooms Howard had occupied were empty. Unluckily the manager was out, but the floor clerk, Miss Todd, was at her desk. She greeted us with the decorous gravity the occasion seemed to demand, and bowed to Mr. Waite.

"You remember me?" he asked her.

"Oh, perfectly, Mr. Waite."

"And that I came here on two succeeding days?"

"Yes, indeed. Mr. Hendrickson brought you up the first day." And she added glibly: "The first day you had the young lady with you. The second day she came again, and the hotel notary came up later. I remember it all very clearly. Miss Gunther sat down there on that chair until you called her in."

"And why?" said Katherine suddenly, "did she wait in the hall? There was a sitting room."

Miss Todd looked slightly surprised.

"That's so," she said. "That's queer, isn't it? Do you remember why, Mr. Waite?"

Mr. Waite however did not remember. He had seen no sitting room. He had been ushered directly from the hall into the bedroom.

"I suppose the nurse was in there," he said impatiently. "If you will open the rooms, Miss Todd—"

Miss Todd was very curious, and I think rather thrilled. She led the way briskly to the sitting room of the suite, unlocked the door and threw open a window or two; but if she had hoped to be asked to remain she was disappointed.

"In which room was Mr. Somers?"

"In there. I'll light the lights."

"Thanks. If you'll close the door as you go out—"

Some of Mr. Waite's irritation had returned. He limped into the bedroom Miss Todd had indicated and stood surveying it.

"I imagine your questions are answered, Mrs. Somers," he said crisply. "Here is the room. You have learned that I came here as I said. If you believe that I came for any other purpose than to draw up a will, I will remind you that I had not spoken ten words to Mr. Somers in my life until that day. I came because I was sent for, and for that reason only."

Katherine moistened her dry lips.

"And my husband was in bed?"

"In this bed. I sat down beside him, and I saw that he looked very ill. It was a dark day, but the lamp was on. I sat down here, as the lamp was on this side of the bed then. I see they have moved it."

There was a curious look in Katherine's face.

"I wonder," she said tensely, "if you mind doing again just what you did then? Can you remember? Try to remember, Mr. Waite! Everything. Every *little* thing."

I could see that her suppressed excitement had its effect on him. He glanced at her, and his voice was not so cold. He walked to the hall door and opened it.

"Let me see," he said. "Yes. Walter Somers was outside the door, in the hall. He opened the door and said: 'Father, Mr. Waite is here.' Then he stepped back and I came in alone. I think he closed the door behind me. Yes, he closed the door.

"I said: 'Well, Mr. Somers, I'm sorry to see you laid up.' He said something about his condition; that he was better, or getting better, and I put down my hat and gloves and got out some paper and my fountain pen. After that it was strictly business. He had the will pretty well thought out, and I suppose I was there only a half hour."

"And that is all?"

"All I can recall."

"He seemed perfectly normal. But he was nervous. I had propped my stick against the table, and once it slipped and fell. I remember that he jumped as though I had hit him. I picked it up and hung it on the doorknob, and—that's funny! That's damned queer."

He was staring at the wall beside the bed.

"They've taken away the door," he said.

"What door?"

"There was a door there by my right hand. It's on the other side of the bed now."

We all stood there, stupidly staring at the door. None of us, I fancy, had the remotest idea of its significance at that moment. It was Katherine who realized it first.

"Are you certain you were in this room, Mr. Waite?"

"I don't know. They all look alike. Of course they are always changing these places about."

And I think to Katherine must go the credit of that discovery, although Inspector Harrison had known it for at least a week. She was very calm, very quiet, as she went into the hall and called Miss Todd again.

"You are certain that this was my husband's bedroom?"

"Oh, yes, indeed, Mrs. Somers."

"And it has not been altered since? No changes have been made?"

"Only the new curtains at the windows."

"Thank you."

Miss Todd retired, her sharp eyes giving us a final survey as she closed the door. Not until she was gone did Katherine move, and then it was to cross the sitting room and glance into the bedroom there. Then she called to us, quietly enough.

"I think this is where you came, Mr. Waite," she said. "To Walter's bedroom, where an accomplice of Walter's impersonated his father and drew that will."

And only then was there a ring of triumph in her tired voice. "I knew it," she said. "I knew it. My poor Howard!"

CHAPTER XXXI

Of the plot which lay behind that discovery we had no knowledge. It was enough at the moment that there had been a conspiracy.

But later on in the day, the initial shock over, our ideas began to crystallize. Who had been the man in the bed? What relation did he bear to the murders? Was he himself the murderer?

None of us, however, gathered in my library that night, believed what was the fact; that the amazing *dénouement* was even then in preparation, and that it was a matter of only a few hours until all our questions were to be answered.

We were silent but more cheerful than we had been for days on end. There was hope now for Jim, and Katherine's relief was written in her face. Jim would be saved and Howard was once again hers to mourn. The frozen look had left her.

Judy too looked better than she had looked for weeks.

She had come in with her eyes bright and her color high, to show me a very nice but extremely small diamond on her engagement finger.

"Isn't it beautiful?" she said.

"It is indeed beautiful," I told her gravely. For it seemed so to me, that symbol of Dick's pride and his essential honesty. And I was proud of Judy, that she wore that bit of stone as a queen might wear a crown.

But talking got us nowhere that night. Again and again we went back to the scene in that hotel bedroom, with no result. It was Judy, with Dick's arm around her and Katherine accepting that as she had accepted the ring, who put forth the theory that the fifty thousand dollar clause which had been put in the will was to be the payment to this unknown for his services.

And it was Dick who followed that scene to its logical conclusion, and who said that a man who could put on a wig and look enough like Howard to deceive Mr. Waite under those circumstances, could easily have fooled Jim at night on the hillside.

Nevertheless, we were as far from the identity of this man as ever.

It was a broiling July night. At ten o'clock Joseph, in his traveling clothes, brought in some lemonade—he was leaving at eleven that night for a short holiday—and I remember that he had hardly gone out when Judy drew up a window shade for air, and suddenly drew back from the window.

"There's a man out there!" she said. "Just outside the window!"

Dick ran out at once. He was gone for some time, and when he came back it was to report that nobody was in sight, but that it was about to storm and that they'd better be on their way. I thought he looked rather odd, but we were all on edge that night and so I said nothing.

I was uneasy after they had gone. I wandered back to the pantry, where Robert was talking with the policeman and waiting for Joseph to come down, and while Robert stayed in the pantry the officer made a round of the house, inside and out. He found nothing, however, and as the storm broke soon after that, Joseph departed to the car by way of the kitchen porch in such a downpour as I have seldom seen.

I did not go up to bed, although it was eleven o'clock. I had a strange feeling of uneasiness, as though something was about to happen, or had happened. And at a little after eleven Jock sat up in the hall and gave tongue to a really dreadful howl.

I do not even now pretend to explain that wail, or that when I went into the hall both dogs were standing with their neck ruffs on end, staring into the dark drawing room.

I had a picture of that, of the incredulous terror in their attitudes; then they turned and bolted into the library, and I am not ashamed to admit that I followed them, and slammed and locked the door.

No, I have no explanation. When a short time later Inspector Harrison arrived and rang the door bell, he found me locked in the library; and it was all he could do to make me open the door.

He was soaking wet, and he looked very weary. He looked dejected, too, although I did not understand that until later on.

"I'm late," he said, "but we've had to cut open a safe deposit box in a bank, and it took some time and some red tape. Then I had another little job—I'm not proud of that. I'm coming to it pretty soon, but I'm not proud of it. Still, maybe it's all for the best. It will save Walter Somers a lot of trouble."

"Walter? He is alive?"

"He is. I've been doing a little nursing now and then, in odd moments! But he's alive. He's going to live. He's conscious, too, since yesterday. And now that you've turned up the story of the will—Waite told me—I hope the family won't prosecute. He tried to do the right thing, and it damn near cost him his life."

He sat back and bit savagely on the end of a rather soggy toothpick.

"Yes," he said, "I've bungled this thing. When I did get on the right track it was pretty late. It was the shooting of Joseph Holmes that started me straight, by the way. But I lost a lot of time, one way and another, and—well, I'll say this, our killer will never kill again."

"You've got him? The murderer?"

"Yes," he said. "Yes—and no."

I sat bolt upright in my excitement.

"Who was it, Inspector? Surely I have a right to know."

"I'm coming to that." He looked at me and smiled quizzically. "But not right off. We'll lead up to it, and then there'll be no shock."

"Shock! Then I know him?"

"You do indeed," he said gravely. "That's why I want to tell you the story first, so you'll understand. We'll call it a sort of psychological preparation. And I'm going to tell the story without telling you his name. We'll call him James C. Norton, because that's the name he used when he rented the safe deposit box. Norton. And up to a quarter to three o'clock today we hadn't a hope of landing him. We knew he was guilty, guilty as hell. We've watched him and followed him, but we hadn't a thing. Then today he went to the Commercial Bank—he had to—and he gave the show away.

"Mind you, he knew he was being watched, or he suspected it. He didn't know I'd found Walter, however. He had half killed Walter and tied him up in an abandoned farmhouse, and for a while he went back there now and then. It wasn't to his interest that Walter die. But later on it *was* to his interest that Walter Somers die. He left him where I found him, left him to die. I want you to remember that.

"Things were getting pretty hot for him, and with Walter dead the story wasn't likely to come out. And I'll say for him, that he held on to the last minute. He knew we had nothing on him. As a matter of fact we didn't, until about seven o'clock tonight.

"I want to give you a picture of this man, Miss Bell. We knew that he was at least moderately tall and stronger than the average. After I learned the story of that little comedy at the Imperial we knew he could act, and that he was a bit of a forger. Also we knew he was quick and catlike on his feet.

"But we knew some other things.

"This man had no heart, had no bowels of compassion. He had instead a lust for money and an infinite capacity for wickedness. Also he had cunning, a cunning so devilish that he had not only covered up his tracks; he had deliberately thrown suspicion on another man by the manufacture of false evidence.

"Such, for instance, was the oil in Jim Blake's car; the use of Jim Blake's name in that deadly visit to New York, and the clothing, expressly arranged to give the impression to the man Parrott that it was Blake; and there was the telephone message using Blake's name. And I say here and now that this man would have let Jim Blake go to the chair with less scruple than I break this toothpick.

"That's the picture of this assassin. I want you to remember it.

"Now I'm going to somebody else. I don't need to give you a picture of her. But she seemed to be in this thing up to the neck. She was, and my hat's off to her. Her name is Mary Martin."

"Mary! What has she done, but damage?"

He smiled again.

"She did her bit, when the truth began to drift in on her. She tried to save Howard Somers, but this—this Norton was too smart for her. She helped to find Walter. And on the night she was seen here in the drive she was running because she knew something. She knew there was going to be another murder, or an attempt at it."

"She knew Joseph was to be killed!"

"She was afraid it would be tried. We're coming to that. But she was in a bad way herself; she suspected what had happened to Walter. She was almost crazy, that girl. So she relaxed her vigilance and—you find Joseph shot."

"What possible interest had Mary Martin in Walter Somers, Inspector?" I asked, bewildered.

"She has a very real interest. She had married him last fall."

He gave me a moment to comprehend that, and then went on more briskly.

"Now let's go back. Let's go back to last summer, to the end of July.

"Walter Somers was in town, and one day he got a note to go to a house on Halkett Street. He went, and he met there this man I'm calling Norton, and a woman named Bassett. The Bassett woman claimed to have been a maid in Margaret Somers' employ in Biarritz, and that Margaret Somers had there given birth to a child."

"Howard Somers' child?" I asked sharply.

"No. I believe that was the plot at first; it was all a plot anyhow. There was no such child. This girl they were passing off was the Bassett woman's own daughter by an earlier marriage. The Bassett woman had remarried. The girl's name was Mary Martin."

"Mary! And she believed it?"

"I think she did believe it for a time. She wanted to believe it. That's natural. But when the plot failed Mrs. Bassett told her the truth. The immediate result, however, was that Walter sent for his father, and his father came here.

"Howard Somers denied the story in toto. He had had no second child by Margaret, and she had borne no child in Europe. The whole story was a lie. But he worked himself into a heart attack over it, and that was the start of the trouble.

"Norton's little plan had failed. But this sickness gave him a new idea. Queer how one criminal thought leads to another. He went to Walter with the scheme about the will, and Walter almost kicked him out. But Walter was in debt, and there was the idea. It got to 'eating him,' as he put it. Then, too, he was already interested in the girl. The girl was straight. She'd believed that story. As a matter of fact, when her mother told her the truth she tried to see Howard Somers at the Imperial, but they would not let her in.

"And there's this to say in Walter's defense; he felt that he had been badly treated, that a half of the estate should have been his. Later on, when his father was dead, he went on to New York to tell the whole story. But they alienated him there, and we have to remember that he wasn't sure his father had been murdered. Mary Martin suspected it, and told him so over the long distance telephone.

"And I'll say this for him. He went to this Norton and Norton denied it. But he laid Norton out cold on general principles, and Norton hated him from that moment. That's what I mean when I say Walter Somers has paid his price. His wife was desperately in love with him, but she loathed the whole imposture. She threatened again and again to uncover it.

"Now about this conspiracy to draw up a fake will. It wasn't Walter Somers' idea, although he helped to put it through, and the cleverness with which that will was put among his father's papers was not his idea either. It was simple enough, at that. Mr. Somers did not alter his mind or his will during that illness, but he did pay some notes of Walter's. In some ways he was a hard man, and he made Walter bring him the canceled notes.

"He meant to keep them. But Walter was afraid Mrs. Somers would find them in case his father died, so he had him endorse the envelope to be returned to him—to Walter—in that case.

"He told all this to Norton, and that was the start of the whole business. Norton suggested that a spurious will could be placed in that envelope and substituted for the notes, and that's what happened. Howard Somers himself carried back to New York and placed among his private papers that bogus will, endorsed in his own hand 'to be given to my son Walter in the event of my death.' It was neat, when you think of it."

"Neat, but wicked, Inspector!"

"Wrong, yes. Still, you must remember that no murder was contemplated. Fraud, yes, although Walter felt justifiable fraud, in a way. But murder, never.

"So the comedy was staged, with the fifty thousand dollars to be this Norton's share, his pay for that imposture, for the study he had made of Howard Somers' signature, and for that bit of comedy where he lay in a bed in a low light, on a day selected because it was dark and gray, and feebly signed that spurious document.

"I haven't been able to learn everything from Walter yet, but in that bit of comedy—and God knows it's the only comedy there is—the Bassett woman in a nurse's uniform played Sarah Gittings. Walter had prepared for that by having her give massage treatments to his father. And Norton was Mr. Somers. I imagine that Norton was the man with the box of flowers the floor clerk remembered. He had long gray hair, she said, and so Norton probably wore into the hotel that day the wig made to resemble Howard Somers' hair.

"That flower box had flowers in it. But it had some other things, make-up and silk pyjamas, a dressing gown, a few bottles and toilet articles to dress the room. That's a guess, but it's pretty accurate.

"It was Walter's room, anyhow. But they locked off the door to the sitting room, and Walter told Sarah Gittings he was having some friends there for cocktails, and to 'stay out.'

"Yes, it looked like a waterproof scheme. The hotel manager himself brings Waite up, and Walter meets him in the hall. Nobody thinks about that door. The notary comes up on the second day and witnesses the signatures. Florence Gunther is brought in from the hall. When it is over the players go away, one at a time, by the service staircase.

"Only one thing slipped. It was Sarah Gittings' custom to go out for a breath of air, and Walter took her place. But the two gray days with rain that were the best for their purposes, the twelfth and thirteenth of August, were bad days for her. She did not go out. She read a novel aloud to Mr. Somers instead, and put that on her record.

"Now let's go on to this last spring, when Sarah met Florence Gunther. She may have remembered seeing her at the Imperial, sitting in the hall, or it may have been pure accident. It's enough for us that they met, that Sarah told her she was with you, and as your connection with the Somers family is well known, that Florence finally mentioned the will.

"Sarah Gittings was incredulous, and after learning the date of the will, she went home and examined her records. She saw then that no such will could have been drawn on those days, and she began to try to reach Mr. Blake. She also finally induced Florence to abstract that copy from the safe, and on Monday the eighteenth of April she arranged to meet Mr. Blake at the Halkett Street house.

"She had already secreted the records in the wood cellar, but that evening she moved them to the cabinet. She had learned the terms of the will that day, and she knew well enough that there had been fraud. Also she knew about that secret compartment in the cabinet. When she took the will from Florence that afternoon she gave her the clock dial directions.

"But she felt safe enough. She had no thought of danger that night, when she left this house.

"Now, I'm going to reconstruct that night of the eighteenth of April. And you must remember that Walter Somers is still very weak, and that he himself can only guess at a part of it.

CHAPTER XXXII

"At five minutes past seven Sarah Gittings left this house, taking the dogs with her. She had the will for safekeeping probably inside her shoe—there had been some purse-snatching in this neighborhood—and she carried in her bag the key to her front door; but she was excited that night, and she forgot to lock her bedroom door.

"She went out the door, and in the drive she found Walter Somers waiting for her. He knew that she frequently took the dogs out at that hour, and this night he knew something else. He knew through Norton, who had his own way of learning things, that she had met Florence that afternoon and received a longish legal envelope from her.

"It looked as though the fat was in the fire.

"After he had talked to her, Walter saw that the game was all up. He threw up his hands and told her he'd go to his father the next day and tell him the whole story. But he begged her not to tell Jim Blake. If his stepmother ever heard this story he was through. She agreed to this.

"But she would not give him the copy of the will. Said she'd left it in the house. And he didn't trust her. She had never liked him. He didn't even believe her.

"But she showed him her hand bag, and the will was not in it.

" 'I'll give it back to you after you've seen your father,' she told him, and she left him standing there in the drive.

"He says, and I believe him, that he never saw her alive again.

"I'm not defending Walter for trying to get into the house and to get the will. He did get in, although he broke the point of his knife in doing so. While he was working at the putty of the door back there he says he heard her whistling and calling for Jock, who appeared to have wandered off. She was, he thought, in or near the Larimer lot, and later on, when his errand had been fruitless and Joseph had helped him to escape from the house, he thinks that he still heard her.

"I imagine he is right about that. The dog had run off, and she hunted him. Then, instead of going on to the house on Halkett Street, she may have been coming back here to telephone and call off that meeting. In any event, perhaps because she was tired with the climbing she had done, on the way back she seems to have sat down on that log to rest.

"And that was where Norton found her, at or about the very time the officer had arrived and the house was being searched. He probably heard the dogs, and so located her. He struck her down from behind, so that she never saw him, and he thought she was dead. Later on, at ten o'clock, he went back to look and she was still living, although unconscious. Then he finished the job. With a knife this time, a knife with a blade approximately four and a half inches long.

"Something scared him about that time, and he ran. He didn't see Blake on the hill, coming back after waiting at the Halkett Street house for her until twenty minutes to ten. He didn't see Blake, but Blake saw him. And now remember this. He—Norton—still had that wig like Howard Somers' own hair, and he was going back to see if that job needed finishing. Also very likely he hadn't got the will that first time. I believe he put that wig on his head before he went back to the lot.

"He didn't know what had happened in the interval. She might have been found, there might be a policeman there. So he put on that disguise of his, and he fooled Jim Blake; evening clothes, longish white hair and so on. It isn't hard, when the story began to come out, to see who Jim Blake thought he saw that night.

"It put him to bed, and it damned near sent him to the chair."

"Then this Norton, or whoever he is, killed her for the will?"

"Partly. Partly, too, because, although Walter Somers was sick of the whole thing, Norton was determined that it go on. It was that determination, that the will stand, that was behind all the other murders.

"If Florence had kept quiet, she might have lived. He may have thought she would. She'd taken that will from the safe, and she might keep quiet about it. But she tried to see you, and that was fatal. Also, there was something else which marked her for death. Sarah had told Walter about her records for those two days, and when repeated searchings of this house didn't turn them up, this Norton concluded that Florence had them.

"Under the pretext of bringing her here to you, he lured her into a car.

"He killed her and searched her, and then he went to the Halkett Street house that night and examined her room. He made the Bassett woman help him. It was Mrs. Bassett the Sanderson woman heard crying.

"But I want to go back to Walter. Joseph helped him out of the house that night, and he got away down the hill behind the garage, dressed and came back here. You were expecting him, but he had to come back anyhow. He had dropped his fountain pen into the air shaft, and it bore his initials.

"He got it, as we know. He was uneasy when Sarah didn't come back, but that's all. He was afraid she'd left the dogs somewhere and gone on to New York. That scared him; he wanted to do his own confessing, and when he went out and heard the dogs in the lot next door he thought she had tied them there. He was pretty well upset, but he went back to the club and played bridge.

"That is Walter's story, and I know that it is true in all the salient points. When Sarah was still missing the next day he was worried, especially when you found she was not in New York.

"But he still didn't believe she was dead, and he never thought of Norton.

"When her body was found, however, he went almost crazy. He went to Norton and Norton was shocked and grieved. Walter just didn't understand it, that's all. And when the sword-stick disappeared he began to suspect Jim Blake.

"Only why would Blake kill her? Had she shown him that will and let him believe it was genuine? And had Blake done it, in a passion of anger or to secure the will? It was the only answer he had, and we have to admit that a good many people thought the same way.

"The only person who didn't was Mary Martin, and she suspected Norton from the start. She'd loathed the scheme from the moment she learned about it, the will and all of it.

"But Florence Gunther's death showed Walter where he stood. I'm not defending him for keeping silent, but it's easy to see how he argued. He could not bring the two women back, and how could he prove that Norton had killed them? Norton was still protesting his innocence, calling on high heaven to show that his hands were clean.

"Then you burned the carpet from the car, and Walter was all at sea. He didn't know where he was.

"But Mary knew, and Norton knew she knew, or suspected. She wasn't safe after that, so we have her taking Joseph's revolver and keeping it by her, and later on we have her going to New York to the Somers' apartment.

"She went out on the Brooklyn Bridge that night and threw the gun into the river. She felt safe, after some pretty awful weeks."

"But why go to the Somers' apartment?" I asked, bewildered.

"Because she saw this. She is quicker than Walter, and she believed what he still didn't want to accept; that Norton was the killer. She saw Norton still holding on, searching Florence's room after her death for the records, searching this house over and over. And by the way, there's your ghost! It may be helpful with your servants!

"She saw too that Mr. Somers would have to go next, before the story of that bogus will was uncovered, and that with Mr. Somers dead Jim Blake would go to the chair. Either that or Wallie would have to tell his story, and even then that mightn't save Blake. Blake mightn't have known that the will was not genuine."

"Inspector," I said gravely, "I want to know who Norton is. I must know. This is—well, it's cruel."

"I think it's kindness," he said. "I want you to realize this man first, as he is. The craft of him, using Jim Blake's name to get to Howard Somers, and even dressing like him; telling Mr. Somers the proofs of Jim's guilt, and promising for a thousand dollars to keep certain things to himself; getting Mr. Somers into his study to write that check, and putting poison into the highball while he is in that study."

"And that is what he did?"

"That is what he did. And I don't mind saying that it was that check, which we found in his box, which completed the case against him. He couldn't bring himself to destroy that check."

He looked at his watch.

"Now—I'll hurry over this—I'm going to Walter Somers again. His father's death drove him frantic. Again he had no proof, but Mary Martin was certain. She had broken the glass and raised the windows—there's an odor to cyanide—and she felt pretty sure it was murder. And if murder came out, the whole story came out. You can see why she tried to prevent that.

"She called Walter on the long distance phone and told him, and he about went crazy. But a confession then was a very grave matter; here were three deaths as a result of that conspiracy, and one of them his own father.

"He compromised with himself. He would see that Jim Blake got off; but if he was acquitted he would let things ride.

"But the verdict was a foregone conclusion. He had to come clean to save Jim, and Norton had to confess. For he knew now that Norton had got the records. He had been over this house and he knew the cabinet. When the clock dial cipher was read in court all Norton had to do was to come here and get them.

"When Walter left the club, that night before the day when he was to go on the stand, he had in his pocket a full confession of the murders. He had taken it with him to force the murderer to sign it. He had determined to get that signature, at the point of a gun if necessary. But he hoped to get it, by letting Norton have a chance to escape. It looked reasonable to him; if Walter went on the stand the next day it was all over anyhow. As to the will, I mean.

"But I ought to say this. He and Norton were definitely out. There had been furious trouble between them, and of course there was the time when Walter had knocked Norton cold. Walter hated the very sight of the other man, and he knew it.

"Walter picked him up in his car; and they drove out of town, Walter talking, the other man listening. Walter was going on the stand the next day, to tell all he knew. He was wary enough; he had his revolver. But Norton, too, was prepared for trouble that night. He was too quick for Walter.

"He knocked him out and nearly killed him, and then he took him to an abandoned farmhouse out on the Warrenville road and left him there, tied. But it wasn't to his advantage that Walter die. He drove the car over the hill where we found it, and he carried off Walter's revolver and locked him up. But he went back now and then, although Walter was in pretty poor shape when I found him.

"With Walter dead, Mary would tell the story, and he was through. He went back now and then, looked after him a bit. Not much. Just enough to keep him alive. But he had not been there for three days when we found him, and he was mighty close to death.

"Of course it's easy to say this now, but the case against Blake never had satisfied me. You know that. I gave you my reasons before. All along there have been some things that didn't quite fit. Why would Jim Blake invent a man in evening dress? Well, the answer to that is easy. He was not inventing it. He *saw* a man in evening dress. But he said this man's face was turned down the hill. Now that's not possible. A man doesn't run rapidly along a bushy hillside in the dark without looking where he is going.

"So I decided that this man, conceding that Mr. Blake saw a man, was some one he knew and wouldn't mention. And after Howard Somers' death, I began to wonder if it wasn't Somers.

"But that didn't get me very far, and to add to the confusion, Joseph is shot. Jim Blake is in jail, Mr. Somers is dead and Walter's missing. And still Joseph gets shot! I'll admit that I thought it possible at the time that Walter had done it. There was some underneath story, and Joseph either suspected or knew something. It was pretty clear to me that Joseph had had to help Walter get out of the house the night he broke in.

"And I had had a theory that Walter knew a good bit about that attack on him at the top of the back stairs.

"Then there were some queer things about the shooting. Joseph was sitting in the pantry with the shades drawn, 'because it was safer,' but he tells some cock and bull story about dropping off to sleep, and that with the kitchen door standing wide open!

"It looked fishy to me, and as I say I thought of Walter Somers. He had had a revolver when he left, and of course at that time I didn't know the rest of the story. So it was for Walter's footprints that I looked the next morning, around the grounds and down the hill. But I didn't find them. I found something that I couldn't make out.

"It looked to me as though a woman had climbed that hill the night before, and gone back the same way. You'll remember that it had been raining, and the ground was soft. Certainly a woman had come up that hillside, walked past the garage and through the shrubbery toward the kitchen door. And she had gone back the same way, except that she went out the front door and around back along the opposite side of the house from where the three of you were.

"But here was the queer thing. It was a heavy-ish woman, moving slowly, and she walked on the outsides of her feet. I'd seen prints like that before.

"Well, I had two choices, and I took the wrong one. Young Carter had been in the house at the time the shot was fired, or close to it; he had a revolver in his car, and he had a knife with the point gone, and that broken blade fitted the bit I'd picked up on the steps back there. And there were other things. He had an interest in that will and he was young and strong. I don't mind saying that I gave him considerable thought.

"It was you yourself who put me on the right track. If it hadn't been for that message of yours about the Bassett woman I believe this murderer, this cold and crafty assassin, would be free tonight, and not where he is.

"But we had to move slowly. We had no proof; we had the story and the motive, but what else? Not a fingerprint, or a track or a weapon! Nothing to hang the case on, and he knew it. We went through his belongings with a fine tooth comb, and found nothing. We could jail him for forging that will, but we wanted him for four murders!"

"Four?"

"Amos was murdered," he said. "He was shoved into the river and he couldn't swim. *Because* he couldn't swim," he amended that. "Four murders and three murderous assaults, and we had nothing.

"Nothing that we could lay our hands on, anyhow. But it came to me one day, sitting by Walter's bed, that if this man would do all he had done for fifty thousand dollars, he'd be likely to have kept that check for a thousand; that if he had, we had him.

"We watched him after that, day and night. And at last he slipped up. He slipped up today. He went today to the Commercial Bank to draw some money. He had an account there in the name of Norton. And he had a box there, too.

"We had the bank open that box tonight, and we found that check there; the check, and the duplicate copy of the will Sarah Gittings carried hidden the night she was killed.

"So we got him. We'd had his house surrounded, and he hadn't a chance. He walked out of that house tonight in a driving storm, and got into a car, the same car he had been using all along; the car he used to visit Howard

Somers and the car in which he had carried Florence Gunther to her death, under pretext of bringing her here to you.

"But he was too quick for us, Miss Bell. That's why I say I bungled the job. He had some cyanide ready. He looked at the car, saw the men in and around it, said, "Well, gentlemen, I see I am not to have my holiday—"

"Holiday! You're not telling me—"

"Quietly, Miss Bell! Why should you be grieved or shocked? What pity have you for this monster, whose very wife crawled out of her deathbed to end his wickedness?"

"He is dead?"

"Yes," he said, "Joseph Holmes is dead."

And with that I believe that I fainted.

The Confession

CHAPTER I

I AM NOT a susceptible woman. I am objective rather than subjective, and a fairly full experience of life has taught me that most of my impressions are from within out rather than the other way about. For instance, obsession at one time a few years ago of a shadowy figure on my right, just beyond the field of vision, was later exposed as the result of a defect in my glasses. In the same way Maggie, my old servant, was during one entire summer haunted by church bells and considered it a personal summons to eternity until it was shown to be in her inner ear.

Yet the Benton house undeniably made me uncomfortable. Perhaps it was because it had remained unchanged for so long. The old horsehair chairs, with their shiny mahogany frames, showed by the slightly worn places in the carpet before them that they had not deviated an inch from their position for many years. The carpets—carpets that reached to the very baseboards and gave under one's feet with the yielding of heavy padding beneath—were bright under beds and wardrobes, while in the centers of the rooms they had faded into the softness of old tapestry.

Maggie, I remember, on our arrival moved a chair from the wall in the library, and immediately put it back again, with a glance to see if I had observed her.

"It's nice and clean, Miss Agnes," she said. "A—I kind of feel that a little dirt would make it more homelike."

"I'm sure I don't see why," I replied, rather sharply, "I've lived in a tolerably clean house most of my life."

Maggie, however, was digging a heel into the padded carpet. She had chosen a sunny place for the experiment, and a small cloud of dust rose like smoke.

"Germs!" she said. "Just what I expected. We'd better bring the vacuum cleaner out from the city, Miss Agnes. Them carpets haven't been lifted for years."

But I paid little attention to her. To Maggie any particle of matter not otherwise classified is a germ, and the prospect of finding dust in that immaculate house was sufficiently thrilling to tide over the strangeness of our first few hours in it.

Once a year I rent a house in the country. When my nephew and niece were children, I did it to take them out of the city during school vacations. Later, when they grew up, it was to be near the country club. But now, with the children married and new families coming along, we were more concerned with dairies than with clubs, and I inquired more carefully about the neighborhood cows than about the neighborhood golf-links. I had really selected the house at Benton Station because there was a most alluring pasture, with a brook running through it, and violets over the banks. It seemed to me that no cow with a conscience could live in those surroundings and give colicky milk.

Then, the house was cheap. Unbelievably cheap. I suspected sewerage at once, but it seemed to be in the best possible order. Indeed, new plumbing had been put in, and extra bathrooms installed. As old Miss Emily Benton lived there alone, with only an old couple to look after her, it looked odd to see three bathrooms, two of them new, on the second floor. Big tubs and showers, although little old Miss Emily could have bathed in the washbowl and have had room to spare.

I faced the agent downstairs in the parlor, after I had gone over the house. Miss Emily Benton had not appeared and I took it she was away.

"Why all those bathrooms?" I demanded. "Does she use them in rotation?"

He shrugged his shoulders.

"She wished to rent the house, Miss Blakiston. The old-fashioned plumbing—"

"But she is giving the house away," I exclaimed. "Those bathrooms have cost much more than she will get out of it. You and I know that the price is absurd."

He smiled at that. "If you wish to pay more, you may, of course. She is a fine woman, Miss Blakiston, but you can never measure a Benton with any yard-stick but their own. The truth is that she wants the house off her hands this summer. I don't know why. It's a good house, and she has lived here all her life. But my instructions, I'll tell you frankly, are to rent it, if I have to give it away."

With which absurd sentence we went out the front door, and I saw the pasture, which decided me.

In view of the fact that I had taken the house for my grandnieces and nephews, it was annoying to find, by the end of June, that I should have to live in it by myself. Willie's boy was having his teeth straightened, and must make daily visits to the dentist, and Jack went to California and took Gertrude and the boys with him.

The first curious thing happened then. I wrote to the agent, saying that I would not use the house, but enclosing a check for its rental, as I had signed the lease. To my surprise, I received in reply a note from Miss Emily herself, very carefully written on thin note paper.

Although it was years since I had seen her, the exquisite neatness of the letter, its careful paragraphing, its margins so accurate as to give the impression that she had drawn a faint margin line with a lead pencil and then erased it—all these were as indicative of Emily Benton as—well, as the letter was not.

As well as I can explain it, the letter was impulsive, almost urgent. Yet the little old lady I remembered was neither of these things. "My dear Miss Blakiston," she wrote. "But I do hope you will use the house. It was because I wanted to be certain that it would be *occupied* this summer that I asked so low a rent for it.

"You may call it a whim if you like, but there are reasons why I wish the house to have a summer tenant. It has, for one thing, never been empty since it was built. It was my father's pride, and his father's before him, that the doors were never locked, even at night. Of course I can not ask a tenant to continue this old custom, but I can ask you to reconsider your decision.

"Will you forgive me for saying that you are so exactly the person I should like to see in the house that I feel I can not give you up? So strongly do I feel this that I would, if I dared, enclose your check and beg you to use the house rent free. Faithfully yours, Emily Benton."

Gracefully worded and carefully written as the letter was, I seemed to feel behind it some stress of feeling, an excitement perhaps, totally out of proportion to its contents. Years before I had met Miss Emily, even then a frail little old lady, her small figure stiffly erect, her eyes cold, her whole bearing one of reserve. The Bentons, for all their open doors, were known in that part of the country as "proud." I can remember, too, how when I was a young girl my mother had regarded the rare invitations to have tea and tiny cakes in the Benton parlor as commands, no less, and had taken the long carriage-ride from the city with complacency. And now Miss Emily, last of the family, had begged me to take the house.

In the end, as has been shown, I agreed. The glamor of the past had perhaps something to do with it. But I have come to a time of life when, failing intimate interests of my own, my neighbors' interests are mine by adoption. To be frank, I came because I was curious. Why, aside from a money consideration, was the Benton house to be occupied by an alien household? It was opposed to every tradition of the family as I had heard of it.

I knew something of the family history: the Reverend Thaddeus Benton, rector of Saint Bartholomew, who had forsaken the frame rectory near the church to build himself the substantial home now being offered me; Miss Emily, his daughter, who must now, I computed, be nearly seventy; and a son whom I recalled faintly as hardly bearing out the Benton traditions of solidity and rectitude.

The Reverend Mr. Benton, I recalled, had taken the stand that his house was his own, and having moved his family into it, had thereafter, save on great occasions, received the congregation individually or *en masse,* in his study at the church. A patriarchal old man, benevolent yet austere, who once, according to a story I had heard in my girlhood, had horsewhipped one of his vestrymen for trifling with the affections of a young married woman in the village!

There was a gap of thirty years in my knowledge of the family. I had indeed forgotten its very existence, when by the chance of a newspaper advertisement I found myself involved vitally in its affairs, playing Providence, indeed, and both fearing and hating my rôle.

Looking back, there are a number of things that appear rather curious. Why, for instance, did Maggie, my old servant, develop such a dislike for the place? It had nothing to do with the house. She had not seen it when she first refused to go. But her reluctance was evident from the beginning.

"I've just got a feeling about it, Miss Agnes," she said. "I can't explain it, any more than I can explain a cold in the head. But it's there."

At first I was inclined to blame Maggie's "feeling" on her knowledge that the house was cheap. She knew it, as she has, I am sure, read all my letters for years. She has a distrust of a bargain. But later I came to believe that there was something more to Maggie's distrust—as though perhaps a wave of uneasiness, spreading from some unknown source, had engulfed her.

Indeed, looking back over the two months I spent in the Benton house, I am inclined to go even further. If thoughts carry, as I am sure they do, then emotions carry. Fear, hope, courage, despair—if the intention of writing a letter to an absent friend can spread itself halfway across the earth, so that as you write the friend writes also, and your letters cross, how much more should big emotions carry? I have had sweep over me such waves of gladness, such gusts of despair, as have shaken me. Yet with no cause for either. They are gone in a moment. Just for an instant, I have caught and made my own another's joy or grief.

The only inexplicable part of this narrative is that Maggie, neither a psychic nor a sensitive type, caught the terror, as I came to call it, before I did. Perhaps it may be explainable by the fact that her mental processes are comparatively simple, her mind an empty slate that shows every mark made on it.

In a way, this is a study in fear.

Maggie's resentment continued through my decision to use the house, through the packing, through the very moving itself. It took the form of a sort of watchful waiting, although at the time we neither of us realized it, and of dislike of the house and its surroundings. It extended itself to the very garden, where she gathered flowers for the table with a ruthlessness that was almost vicious. And, as July went on, and Miss Emily made her occasional visits, as tiny, as delicate as herself, I had a curious conclusion forced on me. Miss Emily returned her antagonism. I was slow to credit it. What secret and even unacknowledged opposition could there be between my downright Maggie and this little old aristocrat with her frail hands and the soft rustle of silk about her?

In Miss Emily, it took the form of—how strange a word to use in connection with her!—of furtive watchfulness. I felt that Maggie's entrance, with nothing more momentous than the tea-tray, set her upright in her chair, put an edge to her soft voice, and absorbed her. She was still attentive to what I said. She agreed or dissented. But back of it all, with her eyes on me, she was watching Maggie.

With Maggie the antagonism took no such subtle form. It showed itself in the second best instead of the best china, and a tendency to weak tea, when Miss Emily took hers very strong. And such was the effect of their mutual watchfulness and suspicion, such perhaps was the influence of the staid old house on me, after a time even that fact, of the strong tea, began to strike me as incongruous. Miss Emily was so consistent, so consistently frail and dainty and so—well, unspotted seems to be the word—and so gentle, yet as time went on I began to feel that she hated Maggie with a real hatred. And there was the strong tea!

Indeed, it was not quite normal, nor was I. For by that time—the middle of July it was before I figured out as much as I have set down in five minutes—by that time I was not certain about the house. It was difficult to say just what I felt about the house. Willie, who came down over a Sunday early in the summer, possibly voiced it when he came down to his breakfast there.

"How did you sleep?" I asked.

"Not very well." He picked up his coffee-cup, and smiled over it rather sheepishly. "To tell the truth, I got to thinking about things—the furniture and all that," he said vaguely. "How many people have sat in the chairs and seen themselves in the mirror and died in the bed, and so on."

Maggie, who was bringing in the toast, gave a sort of low moan, which she turned into a cough.

"There have been twenty-three deaths in it in the last forty years, Mr. Willie," she volunteered. "That's according to the gardener. And more than half died in that room of yours."

"Put down that toast before you drop it, Maggie," I said. "You're shaking all over. And go out and shut the door."

"Very well," she said with a meekness behind which she was both indignant and frightened. "But there is one word I might mention before I go, and that is—cats!"

"Cats!" said Willie, as she slammed the door.

"I think it is only one cat," I observed mildly. "It belongs to Miss Emily, I fancy. It manages to be in a lot of places nearly simultaneously, and Maggie swears it is a dozen."

Willie is not subtle. He is a practical young man with a growing family, and a tendency the last year or two to flesh. But he ate his breakfast thoughtfully.

"Don't you think it's rather isolated?" he asked finally. "Just you three women here?" I had taken Delia, the cook, along.

"We have a telephone," I said, rather loftily. "Although——" I checked myself. Maggie, I felt sure, was listening in the pantry, and I intended to give her wild fancies no encouragement. To utter a thing is, to Maggie, to give it life. By the mere use of the spoken word it ceases to be supposition and becomes fact.

As a matter of fact, my uneasiness about the house resolved itself into an uneasiness about the telephone. It seems less absurd now than it did then.

But I remember what Willie said about it that morning on our way to the church.

"It rings at night, Willie," I said. "And when I go there is no one there."

"So do all telephones," he replied briskly. "It's their greatest weakness."

"Once or twice we have found the thing on the floor in the morning. It couldn't blow over or knock itself down."

"Probably the cat," he said with the patient air of a man arguing with an unreasonable woman. "Of course," he added—we were passing the churchyard then, dominated by what the village called the Benton "mosolem"—"there's a chance that those dead-and-gone Bentons resent anything as modern as a telephone. It might be interesting to see what they would do to a victrola."

"I'm going to tell you something, Willie," I said. "I am *afraid* of the telephone."

He was completely incredulous. I felt rather ridiculous, standing there in the sunlight of that summer Sabbath and making my confession. But I did it.

"I am afraid of it," I repeated. "I'm desperately sure you will never understand. Because I don't. I can hardly force myself to go to it. I hate the very back corner of the hall where it stands, I—"

I saw his expression then, and I stopped, furious with myself. Why had I said it? But more important still, why did I feel it? I had not put it into words before, I had not expected to say it then. But the moment I said it I knew it was true. I had developed an *idée fixe.*

"I have to go downstairs at night and answer it," I added, rather feebly. "It's on my nerves, I think."

"I should think it is," he said, with a note of wonder in his voice. "It doesn't sound like you. A telephone!" But just at the church door he stopped me, a hand on my arm.

"Look here," he said, "don't you suppose it's because you're so dependent on the telephone? You know that if anything goes wrong with it, you're cut off, in a way. And there's another point—you get all your news over it, good and bad." He had difficulty, I think, in finding the words he wanted. "It's—it's vital," he said. "So you attach too much importance to it, and it gets to be an obsession."

"Very likely," I assented. "The whole thing is idiotic, anyhow."

But—was it idiotic?

I am endeavoring to set things down as they seemed to me at the time, not in the light of subsequent events. For, if this narrative has any interest at all, it is a psychological one. I have said that it is a study in fear, but perhaps it would be more accurate to say that it is a study of the mental reaction of crime, of its effects on different minds, more or less remotely connected with it.

That my analysis of my impressions in the church that morning are not colored by subsequent events is proved by the fact that under cover of that date, July 16th, I made the following entry:

"Why do Maggie and Miss Benton distrust each other?"

I realized it even then, although I did not consider it serious, as is evidenced by the fact that I follow it with a recipe for fruit gelatin, copied from the newspaper.

It was a calm and sunny Sunday morning. The church windows were wide open, and a butterfly came in and set the choir boys to giggling. At the end of my pew a stained-glass window to Carlo Benton—the name came like an echo from the forgotten past—sent a shower of colored light over Willie, turned my blue silk to most unspinsterly hues, and threw a sort of summer radiance over Miss Emily herself, in the seat ahead.

She sat quite alone, impeccably neat, even to her profile. She was so orderly, so well balanced, one stitch of her hand-sewed organdy collar was so clearly identical with every other, her very seams, if you can understand it, ran so exactly where they should, that she set me to pulling myself straight. I am rather casual as to seams.

After a time I began to have a curious feeling about her. Her head was toward the rector, standing in a sort of white nimbus of sunlight, but I felt that Miss Emily's entire attention was on our pew, immediately behind her. I find I can not put it into words, unless it was that her back settled into more rigid lines. I glanced along the pew. Willie's face wore a calm and slightly somnolent expression. But Maggie, in her far end—she is very high church and always attends—Maggie's eyes were glued almost fiercely to Miss Emily's back. And just then Miss Emily herself stirred, glanced up at the window, and turning slightly, returned Maggie's glance with one almost as malevolent. I have hesitated over that word. It seems strong now, but at the time it was the one that came into my mind.

When it was over, it was hard to believe that it had happened. And even now, with everything else clear, I do not pretend to explain Maggie's attitude. She knew, in some strange way. But she did not know that she knew—which sounds like nonsense and is as near as I can come to getting it down in words.

Willie left that night, the 16th, and we settled down to quiet days, and, for a time, to undisturbed nights. But on the following Wednesday, by my journal, the telephone commenced to bother me again. Generally speaking, it rang rather early, between eleven o'clock and midnight. But on the following Saturday night I find I have recorded the hour as 2 a.m.

In every instance the experience was identical. The telephone never rang the second time. When I went downstairs to answer it—I did not always go—there was the buzzing of the wire, and there was nothing else. It was on the twenty-fourth that I had the telephone inspected and reported in normal condition, and it is possibly significant that for three days afterward my record shows not a single disturbance.

But I do not regard the strange calls over the telephone as so important as my attitude to them. The plain truth is that my fear of the calls extended itself in a few days to cover the instrument, and more than that, to the part of the house it stood in. Maggie never had this, nor did she recognize it in me. Her fear was a perfectly simple although uncomfortable one, centering around the bedrooms where, in each bed, she nightly saw dead and gone Bentons laid out in all the decorum of the best linen.

On more than one evening she came to the library door, with an expression of mentally looking over her shoulder, and some such dialogue would follow:

"D'you mind if I turn down the bed now, Miss Agnes?"

"It's very early."

"S'almost eight." When she is nervous she cuts verbal corners.

"You know perfectly well that I dislike having the beds disturbed until nine o'clock, Maggie."

"I'm going out."

"You said that last night, but you didn't go."

Silence.

"Now, see here, Maggie, I want you to overcome this feeling of–" I hesitated–"of fear. When you have really seen or heard something, it will be time enough to be nervous."

"Humph!" said Maggie on one of these occasions, and edged into the room. It was growing dusk. "It will be too late then, Miss Agnes. And another thing. You're a brave woman. I don't know as I've seen a braver. But I notice you keep away from the telephone after dark."

The general outcome of these conversations was that, to avoid argument, I permitted the preparation of my room for the night at an earlier and yet earlier hour, until at last it was done the moment I was dressed for dinner.

It is clear to me now that two entirely different sorts of fear actuated us. For by that time I had to acknowledge that there was fear in the house. Even Delia, the cook, had absorbed some of Maggie's terror; possibly traceable to some early impressions of death which connected themselves with a four-post bedstead.

Of the two sorts of fear, Delia's and Maggie's symptoms were subjective. Mine, I still feel, were objective.

It was not long before the beginning of August, and during a lull in the telephone matter, that I began to suspect that the house was being visited at night.

There was nothing I could point to with any certainty as having been disturbed at first. It was a matter of a book misplaced on the table, of my sewing-basket open when I always leave it closed, of a burnt match on the floor, whereas it is one of my orderly habits never to leave burnt matches around. And at last the burnt match became a sort of clue, for I suspected that it had been used to light one of the candles that sat in holders of every sort, on the top of the library shelves.

I tried getting up at night and peering over the banisters, but without result. And I was never sure as to articles that they had been moved. I remained in that doubting and suspicious halfway ground that is worse than certainty. And there was the matter of motive. I could not get away from that.

What possible purpose could an intruder have, for instance, in opening my sewing-basket or moving the dictionary two inches on the center table?

Yet the feeling persisted, and on the second of August I find this entry in my journal:

Right-hand brass, eight inches; left-hand brass, seven inches; carved-wood —Italian—five and three quarters inches each; old glass on mantelpiece—seven inches. And below this, dated the third: Last night, between midnight and daylight, the candle in the glass holder on the right side of the mantel was burned down one and one-half inches.

I should, no doubt, have set a watch on my nightly visitor after making this discovery—and one that was apparently connected with it—nothing less than Delia's report that there were candle-droppings over the border of the library carpet. But I have admitted that this is a study in fear, and a part of it is my own.

I was afraid. I was afraid of the night visitor, but, more than that, I was afraid of the fear. It had become a real thing by that time, something that lurked in the lower back hall waiting to catch me by the throat, to stop my breath, to paralyze me so I could not escape. I never went beyond that point.

Yet I am not a cowardly woman. I have lived alone too long for that. I have closed too many houses at night and gone upstairs in the dark to be afraid of darkness. And even now I can not, looking back, admit that I was afraid of the darkness there, although I resorted to the weak expedient of leaving a short length of candle to burn itself out in the hall when I went up to bed.

I have seen one of Willie's boys waken up at night screaming with a terror he could not describe. Well, it was much like that with me, except that I was awake and horribly ashamed of myself.

On the fourth of August I find in my journal the single word "flour." It recalls both my own cowardice at that time, and an experiment I made. The telephone had not bothered us for several nights, and I began to suspect a connection of this sort: when the telephone rang, there was no night visitor, and *vice versa*. I was not certain.

Delia was setting bread that night in the kitchen, and Maggie was reading a ghost story from the evening paper. There was a fine sifting of flour over the table, and it gave me my idea. When I went up to bed that night, I left a powdering of flour here and there on the lower floor, at the door into the library, a patch by the table, and—going back rather uneasily—one near the telephone.

I was up and downstairs before Maggie the next morning. The patches showed trampling. In the doorway they were almost obliterated, as by the trailing of a garment over them, but by the fireplace there were two prints quite distinct. I knew when I saw them that I had expected the marks of Miss Emily's tiny foot, although I had not admitted it before. But these were not Miss Emily's. They were large, flat, substantial, and one showed a curious marking around the edge that— It was my own! The marking was the knitted side of my bedroom slipper. I had, so far as I could tell, gone downstairs, in the night, investigated the candles, possibly in darkness, and gone back to bed again.

The effect of the discovery on me was—well undermining. In all the uneasiness of the past few weeks I had at least had full confidence in myself. And now that was gone. I began to wonder how much of the things that had troubled me were real, and how many I had made for myself.

To tell the truth, by that time the tension was almost unbearable. My nerves were going, and there was no reason for it. I kept telling myself that. In the mirror I looked white and anxious, and I had a sense of approaching trouble. I caught Maggie watching me, too, and on the seventh I find in my journal the words: "Insanity is often only a formless terror."

On the Sunday morning following that I found three burnt matches in the library fireplace, and one of the candles in the brass holders was almost gone. I sat most of the day in that room, wondering what would happen to me if I lost my mind. I knew that Maggie was watching me, and I made one of those absurd hypotheses to myself that we all do at times. If any of the family came, I would know that she had sent for them, and that I was really deranged! It had been a long day, with a steady summer rain that had not cooled the earth, but only set it steaming. The air was like hot vapor, and my hair clung to my moist forehead. At about four o'clock Maggie started chasing a fly with a folded newspaper. She followed it about the lower floor from room to room, making little harsh noises in her throat when she missed it. The sound of the soft thud of the paper on walls and furniture seemed suddenly more than I could bear.

"For heaven's sake!" I cried. "Stop that noise, Maggie." I felt as though my eyes were starting from my head.

"It's a fly," she said doggedly, and aimed another blow at it. "If I don't kill it, we'll have a million. There, it's on the mantel now. I never—"

I felt that if she raised the paper club once more I should scream. So I got up quickly and caught her wrist. She was so astonished that she let the paper drop, and there we stood, staring at each other. I can still see the way her mouth hung open.

"Don't!" I said. And my voice sounded thick even to my own ears. "Maggie—I can't stand it!"

"My God, Miss Agnes!"

Her tone brought me up sharply. I released her arm.

"I—I'm just nervous, Maggie," I said, and sat down. I was trembling violently.

I was sane. I knew it then as I know it now. But I was not rational. Perhaps to most of us come now and then times when we realize that some act, or some thought, is not balanced, as though, for a moment or an hour, the control was gone from the brain. Or—and I think this was the feeling I had—that some other control was in charge. Not the Agnes Blakiston I knew, but another Agnes Blakiston, perhaps, was exerting a temporary dominance, a hectic, craven, and hateful control.

That is the only outburst I recall. Possibly Maggie may have others stored away. She has a tenacious memory. Certainly it was my nearest approach to violence. But it had the effect of making me set a watch on myself.

Possibly it was coincidence. Probably, however, Maggie had communicated with Willie. But two days later young Martin Sprague, Freda Sprague's son, stopped his car in the drive and came in. He is a nerve specialist, and very good, although I can remember when he came down in his night drawers to one of his mother's dinner-parties.

"Thought I would just run in and see you," he said. "Mother told me you were here. By George, Miss Agnes, you look younger than ever."

"Who told you to come, Martie?" I asked.

"Told me? I don't have to be told to visit an old friend."

Well, he asked himself to lunch, and looked over the house, and decided to ask Miss Emily if she would sell an old Japanese cabinet inlaid with mother of pearl that I would not have had as a gift. And, in the end, I told him my trouble, of the fear that seemed to center around the telephone, and the sleepwalking.

He listened carefully.

"Ever get any bad news over the telephone?" he asked.

One way and another, I said I had had plenty of it. He went over me thoroughly, and was inclined to find my experience with the flour rather amusing than otherwise. "It's rather good, that," he said. "Setting a trap to catch yourself. You'd better have Maggie sleep in your room for a while. Well, it's all pretty plain, Miss Agnes. We bury some things as deep as possible, especially if we don't want to remember that they ever happened. But the mind's a queer thing. It holds on pretty hard, and burying is not destroying. Then we get tired or nervous—maybe just holding the thing down and pretending it is not there makes us nervous—and up it pops, like the ghost of a buried body, and raises hell. You don't mind that, do you?" he added anxiously. "It's exactly what those things do raise."

"But," I demanded irritably, "who rings the telephone at night? I daresay you don't contend that I go out at night and call the house, and then come back and answer the call, do you?"

He looked at me with a maddening smile.

"Are you sure it really rings?" he asked.

And so bad was my nervous condition by that time, so undermined was my self-confidence, that I was not certain! And this in face of the fact that it invariably roused Maggie as well as myself.

On the eleventh of August Miss Emily came to tea. The date does not matter, but by following the chronology of my journal I find I can keep my narrative in proper sequence.

I had felt better that day. So far as I could determine, I had not walked in my sleep again, and there was about Maggie an air of cheerfulness and relief which showed that my condition was more nearly normal than it had been for some time. The fear of the telephone and of the back hall was leaving me, too. Perhaps Martin Sprague's matter-of-fact explanation had helped me. But my own theory had always been the one I recorded at the beginning of this narrative—that I caught and—well, registered is a good word—that I registered an overwhelming fear from some unknown source.

I spied Miss Emily as she got out of the hack that day, a cool little figure clad in a thin black silk dress, with the sheerest possible white collar and cuffs. Her small bonnet with its crêpe veil was faced with white, and her carefully crimped gray hair showed a wavy border beneath it. Mr. Staley, the station hackman, helped her out of the surrey, and handed her the knitting-bag without which she was seldom seen. It was two weeks since she had been there, and she came slowly up the walk, looking from side to side at the perennial borders, then in full August bloom.

She smiled when she saw me in the doorway, and said, with the little anxious pucker between her eyes that was so childish, "Don't you think peonies are better cut down at this time of year?" She took a folded handkerchief from her bag and dabbed at her face, where there was no sign of dust to mar its old freshness. "It gives the lilies a better chance, my dear."

I led her into the house, and she produced a gay bit of knitting, a baby afghan, by the signs. She smiled at me over it.

"I am always one baby behind," she explained and fell to work rapidly. She had lovely hands, and I suspected them of being her one vanity.

Maggie was serving tea with her usual grudging reluctance, and I noticed then that when she was in the room Miss Emily said little or nothing. I thought it probable that she did not approve of conversing before servants, and would have let it go at that, had I not, as I held out Miss Emily's cup, caught her looking at Maggie. I had a swift impression of antagonism again, of alertness and something more. When Maggie went out, Miss Emily turned to me.

"She is very capable, I fancy."

"Very. Entirely too capable."

"She looks sharp," said Miss Emily. It was a long time since I had heard the word so used, but it was very apt. Maggie was indeed sharp. But Miss Emily launched into a general dissertation on servants, and Maggie's sharpness was forgotten.

It was, I think, when she was about to go that I asked her about the telephone.

"Telephone?" she inquired. "Why, no. It has always done very well. Of course, after a heavy snow in the winter, sometimes—"

She had a fashion of leaving her sentences unfinished. They trailed off, without any abrupt break.

"It rings at night."

"Rings?"

"I am called frequently and when I get to the phone, there is no one there."

Some of my irritation doubtless got into my voice, for Miss Emily suddenly drew away and stared at me.

"But—that is very strange. I—"

She had gone pale. I saw that now. And quite suddenly she dropped her knitting-bag. When I restored it to her, she was very calm and poised, but her color had not come back.

"It has always been very satisfactory," she said. "I don't know that it ever—"

She considered, and began again. "Why not just ignore it? If some one is playing a malicious trick on you, the only thing is to ignore it."

Her hands were shaking, although her voice was quiet. I saw that when she tried to tie the ribbons of the bag. And—I wondered at this, in so gentle a soul—there was a hint of anger in her tones. There was an edge to her voice.

That she could be angry was a surprise. And I found that she could also be obstinate. For we came to an *impasse* over the telephone in the next few minutes, and over something so absurd that I was nonplussed. It was over her unqualified refusal to allow me to install a branch wire to my bedroom.

"But," I expostulated, "when one thinks of the convenience, and—"

"I am sorry." Her voice had a note of finality. "I daresay I am old-fashioned, but—I do not like changes. I shall have to ask you not to interfere with the telephone."

I could hardly credit my senses. Her tone was one of reproof, plus decision. It convicted me of an indiscretion. If I had asked to take the roof off and replace it with silk umbrellas, it might have been justified. But to a request to move the telephone!

"Of course, if you feel that way about it," I said, "I shall not touch it."

I dropped the subject, a trifle ruffled, I confess, and went upstairs to fetch a box in which Miss Emily was to carry away some flowers from the garden.

It was when I was coming down the staircase that I saw Maggie. She had carried the hall candlesticks, newly polished, to their places on the table, and was standing, a hand on each one, staring into the old Washington mirror in front of her. From where she was she must have had a full view of Miss Emily in the library. And Maggie was bristling. It was the only word for it.

She was still there when Miss Emily had gone, blowing on the mirror and polishing it. And I took her to task for her unfriendly attitude to the little old lady.

"You practically threw her muffins at her," I said. "And I must speak again about the cups—"

"What does she come snooping around for, anyhow?" she broke in. "Aren't we paying for her house? Didn't she get down on her bended knees and beg us to take it?"

"Is that any reason why we should be uncivil?"

"What I want to know is this," Maggie said truculently. "What right has she to come back, and spy on us? For that's what she's doing, Miss Agnes.

Do you know what she was at when I looked in at her? She was running a finger along the baseboard to see if it was clean! And what's more, I caught her at it once before, in the back hall, when she was pretending to telephone for the station hack."

It was that day, I think, that I put fresh candles in all the holders downstairs. I had made a resolution like this—to renew the candles, and to lock myself in my room and throw the key over the transom to Maggie. If, in the mornings that followed, the candles had been used, it would prove that Martin Sprague was wrong, that even foot-prints could lie, and that some one was investigating the lower floor at night. For while my reason told me that I had been the intruder, my intuition continued to insist that my sleepwalking was a result, not a cause. In a word, I had gone downstairs, because I knew that there had been and might be again, a night visitor.

Yet, there was something of comedy in that night's precautions, after all.

At ten-thirty I was undressed, and Maggie had, with rebellion in every line of her, locked me in. I could hear her, afterwards running along the hall to her own room and slamming the door. Then, a moment later, the telephone rang.

It was too early, I reasoned, for the night calls. It might be anything, a telegram at the station, Willie's boy run over by an automobile, Gertrude's children ill. A dozen possibilities ran through my mind.

And Maggie would not let me out!

"You're not going downstairs," she called, from a safe distance.

"Maggie!" I cried, sharply. And banged at the door. The telephone was ringing steadily. "Come here at once."

"Miss Agnes," she beseeched, "you go to bed and don't listen. There'll be nothing there, for all your trouble," she said, in a quavering voice. "It's nothing human that rings that bell."

Finally, however, she freed me, and I went down the stairs. I had carried down a lamp, and my nerves were vibrating to the rhythm of the bell's shrill summons. But, strangely enough, the fear had left me. I find, as always, that it is difficult to put into words. I did not relish the excursion to the lower floor. I resented the jarring sound of the bell. But the terror was gone.

I went back to the telephone. Something that was living and moving was there. I saw its eyes, lower than mine, reflecting the lamp like twin lights. I was frightened, but still it was not the *fear*. The twin lights leaped forward—and proved to be the eyes of Miss Emily's cat, which had been sleeping on the stand!

I answered the telephone. To my surprise it was Miss Emily herself, a quiet and very dignified voice which apologized for disturbing me at that hour, and went on:

"I feel that I was very abrupt this afternoon, Miss Blakiston. My excuse is that I have always feared change. I have lived in a rut too long, I'm afraid. But of course, if you feel you would like to move the telephone, or put in an upstairs instrument, you may do as you like."

She seemed, having got me there, unwilling to ring off. I got a curious effect of reluctance over the telephone, and there was one phrase that she repeated several times.

"I do not want to influence you. I want you to do just what you think best."

The fear was entirely gone by the time she rang off. I felt, instead, a sort of relaxation that was most comforting. The rear hall, a cul-de-sac of nervousness in the daytime and of horror at night, was suddenly transformed by the light of my lamp into a warm and cheerful refuge from the darkness of the lower floor. The purring of the cat, comfortably settled on the telephone stand, was as cheering as the singing of a kettle on a stove. On the rack near me my garden hat and an old Paisley shawl made a grotesque human effigy.

I sat back in the low wicker chair and surveyed the hallway. Why not, I considered, do away now with the fear of it? If I could conquer it like this at midnight, I need never succumb again to it in the light.

The cat leaped to the stand beside me and stood there waiting. He was an intelligent animal, and I am like a good many spinsters. I am not more fond of cats than other people, but I understand them better. And it seemed to me that he and I were going through some familiar program, of which a part had been neglected. The cat neither sat nor lay, but stood there, waiting.

So at last I fetched the shawl from the rack and made him a bed on the stand. It was what he had been waiting for. I saw that at once. He walked onto it, turned around once, lay down, and closed his eyes.

I took up my vigil. I had been the victim of a fear I was determined to conquer. The house was quiet. Maggie had retired shriveled to bed. The cat slept on the shawl.

And then—I felt the fear returning. It welled up through my tranquillity like a flood, and swept me with it. I wanted to shriek. I was afraid to shriek. I longed to escape. I dared not move. There had been no sound, no motion. Things were as they had been.

It may have been one minute or five that I sat there. I do not know. I only know that I sat with fixed eyes, not even blinking, for fear of even for a second shutting out the sane and visible world about me. A sense of deadness commenced in my hands and worked up my arms. My chest seemed flattened.

Then the telephone bell rang.

The cat leaped to his feet. Somehow I reached forward and took down the receiver.

"Who is it?" I cried, in a voice that was thin, I knew, and unnatural.

The telephone is not a perfect medium. It loses much that we wish to register but, also, it registers much that we wish to lose. Therefore when I say that I distinctly heard a gasp, followed by heavy difficult breathing, over the telephone, I must beg for credence. It is true. Someone at the other end of the line was struggling for breath.

Then there was complete silence. I realized, after a moment, that the circuit had been stealthily cut, and that my conviction was verified by Central's demand, a moment later, of what number I wanted. I was, at first unable to answer her. When I did speak, my voice was shaken.

"What number, please?" she repeated, in a bored tone. There is nothing in all the world so bored as the voice of a small town telephone-operator.

"You called," I said.

"Beg y'pardon. Must have been a mistake," she replied glibly, and cut me off.

CHAPTER II

IT MAY BE SAID, and with truth, that so far I have recorded little but subjective terror, possibly easily explained by my occupancy of an isolated house, plus a few unimportant incidents, capable of various interpretations. But the fear was, and is today as I look back, a real thing. As real—and as difficult to describe—as a chill, for instance. A severe mental chill it was, indeed.

I went upstairs finally to a restless night, and rose early, after only an hour or so of sleep. One thing I was determined on—to find out, if possible, the connection between the terror and the telephone. I breakfasted early, and was dressing to go to the village when I had a visitor, no other than Miss Emily herself. She looked fluttered and perturbed at the unceremonious hour of her visit—she was the soul of convention—and explained, between breaths as it were, that she had come to apologize for the day before. She had hardly slept. I must forgive her. She had been very nervous since her brother's death, and small things upset her.

How much of what I say of Miss Emily depends on my later knowledge, I wonder? Did I notice then that she was watching me furtively, or is it only on looking back that I recall it? I do recall it—the hall door open and a vista of smiling garden beyond, and silhouetted against the sunshine, Miss Emily's frail figure and searching, slightly uplifted face. There was something in her eyes that I had not seen before—a sort of exaltation. She was not, that morning, the Miss Emily who ran a finger along her baseboards to see if we dusted them.

She had walked out, and it had exhausted her. She breathed in little gasps.

"I think," she said at last, "that I must telephone for Mr. Staley. I am never very strong in hot weather."

"Please let me call him for you, Miss Emily."

I am not a young woman, and she was at least sixty-five. But, because she was so small and frail, I felt almost a motherly anxiety for her that morning.

"I think I should like to do it, if you don't mind. We are old friends. He always comes promptly when I call him."

She went back alone, and I waited in the doorway. When she came out, she was smiling, and there was more color in her face.

"He is coming at once. He is always very thoughtful for me."

Now, without any warning, something that had been seething since her breathless arrival took shape in my mind, and became—suspicion. What if it had been Miss Emily who had called me the second time to the telephone, and having established the connection, had waited, breathing hard for—what?

It was fantastic, incredible in the light of that brilliant summer day. I looked at her, dainty and exquisite as ever, her ruchings fresh and white, her very face indicative of decorum and order, her wistful old mouth still rather like a child's, her eyes, always slightly upturned because of her diminutive height, so that she had habitually a look of adoration.

"One of earth's saints," the rector had said to me on Sunday morning. "A good woman, Miss Blakiston, and a sacrifice to an unworthy family."

Suspicion is like the rain. It falls on the just and on the unjust. And that morning I began to suspect Miss Emily. I had no idea of what.

On my mentioning an errand in the village she promptly offered to take me with her in the Staley hack. She had completely altered in manner. The strain was gone. In her soft low voice, as we made our way to the road, she told me the stories of some of the garden flowers.

"The climbing rose over the arch, my dear," she said, "my mother brought from England on her wedding journey. People have taken cuttings from it again and again, but the cuttings never thrive. A bad winter, and they are gone. But this one has lived. Of course now and then it freezes down."

She chattered on, and my suspicions grew more and more shadowy. They would have gone, I think, had not Maggie called me back with a grocery list.

"A sack of flour," she said, "and some green vegetables, and—Miss Agnes, that woman was down on her knees beside the telephone!—and bluing for the laundry, and I guess that's all."

The telephone! It was always the telephone. We drove on down the lane, eyed somnolently by spotted cows and incurious sheep, and all the way Miss Emily talked. She was almost garrulous. She asked the hackman about his family and stopped the vehicle to pick up a peddler, overburdened with his pack. I watched her with amazement. Evidently this was Mr. Staley's Miss Emily. But it was not mine.

But I saw mine, too, that morning. It was when I asked the hackman to put me down at the little telephone building. I thought she put her hand to her throat, although the next moment she was only adjusting the ruching at her neck.

"You—you have decided to have the second telephone put in, then?"

I hesitated. She so obviously did not want it installed. And was I to submit meekly to the fear again, without another effort to vanquish it?

"I think not, dear Miss Emily," I said at last, smiling at her drawn face. "Why should I disturb your lovely old house and its established order?"

"But I want you to do just what you think best," she protested. She had put her hands together. It was almost a supplication.

As to the strange night calls, there was little to be learned. The night operator was in bed. The manager made a note of my complaint, and promised an investigation, which, having had experience with telephone investigations, I felt would lead nowhere. I left the building, with my grocery list in my hand.

The hack was gone, of course. But—I may have imagined it—I thought I saw Miss Emily peering at me from behind the bonnets and hats in the milliner's window.

I did not investigate. The thing was enough on my nerves as it was.

Maggie served me my luncheon in a sort of strained silence. She observed once, as she brought me my tea, that she was giving me notice and intended leaving on the afternoon train. She had, she stated, holding out the sugar-bowl to me at arm's length, stood a great deal in the way of irregular hours from me, seeing as I would read myself to sleep, and let the light burn all night, although very fussy about the gas-bills. But she had reached the end of her tether, and you could grate a lemon on her most anywhere, she was that covered with goose-flesh.

"Goose-flesh about what?" I demanded. "And either throw the sugar to me or come closer."

"I don't know about what," she said sullenly. "I'm just scared."

And for once Maggie and I were in complete harmony. I, too, was "just scared."

We were, however, both of us much nearer a solution of our troubles than we had any idea of. I say solution, although it but substituted one mystery for another. It gave tangibility to the intangible, indeed, but I can not see that our situation was any better. I, for one, found myself in the position of having a problem to solve, and no formula to solve it with.

The afternoon was quiet. Maggie and the cook were in the throes of jelly-making, and I had picked up a narrative history of the county, written most pedantically, although with here and there a touch of heavy lightness, by Miss Emily's father, the Reverend Samuel Thaddeus Benton.

On the fly-leaf she had inscribed, "Written by my dear father during the last year of his life, and published after his death by the parish to which he had given so much of his noble life."

The book left me cold, but the inscription warmed me. Whatever feeling I might have had about Miss Emily died of that inscription. A devoted and self-sacrificing daughter, a woman both loving and beloved, that was the Miss Emily of the dedication to "Fifty Years in Bolivar County."

In the middle of the afternoon Maggie appeared, with a saucer and a tea-spoon. In the saucer she had poured a little of the jelly to test it, and she was blowing on it when she entered. I put down my book.

"Well!" I said. "Don't tell me you're not dressed yet. You've just got about time for the afternoon train."

She gave me an imploring glance over the saucer.

"You might just take a look at this, Miss Agnes," she said. "It jells around the edges, but in the middle—"

"I'll send your trunk tomorrow," I said, "and you'd better let Delia make the jelly alone. You haven't much time, and she says she makes good jelly."

She raised anguished eyes to mine.

"Miss Agnes," she said, "that woman's never made a glass of jelly in her life before. She didn't even know about putting a silver spoon in the tumblers to keep 'em from breaking."

I picked up "Bolivar County" and opened it, but I could see her hands holding the saucer were shaking.

"I'm not going, Miss Agnes," said Maggie. (I had, of course, known she would not. The surprising thing to me is that she never learns this fact, although she gives me notice quite regularly. She always thinks that she is really going, until the last.) "Of course you can let that woman make the jelly, if you want. It's your fruit and sugar. But I'm not going to desert you in your hour of need."

"What do I need?" I demanded. "Jelly?"

But she was past sarcasm. She placed the saucer on a table and rolled her stained hands in her apron.

"That woman," she said, "what was she doing under the telephone stand?"

She almost immediately burst into tears, and it was some time before I caught what she feared. For she was more concrete than I. And she knew now what she was afraid of. It was either a bomb or fire.

"Mark my words, Miss Agnes," she said, "she's going to destroy the place. What made her set out and rent it for almost nothing if she isn't? And I know who rings the telephone at night. It's her."

"What on earth for?" I demanded as ungrammatical and hardly less uneasy than Maggie.

"She wakes us up, so we can get out in time. She's a preacher's daughter. More than likely she draws the line at bloodshed. That's one reason. Maybe there's another. What if by pressing a button somewhere and ringing that bell, it sets off a bomb somewhere?"

"It never has," I observed dryly.

But however absurd Maggie's logic might be, she was firm in her major premise. Miss Emily had been on her hands and knees by the telephone stand, and had, on seeing Maggie, observed that she had dropped the money for the hackman out of her glove.

"Which I don't believe. Her gloves were on the stand. If you'll come back, Miss Agnes, I'll show you how she was."

We made rather an absurd procession, Maggie leading with the saucer, I following, and the cat, appearing from nowhere as usual, bringing up the rear. Maggie placed the jelly on the stand, and dropped on her hands and knees, crawling under the stand, a confused huddle of gingham apron, jelly-stains, and suspicion.

"She had her head down like this," she said, in rather a smothered voice. "I'm her, and you're me. And I says: 'If it's rolled off somewhere I'll find it next time I sweep, and give it back to you.' Well, what d'you think of that! Here it is!"

My attention had been caught by the jelly, now unmistakably solidifying in the center. I moved to the kitchen door to tell Delia to take it off the fire. When I returned, Maggie was digging under the telephone battery-box with a hair-pin and muttering to herself.

"Darnation!" she said, "it's gone under!"

"If you do get it," I reminded her, "it belongs to Miss Emily."

There is a curious strain of cupidity in Maggie. I have never been able to understand it. With her own money she is as free as air. But let her see a chance for illegitimate gain, of finding a penny on the street, of not paying her fare on the cars, of passing a bad quarter, and she is filled with an unholy joy. And so today. The jelly was forgotten. Terror was gone. All that existed for Maggie was a twenty-five-cent piece under a battery-box.

Suddenly she wailed: "It's gone, Miss Agnes. It's clear under!"

"Good heavens, Maggie! What difference does it make?"

"W'you mind if I got the icepick and unscrewed the box?"

My menage is always notoriously short of tools.

I forbade it at once, and ordered her back to the kitchen, and after a final squint along the carpet, head flat, she dragged herself out and to her feet.

"I'll get the jelly off," she said, "and then maybe a hat pin'll reach it. I can see the edge of it."

A loud crack from the kitchen announced that cook had forgotten the silver spoon, and took Maggie off on a jump. I went back to the library and "Bolivar County," and, I must confess, to a nap in my chair.

I was roused by the feeling that some one was staring at me. My eyes focused first on the icepick, then, as I slowly raised them, on Maggie's face, set in hard and uncompromising lines.

"I'd thank you to come with me," she said stiffly.

"Come where?"

"To the telephone."

I groaned inwardly. But, because submission to Maggie's tyranny has become a firm habit with me, I rose. I saw then that she held a dingy quarter in one hand.

Without a word she turned and stalked ahead of me into the hall. It is curious, looking back and remembering that she had then no knowledge of the significance of things, to remember how hard and inexorable her back was. Viewed through the light of what followed, I have never been able to visualize Maggie moving down the hall. It has always been a menacing figure, rather shadowy than real. And the hall itself takes on grotesque proportions, becomes inordinately long, an infinity of hall, fading away into time and distance.

Yet it was only a moment, of course, until I stood by the telephone. Maggie had been at work. The wooden box which covered the battery-jars had been removed, and lay on its side. The battery-jars were uncovered, giving an effect of mystery unveiled, a sort of shamelessness, of destroyed illusion.

Maggie pointed. "There's a paper under one of the jars," she said. "I haven't touched it, but I know well enough what it is."

I have not questioned Maggie on this point, but I am convinced that she expected to find a sort of final summons, of death's visiting-card, for one or the other of us.

The paper was there, a small folded scrap, partially concealed under a jar.

"Them prints was there, too," Maggie said, noncommittally.

The box had accumulated the fluctuant floating particles of months, possibly years—lint from the hall carpet giving it a reddish tinge. And in this light and evanescent deposit, fluttered by a breath, fingers had moved, searched, I am tempted to say groped, although the word seems absurd for anything so small. The imprint of Maggie's coin and of her attempts at salvage were at the edge and quite distinct from the others.

I lifted the jar and picked up the paper. It was folded and refolded until it was not much larger than a thumb-nail, a rather stiff paper crossed with faint blue lines. I am not sure that I would have opened it—it had been so plainly in hiding, and was so obviously not my affair—had not Maggie suddenly gasped and implored me not to look at it. I immediately determined to examine it.

Yet, after I had read it twice, it had hardly made an impression on my mind. There are some things so incredible that the brain automatically rejects them. I looked at the paper. I read it with my eyes. But I did not grasp it.

It was not note paper. It was apparently torn from a tablet of glazed and ruled paper—just such paper, for instance, as Maggie soaks in brandy and places on top of her jelly before tying it up. It had been raggedly torn. The scrap was the full width of the sheet, but only three inches or so deep. It was undated, and this is what it said:

"To Whom it may concern: On the 30th day of May, 1911, I killed a woman (*here*) *in this house. I hope you will not find this until I am dead.*

(*Signed*) EMILY BENTON."

Maggie had read the confession over my shoulder, and I felt her body grow rigid. As for myself, my first sensation was one of acute discomfort—that we should have exposed the confession to the light of day. Neither of us, I am sure, had really grasped it. Maggie put a trembling hand on my arm.

"The brass of her," she said, in a thin, terrified voice. "And sitting in church like the rest of us. Oh, my God, Miss Agnes, put it back!"

I whirled on her, in a fury that was only an outlet for my own shock.

"Once for all, Maggie," I said, "I'll ask you to wait until you are spoken to. And if I hear that you have so much as mentioned this—piece of paper, out you go and never come back."

But she was beyond apprehension. She was literal, too. She saw, not Miss Emily unbelievably associated with a crime, but the crime itself.

"Who d'you suppose it was, Miss Agnes?"

"I don't believe it at all. Some one has placed it here to hurt Miss Emily."

"It's her writing," said Maggie doggedly.

After a time I got rid of her, and sat down to think in the library. Rather I sat down to reason with myself.

For every atom of my brain was clamoring that this thing was true, that my little Miss Emily, exquisite and fine as she was, had done the thing she claimed to have done. It was her own writing, thin, faintly shaded, as neat and as erect as herself. But even that I would not accept, until I had compared it with such bits of hers as I possessed, the note begging me to take the house, the inscription on the fly-leaf of "Fifty Years in Bolivar County."

And here was something I could not quite understand. The writing was all of the same order, but while the confession and the inscription in the book was similar, letter for letter, in the note to me there were differences, a change in the "t" in Benton, a fuller and blacker stroke, a variation in the terminals of the letters—it is hard to particularize.

I spent the remainder of the day in the library, going out for dinner, of course, but returned to my refuge again immediately after. Only in the library am I safe from Maggie. By virtue of her responsibility for my wardrobe, she virtually shares my bedroom, but her respect for books she never reads makes her regard a library as at least semi-holy ground. She dusts books with more caution than china, and her respect for a family Bible is greater than her respect for me.

I spent the evening there, Miss Emily's cat on the divan, and the mysterious confession lying before me under the lamp. At night the variation between it and her note to me concerning the house seemed more pronounced. The note looked more like a clumsy imitation of Miss Emily's own hand. Or —perhaps this is nearer—as if, after writing in a certain way for sixty years, she had tried to change her style.

All my logic ended in one conclusion. She must have known the confession was there. Therefore the chances were that she had placed it there. But it was not so simple as that.

Both crime and confession indicated a degree of impulse that Miss Emily did not possess. I have entirely failed with my picture of Miss Emily if the word violence can be associated with her in any way. Miss Emily was a temple, clean-swept, cold, and empty. She never acted on impulse. Every action, almost every word, seemed the result of thought and deliberation.

Yet, if I could believe my eyes, five years before she had killed a woman in this very house. Possibly in the very room in which I was then sitting.

I find, on looking back, that the terror must have left me that day. It had, for so many weeks, been so much a part of my daily life that I would have missed it had it not been for this new and engrossing interest. I remember that the long French windows of the library reflected the room—like mirrors against the darkness outside, and that once I thought I saw a shadowy movement in one of them, as though a figure moved behind me. But when I turned sharply there was no one there, and Maggie proved to be, as usual after nine o'clock, shut away upstairs.

I was not terrified. And indeed the fear never returned. In all the course of my investigations, I was never again a victim of the unreasoning fright of those earlier days.

My difficulty was that I was asked to believe the unbelievable. It was impossible to reconstruct in that quiet house a scene of violence. It was equally impossible, in view, for instance, of that calm and filial inscription in the history of Bolivar County, to connect Miss Emily with it. She had killed a woman, forsooth! Miss Emily, of the baby afghans, of the weary peddler, of that quiet seat in the church.

Yet I knew now that Miss Emily knew of the confession; knew, at least, of something concealed in that corner of the rear hall which housed the telephone. Had she by chance an enemy who would have done this thing? But to suspect Miss Emily of an enemy was as absurd as to suspect her of a crime.

I was completely at a loss when I put out the lights and prepared to close the house. As I glanced back along the hall, I could not help wondering if the telephone, having given up its secret, would continue its nocturnal alarms. As I stood there, I heard the low growl of thunder and the patter of rain against the windows. Partly out of loneliness, partly out of bravado, I went back to the telephone and tried to call Willie. But the line was out of order.

I slept badly. Shortly after I returned I heard a door slamming repeatedly, which I knew meant an open window somewhere. I got up and went into the hall. There was a cold air coming from somewhere below. But as I stood there it ceased. The door above stopped slamming, and silence reigned again.

Maggie roused me early. The morning sunlight was just creeping into the room, and the air was still cool with the night and fresh-washed by the storm.

"Miss Agnes," she demanded, standing over me, "did you let the cat out last night?"

"I brought him in before I went to bed."

"Humph!" said Maggie. "And did I or did I not wash the doorstep yesterday?"

"You ought to know. You said you did."

"Miss Agnes," Maggie said, "that woman was in this house last night. You can see her footprints as plain as day on the doorstep. And what's more, she stole the cat and let out your mother's Paisley shawl."

Which statements, corrected, proved to be true. My old Paisley shawl was gone from the hall-rack and unquestionably the cat had been on the back doorstep that morning along with the milk bottles. Moreover, one of my fresh candles had been lighted, but had burned for only a moment or two.

That day I had a second visit from young Martin Sprague. The telephone was in working order again, having unaccountably recovered, and I was using it when he came. He watched me quizzically from a position by the newel post, as I rang off.

"I was calling Miss Emily Benton," I explained, "but she is ill."

"Still troubled with telephobia?"

"I have other things to worry me, Martin," I said gravely, and let him into the library.

There I made a clean breast of everything. I omitted nothing. The fear, the strange ringing of the telephone bell; the gasping breathing over it the night before; Miss Emily's visit to it. And, at last, the discovery.

He took the paper when I offered it to him, and examined it carefully by a window. Then he stood looking out and whistling reflectively. At last he turned back to the room.

"It's an unusual story," he said. "But if you'll give me a little time I'll explain it to you. In the first place, let go of the material things for a moment, and let's deal with minds and emotions. You're a sensitive person, Miss Agnes. You catch a lot of impressions that pass most people by. And, first of all, you've been catching fright from two sources."

"Two sources?"

"Two. Maggie is one. She hates the country. She is afraid of old houses. And she sees in this house only the ghosts of people who have died here."

"I pay no attention to Maggie's fears."

"You only think that. But to go further—you have been receiving waves of apprehension from another source—from the little lady, Miss Emily."

"Then you think—"

"Hold on," he said smiling. "I think she wrote that confession. Yes. As a matter of fact, I'm quite sure she did. And she has established a system of espionage on you by means of the telephone. If you had discovered the confession, she knew that there would be a change in your voice, in your manner. If you answered very quickly, as though you had been near the instrument, perhaps in the very act of discovering the paper—don't you get it? And can't you see how her terror affected you even over the wire? Don't you think that, if thought can travel untold distances, fear can? Of course."

"But, Martin!" I exclaimed. "Little Miss Emily a murderess."

He threw up his hands.

"Certainly not," he said. "You're a shrewd woman, Miss Agnes. Do you know that a certain type of woman frequently confesses to a crime she never committed, or had any chance of committing? Look at the police records—confessions of women as to crimes they could only have heard of through the newspapers! I would like to wager that if we had the newspapers of that date that came into this house, we would find a particularly atrocious and mysterious murder being featured—the murder of a woman."

"You do not know her," I maintained doggedly. And drew, as best I could, a sketch of Miss Emily, while he listened attentively.

"A pure neurasthenic type," was his comment. "Older than usual, but that is accountable by the sheltered life she has led. The little Miss Emily is still at heart a girl. And a hysterical girl."

"She has had enough trouble to develop her."

"Trouble! Has she ever had a genuine emotion? Look at this house. She nursed an old father in it, a bedridden mother, a paretic brother, when she should have been having children. Don't you see it, Miss Agnes? All her emotions have had to be mental. Failing them outside, she provided them for herself. This"—he tapped the paper in his hand—"this is one."

I had heard of people confessing to crimes they had never committed, and at the time Martin Sprague at least partly convinced me. He was so sure of himself. And when, that afternoon, he telephoned me from the city to say that he was mailing out some old newspapers, I knew quite well what he had found.

"I've thought of something else, Miss Agnes," he said. "If you'll look it up you will probably find that the little lady had had either a shock sometime before that, or a long pull of nursing. Something, anyhow, to set her nervous system to going in the wrong direction."

Late that afternoon, as it happened, I was enabled to learn something of this from a visiting neighbor, and once again I was forced to acknowledge that he might be right.

The neighbors had not been overcordial. I had gathered, from the first, the impression that the members of the Reverend Samuel Thaddeus Benton's congregation did not fancy an interloper among the sacred relics of the historian of Bolivar County. And I had a corroboration of that impression from my visitor of that afternoon, a Mrs. Graves.

"I've been slow in coming, Miss Blakiston," she said, seating herself primly. "I don't suppose you can understand, but this has always been the Benton place, and it seems strange to us to see new faces here."

I replied, with some asperity, that I had not been anxious to take the house, but that Miss Emily had been so insistent that I had finally done so.

It seemed to me that she flashed a quick glance at me.

"She is quite the most loved person in the valley," she said. "And she loves the place. It is—I cannot imagine why she rented the house. She is far from comfortable where she is."

After a time I gathered that she suspected financial stringency as the cause, and I tried to set her mind at rest.

"It cannot be money," I said. "The rent is absurdly low. The agent wished her to ask more, but she refused."

She sat silent for a time, pulling at the fingers of her white silk gloves.

And when she spoke again it was of the garden. But before she left she returned to Miss Emily.

"She has had a hard life, in a way," she said. "It is only five years since she buried her brother, and her father not long before that. She has broken a great deal since then. Not that the brother—"

"I understand he was a great care."

Mrs. Graves looked about the room, its shelves piled high with the ecclesiastical library of the late clergyman.

"It was not only that," she said. "When he was—all right, he was an atheist. Imagine, in this house! He had the most terrible books, Miss Blakiston. And, of course, when a man believes there is no hereafter, he is apt to lead a wicked life. There is nothing to hold him back."

Her mind was on Miss Emily and her problems. She moved abstractedly toward the door.

"In this very hall," she said, "I helped Miss Emily to pack all his books into a box, and we sent for Mr. Staley—the hackman at the station, you know—and he dumped the whole thing into the river. We went away with him, and how she cheered up when it was done!"

Martin Sprague's newspapers arrived the next morning. They bore a date of two days before the date of the confession, and contained, rather triumphantly outlined in blue pencil, full details of the murder of a young woman by some unknown assassin. It had been a grisly crime, and the paper was filled with details of a most sensational sort.

Had I been asked, I would have said that Miss Emily's clear, slightly upturned eyes had never glanced beyond the merest headlines of such journalistic reports. But in a letter Martin Sprague set forth a precisely opposite view.

"You will probably find," he wrote, "that the little lady is pretty well fed up on such stuff. The calmer and more placid the daily life, the more apt is the secret inner one, in such a circumscribed existence, to be a thriller! You might look over the books in the house. There is a historic case where a young girl swore she had tossed her little brother to a den of lions (although there were no lions near, and little brother was subsequently found asleep in the attic) after reading Fox's Book of Martyrs. Probably the old gentleman has this joke book in his library."

I put down his letter and glanced around the room. Was he right, after all? Did women, rational, truthful, devout women, ever act in this strange manner? And if it was true, was it not in its own way as mysterious as everything else?

I was, for a time that day, strongly influenced by Martin Sprague's conviction. It was, for one thing, easier to believe than that Emily Benton had committed a crime. And, as if to lend color to his assertion, the sunlight, falling onto the dreary bookshelves, picked out and illuminated dull gilt letters on the brown back of a volume. It was Fox's Book of Martyrs!

If I may analyze my sensations at that time, they divided themselves into three parts. The first was fear. That seems to have given away to curiosity, and that at a later period, to an intense anxiety. Of the three, I have no excuse for the second, save the one I gave myself at the time—that Miss Emily could not possibly have done the thing she claimed to have done, and that I must prove her innocence to myself.

With regard to Martin Sprague's theory, I was divided. I wanted him to be right. I wanted him to be wrong. No picture I could visualize of little old Miss Emily conceivably fitted the type he had drawn. On the other hand, nothing about her could possibly confirm the confession as an actual one.

The scrap of paper became, for the time, my universe. Did I close my eyes, I saw it side by side with the inscription in "Fifty Years in Bolivar County," and letter for letter, in the same hand. Did the sun shine, I had it in the light, examining it, reading it. To such a point did it obsess me that I refused to allow Maggie to use a tablet of glazed paper she had found in the kitchen table drawer to tie up the jelly-glasses. It seemed, somehow, horrible to me.

At that time I had no thought of going back five years and trying to trace the accuracy or falsehood of the confession. I should not have known how to go about it. Had such a crime been committed, how to discover it at this late day? Whom in all her sheltered life, could Miss Emily have murdered? In her small world, who could have fallen out and left no sign?

It was impossible, and I knew it. And yet—

Miss Emily was ill. The news came through the grocery boy, who came out every day on a bicycle, and teased the cat and carried away all the pears as fast as they ripened. Maggie brought me the information at luncheon.

"*She's* sick," she said.

There was only one person in both our minds those days.

"Do you mean really ill, or only—"

"The boy says she's breaking up. If you ask me, she caught cold the night she broke in here and took your Paisley shawl. And if you ask my advice, Miss Agnes, you'll get it back again before the heirs step in and claim it. They don't make them shawls nowadays, and she's as like as not to will it to somebody if you don't go after it."

"Maggie," I said quietly, "how do you *know* she has that shawl?"

"How did I know that paper was in the telephone-box?" she countered.

And, indeed, by that time Maggie had convinced herself that she had known all along there was something in the telephone battery-box.

"I've a sort of second sight, Miss Agnes," she added. And, with a shrewdness I found later was partially correct: "She was snooping around to see if you'd found that paper, and it came on to rain; so she took the shawl. I should say," said Maggie, lowering her voice, "that as like as not she's been in this house every night since we came."

That afternoon I cut some of the roses from the arch for Miss Emily, and wrapping them against the sun, carried them to the village. At the last I hesitated. It was so much like prying. I turned aside at the church intending to leave them there for the altar. But I could find no one in the parish house, and no vessel to hold them.

Late in the day I opened a door and stepped into the old church. I knelt for a moment, and then sat back and surveyed the quiet building. It occurred to me that here one could obtain a real conception of the Benton family, and of Miss Emily. The church had been the realest thing in their lives. It had dominated them, obsessed them. When the Reverend Samuel Thaddeus died, they had built him, not a monument, but a parish house. When Carlo Benton died (however did such an ungodly name come to belong to a Benton?) Miss Emily according to the story, had done without fresh mourning and built him a window.

I looked at the window. It was extremely ugly, and very devout. And under it was the dead man's name and two dates, 1860 and 1911.

So Carlo Benton had died the year Miss Emily claimed to have done a murder! Another proof, I reflected that Martin Sprague would say. He had been on her hands for a long time, both well and ill. Small wonder if little Miss Emily had fallen to imagining things, or to confessing them.

I looked at the memorial window once more, and I could almost visualize her gathering up the dead man's hateful books, and getting them as quickly as possible out of the house. Quite possibly there were unmentionable volumes among them—de Maupassant, perhaps Boccaccio. I had a distinct picture, too, of Mrs. Graves, lips primly set, assisting her with hands that fairly itched with the righteousness of her actions.

I still held the roses, and as I left the church I decided to lay them on some grave in the churchyard. I thought it quite likely that roses from the same arch had been frequently used for that purpose. Some very young grave, I said to myself, and found one soon enough, a bit of a rectangle of fresh earth, and a jarful of pansies on it. It lay in the shadow of the Benton mausoleum.

That was how I found that Carlo Benton had died on the 27th of May, 1911.

I cannot claim that the fact at the time had any significance for me, or that I saw in it anything more than another verification of Martin Sprague's solution. But it enabled me to reconstruct the Benton household at the date that had grown so significant. The 30th would have probably been the day after the funeral. Perhaps the nurse was still there. He had had a nurse for months, according to Mrs. Graves. And there would have been the airing that follows long illness and death, the opened windows, the packing up or giving away of clothing, the pauses and silences, the sense of strangeness and quiet, the lowered voices. And there would have been, too, that remorseless packing for destruction of the dead atheist's books.

And some time, during that day or the night that followed, little Miss Emily claimed to have committed her crime.

I went home thoughtfully. At the gate I turned and looked back. The

Benton mausoleum was warm in the sunset, and the rose sprays lay, like outstretched arms, across the tiny grave.

Maggie is amazingly efficient. I am efficient myself, I trust, but I modify it with intelligence. It is not to me a vital matter, for instance, if three dozen glasses of jelly sit on a kitchen table a day or two after they are prepared for retirement to the fruit cellar. I rather like to see them, marshaled in their neat rows, capped with sealing-wax and paper, and armed with labels. But Maggie has neither sentiment nor imagination. Jelly to her is an institution, not an inspiration. It is subject to certain rules and rites, of which not the least is the formal interment in the fruit-closet.

Therefore, after much protesting that night, I agreed to visit the fruit cellar, and select a spot for the temporary entombing of thirty-six jelly tumblers, which would have been thirty-seven had Delia known the efficacy of a silver spoon. I can recall vividly the mental shift from the confession to that domestic excursion, my own impatience, Maggie's grim determination, and the curious *dénouement* of that visit.

CHAPTER III

I HAD THE VERY slightest acquaintance with the basement of the Benton house. I knew it was dry and orderly, and with that my interest in it ceased. It was not cemented, but its hard clay floor was almost as solid as macadam. In one end was built a high potato-bin. In another corner two or three old pews from the church, evidently long discarded and showing weather-stains, as though they had once served as garden benches, were up-ended against the whitewashed wall. The fruit-closet, built in of lumber, occupied one entire end, and was virtually a room, with a door and no windows.

Maggie had, she said, found it locked and had had an itinerant locksmith fit a key to it.

"It's all scrubbed and ready," she said. "I found that preserved melon-rind you had for lunch in a corner. 'Twouldn't of kept much longer, so I took it up and opened it. She's probably got all sorts of stuff spoiling in the locked part. Some folks're like that."

Most of the shelves were open, but now, holding the lamp high, I saw that a closet with a door occupied one end. The door was padlocked. At the time I was interested, but I was, as I remembered, much more occupied with Maggie's sense of *meum* and *tuum*, which I considered deficient, and of a small lecture on other people's melon-rinds, which I delivered as she sullenly put away the jelly.

But that night, after I had gone to bed, the memory of that padlock became strangely insistent. There was nothing psychic about the feeling I had. It was perfectly obvious and simple. The house held, or had held, a secret. Yet it was, above stairs, as open as the day. There was no corner into which I might not peer, except— Why was that portion of the fruit-closet locked?

At two o'clock, finding myself unable to sleep, I got up and put on my dressing-gown and slippers. I had refused to repeat the experiment of being locked in. Then, with a candle and a box of matches, I went downstairs. I had, as I have said, no longer any terror of the lower floor. The cat lay as usual on the table in the back hall. I saw his eyes watching me with their curious unblinking stare, as intelligent as two brass buttons. He rose as my light approached, and I made a bed for him of a cushion from a chair, failing my Paisley shawl.

It was after that that I had the curious sense of being led. It was as though I knew that something awaited my discovery, and that my sole volition was whether I should make that discovery or not. It was there, waiting.

I have no explanation for this. And it is quite possible that I might have had it, to find at the end nothing more significant than root-beer, for instance, or bulbs for the winter garden.

And indeed, at first sight, what awaited me in the locked closet amounted to anti-climax. For when I had broken the rusty padlock open with a hatchet, and had opened the door with nervous fingers, nothing more startling appeared than a number of books. The shelves were piled high with them, a motley crew of all colors, but dark shades predominating.

I went back to bed, sheepishly enough, and wrapped my chilled feet in an extra blanket. Maggie came to the door about the time I was dozing off and said she had heard hammering downstairs in the cellar sometime ago, but she had refused to waken me until the burglars had gone.

"If it *was* burglars," she added, "you're that up-and-ready, Miss Agnes, that I knew if I waked you you'd be downstairs after them. What's a bit of silver to a human life?"

I got her away at last, and she went, muttering something about digging up the cellar floor and finding an uneasy spirit. Then I fell asleep.

I had taken cold that night, and the following morning I spent in bed. At noon Maggie came upstairs, holding at arm's length a book. She kept her face averted, and gave me a slanting and outraged glance.

"This is a nice place we've come to," she said, acidly. "Murder in the telephone and anti-Christ in the fruit cellar!"

"Why, Maggie," I expostulated.

"If these books stay, I go, and that's flat, Miss Agnes," was her *ipse dixit*. She dropped the book on the bed and stalked out, pausing at the door only to throw back, "If this is a clergyman's house, I guess I'd be better out of the church."

I took up the book. It was well-worn, and in the front, in a heavy masculine hand, the owner had written his name—written it large, a bit defiantly, perhaps. It had taken both courage and conviction to bring such a book into that devout household.

I am not quick, mentally, especially when it comes to logical thought. I daresay I am intuitive rather than logical. It was not by any process of reasoning at all, I fancy, that it suddenly seemed strange that there should be books locked away in the cellar. Yet it was strange. For that had been a bookish household. Books were its stock in trade, one may say. Such as I had borrowed from the library had been carefully tended. Torn leaves were neatly repaired. The reference books were alphabetically arranged. And, looking back on my visit to the cellar, I recalled now as inconsistent the disorder of those basement shelves.

I did not reach the truth until, that afternoon, I made a second visit to the cellar. Mrs. Graves had been mistaken. If not all Carlo Benton's proscribed books were hidden there, at least a large portion of his library was piled, in something like confusion, on the shelves. Yet she maintained that they had searched the house, and she herself had been present when the books were packed and taken away to the river.

That afternoon I returned Mrs. Graves's visit. She was at home, and in a sort of flurried neatness that convinced me she had seen me from far up the road. That conviction was increased by the amazing promptness with which a tea-tray followed my entrance. I had given her tea the day she came to see me, and she was not to be outdone. Indeed, I somehow gained the impression that tray and teapot, and even little cakes, had been waiting, day by day, for my anticipated visit.

It was not hard to set her talking of Carlo Benton and his wickedness. She rose to the bait like a hungry fish. Yet I gathered that, beyond his religious views or lack of them, she knew nothing. But on the matter of the books she was firm.

"After the box was ready," she said, "we went to every room and searched it. Miss Emily was set on clearing out every trace. At the last minute I found one called 'The Fallacy of Christianity' slipped down behind the dresser in his room, and we put that in."

It was "The Fallacy of Christianity" that Maggie had brought me that morning.

"It is a most interesting story," I observed. "What delicious tea, Mrs. Graves! And then you fastened up the box and saw it thrown into the river. It was quite a ceremony."

"My dear," Mrs. Graves said solemnly, "it was not a ceremony. It was a rite—a significant rite."

How can I reconcile the thoughts I had that afternoon with my later visit to Miss Emily? The little upper room in the village, dominated and almost filled by an old-fashioned bed, and Miss Emily, frail and delicate and beautifully neat, propped with pillows and holding a fine handkerchief, as fresh as the flutings of her small cap, in her hand. On a small stand beside the bed were her Bible, her spectacles, and her quaint old-fashioned gold watch.

And Miss Emily herself? She was altered, shockingly altered. A certain tenseness had gone, a tenseness that had seemed to uphold her frail body and carry her about. Only her eyes seemed greatly alive, and before I left they, too, had ceased their searching of mine and looked weary and old.

And, at the end of my short visit, I had reluctantly reached this conclusion: either Miss Emily had done the thing she confessed to doing, incredible as it might appear, or she thought she had done it; and the thing was killing her.

She knew I had found the confession. I knew that. It was written large over her. What she had expected me to do God only knows. To stand up and denounce her? To summon the law? I do not know.

She said an extraordinary thing, when at last I rose to go. I believe now that it was to give me my chance to speak. Probably she found the suspense intolerable. But I could not do it. I was too surprised, too perplexed, too—well, afraid of hurting her. I had the feeling, I know, that I must protect her. And that feeling never left me until the end.

"I think you must know, my dear," she said, from her pillows, "that I have your Paisley shawl."

I was breathless. "I thought that, perhaps"—I stumbled.

"It was raining that night," she said in her soft, delicate voice. "I have had it dried and pressed. It is not hurt. I thought you would not mind," she concluded.

"It does not matter at all—not in the least," I said unhappily.

I am quite sure now that she meant me to speak then. I can recall the way she fixed her eyes on me, serene and expectant. She was waiting. But to save my life I could not. And she did not. Had she gone as far as she had the strength to go? Or was this again one of those curious pacts of hers—if I spoke or was silent, it was to be?

I do not know.

I do know that we were both silent and that at last, with a quick breath, she reached out and thumped on the floor with a cane that stood beside the bed until a girl came running up from below stairs.

"Get the shawl, Fanny, dear," said Miss Emily, "and wrap it up for Miss Blakiston."

I wanted desperately, while the girl left the room to obey, to say something helpful, something reassuring. But I could not. My voice failed me. And Miss Emily did not give me another opportunity. She thanked me rather formally for the flowers I had brought from her garden, and let me go at last with the parcel under my arm, without further reference to it. The situation was incredible.

Somehow I had the feeling that Miss Emily would never reopen the subject again. She had given me my chance, at who knows what cost, and I had not taken it. There had been something in her good-by—I can not find words for it, but it was perhaps a finality, an effect of a closed door—that I felt without being able to analyze.

I walked back to the house, refusing the offices of Mr. Staley who met me on the road. I needed to think. But thinking took me nowhere. Only one conclusion stood out as a result of a mile and a half of mental struggle. Something must be done. Miss Emily ought to be helped. She was under a strain that was killing her.

But to help I should know the facts. Only, were there any facts to know? Suppose—just by way of argument, for I did not believe it—that the confession was true; how could I find out anything about it? Five years was a long time. I could not go to the neighbors. They were none too friendly as it was. Besides, the secret, if there was one, was not mine, but was Miss Emily's.

I reached home at last, and smuggled the shawl into the house. I had no intention of explaining its return to Maggie. Yet, small as it was in its way, it offered a problem at once. For Maggie has a penetrating eye and an inquiring nature. I finally decided to take the bull by the horns and hang it in its accustomed place in the hall, where Maggie, finding it at nine o'clock that evening, set up such a series of shrieks and exclamations as surpassed even her own record.

I knitted that evening. It has been my custom for years to knit bedroom slippers for an old ladies' home in which I am interested. Because I can work at them with my eyes shut, through long practise, I find the work soothing. So that evening I knitted at Eliza Klinordlinger's fifth annual right slipper, and tried to develop a course of action.

I began with a major premise—to regard the confession as a real one, until it was proved otherwise. Granted then, that my little old Miss Emily had killed a woman.

1st—Who was the woman?

2nd—Where is the body?

3rd—What was the reason for the crime?

Question two I had a tentative answer for. However horrible and incredible it seemed, it was at least possible that Miss Emily had substituted the body for the books, and that what Mrs. Graves described as a rite had indeed been one. But that brought up a picture I could not face.

And yet—

I called up the local physician, a Doctor Lingard, that night and asked him about Miss Emily's condition. He was quite frank with me.

"It's just a breaking up," he said. "It has come early, because she has had a trying life, and more responsibility than she should have had."

"I have been wondering if a change of scene would not be a good thing," I suggested. But he was almost scornful.

"Change!" he said. "I've been after her to get away for years. She won't leave. I don't believe she has been twelve miles away in thirty years."

"I suppose her brother was a great care," I observed.

It seemed to me that the doctor's hearty voice was a trifle less frank when he replied. But when I rang off I told myself that I, too, was becoming neurasthenic and suspicious. I had, however, learned what I had wanted to know. Miss Emily had had no life outside Bolivar County. The place to look for her story was here, in the immediate vicinity.

That night I made a second visit to the basement. It seemed to me, with those chaotic shelves before me, that something of the haste and terror of a night five years before came back to me, a night when, confronted by the necessity for concealing a crime, the box upstairs had been hurriedly unpacked, its contents hidden here and locked away, and some other content, inert and heavy, had taken the place of the books.

Miss Emily in her high bed, her Bible and spectacles on the stand beside her, her starched pillows, her soft and highbred voice? Or another Miss Emily, panting and terror-stricken, carrying down her armfuls of forbidden books, her slight figure bent under their weight, her ears open for sounds from the silent house? Or that third Miss Emily, Martin Sprague's, a strange wild creature, neither sane nor insane, building a crime out of the fabric of a nightmare? Which was the real Emily Benton?

Or was there another contingency that I had not thought of? Had some secret enemy of Miss Emily's, some hysterical girl from the parish, suffering under a fancied slight, or some dismissed and revengeful servant, taken this strange method of retaliation, done it and then warned the little old lady that her house contained such a paper? I confess that this last thought took hold on me. It offered a way out that I clutched at.

I had an almost frantic feeling by that time that I must know the truth. Suspense was weighing on me. And Maggie, never slow to voice an unpleasant truth, said that night, as she brought the carafe of ice-water to the library, "You're going off the last few days, Miss Agnes." And when I made no reply: "You're sagging around the chin. There's nothing shows age like the chin. If you'd rub a little lemon-juice on at night you'd tighten up some."

I ignored her elaborately, but knew she was right. Heat and sleepless nights and those early days of fear had told on me. And although I usually disregard Maggie's cosmetic suggestions, culled from the beauty columns of the evening paper, a look in the mirror decided me. I went downstairs for the lemon. At least, I thought it was for the lemon. I am not sure. I have come to be uncertain of my motives. It is distinctly possible that, subconsciously, I was making for the cellar all the time. I only know that I landed there, with a lemon in my hand, at something after eleven o'clock.

The books were piled in disorder on the shelves. Their five years of burial had not hurt them beyond a slight dampness of the leaves. No hand, I believe, had touched them since they were taken from the box where Mrs. Graves had helped to pack them. Then, if I were shrewd, I should perhaps have gathered something from their very disorder. But, as a matter of fact, I did not.

I would, quite certainly, have gone away as I came, clueless, had I not attempted to straighten a pile of books, dangerously sagging—like my chin! —and threatening a fall. My effort was rewarded by a veritable Niagara of books. They poured over the edge, a few first, then more, until I stood, it seemed, knee-deep in a raging sea of atheism.

Somewhat grimly I set to work to repair the damage, and one by one I picked them up and restored them. I put them in methodically this time, glancing at each title to place the volume upright. Suddenly, out of the darkness of unbelief, a title caught my eye and held it. "The Handwriting of God." I knew the book. It had fallen into bad company, but its theology was unimpeachable. It did not belong. It–

I opened it. The Reverend Samuel Thaddeus had written his own name in it, in the cramped hand I had grown to know. Evidently its presence there was accidental. I turned it over in my hands, and saw that it was closed down on something, on several things, indeed. They proved to be a small black note-book, a pair of spectacles, a woman's handkerchief.

I stood there looking at them. They might mean nothing but the accidental closing of a book, which was mistakenly placed in bad company, perhaps by Mrs. Graves. I was inclined to doubt her knowledge of religious literature. Or they might mean something more, something I had feared to find.

Armed with the volume, and the lemon forgotten–where the cook found it the next day and made much of the mystery–I went upstairs again.

Viewed in a strong light, the three articles took on real significance. The spectacles I fancied were Miss Emily's. They were, to all appearances, the duplicates of those on her tidy bedside stand. But the handkerchief was not hers. Even without the scent, which had left it, but clung obstinately to the pages of the book, I knew it was not hers. It was florid, embroidered, and cheap. And held close to the light, I made out a laundry-mark in ink on the border. The name was either Wright or Knight.

The note-book was an old one, and covered a period of almost twenty years. It contained dates and cash entries. The entries were nearly all in the Reverend Samuel Thaddeus's hand, but after the date of his death they had been continued in Miss Emily's writing. They varied little, save that the amounts gradually increased toward the end, and the dates were further apart. Thus, in 1898 there were six entries, aggregating five hundred dollars. In 1902–1903 there were no entries at all, but in 1904 there was a single memorandum of a thousand dollars. The entire amount must have been close to twenty-five thousand dollars. There was nothing to show whether it was money saved or money spent, money paid out or come in.

But across the years 1902 and 1903, the Reverend Thaddeus had written diagonally the word "Australia." There was a certain amount of enlightenment there. Carlo Benton had been in Australia during those years. In his "Fifty Years in Bolivar County," the father had rather naively quoted a letter from Carlo Benton in Melbourne. A record, then, in all probability, of sums paid by this harassed old man to a worthless son.

Only the handkerchief refused to be accounted for.

I did not sleep that night. More and more, as I lay wide-eyed through the night, it seemed to me that Miss Emily must be helped, that she was drifting miserably out of life for need of a helping hand.

Once, toward morning, I dozed off, to waken in a state of terror that I recognized as a return of the old fear. But it left me soon, although I lay awake until morning.

That day I made two resolves—to send for Willie and to make a determined effort to see the night telephone-operator. My letter to Willie off, I tried to fill the day until the hour when the night telephone-operator was up and about, late in the afternoon.

The delay was simplified by the arrival of Mrs. Graves, in white silk gloves and a black cotton umbrella as a sunshade. She had lost her air of being afraid I might patronize her, and explained pantingly that she had come on an errand, not to call.

"I'm at my Christmas presents now," she said, "and I've fixed on a bedroom set for Miss Emily. I suppose you won't care if I go right up and measure the dresser-top, will you?"

I took her up, and her sharp eyes roved over the stairs and the upper hall.

"That's where Carlo died," she said. "It's never been used since, unless you—" she had paused, staring into Miss Emily's deserted bedroom. "It's a good thing I came," she said. "The eye's no use to trust to, especially for bureaus."

She looked around the room. There was, at that moment, something tender about her. She even lowered her voice and softened it. It took on, almost comically, the refinements of Miss Emily's own speech.

"Whose photograph is that?" she asked suddenly. "I don't know that I ever saw it before. But it looks familiar, too."

She reflected before it. It was clear that she felt a sort of resentment at not recognizing the young and smiling woman in the old walnut frame, but a moment later she was measuring the dresser-top, her mind set on Christmas benevolence.

However, before she went out, she paused near the photograph.

"It's queer," she said. "I've been in this room about a thousand times, and I've never noticed it before. I suppose you can get so accustomed to a thing that you don't notice it."

As she went out, she turned to me, and I gathered that not only the measurement for a gift had brought her that afternoon.

"About those books," she said. "I run on a lot when I get to talking. I suppose I shouldn't have mentioned them. But I'm sure you'll keep the story to yourself. I've never even told Mr. Graves."

"Of course I shall," I assured her. "But—didn't the hackman see you packing the books?"

"No, indeed. We packed them the afternoon after the funeral, and it was the next day that Staley took them off. He thought it was old bedding and so on, and he hinted to have it given to him. So Miss Emily and I went along to see it was done right."

So I discovered that the box had sat overnight in the Benton house. There remained, if I was to help Miss Emily, to discover what had occurred in those dark hours when the books were taken out and something else substituted.

The total result of my conversation that afternoon on the front porch of the small frame house on a side street with the night telephone-operator was additional mystery.

I was not prepared for it. I had anticipated resentment and possibly insolence. But I had not expected to find fright. Yet the girl was undeniably frightened. I had hardly told her the object of my visit before I realized that she was in a state of almost panic.

"You can understand how I feel," I said. "I have no desire to report the matter, of course. But some one has been calling the house repeatedly at night, listening until I reply, and then hanging up the receiver. It is not accidental. It has happened too often."

"I'm not supposed to give out information about calls."

"But—just think a moment," I went on. "Suppose some one is planning to rob the house, and using this method of finding out if we are there or not?"

"I don't remember anything about the calls you are talking about," she parried, without looking at me. "As busy as I am—"

"Nonsense," I put in, "you know perfectly well what I am talking about. How do I know but that it is the intention of some one to lure me downstairs to the telephone and then murder me?"

"I am sure it is not that," she said. For almost the first time she looked directly at me, and I caught a flash of something—not defiance. It was, indeed, rather like reassurance.

"You see, you *know* it is not that." I felt all at once that she did know who was calling me at night, and why. And, moreover, that she would not tell. If, as I suspected, it was Miss Emily, this girl must be to some extent in her confidence.

"But—suppose for a moment that I think I know who is calling me?" I hesitated. She was a pretty girl, with an amiable face, and more than a suggestion of good breeding and intelligence about her. I made a quick resolve to appeal to her. "My dear child," I said, "I want so very much, if I can, to help some one who is in trouble. But before I can help, I must know that I can help, and I must be sure it is necessary. I wonder if you know what I am talking about?"

"Why don't you go back to the city?" she said suddenly. "Go away and forget all about us here. That would help more than anything."

"But—would it?" I asked gently. "Would my going away help—her?"

To my absolute amazement she began to cry. We had been sitting on a cheap porch seat, side by side, and she turned her back to me and put her head against the arm of the bench.

"She's going to die!" she said shakily. "She's weaker every day. She is slipping away, and no one does anything."

But I got nothing more from her. She had understood me, it was clear, and when at last she stopped crying, she knew well enough that she had betrayed her understanding. But she would not talk. I felt that she was not unfriendly, and that she was uncertain rather than stubborn. In the end I got up, little better off than when I came.

"I'll give you time to think it over," I said. "Not so much about the telephone calls, because you've really answered that. But about Miss Emily. She needs help, and I want to help her. But you tie my hands."

She had a sort of gift for silence. As I grew later on to know Anne Bullard better, I realized that even more. So now she sat silent, and let me talk.

"What I want," I said, "is to have Miss Emily know that I am friendly—that I am willing to do anything to—to show my friendliness. *Anything.*"

"You see," she said, with a kind of dogged patience, "it isn't really up to you, or to me either. It's something else." She hesitated. "She's very obstinate," she added.

When I went away I was aware that her eyes followed me, anxious and thoughtful eyes, with something of Miss Emily's own wide-eyed gaze.

Willie came late the next evening. I had indeed gone upstairs to retire when I heard his car in the drive. When I admitted him, he drew me into the library and gave me a good looking over.

"As I thought!" he said. "Nerves gone, looks gone. I told you Maggie would put a curse on you. What is it?"

So I told him. The telephone he already knew about. The confession he read over twice, and then observed, characteristically, that he would be eternally—I think the word is "hornswoggled."

When I brought out "The Handwriting of God," following Mrs. Graves's story of the books, he looked thoughtful. And indeed by the end of the recital he was very grave.

"Sprague is a lunatic," he said, with conviction. "There was a body, and it went into the river in the packing-case. It is distinctly possible that this Knight—or Wright—woman, who owned the handkerchief, was the victim. However, that's for later on. The plain truth is, that there was a murder, and that Miss Emily is shielding some one else."

And, after all, that was the only immediate result of Willie's visit—a new theory! So that now it stood: there was a crime. There was no crime. Miss Emily had committed it. Miss Emily had not committed it. Miss Emily had confessed it, but some one else had committed it.

For a few hours, however, our attention was distracted from Miss Emily and her concerns by the attempted robbery of the house that night. I knew nothing of it until I heard Willie shouting downstairs. I was deeply asleep, relaxed no doubt by the consciousness that at last there was a man in the house. And, indeed, Maggie slept for the same reason through the entire occurrence.

"Stop, or I'll fire!" Willie repeated, as I sat up in bed.

I knew quite well that he had no weapon. There was not one in the house. But the next moment there was a loud report, either a door slamming or a pistol-shot, and I ran to the head of the stairs.

There was no light below, but a current of cool night air came up the staircase. And suddenly I realized that there was complete silence in the house.

"Willie!" I cried out, in an agony of fright. But he did not reply. And then, suddenly, the telephone rang.

I did not answer it. I know now why it rang, that there was real anxiety behind its summons. But I hardly heard it then. I was convinced that Willie had been shot.

I must have gone noiselessly down the stairs, and at the foot I ran directly into Willie. He was standing there, only a deeper shadow in the blackness, and I had placed my hand over his, as it lay on the newel post, before he knew I was on the staircase. He wheeled sharply, and I felt, to my surprise, that he held a revolver in his hand.

"Willie! What is it?" I said in a low tone.

" 'Sh," he whispered. "Don't move—or speak."

We listened, standing together. There were undoubtedly sounds outside, some one moving about, a hand on a window-catch, and finally not particularly cautious steps at the front door. It swung open. I could hear it creak as it moved slowly on its hinges.

I put a hand out to steady myself by the comfort of Willie's presence before me, between me and that softly-opening door. But Willie was moving forward, crouching down, I fancied, and the memory of that revolver terrified me.

"Don't shoot him, Willie!" I almost shrieked.

"Shoot whom?" said Willie's cool voice, just inside the door.

I knew then, and I went sick all over. Somewhere in the hall between us crouched the man I had taken for Willie, crouched with a revolver in his right hand. The door was still open, I knew, and I could hear Willie fumbling on the hall-stand for matches. I called out something incoherent about not striking a light; but Willie, whistling softly to show how cool he was, struck a match. It was followed instantly by a report, and I closed my eyes.

When I opened them, Willie was standing unhurt, staring over the burning match at the door, which was closed, and I knew that the report had been but the bang of the heavy door.

"What in blazes slammed that door?" he said.

"The burglar, or whatever he is," I said, my voice trembling in spite of me. "He was here, in front of me. I laid my hand on his. He had a revolver in it. When you opened the door, he slipped out past you."

Willie muttered something, and went toward the door. A moment later I was alone again, and the telephone was ringing. I felt my way back along the hall. I touched the cat, which had been sleeping on the telephone stand. He merely turned over.

I have tried, in living that night over again, to record things as they impressed me. For, after all, this is a narrative of motive rather than of incidents, of emotions as against deeds. But at the time, the brief conversation over the telephone seemed to me both horrible and unnatural.

From a great distance a woman's voice said, "Is anything wrong there?"

That was the first question, and I felt quite sure that it was the Bullard girl's voice. That is, looking back from the safety of the next day, I so decided. At the time I had no thought whatever.

"There is nothing wrong," I replied. I do not know why I said it. Surely there was enough wrong, with Willie chasing an armed intruder through the garden.

I thought the connection had been cut, for there was a buzzing on the wire. But a second or so later there came an entirely different voice, one I had never heard before, a plaintive voice, full, I thought, of tears.

"Oh, please," said this voice, "go out and look in your garden, or along the road. Please—quickly!"

"You will have to explain," I said impatiently. "Of course we will go and look, but who is it, and why—"

I was cut off there, definitely, and I could not get "Central's" attention again.

Willie's voice from the veranda boomed through the lower floor. "This is I," he called. "No boiling water, please. I am coming in."

He went into the library and lighted a lamp. He was smiling when I entered, a reassuring smile, but rather a sheepish one, too.

"To think of letting him get by like that!" he said. "The cheapest kind of a trick. He had slammed the door before to make me think he had gone out, and all the time he was inside. And you—why didn't you scream?"

"I thought it was you," I told him.

The library was in chaos. Letters were lying about, papers, books. The drawer of the large desk-table in the center of the room had been drawn out and searched. "Fifty Years in Bolivar County," for instance, was lying on the floor, face down, in a most ignoble position. In one place books had been taken from a recess by the fireplace, revealing a small wall cupboard behind. I had never known of the hiding-place, but a glance into it revealed only a bottle of red ink and the manuscript of a sermon on missions.

Standing in the disorder of the room, I told Willie about the telephone-message. He listened attentively, and at first skeptically.

"Probably a ruse to get us out of the house, but coming a trifle late to be useful," was his comment. But I had read distress in the second voice, and said so. At last he went to the telephone.

"I'll verify it," he explained. "If some one is really anxious, I'll get the car and take a scout around."

But he received no satisfaction from the Bullard girl, who, he reported, listened stoically and then said she was sorry, but she did not remember who had called. On his reminding her that she must have a record, she countered with the flat statement that there had been no call for us that night.

Willie looked thoughtful when he returned to the library. "There's a queer story back of all this," he said. "I think I will get the car and scout around."

"He is armed, Willie," I protested.

"He doesn't want to shoot me, or he could have done it," was his answer. "I'll just take a look around, and come back to report."

It was half-past three by the time he was ready to go. He was, as he observed, rather sketchily clad, but the night was warm. I saw him off, and locked the door behind him. Then I went into the library to wait and to put things to rights while I waited.

The dawn is early in August, and although it was not more than half-past four when Willie came back, it was about daylight by that time. I went to the door and watched him bring the car to a standstill. He shook his head when he saw me.

"Absolutely nothing," he said. "It was a ruse to get me out of the house, of course. I've run the whole way between here and town twice."

"But that could not have taken an hour," I protested.

"No," he said. "I met the doctor—what's his name?—the local M.D. anyhow—footing it out of the village to a case, and I took him to his destination. He has a car, it seems, but it's out of order. Interesting old chap," he added, as I led the way into the house. "Didn't know me from Adam, but opened up when he found who I was."

I had prepared the coffee machine and carried the tray to the library. While I lighted the lamp, he stood, whistling softly, and thoughtfully. At last he said:

"Look here, Aunt Agnes, I think I'm a good bit of a fool, but—sometime this morning I wish you would call up Thomas Jenkins, on the Elmsburg road, and find out if any one is sick there."

But when I stared at him, he only laughed sheepishly. "You can see how your suspicious disposition has undermined and ruined my once trusting nature," he scoffed.

He took his coffee, and then, stripping off his ulster, departed for bed. I stopped to put away the coffee machine, and with Maggie in mind, to hang up his motor-coat. It was then that the flashlight fell out. I picked it up. It was shaped like a revolver.

I stopped in Willie's room on my way to my own, and held it out to him.

"Where did you get that?" I asked.

"Good heavens!" he said, raising himself on his elbow. "It belongs to the doctor. He gave it to me to examine the fan belt. I must have dropped it into my pocket."

And still I was nowhere. Suppose I had touched this flashlight at the foot of the stairs and mistaken it for a revolver. Suppose that the doctor, making his way toward the village and finding himself pursued, had faced about and pretended to be leaving it? Grant, in a word, that Doctor Lingard himself had been our night visitor—what then? Why had he done it? What of the telephone-call, urging me to search the road? Did some one realize what was happening, and take this method of warning us and sending us after the fugitive?

I knew the Thomas Jenkins farm on the Elmsburg road. I had, indeed, bought vegetables and eggs from Mr. Jenkins himself. That morning, as early as I dared, I called the Jenkins farm. Mr. Jenkins himself would bring me three dozen eggs that day. They were a little torn up out there, as Mrs. Jenkins had borne a small daughter at seven a.m.

When I told Willie, he was evidently relieved.

"I'm glad of it," he said heartily. "The doctor's a fine old chap, and I'd hate to think he was mixed up in any shady business."

He was insistent, that day, that I give up the house. He said it was not safe, and I was inclined to agree with him. But although I did not tell him of it, I had even more strongly than ever the impression that something must be done to help Miss Emily, and that I was the one who must do it.

Yet, in the broad light of day, with the sunshine pouring into the rooms, I was compelled to confess that Willie's theory was more than upheld by the facts. First of all was the character of Miss Emily as I read it, sternly conscientious, proud, and yet gentle. Second, there was the connection of the Bullard girl with the case. And third, there was the invader of the night before, an unknown quantity where so much seemed known, where a situation involving Miss Emily alone seemed to call for no one else.

Willie put the matter flatly to me as he stood in the hall, drawing on his driving gloves.

"Do you *want* to follow it up?" he asked. "Isn't it better to let it go? After all, you have only rented the house. You haven't taken over its history, or any responsibility but the rent."

"I think Miss Emily needs to be helped," I said, rather feebly.

"Let her friends help her. She has plenty of them. Besides, isn't it rather a queer way to help her, to try to fasten a murder on her?"

I could not explain what I felt so strongly—that Miss Emily could only be helped by being hurt, that whatever she was concealing, the long concealment was killing her. That I felt in her—it is always difficult to put what I felt about Miss Emily into words—that she both hoped for and dreaded desperately the light of the truth.

But if I was hardly practical when it came to Miss Emily, I was rational enough in other things. It is with no small pride—but without exultation, for in the end it cost too much—that I point to the solution of one issue as my own.

With Willie gone, Maggie and I settled down to the quiet tenure of our days. She informed me, on the morning after that eventful night, that she had not closed an eye after one o'clock! She came into the library and asked me if I could order her some sleeping-powders.

"Fiddlesticks!" I said sharply. "You slept all night. I was up and around the house, and you never knew it."

"Honest to heaven, Miss Agnes, I never slep' at all. I heard a horse gallopin', like it was runnin' off, and it waked me for good."

And after a time I felt that, however mistaken Maggie had been about her night's sleep, she was possibly correct about the horse.

"He started to run about the stable somewhere," she said. "You can smile if you want. That's the heaven's truth. And he came down the drive on the jump and out onto the road."

"We can go and look for hoof-marks," I said, and rose. But Maggie only shook her head.

"It was no real horse, Miss Agnes," she said. "You'll find nothing. Anyhow, I've been and looked. There's not a mark."

But Maggie was wrong. I found hoof-prints in plenty in the turf beside the drive, and a track of them through the lettuce-bed in the garden. More than that, behind the stable I found where a horse had been tied and had broken away. A piece of worn strap still hung there. It was sufficiently clear, then, that whoever had broken into the house had come on horseback and left afoot. But many people in the neighborhood used horses. The clue, if clue it can be called, got me nowhere.

CHAPTER IV

For several days things remained in *statu quo*. Our lives went on evenly. The telephone was at our service, without any of its past vagaries. Maggie's eyes ceased to look as if they were being pushed out from behind, and I ceased to waken at night and listen for untoward signs.

Willie telephoned daily. He was frankly uneasy about my remaining there. "You know something that somebody resents your knowing," he said, a day or two after the night visitor. "It may become very uncomfortable for you."

And, after a day or two, I began to feel that it was being made uncomfortable for me. I am a social being; I like people. In the city my neighborly instinct has died of a sort of brickwall apathy, but in the country it comes to life again. The instinct of gregariousness is as old as the first hamlets, I daresay, when prehistoric man ceased to live in trees, and banded together for protection from the wild beasts that walked the earth.

The village became unfriendly. It was almost a matter of a night. One day the postmistress leaned on the shelf at her window and chatted with me. The next she passed out my letters with hardly a glance. Mrs. Graves did not see me at early communion on Sunday morning. The hackman was busy when I called him. It was intangible, a matter of omission, not commission. The doctor's wife, who had asked me to tea, called up and regretted that she must go to the city that day.

I sat down then and took stock of things. Did the village believe that Miss Emily must be saved from me? Did the village know the story I was trying to learn, and was it determined I should never find out the truth? And, if this were so, was the village right or was I? They would save Miss Emily by concealment, while I felt that concealment had failed, and that only the truth would do. Did the village know, or only suspect? Or was it not the village at all, but one or two people who were determined to drive me away?

My theories were rudely disturbed shortly after that by a visit from Martin Sprague. I fancied that Willie had sent him, but he evaded my question.

"I'd like another look at that slip of paper," he said. "Where do you keep it, by the way?"

"In a safe place," I replied noncommittally, and he laughed. The truth was that I had taken out the removable inner sole of a slipper and had placed it underneath, an excellent hiding-place, but one I did not care to confide to him. When I had brought it downstairs, he read it over again carefully, and then sat back with it in his hand.

"Now tell me about everything," he said.

I did, while he listened attentively. Afterward we walked back to the barn, and I showed him the piece of broken halter still tied there.

He surveyed it without comment, but on the way back to the house he said: "If the village is lined up as you say it is, I suppose it is useless to interview the harness-maker. He has probably repaired that strap, or sold a new one, to whoever— It would be a nice clue to follow up."

"I am not doing detective work," I said shortly. "I am trying to help some one who is dying of anxiety and terror."

He nodded. "I get you," he said. But his tone was not flippant. "The fact is, of course, that the early theory won't hold. There has been a crime, and the little old lady did not commit it. But suppose you find out who did it. How is that going to help her?"

"I don't know, Martin," I said, in a sort of desperation. "But I have the most curious feeling that she is depending on me. The way she spoke the day I saw her, and her eyes and everything; I know you think it nonsense," I finished lamely.

"I think you'd better give up the place and go back to town," he said. But I saw that he watched me carefully, and when at last he got up to go, he put a hand on my shoulder.

"I think you are right, after all," he said. "There are a good many things that can't be reasoned out with any logic we have, but that are true, nevertheless. We call it intuition, but it's really subconscious intelligence. Stay, by all means, if you feel you should."

In the doorway he said: "Remember this, Miss Agnes. Both a crime of violence and a confession like the one in your hand are the products of impulse. They are not, either of them, premeditated. They are not the work, then, of a calculating or cautious nature. Look for a big, emotional type."

It was a day or two after that that I made my visit to Miss Emily. I had stopped once before, to be told with an air of finality that the invalid was asleep. On this occasion I took with me a basket of fruit. I had half expected a refusal, but I was admitted.

The Bullard girl was with Miss Emily. She had, I think, been kneeling beside the bed, and her eyes were red and swollen. But Miss Emily herself was as cool, as dainty and starched and fragile as ever. More so, I thought. She was thinner, and although it was a warm August day, a white silk shawl was wrapped around her shoulders and fastened with an amethyst brooch. In my clasp her thin hand felt hot and dry.

"I have been waiting for you," she said simply.

She looked at Anne Bullard, and the message in her eyes was plain enough. But the girl ignored it. She stood across the bed from me and eyed me steadily.

"My dear," said Miss Emily, in her highbred voice, "if you have anything to do, Miss Blakiston will sit with me for a little while."

"I have nothing to do," said the girl doggedly. Perhaps this is not the word. She had more the look of endurance and supreme patience. There was no sharpness about her, although there was vigilance.

Miss Emily sighed, and I saw her eyes seek the Bible beside her. But she only said gently: "Then sit down, dear. You can work at my knitting if you like. My hands get very tired."

She asked me questions about the house and the garden. The raspberries were usually quite good, and she was rather celebrated for her lettuces. If I had more than I needed, would I mind if Mr. Staley took a few in to the doctor, who was fond of them.

The mention of Doctor Lingard took me back to the night of the burglary. I wondered if to tell Miss Emily would unduly agitate her. I think I would not have told her, but I caught the girl's eye, across the bed, raised from her knitting and fixed on me with a peculiar intensity. Suddenly it seemed to me that Miss Emily was surrounded by a conspiracy of silence, and it roused my antagonism.

"There are plenty of lettuces," I said, "although a few were trampled by a runaway horse the other night. It is rather a curious story."

So I told her of our night visitor. I told it humorously, lightly, touching on my own horror at finding I had been standing with my hand on the burglar's shoulder. But I was sorry for my impulse immediately, for I saw Miss Emily's body grow rigid, and her hands twist together. She did not look at me. She stared fixedly at the girl. Their eyes met.

It was as if Miss Emily asked a question which the girl refused to answer. It was as certain as though it had been a matter of words instead of glances.

It was over in a moment. Miss Bullard went back to her knitting, but Miss Emily lay still.

"I think I should not have told you," I apologized. "I thought it might interest you. Of course nothing whatever was taken, and no damage done—except to the lettuces."

"Anne," said Miss Emily, "will you bring me some fresh water?"

The girl rose reluctantly, but she did not go farther than the top of the staircase, just beyond the door. We heard her calling to some one below, in her clear young voice, to bring the water, and the next moment she was back in the room. But Miss Emily had had the opportunity for one sentence.

"I know now," she said quietly, "that you have found it."

Anne Bullard was watching from the doorway, and it seemed to me, having got so far, I could not retreat. I must go on.

"Miss Bullard," I said. "I would like to have just a short conversation with Miss Emily. It is about a private matter. I am sure you will not mind if I ask you—"

"I shall not go out."

"Anne!" said Miss Emily sharply.

The girl was dogged enough by that time. Both dogged and frightened, I felt. But she stood her ground.

"She is not to be worried about anything," she insisted. "And she's not supposed to have visitors. That's the doctor's orders."

I felt outraged and indignant, but against the stone wall of the girl's presence and her distrust I was helpless. I got up, with as much dignity as I could muster.

"I should have been told that downstairs."

"The woman's a fool," said Anne Bullard, with a sort of suppressed fierceness. She stood aside as, having said good-by to Miss Emily, I went out, and I felt that she hardly breathed until I had got safely to the street.

Looking back, I feel that Emily Benton died at the hands of her friends. For she died, indeed, died in the act of trying to tell me what they had determined she should never tell. Died of kindness and misunderstanding. Died repressed, as she had lived repressed. Yet, I think, died calmly and bravely.

I had made no further attempt to see her, and Maggie and I had taken up again the quiet course of our lives. The telephone did not ring of nights. The cat came and went, spending as I had learned, its days with Miss Emily and its nights with us. I have wondered since how many nights Miss Emily had spent in the low chair in that back hall, where the confession lay hidden, that the cat should feel it could sleep nowhere else.

The days went by, warm days and cooler ones, but rarely rainy ones. The dust from the road settled thick over flowers and shrubbery. The lettuces wilted, and those that stood up in the sun were strong and bitter. By the end of August we were gasping in a hot dryness that cracked the skin and made any but cold food impossible.

Miss Emily lay through it all in her hot upper room in the village, and my attempt, through Doctor Lingard, to coax her back to the house by offering to leave it brought only a negative.

"It would be better for her, you understand," the doctor said, over the telephone. "But she is very determined, and she insists on remaining where she is."

And I believe this was the truth. They would surely have been glad to get rid of me, these friends of Miss Emily's.

I have wondered since what they thought of me, Anne Bullard and the doctor, to have feared me as they did. I look in the mirror, and I see a middle-aged woman, with a determined nose, slightly inquisitive, and what I trust is a humorous mouth, for it has no other virtues. But they feared me. Perhaps long looking for a danger affects the mental vision. Anyhow, by the doctor's orders, I was not allowed to call and see Miss Emily again.

Then, one night, the heat suddenly lifted. One moment I was sitting on the veranda, lifeless and inert, and the next a cool wind, with a hint of rain, had set the shutters to banging and the curtains to flowing, like flags of truce, from the windows. The air was life, energy. I felt revivified.

And something of the same sort must have happened to Miss Emily. She must have sat up among her pillows, her face fanned with the electric breeze, and made her determination to see me. Anne Bullard was at work, and she was free from observation.

It must have been nine o'clock when she left the house, a shaken little figure in black, not as neat as usual, but hooked and buttoned, for all that, with no one will ever know what agony of old hands.

She was two hours and a half getting to the house, and the rain came at ten o'clock. By half after eleven, when the doorbell rang, she was a sodden mass of wet garments, and her teeth were chattering when I led her into the library.

She could not talk. The thing she had come to say was totally beyond her. I put her to bed in her own room. And two days later she died.

I made no protest when Anne Bullard presented herself at the door the morning after Miss Emily arrived, and, walking into the house, took sleepless charge of the sickroom. And I made no reference save once to the reason for the tragedy. That was the night Miss Emily died.

Anne Bullard had called to me that she feared there was a change, and I went into the sickroom. There was a change, and I could only shake my head. She burst out at me then.

"If only you had never taken this house!" she said. "You people with money, you think there is nothing you can not have. You came, and now look!"

"Anne," I said with a bitterness I could not conceal, "Miss Emily is not young, and I think she is ready to go. But she has been killed by her friends. I wanted to help, but they would not allow me to."

Towards morning there was nothing more to be done, and we sat together, listening to the stertorous breathing from the bed. Maggie, who had been up all night, had given me notice at three in the morning, and was upstairs packing her trunk.

I went into my room, and brought back Miss Emily's confession.

"Isn't it time," I said, "to tell me about this? I ought to know, I think, before she goes. If it is not true, you owe it to her, I think." But she shook her head.

I looked at the confession, and from it to Miss Emily's pinched old face.

"To whom it may concern: On the 30th day of May, 1911, I killed a woman (here) in this house. I hope you will not find this until I am dead.
(*Signed*) EMILY BENTON."

Anne was watching me. I went to the mantel and got a match, and then, standing near the bed, I lighted it and touched it to the paper. It burned slowly, a thin blue semicircle of fire that ate its way slowly across until there was but the corner I held. I dropped it into the fireplace and watched it turn to black ash.

I may have fancied it—I am always fancying things about Miss Emily—I will always think that she knew. She drew a longer, quieter breath, and her eyes, fixed and staring, closed. I think she died in the first sleep she had had in twenty-four hours.

I had expected Anne Bullard to show emotion, for no one could doubt her attachment to Miss Emily. But she only stood stoically by the bed for a moment and then, turning swiftly, went to the wall opposite and took down from the wall the walnut-framed photograph Mrs. Graves had commented on.

Anne Bullard stood with the picture in her hand, looking at it. And suddenly she broke into sobs. It was stormy weeping, and I got the impression that she wept, not for Miss Emily, but for many other things—as though the piled-up grief of years had broken out at last.

She took the photograph away, and I never saw it again.

Miss Emily was buried from her home. I obliterated myself, and her friends, who were, I felt, her murderers, came in and took charge. They paid me the tribute of much politeness, but no cordiality, and I think they felt toward me as I felt toward them. They blamed me with the whole affair.

She left her property all to Anne Bullard, to the astonished rage of the congregation, which had expected the return of its dimes and quarters, no doubt in the shape of a new altar, or perhaps an organ.

"Not a cent to keep up the mausoleum or anything," Mrs. Graves confided in me. "And nothing to the church. All to that telephone-girl, who comes from no one knows where! It's enough to make her father turn over in his grave. It has set people talking, I can tell you."

Maggie's mental state during the days preceding the funeral was curious. She coupled the most meticulous care as to the preparations for the ceremony, and a sort of loving gentleness when she decked Miss Emily's small old frame for its last rites, with suspicion and hatred of Miss Emily living. And this suspicion she held also against Anne Bullard.

Yet she did not want to leave the house. I do not know just what she expected to find. We were cleaning up preparatory to going back to the city, and I felt that at least a part of Maggie's enthusiasm for corners was due to a hope of locating more concealed papers. She was rather less than polite to the Bullard girl, who was staying on at my invitation—because the village was now flagrantly unfriendly and suspicious of her. And for some strange reason, the fact that Miss Emily's cat followed Anne everywhere convinced Maggie that her suspicions were justified.

"It's like this, Miss Agnes," she said one morning, leaning on the handle of a floor brush. "She had some power over the old lady, and that's how she got the property. And I am saying nothing, but she's no Christian, that girl. To see her and that cat going out night after night, both snooping along on their tiptoes—it ain't normal."

I had several visits from Martin Sprague since Miss Emily's death, and after a time I realized that he was interested in Anne. She was quite attractive in her mourning clothes, and there was something about her, not in feature, but in neatness and in the way her things had of, well, staying in place, that reminded me of Miss Emily herself. It was rather surprising, too, to see the way she fitted into her new surroundings and circumstances.

But I did not approve of Martin's attraction to her. She had volunteered no information about herself, she apparently had no people. She was a lady, I felt, although, with the exception of her new mourning, her clothing was shabby and her linen even coarse.

She held the key to the confession. I knew that. And I had no more hope of getting it from her than I had from the cat. So I prepared to go back to the city, with the mystery unsolved. It seemed a pity, when I had got so far with it. I had reconstructed a situation out of such bricks as I had, the books in the cellar, Mrs. Graves's story of the river, the confession, possibly the note-book and the handkerchief. I had even some material left over in the form of the night intruder, who may or may not have been the doctor. And then, having got so far, I had had to stop for lack of other bricks.

A day or two before I went back to the city, Maggie came to me with a folded handkerchief in her hand.

"Is that yours?" she asked.

I disclaimed it. It was not very fine, and looked rather yellow.

"S'got a name on it," Maggie volunteered. "Wright, I think it is. 'Tain't hers, unless she's picked it up somewhere. It's just come out of the wash."

Maggie's eyes were snapping with suspicion. "There ain't any Wrights around here, Miss Agnes," she said. "I sh'd say she's here under a false name. Wright's likely hers."

In tracing the mystery of the confession, I find that three apparently disconnected discoveries paved the way to its solution. Of these the handkerchief came first.

I was inclined to think that in some manner the handkerchief I had found in the book in the cellar had got into the wash. But it was where I had placed it for safety, in the wall-closet in the library. I brought it out and compared the two. They were unlike, save in the one regard. The name "Wright" was clear enough on the one Maggie had found. With it as a guide, the other name was easily seen to be the same. Moreover, both had been marked by the same hand.

Yet, on Anne Bullard being shown the one Maggie had found, she disclaimed it. "Don't you think some one dropped it at the funeral?" she asked.

But, I thought, as I turned away, that she took a step toward me. When I stopped, however, and faced about, she was intent on something outside the window.

And so it went. I got nowhere. And now, by way of complication, I felt my sympathy for Anne's loneliness turning to genuine interest. She was so stoical, so repressed, and so lonely. And she was tremendously proud. Her pride was vaguely reminiscent of Miss Emily's. She bore her ostracism almost fiercely, yet there were times when I felt her eyes on me, singularly gentle and appealing. Yet she volunteered nothing about herself.

I intended to finish the history of Bolivar County before I left. I dislike not finishing a book. Besides, this one fascinated me—the smug complacence and almost loud virtue of the author, his satisfaction in Bolivar County, and his small hits at the world outside, his patronage to those not of it. And always, when I began to read, I turned to the inscription in Miss Emily's hand, the hand of the confession—and I wondered if she had really believed it all.

So on this day I found the name Bullard in the book. It had belonged to the Reverend Samuel Thaddeus's grandmother, and he distinctly stated that she was the last of her line. He inferred, indeed, that since the line was to end, it had chosen a fitting finish in his immediate progenitor.

That night, at dinner, I said, "Anne, are there any Bullards in this neighborhood now?"

"I have never heard of any. But I have not been here long."

"It is not a common name," I persisted.

But she received my statement in silence. She had, as I have said, rather a gift for silence.

That afternoon I was wandering about the garden snipping faded roses with Miss Emily's garden shears, when I saw Maggie coming swiftly toward me. When she caught my eye, she beckoned to me. "Walk quiet, Miss Agnes," she said, "and don't say I didn't warn you. She's in the library."

So, feeling hatefully like a spy, I went quietly over the lawn toward the library windows. They were long ones, to the floor, and at first I made out nothing. Then I saw Anne. She was on her knees, following the border of the carpet with fingers that examined it, inch by inch.

She turned, as if she felt our eyes on her, and saw us. I shall never forget her face. She looked stricken. I turned away. There was something in her eyes that made me think of Miss Emily, lying among her pillows and waiting for me to say the thing she was dreading to hear.

I sent Maggie away with a gesture. There was something in her pursed lips that threatened danger. For I felt then as if I had always known it and only just realized I knew it, that somewhere in that room lay the answer to all questions; lay Miss Emily's secret. And I did not wish to learn it. It was better to go on wondering, to question and doubt and decide and decide again. I was, I think, in a state of nervous terror by that time, terror and apprehension.

While Miss Emily lived, I had hoped to help. But now it seemed too hatefully like accusing when she could not defend herself. And there is another element that I am bound to acknowledge. There was an element of jealousy of Anne Bullard. Both of us had tried to help Miss Emily. She had foiled my attempt in her own endeavor, a mistaken endeavor, I felt. But there was now to be no blemish on my efforts. I would no longer pry or question or watch. It was too late.

In a curious fashion, each of us wished, I think, to prove the quality of her tenderness for the little old lady who was gone beyond all human tenderness.

So that evening, after dinner, I faced Anne in the library.

"Why not let things be as they are, Anne?" I asked. "It can do no good. Whatever it is, and I do not know, why not let things rest?"

"Some one may find it," she replied. "Some one who does not care, as I—as we care."

"Are you sure there is something?"

"She told me, near the last. Only I don't know just where it is."

"And if you find it?"

"It is a letter. I shall burn it without reading. Although," she drew a long breath, "I know what it contains."

"If in any way it comes into my hands," I assured her, "I shall let you know. And I shall not read it."

She looked thoughtful rather than grateful.

"I hardly know," she said. "I think she would want you to read it if it came to you. It explains so much. And it was a part of her plan. You know, of course, that she had a plan. It was a sort of arrangement"—she hesitated—"it was a sort of pact she made with God, if you know what I mean."

That night Maggie found the letter.

I had gone upstairs, and Anne was, I think, already asleep. I heard what sounded like distant hammering, and I went to the door. Some one was in the library below. The light was shining out into the hall, and my discovery of that was followed almost immediately by the faint splintering of wood. Rather outraged than alarmed, I went back for my dressing-gown, and as I left the room, I confronted Maggie in the hallway. She had an envelope in one hand, and a hatchet in the other.

"I found it," she said briefly.

She held it out, and I took it. On the outside, in Miss Emily's writing, it said, "To whom it may concern." It was sealed.

I turned it over in my hand, while Maggie talked.

"When I saw that girl crawling around," she said, "seems to me I remembered all at once seeing Miss Emily, that day I found her, running her finger along the baseboard. Says I to myself, there's something more hidden, and she don't know where it is. But I do. So I lifted the baseboard, and this was behind it."

Anne heard her from her room, and she went out soon afterward. I heard her going down the stairs and called to her. But she did not answer. I closed the door on Maggie and stood in my room, staring at the envelope.

I have wondered since whether Miss Emily, had she lived, would have put the responsibility on Providence for the discovery of her pitiful story. So many of us blame the remorseless hand of destiny for what is so manifestly our own doing. It was her own anxiety, surely, that led to the discovery in each instance, yet I am certain that old Emily Benton died, convinced that a higher hand than any on earth had directed the discovery of the confession.

Miss Emily has been dead for more than a year now. To publish the letter can do her no harm. In a way, too, I feel, it may be the fulfilment of that strange pact she made. For just as discovery was the thing she most dreaded, so she felt that by paying her penalty here she would be saved something beyond—that sort of spiritual bookkeeping which most of us call religion.

Anne Sprague—she is married now to Martin—has, I think, some of Miss Emily's feeling about it, although she denies it. But I am sure that in consenting to the recording of Miss Emily's story, she feels that she is doing what that gentle fatalist would call following the hand of Providence.

I read the letter that night in the library, where the light was good. It was a narrative, not a letter, strictly speaking. It began abruptly.

"*I must set down this thing as it happened. I shall write it fully, because I must get it off my mind. I find that I am always composing it, and that my lips move when I walk along the street or even when I am sitting in church. How terrible if I should some day speak it aloud. My great-grandmother was a* Catholic. *She was a* Bullard. *Perhaps it is from her that I have this overwhelming impulse to confession. And lately I have been terrified. I must tell it, or I shall shriek it out some day, in the church, during the Litany. 'From battle and murder, and from sudden death,* Good Lord deliver us.' "

(There was a space here. When the writing began again, time had elapsed. The ink was different, the writing more controlled.)

"*What a terrible thing hate is. It is a poison. It penetrates the mind and the body and changes everything. I, who once thought I could hate no one, now find that hate is my daily life, my getting up and lying down, my sleep, my waking.*

"'*From hatred, envy, and malice, and all uncharitableness,* Good Lord, deliver us.'

"*Must one suffer twice for the same thing? Is it not true that we pay but one penalty? Surely we pay either here or beyond, but not both. Oh, not both!*

"*Will this ever be found? Where shall I hide it? For I have the feeling that I must hide it, not destroy it—as the Catholic buries his sin with the priest. My father once said that it is the healthful humiliation of the confessional that is its reason for existing. If humiliation be a virtue—*"

I have copied the confession to this point, but I find I can not go on. She was so merciless to herself, so hideously calm, so exact as to dates and hours. She had laid her life on the table and dissected it—for the Almighty!

I heard the story that night gently told, and somehow I feel that that is the version by which Miss Emily will be judged.

"If humiliation be a virtue—" I read and was about to turn the page, when I heard Anne in the hall. She was not alone. I recognized Doctor Lingard's voice.

Five minutes later I was sitting opposite him, almost knee to knee, and he was telling me how Miss Emily had come to commit her crime. Anne Bullard was there, standing on the hearth rug. She kept her eyes on me, and after a time I realized that these two simple people feared me, feared for Miss Emily's gentle memory, feared that I—good heaven!—would make the thing public.

"First of all, Miss Blakiston," said the doctor, "one must have known the family to realize the situation—its pride in its own uprightness. The virtue of the name, what it stood for in Bolivar County. She was raised on that. A Benton could do no wrong, because a Benton would do no wrong.

"But there is another side, also. I doubt if any girl was ever raised as Miss Emily was. She—well, she knew nothing. At fifty she was as childlike and innocent as she was at ten. She had practically never heard of vice. The ugly things, for her, did not exist.

"And, all the time, there was a deep and strong nature underneath. She should have married and had children, but there was no one here for her to marry. I," he smiled faintly, "I asked for her myself, and was forbidden the house for years as a result.

"You have heard of the brother? But of course you have. I know you have found the books. Such an existence as the family life here was bound to have its reactions. Carlo was a reaction. Twenty-five years ago he ran away with a girl from the village. He did not marry her. I believe he was willing at one time, but his father opposed it violently. It would have been to recognize a thing he refused to recognize." He turned suddenly to Anne. "Don't you think this is going to be painful?" he asked.

"Why? I know it all."

"Very well. This girl—the one Carlo ran away with—determined to make the family pay for that refusal. She made them actually pay, year by year. Emily knew about it. She had to pinch to make the payments. The father sat in a sort of detached position, in the center of Bolivar County, and let her bear the brunt of it. I shall never forget the day she learned there was a child. It—well, it sickened her. She had not known about those things. And I imagine, if we could know, that that was the beginning of things.

"And all the time there was the necessity for secrecy. She had never known deceit, and now she was obliged to practice it constantly. She had no one to talk to. Her father, beyond making entries of the amounts paid to the woman in the case, had nothing to do with it. She bore it all, year after year. And it ate, like a cancer.

"Remember, I never knew. I, who would have done anything for her—she never told me. Carlo lived hard and came back to die. The father went. She nursed them both. I came every day, and I never suspected. Only, now and then, I wondered about her. She looked *burned*. I don't know any other word.

"Then, the night after Carlo was buried, she telephoned me. It was eleven o'clock. She met me, out there in the hall, and she said, 'John, I have killed somebody.'

"I thought she was out of her mind. But she opened the door, and—"

He turned and glanced at Anne.

"Please!" she said.

"It was Anne's mother. You have guessed it about Anne by now, of course. It seems that the funeral had taken the money for the payment that was due, and there had been a threat of exposure. And Emily had reached the breaking-point. I believe what she said—that she had no intention even of striking her. You can't take the act itself. You have to take twenty-five years into account. Anyhow, she picked up a chair and knocked the woman down. And it killed her." He ran his fingers through his heavy hair. "It should not have killed her," he reflected. "There must have been some other weakness, heart or something. I don't know. But it was a heavy chair. I don't see how Emily—"

His voice trailed off.

"There we were," he said, with a long breath. "Poor Emily, and the other poor soul, neither of them fundamentally at fault, both victims."

"I know about the books," I put in hastily. I could not have him going over that again.

"You knew that, too!" He gazed at me.

"Poor Emily!" he said. "She tried to atone. She brought Anne here, and told her the whole story. It was a bad time—all round. But at last Anne saw the light. The only one who would not see the light was Emily. And at last she hit on this confession idea. I suspected it when she rented the house. When I accused her of it, she said: "I have given it to Providence to decide. If the confession is found, I shall know I am to suffer. And I shall not lift a hand to save myself."

So it went through the hours. Her fear, which I still think was the terror that communicated itself to me; the various clues, which she, poor victim, had overlooked; the articles laid carelessly in the book she had been reading and accidentally hidden with her brother's forbidden literature; the books themselves, with all of five years to destroy them, and left untouched; her own anxiety about the confession in the telephone-box, which led to our finding it; her espionage of the house by means of the telephone; the doctor's night visit in search of the confession; the daily penance for five years of the dead woman's photograph in her room—all of these—and her occasional weakenings, poor soul, when she tried to change her handwriting against discovery, and refused to allow the second telephone to be installed.

How clear it was! How, in a way, inevitable! And, too, how really best for her it had turned out. For she had made a pact, and she died believing that discovery here had come, and would take the place of punishment beyond.

Martin Sprague came the next day. I was in the library alone, and he was with Anne in the garden, when Maggie came into the room with a saucer of crab-apple jelly.

"I wish you'd look at this," she said. "If it's cooked too much, it gets tough and—" She straightened suddenly and stood staring out through a window.

"I'd thank you to look out and see the goings-on in our garden," she said sharply. "In broad daylight, too. I—"

But I did not hear what else Maggie had to say. I glanced out, and Martin had raised the girl's face to his and was kissing her, gently and very tenderly.

And then—and again, as with fear, it is hard to put into words—I felt come over me such a wave of contentment and happiness as made me close my eyes with the sheer relief and joy of it. All was well. The past was past, and out of its mistakes had come a beautiful thing. And, like the fear, this joy was not mine. It came to me. I picked it up—a thought without words.

Sometimes I think about it, and I wonder—did little Miss Emily know?

The Red Lamp

Introduction to the Journal of William A. Porter, A.B., M.A., Ph.D., Litt.D., etc.

June 30, 19—

A FEW WEEKS AGO, at a dinner, a discussion arose as to the unfinished dramas recorded in the daily press. The argument was, if I remember correctly, that they give us the beginning of many stories, and the endings of as many more. But that what followed those beginnings, or preceded those endings, was seldom or never told.

It was Pettingill, of all persons, who turned the attention of the table to me.

"Take that curious case of yours, Porter," he said. "Not yours, of course, but near your summer place two years ago. What ever happened there? Grace and I used to sit up all night to see who would get the morning paper first; then—it quit on us. That's all. Quit on us." He surveyed the table with an aggrieved air.

Helena Lear glanced across at me maliciously.

"Do tell us, Willie," she said. She is the only person in the world who calls me Willie. "And give us all the horrible details. You know, I have always had a sneaking belief that you did the things yourself!"

Under cover of the laugh that went up, I glanced at my wife. She was sitting erect and unsmiling, her face drained of all its color, staring across the flowers and candles into the semidarkness above the buffet. As though she saw something.

I do not know; I never shall know, probably. I saw little Pettingill watching her unobtrusively, and following her eyes to the space over the buffet behind me, but I did not turn around. Possibly it was only the memories aroused by that frivolous conversation which made me feel, for a moment, that there was a cold wind eddying behind my back—

It occurred to me then that many people throughout the country had been intensely interested in our Oakville drama, and had been left with that same irritating sense of noncompletion. But not only that. At least three of the women had heard me make that absurd statement of mine, relative to the circle enclosing a triangle. There were more than Helena Lear, undoubtedly, who had remembered it when, early in July, the newspapers had announced the finding of that diabolical symbol along with the bodies of the slain sheep.

It seemed to me that it might be a duty I owed to myself as well as to the University, to clarify the matter; to complete the incomplete; to present to them the entire story with its amazing climax, and in effect to say to them and to the world at large, "This is what happened. As you see, the problem is solved, and here is your answer. But do not blame me if here and there is found an unknown factor in the equation; an X we do not know what to do with, but without which there would have been no solution. I can show you the X. I have used it. But I cannot explain it."

As will be seen, I have taken the portion of my journal extending from June 16th, to September 10th of that year. Before that period, and after it, it is merely the day-by-day record of an uneventful life. Rather more fully detailed, since like Pepys I have used it as a reservoir into which to pour much of that residue which remains in a man's mind over and above the little he gives out each day. Rather more fully detailed, too, since I keep it in shorthand, an accomplishment acquired in my student days, and used not to ensure the privacy of the diary itself, although I think my dear wife so believes, but to enable me, frankly, to exercise that taste for writing which exists in all of us whose business is English literature.

Show me any man who teaches literature, and I will show you a man thwarted. For it is our universal, hidden conviction that we, too, could write, were it not for the necessity of earning our daily bread. We start in as writers, only temporarily sidetracked. "Some day—" we say to ourselves, and go to our daily task of Milton or Dryden or Pope as those who, seeking the beauties of the country, must travel through a business thoroughfare to get there.

But time goes by, and still we do not write. We find, as life goes on, that all the great thoughts have already been recorded; that there is not much to say that has not been already said. And, because we are always staring at the stars, we learn the shortness of our arms.

We find a vicarious consolation in turning out, now and then, a man who is not daunted by tradition, and who puts his old wine into new bottles. We read papers before small and critical societies. And we sometimes keep journals.

And so—this journal. Much the same as when, under stress of violent excitement or in the peaceful interludes, I went to it as one goes to a friend, secure against betrayal. Here and there I have detailed more fully conversations which have seemed to bear on the mystery; now and again I have rounded a sentence. But in the main it remains as it was, the daily history of that strange series of events which culminated so dramatically on the night of September 10th in the paneled room of the main house at Twin Hollows.

Of this house itself, since it figures so largely in the narrative, a few words should be said. The main portion of it, the hall which extended from the terrace toward the sea through to the rear and the drive, the paneled den and the large library in front of it are very old. To this portion, in the seventies, had been added across the hall, by some long-forgotten builder, a dining-room opposite the library and facing the sea, pantries, kitchen, laundry, and beyond the laundry a nondescript room originally built as a gun room and still containing the gun cases on the walls.

In later years the gun room, still so called, had fallen from its previous dignity and served divers purposes. In my Uncle Horace's time old Thomas, the gardener, used it on occasion as a potting-room. And on wet days washing was hung up in it to dry. But it remained the "gun room," and so figures in this narrative.

In the rebuilding considerable judgment had been shown, and the broad white structure, with its colonial columns to the roof, makes a handsome appearance from the bay. It stands on a slight rise, facing the water, and its lawn extends to the edge of the salt marsh which divides it from the sea.

This is Twin Hollows. A place restful and beautiful to the eye; a gentleman's home, with its larkspurs and zinnias, its roses and its sundial, its broad terrace, its great sheltered porch, and its old paneling. Some lovely woman should sweep down its wide polished staircase or, armed with basket and shears, should cut roses in the garden with its sundial—that sundial where I stood the night the bell clanged. But it stands idle. It will, so long as I live, always stand idle.

Of my Uncle Horace, who also figures largely in the journal, a few words are necessary. He graduated from this University. He had died suddenly in June of the year before the journal takes up the narrative, presumably of cardiac asthma, from which he had long suffered. A gentleman and a scholar, an essential solitary, there had been no real intimacy between us. Once in a while I passed a week-end in the country with him, and until the summer of the narrative, my chief memory of him had been of a rather small and truculent elderly gentleman, with the dry, sharp cough of the heart sufferer, pacing the terrace beneath my window at night in the endless search of the asthmatic for air, and smoking for relief some particularly obnoxious brand of herbal cigarette.

Until the summer of the narrative—

Ever since I have been considering the making public of the journal, I have been asking myself this question, as one which will undoubtedly be asked when the book is published. What effect have the events of that summer had on my previous convictions?

Have I changed? Do I now believe that death is but a veil, and that through that veil we may now and then, as through a glass, see darkly?

I can only answer that as time has gone on I find they have exerted no permanent effect whatever. I am still profoundly agnostic. My wife and I have emerged from it, I imagine, as one emerges from a seance room where the phenomena have been particularly puzzling; that is, bewildered and half convinced for the moment, but without any change in our fundamental incredulity.

The truth is that if these things be, they are too great for our human comprehension; the revolution demanded in our ideas of the universe is too basic. And, as the journal will show, too dangerous.

All houses in which men have lived and suffered and died are haunted houses, I have written somewhere in the journal. And if thoughts are entities, which may impress themselves on their surroundings, perhaps this is true.

But dare I go further? Restate my conviction at the time that the solution of our crimes had been facilitated by assistance from some unseen source? And that, having achieved its purpose, this force forthwith departed from us? I do not know.

The X remains unsolved.

But I admit that more than once, during the recent editing of this journal for publication, I have wakened at night covered with a cold sweat, from a dream in which I am once more standing in the den of the house at Twin Hollows, the red lamp lighted behind me, and am looking out into the hall at a dim figure standing at the foot of the staircase.

A figure which could not possibly be there. But was there.

(Signed)

WILLIAM A. PORTER

June 16th.

COMMENCEMENT WEEK is over at last, thank heaven, and with no more than the usual casualties. Defeated at the ball game, 9–6. Lear down with ptomaine, result of bad ice cream somewhere or other. Usual reunions of old boys, with porters staggering under the suitcases, which seem to grow heavier each year.

Nevertheless, the very old 'uns always give me a lump in the throat, and I fancy there was a considerable amount of *globus hystericus* as Uncle Horace's class marched onto the field on Class Day. Only eight of them this year, Uncle Horace being missing. Poor old boy!

Which reminds me that Jane thought she saw him with the others as they marched in. Wonderful woman, Jane! No imagination ordinarily, meticulous mind and only a faint sense of humor. Yet she drags poor old Horace out of his year-old grave and marches him onto the field, and then becomes slightly sulky with me when I laugh!

"I told you to bring your glasses, my dear," I said.

"How many men are in that group?" she demanded tensely.

"Eight. And, for heaven's sake, lower your voice."

"I see nine, William," she said quietly. And when she stood up to take her usual snapshots of the alumni procession she was trembling.

A curious woman, Jane.

So another year is over, and what have I to show for it? A small addition to my account in the savings bank, a volume or two of this uneventful diary, some hundreds of men who perhaps know the Cavalier Poets and perhaps not, and some few who have now an inkling that English literature did not begin with Shakespeare.

What have I to look forward to? Three months of uneventful summering, perhaps at Twin Hollows—if Larkin ever gets the estate settled—and then the old round again. Milton and Dryden and Pope. Addison and Swift.

"Mr. Sims, have you any idea who wrote the Ancient Mariner? Or have you by chance ever heard of the Ancient Mariner?"

"Wordsworth, I believe, sir."

Yet I am not so much discontented as afraid of sinking into a lethargy of smug iconoclasm. It is bad for the soul to cease to expect grapes of a thistle, for the next stage is to be "old and a cynic; a carrion crow," like the old man in Prince Otto, with rotten eggs the burthen of my song.

Yet what is it that I want? My little rut is comfortable; so long have I lain in it that now my very body has conformed. I fit my easy chair beside my reading lamp; my thumbs are broadened with much holding of books. *I depend on my tea.*

Yesterday, calling on Lear, I must have voiced my uneasiness, for he at once suggested a hobby. His bed was littered with mutilated envelopes.

"Nothing like it," he said. "It's the safety valve of middle life, and the solace of age."

"I'm not quite sure I want a safety valve," I said, and I fancied he looked at me suspiciously.

A hobby! Shall I gather postage stamps, and inquire of a letter not from whom it comes, but from where? Or adopt Jane's camera, and take little pictures of unimportant folk doing uninteresting things? Or go, as Lear finally suggested, afishing? Is it to be my greatest adventure to pull a fish out of the water and watch it drown with wide-opened mouth, in the air? Ah, me!

"Greatest rest in the world for the brain," Lear said. "Fishing."

"I'm not sure I want a rest for my brain," I protested. "I dare say what I need is a complete change."

"Well, try ptomaine," he said dryly, and with that I went away.

But I dare say Lear is right. The prospect of my three months' vacation has gone to my head somewhat. And I dare say, too, that I am much like the solitary water beetle Jock found on the kitchen floor last night. That is, willing enough to leave my snug spot behind the warm pipes of life until danger threatens, or discomfort, and then all for scurrying back, atremble, into unexciting security again.

June 17th.

AFTER ALL, security has its points.

I am the object of a certain amount of suspicion today on the part of my household! There is no place in the world, I imagine, for a philosopher with a sense of humor, a new leisure, and an inquiring turn of mind! In fact, I sometimes wonder whether any philosopher belongs in the present day and generation. These are times of action. Men think and then act; sometimes, indeed, they simply act.

But a philosopher, of course, should only think.

And all this because last night I set Jane's clock forward one hour. Because, forsooth, I had determined to cease casting my eyes out on the world, and to study intensively that small domain of my own which lies beyond the drain pipe!

During some nine months of the year I bring home to Jane from the lecture room the mere husk of a man; exhausted with the endeavor to implant one single thought into a brain where it will germinate, I sink into my easy chair and accept the life of my household. Tea. Dinner. A book. Bed. And this is my life. My existence, rather.

But with the close of the spring term I find a faint life stirring within me.

"Isn't this a new tea?" I will say.

"You have been drinking it all winter," Jane will reply, rather shortly.

Yesterday was my first free day, and last night I wandered about the house, looking over my possessions and rediscovering them.

"You've had the sofa done over, my dear."

"Before Christmas," Jane replied, and glanced at me. In return I glanced at Jane.

It dawns on a man now and then that he knows very little about his wife. He knows, of course, the surface attributes of her mind, her sense of order—Jane is orderly—her thrift, and Jane is thrifty. She has had to be! But it came to me suddenly that I knew very little of Jane, after all.

She is making one of those endless bits of tapestry, which some day she will put on the seat of a chair, and thereafter I shall not be expected to sit in that chair. But it is not a work which requires profound attention. She was working at it at the moment, her head bent, her face impassive.

"What are you thinking about, Jane?" I asked her.

"I really wasn't thinking at all."

I dare say from that I fell to speculating on Jane's mind, and that does not imply a criticism. Rather on the contrary, for Jane has an excellent mental equipment. But I am sometimes aware that she possesses certain qualities I do not possess. For example, it would be impossible for me to imagine, as Jane did on Class Day, that I saw Uncle Horace. Although, like all men with defective vision, I have occasional optical illusions. But it is equally impossible for me to deny that she did see Uncle Horace, and there has been a certain subtle change in her since which convinces me of her sincerity.

What, then, I considered, is the difference between Jane's mind and my own? She has some curious ability, which she hides like one of the seven deadly sins, and which makes her at times a difficult person with whom to live.

I have already recorded in this journal that one occasion in my life when at the reunion of my class, some wag proposed mixing all that was left of the various liquors in the punch bowl and drinking a stirrup cup out of it, and the fact that I was extremely dizzy on my way home.

But I did not record, I think, the fact that after I had quietly entered the house and got myself to bed, Jane came into my room.

"Oh! So you are back!" she said.

"Certainly I am back, my dear."

It seemed unnecessary to state that neither she nor the doorway in which she stood seemed entirely steady at the moment, nor did I so state. But perhaps it was not necessary, for after eyeing me coldly for a moment, she said, "Were you supporting the chapel half an hour ago, William, or was it supporting you?"

"I don't know what you are talking about!"

"Don't you?" she observed, and retired quietly, after removing my shoes from the top of my bookcase.

But the humiliating fact remains that I *had* stopped for a moment's rest beside the chapel, and that somehow Jane knew it.

Or take again that incident already recorded in this journal, under the date of June 28th of last year, when she wakened me at seven o'clock and said she had seen Uncle Horace lying dead on the floor of the library at Twin Hollows.

"Dreams," I said drowsily, "are simply wish fulfillments. Go on back to bed, my dear. The old boy's all right."

"I wasn't asleep," she said quietly. "And you will have a telephone message soon telling you I was not."

And so true was this that she had hardly ceased speaking before Annie Cochran called up to tell us she had found him, at seven o'clock, dead on the library floor.

(Note: In preparing these notes for publication one thing occurs to me very strongly, and that is this. It is curious that my wife's vision, or whatever it may be called, did not occur until some hours after the death. If there came some mental call to her, why not when he was *in extremis*? Not only would it have helped us greatly in the mystery which was so soon to develop, but it would have been more true to the usual type of such phenomena. In this case, if we are to admit anything but coincidence, it is easier to accept the fact that we are dealing with mental telepathy. In other words, that the servant Annie Cochran, who actually found the body at seven in the morning, at once thought of Jane and so flashed the scene to her.

But I admit that this is merely explaining one mystery with another.)

So I was reflecting, as Jane pushed her needle through her tapestry, slow, infinitely plodding and absolutely composed. What portion of Jane, then, wandered out at night, and saw me with a death grip on the chapel wall? Or, with a fine contempt of distance and a house she loathed, went to Twin Hollows and found Uncle Horace on the floor?

It was an interesting thought, and I played with it out of sheer joy in idleness. The Jane, then, whom I could reach out and touch at night, might only be the shell of Jane, while the real Jane might be off on some spirit adventure of her own! I considered this. It has, one must admit, its possibilities. And just then she glanced up at me.

"What are you thinking about?" she asked.

"My dear," I said gravely, "I am worrying."

"What about?"

"About you."

"I'm all right," she said. "Although of course I'd like to get away somewhere."

"That's precisely what I'm worrying about!" I observed, and she looked puzzled but said nothing.

I went back to Jane's mind, with a volume of Von Humboldt unnoticed on my knee. Had she true clairvoyance, whatever that may mean? Or was telepathy the answer? She is Scotch, and the Scots sometimes claim what is called "second sight." I know that in her heart she believes she has this curious gift. She was, they say, a queer child, seeing and hearing things unseen and unheard by others. And I know she fears and hates it; it is somehow irreligious to her.

But—has she?

No immediate answer being forthcoming, I went back to my book, and very soon I happened on the following paragraph: *A presumptuous skepticism which rejects facts without examining them to see if they are real, is more blameworthy than an irrational credulity.*

It was, in a way, a challenge, but there were no facts to examine. I could believe that Jane is merely a fine recording instrument on which telepathic impressions are recorded, or I could accept that she is able to leave that still lovely but slightly matronly body of hers on occasion and travel on the wings of space. But, because my interest was aroused, I consulted the dictionary on clairvoyance, and found that it was the faculty of being able to perceive objects without the customary use of the senses.

It was "vision without eyes."

Even then—on so small a base does one's comfort behind the pipe sometimes depend—all would have been well had not Clara entered with the dish of fruit which is my method of telling the seasons; the winter orange and banana gradually giving way to the early berries which mark the spring, and so on. And with that Jane looked at the clock.

That glance was at once my downfall and my triumph. For it occurred to me then to make a simple experiment, and to "examine the facts."

Jane, I argued, *rises by her bedroom clock every morning, and punctually to the minute. But Jane does not look at her clock. Then, if I set it forward one hour—*

And set it forward one hour I did, after Jane was asleep. And at the moment its hands indicated seven-thirty, although it was but half past six, did Jane open her eyes, rise from her bed without so much as a glance toward the clock, and call her household.

So Jane saw her clock without eyes, Clara has been sulky all day, and I am in extreme disfavor.

"Really, William," Jane said with a sigh this afternoon, "you are very difficult in the holidays."

"Difficult?"

"You know perfectly well you turned my clock on."

"Why in the world should I turn your clock on?"

"It is your idea of being funny, I dare say."

"It isn't funny to be wakened an hour too soon, my dear."

But she is suspicious of me, and cold toward me. Thus I suffer the usual lot of the seeker after truth. And Jane, my dear Jane, can see without her eyes. But she cannot understand why I turned her clock on for all her curious ability. Nor, after eating the burned biscuits Clara served tonight, can I.

But if Jane can see without her eyes, if she can perceive objects not visible to those of us who depend on the usual senses, then is one to admit that she saw Uncle Horace, as she said she did, marching at the head of his class procession last Tuesday?

June 18th.

I FEEL TONIGHT rather like the man who had caught a bull by the tail and daren't let go. And yet I am certain there is a perfectly natural explanation.

The difficulty is that I cannot very well go to Jane about it. If it is what it appears to be, and not a double exposure, it will frighten her. If it *is* a double exposure, she will wonder at my inquiry, and think I am watching her. She has not, even today, quite forgotten the clock.

But certain things are very curious; she thought she saw Uncle Horace marching onto the field with his class. So much did this upset her that, when she stood up to take her picture, the camera shook in her hands. Then she takes the picture, and instead of the eight old men of the class there are nine.

And she knows it. Why else would she hide the print, and pretend that she had mislaid it? It was that fact which made me suspicious.

"I'll look them up for you later, William," she said. "You aren't in a hurry, are you?"

"In the bright lexicon of vacation there is no such word as hurry," I observed brightly. And she who usually smiles at my feeblest effort turned abruptly away.

So Jane had lost her picture. Jane, whose closets are marvels of mathematical exactness, who keeps my clothing so exactly that I can find it in the dark, save for that one incident, duly noted in this journal, when I unfolded a washcloth at the president's dinner, having taken it from my handkerchief box.

And shortly after Jane went out for a walk, Jane who never exercises save about her household. Poor Jane, I feel tonight, face to face with the inexplicable and hiding it like one of the seven deadly sins.

There are nine men in the picture; there is no getting away from it. And there is no denying, either, a faint difference in the ninth figure, a sort of shadowiness, a lack of definition. Under Jane's reading-glass it gains nothing. The features, owing to the distance, are indistinct, but if one could imagine the ghost of old Horace, in his brocaded dressing-gown and slightly stooped to cough, in that blare of noise, shouting, and sunshine, it is there.

Later: I have shown the picture to Lear, and he says it is undoubtedly a case of double exposure.

"What else could it be?" he said, with that peculiar irritation induced in some people by any suggestion of the supernatural.

"I don't think she ever took a picture of him in her life."

"Well, somebody has," he said, and handed the print back to me. "If you don't believe me, show it to Cameron. He's a shark on that sort of thing."

(Note: Cameron, Exchange Professor of Physics, at our University. A member of the Society for Psychical Research, and known, I understand, among the students as "Spooks" Cameron.)

But I have not shown it to Cameron, and I do not intend to. I hardly know the man, for one thing. And for another, Lear is right. The University looks with suspicion on the few among the faculty who have on occasion dabbled with such matters.

"Personally," he said, "I think it's a double exposure. But whether it is or not I'm damned certain of one thing, the less said about it the better."

June 19th.

CURIOUS, when one begins to think on a subject, how it sometimes comes up in the most unexpected places.

I dropped into the dining-room for tea this afternoon after Jane's bridge party, to find Jane looking uncomfortable and an animated conversation on spiritualism going on, with Helena Lear leading it.

"Ah!" she said when she saw me. "Here comes our cynic. I suppose you don't believe in automatic writing, either?"

"I should," I replied gravely. "I have seen as many as fifty men taking notes while in a trance in my lecture room."

"Nor in spirits?"

"Certainly I do. And in the Smoke of Prophecy, and the Powder of Death."

She looked rather blank, and Jane flushed a trifle.

"What is more," I said, a trifle carried away by the tenseness of the room, perhaps, "I know that if I take a piece of chalk—have you any chalk, Jane?—and draw on the floor here the magic circle, and a triangle within it, no evil spirits can approach me. Get the chalk, dear; I promise I shall not be disturbed by so much as one demon."

In the laughter which followed the subject was dropped. But Helena Lear, when she gave me my tea, eyed me with amusement.

"You and your circle!" she said. "Don't you know that half these women more than half believe you?"

"And don't you?"

"You don't believe yourself."

"Still," I said, remembering Von Humboldt, "I am not an out-and-out skeptic. I will admit that Jock there, who is acting as a vacuum cleaner under the table, can hear and see and smell things that I cannot. But I do not therefore believe he communicates with the spirit world."

"But he sees things you don't see. You admit that."

"Certainly. He may see farther into the spectrum than I do."

"Then *what* does he see?" she said triumphantly.

A fortunate digression enabled me to escape with a whole skin, but I think there was something rather quizzical in her smiling farewell. After all, if Jock does see things I do not, what does he see? I'm blessed if I know.

June 20th.

JANE KNOWS that I have seen the picture, and that I know it lies behind her refusal to go to Twin Hollows for the summer. When I came back from Larkin's office today, the final papers having been signed, I could see her almost physically bracing herself.

"So it's all set, my dear," I said. "And if we can get Annie Cochran to clean the place a bit–"

"Would you mind so very much," she asked, almost wistfully, "if we don't go there?"

"But it's all settled. Edith is coming back on purpose."

(Note: The "Edith" of the journal is my niece, who makes her home with us. At this time she was absent on a round of house parties. A very lovely and popular girl, of whom more hereafter.)

"It's too large for us," said Jane. "I need a rest in the summer, not a big house to care for."

And there was a certain definiteness in her statement which ended the conversation. As a result, and following our usual course when there is a difference between us, we have taken refuge in polite silence all day, the familiar armed neutrality of marriage. An uncomfortable state of affairs, and aggravated by Edith's absence. When she is here her bright talk fills in the gaps, and in the end she forces a *rapprochement*.

Lear has told Cameron about the picture. I met Cameron while taking Jock for his evening walk tonight, and he reintroduced himself to me. After today's repression I fear I was a bit talkative, but he was a good listener. Evidently he has a certain understanding of Jane's refusal to go to Twin Hollows, although he said very little.

"Houses are curious, sometimes," was his comment.

But on the matter of the picture he was frankly interested.

"There is," he said, "a certain weight in the evidence for psychic photography, Mr. Porter. Of course, it is absurd to claim that all the curious photographs–and thousands of them come to me–are produced by discarnate intelligences. But there is something; I don't know just what."

Jane has gone to bed, still politely silent, and I am left alone to wrestle with my two problems; where to spend the summer, and why Jane finds the house at Twin Hollows what Cameron describes as curious.

A mild term, that, for Jane's feeling about the house. Actually she hates it. Has always hated it. She has had no pride in our acquisition of it; she has even steadfastly refused to bring away from it any of that early American furniture with which old Horace had filled it.

Yet she collects early American furniture. I write tonight at an utterly inadequate early American desk, because of this taste of hers. Jock has at this moment curled his long length on the hard seat of a Windsor chair, because of it! And yet she will have none of Uncle Horace's really fine collection.

Nor is she of the type to listen to Annie Cochran's story that the old portion of the house is haunted by the man killed there.

(Note: An old story and not authenticated, of the shooting of a man many years ago as he hid to escape the Excise. As a matter of fact, none of our later experiences in the house bore out this particular tradition at all.)

If she has a distaste for it, it may possibly relate to the occupancy of the house by the Riggs woman before Uncle Horace bought it. But even here I am doubtful, for Mrs. Riggs was caught in most unblushing fraud and entirely discredited as a medium.

June 21st.

EDITH IS BACK. She came in this morning, kissed Jock, Jane, and myself, Jock first, demanded an enormous breakfast and all the hot water in the house, and descended gaily a half hour later to the table, in her usual aura of bath salts, bath powder, and sunshine.

"Well," she said, attacking her melon, "and when do we go to the haunted house?"

"Ask your aunt."

She glanced at me and then shrewdly at Jane.

"Good heavens!" she said. "Don't tell me there's any question about it?"

"It isn't decided yet," Jane said uneasily. "It's a big house, Edith, and–"

"All the more reason for taking it," said Edith, and having finished her melon flung out her pretty arms. "Grass," she said, "*and* flowers, *and* the sea. I shall swim," she went on. "And old Father William shall fish, and Jane shall sew a fine seam. And at night the ghosts shall walk. And everything will be lovely."

She turned to me.

"You do believe in ghosts, don't you, Father William?"

And somehow even Jane caught some of the infection of her gaiety. "Ask him about the triangle in a circle," she said.

"What's that?" Edith inquired.

"The triangle in a circle, drawn around you, will keep off demons," I explained gravely. "Surely you know that?"

"How–convenient!"

"And that the skins of four frogs, killed on a moonless night, will make one invisible if worn as a cap? And that the spirits obey Solomon's seal–not the plant, of course! And that if you eat a stew of the eyes of a vulture, and the ear tufts of an owl, you will be wise beyond all dreams of wisdom?"

"Who wants to be wise?" said Edith. "But go on. I love to hear you."

"Very well," I agreed, with an eye on Jane. "Now, take the figure five. Five is the magic number, not seven. We have five fingers, five toes, five senses. There are five points to a star. Perhaps you noticed my wild excitement when my automobile license this year was 555."

Jane got up, and I saw that my nonsense had had its effect. She was smiling, for the first time in days.

"If you care to go out and look at the house tomorrow, William," she said, "I will go."

And perhaps Edith had sensed a situation she did not understand, for she kissed her, and as I left the room I heard her requesting Jane to bring back with her marketing some frog skins and the ear tufts of an owl.

So this afternoon things are looking brighter. And thus does man deceive himself! Only three days ago I was filled with vague yearnings and aspirations; I recorded here that my little rut was comfortable, but that I feared it. I wrote, *Was my greatest adventure to be to drag a fish out of the water, and watch it drown, openmouthed, in the air?*

And yet, at the mere thought of not going to Twin Hollows, of being thrown on the mercies of some Mountain House, or set on a horse in the far West, I have been frightened almost into a panic.

The water beetle indeed.

The town is very quiet tonight. The annual student exodus is almost over, although still an occasional truck goes by, piled high with trunks. The Lears intend to stay. Sulzer and Mackintyre are off for the Scottish Lakes, and Cameron, I hear, is going soon to the Adirondacks, where he spends his summer in a boat, and minus ghosts, I dare say.

I have mailed him the picture today, and can only hope Jane does not miss it.

One wonders about men like Cameron. Slight, almost negligible, as is my acquaintance with him—I would not know him in a crowd, even now—there is something of Scottish dourness in him. He neither smokes nor drinks; he lives austerely and alone. He has a reputation as a relentless investigator; it was he who exposed the hauntings at the house on Sabbathday Lake, in Massachusetts.

But he is a believer. That is, he believes in conscious survival after death, and I suspect that he has his own small group here. Among them little Pettingill. It would be a humiliating thought, for me, to feel that after I "passed over," as they say, little Pettingill might hale me to him, in the light of a red lamp, and request me to lift a table!

Warren Halliday is on the veranda with Edith. I can hear her bubbling laughter, and his quiet, deep voice. After all, I dare say we must make up our minds to lose her sometime, but it hurts.

But it will not be soon. He has not a penny to bless himself with, nor has she. I think, if I were very rich, I would provide an endowment fund for lovers.

But something is wrong with our university system. It takes too long to put a man on a wife-supporting basis. Halliday is twenty-six; he lost two years in the war, and he has another year of law. Truly, Edith will need the eyes of a vulture and the ear tufts of an owl.

June 22nd.

ALL HOUSES *in which men have lived and suffered and died are haunted houses.* But, then, all houses are haunted. Why, then, did Jock refuse to enter the house at Twin Hollows today, but crawled under the automobile and remained there, a picture of craven terror, until our departure?

This old house where I am writing tonight, undoubtedly it has seen the passing of more than one human soul. Yet Jock moves through it unconcernedly, his stump of a tail proudly upraised, his head unbowed. His attitude tonight, too, is even slightly more flamboyant than usual, as though to testify that although he may have given the impression of terror during the day, we are laboring under a misapprehension. He but sought the shelter of the car for coolness.

"He may see farther into the spectrum than I do," I said to Helena Lear the other day, and she countered, "Yes. But *what* does he see?"

Old Thomas met us in Oakville with the keys, and we drove out to the house. I sensed in Jane a reluctance to enter, but she fought it back bravely, and we examined it with a view to our own occupancy. It is in excellent condition and repair, although the white covers over the library furniture and in the den behind gave those rooms a rather ghostly appearance. Jane, I saw, gave only a cursory glance into those rooms, and soon after, pleading the chill inside, moved out into the sunlight.

Edith, however, was enchanted with it all, and said so. She danced through the house, shamelessly courting old Thomas, selecting bedrooms for us all, and peering into closets, and I caught up with her at last on the second floor, looking at the boathouse on the beach beyond the marsh.

"What's above it?" she asked. "Rooms?"

"When the old sloop was in commission, the captain slept there," I told her.

"How many rooms?"

"Two, I think, and a sort of kitchenette."

"Are they furnished?"

Old Thomas, being appealed to, said they were, and Edith's face assumed that air of mysterious calculation which I have learned to associate with what she calls "an idea." Whatever it was, however, she kept it to herself, and I left her selecting a bedroom for herself, and putting into it sufficient thought to have served a better purpose.

Her surroundings and belongings are very important to her; and yet I believe she is in love with young Halliday, who can, so far as I see, give her neither.

It is a curious thing, to go into a house left, as Twin Hollows has been, without change since old Horace died, and not to find him there; his big armchair near the fireplace in the library, his very pens still on the flat-topped desk which is the only modern piece in the room, the books he was reading still in the desk rack. I had a curious feeling today that if I raised my voice, I would hear the little cough which was so often his preliminary to speech, from the den beyond.

The den, too, is unchanged. (Note: From an ugly room, the original kitchen of the old house, he had made it a sort of treasure house of early

American old pewter, brought over perhaps in ships which had anchored in the very bay outside; of early framed charters and deeds of land, signed by English kings and hung on the walls above the old paneling, which he himself had found somewhere and installed; of quaint chairs, a settle, and an old chest, hooked rugs on the floors, and old glass candlesticks.)

I threw back the covering which protected the desk top, and sat down at it. Just there, in all probability, he had been sitting when the fatal attack took place. He may have felt it coming on, but there was no one to call, poor old chap. We had not been overly close, but the thought of him, writing, perhaps, or reading, the sudden consciousness that all was not well, an instant of comprehension, and then the end—it got me, rather.

I think he had been reading. Among the other books on the desk was the one with a scrap of paper thrust in it to mark the place, and a pencil line drawn on the margin of the page to mark a paragraph. But it gives me rather a new line on him. I had always thought that his purchase of a house locally reputed to be haunted, a reputation considerably enhanced by the Riggs woman's tenancy, was a rather magnificent gesture of pure Calvinism.

But tonight I am wondering. The marked paragraph is in a book entitled *Eugenia Riggs and the Oakville Phenomena,* and I have brought it home with me. It is a creepy sort of thing, and I find myself looking back over my shoulder as I copy it into this record.

It is to be borne in mind that the room was always subjected to the most careful preliminary examination. Its walls were plastered, and no doors or windows (see photograph) were near the cabinet. As an additional precaution strings of small bells were placed across all possible entrances and exits, which were also closed and locked.

It is also to be remembered that the medium herself was always willing to be searched, and this was frequently done by Madame B—. This had been done on the night when the hand was distinctly seen by all present, reaching out and touching those nearest, on the shoulder, and later making the impression in the pan of soft putty left in the cabinet.

It is to be borne in mind, too, that, except when the controls rapped for no light, there was always sufficient illumination for us to see the medium clearly. A small red lamp was found to offer least disturbance and was customarily used.

There was occasional fraud, but THERE WERE ALSO GENUINE PHENOMENA.

The last few words are in capitals.

So tonight I am wondering. Does one find, as life goes on, that the lonely human spirit revolts at the thought of eternal peace, and craves a relief in action in the life beyond? Would I not myself, for instance, prefer even coming back and lifting little Pettingill's table to the unadulterated society of the saints?

June 23rd.

THERE IS a division in my family. Edith has come out with her plan, which is to "spread out," as she puts it, in the main house at Twin Hollows, and to let Warren Halliday spend his vacation at the boathouse!

"*Renting* it to him, I suppose?" I inquired over my breakfast bacon.

"Renting it?" she said indignantly. "You wouldn't have the nerve to ask money for that tumble-down place, would you? And, anyhow, you can't get blood out of a stone."

There is a terrible frankness about Edith at times.

But Jane is as equally determined not to occupy the house at any cost. It was written all over her yesterday, and there is still an ominous set look about her mouth. Between them I am more or less trimming skiff.

If Jane would be more open it would be easier; if she would only come to me and say that she is afraid of the house I think I could reassure her. It may be that that silly photograph is still in her mind. But why would she not even stay in the house yesterday? She went out into the garden and picked some of its neglected flowers instead.

"It's a pity not to use them," she said, and then looked at me with such a white and pitiful face that I put my arm around her.

"I must have been a very bad husband," I said, "if you think I am going to force you to live here. Who am I," I added, "against you and Jock?"

But she did not smile.

"If you want to come here," she said, making what I felt was a painful concession, "why couldn't we live at the Lodge? It is really quite sweet. And we could rent this."

"Would that be quite moral, under the circumstances? I'm not asking the circumstances," I added hastily. "I'm simply putting the question."

"We could ask a lower rent."

There is, I sometimes think, a fundamental difference in the ethical views of men and women. To Jane it is quite proper to let a house with what she believes is a most undesirable quality, if she lowers the price. She does not suggest advertising. *One house, furnished, reputed to be haunted.* On the contrary, she proposes to entice tenants with a lower rent, and once having got them there, to be able to say, in effect, "What would you? The house is cheap. True, it has certain disadvantages; I am sorry you have been bothered. But you have saved money."

Aside from this viewpoint, however, the idea is sound enough. We can be comfortable at the Lodge. And—let me always be frank in this journal—I may have my occasional yearnings for adventure, but they have their limitations, and the talk Edith has reported as taking place between old Thomas and herself yesterday after I left them has revealed them to myself.

Edith, on the contrary, finds the situation "really thrilling."

"It's a good house, yes'm," said Thomas. "For them as likes it. I wouldn't be caught dead in it at night myself."

"I hope you never will be," said Edith.

"It ain't nothing you can put your finger on," said Thomas. "It's just knocks and raps, and doors opening and closing. But I say that's enough."

"It sounds like plenty," said Edith. "Of course it may be rats."

"It's a right husky rat that'll open a closed door, and I ain't yet seen a rat that could move a chair. Besides, I ain't ever heard that rats are partial to a red light."

"Now see here, Thomas," Edith reports herself as saying, "either you've said too much or you've said too little. What about a red light? Nothing scandalous, I hope!"

Stripped of further trimming, it appears that some two years ago a small red lamp was installed in the den at Twin Hollows, and is now still there, Thomas having declined to destroy it for fear of some dire and mysterious vengeance.

"Not for light, as far as I could see, miss," he said. "I never seen him read by it. But put in it was, and the night it first came Annie Cochran said something came into her room and pulled the covers off her bed."

"How—shameless!" said Edith.

"More than that," he went on stolidly, "the furniture was moving through the house all night, and the next morning she found the teakettle sitting in the pantry, and tea had been made in the teapot."

"But surely she did not begrudge the poor things their tea, Thomas? It must be thirsty work, moving furniture and chasing about rapping on things."

"She's left the kettle on the stove, and there it was," he said, doggedly.

Like the lady who said to the judge that she had "just sort of lost her taste" for her husband, I begin to lose my taste for this lamp. But one wonders whether its evil reputation is not a survival from the days of Mrs. Riggs, when *a small red lamp was found to offer least disturbance, and was customarily used.*

June 24th.

EDITH HAS LOST and Jane has won. We shall spend the summer at the Lodge.

But I feel that Jane's victory brings her no particular pleasure, that even to go to the Lodge is a concession she is making against some hidden apprehension. Yet to show just how baseless are most of these things, this morning Clara had been in a low mood, and I heard Jane inquire the reason.

"I dreamed last night that I'd lost a tooth," said Clara. "That's a sign of death, sure, Mrs. Porter."

Edith, however, has won in one way. Warren Halliday is to have the boathouse.

We motored out together today, I to look over the Lodge more carefully, and Halliday to inspect his prospective quarters. He is thoroughly likable, a nice, clean-cut young fellow, not too handsome but manly and with a good war record, and badly cut up at his failure to find a job for the summer.

"I'd do anything," he said. "Sell neckties if necessary! But I can't even land that. Although"—he forced a grin—"I have a nice taste in neckties!"

On the way out I told him something of the history of the house, and a little—very little—of Jane's nervousness concerning it.

"Of course," he said, "it's all nonsense. But a surprising number of people are going bugs on it."

"Darned uncomfortable nonsense, too."

"It's not only that, sir. It's dangerous. Imagine what a general conviction of this sort would do. Think of the fellows who find things getting a bit thick for them here, and how quickly they'd hop out of it! Think of the crimes it would cause. And take wars. Nobody would care whether he lived or not. Talk about civilization going! Why, the whole populace would go!"

In view of that conversation, it was interesting later that day, at the Lodge, to have old Thomas intimate that Uncle Horace had not died a natural death, but had "seen something" which had caused it.

As a matter of fact, he brought out certain rather curious facts, which appear to have been somehow overlooked, or at least considered unimportant, at the inquest.

For instance, he had been writing at his desk when the attack came on. His pen was found on the floor. But there was no sign of what he had been writing, save for a mark on the fresh blotter, as if he had blotted something there. The most curious thing, however, according to old Thomas, was the matter of lights.

When Annie Cochran found him the following morning, on the floor beside his desk, all the lights were out, including his desk lamp.

"But the red lamp was going in the den," said old Thomas. "It didn't make much light, so nobody noticed it until the doctor came. He saw it right off. I leave it to you, what shut off that desk lamp?"

I rather gather from Thomas that the ill repute of the red lamp has spread over the countryside. The house had a bad reputation to start with, which Mrs. Riggs's tenancy did nothing to redeem, and now comes Annie Cochran and her red lamp, and a fairly poor outlook so far as renting the property is concerned.

There has been, according to Thomas, considerable interest as to whether we will inhabit the house or not, and if ever I saw relief in a man's face it was in his when I announced the decision. As Halliday observes, it would be interesting to know if either Annie Cochran or Thomas has ever heard that red is the best light for so-called psychic phenomena.

The Lodge proves to be weatherproof and in good condition, and the boathouse quite livable, with the addition of a few things from the main house.

It will need thorough screening, however, on account of the mosquitoes.

(Note: It is necessary, for the sake of the narrative, to describe the boathouse. It is built up on piles which raise it above tide level, and the dory and canoe belonging to the house are stored in the lower portion of it in winter. The old sloop, however, not in commission for several years, was at this time anchored to a buoy about a hundred yards out in the bay, and showed the buffetings of wind and tide.

Across the salt marsh, from the foot of the lawn, extended a raised wooden runway which led to the boathouse and the beach. This walk also prolongs itself into a sort of ramshackle pier, from which a runway extends to a wooden float. At the time of our visit examination showed the float badly in need of repair, a number of the barrels which supported it having more or less gone to pieces.

It was, as will be seen, during Halliday's repair of this float that he made that discovery which was later to see the commencement of my troubles.)

All in all, Jane's scheme is practical, although Edith is frankly disappointed.

"I would have looked so sweet on that terrace!" she said, and made a dreadful face at me.

I have asked her to say nothing to Jane about old Thomas's ravings, as she calls them. She has agreed, but accuses me of extreme terror, and maintains that I am merely putting the responsibility on Jane.

"You know perfectly well," she says, "that you believe in ghosts. And if you rent that house old Horace *ought* to come back and haunt you."

But she is secretly pleased. She sees herself in the cottage, in a bungalow apron, presenting a picture of lovely but humble domesticity to young Halliday, and thus forcing his hand. For if I know anything of Edith, she is going to marry him. And if I know anything of Halliday, he is going to marry nobody he cannot support.

It may be an interesting summer.

Curious about that lamp on the desk, the night the poor old chap passed out. Of course, he might have turned it out and risen to go upstairs when he felt the attack coming on. But wouldn't he have laid the pen down first? One would do that automatically.

It's a pity the blotting-pad has been destroyed.

June 25th.

THE LAST, or almost the last, word Uncle Horace wrote the night of his death was *danger*.

But how much significance am I to attach to that? We speak of the danger of taking cold, of levity in the lecture room, of combining lobster and ice cream. To poor old Horace there would have been danger in overexertion; in that sense of the word he was always in danger. But it was not a word he was apt to use lightly.

Yet what conceivable danger could have threatened him?

This morning, clearing my desk preparatory to our exodus, I resorted to an old trick of mine. I turned over my large desk blotter and presented a fresh and unblemished side to the world. It came to me then that thus probably since the invention of blotters had neatness been established with a minimum of effort, and that it might have been resorted to by Annie Cochran.

After luncheon I started to Twin Hollows with the back of the car piled high with a varied assortment of breakable toilet articles, a lamp or two, and a certain number of dishes. The Lodge was open, and Annie Cochran vigorously cleaning it, and having deposited my fragile load there, I wandered up to the house.

Thomas was cutting the lawn, with a mare borrowed for the purpose, pulling the old horse mower, and the Oakville constable, Starr, who is also the local carpenter, was replacing old boards with new on the raised walk to the beach. What with the sunlight, the *put-put* of a two-cycle engine in a passing motorboat, a flock of knockabouts and sloops poised on the water like great butterflies, and the human activities about, the absurdity of abandoning the old house to some unappreciative tenant grew on me.

"Hear you're going to live in the Lodge," said Starr, spitting over the rail.

"Mrs. Porter feels the main house is too large for us."

He eyed me sharply.

"Yes," he said. "Pretty big house. Well, I'm in a dollar on it."

"A dollar?"

"I bet you'd never live in it," he said, and there was a furtive gleam of amusement in his eyes as he marked a board preparatory to sawing it.

"It's my opinion, Starr," I said, "that you people around here have talked this place into disrepute."

"Maybe we have," he said, noncommittally.

"Mr. Horace Porter lived there for twenty years."

"And *died* there," he reminded me.

"Of chronic heart trouble."

"So the doctor says."

"But you don't think so?"

"I know he had got a right forcible knock on the head, too."

"I thought that came from his fall."

"Well, it may have," he said, and signified the end of the conversation by falling to work with his saw. I waited, but he evidently felt he had said enough, and his further speech was guarded in the extreme. He didn't know whether Mr. Porter had been writing or not when it happened. No, he'd been the first to get there, and he had seen no paper.

Asked if he had had any reason, any experience of his own, to make him wager we would not live in the house, he only shook his head. But as I started back he called after me.

"I don't know as there's any truth in it," he said. "But they do say, on still nights, that he's been heard coughing around the place. I ain't ever heard it myself."

So Thomas thinks that Uncle Horace was frightened to death, and Starr intimates that he was murdered, and all this was seething in the minds of these country people a year ago, without it reaching me at all. There had been no inquest; simply, as I recall, Doctor Hayward notifying the coroner by telephone, and giving organic heart disease as the cause.

I was, I admit, startled this morning as I turned back to the main house. But I knew the tendency of small inbred communities to feed on themselves, for lack of outside nutriment, and by the time I had reached the terrace I was putting Starr's statement about a blow in the same class with the cough heard at night. I stood looking out over the sweep of lawn, and the words occurred to me of that other ancient Horace, confirmed city dweller that he was.

There was ever among the number of my wishes, a portion of ground, not over large, in which was a garden and a fountain, with a continual stream close to my house, and a little woodland besides. The gods have done more abundantly, and better for me, than this.

So I felt that the gods had done even better for me than I had thought. My little woodland, to my left as I faced the sea, covered thirty acres, extending beyond Robinson's Point; true, I had no fountain, but I had a garden of sorts. And I had a ship, which apparently the old Roman had never dreamed of. The old sloop bobbed and swung in the wash of a passing tug.

I turned and went into the house to find that Annie Cochran had turned the blotter and that almost the last word the poor old boy had written had been *danger*.

June 26th.

WOMEN ARE curious creatures. Throughout the winter it is of vital importance to Jane that her teacups are old Chelsea, and that the mirror over the hall table is pure early colonial, even if it does raise my right eye an inch or so. The Queen Anne chairs in her bedroom, the Adam sideboard in the dining-room, apparently divide her affection with me, and she has been known to make considerably more fuss over a scratch on the Sheraton cabinet than over a similar injury to myself.

We are settled tonight in the Lodge, and whatever Edith may say as to its romantic outside appearance, within it is frankly hideous. It is all a cottage should not be. From the old parlor organ downstairs to beds that dip in the center above, it is atrocious. Yet tonight Jane is a happy woman.

Can it be that women require rest from their possessions, as, for instance, I do from my dinner clothes? That it gives them the same sense of freedom to don, speaking figuratively, a parlor organ and the cheapest of other furnishings, as it does me to put on my ancient fishing-garments?

Or is Jane simply relieved?

I confess that tonight with Larkin's advertisement for the other house before me, I feel not only in the position of a man attempting to sell a gold brick, but that I have a secret hankering for the gold brick myself.

For rent for the season, large, handsomely furnished house on bay three miles from Oakville. Beautiful location. Thirty-two acres, landscaped. Flower and kitchen gardens. Low rental.

Yet I dare say we shall do well enough. After all, there comes a time when ambition ceases to burn, or romance to stir, and the highest cry of the human heart is for peace. Here, I feel, is peace.

I have brought with me those books which all the year I have promised myself to read, so that my small room overflows with them; a spare notebook or two for this journal, to be filled probably with the weights of fish and the readings of the barometer; Jane for solid affection, Edith for the joy of life, and Jock for companionship.

But the latter I am questioning tonight. Jock has deserted me. He will not occupy the window seat of my room, although his comforter is neatly spread upon it. When I showed it to him he leaped up obediently, then glanced out the window toward the main house, emitted a long and melancholy howl, and with an air of firmness not to be gainsaid, retired under the bed in Jane's room, which faces toward the highroad. Nor could I later coax him past the main house for a moonlight stroll upon the beach.

He joined me there later, having reached it by some devious route of his own through the marsh, but without enthusiasm.

Later: There has been wild excitement here, and only now have we quieted down. It is clear that already Clara has heard some of the local talk.

At eleven o'clock we heard wild screams from Clara's attic bedroom, and all three of us arrived there in varying stages of undress. Clara was outside her door, which was closed, and was hysterically shrieking that there was a blue light under her bed.

I opened the door, entered the room, which was dark, and stooped down. There *was* a blue light there, luminous and spectral, and my very scalp prickled. I think, had it not been for the women outside, I would have howled like a dog. And the worst of it was that it had an eye, a large staring eye that gazed at me with all the concentrated malevolence in the world.

It was a moment before I could say in an unshaken voice, "Turn on the lights, somebody."

There was a delay until the switch was found, and for that moment the blue light stared at me and I at it. I heard Edith flop down on the floor beside me and give a little yelp, and Clara sniveling outside and saying she would never go into that room again. Never.

Then Jane turned on the lights, and I saw under the bed the large phosphorescent head of a dead fish, brought by Jock from the beach and carefully cached there!

June 27th.

I HAVE FOUND Uncle Horace's letter, and in a manner so curious that there can be, it seems to me, but two interpretations of it. One is that, somehow, I have had all along a subconscious knowledge of its presence behind the drawer. But I hesitate to accept that. I am orderly by instinct, and when I went over the desk after his death, the merest indication of a paper caught behind the drawer would have sent me after it.

The other explanation is that I received a telepathic message. It came, as I fancy such messages must come, not from outside but from within. I heard nothing; it welled up, above the incoherent and vague wanderings of a mind not definitely in action, in a clear-cut and definite form. *Take out the bottom drawer on the right.*

But if I am to accept telepathy, I am to believe that I am not alone in my knowledge of this letter. Yet considering the tone of it, the awful possibility it indicates, who could have such a knowledge and yet keep it to himself?

How did it get behind the drawer? If the brownish smudge on the corner turns out to be blood, and I think it is, then it was placed in the drawer after he died. Annie Cochran and Thomas both deny having seen any paper about. The doctor, perhaps? But would he not have read it first?

It had been crumpled into a ball and thrown into the drawer, and the subsequent opening of the drawer had pushed it back, out of sight. So much is clear.

But–after he fell!

Suppose–and in the privacy of this journal I may surely let my imagination wander–suppose, then, that some other hand picked up this paper, ignorant of its contents, and in a hurried attempt to put the room in order, flung it into the drawer? Or toward the wastebasket beside it, and it fell short? Suppose, in a word, that he was not alone when he died? Suppose that some other hand, again, turned out the desk light and the others, and somehow overlooked the dim-red lamp in the next room, or left it to see the way to escape?

I must not let my nerves run away with me. Murder is an ugly word, and, after all, we have Hayward's verdict of death by heart failure. But a sufficient shock, or a blow, might have brought that on. Fright, even, for the poor old chap was frightened when he wrote that letter. Trembling but uncompromising. That was like him.

I realize fully the unpleasantness of my own situation; even, if you are consistent, its danger. But–

But what? But in spite of this I shall do as I have threatened, probably.

I am profoundly moved tonight. We did not love one another, but he was old and alone, and menaced by some monstrous wickedness. Just what that wickedness was no one can say, but I fully believe tonight that he died of it.

This morning I went with Edith to the main house, she to select some odds and ends for the boathouse, against Halliday's coming, and I to clear out the library desk, to have it moved to the Lodge.

Edith was in high spirits as I unlocked the front door, and was gravely telling Thomas, who accompanied us, that we had seen a blue light under Clara's bed the night before. But he expressed no surprise.

"Plenty of them, folks tell me," he said. "First time I've heard of them in the Lodge, though."

"Oh!" said Edith, slightly daunted. "So there are lights, too."

"Yes'm," he replied. "Annie Cochran, she had one here, used to hang around the shower bath off the gun room. And there used to be plenty outside. Fellows setting trawl out in the bay used to see them over the swamp."

"Marsh gas," I suggested.

"Maybe," he said, with his take-it or leave-it attitude, and we went into the house.

There Edith and Thomas left me, and I opened the shutters of the library and sat down at the desk. I could hear Edith insisting on seeing the shower bath off the gun room. Then their voices died away, and I began to go through the desk once more. All important papers had been taken away after the death, and the drawers contained the usual riffraff of such depositories, old keys, ancient checkbooks, their stubs filled in Uncle Horace's neat hand.

Naturally, I was thinking of him. More or less, I was concentrated on him, if this is any comfort to my spiritualistic friends. He had, indeed, fallen out of the very chair in which I sat when he was stricken, and had apparently cut his head badly on the corner of the desk. All this was in my mind, as I closed the last drawer and surveyed the heap of rubbish on the desk.

I suppose I was subconsciously reconstructing the night of his death, when he had penned that word *danger* which now lay, clearly outlined in reverse, on the blotter. And that when I wandered into the den, looking for a place to store what Lear calls the detritus piled up on the desk, I was still thinking of it. But I cannot feel that my entrance into the room, or my idly switching on the red lamp which stood there, had the slightest connection with the message I seemed at that moment to receive: *Take out the bottom drawer on the right.*

I have heard people who believe in this sort of thing emphasize the peculiar insistence of the messages, and this was true in this case. I do not recall that there was any question in my mind, either, as to which bottom drawer on the right I was to remove. But I must record here a rather curious incident which my spiritualistic friends would add to the picture as proof positive of its other-earth origin.

Edith came back. I could hear her in the library.

"I've found Annie Cochran's blue light," she called. "A piece of phosphorescent wood. No wonder this neighborhood's haunted!" Then she came into the doorway, with Thomas behind her, and suddenly stopped.

"Why!" she said. "What funny shadows!"

"Shadows?"

Then she laughed and ran her fingers across her eyes.

"My error," she said. "When I came in I seemed to see a sort of cloud under the ceiling. It's gone now."

Old Thomas stood by, quietly.

"Lots of folks have seen them shadows," he said. "Some say they're red and some brown. I ain't ever seen them myself, so I can't say." He turned to go. "Maybe it's phosphorescence!" he said, and went away with a sort of hideous silent mirth shaking him.

Behind the drawer I found the letter.

(Note: I made no copy of the letter in the original journal, so I give it here.)

Unfinished letter of Mr. Horace Porter, addressed to someone unknown, and dated the day of his death, June 27th of the preceding year:

I am writing this in great distress of mind, and in what I feel is a righteous anger. It is incredible to me that you cannot see the wickedness of the course you have proposed.

In all earnestness I appeal to you to consider the enormity of the idea. Your failure to comprehend my own attitude to it, however, makes me believe that you may be tempted to go on with it. In that case I shall feel it my duty, not only to go to the police but to warn society in general.

I realize fully the unpleasantness of my own situation; even, if you are consistent, its danger. But—

The letter had not been finished.

June 28th.

I SLEPT VERY LITTLE last night, and this morning made an excuse to go up to town with the letter. Larkin had telephoned me that he had an inquiry on the house through Cameron, and this gave me a pretext. Jane at first wished to go with me, but Edith coaxed her into helping with the rooms over the boathouse, and I finally got away.

Larkin is impressed with the letter, but does not necessarily see its connection with Uncle Horace's death.

"After all," he said, "you've got your medical man's statement that he died of heart failure. Suppose he *was* scared to death? That isn't a crime in law. And you've got to remember the old gentleman was pretty much of a pepper pot. He attacked me almost as violently as that once for my politics!"

"He didn't threaten you with the police, did he?"

"No; he recommended a sanitarium, I think. You haven't an idea who it's meant for, you say?"

"Not the slightest. He hadn't any friends, intimates, so far as I know. The Livingstones, very decent people with a big place about six miles from him, his doctor, and myself—that's about all."

"'Enormity of the idea,'" he read again. "Of course that might be this thing the press is always scaring up, the death ray. Some fellow with a bee in his bonnet, you may be sure."

"That wouldn't imply danger to himself."

"Any fellow with a bee in his bonnet is dangerous," he said, and gave me back the letter.

"Of course," he went on, "you've made a nice point about the stain on the corner. If it's blood, it's hardly likely he got up again and put it where you found it. But I think you'll find the servant there, what's her name, picked it up in her excitement and threw it into the drawer. People don't always know what they do at such times. However, if you like, I'll have that stain tested and see what it is."

I tore off the corner, and left him putting it carefully into an envelope. He glanced up as I prepared to go.

"What's this I hear about your keeping off demons by drawing some sort of a cabalistic design around yourself?" he asked. "You'd better let me in on it; I need a refuge now and then."

Which proves that a man may shout the eternal virtues and be unheard forever, but if he babble nonsense in a wilderness it will travel around the world.

Nevertheless, I am the better for the talk with him. I have been too closely consorting with my womankind, probably; the most virile man can become effeminized in time. And Larkin's attitude as to renting the house is an eminently sane one.

"Rent it without saying anything," he said, "and ten to one whoever takes it will have a peaceable summer. But do as you suggest, tell the tenant the place has the reputation of being haunted, and ghosts will be as thick as mosquitoes from the start."

He has asked for some photographs of the property, and I have promised them for the day after tomorrow.

We have settled down into our routine here very comfortably. Our eggs and milk are brought each morning by a buxom farmer's daughter, one Maggie Morrison, a sturdy red-cheeked girl who drives in a small truck, and backs and turns before the Lodge rather than circle around the main house.

"Surely," I said to her yesterday, "you aren't afraid of the place in daylight?"

"Not afraid," she said, "but it gives me the shivers." And weakened that somewhat by her statement that she never liked a place where there had been a death. Yet she handles callously the cold corpses of her chickens, pulling up their poor rigid wings to show the tenderness of the dead skin beneath, and bending their stilled breastbones to prove that they have died young!

With the lawns cut and the shrubbery trimmed, the place grows increasingly lovely. At low tide the beach is covered with odds and ends from the mysterious life of the sea, red and white starfish, sea urchins, and disintegrated jelly fish. Sea gulls pick up mussels, hover over a flat-topped rock, drop them onto its surface, and then swoop down upon the broken shell, with a warning cry to other gulls to keep away.

So clear was the water this afternoon that, rowing to the old sloop, I could see the barnacles encrusting it, and the long strings of kelp which hang from it like green and matted hair. Edith, bare-armed and slim in the canoe, paddled around it appraisingly.

"Needs a shave and a haircut," she decided.

The boathouse is ready for young Halliday. She has put in it a great deal of love and one or two of my most treasured personal possessions.

"That isn't by any chance my smoking-stand?"

"But you aren't going to smoke much this summer, Father William," she says, and tucks a hand into my arm. "I heard you say so yourself."

It has a sitting-room, bedroom, and kitchenette, but no bath.

"He can use the sea," says Edith easily. "And take a cake of soap in with him."

"And wash himself ashore," I suggest, and am frowned down, probably as too old for such ribaldry.

Jane is very serene. Now and then, as she sits on our small veranda with her tapestry, I see her raise her eyes and glance toward the other house, but she does not mention it, nor do I. I notice that, like Maggie Morrison, she does not go very near to it, but she appears to have adopted an attitude of *laissez faire*.

But she absolutely refused to take the pictures of the house Larkin asks for. Not that she put it like that.

"I haven't had any luck with the camera lately," she said. "You take them, or let Edith do it."

The result of the collaboration, which followed early this afternoon is still in doubt. Jane intends to develop and print them this evening.

And so our life goes on. We retire early, I generally slightly scented from the cold cream of Edith's good-night kiss. Clara, too, goes up early, probably looking under her bed before retiring into it. And Jane sits and sews while I make my nightly entry in this journal; she is, I think, both jealous and faintly suspicious of it!

At ten o'clock or so we let Jock out, and he looks toward the main house and then turns out the gates and into the highroad, where for a half hour or so he chases rabbits and possibly looks for a bear. At ten-thirty he scratches at the door, and we admit him and go up to bed. Behind the drain pipe!

Later: I have just had a surprise amounting to shock. Jane finds she has forgotten the black lantern with a red slide which she uses in the mysterious rites of developing pictures, and suggests that we go to the other house and use the red lamp there.

"But I can bring it here."

"I am through being silly about the other house, William," she says with an air of resolution. "Anyhow, the pantry there is better, and you can sit in the kitchen. Bring a book or something."

She has, poor Jane, very much the air of Helena Lear's kitten the day Jock cornered it and it came out resolutely and looked him in the eye. In effect, Jane is going out to meet her bugaboo and stare it down.

June 29th.

JANE IS IN BED TODAY, and I am not all I might be, although I managed to get an indifferent print or two to Larkin this morning.

It is well enough for cold-blooded and nerveless individuals to speak of fear as a survival of that time when, in our savage state, we were surrounded by enemies, dangers, and a thousand portents in skies we could not comprehend, and to insist that when knowledge comes in at the door, fear and superstition fly out of the window.

It is only in his head that man is heroic; in the pit of his stomach he is always a coward.

Yet, stripped of its trimmings,—the empty, echoing house, its reputation, and my own private thoughts about its possible tragedy, the incident loses much of its terror; is capable, indeed, of a quite normal explanation.

That is, that Jane either saw someone outside the pantry window, or was the victim of a subjective image of her own producing.

To put the affair in consecutive shape.

At eleven o'clock I had moved the red lamp from the den in the other house to the pantry and there connected it. I also lighted the kitchen, and established myself there with *The Life and Times of Cavour*, a book which I considered safe and sufficiently unexciting under the circumstances.

Jane seemed to be going very well beyond the pantry door, and after a time I ceased the reassuring whistling with which I had been affirming my continued presence within call, and grew absorbed in my book.

It must have been 11:15 when she called out to me sharply to know where a cold wind was coming from, and although I felt no such air I closed the kitchen door. It was within a couple of minutes of that, or thereabouts, that I suddenly heard her give a low moan, and the next instant there was the crash of a falling body.

When I opened the pantry door I found her in a dead faint, underneath the window. When she revived, she maintained that she had seen Uncle Horace.

Her statement runs about as follows: She had not felt particularly uneasy on entering the house, "although I had expected to," she admits. Nor at the beginning of operations in the pantry. The cold air, however, had had a peculiar quality to it; it "froze" her, she says; she felt rigid with it.

And it continued after she heard me close the kitchen door.

This wind, she says, was not only so cold that she called to me, but she had an impression that it was coming from somewhere near at hand, and she seemed to see the curtains blowing out at the window. The lower sash was down, as she could tell by the reflection of the red lamp in it, but she went to the window to see if the upper sash had been lowered.

With the darkness outside, the glass had become a sort of mirror, and she said her own figure in it startled her for a moment. She stood staring at it, when she realized that she was not alone in the room. Clearly reflected, behind and over her right shoulder, was a face.

It disappeared almost immediately, and I have my own private doubts about her recognition of it as Uncle Horace which I believe is *post facto.* But I am obliged to admit that Jane saw something, either outside the window and looking in, or the creation of her own excited fancy.

As soon as I could leave her I went outside, but I could find no one there, and this morning I find that my own footprints under the window have entirely obliterated anything else that may have been there.

Jane herself believes it was Uncle Horace, but I cannot find that she received anything more than an indistinct impression of a face. She rather startled me this morning, however, by asking me if I had ever thought that Uncle Horace had not died a natural death.

"Why in the world should I think such a thing?"

But pressed for an explanation she merely said she had heard that the spirits of those who have died violent deaths are more likely to appear than of others who have passed peaceably away; that the desire to acquaint the world with the circumstances of the tragedy is overwhelming!

What seems much more likely is that she has caught from me, with that queer gift of hers, some inkling of my own anxiety.

Larkin's report from the laboratory shows that the stain on the corner of the letter is human blood. Moreover, that it is about a year old, and that it is the imprint of a human finger, but is too badly blurred for identification, as it was made while the blood was fresh.

Larkin watched me while I read the report.

"You see?" I said. "It is human blood."

"What else did you expect it to be?"

"Still, it shows something."

"Certainly it does," he agreed easily. "It may even show a crime, for all I know. But where do you go from there? That fingerprint is valueless. Say there was a crime—where's your criminal? You can't go through the world rounding up all the individuals society ought to be warned against."

"No," I said, rather feebly. "No, I dare say not."

He went with me to the door of his office, and put his hand on my shoulder.

"Go on out to the country and forget about it," he advised. "You're looking rather shot, Porter. Draw your magic circle or whatever it is about your cottage, and retire inside it! Whatever happened there last year, it's too late to do anything about it now."

He is right. I shall get out my fishing-gear tomorrow and perhaps Edith will spare me young Halliday now and then. He is, she said the other day in the inelegant vernacular of present-day youth, "about as psychic as a doorknob."

June 30th.

I HAVE BEEN BROUGHT TODAY, for the first time, into active contact with the feeling of the country people against my house, and especially against the red lamp. It is an amazing situation.

Thomas came to the doorway this morning while I was at breakfast, followed by Starr the constable, who remained somewhat uneasily behind him. It developed that half a dozen sheep, in a meadow beyond Robinson's Point, were found the night before last with their throats cut. The farmer who owned them heard them milling about and ran out, and he declares he saw a dark figure dart out of the field and run into my woods at the head of Robinson's Point.

It appears that the farmer, whose name is Nylie, abandoned the pursuit as soon as he saw where the fugitive was headed, and went back to his dead sheep. They were neatly laid out in a row.

"At what time was all this?" I asked.

"Eleven o'clock, or thereabouts."

"How about a dog?" I asked. "They kill sheep, don't they? Catch them by the throat or something?"

"They don't stab them with a knife. Not around here, anyhow," said Starr.

The ostensible object of the visit was to ask if we had been disturbed that night, and for some reason or other I did not at once connect the situation with Jane's curious experience.

"No," I said. "You'll probably find that Nylie has an enemy somewhere, some hand he has discharged, perhaps."

Starr took himself away very soon after that, but before he left he exchanged a glance with Thomas, and I had a feeling that something lay behind this morning visit. It was not long before Thomas brought it out. It appears that Nylie ran after the figure to the edge of the woods, and there stood hesitating. The woods, I gather, share in the ill repute of the house. And as he stood there, although everyone knew the house was empty, he distinctly saw the evil glow of the red lamp from it!

I dare say Jane is right, and my sense of humor is perverted, but I could not resist the opportunity of baiting Thomas. In which I realize now I made a tactical error.

"Really?" I said. "Nylie was certain of that, was he?"

"Saw it as plain as I see you," said Thomas. "I know you don't believe me—"

"But I do believe you. What about the red lamp?"

"Well," he said, "it's pretty well known about these parts that that lamp ain't healthy. Some say one thing and some say another, but most folks is agreed on that."

"Still, I don't see how it could kill sheep, do you?"

And even now I do not distinctly see the connection. I imagine the local belief is that the lamp exerts some malign influence, possibly even that it liberates some sinister spirit. Not, I imagine, that this is ever put into words. The nearest they come to that is the statement that the lamp is not "healthy," and that "George" has come back.

At least that is all that I can make out of that strange mixture of hysteria, superstitious fears, and local mishaps to which Thomas gave birth in the next ten minutes or so. It began with Annie Cochran in the house after the lamp came, and gradually extended into the countryside; cows had mysteriously and prematurely calved; a meteorite had dropped into a field near by; a fisherman's boat had been found empty in the bay on a quiet day and its owner never seen again; blight, pestilence, and death had visited the community, equaled only in its history by the last few months of Mrs. Riggs's occupancy of the house. And the tradition was that Mrs. Riggs had used a red lamp to call her particular spirit.

" 'George' was his name," said Thomas, "and by and large he gave us a lot of trouble."

"Let me get this, Thomas," I said. "You mean that you think this 'George' has come back?"

"I'm not saying that," he said with his usual caution. "But there's some talk of it."

"And killed those sheep?"

"I'm not saying that, either. But there's not a man, woman, or child around these parts would have gone into those woods night before last, heading for the big house."

I felt that I had gone far enough, and I proceeded to explain the lighting of the lamp that night. But, although I saw that he believed me readily enough, it did not for a moment alter his attitude toward the red lamp.

"And, as a matter of fact," I concluded, "I think Mrs. Porter actually saw the man Nylie chased, looking in through the pantry window."

"That'll have been George, all right," said Thomas, and creaked heavily out of the room.

To leaven the gloom of the morning, Halliday arrived today in boisterous high spirits, broken with a sort of husky emotion when he saw his quarters.

"It's so good of you all," he said, and although the words were to Jane the look was for Edith.

We all escorted him down, Thomas carrying his kit bag, I his overcoat, Jock the newspaper, and Warren himself staggering under a box of groceries and the canned goods on which he apparently intends to subsist. He has definitely refused Jane's offer to take his meals at our table.

"I'm the world's best cook with a can opener," he said boastfully. "And when bacon and beans begin to pall on me, I'll come up for a handout."

We stood around, Edith with entire shamelessness, while he unpacked and settled them. She herself insisted on arranging the top of the chest of drawers, and I saw her there, handling his hairbrushes caressingly. Poor little Edith, so frankly in love, so ready to believe that love is enough, and that such things as she has always taken for granted, food and shelter, will automatically follow in its train.

Afterward we had tea on the narrow veranda over the water, and Halliday examined the old sloop with a professional eye.

"Pretty well out of condition, I'm afraid."

"Any boat's a good boat, sir," he said with his quick smile. "You shall be the skipper, and I'll be the midshipmite, the bo'sun tight, and the crew of the—what's its name, anyhow?"

There followed a prolonged dispute between Edith and the new crew as to a name for the sloop, which was compromised by their announcing that it was to be called *The Cheese.*

"Why? It has no holes in it," I protested.

"Because it's to have a skipper in it," said Edith conclusively.

After the women left we sat on the small veranda which surrounds the boathouse on three sides, and smoked. He told me his circumstances; he has exactly enough money to finish his course which will take another year. At the end of that time he is to have a junior partnership in a law firm in Boston.

"But you know what that means, at first," he said. "A sort of sublimated clerical job. It will be a long time before I am independent."

Before he could marry, was what he meant. And again I thought of my endowment fund for lovers. There are so many funds for preserving human life, and so few to make it worth the preserving. But I must talk to Edith. It is no use making the boy more unhappy than he is, or breaking down the restraints he is clearly putting on himself.

"I lost two years in the war," he said. "That threw me back, you see."

"I dare say it was not lost."

"No," he agreed. "I suppose a man must gain something by a thing like that, if he survives."

From that to the stories about the main house, and to Thomas's recital this morning, was not a long step, nor from that to the history of the house itself and to Mrs. Riggs.

"Curious," he said, "how these people rise, prosper, and then are found fraudulent, without discrediting the next generation of their kind. Eventually they are all caught between bases, and it begins all over again."

But the red lamp interested him.

"Some night, sir," he suggested, "you and I might go up there and try rubbing the thing; see if we can evoke the genii."

About 8:30 tonight I took Jock and walked to Nylie's farm, where the sheep had been killed. I found the field, and wandered idly in. To my surprise, a man with a shotgun rose from a fence corner and confronted me, and Jock's hair rose as he prepared to spring.

"What do you want here?" he demanded suspiciously.

"Go easy with that gun," I said. "My name's Porter, and I'm out for a stroll. That's all."

He apologized gruffly, while I held Jock by the collar, and even condescended to point out where the dead sheep had been found, but there was certainly no cordiality in his manner, and even a trace of hostility.

July 1st.

MORE SHEEP were killed last night. The Livingstones have lost a dozen of their blooded stock, and several farmers have suffered.

In each case the method is the same; the sheep are neatly stabbed in the jugular vein and then as neatly laid out in a row.

We are buying no mutton from the local butcher!

I assured Thomas this morning that I had not lighted the red lamp again, but he did not smile. He is quite capable of believing, I dare say, that I have summoned a demon I cannot control.

But he tells me that a county detective from town, sent by the sheriff, is coming out to look into the matter. And there is a certain relief in this. It seems to me that we have to do with some form of religious mania, symbolistic in its manifestation. The sheep is the ancient sacrifice of many faiths.

This belief is strengthened by Thomas's statement that in each case save the first one there has been left on a near-by rock or, in one instance, on a fence, a small cabalistic design roughly drawn in chalk.

8:00 p.m. I feel like a man who has dreamed of some horrible or grotesque figure, and wakes to find it perched on his bedpost.

The detective sent by Benchley, the sheriff, has just been here, a man named Greenough, a heavy-set individual with a pleasant enough manner and a damnable smile, behind which he conceals a considerable amount of shrewdness.

He had, of course, gathered together the local superstitions, and he was inclined to be facetious concerning my ownership of the red lamp. But he was serious enough about the business that had brought him.

"It's probably psychopathic," he said, "and the psychopath is a poor individual to let loose in any community, especially when he's got a knife."

My own suggestion of religious mania seemed to interest him.

"It's possible," he said. "It's a queer time in the world, Mr. Porter. People seem ready to do anything, think anything, to escape reality. And from that to delusional insanity isn't very far."

I suppose I looked surprised at that, for he smiled.

"I read a good bit," he said, "and my kind of work is about nine-tenths psychology, anyhow. You've got to know what your criminal was thinking, and then try to think like him. The third degree is nothing but applied psychology." He smiled again. "But that's a long way from sheep-killing. Now I'll ask you something. Did you ever hear of a circle, with a triangle inside it?"

I suppose I started, and I had a quick impression that his eyes were on me, shrewdly speculative behind his glasses. But the next moment he had reached into his pocket and drawn out a pencil and an envelope. "Like this," he said and, drawing the infernal symbol slowly and painstakingly, held it out to me.

To save my life I could not keep my hand steady; the envelope visibly quivered, and I saw his eyes on it.

"What do you mean, hear of it?" I asked. And then it came to me suddenly that that ridiculous statement of mine had somehow got to the fellow's ears, and that he was quietly hoaxing me. "Good Lord!" I said, and groaned. "So you've happened on that, too!"

"So you know something about it?" he said quietly, and leaned forward. "Now do you mind telling me what you know?"

He had not been hoaxing me. There was a curious significance in his manner, in the way he was looking at me, and it persisted while I told my absurd story. Told it badly, I realize, and haltingly; that I had picked up a book on Black Magic somewhere or other, and had as promptly forgotten it, save for one or two catch phrases and that infernal symbol of a triangle in a circle; how I had foolishly repeated them to a group of women, and now seemed likely never to hear the last of it.

"As I gather, the Lear woman has spread it all over town," I said. "She dabbles in spiritualism, or something, and it seems to have appealed to her imagination." I thought of Cameron, too—to whom I'd sent the picture.

"It has certainly appealed to somebody's imagination," he said. "That's the mark our friend the sheep killer has been leaving."

He was very cordial as he picked up his hat and prepared to depart. He was sorry to have had to trouble me; nice little place I had there. He understood I was fighting shy of the other house. He would do the same thing; he didn't believe in ghosts, but he was afraid of them.

And so out onto the drive, leaving me with a full and firm conviction that he suspects me of killing some forty odd sheep in the last few nights, probably in the celebration of some Black Mass of my own psychopathic revising.

July 2nd.

LARKIN THINKS he has rented the house. I made a telephone message from him the excuse to go to town this morning. Mr. Bethel was not present, but his secretary was, a thin boy with bad skin and with his hair pomaded until it looks as though it is painted on his head. He smoked one cigarette after another as we talked.

If tomorrow is fair, Mr. Bethel will motor out and look over the property. It appears that he is in feeble health. If it is not, Gordon, the secretary, will come alone. It develops that, although the boy is a local product, and not one to be particularly proud of, Mr. Bethel comes from the West; Cameron's note to Larkin merely introduced him, but assumed no responsibility. As, however, he offers the rent in advance, the matter of references becomes, as Larkin says, an unimportant detail.

I get the impression from the secretary that the old man is writing a book, and wishes to be undisturbed, and if his choice of a secretary fairly represents him, he will be.

From Larkin I learned that he had heard of the circle in a triangle from Helena Lear herself, at a dinner table, and that he has no idea that it is at all widespread. He regards the use of it by the sheep killer as purely coincidence, which greatly cheers me.

Nevertheless, I went to the Lears' and lunched there. Helena has agreed to spread the thing no farther, and I came away with a great sense of relief. Into the bargain, Lear tells me that Cameron, after studying the photograph I sent him, is inclined to think it is the result of a double exposure.

"Double exposures or a thought image," Lear says. "He has had some success himself in getting curious forms on a sensitized plate. Got the number five once, after concentrating on it for an hour! I asked him about Doyle's fairies, but he only laughed."

All in all, I feel today that I was unduly apprehensive last night. The weather is magnificent; Edith has been holding nails for young Halliday today while he repairs the float. Jane has taken over from Thomas the care of the flower beds around the cottage, and has been busy there all afternoon with a weed puller and a hoe, and I have found the sails for the sloop, mildewed but usable, in the attic of the Lodge.

No more sheep were killed last night. I understand Greenough has put guards on all the near-by flocks, and advised outlying farms to do the same thing. Maggie Morrison told us this morning that they were doing it, but in, I gathered, a half-hearted manner. Most of them believe that, by his very nature, the marauder is impervious to shot and shell.

"Joe Willing," she says, "saw something moving around his cow barn a night or so ago, and he fired right into it. But when he ran up there was nothing there."

One curious thing, however, has been brought in by Starr, who stopped on his way past today. In a meadow not far from the Livingstone place two large stones, which had lain there for years, have been moved together and stood on their edges, and a flat slab of rock laid across them. On top of this, when it was found, there lay a small heap of fine sand.

One can figure, of course, that here is an altar, erected by the same unbalanced mind which has been killing the sheep. But no offering has yet been laid on it.

Later: Halliday spent the evening here, and I walked back with him. He tells me that on his first night in the boathouse, he saw a light moving over the salt marsh, about three hundred feet away.

He was sitting on the small balcony of the boathouse, which surrounds it on three sides, and glancing toward the marsh, saw a light there. It seemed to float above the marsh at a distance of three or four feet, and was intermittent.

At first he thought it was someone on the way to the beach, with a flashlight or a lantern, and he watched with some curiosity. Earlier in the evening he had himself walked along the edge of the swamp and decided it was not passable. But halfway through the marsh the light stopped and then disappeared.

"I decided the chap, whoever it was, was in trouble," he said, "so I called to him. But there was no answer, and the light didn't appear again."

"Marsh gas, probably," I explained. "Methane, C.H., of course."

"Marsh gas burns with a thin blue flame, doesn't it? This was a small light, rather white. I waited an hour or so, but it didn't show again."

I have, since my return, looked up the book on the Oakville phenomena which I discovered on the desk of the main house. It is not significant, but it is interesting, to find that Mrs. Riggs produced fleeting lights, sometimes of a bluish-green, from the cabinet, again a sparkling point which generally localized itself near her head. But I cannot find any record of a light persisting for any length of time, or following a definite course.

July 3rd.

THE HOUSE is rented. As it rained this morning, the secretary came alone, and seemed very well satisfied.

But at the last moment my conscience began to worry me, and perhaps, too, for none of our motives are unmixed, I was afraid he suspected something. He made some observation about the rent being low for a property of that size, and glanced at me as he said it, so I plunged.

"I think I'd better be honest with you, even if it costs me money," I said. "The house is cheap because it—well, it isn't an easy house to rent."

"Too lonely, eh?"

"Partly that, and partly because—a portion of the house is very old, and there have been some stories about it circulating in the neighborhood for years."

"Ghost stories?"

"You can call them that."

He seemed to be amused, rather than alarmed. He grinned broadly and took out a cigarette.

"Ghosts won't bother me any," he said rather boastfully. "What kind of a ghost?"

"I don't believe anyone claims to have seen anything. The reports are mostly of raps and various noises."

He seemed to take a peculiar, almost a furtive, enjoyment out of my statement, my confession, rather.

"Hot dog!" he said. "Well, raps won't bother me, and Mr. Bethel's got a deaf ear; he can turn that up at night if they worry him."

So the house is rented, unless something unexpected turns up, and I have done my part. But I confess to an extreme distaste for the secretary, and Edith may find herself with a small problem on her hands. For just before we left he spied her on the float, and gave her a careful inspection.

"That looks pretty good to me," he said. And although his gesture embraced the water front his eyes were on her.

I have arranged with Annie Cochran, following Gordon's query about a servant, to resume her old position at the main house. She refuses to remain after dark, but I presume this will be satisfactory. She will also commence tomorrow to get the house in readiness.

With that strange swiftness with which news travels in the country, already the word has gone out that the place is rented, and I lay to that our sudden popularity this afternoon. The first to arrive was Doctor Hayward, as nervous and jerky as ever, fiddling with his collar, and when for a moment excluded from the talk, gnawing abstractedly at his finger ends. Nothing escapes the man; I sometimes feel that he goes about on his rounds, collecting gossip as assiduously as he disperses the medicines he puts up in his small dispensary, and that his mind is similarly stocked with it, put up neatly on shelves and in order, so that he can conveniently put his hand on it.

He addressed himself mostly to Jane—there is a certain type of medical man who wins his way into families by the favor of women, and is more at his ease with them than with its menfolk—and only beat a circuitous route to the subject uppermost in his mind, which clearly was that an elderly invalid had taken Twin Hollows and would probably require a physician.

In the course of this roundabout talk, however, I came finally to the conclusion that, like the detective, he was watching me. And, as had happened with Greenough, I became absurdly self-conscious. The very knowledge that, the moment I looked away, his eyes slid to me and there remained, made me awkward. As a result I upset my teacup, and while Jane was hurrying for a cloth to repair the damage, he said, "Pretty nervous, aren't you?"

"Not particularly. But I happen to specialize in upsetting teacups."

"How are you sleeping?"

"Like a top," I assured him with a certain truculence, I dare say. But he is fairly thick-skinned. He passed it over by giving his collar a twitch.

"Dream any?" he inquired.

By heaven! The fellow was not only watching me; he was analyzing me. And with that peculiar perverse humor which, I feel tonight, may get me into trouble yet, I answered. I who seldom dream, and then the benign dreams of an uneventful life and an easy conscience, I answered, "Horribly!"

He leaned back and took to biting a finger, staring at me over it. "What do you mean by 'horribly'?" he inquired. But some gleam of reason came to me then, and I laughed.

"Sorry, Hayward," I said, "I couldn't resist it. I never dream, at least nothing I can remember. But you were being so professional—"

Jane's return prevented the apology which was on his lips, and he went back to the local gossip. Once I mentioned the matter of the sheep, but he rather dexterously side-stepped it, and finally brought the talk around to the renting of the house. But I am confident that Greenough has been to him about me, and has asked him to give him an opinion on my mental balance.

I was on guard after that; determined to exhibit myself in my most rational manner. But there is something upsetting in the mere thought that one's sanity is being brought into question. One's usually automatic acts become self-conscious ones. And tonight I could laugh, if I were not somewhat disturbed by it, at the care with which I placed my cigarette on the saucer of my teacup and flung the silver spoon into the grate; at the sudden comprehension of what I had done, and my wild leap to recover the spoon; and at Hayward's intent expression as I turned from the fireplace with the spoon in my hand, and muttered something about being the original man who put his umbrella to bed and stood himself in the corner. He was too absorbed to smile.

He left finally, when the Livingstones arrived.

"You must take good care of this fine husband of yours, Mrs. Porter," he said, holding her hand in the paternal fashion of his type. "He's probably been overdoing it a bit." The result of which is that Jane herself has taken to watching me quietly, over her tapestry, and that she suggested this evening that I take a course of bromide for my nerves.

Irritated at Hayward as I was, and annoyed at myself, I saw him to his car, and asked him the question which has been in the back of my mind ever since I found the letter in the library desk.

"By the way," I said, "you knew my Uncle Horace pretty well. Better than I did, in recent years. Did he have many friends—I mean, locally?"

He straightened his tie with a jerk.

"He had no intimates at all, so far as I know. I knew him as well as anybody. He rather liked Mrs. Livingstone, but he had no use for Livingstone himself."

"Well, I'll change the question. Do you know of any quarrel he had had, shortly before he died?"

"That's easier. He quarreled with a good many people. I imagine you know that as well as I do."

"He never mentioned to you that he had had a definite difference of opinion with anyone?"

Looking back tonight over that conversation, I am inclined to think that he had an answer for that question, and that he almost gave it. But he changed his mind. The purpose of his visit must have come to him, Greenough's story about that idiotic circle and my own lame explanation of it, and all the outrageous mess in which I had involved myself.

"I'd like to know why you ask me that," he said instead.

"He had never talked to you about calling on the police, in some emergency?"

"Never. I see what you're driving at, Porter," he added. "I admit, I had some thought of that myself at the time. But the autopsy showed the cause of death, all right. He wasn't murdered."

"The blow on the head had nothing to do with it, then?"

He glanced at me quickly.

"If it *was* a blow," he said, "it didn't help matters any, of course. But

I prefer to think that the head injury was received as he fell." He hesitated. "Don't you?"

"Naturally," I agreed.

But there was a significance in that pause of his, followed by "Don't you?" which has stayed with me ever since. It was almost as though, in view of Greenough's visit to him and my own questions, I had been somehow responsible for the poor old boy's death, and was seeking reassurance.

1:00 a.m. I am not able to sleep, and so, recipient of all my repressions, I come to you. I have repeated my little formula over and over, as some people count sheep. "Milton and Dryden and Pope." "Milton and Dryden and Pope," but without result. Yet I have seen whole classrooms succumb to the soporific effect of that or some similar phrase in the early hours of a bright morning.

I have even been out, in dressing-gown and slippers, and wandered a way down the main road, where I was surprised by a countryman with a truckload of produce and probably recognized. If any more sheep are killed tonight!

What am I to think about this red-lamp business?

Into every situation it insistently intrudes itself. It was burning when old Horace died; I had turned it on in the closed and shuttered den the day I received that curious message about the letter; Jane lights it to develop the pictures of the house for Larkin, and Nylie's sheep are killed. What is more, Jane sees a face, either outside the window or behind her in the pantry. From the moment of its entrance into the house, after eighteen years of quiet, the old stories of hauntings are revived, raps are heard, footsteps wander about, and furniture appears to move.

Is Greenough right, and am I ready for the psychopathic ward of some hospital? Is this accumulation of evidence actual, or have I imagined it? And yet I am sane enough, apparently. I listen, and I hear the familiar sounds of nighttime here, Jock moving about uneasily in Jane's bedroom next to mine; the rhythmic creaking of the runway to the float, as the wash of the tide swings it to and fro on its rollers. I hear no voices whispering.

Yet Mrs. Livingstone was most explicit this afternoon. She clearly has no nerves, being complacent with the complacence of fat rapidly gained in middle age, and no imagination, or she would have taken lemon in her tea, and no sugar. But she sat there, ignoring little Livingstone's attempts to change the subject, and soberly warned me against renting the house.

Jane's face was a study. So far I had been able to keep from her much of the local gossip about the house, and all of the talk about the red lamp. But now she heard it all, garnished and embellished, and I caught her eyes fixed on me piteously.

"Is it too late, William?" she asked. "Must we rent it now?"

"It's all signed, sealed, and delivered, my dear," I said. "But all is not lost. Tomorrow morning I shall take my little hatchet and smash that lamp to kingdom come."

Mrs. Livingstone took a slice of cake.

"I'm sure you have my permission," she said, "and as I gave it to your Uncle Horace, I dare say I have a right to say so."

"Perhaps you would like to have it back?"

"God forbid!" she said quickly.

"Oh, for heaven's sake," Livingstone put in irritably, "let's talk about something else. Mrs. Porter, will you show me your garden?"

I had a feeling that his wife had wanted just this, perhaps had given him some secret signal, for she settled back the moment they had gone and, so to speak, opened fire.

"You're not a spiritist, Mr. Porter?"

"'I am a cynic; I am a carrion crow,'" I quoted. But I saw the words had no meaning for her. She may have felt some underlying amusement in them, however, for she stiffened somewhat, and rather abruptly changed her point of attack.

"I have often wondered," she said slowly, "whether you have ever considered your uncle's death as—unusual."

"You mean that you do?"

"Personally," she said, looking directly at me, "I think he was frightened to death." She hesitated. She gave me the impression of venturing on ground which was unpleasant to her. "Either that or—" She abandoned that, and began again, hurriedly.

"My husband dislikes the subject," she said. "But I will tell you why I believe what I do, and you can see what you can make of it. You remember that Mrs. Porter was not well when you both came out, the day he was found dead, and toward evening you took her home? Well, Annie Cochran would not stay alone that night, and I stayed with her. It was very—curious."

"Just what do you mean by curious?"

"That there was somebody in the house that night, or something."

"And you don't believe it was somebody?"

"I don't know what I believe," she said, rather breathlessly. "I suppose, since you claim to be a cynic you will laugh, but I have to tell you just the same."

Stripping her narrative to the skeleton, she had been skeptical before, but that night the house had been strangely uncanny. They had sat in the kitchen with all the lights on, and at two o'clock in the morning she distinctly heard somebody walking in the hall overhead, on the second floor. Doors seemed to open and shut, and finally, on a crash from somewhere in the dining-room, "like a doubled fist striking the table," Annie Cochran had bolted outside and stayed there. At dawn she came back, and said she had distinctly seen a ball of light floating in the room over the den, shortly after she went out.

"And was the red lamp lighted, while all this was going on?"

"That's one of the most curious things about it. It was not, when I made a round of that floor early in the evening. But it was going at dawn."

There is, of course, one thing I can do. I can meet Mr. Bethel when he arrives and lay my cards on the table. It will take all my courage; I know how I should feel if I had taken a house, and at the moment of my arrival a wild-eyed owner came to turn me away, on the ground that his house is haunted. Or, we will say, subject to inexplicable nocturnal visits.

Shall I take Halliday into my confidence? I need a fresh brain on the matter, certainly. Someone who will see that the local connection of the murdered sheep with the red lamp, and so with old Horace's death, is the absurdity it must be.

July 4th.

A QUIET FOURTH, but in spite of all precautions, more sheep were killed last night, and in fear of my life I have been expecting a visit from Greenough this morning. But perhaps old Morrison—it looked like the Morrison truck—did not recognize me last night.

But to make things more unpleasant all around, the fellow this time did not leave his infernal chalk mark! One can imagine Greenough straightening from his investigation and deciding that his recent talk with me has put me on my guard. Heigh-ho!

The neighborhood is in a wild state of alarm. The failure of the detective from town to stop the killings has probably added to the superstitious fears which seem mixed up in it. But the more intelligent farmers have got out their rifles and duck guns, and there will be short shrift for the fellow if he is seen at work.

Public opinion appears to be divided between a demon and a dangerous lunatic at large.

Otherwise, I have recovered from last night's hysteria. The cleaning of the house for Mr. Bethel begins today, and I have decided to let it go on. If on hearing my story he decides not to stay no harm will be done; if he remains, it is in order for him.

Jane said at breakfast, "Are you letting him come, William?"

"I shall tell him all I know, my dear. After that it is up to him."

"But is it? Suppose something happens to him?"

"What on earth could happen?" I inquired irritably. "He doesn't need to light that silly lamp. Anyhow, I'm going to destroy it. And as for the other matter, the sheep, the fellow is sticking to sheep, thank God."

But I am not so certain, just now, as to destroying the lamp. This is the result of a conversation with Annie Cochran, as I admitted her, armed with broom and pail, to the house this morning.

She represents, I imagine, the lowest grade of local intelligence, and I dare say she is responsible for much of the superstitious fear of the lamp. But, after all, her attitude represents that of a part of the community, and if I destroy the lamp I shall undoubtedly be held responsible for any local tragedies for the next lifetime or two.

In a word, Annie Cochran not only believes that the lamp houses a demon; she believes that to smash the lamp will liberate that demon in perpetuity.

Incredible? Yet who am I to laugh at this, who went arunning to Lear with a double-exposure photograph, and have been secretly annoyed that little Pettingill has never asked me to one of his table-tipping seances? Or who have, in deference to Annie Cochran and her kind, most carefully locked away the red lamp in an attic closet of the other house, there to contain its devil unreleased. Or who am, at this moment, somewhat oppressed by a so-called spirit message I have just received, forwarded to me by Cameron's secretary.

It is a difference of degree, not of kind.

This is my first letter from the spirit world, and it comes via Salem, Ohio! I have had a curious message or two, witness the unknown correspondent who for several years at intervals sent me a playing-card in an envelope, so that it was nothing unusual for me to receive the deuce of spades with my bacon and eggs, or the knave of diamonds for tea. But this one stands in a class by itself. It has, in Mr. Cameron's absence, been forwarded to me by his secretary.

My dear Mr. Porter:

In Mr. Cameron's absence on his vacation I am forwarding the enclosed message at the request of the writer, who appears to have considerable faith in our ability to locate the person for whom it is intended!

We have had no previous correspondence with the young lady. At least I can find none in our files. But I know you will not mind my saying, in Mr. Cameron's absence, that he has always regarded these Ouija-board communications as purely subconscious in origin; in other words, as unconscious fraud.

The enclosed note is very long, and fully detailed. Even the arrangement of the furniture in the room is described, and the lighting of it. How she came to omit a red lamp I cannot tell; I have somehow grown to expect one! But no amount of light handling of the matter on my part can alter the fact that I am not as comfortable about the thing as I might be. The damnable accuracy of it is in itself disconcerting. The name is right, even to my initial; I am living in a lodge, which even my own subconscious mind could hardly have anticipated a few days ago. And I am warned of danger, on a morning when I feel that danger is, as Edith would say, my middle name.

According to the writer, she and the other sitter, who she naïvely explains was her fiancé, received twice the name, William A. Porter. Assured then that they had it accurately, the "control" spelled out as follows:

Advise you and Jane to go elsewhere. Lodge dangerous.

It sounds, I admit, like a telegraphic message, with one word to spare. One rather looks for the word *love,* so often added to get full value for one's money. But it is a definite warning for all that.

So the Lodge is dangerous, and Jane and I advised to go elsewhere. Heaven knows I'd like nothing better.

Our love story goes on, and I am as helpless there as in other directions;

Edith proffering herself simply and sweetly, in a thousand small coquetries and as many unstudied allurements, and young Halliday gravely adoring her, and holding back.

Today, along with the rest of the summer colony, they made a pilgrimage in the car to the scenes of the various meadow tragedies, ending up with the stone altar and I suspect matters came very nearly to a head between them, for Edith was very talkative on their return, and Halliday very quiet and a trifle pale.

And tonight, sitting on the veranda of the boathouse, while the boy set off Roman candles and skyrockets over the water, Edith asked me how I thought she could earn some money.

"Earn money?" I said. "What on earth for? I've never known you to think about money before."

"Well, I'm thinking about it now," she said briefly, and relapsed into silence, from which she roused in a moment or so to state that money was a pest, and if she were making a world she'd have none in it.

I found my position slightly delicate, but I ventured to suggest that no man worth his salt would care to have his wife support him. She ignored that completely, however, and said she was thinking of writing a book. A book, she said, would bring in a great deal of money, and "nobody would need to worry about anything."

"And you could get it published, Father William," she said. "Everybody knows who you are. And you could correct the spelling, couldn't you? That's the only thing that's really worrying me."

And I honestly believe the child is trying it. Her light is still going tonight as I can see under her door.

July 5th.

The sheriff has offered a thousand dollars reward for the apprehension and conviction of the sheep killer. A notice to that effect is neatly tacked on a post outside our gates, and must rather appeal to Greenough's sense of humor, if he has any. I understand Livingstone is privately offering another five hundred.

Mr. Bethel and his secretary arrive tomorrow, and the house is about ready for them, in spite of the fact that Annie Cochran moves about it, unoccupied as it is, like a scared rabbit. I shall see him at once on his arrival.

Halliday will finish the float today, and I understand he intends then to start on the sloop. He has found a way to address me, instead of the formal "sir" of the first day or two, and now calls me "skipper."

He is visibly more cheerful since yesterday. However hopeless the future looks, he must, during that "showdown" yesterday, as Edith would undoubtedly call it, have been fairly assured of her love for him. Today I overheard a conversation between him and Clara.

"Well, I must be getting on," he said. "It's my wash day."

"Wash day, is it?" she commented skeptically. "I'd like to see your clothes after *you* wash them."

"Who said anything about clothes?" he demanded. "It's my dishwashing day. I always do them every Monday morning."

I watched him go down the drive, his head virtuously erect and Jock, who adores him, bidding him a reluctant good-by. He will not follow him in that direction.

The boy wheedles Clara out of food, too, while Jane stands by and smiles. Passing the pantry window yesterday I saw him stop abruptly and stare at the table inside.

"I beg your pardon, Clara," he said, "but are those *custard* pies?"

"They are. And you needn't be thinking—"

"Real, honest-to-goodness custard pies?"

"That's what the cookbook calls them."

"Would you mind if I came a little closer, Clara?" he inquired. "I have heard of them, but it is so long since I have seen one, let alone tasted it—"

"They're too fresh to cut," said Clara, weakening, one could see, by inches.

"But I could come back," he said gently. "I could go and sit in my lonely boathouse, surrounded by the cans I live out of, and think about them. And later I could come back, you know."

And although he did not come back, a half hour later I saw Clara carrying one down to him, neatly covered with a napkin.

Today, for the first time, I have taken him fully into my confidence. I had been halfway debating it, but the matter of the dressing-gown decided it.

(Note: I find that in the original journal I made no note of this incident. The facts are as follows):

At Jane's suggestion I proceeded to the main house, to remove such of Uncle Horace's clothing as remained in the closets and so on, to a trunk in the attic. Since the night of her experience in the pantry she had not entered the house. Armed with a package of moth-preventive, I was on my way when I met Halliday, and he returned with me.

We worked quietly, for there is something depressing in the emptiness of such garments, and in their mute reminder that sooner or later we must all shed the clothing that we call the flesh.

I said something of this and the boy gave me rather a twisted smile.

"It can't be so bad," he said. "Not worse than things are here sometimes, anyhow. And as Burroughs said—wasn't it Burroughs?—'the dead do not lie in the grave, lamenting there is no immortality.' "

"Then you don't believe in immortality?"

"I don't know what I believe," he replied. "I know it isn't any use telling us we're going to be happy in the next world, to make up for our being miserable in this."

It was shortly after this that I located the dressing-gown which poor old

Horace was wearing when he was found, and discovered that there were bloodstains on it near the hem.

"I'm going to ask you something," I said to Halliday. "A man dies of heart failure, and as he falls strikes his head, so that it bleeds. He lies there, from some time in the evening until seven o'clock in the morning. There wouldn't be much blood, would there?"

"Hardly any, I should say."

"And none in this location, I imagine."

I showed it to him, and he looked at me curiously.

"I'm afraid I don't get it, skipper," he said. "You mean, he moved, afterward?"

"If you want to know exactly what I mean, I believe the poor old chap was knocked down, that he got up and managed to dispose of something he had in his hand, something he didn't want seen, and that *after that* his heart failed."

He picked up the dressing-gown and carried it to the window.

"Tell me about it," he said quietly.

As neither one of us knows anything about the heart, or what occurs when a fatal seizure attacks it, it is possible Halliday is right. That is, that feeling ill he got up, crumpled the letter in his hand, turned out the desk light, and then fell. But that he recovered himself and managed to drag himself to his feet again, when the full force of the seizure came, and he fell once more, not to rise.

"There is no real reason to believe that he was not alone," he said. "Nor even that he 'saw something,' as Mrs. Livingstone intimates."

But the letter I had found in the drawer interests him. He has made a copy of it, and taken it home to study.

I appeal to you to consider the enormity of the idea. Your failure to comprehend my own attitude to it, however, makes me believe that you may be tempted to go on with it. In that case I shall feel it my duty, not only to go to the police but to warn society in general.

I realize fully the unpleasantness of my own situation; even, if you are consistent, its danger. But–

"But–what?" said Halliday. "'But I shall do what I have threatened, if *you go on with it.*'" He glanced up at me. "It doesn't sound like sheep-killing, does it?"

"No," I was obliged to admit. "It does not."

July 6th.

I AM IN A FAIR WAY to go to jail if things keep on as they have been going! And not only for sheep-killing. If we have not had a tragedy here, certainly today there is every indication of it. And with the fatality which has attended me for the past week or so, I have managed to get myself involved in it.

Last night a youth named Carroway, sworn in by Starr a few days ago as deputy constable, was assigned to the highroad behind our property as his beat. He was armed against the sheep killer with a .30-30 Winchester, which was found this morning in the hedge not far from our gates.

Nothing is known of his movements from nine o'clock, when he went on duty, until a few minutes after midnight, when he appeared breathless on the town slip, minus his rifle and, jumping into a motor launch moored at the float, started off into the bay.

Peter Geiss, an old fisherman, was smoking his pipe on the slip at the time, but Peter is deaf, and although Carroway shouted something the old man did not hear it. There is, however, an intermediate clue here, for on his way Carroway had run into the Bennett House, and told the night clerk there to awaken Greenough and get him to our float; that the sheep killer had taken a boat there and was somewhere out on the water.

The deputy's idea was probably to drive the fugitive back to the shore, and as there are, due to the marshes, but few landing-places there, he seems so far as I can make out to have figured that the unknown would be forced back to our slip.

Greenough appears to have lost no time. He threw an overcoat over his pajamas, took his revolver, and commandeering a car in the street, was on our pier before Carroway had been on the water ten minutes. And here, with that fatality which has recently pursued me, he found me returning from the float!

There are times when misfortune apparently picks up some hapless individual as her victim and, perhaps for the good of his soul, hammers him on this side and on that until he himself begins to think he has deserved it. He is guilty of something; he knows not what.

I was a guilty man as I faced Greenough! And yet the scene must have had its elements of humor. I, rather shaken already with the night air, my teeth rattling, and this ghostly figure suddenly appearing on the runway above me and turning my knees to water; a terror which only changed in quality when this ghost instructed me to put up my hands.

But I knew the voice, and I managed as debonair a manner as was possible under the circumstances.

"Nothing in them but a flashlight," I said. "However, if you insist—"

He seemed to hesitate. Then he laughed a little, not too pleasantly, and came down the runway to me.

"Out rather late, aren't you, Mr. Porter?" he asked.

It was my turn to hesitate.

"I came down to pull the canoe up onto the float," I said finally. "Mrs. Porter thought the sea was rising."

"Sounds quiet enough to me," he retorted and turning on his flash, he ran it over the surface of the water, which was as still as a millpond, and onto the canoe, which lay bottom up and still dripping, on the float.

It is indicative of the whole situation, I think, that he lighted the flash. He was no longer lurking in the dark, waiting for the motorboat to drive the marauder ashore. That marauder, in the shape of a shivering professor of English literature, slightly unbalanced mentally, was before him.

Then he seemed to be listening, and knowing the story this morning, I dare say he was listening for the beat of the motor engine. There was no sound, and this, I imagine, puzzled him, as it is puzzling the entire community today. I am myself not particularly observant, and any testimony I might give would, under the circumstances, be discredited in advance. But my own impression is that there was the sound of an engine from somewhere on the bay as I crossed the lawn, and that it had ceased before I reached the water's edge.

Greenough was frankly puzzled. He had, one perceives, a problem on his hands. He wanted Carroway to come in and identify me, for without that identification he was helpless. And somewhere out on the water was Carroway, possibly with a stalled engine. He put his hands to his mouth and called.

"Hi, Bob!" he yelled. "*Bob.*"

But there was no answer, except that Halliday came running out and asked what the trouble was. Greenough was thoroughly irritated; he lapsed into a sulky, watchful silence, and offered no objection when I shiveringly suggested that I go back to my bed. I left them both there, Halliday preparing to row out and locate the launch if possible, and came back to the Lodge.

This morning I learn that Carroway's boat was found by Greenough who had a fast launch with a searchlight, at one o'clock this morning, drifting out with the tide and about two miles from land. It was empty, and no sign of young Carroway was found. As it trailed no dory, our mystery has apparently become a tragedy.

And I am under suspicion. I have put that down, and sitting back have stared at it. It is true. And suppose what I am expecting at any moment takes place, and Greenough comes into the drive, to confront me with the damnable mass of evidence he has put together, the circle enclosing the triangle; the fact that the sheep-killing did not commence until after our arrival at the Lodge; the night Morrison, driving his truckload of produce, saw me on the road; and most of all, with last night!

Suppose I tell him the actual fact? That my wife has some curious power, and that in obedience to it she last night roused me from a virtuous sleep, to tell me she had clairvoyantly seen a man taking a boat from our float, and that I must immediately go down; that there was, she felt, something terribly wrong? Suppose I told him that, which is exactly the fact? And also that, once there, I found that Edith had left the canoe in the water, and that I had, like the careful individual I am, drawn it up out of harm's way? Will he believe that? I wonder—

Quite aside from my unwillingness to drag Jane into this, particularly as the possessor of a faculty which she herself only reluctantly reveals even to me, is my conviction that such a story, soberly told, would only increase Greenough's suspicion of my sanity.

And as if to add to the precariousness of the situation, Halliday himself in all innocence has added another damning factor; gave it, indeed, to the detective last night.

Yesterday, it appears, in repairing the float, he found a new and razor-sharp knife between the top of one of the barrels and the planks which made the flooring.

"I didn't tell you, skipper," he says, "because I was afraid of alarming you. And, of course, there might have been some simple explanation. Starr might have dropped it, during his carpentering."

He was first amused and then infuriated by the web which seems to be closing around me.

"Of course they can't do anything," he says, "unless they catch you in the act."

But the unconscious humor of that statement set me laughing, and after a moment he saw it and grinned sheepishly. "You know what I mean," he said. "And in one way, if you can stand it, it's not a bad thing."

Pressed for an explanation, it appears that he had been thinking of going after the reward himself, and that this matter of Carroway has decided him.

"Reward or no reward," he said, quietly, "I've had a bit of training; they put me in the Intelligence in Germany, during the occupation. And of course the way to catch a criminal is to keep him from knowing who's after him. Then again, if he learns the police are watching you—and he may—he's watching *them*, you know—it may make him a bit reckless. You never can tell."

But he has a third reason, although he has not mentioned it. He is chivalrously determined to protect me, and through me, Edith.

July 7th.

ANOTHER DAY has gone by, and I am still at large. Free, I suppose in order that I may eventually again sally forth, some dark night, with my piece of chalk and another knife—for has not Greenough my original one?—to kill more sheep; if indeed there be any remaining for slaughter; or to stab and throw overboard another hapless boatman.

To save my life, I cannot prevent my absurd situation from coloring my actions. I constantly remind myself of the centipede which, on being asked how it used its many legs, became suddenly conscious of them and fell over into the ditch.

For example, at breakfast this morning I gravely poured some coffee into Jock's saucer, instead of the leftover cream from the breakfast table. And Edith caught me in the act.

"Nobody home," she announced. "Poor old dear, so nice and once so intelligent! It is sad," she said to Jane, "to see his mind failing him by inches. But his heart is all right. If the worst comes to the worst—"

"Don't talk about my mind," I snapped, and then was sorry for it. "I don't feel humorous at breakfast, my dear," I said. "I'm sorry."

But the plain truth is that I am sadly upset. Even what before seemed a plain and obvious duty, to go to the other house tonight and tell Mr. Bethel on his arrival the exact situation, has been all day a matter for most anxious thought. It had seemed quite simple before. I would say to him, "Sir, I have rented you this house. True, I warned your secretary of certain unpleasant qualities it is supposed to have, but I must also warn you. The building is reported to be haunted. I do not believe this, nor I dare say will you, but I feel that I must tell you."

Or again:

"There is also a popular—or unpopular—idea that some recent sheep-killings around the vicinity are somehow connected with this haunting. The police do not think so, but the more ignorant of the natives do. If this alarms you, I am prepared to pay back your money to you."

Not quite in this fashion but with a similar candor, I have been prepared to clarify my relations with my new tenant. But now what happens? Will Greenough, for instance, credit my entire disinterestedness? Will he not rather believe that I have given but one more evidence of my essential lunacy? Would I not myself, only a few weeks ago, have distrusted any individual who came to me with such a tale?

After all, I have told young Gordon. At least I have that to my comfort if anything happens. But what am I writing? What can happen? "It is sad," says Edith cheerfully, "to see his mind failing him by inches." Perhaps it is.

I have seen Bethel, and I have not told him. He gives me every impression, in spite of his infirmity, of being able to look after himself, and after tonight's experience he is welcome to do so. Let him have his raps and his footsteps; let him find his teakettle on the floor, and his faces in the pantry. Let him freeze in cold airs or stew in his own juice. I have done my part.

His car drove in at eight-thirty, and I followed it along the drive. True to her agreement, Annie Cochran had only waited until seven and then had taken a firm departure, and I dare say this threw him into the execrable temper in which I found him. The secretary had assisted him into the house, and I found him in the library, with only one lamp going, huddled in a chair among a clutter of wraps, and introduced myself. He barely acknowledged it.

"Where the devil's the servant?" he barked at me. "I thought there was a woman, or somebody."

"There is a very good woman," I said, "but she goes home before dark. That is," I corrected myself, "she leaves early. I told your secretary that."

"Do you suppose she's left a fire? Gordon!" he called. "Go and see if there's a fire. I want some hot water."

He fumbled in a pocket and brought out what I fancy was a beef cube or some similar concoction, and sat with it in his hand.

"Which way does the house face?" he asked suddenly.

"East. Toward the bay."

"Then I want a back room. Don't like the morning sun. Don't like anything in the morning," he added, and peered up at me through his spectacles.

Young Gordon returned then with a cup of hot water and a spoon, and

Mr. Bethel favored me with little or no further attention. He has but one usable hand, and the secretary held the cup while he stirred the tablet in it.

Only once did he favor me with direct speech during this proceeding. He glanced up as I stood—he had not asked me to sit down—and said, "Been having some sheep-killing around here lately, haven't you?"

I may have flushed slightly, but I doubt if he could see it, although his eyes were on me. "Yes," I admitted.

"Saw it in the papers," he said, and went back to his broth.

Then if ever was my time to plunge, but to save my life I could not do it. That truculent, childish old man, one leg stretched out before him in the relaxation of partial paralysis, one hand contracted in his lap with the tonic spasm of his condition, taking soup under the direction of a pasty-faced boy who grinned at me above his white head, was no recipient of such information as I had to give. And he allowed me no further opportunity; the cup empty, he indicated that he wished to go upstairs, and with a nod in my direction he shuffled out, Gordon supporting him on the infirm side.

I had had some notion of offering my assistance, but I felt that this recognition of his condition would only annoy him; obvious as it was, he had not mentioned it to me, and I guessed that it was a cross borne not only without fortitude, but with a continuing resentment. I followed them to the foot of the stairs however, and part way up, pausing for breath, he must have suspected my presence there for he turned and looked down.

"What do you think is behind this sheep-killing?" he said. Just that. Not good night. Nothing whatever about the house; nothing about my presence or my approaching departure. "Who's killed them?" he rasped.

"Some maniac, probably."

"A maniac!" he barked, and steadying himself by Gordon, twisted around so he could see me better. "Religious tomfoolery, eh? The Blood of the Lamb!"

He cackled dryly, staring down at me. Then he turned, without another word, and went on up and out of my sight.

July 8th.

On Halliday's advice I am not leaving the property, and whenever it is humanly possible, I am in sight of Thomas. Thus today I have been weeding Jane's flower beds for her, and with the garage doors open have been ostentatiously oiling the car. Tonight, too, I have drawn the table in my room to the window and am there making this day's entry, in full view of any observer who chances to take any interest in my movements.

I am, I am convinced, under espionage. Old Thomas is too frequently in view, as he patters around his daylight tasks, and tonight I have a distinct impression that some observer who takes an interest in my movements is outside, watching my window. Jock believes this, also. He is restless, moving from the passage into my room and back again, and twice, standing near me, the short ruff on the back of his neck has risen.

Halliday brought me today further details about Carroway's disappearance.

"The hotel clerk ran down to the piers," he says, "and he heard the engine going for some time. The boat didn't start up the beach, but out into the bay, as if Carroway felt the other man had a good start on him, and was trying to cross the bay. Then he either lost the sound of the engine, or it stopped.

"He waited on the slip for a half hour or so and then went back to the hotel. Greenough came in about that time and called up Starr, and they went together to the town slip. But Carroway hadn't shown up, and after a time Greenough decided to go out after him.

"They found the boat pretty well out in the bay—the tide was going out—and empty. They looked around, as well as they could, then Starr got into it and brought it back. But here's the part they're not telling. Peter Geiss says Greenough got some waste and wiped something off the top of the engine box."

"He didn't see what it was?"

"They wouldn't let him near the boat, but he says it was the circle again."

Of any other details there are apparently none. Bob Carroway has apparently gone the way of all flesh, poor lad. And while Greenough or some emissary of his watches me from my own drive, the murderer is perhaps concocting some further deviltry.

In the meantime a veritable panic has, according to Halliday, seized the countryside, and of this we have certain evidence ourselves. The road beyond the Lodge gates, usually a procession of twin lights, is tonight dark and silent. No motorboats with returning picnic parties rumble across the water, throwing us now and then a bit of song. The fishermen, starting out at three in the morning, are going armed and in fear of their lives. And each man suspects the other.

My own position is as unpleasant as possible. Today Jane said to me, "I wish you would get a meat knife in Oakville today, William."

"What do you mean by a meat knife?"

"Just a good sharp knife," she said, "with a long blade."

"My dear," I said, "anyone buying such a knife in Oakville today would be put into jail at once. Personally, I need razor blades, but I shall grow a beard like the sloop's before I purchase any."

"You could send for one, in town."

And I could not tell her that such a proceeding would be even worse than the other.

Jane's own attitude these days is curious. She is quite convinced, for instance, that she had a premonition of Carroway's death the night she sent me to the slip. As she has no idea that this premonition of hers may be most unpleasant in its consequences to me, today I got her to talk about it.

"Just how did it come?"

"I don't know. I had been asleep, I think. Yes, I know I had. I wakened, anyhow, and I seemed to be looking at the slip. There was somebody there, kneeling."

"Kneeling? Saying his prayers, you mean?" with a recollection of the altar.

"I think he was feeling for something, under the float."

There is a certain circumstantial quality to this, one must admit. He had been seen and was being followed, and his knife for some reason was still where he had left it. Or rather, it was not there, since Halliday had that day found it and taken it away. Had it not been for that, poor Carroway might have met his end there on our slip, and not later. But the knife was gone, and there was nothing left but flight.

Just where that flight began no one can say. It seems incredible that he had left his boat moored directly below our boathouse, with Halliday so close at hand. It seems more likely that he ran up the beach a way, and that—well, *de mortuis nil nisi bonum*. Perhaps I am wrong, but it seems to me that Carroway could more easily have followed him by one of the rowboats from our slip, than follow the method he did, with the loss of time involved.

Still, I myself would not have started out unarmed after a killer, even of sheep, unless I had first raised the alarm and was fairly sure of assistance to follow.

"But I don't see," I said to Jane, "why you felt that there was anything ominous in this dream of yours, or whatever it was."

"I never have them without a reason."

"But that night when you so unjustly accused me of holding up the chapel wall—"

"There was a reason there," she said coldly. "I thought it quite likely I might have to go and get you."

There may be one comfort to the superstitious in all this; not once since the night when we lighted the red lamp in the pantry, has it—

Midnight: I have just had rather a curious experience, and I am still considerably shaken.

I had no more than written the above words when I glanced out the window, and distinctly saw a small red light through the window of the den in the main house.

My first thought, so certain was I that the lamp was carefully hidden in the attic, was of fire. Long before, I had seen Mr. Bethel's light, in the room above it, go out, and soon after that young Gordon's had been likewise extinguished.

I went quickly to my window and leaned out. So dark is the night that it hangs outside like an opaque curtain, and as the light almost immediately disappeared, I was left staring into this void, when suddenly Jock on the staircase landing gave vent to an unearthly howl.

The next moment I heard, under the trees and toward the house, the short dry cough of cardiac asthma, and smelled the queer, unmistakable odor of Uncle Horace's herbal cigarette.

I have reasoned with myself for the last ten minutes or so. All the evidence is against me; Greenough may be watching me, or having me watched, and some poor devil out under the trees is suffering from the night air. Or old Mr. Bethel, unable to sleep, has somehow dragged himself out for a midnight airing under the trees.

But I saw the lamp. And it is locked in the attic. I myself put it there, and at this moment have the key.

July 9th.

I MADE AN EXCUSE this morning to Annie Cochran, and she slipped me up the kitchen staircase of the other house and so to the attic. The lamp was as I had left it and the closet locked, and today I am asking myself whether, with that curious lack of perspective one finds at night, I did not see instead of the lamp far away, the lighted end of a cigar close at hand.

Annie's report on my tenants is satisfactory on the whole. She doesn't much care for the secretary, but the old man's "bark is worse than his bite." He comes down in the morning, or is helped down, to his breakfast, and she cuts his food for him—he seems to dislike the boy's doing it—reads the paper, and then goes to work.

"To work?" I asked. "What sort of work?"

"He's writing a book."

But it appears that he is writing it only in the nonliteral sense. He is dictating a book. And it also appears that he has chosen this place because of its isolation, and Annie's orders are that he receives no visitors.

But it also appears that young Gordon is perhaps not as courageous as he made out to me when he came to look over the house, and that he has been "hearing things."

"What sort of things?"

"He didn't say. But he asked me this morning if I'd been in the house last night. 'If you find me here at night, it'll be because I'm paralyzed and can't move,' I said, 'and if you take my advice, you'll not go round hunting if you hear anything.'"

"That must have cheered him considerably."

"I don't know about that. He just looked at me and said, 'What's the game, anyhow? I'll bet a dollar you're in on it.'"

Edith has sprung a surprise on us all. I have noticed for a day or two that she has been taking a keen interest in the mail; yet Edith's mail, with Halliday here, is largely a matter of delicate paper and the large square handwriting of the modern young woman, and has dealt this summer largely with reports on house parties, summer resorts, and various young men who seem recognizable to her under such cognomens as Chick, Bud, and Curley.

This morning, however, her mail included a businesslike envelope, and she flung the white, rose, and mauve heap aside and pounced on it. A moment later she got up and coming around the table to me, gravely kissed that portion of my head which is gradually emerging, like a shore on an ebb tide, from my hair.

"As one literary artist to another," she said, "I salute you." And placed before me a check for twenty dollars.

She has written a feature article on our sheep-killing, and has sold it.

"And it took me only two hours," she says triumphantly. After that she was rather silent, computing I dare say how much she can earn, giving four hours a day to it for six days a week. At the rate, then, of ten thousand a year!

"Considerably more than I receive, Edith," I said gravely, and I saw I had been right by the way she started.

She set off at once for the boathouse, but came back later considerably crestfallen, and poured out her troubles to me.

"If he had anything he would give it to me," she wailed. "If I can write and make money—"

"You can't fight the masculine instinct, my dear, to support its woman; not be kept by her."

"And wait for years and years to do it!" she said. "The best years of our lives going by, and—nothing."

"Besides, have you considered this? You will not always find subjects as salable as this one has been."

"Subjects!" she said scornfully. "Why, this place is full of them."

The result of which has been on my part all day an uneasy apprehension as to what she will choose next. Nor am I made easier by a question she asked me just before dinner.

"What became of the Riggs woman?" she asked. "Do you suppose she's still around here?"

"I imagine not. Why?"

"I just wondered," she said, and wandered to that particular corner of the veranda from which she has a distant but apparently satisfactory view of the boathouse.

Perhaps Halliday is right. (Note: In his suggestion that Jane and I take the sloop and go down the coast for a few days.) If any sheep are killed in my absence, or anything more serious should happen, it will serve to rout Greenough's absurd determination to involve me, and provide a complete alibi. At the same time, it will be rest and recreation for Jane, and it may put me in a better frame of mind.

Peter Geiss, he thinks, would go with us as captain and bunk under a pup tent, leaving the cabin to Jane and myself.

(*On board the sloop*) *July 10th.*

AMAZING, THE CELERITY with which youth thinks and acts. Tonight Jane and I—and Peter Geiss—are rolling gently to our anchor in Bass Cove, close enough in to be quiet and far enough out to escape the mosquitoes. And yet only yesterday the plan was an amorphous thing, floating in the air between Halliday and myself, a mere ghost of an idea, without material substance.

I am glad to sit in my wicker chair, this journal on my knee, and rest my body. I have indeed earned my night's repose. Now and then I reach out a languid hand and touch a fishing-line, one end of which is tied to the arm of my chair, the other extending into those mysterious depths from which I hope to lure tomorrow's breakfast.

The sloop is tidy. Is even fairly seaworthy. Her bottom has today been scrubbed with a broom, and her sails, slightly mildewed, still present from a distance a certain impressiveness.

"What," I shout at Peter Geiss, "is that small sail in front? Forward, I mean."

"How's that?"

"The sail there, what's its name?" I say, pointing. "*Name?*"

"I'll say it's a shame," he says. "Canvas on this boat cost the old gentleman a lot of money."

By and by, however, I learn the jib and the flying jib. Also that sea water is an unsatisfactory cleansing medium, as witness the supper dishes.

"Why," I demanded of Jane, "did Nausicaä wash her garments in the sea, when there was a river at hand?"

"I haven't an idea," she says absently, her eyes on her alcohol cooking-stove. "They weren't overly clean in those days, were they?"

But I think my dear Jane is exceedingly uncertain as to just what days were those of Nausicaä.

We have a small cabin, with four bunks in it, and two of these are now neatly and geometrically made up, ready for the night. In Jane's small closet there is food of all sorts, neat rows of tins and wax-paper packages. If we are washed out to sea we can, I imagine, live indefinitely on deviled ham, sardines, and cheese. And I have always my fishing-line.

Ah! A tug at it!

July 11th.

I HAVE BEEN PLAYING solitaire today, as a cover for my thoughts. For this, I take it, is the great virtue of solitaire, that it insures against frivolous interruption, while at the same time leaving the mind free to wander where it will.

My worries are dropping from me. Helena Lear is with Edith, and no doubt Halliday is camped on their doorstep, as vigilant as a watchdog, and certainly more dependable than Jock. I can see, too, with better perspective how absurd my anxiety has been as to Greenough. It is his business to believe every man guilty until he has proved himself innocent. And am I not now in the act of proving my innocence?

But my problem remains. And trying to solve it is like playing solitaire with a card missing. I have, we will say, lost the knave of clubs out of my pack, and without it the game cannot go on.

Halliday, I know, believes that there is a possible connection between the killer and Uncle Horace's letter. He believes, in other words, that some curious and perhaps monstrous idea lies behind the sheep-killing, and that it may be the same idea to which the letter refers.

"There is something behind it," he asserts. "Something so vital to the man who believes it that he is ready to kill—has killed certainly once and possibly twice—to protect it."

But the nature of the idea, or conviction, he nobly evades.

"And this monstrous idea was to kill sheep, and build a stone altar?"

"How do we know that isn't merely a propitiatory sacrifice, skipper? A sort of preliminary to the real thing?"

"And what is to be the real thing?"

"What is the wickedest crime you can name, against society?"

"The taking of human life."

"Exactly."

But this, as he says, is as far as he goes. He is, however, careful to say that his theory has got him somewhere; that is, that there is a definite idea behind what has been happening.

"An insane one, then."

"Not necessarily," he objects. "Your Uncle Horace didn't write that letter to a man he considered insane."

Peter Geiss has his own theory about poor Carroway's death. Carroway, he says, probably located the boat; he could do that by cutting off his engine and listening for the oars. Then, in black darkness, he steered toward it, probably with the idea of driving the fellow back. But Peter does not think that Carroway would have closed in on the murderer, unarmed as he was.

"The chances are," he said today, "that the fellow crept up on him, quiet-like, and leaped into the launch."

"But he was unarmed, too," I said, remembering the knife under our slip.

It seemed to me that Peter not only heard that with surprising distinctness, but that he shot a stealthy glance at me.

"He had an oar," he said, and fell back into his customary taciturnity.

The nights are wonderful. I have brought my mattress out of the cabin, and shall sleep tonight face up to the stars. We are anchored in Pirate Harbor, that small enclosed anchorage the shore of which has been so frequently dug for treasure that it is pitted like a pock-marked face.

In our forerigging hangs our riding light. It should be white, but as in a burst of energy this evening I scraped a supper plate over the side, I also scraped off the lantern. So it is red, our red sailing light. It reminds me of the lamp at home. I think about light in general. What do I know about light, anyhow? That it is a wave, a vibration, and that only within a certain fixed range can it be perceived by my human sensorium; that, below the infrared, and above the ultraviolet, are waves our human eye cannot perceive. Then, all around us are things to which our human senses do not react. How far dare I extend that? From invisible things to invisible beings is not so far, I dare say.

What is reality and what is not? Only what we can see, hear, touch, or taste? But that is absurd. Thought is reality; perhaps the only reality.

But can thought exist independent of the body? The spiritists believe it can. And undoubtedly the universe is full of unheard sounds; all the noises in the world go echoing around our unhearing ears for centuries, and then comes the radio and begins to pick them up for us.

But the radio requires a peculiar sort of receiving instrument, and so with the sights and sounds beyond our normal ken. Jane may be such an instrument. So for all I know may be Peter Geiss, snoring in his pup tent. Even myself—

(Note: I fell asleep here, and the entry is incomplete.)

July 12th.

JUST WHAT did Peter Geiss see last night?

If I were asked to name, in order of their psychic quality, the three persons on this boat, I would put Jane first and Peter last.

He is a materialist. Not for him the interesting abstractions, the controversial problems of the universe. The life of the mind, the questions of the soul, are hidden from him. His food, his tobacco, the direction of the wind, the state of the tide, these cover the field of his speculations and anxieties. And yet—Peter saw something last night.

It was about one o'clock in the morning, and he had wakened and crawled out of his pup tent, with, according to him "the feeling that we were in for a blow. There was a cold wind across my feet."

So he rose, and he saw that our red lantern was burning low, and gingerly stepping across me, reached into a locker for the oil can. When he straightened up he saw a shadowy figure standing in the bow of the boat, directly under the lantern.

He thought at first that it was I, but the next moment he had stumbled across me as I lay supine, and the oil can fell and went arolling. The noise did not disturb the figure, and Peter gave a long look at it before he howled like a hyena and brought me up all standing.

It was only then that it disappeared. "Just blew to windward," according to Peter. I never saw it at all.

Peter did not go to bed again all night, but sat huddled by the wheel, staring forward, a queer old figure of terror without hope. And I admit I was not much better.

For Peter says that it was that of a man in a dressing-gown, and that "it looked like the old gentleman." By which he means my Uncle Horace.

July 13th.

ELLIS LANDING.

We have had bad news, and are preparing to land and take a motor back. Edith wires that Halliday has been hurt. She gives no details.

July 14th.

HALLIDAY'S CONDITION is not critical, thank God. We found him (Note: in my bedroom here at the Lodge) with Edith and Helena fussing over him, and with his collarbone broken, the result, not of the attack but of his ditching the car.

For he is the indirect victim of an attack.

On the evening of the 12th he was on his way to the station at Oakville to meet Helena Lear and Edith, who were in town on some mysterious feminine errand which detained them until the late train.

At eleven o'clock, then, he took the car and started off, and as he was early took the longer route through the back country. The one by Sanger's Mill and the Livingstone place. It was near the drive into the Livingstones' that a man carrying a sawed-off shotgun stopped the car and asked for a lift into town. He was, he said, one of Starr's special deputies, watching for the sheep killer.

It was very dark, and he could only see the outlines of the deputy. But as, all along, he had come across men similarly armed—"The fence corners were full of them," he says—he thought nothing of it, and told the fellow to jump in.

"I hadn't seen him," he said, "but I got an impression of him. You know what I mean. A heavy square type, and he got into the car like that, slowly and deliberately. I think he had a cigar in his mouth, not lighted; he talked like it anyhow."

Once in the car the man was taciturn. Halliday spoke once or twice, and got only a sort of grunt in reply, and finally he began to be uneasy. He had, he says, the feeling that the fellow's whole body was taut, and that his silence was covering some sort of stealthy motion, "or something," he adds, rather vaguely.

"And, of course, he had his gun. Lying across his knees as well as I could make out."

They had gone about a mile by that time, and then Halliday began to smell a queer odor.

"He was not trying to anesthetize me." He is certain. "He'd had it in his pocket, and something had gone wrong; the cork came out, perhaps. Anyhow, all at once it struck me that ether was a queer thing for one of Starr's deputies to be carrying, and I felt I was in for trouble."

He took his left hand quietly from the steering-wheel, and began to fumble in the pocket where he had put his revolver. And although he is confident he made no sound, the fellow must have had ears like a bat, for just then Halliday saw him raise the gun, and as he ducked forward the barrel of it hit the seat back behind him with a sickening thud.

But he had somehow turned the wheel of the car, and the next moment it had left the road. Halliday made a clutch at it, but it was too late; he saw, as the car swung, the lights of another car ahead and coming toward them; then they struck a fence, and the machine turned over.

He had been found, by the people in the other car, unconscious in the wreckage, and brought to the Lodge. No sign of the other man was discovered.

But this story, curious and ominous as it is, is as nothing to my sensations today when I visited my small garage, where my car is awaiting insurance adjustment before undergoing repairs.

The point of the matter is this. Greenough has already been to see our invalid, and has assured him that he has been the victim of an ordinary attempt at a holdup.

"Only difference is," he told Halliday, "that our men around with weapons gave the fellow a chance to carry his gun openly. Gave him a good excuse for a lift, too. Most people around here now aren't stopping their cars for anything or anybody. But of course they'd pick up a deputy."

"I'm not as familiar with crime as you are," Halliday had responded. "But is ether part of the modern holdup outfit?"

"It's pretty hard to name offhand anything they don't use," said Greenough, imperturbably. "From women's stockings up."

Which was, I imagine, a bit of unconscious humor.

So Greenough dismisses the possibility of any connection between Halliday's trouble and the unknown malefactor; in a word, my absence has probably not altered his suspicion of me a particle. Or had not, for within the next half hour I propose to show him that an absolute connection exists between the two.

On the right-hand cushion of my car, which during the salvaging of it was thrown upside down into the rear, there is marked an infinitesimal circle in chalk, enclosing a crude triangle. I have sent for Greenough.

Later: Truly the way of the innocent is hard.

Doctor Hayward was making his afternoon call on Halliday when the detective came, and as I feel confident that the doctor is in Greenough's confidence I was glad to spring my little bombshell on them both at the same time. But tonight I am feeling much like Bunyan's Man in an Iron Cage. "I am now a man of despair, and am shut up in it."

Edith was on the veranda when the detective came, and young Gordon was with her. During our absence he has struck up with her an acquaintance of sorts, but she dislikes him extremely. She has, Jane tells me, nicknamed him Shifty.

As Hayward was still upstairs, I sparred politely with Greenough for a few minutes. We had had good weather for the trip; fishing was only fair. It was too bad to be brought back as we were. Yes, but if things like that were going on, it was better to be on the ground. "What sort of things?" he asked.

"We have had two murderous attacks, haven't we? One successful, and one not."

"So you class this little affair of young Halliday's with the other?"

"Don't you?"

"Not until I've got something that ties them together, Mr. Porter."

Hayward had come in and stood inside the doorway, gnawing at his fingers and listening.

"But if you found something *did* tie them together?"

"For instance?"

"I'm going to ask you something. Was there or was there not something drawn on top of the engine box of the boat from which Carroway disappeared?"

"How do you know that?" he shot at me. And like a fool I said, thinking to protect Peter Geiss, "That doesn't matter, does it? It's the fact I'm after."

"Suppose there were. What would that prove?"

"And suppose I can show you another, and similar mark on my car, made there by Halliday's assailant before he struck at him?"

It was then that Greenough smiled horribly, damnably.

"It's there, is it?" he said, and looked up at Hayward.

"It is there."

He got up, the remains of that smile still plastered on his face, and confronted me.

"That's curious," he said. "I examined that car in the ditch, before they moved it, Mr. Porter. And I've been over it here with the doctor, since. If there's anything there of the sort you describe, it's been put there since yesterday afternoon."

And then I saw where I stood. They believed that, finding Halliday assaulted during my absence, I was attempting to link that assault with the sheep-killing and with Carroway's death, and turn it to my own advantage. In other words, to prove that the reign of terror had gone on in my absence!

A drowning man, swimming exhaustedly toward a log which sinks when he touches it, must have much the same sensation that I had, as I stood there facing Greenough's vile smile and the doctor's searching gaze.

"You can go out and look," I said feebly. "It's there."

I did not go with them. I heard Edith and Gordon follow them out, and then I sat down and faced my situation.

And indeed it has passed the point of philosophical endurance. Even if Carroway's body is not found and no charge of murder can be brought, it is not hard to see what power lies in this detective's hands, backed by his conviction of my guilt. He may not imprison me, but he can cost me my reputation, even my position in the University. He can hound me out of the only life I know and am fitted for, the warm place behind the drain pipe.

It is well enough for Halliday to say that we can assume a counteroffensive. When? With him temporarily crippled, and every act of mine watched and questioned? And, even with all other things equal, how?

Nor do I see, as he does, any possible clue in young Gordon finding the chalk with which the drawing was done, behind the lawn roller in the garage, a fact which Edith reported after Hayward and Greenough had gone, or in the scrap of paper in which it was wrapped when found. For one thing,

Edith's memory as to what was on the paper may be at fault. Naturally, not knowing my situation, she would observe it only casually.

According to Clara, the only persons visiting the car after it was brought back yesterday morning were Annie Cochran and Thomas, who were there when it was returned; Greenough, who spent some time there while the doctor made his call on Halliday; the doctor himself, who wandered in later to look at it; young Gordon, who she says showed particular interest in it and a sort of ghoulish amusement, and the Livingstones. Or rather, Livingstone only, who appears to have stood in the doorway smoking and surveying it while his wife carried up to the invalid a jar of jellied broth.

But as the garage door was unlocked all night, such speculation is purely futile.

Edith suggests malicious mischief.

"The village children are chalking up circles with triangles all over the fences," she says, "and old Starr came out here yesterday with one between his shoulders. He almost had a stroke when I told him."

Her explanation of the paper found about the chalk and what was on it is equally simple. That in itself, she concludes, proves her contention. "It looked as if children had been playing with a typewriter," she says. And she has reproduced it from memory, as nearly as possible, Greenough having carried it off with him.

It was done, she says, on a typewriter in a curious jumble of capitals and small letters, and the paper was perforated at the side, as if it were from a loose-leaf notebook. Also, it had been torn, so that only a portion of the typing remained.

This portion was, according to her, as follows:

GeLTr, K. 28.

(Note: As will be seen, Edith's memory was extremely good. She made only one error in the cipher. The final number, 28, should, of course, have been 24.)

Tonight I have had a long talk with Halliday. It appears that the time of Peter Geiss's apparition almost exactly coincides with the attack. This however, does not impress Halliday as it does me.

"You have to remember, skipper," he says, "that old Geiss has been scared almost out of his wits the last few weeks. And the Carroway affair has carried the terror right out onto his domain, which is the water."

"Then why didn't he see Carroway?"

"Search me," he said, with a shrug that set him wincing. "What's bothering me is why doesn't anybody see Carroway? Eight days, and no body found yet."

When I left him a few minutes ago, he had Edith's memory copy of the paper in the garage, and was propped up in bed with a pencil.

"If we had the original we'd be better off," he said. "It oughtn't to be hard to find the typewriter in the vicinity that wrote it. And if Greenough isn't crazy with the heat he's looking for it now."

I glanced at my own portable machine, sitting on the table, and he followed my eyes and smiled.

"You've got your best alibi right there," he said, "if this turns out to be a cipher. And I think it is."

He has, it appears, some small knowledge of ciphers, and from the mixture of capitals and small letters he believes he recognizes this one. But it requires a key word, or two key words.

"Even without it," he says, "it could be solved, possibly, if I had enough of it. But with only this scrap— And I don't get the number added to it."

The idea of this type of cipher, I gather, is to take a word, or two words, containing thirteen letters of the alphabet, no one used twice. Written first in small or lower-case size these letters represent the first thirteen letters of the alphabet. The same word or words repeated in capitals becomes the second half of the alphabet.

Thus the words *subnormal diet* becomes a key in this fashion:

s u b n o r m a l d i e t   S U B N O R M A L D I E T
a b c d e f g h i j k l m   n o p q r s t u v w x y z

But as *subnormal diet* was the only key phrase we could think of, and as it obviously did not fit, I left him still biting the end of his pencil, and came to complete this record.

Renan said that the man who has time to keep a private diary has never understood the immensity of the universe. But I reply to Renan that the man in my position, who does not keep a private diary and thus let off his surplus thoughts, is liable to burst into minute fragments and scatter over the said immensity of the universe!

Sunday, July 15th.

THE ONE PLEASURE that never palls is the pleasure of not going to church.

Again, as I recorded once before, a quiet morning and I am still at large. Jane has gone. Sometimes I suspect Jane of throwing a sop to Providence in this matter of church-going; almost, one might say, of bargaining with the Almighty. "I will do thus and so," says Jane to herself, "and in return I have a right to ask thus and so."

Yet she asks little enough; a quiet life, peace, and if not active happiness, that resignation which after the hot days of youth are over, passes for contentment. And as she went out this morning, demurely dressed in the Sabbatical restraint which is a part of her bargain, I felt rather than said a small prayer for her; that she who asks so little may keep what she has.

And Jane is worried. She knows nothing, but she suspects everything. By that, I mean that she is somehow aware, after her own curious fashion, that there is something wrong with her world. She watches me, when I am not looking at her. She has an odd, rather furtive, dislike of Doctor Hayward. And she is almost criminally forwarding Edith's love affair.

Since Halliday was brought here Jane and I have shared her bedroom, and this morning, buttoning my collar, I said, "The sooner that boy goes back to the boathouse, the better."

"Why?" she demanded, almost militantly.

"Well, if you can't see what's going on under your eyes, my dear—"

"I don't see why it shouldn't go on. There's not too much love in the world."

"Nor enough bread and cheese."

"We didn't have very much when we started, William," she said, looking up at me wistfully.

"And we haven't much more now," I said, and kissed her.

But the plain truth is that Jane's nerves are shaken. She wants Edith settled; she would like nothing better than a speedy marriage, if that would take us back to the city at once. All her old hatred and distrust of this place have been steadily reviving, and the attack on Halliday has about eaten away her resistance.

All life is the resistance of an undiscoverable principle against unceasing forces. And my poor Jane, after years of protected life, is only discovering those unceasing forces.

Later: Poor Carroway's body has been found. The tide was unusually low at two this afternoon and a yawl from Bass Cove, crossing the bay, saw it floating face down, and recovered it, not without difficulty. The poor lad had been tied with the end of an anchor rope, and the anchor thrown over with him. Thus for days the body has been only a few feet beneath the surface, floating at the end of its tragic tether.

From the doctor, making his afternoon call here, we heard the details. He was summoned as soon as the body was brought in, and made a hasty examination. From that it appears that Carroway was beaten over the head first and then thrown into the sea.

"He was probably dead before he touched the water," is Hayward's opinion. "Of course, the autopsy will tell that. If there is no water in the middle ear or the lungs, we can be certain."

But from Peter Geiss, who wandered in this afternoon after salvaging certain of his personal possessions from the sloop, we learned other facts. Thus, Peter declares that the man who killed Carroway was a sailor, or at least knew how to use a rope, sailor-fashion.

And as Halliday said to me, aside, this was cheering news, for my best friend could not accuse me of any nautical knowledge.

The body, it seems, was tied with two half hitches around the wrists; from there the rope extended to the ankle, with similar half hitches, and to these ends, again, the anchor had been affixed. To my query as to whether such a proceeding would not take considerable time Peter says not.

"Two half hitches is about the quickest and easiest tie there is," he assures me, "and the best to hold. If it slips one way it holds another."

There is, it seems to me, a certain relish in Peter's account of these gruesome details; a gusto in the telling. Like the ancient Greeks, Peter's literature is purely oral, and he has by accident stumbled on an epic.

But the recovery of the body has roused the neighborhood to fever heat. There have been those, up to now, who have half believed that Carroway had been the victim of an accident; had somehow stumbled and fallen overboard, and to prove this they brought out the fact that, like many of the men on the waterside, he could not swim.

There were others, too, who still inclined to the belief that some supernatural influence had been at work; that Carroway, indeed, had been the victim of some other-world foul play. But even these superstitious folk cannot now blame the red lamp. Carroway has been murdered, by hands which wielded the oar that struck him, and which tied the half hitches which "if they slipped one way, held the other."

The anchor presents the only possible clue, and that is a feeble one. There was no anchor in the boat Carroway took out. On the other hand, there is a sort of halfhearted recognition of it by Doctor Hayward as one stolen from his small knockabout sometime late in June.

"Of course, all these anchors are as like as peas," he said this afternoon, "but the boys down at the wharf say it's mine, and they can tell two fishhooks apart, same size and same kind."

The county authorities have finally roused themselves and the sheriff, Benchley, is in Oakville. Under the excuse of examining our float Greenough brought him out, and Halliday dressed and went with them, to show where he had found the knife. On their return they stopped in and looked at my car.

When Halliday came back he was grave and quiet. In vain did Edith try to coax him into his usual lightheartedness. While I have no idea as to what happened, I can make a fair guess, for he announced at supper that he was through playing the invalid.

"It's time for me to be up and about," he said.

Benchley has increased the county's reward to twenty-five hundred dollars, and this with Livingstone's makes three thousand. As a result, until twilight frightened them back to their hearths, the vicinity was filled this afternoon with amateur detectives. According to Annie Cochran, one of them was skulking around the hedge of the main house when Mr. Bethel saw him and drove him off.

Just what that irritable and exclusive gentleman makes of the situation, I do not know. He must have learned, through Gordon, of our trouble here, but he makes no sign. Now and then, but not often, I see him on the terrace, and if he acknowledges my finger to my cap, I do not see it.

He is so consistently unpleasant that one must respect it, as consistency of any sort is respected.

My own position is rather strengthened than weakened by today's developments, and I imagine Greenough himself is somewhat at sea. Not only am I no sailor, and obviously no sailor, but I am not a physically muscular man. In the pursuit of English literature the wear and tear is on trouser seats rather than on muscles; in ten years my one annual physical orgy has been putting up the fly screens each April.

I could no more strangle a man than I could bulldog a steer.

And unless Greenough is more beset with prejudices and theory than I think he is, he must know this. He has, in addition, a slowly growing list of qualifications, all of which the murderer must possess, and few of which are mine. Thus:

The murderer is physically strong. I am not. The murderer (or at least Halliday's assailant) wore a soft, dark hat, well pulled down. I have here in the country a golf cap and a summer straw. No other. The murderer had a sailor's knowledge of a rope. I haven't the slightest knowledge of a rope, except that it is used on Mondays to hang out the washing.

On only two points do I plead guilty, and there with reservations. For the murderer shows a knowledge of the countryside, not only equal to my own, but better. And Halliday says he got into the car as would a man of middle life, rather than youth. I am middle-aged–if that be not the next period just ahead and never quite reached, until some day we waken to find that we have passed it in the night and are now old, and taking an ingenuous pride in that age.

July 16th.

I AM FACING an unusual quandary, which is–shall I or shall I not attend poor Carroway's funeral tomorrow? What is the customary etiquette under the circumstances? Does the suspected agent of the death remain decorously absent, the only one in the entire neighborhood so missing? Or does he go, with a countenance carefully set to show exactly the polite amount of concern, and be suspected as the dog returning to his vomit?

There is an old theory–I would like to question Greenough about it, if I dared–that your true murderer has an avid curiosity as to the work of his hands; that, against all prudence, he returns to it. Under these circumstances, what shall I do?

Compromise, probably, send more flowers than I can afford, and stay at home. The same sort of compromise which I effected with my soul yesterday, when I gave Jane a rather larger amount than usual for the collection plate.

One of the reporters who has been hanging around the vicinity since the recovery of the body approached me today on a possible connection between the murder and the attack on Halliday. I found him coming out of the garage, but as Greenough had carefully erased the symbol on the seat cushion, I doubt if he had found anything valuable.

He pried me with polite questions, but I evaded him as well as I could. "But don't you, personally, believe there is some connection?" he insisted.

"I should have to have some proof of such a connection."

"And you have none?" he asked, eyeing me closely.

"I imagine you know at least as much about it as I do. Have you found any?"

Perhaps my attitude had annoyed him, or perhaps he merely had the discoverer's pride in achievement, for he put away the handful of yellow paper, on which he had made no notes, and smiled.

"I haven't found any connection," he said. "But I have found something your detectives missed, Mr. Porter. I have found where the fellow hid after the crash, when the other car was rescuing Mr. Halliday."

But the odd part of that discovery to my mind is not that hiding-place, nor Greenough's failure to locate it. As a matter of fact, I doubt if Greenough has ever looked for it. He seems to have taken for granted that Halliday's assailant merely escaped the wreck and made off in the dark.

No. The point that strikes me, and struck Halliday when I told him is the intimate knowledge of that location shown, and the quickness with which he took advantage of it.

(Note: In view of what we now know, I imagine this is an error. The chances seem to be that he was thrown near the mouth of the culvert, and that the lights of the oncoming car showed it to him.)

Crossing the road, according to the reporter, and about fifteen feet from where the car was ditched, is a small culvert. Hardly a culvert, either, but a largish clay pipe designed to carry the drainage of the higher fields on one side to the lower on the other.

"Have you searched this pipe?" I asked.

"I looked in. If I'd had a pair of overalls I'd have gone in. But as the only clothes I have with me are on me–" He smiled again. "It's a good job for a ferret," he said.

He gave me up reluctantly, at last, and prepared to go.

"So you think it's only an ordinary case of holdup?" he asked.

"I think it's a damned unpleasant case of holdup," I replied, and he went away. But I have been thinking of his phrase since his departure.

How much of the present world disorganization lies in that very use of the word *ordinary!* Time was when no holdup was ordinary, and an act of physical violence or a murder caused a shock that swept us all. Is it true, then, that one cannot turn the minds of a people to killing, as in the recent war, and then expect them at once, when the crisis is over, to regard life as precious? And is this the reason Greenough spoke of its being a "queer time in the world"?

Is every criminal, then, merely seeking escape from reality?

But why the word *criminal?* Was not I myself seeking to escape it, when on June 16th I wrote in this very journal:

Yet what is it that I want? My little rut is comfortable; so long have I lain in it that now my very body has conformed.

For the rest of this afternoon, I have made my will! *To my dearly beloved wife, Jane Porter, I bequeath, etc.*

There is something strangely comforting in making a will; it is as if one has completed the last rites, and now, with such complacence as may be, faces whatever is to come. Like Ishmael in *Moby Dick*, I survive myself; my death and burial are locked up in my desk. I am *like a quiet ghost with a clear conscience, sitting inside the bars of a snug family vault.*

A ghost, too, I begin to feel, among other ghosts.

Ignore it as I will, there is a certain weight in the slowly accumulating mass of evidence at my disposal, a weight and a consistency which have commenced to influence me. I am bound to admit that, if I were able to conceive of the survival of intelligence beyond death, I could also conceive that poor old Horace has been on hand during some of our recent experiences.

Not Thomas's "George," the spirit evoked by Mrs. Riggs and still surviving in the lamp; not some malicious demon, frightening honest folk by ringing bells and pinching women in the dark. But a mind like my own, only greater in its wider knowledge, and painfully trying in its bodiless state to communicate that knowledge to me.

The sum total of evidence is rather startling.

(a) Jane's photograph, taken on Class Day.

(b) Jock's refusal to enter the main house, persisted in to this time.

(c) My own curious telepathic message, relative to the letter.

(d) Jane's experience under the red lamp in the pantry. (Doubtful.)

(e) Halliday's lights over the marsh. (Again doubtful. It may have been the unknown, finding the boathouse occupied and seeking a way to the beach.)

(f) My own experience in hearing Uncle Horace's peculiar cough and smelling the odor of his asthmatic pastilles, or cigarettes.

(g) Jock's peculiar conduct at the same time.

(h) Peter Geiss's vision on the sloop, and his identification of it. (Yet Peter is a staunch supporter of "George." Had he been looking for such a visitation would he not naturally have seen George?)

(i) And the fact that this vision corresponds in time with the attack on Halliday.

In this attempt to refresh my memory I have not included Jane's premonition the night Carroway was murdered, or her dislike and distrust of the house. Nor have I included the vague stories of haunting told by Mrs. Livingstone, Annie Cochran, or Thomas. Of the latter, they are not only beyond my personal experience or contact, but they are, if the word may be used in such a connection, apparently without motive.

With Jane, too, I feel that a faculty which enabled her to rise in the morning without seeing her clock, may be extended further without touching the supernatural. I grant her a strange power, possessed doubtless by many criminals and a few human beings, of being able to see and hear what cannot be seen and heard by normal eyes and ears. But as I grant this same faculty to Jock, it seems to me to be rather a question of ordinary limitations than of a peephole, as I may put it, into another world.

On the other hand, I must not disregard the fact that Jane seems an essential part of the phenomena which I have recorded. On the two occasions when I have had the strongest impression of some disembodied presence, she has been asleep near by. In the case of the photograph, it was Jane who operated the camera; in the pantry of the main house, it was Jane who saw the face behind her, reflected in the window. And so on.

I am driven to wondering if, in some states, Jane herself does not provide the medium for these manifestations. Whether she does not throw off some excess of vital matter, in which the poor naked and disembodied intelligence may clothe itself.

But that is to accept the whole theory of spiritism, and I am not prepared to do that; to travel with Cameron and little Pettingill, weighing the dying with the one and claiming that the purely chemical loss of weight is the weight of the soul; and sitting in the dark with the other, asking nonphysical intelligences to commit various physical acts! Putting their belief in eternity into the grasping hands of a paid medium, and seeing God in the pulling of a black thread.

Which reminds me of an amusing conversation at luncheon today, Halliday's last meal with us before returning to the boathouse.

"What becomes of all the mediums?" Edith asked suddenly, apropos of nothing at all.

"What becomes of all the hairpins, and dead birds?" I asked, not too originally.

"But it is queer," she persisted. "These women come and make a *furore*. Then all at once they disappear."

"They get discovered and then quit," Halliday said. "And, of course, even a medium must die in time. Not that they actually die, of course. They simply go into the fourth dimension."

"And what's the fourth dimension?"

"Why, don't you know?" he asked. "The simplest thing in the world. It's the cube of a cube. And once you get into it you can turn yourself inside out like a glove. Not that I see any particular use in that, but it might be interesting."

Edith, it appears, intends to write an article on mediums!

July 17th.

I DO NOT LIKE young Gordon. He has little enough time to himself—only, I gather, an hour or so after luncheon, while Mr. Bethel sleeps—but he spends that here, if possible.

Edith snubs him, but he is as thick-skinned as one of the porpoises which rolls itself in the bay.

"Why, if you're so clever," I overheard her today, "don't you go out and do something? Use your brains."

"It takes brains to do what I'm doing," he said, "and don't you forget it."

But as to what he is doing he is discreetly silent. There is a book under way, but he parries any attempt to discuss it. Also, he seems to delight in investing Mr. Bethel with a considerable amount of mystery.

"The boss is having one of his fits today," he will say.

"What sort of fits?"

"That would be telling," he says craftily, and ostentatiously changes the subject.

Edith, who has a very feminine curiosity, has questioned Annie Cochran but without much result. The "fit" days, so far as we can make out, are merely days when the invalid is less well than others, and mostly keeps his bed. Annie Cochran, however, has her own explanation of them; she believes that those days follow nights when "George" has been particularly active, and when presumably Mr. Bethel has not been sleeping on his good ear.

And as proof of this, she produces the fact that twice now, having left her teakettle empty on top of the stove, she has found it full in the morning. As Mr. Bethel cannot get downstairs unassisted, and as the secretary has always stoutly maintained that he has not left his room all night, Annie Cochran falls back on "George"; and, one must admit, not without reason.

Poor Carroway was laid away yesterday, after the largest funeral in the history of these parts. And so ends one chapter in our drama. Ends, that is, for him. What is to come after, no one can say.

One thing has tended somewhat to relieve the local strain. No sheep have been killed for eighteen days, and the altar in the field still remains without oblation. There are, I believe, one or two summer people who still make it the objective of an early-morning excursion, hoping to find on it who knows what horrid sacrifice. But they have only their walk for their pains.

Maggie Morrison, who passes it every morning in her truck, makes a daily report of it to Clara, and so it filters to the family.

"Clara says the altar is still empty."

"I suspect her of longing to lay a chicken on it, herself. There is something pantheistic about her."

Jane—or Edith, as it may be—is silent, reflecting on the meaning of pantheistic.

It is Maggie, too, who brings us much of our local news. Today, for instance, she informs us that the detective has gone away, "bag and baggage," from the hotel, and probably this accounts for the lighter tone of this entry. I am reprieved, at least until some other sheep are killed.

Later: Halliday and I, late this afternoon, made an examination of the culvert, or pipe, in which our unknown hid after the accident. We chose a late hour, in order to avoid the procession of cars which winds along our back roads—the farther back the better—during the afternoons.

In this we were successful, for although, like my own, the general sentiment is one of reprieve, there are few still who will trust themselves out after twilight. Mr. Logan, the rector of the Oakville Episcopal Church, Saint Jude's, had an experience in point the other night. Calling late on a dying parishioner he ran out of gasoline on the main road, some six miles from home. He endeavored to stop various cars as they flew past, but in the general terror no one would pick him up, and after being fired at by one excited motorist he gave it up and walked back to the rectory.

We must have presented a curious study for any observer, working with guilty haste, and I in particular emerging from the pipe covered with mud and a heterogeneous collection of leaves and grasses. Not only was Halliday too broad in the shoulders for easy access, but his injury forbade the necessary gymnastics. There was a time when, half in and half out of the pipe, I could hear him laughing consumedly.

But I found nothing, save that undoubtedly someone had preceded me into it. A man skilled in such matters might have read a story into the various marks and depressions, but they were not for me.

I retreated, inch by inch, and was again free as to my legs but a prisoner as to the remainder of my body, when Halliday called that a car was coming. I had three choices; one was to remain in my present shameful state; another was to emerge and face the public eye, looking as though I had been tarred and feathered; and the third was to retire into my burrow.

I retired. With that peculiar venom with which fate has been pursuing me, the car stopped over me, and Starr spoke.

"Looking over the scene of your trouble?" he said.

"Looking for the clues you fellows can't find," Halliday retorted easily.

I could hear Starr snort, and then chuckle dryly as he let in his clutch again. "I'll give you a dollar for every clue you find," he called, and the car moved on.

When Halliday gave me the signal I emerged feebly into the open air, and stood upright. "That was a narrow squeak," I said.

But he was looking after the disappearing car. "Yes," he said. "But I think it was a mistake. I should have told him you were there."

The net result of the search was not encouraging. True, Halliday picked up, outside the pipe, half of the lens of an eyeglass, but there is no proof that it belonged to his assailant. On the other hand, I myself had made a discovery of a certain amount of importance. Halliday had said that the man he had picked up had seemed to be a heavy man, broadly and squarely built.

But my experience showed me that no very heavy man could have entered the pipe. We have, in effect, to recast our picture of the murderer; a man of medium size, we will say, compactly if muscularly built.

Tonight, sitting down to make this entry, I have missed my fountain pen, and as it has my initials on it we must recover it tomorrow if possible. It would be extremely unpleasant under the circumstances for Starr, for instance, in a burst of zeal to find it in the pipe.

True, Peter Geiss could swear that, at the moment Halliday was attacked he and I were looking for a ghost in the forerigging of the sloop. But I am at this disadvantage, that they give me no opportunity to defend myself, for they make no accusation. Their method is that damnable one of watchful waiting; Greenough's psychological idea that, given enough rope a criminal will hang himself.

July 18th.

EDITH AND HALLIDAY went this morning to recover my fountain pen, Edith in spite of our protests determined to crawl into the pipe for it. To this end she put on my mechanic's overalls in which I oil and grease my car, and very sweet indeed she looked in them.

But the pen was not there. She found the cap of it, embedded in the mud, but not the pen itself. It looks as though Starr has lost no time!

Edith, I believe, suspects something. There is a growing gravity and maturity in her; she tries to show me, by small caresses and attentions, that she believes in me and loves me. But she knows that there is something wrong.

And she has, I think, quarreled with Halliday. There was nothing on the surface to show it, on their return today, but he declined her invitation to luncheon and went off, whistling rather ostentatiously, to his bacon and beans at the boathouse. This afternoon, while Mr. Bethel slept, she accepted young Gordon's invitation to go canoeing, and had the audacity to take the canoe, so to speak, from under poor Halliday's nose. According to Jane, she needs a good shaking.

There is, I understand, no definite engagement between them.

"Much as I—care for her," Halliday said to me, while he was still invalided here, "and I guess you know how it is with me, skipper—I'm not going to tie her down until I've something to offer her besides myself. She's young, and I'm not going to take that advantage of her."

"But you do care for her?"

"Care for her? Oh, my God!" he said, and groaned, poor lad.

Three years, he has figured, maybe four. "Three with luck." And what Edith cannot understand is that he does not dare trust himself for that length of time. The urge that is in him is so different from hers; sentiment and attachment on her side, and strong young passion on his. Heigh-ho!

When one thinks that a mere ten thousand dollars or so would stop all these heartaches, and that there are men to whom ten thousand dollars is only a new car, well—heigh-ho again!

I must not forget to enter that Halliday last night believes he saw the red lamp burning in the den behind the library of the main house. He told me the details this morning as he waited for Edith to don my overalls.

It was his first night, after his accident, at the boathouse, and he could not sleep.

"I had a good bit of pain," he said, "and at one o'clock I got up and went outside. There was a sort of dull-red light coming from the windows of the library of the other house, and I watched it for a while. It was extremely faint, and at first I thought it might be a fire; then, as it didn't grow any, I saw it must be a light of some sort."

He knew the stories of the red lamp, but he also knew I had locked it away, so after a time he started up toward the house. He was about halfway up the lawn when it went out, suddenly, and left him staring.

But he was curious, and he went on. He made a complete circuit of the building, but there was no movement or sound from within, and so he turned and went back again. He believes the light was in the den, not the library, for he saw only a diffused reddish glare, as though it came from behind. He could not, through any of the three long French windows which open onto the terrace, see the source of that glare.

Here, then, is corroboration of my own impression of some few nights ago, but with a difference. For I saw the light itself, a momentary flash as though a breeze had for an instant pushed open the heavy curtains at the den windows, and then had let them fall again.

I am convinced that young Gordon has never seen the light, or he would have spoken of it. He is fluent enough about what he calls the "spooky" quality of the house. It is unlikely that Mr. Bethel, imprisoned in his upper room, can have any knowledge of it. Yet here we have two dispassionate observers, seeing at different times and under different circumstances, a light apparently of spontaneous origin and no known cause.

Cameron says (Note: *Experiments in Psychical Phenomena,* a book I had sent for some days before.) that the production of lights is very common; he quotes the appearance of bluish-green lights in the experiments with Mary Outland, the brilliant starlike white lights of Mrs. Riggs, and the luminous effulgence which was frequently seen hanging over the head of the Polish medium, Markowitz.

But in no case is the production of red light mentioned, and in every instance this spontaneous production of light is in the presence of a medium.

In the case of Markowitz, for instance, I find on referring to him:

Following the appearance of the effulgence, usually came the materialization. Sometimes there emerged from between the curtains of the cabinet, while the medium was in sight and securely held, a large white face; again it would be a small hand and arm which apparently came, not from between the curtains, but through the material itself.

But this is no field of conjecture for a man about to go to bed. My nerves are not at their best, anyhow, and in spite of myself, I find that from behind the slight breeze which is waving my curtains, I am expecting something extremely unpleasant to appear.

July 19th.

A SUDDEN and terrifying storm outside. Above the howling of the wind I can hear the surf beating against the shore. Halliday reports, over the telephone, that the float is in danger and that the runway has broken loose. But there is nothing to do. I have just been out, and I do not propose to be soaked again.

(Note: The approach of the storm had made Jane very nervous, and I had driven in to Doctor Hayward's for a sleeping-medicine for her.)

Jock is as bad as Jane, and should have a narcotic, also! He is moving uneasily from place to place, now and then emitting a dismal howl, and Clara is sitting forlornly at the foot of the staircase, under the impression that it is the only place free from metal in the house, and thus less likely to attract the lightning.

It is indeed a night for dark deeds. And for dark thought.

I wonder if I have any justification for my suspicions? Why should Hayward, preparing to go out to an obstetric case, start me along a new and probably unjustified line of thought? Surely, of all men in the world, he has the best right to carry ether. I must be careful not to do as Greenough has done, allow my necessity for finding the guilty man to run away with my judgment.

And yet, in spite of myself, I cannot help feeling that Hayward fulfills many of the requirements. He alone, of all the people hereabout, is free to move about the country at night without suspicion. He knew Uncle Horace "as well as anybody." He is—and God forgive me if I am wrong—enough of a sailor to know and use the half hitch.

There are other points, also. He is about my age, if anything older, but he is a muscular man. And he is, like all general practitioners in the country, by way of being a surgeon, also. He would know how to find the jugular vein of a sheep.

I have reread this. Possibly Greenough is right, after all, and I am a trifle mad. For why sheep? Sheep and a stone altar! And only an hour or so ago he was saying to me, in his professional voice, "Tell her to take plenty of water with it, and not to be impatient. These things take an hour or so to get in their work."

In all earnestness I appeal to you to consider the enormity of the idea, wrote poor old Horace, more than a year ago. But while killing sheep is unpleasant, even sad, there is no particular enormity in it. I pass by a leg of springtime lamb without considering that a tragedy lies behind it. The murder of Carroway, too, cannot come under the strictures of that letter; it was done as a matter of protection.

Nearest of all to the possibilities suggested by the letter comes the attack on Halliday, and if the sheep killer did that, why not have put his devilish symbol on the car during that silent ride of a mile before he prepared to strike?

Why have crept in later and done it?

But here again—the doctor had access to the car, after Greenough had examined it. He went in alone, according to Clara, and was there some time.

Was it, then, the doctor's typewriter which wrote the cipher over which Halliday has been puzzling? The *GeLTr, K. 28?*

July 20th.

MAGGIE MORRISON disappeared last night; disappeared as completely as though she had been wiped from the face of the earth by the storm.

Livingstone telephoned me the facts at seven this morning, and Halliday and I took the car and went over. We have been out with the searching party all day, but without result.

After luncheon young Gordon joined us, sent by Mr. Bethel, who had not heard the news until that hour. It was all we three could do to keep Edith from starting out, also, but it was not work for a woman.

Tonight the search is still going on. Starr has sworn in more deputies, and the entire countryside is aroused.

Jane has been ill all day, and has kept her bed.

July 21st.

NO TRACE of the unfortunate girl tonight, and all hope of finding her alive is slowly being abandoned.

I can now record such facts as we know, relative to the mystery.

The girl went in to Oakville yesterday to do some shopping, and remained for dinner with Thomas and his wife. In spite of Thomas's prophecy of a storm she insisted on staying over for a moving picture, and it was therefore ten-thirty when, alone in the farm truck, she started out of town.

Nothing more is known of her movements, save that she got as far as the Hilburn Road, about two hundred yards beyond the Livingstones' gate. The truck was found there yesterday morning at daylight by an early laborer on the Morrison farm, who, however, thought that she had abandoned it there during the storm the night before, and neglected to report it.

At the farmhouse itself there was no uneasiness, as the family supposed the girl had remained in town. But when the hour came for her to start out with her milk delivery, and she had not arrived, inquiries were set on foot.

The truck shows no signs of any struggle, and that robbery was not the motive of whatever has happened is shown by the fact that the missing girl's pocketbook was found behind the seat of the truck, where she usually placed it.

Greenough and the sheriff were on the ground when we got there, as well as a small knot of country folk, kept at a distance by a deputy or two, and already a small posse, hastily recruited, was beating the woods near by. Such clues as there may have been, however, had been obliterated by the storm. There is no trace of the dreaded symbol in chalk.

Halliday has reconstructed the story, in view of his own experience.

"The fellow was waiting," he said, "and hailed her, as he hailed me. He knew nobody would pass a man caught out in a storm like that. He got in, and of course she hadn't a chance in the world."

He does not therefore agree with the general conviction, that we are dealing with a sexual crime. And that word *general* does not include all of the population; there are many, I understand, among the more ignorant who have put together the almost uncanny violence of the elements that night, a night indeed for demons, and the complete disappearance of the unfortunate girl, and are building out of it and their own superstitious fears a theory that the girl's body will never be found; that she has been, indeed, spirited away.

It has its elements of strangeness, at that. Possibly five hundred men and boys have been searching steadily since yesterday morning; the back country, where it happened, is fairly open; the sea, with its salt marshes, both of which would give unlimited opportunity for concealment, is fully six miles by road from where the truck was found.

Much talk is going around as to a story from the lighthouse on the extreme tip of Robinson's Point today. As is to be expected, the superstitious are making considerable capital of it. And I myself am not disposed to dismiss it without considerable thought.

The story is as follows:

On the night of the tragedy, a flying night bird of some sort broke one of those windows of the lighthouse which protect the light itself. The keeper and the second keeper repaired it as best they could, but the terrific gusts of the wind made them uneasy, and they remained on watch.

(Note: In lighthouses of a certain type there is a small aperture, running down through the successive floors of the building, and through which, as the light revolves, the weights of the clockwork mechanism of the lamp slowly descend.

It should also be said that the Robinson's Point light is a red flash, timed at ten seconds.)

They sat, high in the air, in the room just beneath the light, now and then glancing up to see that all was well. The storm increased in violence, and as the sea came up the surf beat on the rocks below with a crashing only equaled by the thunder itself. As is usual in the high tide of the full moon, the low portion of the point to landward, and the keepers' houses, the engine shed, boathouse, and oil storage tank were soon cut off from the mainland by a strip of angry ocean.

Nevertheless, they were comfortable enough, and the underkeeper had actually fallen asleep, at eleven o'clock, when there came a sudden lull in the storm. It was that time, which I well remember, when there came one of those ominous and quivering pauses in the attack which seem, not a promise of peace, but a gathering together of all the powers of wind, sea, and sky for one final and tremendous effort.

And in that pause Ward, the lightkeeper, heard something below in the tower. He touched his assistant on the shoulder and he sat up. Both of them then distinctly heard footsteps on the lowest flight of stairs, five floors below.

They were alone in the tower, cut off from the mainland by a rushing strip of tide; and no boat could have landed through the surf. And outside was that unearthly quiet which was more sinister than the storm itself.

Neither one of them moved or spoke, but the keeper remembers that, as the steps came on inexorably, a cold air began to eddy around the small circular room, and that he looked up at the red light apprehensively.

The act, one sees, was the habit of a lifetime. Even then, with his body fairly frozen with terror of what was on the staircase, he looked up.

At the top of the second flight the steps paused, and both keepers drew a breath. Then they heard a small dry cough, and the steps recommenced on the third level.

Up and up. The stairs curved round the inside wall of the tower, and they knew they would not see what was climbing until it was fairly on them. They sat there, their eyes glued to the door, and heard the steps coming up the last round. Whatever it was, it was on them. It reached the top, and the next step would bring it into view.

Then the storm burst again, in an explosion that fairly set the tower rocking, and simultaneously the electric lights in the room went out.

It was then that the assistant keeper swears that something touched him; something cold; but there seems to be no doubt, whether that is true or not, that the whole room was filled with a cold eddying wind referred to before.

I prefer to trust the head keeper's statement. Ward is an unemotional type, and this is what he says.

"I was scared enough, but when the lights went out I looked up at the lamp. It's an oil burner, and it was all right. Old Faithful, we call it. Well, you have to understand that we weren't entirely in the dark, even then; some of the red light from above came down, and I could see where Jim was standing. I couldn't see him, y'understand, but I could see where he was. And there was a third party in the room, over near the stair door. That is, he was there one minute; the next he was gone."

They did not make an immediate investigation. True to their type, they ran up and inspected the lamp, but it was "sitting pretty," as Ward says. They had candles, for it was not unusual for storms to put the Oakville light company out of service, and keeping close together they went down through the successive floors of the tower. They found nothing, and the outer door was still closed and bolted.

In view of so detailed and corroborative a statement, the final support of my early skepticism has had a severe blow.

What would be the change, should we enter another world, with the same faculties we have now, but no limitations in their use? For after all, it is the brain that sees, and the human eye is only a faulty window, which shows us but a tiny portion of the universe; the ear hears only a modicum of sound. To carry with us that strange thing of which the brain is only an instrument for our poor physical use, and thus to hear all things, see all things, perhaps even know all things.

And thus equipped with limitless faculties, who would dare to leave out the emotions? To sorrow, then, to love, even perhaps to hate. And who shall laugh at the poor ghost who, knowing and suffering all things, makes its desperate attempt to avert a wickedness? To convey, through the thick mantle of the flesh, a knowledge that is not conveyable. To stand by, wringing its pale amorphous hands, while crimes go on and unnecessary wretchedness inhabits the earth?

Nothing bodily accounts for personality. Back of everything physical, and greater than anything physical, is the mind. And mind is not an attribute of matter.

July 22nd.

THE BODY has not been found, and the sheriff has raised the reward to five thousand dollars. This with Livingstone's original five hundred for the sheep killer, which is to go to the finder of the murderer as being in all probability the same individual, raises the reward to fifty-five hundred dollars.

Today, however, certain information acquired by Halliday has shifted the scene of the search to the salt marshes and the bay, and tonight, as I glance from my window I can see lanterns moving in the marsh beyond the main house, and up and down the shore. Jane has made coffee, and those of the searchers who come up this way from the beach have been stopping in.

Every bit of woodland in the county, according to the sheriff, has been beaten without result, and tomorrow they will drag the bay.

We get a curious reaction from the men who are searching. The police, of course, see in it nothing unusual, and are prosecuting the case with vigor. But the fishermen, always a superstitious crowd, seem to me only halfhearted in the search.

The story from the lighthouse has convinced them once more of the diabolical nature of whatever is at work among us, and there is current also a tale from some passing motorist that the red lamp was burning in the main house at midnight the night of the 19th.

Coming up from our salt marsh, there is more than one who has made a wide detour to avoid the other house.

Halliday's discovery, made today, is as follows: He calculated just how far the truck would have to go after it was hailed, before it stopped, and went back to that point, which was not far from the entrance to the Livingstone drive. Already the crowd of searchers and sensation hunters had pretty well destroyed any clue that might have been left, but about twenty yards from the gates he found marks in the mud indicating that, not only had the truck been backed to that point, but it had been turned there and headed back toward Oakville and the bay.

Just where it left the road again, if at all, is a question. I believe Halliday has taken a scraping from the wheels and proposes to have it analyzed. He finds something suspicious in it. I cannot say what.

I have spent today reorganizing my household. None of the women, including Clara, are to leave it after nightfall unaccompanied, and although no entrance into any house has yet been attempted, Halliday and I have spent the late afternoon tightening window locks and adding new bolts where they are necessary.

I took advantage of the opportunity to tell Halliday my suspicions about the doctor. He was so astonished that he let go of the window sash, dropping it on my fingers.

"The doctor!" he said. "Never in this world, skipper."

And when I had put forth all my evidence he was still skeptical.

"I admit, of course, that the weight of it is rather startling," he said slowly. "But it wasn't the doctor I picked up. I'd know him, even in the dark."

"I'm not so certain of that, Halliday. But I think Maggie Morrison would have."

"Meaning?"

"That I don't believe she would have stopped that truck at night for anyone she didn't know. You have to consider the character of the girl; she was as timid as a rabbit about some things. Superstitious, too. I say she would have gone by, after your experience, unless she had had a particular reason for stopping. And I still think she recognized this man, possibly by the lightning, which was practically incessant, and so she stopped."

"You're right in one thing, probably," he said. "She had a reason for stopping."

Edith has been recalcitrant about not leaving the house in the evening, but has finally agreed to it.

"I can write," she says resignedly. "I haven't really buckled down to it yet."

But nothing is more clear than that Edith's dreams of opulence are slowly fading. Her article on "The Beach at Low Tide" has been returned to her, and the Morrison mystery is being covered as spot news by those who are doing it as a part of the day's work, and on a salary basis.

Jane has entirely recovered, and has today resumed work on her tapestry, with us a barometer of normality. She has even agreed to dine at the Livingstones' tonight, not particularly to my delight.

"Come over and dine," Mrs. Livingstone telephoned, "and let's have a little bridge. I've had the horrors for three days."

"You don't object to my wearing my revolver, as a part of my evening outfit?"

"Everybody's doing it," she said. "This house has been turned into an arsenal."

But in the midst of death we are in life. Clara, going to turn down my bed last night, saw two feet projecting from beneath it, and let out a series of wild shrieks.

Needless to say, they were my boots, hastily discarded for a pair of dry ones.

Later: Doctor Hayward stopped in this evening for a final professional visit to Jane, and on an impulse I showed him Uncle Horace's letter. I may be mistaken, but it seemed to me that, under pretense of reading it a second time, he was playing for time.

"Curious!" he said, when he passed it back to me. "What do you make of it?"

"The last part of it is fairly clear. He was in danger, and knew it."

"But the rest of it?" he said. "What does he say? The wickedness of the idea. What idea?"

"You haven't any opinion on that, yourself?"

"No," he said slowly. "I can't say that I have."

The tension, or whatever it was, seemed to relax then. "As a matter of fact," he said, "I thought it was addressed to me, when I commenced it. We'd had a long argument not long before his death, on euthanasia. I believed in putting the unfit out of the world; he didn't. But of course the end of it settles that."

He laughed again, bit the end of a thumb, hesitated, and then got his hat. "Danger!" he said. "And the police! No, that wasn't for me."

"And you still believe he died of heart disease?"

"It was his heart, all right," he said and, going out, climbed heavily into his car. He seemed abstracted, and made no reply to my good night.

I can read into this what I like. His manner was not that of a guilty man; on the other hand, it was not entirely natural, either. He was both watchful and self-conscious. And I do not believe he read the letter twice.

One of the evening newspapers tonight prints a Photostatic copy of the cipher found in our garage, and offers a prize for its solution.

Edith's memory is shown to have been faulty in only one particular. The cipher, as published reads:

GeLTr, K. 24.

July 23rd.

MRS. LIVINGSTONE has given me something to think about.

The dinner went off very well. A trifle too much food and service, according to Jane, for a meal *en famille* in the country.

"One can see they have not always had money," says Jane, with the calm superiority of one who has never had it.

But the bridge was irritating. It is always a mistake to seat four people at a table, and place cards before them when their minds are full of another and totally different matter. This: I would deal and bid a spade, for example, and wait patiently for Livingstone to sort his cards. In the pause, conversation between the women would be going on. Finally Livingstone would say, "Who dealt?"

"I did," I reply, as patiently as possible. "And bid a spade."

"A heart," from him.

"You'll have to say two hearts."

"All right," he assents reluctantly. "Two hearts."

Then we wait. Mrs. Livingstone finishes what she is saying and picks up her cards.

"Let's see," she says, "did anybody do anything?"

"I dealt," I say, "and bid—"

"It wasn't your deal, was it? I'm perfectly sure I dealt that last hand."

"We have the blue cards," I explain. "Now I have bid a spade, and Mr. Livingstone has bid two hearts. If you want to declare anything—"

"I don't," she says promptly, and starts laying out the dummy. We restrain her by main force, and Jane looks bewildered.

"I'm afraid I'm a little mixed," she says. "You bid two spades, Mr. Livingstone?"

After two hours of that sort of thing last night I was ready to go out and bite a hole in one of the porch pillars. But Jane at that point tactfully ended the game and saved my reason.

Nevertheless, the evening was not without a peculiar interest of its own. While Mr. Livingstone took Jane to see his hothouses I had a few moments alone with his wife, and I received what is to me a new angle on the whole mysterious business.

We were in the library, and I was wandering around looking at Livingstone's books. They were the usual uncut editions a man thinks he should have on his shelves, but reserves for his old age to read; Darwin, Huxley, and Haeckel, De Maupassant (in English), Tennyson, Wordsworth, and Shelley, and, of course, Emerson, among others.

In one corner, however, was a large and well-worn collection of books of an entirely different character. They were, as a matter of fact, books on psychic subjects, and as I glanced up from them Mrs. Livingstone was watching me gravely.

"If you do not know what you believe on these matters," I said, "you must certainly know the opinions of others."

"And you?" she said. "Are you still a cynic? A carrion crow?" I turned and faced her.

"I don't know what I am."

"Ah! You have heard the lighthouse story?"

"Yes."

She said nothing for a moment, then: "What about your new tenant? Your Mr. Bethel? Has he made any complaint?"

"Not yet. As a matter of fact I have talked to him only once."

"And that was?"

"Mostly about hot water and a beef cube," I admitted. "And the direction in which the house faces. He struck me as an extremely irritable and material type."

"'Irritable and material,'" she repeated thoughtfully. "And yet I suppose you know they are saying that he is using the red lamp."

"The red lamp is locked away. So far as I know, he doesn't even suspect its existence."

For some reason or other that puzzled her.

"But it's been seen burning," she protested, after a blank pause.

"It is locked in a closet on the upper floor, Mrs. Livingstone, and I have the key. What is more, I heard that story some time ago, and investigated. So far as I can tell, it has not been disturbed since I put it there. Of course, he may have brought another similar lamp, but that's going rather far, isn't it?"

"Annie Cochran would know."

"I'll ask her, if you like. But privately, I believe that if she so much as saw such a lamp, she would run shrieking from the place."

She picked up some knitting at her elbow and worked at it thoughtfully.

"You have changed since I last talked to you," she said at last. "What has brought about that change, Mr. Porter?"

"A good bit has happened since then."

She looked up at me searchingly.

"Including the lighthouse."

"Including the lighthouse," I agreed, soberly. It was then she put down her knitting.

"Why has he come back?" she asked, watching me intently. "Why is he earth-bound? Have you no idea?"

"I haven't an idea what you mean by earth-bound."

"Just what I appear to mean, and you know it," she said.

But after a moment, during which she continued her curiously searching gaze at me, she picked up her work again, with a smile.

"There is always a reason," she said. "You can laugh if you like; Liv does. But I know what I know. There is always a reason when they come back like this. A very good reason."

But beyond that she refused to go. Whether she has an inkling of this "reason" to which she attributes what she refers to as his "coming back" I have no idea.

The conversation, as I record it, seems as extraordinary as the entire situation; two intelligent people, a man and a woman, discussing the return of a spirit to earth, much as they might that of a friend from Europe.

"What brought him back?"

"Goodness knows! Some sort of business, perhaps."

Some of the humor of the thing occurred to me on the way home and, with no disrespect, I chuckled.

"What in the world are you laughing at?" Jane demanded.

"Sheer relief that that's over," I said.

It was then that Jane made the remark about the Livingstones not always having had money.

July 24th.

THE TRUCK, according to Halliday's analysis, had been driven through heavy leaf mold. But a second drenching rain toward morning, and still continuing, discourages him. Into the bargain, the cars of searchers and summer tourists alike have made it practically impossible to identify any trail.

He has given his information and the result of the report to Greenough, but that gentleman appears to think he requires no assistance.

"If you amateurs would keep out," he grumbled, "we would get somewhere with this case. Some day one of you is going to be missing, and I'll have more trouble on my hands."

From which one may gather that Mr. Greenough feels that we are not through with the situation.

Greenough himself is frankly puzzled. Whether his espionage of me assures him that my single excursion the night of the tragedy was to Doctor Hayward's office and back again, or whether he believes that this new catastrophe bears no relation to the sheep-killing, I do not know.

But the fact remains that, when we met today, he showed me more civility than he has shown in our casual encounters recently. But I have reason to believe that I am still being carefully watched, especially at night, and that his vigilance has increased since the loss of my fountain pen.

He has, in his mind, definitely connected me with Carroway and it is, I dare say, only needed to establish some connection between this recent mystery and the ones that have preceded it, to set him at my heels again.

As a matter of fact, until the body is found or some such connection is established, he has no case in law against anybody, according to Halliday.

"There can be no murder without a body," says Halliday. "The law of corpus delicti, you know. He either has to find the Morrison girl, or failing that, pin his case to Carroway."

He (Halliday) and Edith have taken the car and gone out this evening. Jane is very uneasy, but I feel that they will be safe enough.

The best time to travel is immediately after a railroad accident.

July 25th.

AND NOW where are we?

We can no longer doubt that the same hand which throttled Carroway and attacked Halliday, has brought about the disappearance and almost certain murder of Maggie Morrison.

Halliday knows it. Edith knows it. I know it. But what use are we to make of our knowledge? What effect, for instance, will it have on my own serio-comic position? Could Greenough arrest me on suspicion? Although Halliday laughs at that, he is, I think, a trifle uncertain. He feels, as I do, that before long Greenough will have to satisfy the public by an arrest of some sort, and that I am the only person against whom he has the shadow of a case.

We held a three-cornered conference at the boathouse this afternoon, while Jane slept after luncheon, and for the first time Edith was taken fully into our confidence. She went a trifle pale, but she slipped a hand into mine as a vote of confidence.

"You," she said, "the gentlest soul on earth, hiding a knife under that float there, and going out at night in a boat to kill somebody! Why, you can't even row a boat properly!"

The small laugh which followed helped us all.

What developed last night is as follows: Halliday got out of the car at the spot where the truck was found, and had Edith go back and approach slowly, along the road from town. Approximately, the conditions were the same as those of the night of the disappearance, save that no rain was falling.

Halliday, it appears, was searching for that spot, back among the trees, where the unknown had waited, secure from observation but still able to see the truck's lights far enough away to be able to run out and hail it before it had passed.

After two or three experiments he found the proper location, and there commenced a sort of intensive search with the pocket flash, with Edith in the car, to warn him of any approach, and the lights out.

(Note: Perhaps it is well to record here a conversation with Halliday, which took place a day or so before.

In that, I recall, he stated that the first man who takes a case blazes the trail for any others who may come after. The situation more or less crystallizes under his handling of it. This he claims is the weakness of the French system which follows one direction until it ends in a blind alley, before it takes up another, and the strength of Scotland Yard, where into a central office is brought from varying sources all collectible material, which is there assorted and clarified.

"Greenough's mistake here," he said, "is that he has directed all his efforts toward finding the body, under the impression that that will yield the necessary clues. That's all well enough, but time is going by, has gone by, and he has nobody. And in the meantime rain is wiping out some possible clues, and the murderer himself is free to pick up the others."

He insisted that there would be clues, of one sort or another.

"There is no such thing as a perfect crime," he said, "and of course the general idea that a clue is some mysterious phenomenon which it requires superhuman powers to understand, is all bosh. Clues are practically always trivial, because it is only the trivial things the criminal overlooks. He takes care of the big ones."

It may be as well to add, too, that the reason he did not make this investigation earlier was that, until the search shifted to the sea and the marshes, the vicinity where the truck was found was still the focal point, and was rarely without its constable, or its group of curious onlookers.)

Not under the tree he had selected, but perhaps a dozen feet away from it, he found, well trampled into the ground, a small screw cap, made of tin; exactly similar, he tells me, to those used on the cans of certain makes of ether, and underneath which there is a cork.

"In my case, he was unlucky," he explains. "He went through the same procedure, and took the cap off before he hailed me, but the cork came out. He had better luck this last time."

As to his discovery of the murderer's infernal symbol, he is more reticent. He had some sort of a "hunch" to examine the trees themselves, he says simply.

"What do you mean by a 'hunch'?"

"I don't know. Just an idea, I suppose."

"You thought there might be something on a tree?"

"I don't know that I thought about it at all, skipper. I just turned the flash up, and there it was."

Perhaps I am wrong, but his explanation does not quite satisfy me, nor, I think, does it satisfy himself. With all his keen intelligence he is strictly conventional; I think he believes it would somehow invalidate his manhood to confess that his "hunch" might have been a guidance by some unseen source.

But the triangle enclosed in a circle was there, on a tree only thirty feet back from the road.

July 26th.

ANNIE COCHRAN says absolutely that there is neither a red lamp nor a red lantern in the other house.

I stopped her this morning and asked her.

The day has brought no developments in the Morrison case, which has settled down more or less into a routine. The searchers are fewer each day; the fishermen have gone back to their nets and trawls, and today will probably see the last of the attempts to drag likely spots on the bay.

There are many now who'd believe that this time the anchor rope is shorter, and that the body, securely anchored to the ooze at the bottom of the bay, will not be uncovered by the lowest tide.

But if the day has brought no developments outside, it has brought one or two to us here.

For one thing, the morning mail returned to me through the dead-letter office my letter of thanks to the young woman in Salem, Ohio, an event which would puzzle me more, did I not suspect the lady of using a fictitious name, for all her apparent frankness.

For another, Jane has at last unbosomed herself. She maintains that on the night of the nineteenth she saw Maggie Morrison, clairvoyantly. Rather, on the morning of the twentieth, for granted that she has actually had another of her curious psychic experiences, there is a discrepancy in time here as marked as the interval between Uncle Horace's death and her vision of him lying on the library floor.

Maggie Morrison disappeared presumably at eleven o'clock the night of the nineteenth; Jane's vision occurred at three the morning of the twentieth, or four hours later.

This morning, at eleven o'clock, Jane left the cottage for the first time in days, giving as an excuse that she meant to look over Warren Halliday's clothing and bring back such as required mending.

"I need a little attention of that sort myself," I observed. "I don't mind competing with a tapestry—after all, that is art, and what am I to art?—but I resent competing with a younger and handsomer man."

She gave me the smile with which every wife greets an old familiar jocularity of every husband, and left me to my reading.

When an hour, however, had gone by and she had not returned, I began to grow uneasy. Halliday, I knew, was out on the bay, and in such times as these any small deviation from the normal is upsetting. I started after her, therefore, and was startled not to find her in the living-quarters or on the veranda. But when I called she answered from below, and going down I found her among the boats.

"Well!" I said. "And are you going fishing?"

"I was just wandering about," she said. "There's another boat, isn't there?"

"Halliday's out in it. Why?"

But she pretended not to hear me, and went up the steps again. Even then she made various excuses not to leave at once. She went inside, and I could hear her straightening the small living-room. When there was nothing more to do she came out again.

"I don't think he has cooked a thing since it happened," she said. "Suppose we wait for him, and take him back to luncheon?"

She is no actress, is Jane, and it began to dawn on me that she was determined to wait for Halliday's return, and that she had one of her hidden reasons for it. It was there, sitting on the boathouse veranda, that she finally told her story, which is detailed in the extreme.

"You remember," she said, "the night of Maggie's disappearance, that a storm was threatening, and that I was nervous. I felt queer—I can't describe it, William. I had a sort of premonition, I think; anyhow, I didn't want to go to bed, and when I told you that you started off to Doctor Hayward's for a powder."

"You had meant deliberately to stay awake?"

"Yes. Once in a while something terrifies me, and I am afraid even to wink for fear something happens while my eyes are closed. It was like that.

"Edith was writing something or other, shut in her room, and after you had gone the storm began to come up, and I felt queer and jumpy. I went around the windows downstairs, and then went into the living-room and sat down to wait for you."

"Let's see. What time was that?"

"It must have been ten o'clock; maybe a little later. Then—I hate to tell you this, William. It sounds so silly."

"I've been thinking some pretty foolish things myself, lately, my dear," I said, gravely. "Go ahead."

"Jock was very strange, from the moment we went in there. He sat and stared at that old parlor organ. I—"

"At the parlor organ! What in the world—"

"At the parlor organ," she said positively. "Or rather, above and behind it, where it sits across the corner. And after a while, I thought I saw something there."

"What sort of 'something'?"

"I can't tell you," she said, and shivered. "That is it wasn't really anything. It was like a mist. I could just tell there was something there, and then Jock lifted up his head and howled at it, and—I don't even remember getting upstairs, William."

Now, so far, this runs fairly true to form; the usual strange combination of the grotesque—witness the parlor organ!—overstrained nerves due to the approach of an electrical storm, and Jock, absently staring at nothing at all and preparing to give the storm howl for howl.

It is the remainder of Jane's story which seems worthy of consideration, in view of her previous average of hits.

She went to sleep, sinking fathoms deep into unconsciousness, but at three o'clock she wakened, suddenly and fully, and sat up in her bed. But she was not in a bed at all. She was in a boat, and Maggie Morrison also was in it, lying at her feet. After a time—she has no idea how long—the vision faded, and she was still sitting up in her bed.

Such details as I can draw from her are as follows:

"Did you see Uncle Horace in the same way?"

"Wakening out of a sleep? Yes."

"Was there the same sort of light?"

"Not a light exactly. It doesn't come from anywhere. I can't describe it exactly; the things I see are luminous."

She has, however, her strict limitations; she speaks of a boat, but whether it was quiet or in motion she has no idea; asked if she and the girl were alone, she thinks not, but can give no reason for so thinking. Asked as to why she believed the girl was dead, she says, "I *felt* that she was dead," and then qualifies that by adding, "Besides, I never have these visions unless someone has died."

This, like most broad statements, is an error, but in this case the general developments bear her out. I myself believe that, if she saw the Morrison girl at all, she saw her dead, as she says.

She saw no rope on the body or in the boat, and there was no sign of injury on the girl.

"She looked very peaceful," says Jane, and sets me to shuddering.

On one point, however, she is entirely definite. She maintains that there were pieces of cloth tied around the oarlocks of the boat. "White cloth," she adds, as an afterthought.

"Why cloth?"

"To keep the oars from making a noise," says my Jane, who has been in a rowboat perhaps a half-dozen times in all her life!

We sat on the veranda while Halliday came in with the boat; he had been out, I dare say, on some scouting business of his own, and I confess to a sort of terror that by some unlucky chance we might find the oarlocks of this very boat, wrapped with white cloth, "to keep the oars from making a noise." But they showed no stigma of crime.

"Why," I said to Jane, as Halliday tied his boat and came with his splendid stride up the runway, "why did you come down here to look at *our* boats, my dear?"

She showed a faint distress.

"I don't know, William. I just had a feeling that I had to come."

I have not asked her why she has suppressed this experience for so long. Carrying it down with her to pour my breakfast coffee, going with it through the day, and at night mounting the stairs with it and so to bed. Brushing her hair meticulously, and settling Jock for the night; going in to kiss Edith and tuck her into her fresh white bed, and then closing her door and shutting herself away with it for the night. And always with the guilty feeling that she was withholding that which should be known.

For she no more doubts that Maggie Morrison was killed and thrown into the sea from a boat with muffled oarlocks, than she doubts her own existence. But coupled with that certainty has been her dread of possible publicity, and that ever present feeling of hers that whatever power she has is somehow shameful.

My poor Jane.

July 27th.

THE BLOW has fallen again, and this time almost at our very door. That it is not murder is not due to any lack of intention, but to weakness in execution. I have spent a large portion of the day in urging Edith and Jane to go back to town, but without result.

"Not unless you go," Jane said firmly, and Edith and I exchanged glances.

As a matter of fact, last night's events have left me in a more precarious position than before, and I feel that any move on my part would only precipitate matters. Greenough has given out a statement to the reporters that an early arrest may be expected, and I do not for the life of me understand why he has not pounced already.

I imagine the only thing that has saved me, so far, has been the single fact that Peter Geiss knows I was on the sloop the night and hour when Halliday was attacked. That puzzles him.

To record last night's strange affair in sequence:

I could not sleep, a condition which is growing chronic with me lately, and at or about midnight I went downstairs and outside. The night was extremely dark; I paced back and forward along the drive, keeping at first close to the Lodge, but gradually extending my steps as I grew accustomed to the darkness.

After twenty minutes or so of this, and at the extreme of my swing toward the other house, I heard some sort of movement in that direction, and stopped to listen. It was a cautious disturbance of the shrubbery, and I swung in among the trees and stood listening. It was not repeated, however, and I turned to go back.

I had, however, lost my way, and for some brief time I floundered about. At last I found the sundial, by striking against it, and thus orienting myself, turned about and struck back toward the Lodge.

I had not gone ten feet before I heard the bell ringing.

(Note: A large bell on the kitchen porch of the main house and used in times before the telephone was installed, to summon the gardener. It is rung by pulling a rope attached to it.)

It rang sharply twice and then abruptly stopped, and the sudden silence seemed somehow ominous, like the stillness after a shriek.

There were no lights in the main house, and no further sounds came from it. I dare say at such times one does not think; one acts automatically. Someone has said, "With the spinal cord. Not the brain." I do not recall thinking at all, but I do recall trying to feel my way through the trees, and that I ran into one and was partially stunned for an instant.

The house was still completely dark and silent. I felt my way with more caution, skirted the shrubbery, and at last found the railing leading up the steps to the kitchen. Here I was on safer ground, and I crossed the small porch to the door with increased confidence, only to stumble over something and almost fall. I knew at once what it was, and I felt suddenly ill, although my brain was as active as ever in my life. "In the pit of his stomach man is always a coward." But I found some matches in my dressing-gown pocket and, striking one, bent over a figure lying prone at my feet. It was young Gordon, unconscious and bleeding from a blow on the head, and securely tied with a rope. I was still stooping over him, fumbling for another match, when a flashlight shone in my face, fairly blinding me. It played on me for a moment, and then on the boy stretched on the floor and now slightly moving.

"What's happened?" said a voice from behind it, and with relief I recognized it as the doctor's.

"He's hurt," I said, rising dizzily. "Struck on the head, I think."

"Open the door there and turn on the lights. I'll carry him in."

I did as he told me, being still somewhat unsteady, and as he laid the boy on the floor and straightened I was aware that his eyes, as they rested on me, were hostile and suspicious.

Immediately, however, he went to work on the boy, examining him first and then removing the rope.

"He's only stunned," he said, and leaving him lying as he was, began to move about the room. Just inside the door was the poker from the kitchen range, and this, with the rope, he laid aside carefully. Then he went outside, and with his flash examined the bell.

"Just where were you, Porter, when this happened?" he asked.

"In the grounds, by the sundial. I couldn't sleep. When I heard the bell I came on a run."

"It was the boy who pulled the bell?"

"I haven't an idea."

He went back to his patient, and examined the wound in the scalp more carefully. After that he dressed it, the boy by that time moving about and groaning, but still only partially conscious. I gave such help as I could, getting water and so on, and when the dressing was done the doctor disappeared and returned with a cushion. Keeping the boy supine, he slipped it under his head. Then he straightened.

"You'd better notify the old man," he said. "I'll stay here, if you don't mind."

And from the look he gave me, I gathered that he had no intention of leaving me with the boy.

I made my way upstairs to the room over the den, and knocked for some time before I was heard. Then Mr. Bethel called out, startled, and I asked if I could come in. I heard him making heavy work of getting out of bed, and finally he shot the bolt and, opening the door an inch or two, glared out at me.

"What the devil's the matter?"

"Nothing serious," I said. "There's been a little trouble downstairs, and we thought you'd better be told."

"A fire!"

"Not a fire," I reassured him, and gave him a brief account of what had occurred.

He was not particularly gracious; demanded to know what the boy was doing outside at that hour, and seemed to feel that, with a doctor already in the house, his responsibility was ended. As there was actually nothing he could do, I helped him back to his bed and left him sitting on the side, an unpleasant but helpless figure.

As I went out he asked me to bring him a cup of hot water!

The boy was conscious when I went back to the kitchen, staring around him, and particularly concentrating on the doctor and myself. He put his hand to his head and felt the bandage.

"Where'd I get that?" he asked thickly.

After a time he tried to get up, and the doctor put him into a chair. "Now, Gordon," he said, "what happened to you? Try and think."

"He hit me," he said finally. "The dirty devil!"

"Who hit you?"

But he was still too dazed for coherent thought. He improved rapidly after that, however, although he complained of severe headache. He became garrulous, too, as happens after concussion, but out of his maunderings we were able to secure a fairly connected story.

He had been unable to sleep, because of certain noises in his room. He glanced at me. "You were right, old dear," he said elegantly, "when you said the place has an unpleasant reputation. I'll tell the world it's unpleasant."

He had got up, and gone down to the kitchen for something to eat.

After that, reluctant to go up to his room again, he had wandered out onto the kitchen steps and sat there. It was then that he heard someone stealthily approaching the house.

He listened, and finally he heard a window of the old gun room next to the laundry being raised. He stared that way, and insists he saw a dark figure there. The next moment it was gone, and he was certain there was someone in the house.

He had, apparently, turned to enter the house and head off the intruder, but was struck down in the doorway. On the matter of ringing the bell he was rather vague at first, not remembering that he had done so, but later saying he had had his hand on the rope, when the blow came.

Hayward listened to this intently. Then he turned to me.

"And you were where, Porter?"

"By the sundial. On the other side of it. I had started toward home."

"Do you mean to say that, after that bell rang, this man Gordon speaks of had time to tie him and escape, before you got here?"

"I've told you the facts. It isn't a simple matter to get here from the sundial, in the dark."

I remembered the hot water then, and finding some in the teakettle carried it up to Mr. Bethel. He showed me more civility this time, inquired after the boy, and even offered his pocket flask, lying on his bedside table. There was a revolver beside it, and he saw me glance at it and smiled grimly.

"What with the sounds inside your house, and the things that are happening outside, I think it best to be prepared for anything."

So, in spite of young Gordon's prophecy, he, too, has been hearing things.

In spite of the doctor's attitude and my own fears, I cannot see today that a dispassionate examination of the evidence would really involve me.

Gordon saw a man enter the gun-room window, and was attacked from the kitchen by that man. It must be perfectly evident to Greenough, on hearing the doctor's story, that had I for any reason desired to make some nefarious entrance into the house, I need not have resorted to a window. I have keys to every door, and can produce them.

Thomas, however, who seems to have his own methods of acquiring information, today tells a fact which, in my ignorance of such matters, I had not noticed last night. He states that the doctor reports the boy as having been tied in the same manner as poor Carroway; in two half hitches around the wrists, a turn or two about the body and arms, and ending in two half hitches at the ankles.

The rope, it appears, was not brought for the purpose, but had been left lying on the top of Annie Cochran's laundry basket in the kitchen, when she went home last night.

Later: Greenough and Doctor Hayward have driven past, on their way to the main house. I have telephoned to Halliday, and he is on his way here. I may need him.

July 28th.

AFTER ALL, things passed off yesterday better than I had hoped. The detective concedes that, while in daylight it is a simple matter to reach the main house from the sundial, it is not an easy one at night. And I think he was puzzled when I said, "After all, the real mystery to me is how Doctor Hayward, who says he was passing on the main road in his car, could reach the house so soon after I did."

"He had his car."

"But he didn't drive in. You left it outside the Lodge gates, doctor, didn't you?"

"I didn't know just where the bell was ringing."

"But you knew there was such a bell on the main house. Everyone around here knows that. Even at that, you made very good time. I had only had time to light one match and see the boy, when you turned your flashlight on me."

I imagine, and Halliday agrees with me, that whatever Greenough had in mind when he came, the new element thus introduced caused him to hesitate. And to add to his hesitation, the doctor, from the breezy unctuousness of his entrance, took to switching and gnawing his finger tips.

"I don't suppose you are intimating that I knocked the boy down, Porter," he said, "but it sounds like it. As a matter of fact, I didn't even know him; never saw him, to my knowledge, until last night."

"I'm not intimating anything. I'm in a peculiar position; that's all. And you have been considerably more than intimating that I was where I had no business to be last night. I had, you see, exactly as much reason to be there as you had. Rather more, I imagine."

I was, perhaps, a trifle excited, but heaven knows I had a right to be.

"I know what you have in your mind, Mr. Greenough, and I'm glad to have this chance to lay my cards on the table. Ask my wife why I was on the float, the night Carroway was killed in the bay. She'll tell you I was in bed, until she roused me and sent me down to the beach. Ask Peter Geiss where I was at the hour when Halliday was attacked; he can tell you. Ask the newspaper reporter who told me, right here, about that culvert under the road where Halliday's car overturned; and ask Halliday himself about our excursion to examine it, and my losing my fountain pen there. And then ask yourself if I would open the gun-room window of the main house to make an entrance when I have in this desk a key to every door in the place."

Greenough smiled dryly.

"That's a pretty strong defense, considering that you haven't been accused," he said. "As a matter of fact, we hadn't found your fountain pen, Mr. Porter. I'm afraid we overlooked something there!"

Since they have gone, I feel, although he has not said so, that Halliday believes I have made a tactical error. And I dare say, in one way, I may have. I have given my defense to the opposition, and not only that; I realize that my list of witnesses is painfully weak; my wife, my niece's fiancé, and Peter Geiss!

And Peter Geiss, by local repute, is, like some of the weak sisters of the world, to be bought with a price.

Nevertheless, I feel a great sense of relief. I have at least made a hole in that web of circumstantial evidence which has seemed to be closing around me, and sent the detective scurrying back to the center of it again, to spin such new threads as he is able.

July 29th.

TODAY has been quiet. Those constant reminders of the latest tragedy, the boats dragging the bay, have disappeared, and once more we see gay little picnic parties, chugging across the water to Robinson's Point or thereabouts, laden with hampers and, I dare say, with flasks.

Edith came down to luncheon in her best pink frock, with a hat to match, and made shameless eyes at me during that meal. The cause of this sudden attention developed later, when she took the car—and Halliday—and went to the lighthouse. Over the purpose behind this unexpected display of interest in our coast guard service she draws a discreet veil.

For the rest of the day, there is nothing to record. Jane and I took a brief walk this afternoon, and noticed a man clearing the woods on Nylie's farm, across the road. We stopped and watched him for a time, and he seemed curiously inexpert at the job. But perhaps I am too ready to suspect Greenough's fine hand in everything I see.

I confess, however, to a certain unholy joy when Jock made a most ungentlemanly attack on him, and was only called off with real difficulty.

Young Gordon, although still confined to his room, is up and about again.

Today I asked Hayward, who had been to see him, if I might visit him, but he shook his head.

"He is still in an excitable condition," he said. "Better give him a day or two more."

As, however, Annie Cochran reports him in excellent shape, although moody and irritable, I can only feel that the doctor has his own reasons for keeping me away from him. At the same time, I must be careful not to allow suspicion to carry me too far. Mr. Bethel states flatly that the boy has no idea of who attacked him and himself suggests Thomas!

My talk with Mr. Bethel last night was interesting and not without an unusual quality of its own. He chose to be civil, and rather more than that. I felt that the alarm of my entrance once over, he not only greeted me with a sense of relief, but kept me as long as possible. And he voiced something of the sort before I left.

"My infirmity cuts me off from my kind," he said. "I am dependent on the indulgence of others, and that is a poor thing."

As it was the first time he had referred to his condition, I ventured to ask how he managed without Gordon. It seemed to me that the small laugh he gave was ironical.

"Paid solicitude!" he said. "I can manage without it. I make heavy weather of it, but I manage." My offer to assist him upstairs before I left, however, met with a decided negative. He was not going up yet; when he did, it would be a slow process, but he had done it the last night or so, "somehow." My last impression of him is of a helpless and yet indefinably militant figure in a dimly lighted room, sitting upright in his chair, one withered hand palm upward, on his knee, and the other not too far from the revolver.

I am puzzled over that picture, as I am over the one which I saw from the terrace window, as I approached. He gave the same impression then as he did when I left, of a man waiting for something.

As I looked in at him, he was facing toward the hall and the dining-room door, directly across, with a concentration so great that my light tap at first did not reach his ears. And during the entire conversation which followed, every now and again I was conscious of a sudden abstraction on his part, an intent listening, that made me nervous in spite of myself.

But the conversation was both interesting and enlightening. He was, through the secretary and Annie Cochran, acquainted with the general outline of what has been going on, and even of the stories current about the house itself, especially as to the red lamp.

"I dare say my statement that the red lamp is locked away," he said whimsically, "would not greatly assist the situation. As I understand it, they would simply say that this was some further evidence of its abnormal powers."

I gather that, like young Gordon, he has heard certain sounds in the house at night, but does not intend to be stampeded by them, to use his own words. He has some theory of a disturbance of molecular activity, by some undiscovered natural law, which I could not follow closely. But in the discussion of superstition in general which followed, I was a trifle disconcerted to find him laying much of it to the Christian religion; that our present theology had given birth to the widespread belief in evil spirits and in sorcery. He went even further, and classed the adoration of saints as polytheism, and the worship of sacred relics as fetishism.

Strangely though, I had at that moment one of those curious sensations which I have heard referred to as a failure of the two sides of the brain to synchronize.

(Note: Lear, who has read this, advises me that this is now an exploded idea, and that only one side of the human brain functions at all.)

I had the feeling that sometime, somewhere, eons ago, I had sat in a dimly lighted room and heard those same words. And that I had had the same instinctive revolt from them.

But the impression was fleeting and, seeing perhaps that our views did not coincide, he added that I must not believe that he disregarded the spiritual side of the individual, or of the universe. And he quoted Virgil's *Spiritus inter alit* with a certain unction.

"Soul animating matter!" he said. "It is a great thought, Mr. Porter. And I have reached that time in life when what is to come is assuming more importance than that which has gone."

Then he dismissed the subject, and went back again to the local situation, this time taking up the crimes themselves. He sees no necessary connection between the disappearance of Maggie Morrison and the tragedy of Carroway, and on this I did not enlighten him. On his saying, however, that in my place he would not feel safe in keeping Jane and Edith here, I told him at some length of my own involvement, and this brought about a discussion of Greenough and his methods.

He smiled dryly over my account of the detective's psychological attitude.

"Psychology," he said, "the study of men and motives, is a science in itself. With all due respect to the gentleman in question, I imagine that his chief psychological resource would be that portion of the third degree which consists in knocking a man unconscious, and then obtaining his confession before he has entirely recovered his senses. I would rather trust your young friend at the boathouse. At least he appears to be using a certain independence of thought."

He broke off there, as he had once or twice before, and seemed again to be listening. But in a moment he picked up the talk again. The mention of unconsciousness had brought Gordon to my mind, and his first words on recovering. It was then that I inquired if the secretary had recognized, or thought he recognized, his assailant that night, and that Mr. Bethel replied in the negative.

"At least," he said, "he has not said so to me. But he is a queer boy; moody and sometimes sullen. A good secretary, but an indifferent companion."

As to the strange affair of the attack on Gordon, he himself with Annie Cochran's assistance, examined the gun room the next morning. The lock of the window was broken, but he fancied that was a matter of old standing. He was having it repaired.

"The boy's story seems to be borne out by the facts," he said. "There were indications, as you probably know, that someone had entered by the window. But what strikes me as strange is that whoever did so should have known his way so well. Gordon says no light was turned on, yet this fellow puts his hand on the only weapon about, the poker, without difficulty." He turned and glanced at me. "How long have you known Thomas, the gardener?" he asked.

"Too long to think he would do a thing like that," I said, rather warmly.

"I dare say. And, although I think Thomas is not fond of Gordon, that would be carrying a distaste rather far, I imagine."

He has no anxiety for himself, or at least so he said; I am personally not so certain. For as I looked back from the terrace on my way out, he was once more facing toward the hall, and—I somehow felt—watching it.

July 30th.

I HAVE today borrowed some of Mrs. Livingstone's books on psychic research, and intend to go into them thoroughly. If there is any proof in a mass of evidence, it is certainly here.

On the other hand, one must remember that the hope of survival is the strongest desire of the human heart. How many, if they felt that this life was all, would care to go on with it?

Analyzing my last night's experience, however, I can find nothing in my mind before I went to sleep, to account for it. I ate a light dinner, and spent the evening after Jane retired, with this journal. The night was quiet, and my last waking thought was concerning the woodcutter across the road, who seems so singularly inactive except when someone leaves the Lodge, or appears at one of its windows.

One thing I have traced, however. It is distinctly possible that the herbal, aromatic odor I noticed at the end of the experience was due to the leaves he collected yesterday, and which I find have smoldered throughout the night.

It was after midnight when, just as I was dozing off, Jane came to my door and asked me if I would mind sleeping in her room.

"I can fix you a bed on the couch," she said, avoiding my eyes. "I'm nervous tonight, for some reason."

I went at once, trailing my bedding with me, and while she prepared the couch I observed her. She was very white, and I saw that her hands were shaking, but she refused my offer of some brandy with her usual evasive answer.

"I'm all right," she said. "I just don't like being alone."

She fell asleep almost at once, like one exhausted, but the change of beds had fully roused me, and I lay for some time staring into the darkness. I do not know when it was that I began to have the feeling that we were not alone in the room, but I imagine fully half an hour had passed.

I saw nothing, but I had the sensation of being stealthily watched, and with it something of horror rather than of fear. I was rigid with it. Then something seemed to tug at my coverings, and the next moment they had slid to the floor. Almost immediately after that there came a rush of air through the room, a curtain billowed over my face, and the door into the hall swung open. Then all was silent, save for a low whine from Jock, outside in the hall.

How much of this today to allot to my nerves I do not know. Undoubtedly Jane's nervousness had affected me; equally undoubtedly bedclothing has a tendency to slip from a couch. I have quietly experimented today. A gale of wind would blow out a curtain and open an unlatched door.

On the other hand, I am as certain today as I have been certain of anything recently, that I had bolted the door when I entered the room. But it was not bolted in the morning.

If I have indeed actually had a psychic experience, it seems singularly purposeless. Up to this time I have imagined, correctly or not, that these inexplicable occurrences have had a concealed but definite objective, if such a phrase may be used. But in this case there is apparently nothing.

Otherwise the night was quiet, without new developments. Greenough continues his work, handicapped by the usual difficulty besetting a detective in the country, that his every move is known and watched. Jane herself wakened this morning, after a quiet sleep, and although she is languid, the present intense heat may easily account for that.

We have had, however, a development of our own, and this from Edith!

It appears that this morning, seeing Doctor Hayward pass on his round of morning calls, she went to his office and, on his housekeeper reporting him out, asked permission to go into his office and there leave him a note.

"A note?" I inquired. "What sort of a note?"

"Any sort of note," said Edith. "As it happens, I asked him to tea tomorrow. It was all I could think of."

But what she really did was to type a few lines on his typewriter, tear the paper out, and put it in the small vanity case which is as much a part of her as the nose she powders from it.

(As a net result of which audacious performance Halliday now informs me that the cipher words were not written on the doctor's machine.)

A careful comparison under a magnifying glass shows this so that even I can recognize it. So there we are again.

If we are to believe that the chalk which marked my car was brought in that paper, we must grant that the doctor did not mark the car. Or in other words, that our contraoffensive is not to be launched, as yet, and that our only course is to continue rather ignominiously in our trenches.

July 31st.

HALLIDAY has found the boat.

At least he has found a boat which answers Jane's description. Today he took me to see it.

It lies in the small creek which extends through the marsh half a mile north of the boathouse, and just beyond Robinson's Point.

(Note: This creek is really a narrow estuary from the bay, almost entirely overgrown and its entrance hidden by reeds, and is only a few hundred feet in length. At its upper end, where the boat lay, the swamp ends and woodland commences. Although on another estate, the woodland is a continuation of our own.)

The boat, evidently an old and abandoned one, gives some evidence of recent use. That is, although it contains some water, there is very little, whereas, as Halliday says, after the recent rains it might well be full.

The oarlocks are wrapped with dingy white cloth, and to prevent their being stolen, or the boat taken away, the oars had been skillfully hidden in the marsh. Halliday located them but left them as they were; but with his penknife he cut away a small bit of the muffling on the oarlock, for later possible identification.

During the search for the Morrison girl undoubtedly this boat was discovered and examined; there are numerous footprints on the bank which effectually prevent any clue being discovered among them. But the discovery of an entirely seaworthy boat, in so remote a location, with only the lighthouse in sight and that at a considerable distance, is in itself suspicious.

It was in this boat, Halliday believes, that the murderer fled onto the bay from our slip the night Carroway discovered him, and from it, too, that he later climbed into Carroway's launch and attacked him.

Small wonder that the boy's face set hard as he examined it.

Yet, for one must find some humor nowadays or go mad, there was something humorous in the careful indirection by which we reached it. We made rather ostentatious preparations to go fishing. Halliday working with hooks and sinkers, and I hopelessly entangled in coils of line.

Later, we rowed across the bay and anchored by the whistle buoy, where we fished assiduously for some time. Our approach to the mouth of the creek was therefore of a most desultory sort, but once around Robinson's Point, we abandoned caution and rowed rapidly.

The mouth of the creek was well closed with water weeds, but we poled the boat through them and over a shoal, into the deeper water beyond. Then, with a look around, we settled to the oars again.

Had Greenough been able to see us, from start to finish, he would have had some basis for his suspicions of me.

Whether Halliday's later discovery has any significance or not we are not certain. Believing that, on the night of the girl's murder she was brought in the truck to the water front, and coupling this with the finding of the boat, he left me sheltered from observation in the woodland and started through it toward the main road.

In a half hour or so he came back again, and reported that he had found the track of wheels driven through the woods, and that in one place a barbed-wire fence had been taken down and boards placed over it, to permit the passage of a car across it.

This is, I imagine, fairly presumptive evidence, although it brings us no nearer the identity of the criminal than we were before. And it has this disadvantage, that the villagers have always exerted a right of pre-emption over the fallen timber in the woods hereabout, as I know to my cost, and that the trail may be nothing more nor less than that of some thrifty individual, seeking fuel for his cooking-stove.

One thing, however, may be valuable. Edith, who knows a number of unsuspected housewifely things, insists that the strips which wrapped the oarlocks are of a fine grade of material.

"Look for somebody," she says, "who uses linen sheets on his bed, and doesn't care what they cost."

From which I gather, among other things, that our little Edith has been pricing the equipment of a home.

Tonight that old sea chest which in the boathouse holds on its top the law books which were to occupy Halliday's leisure this summer, and which so far seem to be used chiefly to hold open his doors on windy days—the old sea chest contains to date the four clues which are our sole ammunition in the putative expedition against Greenough. They are:

(a) Half of a broken lens from a pair of eyeglasses.

(b) A scrap of paper, containing a cryptic bit of typing in large and small letters.

(c) The small cap of an ether can.

(d) A fragment of white cloth.

Had it not been for Halliday's unwittingly placing a weapon in the enemy's hands we should also have had:

(e) A very sharp knife, with a plain wooden handle and a blade approximately six inches long.

August 1st.

I AM NOW CONVINCED that any attempt to solve these crimes by the discovery of an underlying motive is a mistake. Nor will Greenough's study of psychology help him here, unless he be expert in its psychopathic developments.

One cannot piece together into a rational whole the fragmentary impulses of a lunatic.

An incendiary fire was started beneath the boathouse last night, or rather toward morning. An assortment of what was apparently oil-soaked waste was placed in one of the pails from the sloop, and a candle lighted and placed in it. Over this was laid such lumber as was left from the repair of the pier.

Had Halliday been asleep the entire building might have burned. As it happened, he had been in the woods near where we found the boat, on a chance that its proprietor might pay it a visit. He discovered the fire from some distance and, by hard running, reached it in time to extinguish it.

He notified Greenough early this morning, but that gentleman was extremely noncommittal. He stood with his hands in his pockets, kicking over the ashes of the fire.

"What's the big idea, Mr. Halliday?" he inquired.

"I don't get that," said Halliday, belligerently.

"Don't you?" said Greenough and, after kicking the ashes once more, took an unruffled departure.

The best we can make of that is that the detective believes the whole thing a clumsy but concerted plan, on Halliday's part and mine; that we have endeavored to show that, although his watchers would be able to testify that I had not left the house last night, the unknown is still at work.

Nor can I entirely blame him for that. Whoever built the fire knew that Halliday was out at the time. But Halliday could not so state without betraying his knowledge of the boat, a matter he wishes to keep to himself as long as possible.

Small wonder that the detective, estimating from its charred remains the amount of lumber heaped over the flame, was skeptical.

"You are a good sleeper, Mr. Halliday!" he observed.

A new month begins today, and, like Pepys, it behooves me to take stock of myself. In spite of my best endeavors, some of my anxiety has crept into this record during the last month; and not always anxiety for myself. Alone, I could take off my coat and fight this thing out, but I am handicapped by Edith and Jane.

Edith will not go and leave Halliday; Jane will not consider abandoning me here, although she has no idea of the true situation.

"If you want to go back to town," she says, "I'll go, too, of course. But if you are talking about staying here alone, for some silly reason, I won't even consider it. You wouldn't have a clean shirt, after the first week."

But, even if I felt that no action would be precipitated by the police, in case of such a move, I have a responsibility I cannot evade. The responsibility to my tenant.

I have, by a reduced rent and an alluring advertisement, brought here an elderly paralytic and his young secretary. And, evade the issue as I may, the fact remains that the last two acts of violence have been on my property. From the beginning, indeed, the most casual survey of the situation shows me that Twin Hollows has been a sort of focal point. It was on this property that Nylie saw the sheep killer hunt sanctuary; not on it, but adjacent to it, is still hidden the boat; and it was from my own float that he first escaped from Carroway and later killed him; it was even very possibly his flashlight that Halliday saw, the night of his arrival when, finding the boathouse occupied, he worked his way through the salt marsh toward the sea.

More recently the radius of his activity has been narrowed to the property itself. The secretary sees him outside a window; he enters the house and attacks him from within. And a few days later, possibly having overseen Halliday's discovery of his boat, he attempts to drive him away by setting fire to the boathouse.

I am tempted to ask Mr. Bethel to cancel his lease; to return him his money, entire, and relieve me of responsibility.

What would he say, I wonder?

August 2nd.

I WRITE AND READ, and now and then make a fugitive excursion into Jane's room, from behind her curtains to watch my watcher at work. In spite of himself he has achieved something, and will doubtless go back to the city somewhat the better for an unexpectedly athletic summer.

I have been reading Mrs. Livingstone's books, and a pretty lot of nonsense I find them. If there is anything in this question of survival, surely we cannot expect to find it in physical phenomena. Why not better accept that the nervous force which actuates the body may, in certain individuals, extend beyond the periphery of that body?

Nevertheless, it is as well that I brought away from the other house the book I found there on the desk, on *Eugenia Riggs and the Oakville Phenomena*. It is no reading for Mr. Bethel, under the circumstances.

One finds, for instance, that the small paneled room which we call the den was used for her seances. That paneling in itself sounds suspicious. But stop! It was not paneled at that time; I recall when poor old Horace found that oak paneling and gleefully installed it in what had been the old kitchen of the original farm house.

An investigation, made just now, has supplemented my memory. The photograph (Note: Plate I, *Eugenia Riggs and the Oakville Phenomena*) shows a plastered wall, and one or two crude water colors on it. Possibly the spirit paintings of the text.

It also shows that the cabinet, so called, was not a cabinet at all, but a dark curtain on a heavy pole, which extends across a blank corner. In the picture these curtains are thrown back, showing a small stand on which are the stage properties of "George," a bell, a pan of something, a glass, and a small bunch of flowers. On the floor, ready for his ghostly hand, is a guitar. The wall is certainly plastered.

An inset shows the pan, set on its edge to allow photography, and with the title: *Imprint of hand in putty. Notice lack of usual whorls and ridges.* But in spite of this rather militant caption, I find I am unimpressed. Rather am I wondering whether somewhere in the background there was not a Mr. Riggs, with a short, broad thumb and a bent little finger, who was not ignorant of the lack of the usual whorls and ridges in a pair of rubber gloves.

But it is no book for Mr. Bethel. Mrs. Riggs meets Markowitz on his own ground and fairly beats him. True, he produces a broad face and an arm which comes through the soiled stuff of the curtain. But she does that, and more; she shows, under very dim red light—and anyone who has tried to see by it knows how negligible that is—hands which may be touched and held.

"The hand," says one witness, "came out from the cabinet and advanced toward me. I could see no body, but the billowing of the curtain indicated some unearthly presence behind it. I asked permission to touch it and the medium agreed, provided I did it without force. I then took the hand and held it for a perceptible moment, when it seemed to dissolve away and slip from my grasp."

One may be sure it dissolved away! And that as speedily as possible.

But, considering that plastered wall, the entire evidence in the book, gathered together, forms a surprising whole. One must take off one's hat to the Riggs family, provided there were two of them, or to whosoever assisted the lady. Especially since the windows were "shuttered and bolted, and small strings of bells, which would ring at the slightest touch, were hung across them."

One does not wonder, since Annie Cochran probably had access to the book, that she found her teakettle moved about, and had her bedclothing shamelessly taken from her.

HALLIDAY, who is an early riser, burst in on us this morning at the breakfast table, fairly bristling with excitement.

"Good morning, everybody!" he sang out. "And how about a picnic today? Ginger ale and fried chicken, I to provide the ginger ale?"

"Sit down, man, and pull yourself together," Edith said, eyeing him. "William, fetch the aromatic spirits of ammonia. He will be all right presently."

"What do I receive for a piece of very cheering news?" he demanded.

"Who's to judge whether it's cheering or not?"

"Well, I leave it to all of you," he said. "Greenough's gone. Benchley came over yesterday and threw him off the case. At least, that's what they say at the post office. Thirteen days he's been fooling around, and he couldn't get over the hump."

"If only he had stayed a little longer," Edith said regretfully, "and somebody had killed him! It's rotten bad luck, that's all."

The conversation had little or no meaning for Jane. She was, I could see, puzzled by our excitement and unable to understand our relief. "Surely they have left somebody," she said. "We ought not to be left without protection. Who knows when something will break out again, and then where are we?"

"Where indeed?" said Halliday, and he and Edith two-stepped into the living-room, where Edith sat down at the organ and played execrably a few bars of "Shall We Gather at the River?"

"Latest song hit," she called. "Words and music here, twenty-five cents."

"I think you are all a trifle mad," Jane said, and went out to do her morning ordering.

The move is a totally unexpected one. Yesterday, as Halliday said, the sheriff came over to the hotel and was closeted for an hour or two with Greenough. A bellboy reports that, on carrying some cracked ice to the room, he found Greenough sitting morosely by a table, and Benchley at the window, staring out. Half an hour later the sheriff left, passing out of the hotel without so much as a nod to anyone, and within the hour Greenough was paying his bill in the lobby and ordering a car to take him to the train.

Our own relief is enormous, but there is much grumbling among the summer folk as well as the natives. Starr is the usual variety of small-town constable, and it seems extraordinary that the case should be left in his care. It is, of course, possible that another man is to be sent in Greenough's place, but if so we have no intimation of it.

Later: Incredible, the rapidity with which news circulates here. The immediate result of Greenough's departure has been rather to revive the interest in the situation than otherwise. I dare say as long as the police were on the case the people more or less lay back and depended on them; now they are thrown once more onto their own resources, and a variety of opinions and even of clues are being exchanged at the central clearing-house, the post office. Thus:

This morning the cows of a man named Vaughan were found huddled in a corner of the field, giving every evidence of having been run to death during the night.

(To the common-sense suggestion of a dog being the culprit, pitying glances.)

A stranger three days ago tried to buy a large knife in the hardware store.

(Later shown to be the Livingstones' new butler seeking a carving-knife.)

The second keeper at the lighthouse has resigned, declaring the tower is haunted.

(This is true, so far as the resignation goes. He has, it appears, asked to be transferred. But Ward says there has been no repetition of the strange affair the night of the storm.)

A car driven recklessly and without lights has been seen twice near the Hilburn Road, both times after midnight.

(There seems a certain authenticity in this; the car, however, shows its lights until fairly close to another car, when it shuts them off entirely. There may be, of course, some defect in the dimmers.)

My own relief is beyond words. Looking in my shaving-mirror today, I am startled at the change in me the last few weeks. The Lears are coming out to dinner tonight. More power to them.

August 4th.

THE PARTY last night was a great success. Lear had brought me out a bottle of claret, and with candles on the table and six wineglasses, hastily borrowed from Annie Cochran at the main house, we took on quite a festive air. Lear looked a trifle puzzled when, at Edith's suggestion, she, Halliday, and myself drank to "the absent one!" But otherwise all was well.

We divided after the meal, Jane and Helena to talk, Edith and Halliday for the boathouse and a canoe, and Lear and I to pace the drive with our cigars.

Lear's quiet face and general dependability, and perhaps the need of a fresh mind on the conditions here, impelled me to tell my story, to which he listened without interruption.

His opinion is that we have to do with a homicidal maniac, and that the sheep-killing was preliminary to the rest, "a propitiation," he puts it.

"Of course, I am no psychiatrist," he said, "but what other explanation have you?"

"None at all," I admitted. "Of course, if I meant to commit a series of crimes, I might find it useful to establish my insanity first. I doubt if any jury, once convinced that the murderer and the sheep killer are the same, would doubt his essential lunacy."

"On the other hand," Lear said, in his cold academic voice, "the man who sets out to commit such a series of crimes as this *is* unbalanced. He doesn't have to kill sheep to make a plea of that sort. He may present an entirely rational face to the world, but something has slipped, you can depend on it."

The supernatural angle of the case he put aside with a gesture.

"I won't even argue it," he said. "There may be something to it; I'm not denying that. But it's not stuff to be meddled with; when the Lord means to open that veil He will do it. And I am no peeping Tom."

He said further that Helena has taken up the Ouija board, and sits for hours "with anyone she can entrap," getting absurd messages which sound well and mean nothing.

"In your place," he said, "I would forget it. If you get really to the point where you think you have something, send for Cameron and let him look into it. But keep out of it yourself, Porter. It's bad medicine."

I took them to the eleven-o'clock train, and have only just returned. But I think it would amuse Lear, in spite of his hands-off attitude, to know that as I drove into the garage and shut off the lights and the engine, in the very act of getting out of the car I heard once more that peculiar dry cough, the faint, slow footfall, and smelled again that curious herbal odor which I shall, all the days of my life, associate with my Uncle Horace.

So unexpected was it, coming on top of the happiest evening of the summer, that I stood for a moment immovable. Then I leaped from the terrifying darkness of the garage out into the moonlight, and there confronted young Gordon, standing outside and quietly smoking.

"Hello!" I said, when I could speak. "Out again, I see."

"Yes. That place gets my goat," he replied. "I guess I'm jumpy, since the other night."

He looked badly, and I asked him if he cared to sit down before starting back. But he refused.

"I'll get hell if he finds I've left the house," he said elegantly.

I turned and walked back with him toward the house, and seeing him secretly amused about something, asked him what it was, whereupon he said that he was thinking of the way I had shot out of the garage.

"Put something over on you there, didn't I?"

"You startled me. What do you mean?"

"I guess you know," he said, with his sidelong glance. "That cough."

"You mean, the lighthouse story?"

He fell again into one of his secret convulsions of mirth.

"No, I don't mean the lighthouse," he said and, turning abruptly, struck off through the trees.

I can take from this as much or as little as I will. Is it possible that Gordon has heard the cough in the house, and associates it with the other sounds of which he has complained to Annie Cochran? Or has he merely been told of it, and with his perverted idea of humor, been deliberately alarming me with it?

If I am to believe my recent reading, according to tradition the discarnate frequently do, after death, the things they did most frequently in life; your hunter returns on horseback, and is seen alone on country roads; ladies of ancient time who lighted themselves to bed with candles seem to go on perennially retiring to God knows what unearthly couch, with the same everlasting candle in their hands.

But to record, in all seriousness, the possibility that they carry with them, without the flesh, the weaknesses of that flesh, is beyond my power of credulity.

August 5th.

I RETURNED the wineglasses to Annie Cochran this morning, and as a result have been attempting ever since to reconcile what she says with the facts as we know them.

Annie Cochran declared that young Gordon has been in the habit of slipping out of the house at night; that he commenced to do it shortly after his arrival, and has done it ever since; that, indeed, he was not sitting on the kitchen steps before he was attacked, but had been out in the car, and was trying to get back into the house.

She also believes that Mr. Bethel suspects it, and has been on the alert, especially since the night of the attack.

"There's been bad blood between them, ever since that night," she said. "They talk a bit when I'm in the dining-room, but once I'm out of it, they're glum as oysters."

She also suspects Mr. Bethel of being afraid of Gordon. On the nights when she assisted him upstairs, while the secretary was still invalided, she always heard him bolt his door as soon as he was inside.

"And the nights he stayed down," she added, "he had me bring down that revolver of his. He laid it to the fellow who got in by the gun-room window, but I've got my own ideas about it."

Her reasons for not telling the detective are peculiarly feminine. He had antagonized her earlier by some highhanded method of his own, and "he was getting paid for finding things out. I wasn't."

But her other reason is curious, and shows a depth of loyalty to me which is unexpected and rather touching.

"I didn't see the use of dragging this place in," she says. "It's got a bad enough name already. And there's a lot of talk going on; some of it makes me sick."

From the way she avoided my eyes and rattled at her stove, I am left to conjecture that my woodcutter—who, by the way, is missing today—has not passed unnoticed, and that possibly either Starr or Nylie has been talking. Probably Nylie. In any event, Annie Cochran, and very likely the entire vicinity, has evidently known that I have been under surveillance; a miserable thought, only relieved by Annie's loyalty.

"What makes you think he had been off the place, the night he was hurt?"

"He said he couldn't sleep, didn't he? And he got up and went downstairs to get something to eat, and then went outside?"

"So he said."

"Well, as far as I can make out, he was dressed from top to toe. He didn't need to do that to get down to the pantry."

And we had missed that! Hayward, Greenough, and I had checked up that story, according to our several abilities, and had never noticed that discrepancy. "I sent his clothes to be cleaned the next day," she said, "and I noticed it then."

But her real contribution, if I may call it that, lay in the garage, and after tiptoeing to the hall and listening to the sound of Mr. Bethel's dictation from within, she drew me outside.

(Note: The small garage for the main house sits behind the kitchen, and not far from the kitchen door. There are two methods of access to it, one by the drive past the Lodge, which curves around the house, and the other by what we knew as "the lane," a dirt road leading through the woodland, which extends toward Robinson's Point, and which strikes the macadam highway further along.)

"So far as I know," she said, "that car's only been out twice since they came, and that was to take Thomas home one time, and me another, the night of the storm. But it's been out, just the same."

"Wouldn't the old man hear it?"

"He might and he mightn't. Suppose it was rolled along the lane and started? He wouldn't hear it there, would he?"

To support her contention she showed me a number of marks in the lane, certainly suspicious but by no means evidential. It is nothing unusual for motorists to strike into the woodland along the lane, under the impression that it is a public road, and to be brought up all standing at the house.

But against all this, at least as pointing to young Gordon as our possible criminal, is what is to me an insuperable obstacle. We know that the crimes are connected with the killing of the sheep. It is not possible to doubt this. And the sheep were killed and the altar built before Mr. Bethel brought Gordon into the neighborhood. Annie Cochran has a certain support for her contention, but not enough.

And she dislikes the boy extremely. Probably she unwittingly revealed the reason for her attack on him just before I left.

"There's something wrong about him," she said. "When a man's dishonest he thinks everybody else is."

"Surely he doesn't say that about you."

"Well, he's taken to locking his room and carrying the key about with him. I never took a thing of anybody else's in my life."

As Halliday went to town early today, taking the scrap of paper with the cipher to an expert he knows there, I have not been able to discuss this new angle with him. Quite aside from the discrepancy in dates, however, Gordon not arriving until after the reign of terror was well under way, the chief stumbling-block is the attack on the boy himself.

Suppose the boy does slip out at night, and take the car? He is young, and I imagine pretty much a prisoner all day. He takes dictation all morning, types after luncheon while Mr. Bethel sleeps, and at four o'clock again is ready with his book and pencil. The few moments he has spent with Edith now and then are plainly stolen.

August 6th.

HALLIDAY'S EXPERT was not particularly helpful, I gather. We have this to our advantage, however, if advantage it be; the typing was done on a Remington machine.

As I had expected, he does not take Annie Cochran's story very seriously, but he bases his skepticism rather on the beginning of the terror before the boy came, than on the attack on the boy himself.

"After all," he says, "how do we know that it wasn't the old man himself who knocked him out? I imagine he has considerable strength in that one arm of his."

"It's difficult, but I'll suppose it."

"Suppose the old chap heard him outside," he went on, "trying to get back into the house, and thought it was somebody else. The killer, we'll say. He'd be pretty well justified in banging him on the head with a poker."

"Granting he could have got there, which I doubt, how could he have tied him?"

"One point for you!" he said. "And one more theory hanged with its own rope. Still, you'll admit it's a nice idea to play with; Mr. Bethel kills a burglar with a poker, sees it is his secretary, rings the bell and calls help, and then gets up to his room and pretends to be asleep."

"It was Gordon who rang the bell."

"Oh, well, have it your own way!" he said disgustedly. "But it was a pretty thing while it lasted. And it's my opinion still that there is more in it than meets the eye."

Aside from this blind alley, up which Annie Cochran started us, we are all more nearly normal than we have been since the early days of the summer. I rise, shave, and bathe and go to my breakfast, no longer with the feeling that it may be, figuratively speaking, my last.

Jane is at the table, fresh in the crisp ginghams she affects, and which in their turn are no crisper than the bacon. She must have been sadly puzzled the last few weeks; she shows such evident relief now. Sometime during the meal Edith, who has been awaiting her turn at our solitary tub, breezes into the room surrounded by her usual aura, pats Jock, kisses Jane, and takes from me the society portion of the morning paper, after a casual glance at the mail. Any step outside, Thomas preparing to wash the veranda, or the boy who has taken poor Maggie's place, brings a faint color to her face. But in case it turns out to be Halliday, she is cavalier in the extreme.

"Morning," she says airily, and it may be adds, "Where on earth did you get that shirt?"

"What's the matter with this shirt?"

"Nothing at all," she says, resuming her breakfast. "I just thought maybe someone had given it to you. It isn't exactly the sort of shirt one buys, is it?"

Her glance appeals to me; I am for a moment the arbiter between them.

"It is a perfectly good shirt," I say with decision, and am accused of sex solidarity and poor taste, both apparently equal sins in Edith's eyes.

It is the apotheosis of the trivial; small things once more make up our lives, and we find pleasure in them. Clara brings in more bacon, catches a reflection of our morning cheerfulness and smiles with us, and even Jock, hearing unaccustomed laughter, joins in with sharp staccato barks.

We are not worried by the uncertainty of the prospect before us; the long period ahead of Edith and Halliday before they can marry; that next year, and the year after that, and God knows how many years to come, I shall be pouring the priceless treasures of the English language into ears that will not hear; that my vacation is more than half over, and that its net result so far is a loss to me of some odd pounds of weight.

We are once more safely behind the drain pipe.

August 7th.

Edith has today received the large sum of ten dollars for the lighthouse story. While she is still far from the opulence she has anticipated, there has been great excitement here today, on receipt of the check.

She has kept a carbon copy, and has let me read it. It is well enough done, in her breezy fashion, but I find she has used the story of the so-called ghost at Twin Hollows as a basis to work from, and that she uses my name as the owner of the property. Quite aside from a distaste for seeing my name in print, I feel that the mere fact of its publication will give it a substantiality it has hitherto lacked.

It is characteristic of the average mind often to question what it hears, but to believe wholeheartedly what it reads.

I find that Halliday has been quietly working along the lines opened up by Annie Cochran. He is convinced that Gordon has been going out at nights, clandestinely, and using the car to do so.

"I don't blame him for that," he said today. "The car's there, and not being used. And—I'm not keen about Gordon—but from such views as I have had of Mr. Bethel, a little of him would go a long way. Gordon's disconnected the speedometer, by the way. But there's something else."

He thinks it was Gordon who set fire to the boathouse. He found a bit of waste outside the garage, hanging on a limb of blue spruce there, and a similar scrap on the raised walk over the marsh to the boathouse.

"Of course that isn't evidence, skipper," he said, "except as a trout in the milk might be. But the stuff's there, and it needs some thinking about."

"But why?" I asked. "There has to be a reason."

"I can go a long way for one," he said thoughtfully, "and imagine he knows I've been working on the case and wants to get rid of me. But I grant that's not good. Burning me out wouldn't do that, unless he hoped I was inside! But that is to imply that he is guilty of the crimes, and I don't believe it."

But he added, as an afterthought, "There's one curious thing, though. That is, it may be curious; I'm not sure. The machine he's using is a Remington."

August 8th.

THIS HAS BEEN a nerve-racking day. I for one am willing to cry quits, to compromise with crime, and to say, in effect, that if the murderer leaves us alone we will not disturb him.

And yet the reason for my moral surrender does not lie in any event today on which I can place my hand. I cannot say that for this reason, or for that, I am through. Discouraged. Ready to go to the mountains and come back from a walk with a withered bunch of wild flowers held in my clenched hand, or to sit on some piazza with my after-dinner cigar and talk politics in the presence of the universe. Or to go back to town and help Jane select a new wallpaper for my study.

My condition probably arises from sheer confusion. For the life of me I cannot see where the results of Halliday's search can lead us, nor, I think, does he.

Edith this morning, at Halliday's request, telephoned to Gordon and asked him to lunch with us. He accepted, after a brief hesitation, and promptly at one o'clock came down the drive, clad in white flannels and with an additional dose of pomade on his hair.

Whether he was suspicious or not we cannot tell. I know that, watching him from a window, part way down the drive he came to a dead stop and then turned, as if he had some idea of going back on some pretext or other. But he evidently thought better of it, looked at his watch, and came on again.

He made a poor impression on us, furtively watching Jane's choice of fork or spoon and otherwise bestowing most of his attention on Edith. Such attention, that is, as he bestowed on anybody at the beginning. He was what a novelist loves to call distrait, although any question about himself roused him to a faint enthusiasm. He has, I suspect, an inordinate vanity.

"I'm a sort of wanderer," he said once, apropos of some question or statement of mine. "I stay in a place long enough to look about me and then I get the itch to move on. Restless," he added.

And restless he was. From where he sat he had his back to the windows, but more than once he managed to turn and look out. I had the feeling that the small room enclosed him too much; that he felt somehow trapped. And more than once I found his eyes on me, and felt that he suspected me of some purpose he was attempting to discover.

His nervousness finally infected me, and even Jane began to show signs of distress. The small lunch party, for some reason she could not understand, was going badly. Only Edith played up well; she pushed back her plate at last, and with her elbows on the table and her chin in her hands, said, "And now, tell us about the night you were hurt."

He was lighting a cigarette at the moment, and he halted, the match held in mid-air, and glanced from her to me.

"I'll do that," he said, with his twisted smile, "if Mr. Porter will tell me how he and the doctor both happened to be such Johnnies on the spot."

But he carried that no further, and although the covert insolence of the speech brought the color to Edith's face, she continued to smile.

"There isn't much to tell," he went on. "The fellow got into the house all right; I turned to go in by the door and head him off, and that's all I remember."

"But you rang the bell first, didn't you?"

Whether because he hated to acknowledge that call for help, or for some reason none of us can determine tonight, he hesitated.

"Yes," he said finally. "I was pretty well excited, but I suppose I did."

On the subject of the house itself he was more fluent, showing a considerable curiosity as to its history, and inquiring with more particularity than delicacy as to the circumstances surrounding Uncle Horace's death.

"The Cochran woman has a line of talk about it," he gave as his explanation. "Seems to think he was done in, or something."

I told him of the doctor's verdict of heart failure, and he seemed to be considering that. But almost immediately he asked me if I had tried hearing the bell as far away as the highroad, "with a motor engine going."

"I don't believe it could be done," he said, with his sideways glance at me. "He's got good ears, the doctor."

He said something before he left about looking for another job, as this one was too confining, and the old man not easy to live with. "I only took it for the summer," he said, "and I'm about fed up with it. It's too confining. And he'd let that car of his rot before he'd let me take it out."

With which clumsy attempt to alibi himself regarding the car, he took his departure. Edith believes that in some manner he knows that the car has been examined, and she may be right.

Halliday's investigation of his room during his absence proceeded without difficulty. With my keys and Annie Cochran's connivance he made an easy entry, Mr. Bethel having retired for his after-luncheon siesta.

At first glance the room offered nothing, and leaving Annie Cochran on guard outside, under pretense of cleaning the passage, Halliday made a more intensive search. The bed disclosed nothing, nor did the closet; his suitcase was locked, and over it Halliday spent more time than was entirely safe.

"Toward the end," he says, "I was pretty shaky. I kept thinking I heard him, and of course the more I hurried the more I bungled the thing."

He got it open at last without breaking the lock, and found in it the notebook.

(Note: I find I have given no description of the notebook in the original journal. As it played a considerable part in the approaching tragedy, it deserves some attention.

It was a small, compact volume of the loose-leaf type, a sort of diary, but not regularly kept. Most of the entries, due to the complication of the cipher, were very brief. One or two, however, occupied almost a page, and all of them had been typed.

Needless to say, the cipher was the one we had found on the scrap of paper picked up in my garage.)

The discovery of the notebook with its cipher sent his excitement to fever pitch. He ran through it for the code word, but was unable to find it. Then, replacing the book and leaving the suitcase as he had found it, he set to work more carefully on the room itself.

The coil of rope and the knife were behind a row of books on the bookshelf, a packet of typing-paper and a box of carbon sheets thrown over them with apparent casualness, to conceal them still further.

So closely had he calculated the time that he had barely restored them to their places when Gordon slammed the entrance door downstairs, and he says, "If he had come straight up we'd have been caught. I could have got out, but I don't believe I could have locked the door. But he stopped there a second or two, and I just made it."

He had not time to make the back staircase, however. Annie Cochran opened the linen-closet door, and he bolted in there. He heard Gordon unlock his room and enter it, and almost immediately reappear and demand of Annie Cochran if she had been in it during his absence. An angry dispute followed, within a foot or two of the linen closet, not the less acrimonious because of its lowered voices, and of an almost hysterical quality in Gordon's.

Every particle of his veneer had dropped from him, and the threats he made if he should find she had been in his room are not even to be recorded here.

And now, once again, where are we? We have, as against Gordon:

(a) The knife and the coil of rope.

(b) Our belief that he uses the car, clandestinely, at night.

(c) At least an indication that he set the fire under the boathouse.

(d) The cipher, found in my garage.

(e) The notebook, in the same cipher. A man does not record his thoughts in this manner, unless he wishes to keep them hidden.

(f) The linen strips muffling the oarlocks, and suggested to Halliday today by his place of concealment. The inventory of the main house shows a certain number of linen sheets. If one is missing it will prove a strong factor in connecting him with the boat.

(g) The locking of his bedroom.

(h) Last and not least, an unpleasant personality. Halliday uses the word *degenerate*, but I am not prepared to go so far.

As against all this, however, we have:

(a) The attack on him at the kitchen door, and the manner in which he was tied, corresponding to the rope about Carroway.

(b) The sheep-killing and murder of Carroway, taking place as they did before his arrival.

(c) The fact that Halliday cannot identify him as the man he picked up in his car.

(d) The distinguishing mark by which the criminal has signed his crimes, so to speak, is the circle and triangle, drawn in chalk; while this is not vital, Halliday found no chalk in the room.

I have put to Halliday the boy's veiled inquiry about the doctor. It is impossible for us to experiment with the bell, but he thinks it could be distinctly heard from the main road.

On the other hand, the arrival of Hayward on the scene almost as soon as I had got there is extremely puzzling. We have tonight paced off the distance, in view of my statement that I had lighted only one match when the doctor's flashlight was turned on me.

There seems to be no doubt that Hayward was on the property that night. But I do not accept the possibility, suggested by Halliday, that as he was in Greenough's confidence he had been watching me. A man does not, I imagine, go out on such an errand with his medical bag in his hand, and the doctor had carried his bag. I recall distinctly his taking from it the dressings for Gordon's head.

August 9th.

Leonardo da Vinci said: "Patience serves as a protection against wrongs as clothes do against cold. For if you put on more cloth as the cold increases it will have no power to hurt you."

But I have put on all the extra patience I can find in my mental closet, and I am still uncomfortable.

Whether Jane has noticed our ostracism I do not know, but I have, and so, I think, has Edith. So marked has it become that today I greeted Mrs. Livingstone with a warmth that slightly puzzled her.

Nothing else new today. Halliday watched the main house last night, but no one left it. Annie Cochran reports that Mr. Bethel is suspicious of Gordon, and that the feud between them still continues. He declines the secretary's assistance as much as possible.

That he is not certain, however, is shown by the care with which he now has the house locked up at night.

"He waits in the library," she says, "until I've locked all the doors and windows. Then I bring him the keys, except the one to the kitchen door. He lets me have that to get in with in the morning."

He is showing considerable courage, to my mind.

Mrs. Livingstone was slightly ruffled on her arrival. It appears she had tried to leave her cards and Livingstone's on the old gentleman at the main house, but was finally compelled to put them under the door, although she could hear voices in the library.

But she recovered sufficiently to tell us a new story, illustrative of the general state of the local mind. She says that three nights ago Hadly, who keeps the hardware store in Oakville, when passing the cemetery where Carroway is buried, saw a figure walking slowly past the grave. It stopped, looked at the mound, and then moved on, fading into nothing at the clump of evergreens beyond it.

Hadly seems to have made no further investigation!

It is unfortunate, however, that Edith's story appeared today, evidently syndicated and receiving wide publicity. The confirmation is sufficient to send off most of the summer visitors, looking back over their shoulders, like Hadly, as they run.

August 10th.

AT MIDNIGHT last night Halliday wakened me by throwing pebbles against the screen of my window. He was standing close underneath, and asked me to put on something and work my way quietly toward the other house.

"What's wrong?" I asked.

"He's getting ready to go out, I think. He put his light out at eleven, and turned it on again a few minutes ago."

Halliday moved away, and as quickly as possible I dressed and followed him. He was under the trees, waiting, when I joined him, and together we worked quietly across the garden and toward the garage, coming out beyond it, toward the lane. Here, while concealed ourselves, we had a full view of the house, but the light was out again and for a time it looked as though nothing more were to happen.

Halliday's plan was as follows: In case Gordon took the car, I was to follow it on foot at a safe distance as he went along the lane, while Halliday himself ran for my car. He would meet me at the fork in the road, and I would be able to tell him which of the two roads Gordon had taken.

We stood together, well hidden in the shrubbery, for some time. A slight wind had come up, and we could hear small waves lapping against the piles of the pier, and the monotonous wail of the whistling buoy beyond Robinson's Point, always an eerie sound. Halliday, who has not had much sleep for a night or two, fell to yawning, and I was not much better off, when I heard some sort of stealthy movement in the woodland to our left. I touched Halliday on the arm, to find him rigid and bending forward, staring toward the house.

"He's coming," he said. "Quiet!" The boy was raising his window screen, with all possible caution. Even when it was accomplished he stood so long, probably listening and watching, that I began to think he had changed his mind and gone back to bed, but as events showed, he had done nothing of the sort.

Up to this moment I had not suspected the use of the rope, although I believe Halliday had. I know my gaze was fixed on the kitchen door, with now and then a glance at the windows of the laundry and the gun room; or rather, in their direction. The darkness was extreme. But now I heard a faint scraping against the wall of the house itself and realized that he was coming down by means of the rope.

His coming was as stealthy as the preliminaries had been. He was probably halfway down, coming hand over hand before I had interpreted the sound.

I was not even aware that he had reached the ground, when I saw him, a blacker shadow among other shadows, near at hand. But he did not come directly toward the garage; he walked along under the walls of the west wing to the gun-room window and stood there. Then, with extreme caution, he raised it an inch or two, as if to reassure himself that it had been unlocked from within, and closed it again.

From there, with somewhat less caution, he moved to the corner of the house and seemed to be surveying the water front and the boathouse. We had our only real view of him then, as he stood silhouetted on the top of the rise. (Note: The main house stands, as I think I have already recorded, rather higher than the remainder of the property.) But suddenly something alarmed him. Neither Halliday nor I saw or heard anything, but evidently he did, and realized, too, his exposed position.

He dropped to the ground. So unexpected was his sudden disappearance, that I gasped; it was not until I heard him creeping along the ground that I understood his maneuver. He lost no time in his retreat, nor did he attempt to use the rope again. He raised the unlocked window, crept over the sill, and closed it again, all with surprising rapidity and silence, and sooner than we could have expected we heard him drawing up the rope from his room overhead.

No interpretation of this is possible without taking into consideration the really horrible stealth of the boy's manner. He was engaged on some nefarious business of his own, whether we can connect that with the crimes or not.

As to the extremely dramatic manner in which he chose to escape from the house, when he had already unlocked the gun-room window, Halliday is divided between two theories, of which he himself favors the second.

"He may be merely dramatizing himself; you'll find a certain type of degenerate mind which is always acting for its own benefit. Or—and this is more likely—our old friend Bethel is suspicious and is watching him. The old man's door commands his. He locks his door from the inside, uses his rope, and is free to go where he pleases.

"But," he added, after a pause, "he unlocks the gun-room window, too, so he can beat a retreat if he has to. That's the best I can do, and if it isn't correct it ought to be!"

Today I am convinced beyond doubt that Gordon is our criminal, and I think even Halliday is shaken. I am no detective, but it seems to me that the boy, coming here during the height of the excitement about the sheep killer and young Carroway, found the way already paved for a career of secret crime, and adopting the methods and the symbol of some still undiscovered religious maniac, has carried on, one may say, under his banner.

My psychiatric friends have discussed with me the neurotic aftermath of the war; the search for the sensational, the wooing of fugitive and secret pleasures, often brutal and violent; and the apotheosis of the criminal. They quote, too, Von Krafft-Ebing's theory that the instinct to kill is purely a legacy from the past, atavistic and more or less nondeliberate. In other words, that killing is inherent in all of us, and that to the ill-balanced the destruction of the artificial inhibition, from any cause, turns them loose on the world, hereditary slayers and doers of violence.

It would, accepting that, be possible to see in young Gordon the heir, not only to his own past, but to the crimes which preceded his arrival here; to see also that gradual process of identification by which he assumed his predecessor's attributes and even the symbol by which he signed his deeds. I believe that in such cases the mental degeneration sometimes continues to the point of complete loss of personality; in that case, accepting this theory, it may even be that the boy now believes that he killed Carroway, and takes a secret and gloating pleasure in it.

A theory which I shall be happy to place at Greenough's disposal, if the opportunity arrives. It should be one after his own heart.

Certainly one fact at least supports the idea. Halliday may be right, and the attack on him not have been made by Gordon. But there seems no reason to doubt that, sometime on the day before we got back, he crept into my garage and put the infernal symbol where we found it.

We have discussed today at some length the desirability of notifying the police once more. But our recent experience with them is not reassuring. On the other hand, I feel strongly that Mr. Bethel should be warned. But Halliday argues against it.

"He knows something already," he says. "He is on guard, and the boy knows it. Then you have to remember that the game, so far, has been to strike in the dark, and run. That is, if you are correct, skipper, and it *is* a game, without motive."

Probably he is right. There would be little chance for him if he attacked the old man; he is too well known to be on bad terms with him. Such a warning, also, might alarm Mr. Bethel to the point of getting rid of him, and after all the only chance we have is to let him go a certain length, and then, with our proofs, call in the police.

But I am very uneasy tonight as I make this entry. I have not Halliday's easy optimism that he "won't get away with anything without our knowing it."

August 11th.

TODAY IS BRIGHT AND SUNNY, and I am in a better mood. Edith came down this morning to an enormous stack of mail, and stared at it incredulously.

"Great heavens," she said, "not *bills!*"

As it turned out, however, they were not bills. Her article has brought out a curious fact; almost everybody has a ghost story, and is anxious to tell it to somebody else; even the most incredulous of us, apparently, has some incident stored in his memory not capable of explanation. And a visible percentage of these victims of thrills and shivers have written to her about the ghost in the light tower.

She and Halliday are reading them on the veranda at this moment. Each has a heap of them, and such bits as this are to be heard:

"Here's a wonder," says Halliday. "Hold my hand, won't you, while I read it to you? There's some ghostly thing touching my neck at this minute."

"It's a spider," says Edith coolly. "You can wait. Listen to this!" And so on.

Which reminds me that I had a visit last night from "Cuckoo" Hadly, our village Don Juan, who sells hardware over his counter to pretty village matrons, and who was dubbed "Cuckoo" some years ago by a summer visitor who saw a resemblance to Byron in him, and evidently knew the quotation.

(Note: "The cuckoo shows melancholia, not madness. Like Byron, he goes about wailing his sad lot, and now and then dropping an egg into someone else's nest.")

Hadly was slightly sheepish. He knows, and he knows I know, that his road home at night lies nowhere near the cemetery. At the same time, he had something to tell me, and was determined to go through with it.

"I guess you've heard the story, Mr. Porter," he said. "I don't suppose I'll ever hear the last of it. But there's a mistake being made, and I thought if Miss Edith was going to write it up, we'd better have it straight."

It appears, then, that it was not near Carroway's grave that Hadly saw the figure, but in the old part of the cemetery, and that there are some facts which he has not given out.

The cemetery is surrounded by a white fence, and inside it is shrubbery. Hadly, it seems, was not alone, but was standing in the road, "talking to a friend." If, as I imagine, the friend was a woman, it was surely a safe place for the rendezvous!

It was the "friend" who saw the light, and who accounts for the suppression of this portion of the tale. It shone through the shrubbery, a small blue-white light about two feet from the ground, and directly in front of the headstone of one George Pierce, who died in the late seventeen hundreds.

Hadly did not see the light, but the "friend" persisting, he crept through the shrubbery to take a look around. It was then that he saw the figure, moving slowly and deliberately toward the trees.

He seems to have no doubt that he saw an apparition, or that the information belongs to me, the reason he gives for the latter being that George Pierce is the gentleman who was, according to local tradition, shot and killed while attempting to escape the Excise in the old farmhouse which is now a part of Twin Hollows.

I have entered this here, because the day seems given over to the supernatural. We have breakfasted with the spirit world, and seem about to lunch with it.

Everything continues quiet at the other house.

Jane and I today returned the Livingstones' call. Although it seems absurd, I have never quite abandoned the hope of finding, in Uncle Horace's unfinished letter, a clue to the present mystery.

I therefore took it with me, hoping for an opportunity to show it to Mrs. Livingstone. But none came. Doctor Hayward was there when we arrived and remained after we left. Perhaps, because my own world is awry, I think the universe is so.

But it seemed to me that we were shown in to what almost amounted to a situation; that Livingstone, usually dapper and calm, was flushed, and that Mrs. Livingstone was on the verge of tears. The doctor, standing by the window, hardly acknowledged our entrance, and remained standing, glowering and biting his fingers, until we left.

He is, I understand, soon to leave for a holiday.

August 12th.

(No entry.)

August 13th.

(No entry.)

August 14th.

TOMORROW Hayward says I shall be able to see Greenough; the first intimation I have had that he is back in the neighborhood.

But I feel that my consciousness of my own innocence will be as nothing against Greenough's sheer determination to prove me guilty. And yet, guilty of what? Of a bullet buried in the floor of my own house, and a broken window! We have had no further crime. Nothing is altered, save my own feeling that a net is closing around me, and that some malignant fate is sitting spider-fashion in the center of it, waiting to pounce on me and destroy me.

Yesterday, being allowed to read, I found that with the single exception of the red light, my experience is fairly true to type in such matters; thousands of people have apparently gone through the same sort of thing, and have been neither the better nor the worse for it afterward.

They saw, they believed, and then dismissed it, to be dug up out of their memories later to assist somebody to write a book, or to entertain a dinner table. But in my case, what?

My only hope, apparently, is to convince Greenough that I saw this thing; to show him the steps by which I was led to fire the shot; to put him, if I can, in my place for an hour or two.

Suppose, like a lawyer preparing a brief, I make my statement here, and tomorrow read it to him? At least I can make this entry full and explicit. It passes the time, and he may be willing to listen.

This is the 14th. It was, then, the early evening of the 11th, when Annie Cochran stopped at the Lodge on her way home and asked to see me at the kitchen door.

"I'm leaving, Mr. Porter," she said. "I don't like to make trouble for you, but I can't stand that secretary."

"What has he done, Annie?"

"Done!" she said, and sniffed. "He's watching me, for one thing. I never go upstairs but he's at my heels. But that's not all. He's going to make trouble for Mr. Bethel. You mark my words. And Mr. Bethel knows it; he's scared tonight."

There had been a quarrel, she said, at dinner, carefully camouflaged while she was in the room, but breaking out again the moment she left it. So far as she could make out, it had to do with the secretary's leaving the house at night, and his insistence that he go out when and how he liked. But there was something beneath that, she thought. "That wasn't enough for the fuss they were making," she said. "There was murder in that boy's face, Mr. Porter."

Mr. Bethel, she thought, was trying to quiet him, but he refused to be quieted. Finally Gordon got up and flung open the pantry door, finding her inside it, and he said, according to her, "Listening, are you? Well, you'd better watch out, or you'll get something you don't expect." Then he went into the hall, got his hat, and slammed out of the house, leaving the paralytic sunk in his chair.

"He's gone? Where?"

"He didn't say. He just took the car and went."

She was uneasy; she had construed what he said as a threat against her of a serious sort, and I drove her into Oakville myself. On the way I tried to persuade her to return to her employment for a time at least, on the ground that we might need her, and she finally agreed.

It was perhaps nine o'clock when I returned, to find the rector and his wife calling, and to sit through an hour and a half of gently unctuous conversation, while my uneasiness constantly increased, and my sense of guilt and responsibility. If we had warned the old man he would have been at least prepared to take care of himself in an emergency, but we had foolishly kept our knowledge to ourselves, and even allowing for exaggeration on Annie Cochran's part, there seemed no doubt that such an emergency might be at hand.

At 10:30 our visitors took their departure, and leaving Jane prepared to retire and Edith to answer some of her letters, I wandered with apparent aimlessness down to the boathouse. Halliday was not there, and as the dory was missing I knew he was somewhere out on the water. After waiting until eleven, my restlessness was extreme and I walked up and around the main house, to find the garage doors open and the car still out.

Had there been any indication of life in the building, I think I would have wakened Mr. Bethel and warned him; stayed with him, perhaps, until that murderous young devil was safely settled for the night. But his room was dark and his windows closed, so I thought better of it. But I did ascertain that the gun-room windows were locked, and that if the boy effected an entrance at all, it would be by some less surreptitious method.

Thus reassured, I went back to the boathouse, and soon after, Halliday rowed quietly in and tied the dory. He had rowed up, he said, to see if the boat was still there. It had not been disturbed, so far as he could tell.

I told him my story, but he was less anxious than I had expected.

"It's not the game," he said. "If Gordon is the killer, we've got to consider that he doesn't kill out of anger. That's different. He's cool and deliberate; he plans his stuff ahead and goes through with it. I don't even think he gets any thrill out of crime itself; the real secret joy is in baffling discovery. And he knows this—after the quarrel tonight, if old Bethel fell down the stairs and broke his neck, he would be blamed for it."

But he thrust his service revolver in his pocket nevertheless, and we started toward the house, with no particular plan in mind, but a fixed determination to protect Mr. Bethel "in case of any trouble," as Halliday put it.

We had almost reached the end of the walk over the marsh when he halted suddenly and stared to the right.

"There was a light over there," he said. "In the woods. Wait a minute; maybe it will show again."

It did show, above the head of Robinson's Point apparently, in that lonely strip of woodland which leads to the hiding-place of the boat.

(Note: In explanation of our conclusion, that we had seen one of the lights of the car as Gordon drove down through the trees, I can only give again the difficulty of distinguishing at night a small light comparatively close at hand from a large one some distance away.)

Halliday watched it, and then passed his revolver to me, first taking off the safety catch.

"Don't fall over anything," he warned me. "And don't shoot until you see the whites of his eyes! I'm going over there, skipper."

He set off on a steady lope, heading for the light but obliged to make a long detour around the marsh. I myself, holding the revolver gingerly, started on to the house.

I was feeling, comparatively speaking, relaxed. I felt, as did Halliday, that Gordon was near Robinson's Point; my duty, as I saw it, was simply to stand guard until Halliday returned and we could make some plan; in case of trouble later to get into the house, if possible.

This thought, that we might want to get into the house, bothered me. My keys were at the Lodge, and I could hardly hope to secure them without disturbing Jane. I made, as a result, another round of the windows, and was brought up short by the fact that one of the gun-room windows, certainly closed and locked before, now stood open.

It was the more startling, because I had but that moment ascertained that the garage doors still stood wide, and that the car was still missing.

I dare say every man has occasional doubts of his physical courage; I know that on reading of the sinking of the Titanic, I was obsessed with the fear that I might have fought like a demon to get into a lifeboat. But I dare say, too, that every man has a sort of spare reservoir of courage, on which he can draw in the emergency, when it comes. Yet I shall not pretend, even to myself, that I pulled up my shoulders, examined my weapon, and then boldly entered that window.

I crawled in, with knees that shook under me and a definite nausea in the pit of my stomach. And to make matters worse there was a slow footstep somewhere near, which I was a second or so in identifying as a drip from the old shower next door.

I had no doubt whatever that Gordon had returned, and the very fact that he had come without the car made that return sinister. I groped for the door into the passage and stood there listening, but there was no sound whatever, save the leak of the tap; I remember that as I passed the open door of the shower room I looked in, and a gleaming eye nearly lost me my equilibrium, until I remembered Edith's piece of phosphorescent wood. All this, it must be noted, was in complete darkness.

I reached the dining-room without incident, and there a new thought struck me. Annie Cochran had represented the old gentleman as distinctly alarmed, and I myself had seen him some time before, more or less on guard, with a revolver. Suppose he saw a strange figure emerge from his dining-room and start up the staircase? It seemed to me that he would have every right to shoot me first and investigate me afterward.

It was while I hesitated there, near the sideboard, that I was first conscious of a cold air blowing around me. So distinct was it that my first thought was that some stealthy movement had opened the door to the passage behind me. Almost immediately on that there was a tremendous crash as though some heavy object had struck the dining-room table, and following that the door into the hall burst open, slamming back against the wall outside. This was followed by complete silence.

So shaken were my nerves by all this that my next consecutive thinking found me once more in the gun room, ready to beat a retreat. But here I managed somehow to pull myself together, and to return to my original errand in the house. Convinced that the slamming of the door would have roused Mr. Bethel—if indeed anything were to rouse him again; and by this time, shaken as I was, I was prepared for the worst—the main staircase was not feasible.

I made my way, therefore, into the passage again to the servants' staircase and crept up it, one stair at a time, with the revolver clutched in my hand.

I have no idea how long all this took. Possibly ten minutes from the time I entered the house. Perhaps even more. I was subconsciously aware, I know, that it was too soon to look for Halliday's return, and in a way I was playing for time.

At the top of the kitchen staircase was a door, opening onto the main hall, and this I cautiously opened.

Save for the ticking of the tall clock on the staircase landing the house was entirely silent. The silence and the closed door gave me back my ebbing courage, and I advanced a step or two along the hall. Here I was close to Gordon's room, and I felt for and tried the knob carefully. It was locked, and listening outside I could hear no movement from within. The relief I gathered from this was enormous, and although my position was still unpleasant enough, the fear of tragedy began to leave me.

There remained, I figured, merely to ascertain that Mr. Bethel's door was closed and locked, and I could beat a retreat which I felt was by no means ignominious. I made my way, therefore, to his door and tried it. It was fastened, also, and I heard him move within; the heavy creak of his bed spring, no doubt as he lay uneasily awake, waiting for the boy's return.

I hesitated there, wondering whether to call to him and tell him he was not alone and helpless, or to retire, satisfied that he was awake and prepared for any trouble that might come. But there were no further sounds from beyond the door, and I turned away and prepared to retrace my steps.

It was then that I became conscious of a light somewhere below. Not a light, rather, but where before had been absolute darkness there was now something else; a faint illumination which outlined the staircase well, and which was reddish in color.

(Note: It is worthy of consideration that when, later on, Halliday and I made our experiment with the red lamp, lighting it in the den and opening the door into the corridor, we secured much the same effect, save that in the experiment the resulting glow seemed stronger than the one recorded here.)

And I will swear that a figure was standing at the foot of the stairs, apparently facing toward me and looking up. Or rather, not a figure, but a face; the light was so faint that no portions of the body were visible. I will swear that it moved, not toward the dining-room and a possible exit by the window of the gun room, as Halliday suggests, but still upturned, toward the library, and that within a foot or two of that door it disappeared.

I will swear that the red glow persisted for a moment or so after that disappeared and then slowly faded away. And I will also swear that I had no more intention of firing my revolver at that figure than I had of leaping down the staircase after it. Mr. Greenough would have done no less, in my situation, and might very possibly have done considerably more. The first knowledge that I had pulled the trigger came with the sound of the shot itself. I was certainly not aiming at the figure. If Mr. Greenough examines the mark left by the bullet, he will find, as Halliday and I did, that my bullet went almost directly down, and is embedded in the baseboard of the hall, near the den door.

As a matter of fact, the whole sequence of events, ending with the shot, had stunned me. I heard Mr. Bethel in his room, calling out, and someone outside shouting from the terrace. Almost immediately there was a crash of breaking glass in the library, as Halliday smashed a window with a porch chair, and the next moment was in the house and fumbling for the light switch inside the library door.

When he ran into the hall I told him what had happened, and he immediately set about his search. As Mr. Bethel was still demanding, beyond his door, to know what was wrong, I went back to reassure him, but it required some time to induce him to unlock the door. Thus it was Halliday who made the first investigation downstairs.

He is confident no one escaped from the library, unless in that brief time while he was feeling for a light. But it is to be remembered that the floor near the window was covered with broken glass; no escape by that method could have been noiseless. At the same time, any theory of departure by the windows of the den is impossible, since we found all these windows closed and locked on the inside.

I am convinced that the intruder was not the secretary. As a matter of fact, he drove in a half hour later, saw the lights in the house, and hammered for admission, and surveyed our group in the hall with an amazement which, under any other circumstances, would be humorous. And I am also convinced that it was not the doctor. Mr. Bethel showing signs of collapse, Halliday telephoned to Hayward. He replied at once. Had he been at the house that night, he could not have made it.

I have no explanation whatever of the fact that Halliday and Hayward later on found the gun-room window closed and locked, save that the intruder may have entered by it while I was working my way into the dining-room; and that the cold air, the crash at the table, and the bursting open of the door in the hall, which so alarmed me, may have marked his passage through the room.

At the same time, no statement of the situation that night should fail to point out, loath as I am to believe in the supernatural, that for many years this house has had a reputation for similar phenomena; the bursting open of the door and the cold wind are merely repetitions of many similar unexplained occurrences. So, also, is the reddish color of the light I saw.

The disappearance of the figure and the blank darkness which followed that disappearance are difficult to account for, under any natural law at present known. I am not a spiritist, but it is to be remembered that only a second or so elapsed between Mr. Halliday's entrance by the broken window and his turning on of the lights.

Neither he nor I heard in that interval any movement; yet an escape over the broken glass of the window would certainly have made some sound. As I have said, the windows in the den were found to be closed and locked on the inside.

(End of memorandum for Mr. Greenough.)

August 15th.

Up today, but not allowed out of my room. Jock spends most of his time with me, whether from devotion or interest in the appetizing trays Jane sends up, I am slightly uncertain.

Edith suspects the latter, and has taken to calling him old dog Tray. She reproaches me bitterly for my faculty of getting myself into difficult situations, and quoted to me today those immortal words of Lewis Carroll, with a small amendment of her own.

" 'You are old, Father William,' his young niece said.

'And your hair has become very white.

'And yet you incessantly stand on your head.

'Do you think, at your age, it is right?' "

In preparation for the detective's visit she has laid out my best silk pajamas, and her reason for doing so sounds like her.

"No man is really at his best without his trousers," she observed. "But there's a sort of moral support about silk pajamas. It puts you out of the housebreaking class, anyhow."

"Not at all," I retorted. "Only our best housebreakers can afford them, these days."

But it shows her strength and my weakness, that I am now wearing them.

Greenough has come and gone. What he thinks of things now I cannot say, but at least I am, as I have had occasion more than once to record here, still at liberty. The fact that the revolver I used was Halliday's, and Halliday's supporting statement, no doubt are in my favor.

At the same time, it is clear that, although he listened carefully to my preliminary statement relative to our suspicions against Gordon, he was not greatly impressed by it.

"How did you and Mr. Halliday reconcile that theory with the sheep-killing?" he asked, when I had finished. "He wasn't here then, was he?"

"No. That has puzzled us, of course."

"Then again," he went on, eyeing me, "he himself was knocked down and tied. I don't suppose you accuse him of that, too?"

"I've told you," I said impatiently, "that we haven't a case; it's a theory. That's all. Take for instance that rope—"

"Oh, come, now, Mr. Porter! I've slipped out of my room at night over a woodshed; so have you, probably."

Coming down to the night of the 11th, he listened to my written statement without comment, save that he smiled somewhat over what he called my "ingenious conclusion." He also passed lightly over my picture of what followed; of Halliday's entrance, of Bethel brought down and sitting huddled in a chair in the library, somewhat dazed and showing signs of collapse. And of Gordon's return and our sudden realization of my predicament.

"Just what predicament?"

"I was in the house because I knew Gordon had a rope and a knife in his room. If we let him up there, and he did away with them, it left me in pretty poor shape."

"So you kept him downstairs! By force, he says."

"I wouldn't call it force. But we were three to his one, of course."

"In other words, you telephoned to the doctor, but you didn't telephone to Starr until Gordon came in and found you there."

"If you want to put it that way, yes."

"You broke into the house and found somebody there who had no business there. But you didn't think of calling on the police."

"What I felt we needed was not a policeman, but a medium."

He condescended to smile at that, but he was back to the matter again like a needle to the pole.

"Gordon says that Hayward and Halliday went off somewhere, after telephoning Starr, and that you held the gun on him. Is that correct?"

"I still had the revolver. I didn't point it at him, if that's what you mean. As for Halliday and Hayward, they were going through the house. That's all."

"And they found the gun-room window closed and locked?"

"So they say. I wasn't present."

"How do you account for that, if that's the way you entered?"

"I don't account for it."

"I suppose you have keys to the house?"

"I have."

"But you entered by this window?"

"Great heavens, man!" I said impatiently. "I don't carry those keys with me. I wasn't trying to get into the house. I went in because the window was open. And if you think I liked doing it, I'm here to tell you I didn't."

"You can't account for the window being locked, later?"

"I cannot. Why should I have locked it, if that's what you are trying to intimate? I had to get out again."

He abandoned that for the time.

"The point is this, Mr. Porter," he said. "You and Halliday have laid considerable emphasis on that knife. It was because Gordon had it that you were in the house, I understand."

"Had it and might use it," I amended.

"It was, in your opinion, either on him or in the room upstairs. But as it turned out, it was neither on him nor in his room. He denies ever owning such a knife."

"Halliday saw it. He's lying."

"It's your belief, then, that on this murderous errand of his, which was to end up at the house, he disposed of the very weapon which you had expected him to use?"

"I haven't said that, but I think it probable."

"Why? Why should he? He could have had no idea the house was to be entered, or his room searched. He came back, smoking a cigarette I understand, to find you and Halliday in the hall, a window broken, and a bullet imbedded in the floor. That doesn't sound like a man who has been out hiding the evidences of his crimes."

He asked me abruptly after that how long I had known Halliday, and his relationship to the family. Then he attacked Halliday's statement that he thought he had seen the lights of a car by Robinson's Point, and had started for that.

"Mr. Halliday," he said, "says that he believed that this car was Mr. Bethel's and started toward it, giving you his revolver and leaving you alone; that he found no car there, and turned back. To support this statement, he says that a boat, lying in the creek there, had excited his suspicions because the oarlocks were wrapped. Muffled oarlocks are not uncommon things."

"The position of the boat was suspicious."

"Perhaps," he said. "But that was a matter for me to determine, not Mr. Halliday. As to the strips he maintains were wrapped around the oarlocks, I am not saying they were not there; but I am saying that they were gone when I went over the next morning to examine the boat."

What he had hoped to gain by that I do not know. He shifted rapidly, perhaps in the hope of somehow trapping me; our reasons for hoping to connect Gordon with the crimes, since one of them had taken place before his arrival; when I had first missed my fountain pen; exactly where I was standing when the revolver was fired; when I had taken off the safety catch; where I was when Halliday broke the window. And from that, without a pause, back to the gun-room window and had me repeat my story about finding it open, and entering by it.

"Yet you thought," he said, "that this boy, whom you consider a degenerate and a murderer, was inside. In a few minutes you expected Halliday back, but you did not wait for him. Is that right?"

"It is."

"Then you thought, in all probability, that the boy had this knife with him."

"I didn't think about it at all," I said. "If I had, I'm not sure I would have gone in."

"But later on the boy returns, and you won't let him upstairs, because the knife is there. Is that right?"

Looking back over the interview, he seemed to be anxious to break down my story, rather than to be following any idea of his own. Halliday stated it fairly well when I reported the examination to him.

"He's got nothing," he said. "Nothing but you. And that's where his system breaks down; it might work, if you were guilty, but it isn't worth a tinker's dam, since you're not."

One rather curious thing he added, however, in view of Greenough's questions about the knife.

(Note: I was not present when Starr followed by Gordon, Halliday, and Doctor Hayward, went upstairs to examine Gordon's room.

During the interval of waiting for the constable I had been conscious of an approaching nervous chill, the beginning of the illness which laid me up for the following three days.)

"Gordon was as surprised as I was," he says, "when Starr didn't find the knife. It was too good to be true; he could hardly believe it."

August 16th.

DOWNSTAIRS today for the first time.

As I had expected, Mr. Bethel intends to give up the house. He has so notified Thomas and Annie Cochran, and has sent me a note asking me to see him tonight.

The note was left by Gordon, and as I happened to be in the hall, it was I who received it.

He stiffened when he saw me, it being our first encounter since the other night.

"Mr. Bethel sent this," he said briefly, and started to go. On the veranda, however, he stopped and turned around. "Pretty dirty work the other night," he said, watching me. "And I'm not forgetting it."

He waited, apparently expecting a reply. On receiving none he stood studying me for a moment—a most uncomfortable moment for me. Then he smiled, his curious sneering smile.

"I'm not afraid, you know," he said. "I can take care of myself. I'm not worrying."

He thrust his hands into his pockets and turned, not toward the other house, but toward the road. Near the gates he began to whistle, and thus theatrically assuring me that he was at his ease, started toward Oakville.

I have learned today that he is leaving Mr. Bethel, and has gone to the city to look for another position.

The boy puzzles me. Here I am, more or less a specialist in boys; for more years than I care to remember I have known them, collectively and individually, but here is a new type.

He is weak; compared to that prognathous portion of Halliday's face, for instance, he has no lower jaw. He completely lacks personality; he could, according to somebody's description of a similar type, be stood up against a whitewashed wall and erased with a good rubber. He is, one would say, almost too weak to be vicious.

But nature apparently gives to these otherwise defenseless creatures of hers a sort of low cunning with which to protect themselves. He has that cunning.

He is not in love with Edith, I think, although that vain young woman probably believes that he is. He is interested in her, as the only young and feminine creature within his present milieu; for the same reason he hates Halliday, quite apart from the other night, as representing what he is not and would like to be. At the same time, he hates the world because he feels himself incapable of coping with it.

But just how far does he carry this secret longing of his to escape his own inferiority? To the length of crime? Granted the desire so to escape it, has he the ability? Can he make his possible dream of being a master criminal come true? I think not.

Other things go on much as before. Greenough after three days of no further discoveries has gone again. The situation at the main house the other night has, thank God, not reached the press. The boat, with the mufflings gone from the oarlocks, still lies in the creek beyond Robinson's Point, and the sole proof of such muffling, if the point is even brought up again, lies in the boathouse along with the broken lens, the bit of Gordon's cipher, and the small screw cap of an ether can.

Our lovers move about their ordinary duties with an eye out, as one may say, each for the other. Vague as the future is, they have each other, and only this morning I saw Edith with a basket of mending, from which looked forth what greatly resembled a masculine undergarment in need of buttons. Shades of many years ago, when each sex politely assumed that the other went, so to speak, undergarmentless!

They cannot turn the clock on. But there are times when there is a sort of despair in Halliday's face, and sometimes I see Edith sitting alone, her hands folded, looking three or four years ahead with a sort of tragic patience. So much, she seems to think, may happen in three or four years.

She asked him, the other day, out of a clear sky, if he had been gone over by a doctor recently.

And the reward, on which she had so blithely counted, seems as far away as ever. As far away as her dreams of earning a fortune with her pen. She has had another rejection or two, and the heart has gone out of her.

But she has had her moment. Mail still continues to come in. Which reminds me that she received a curious letter yesterday. Because it may be construed to have a bearing on our situation I record it here, but as a matter of fact, one must make certain allowances; Edith's articles used my name in full, and a small amount of investigation by the professional mediumistic underground would supply some of the remainder. The Jane, for example, is quite easily accounted for.

But the remainder leaves me considerably puzzled. The boat, for instance. And that strange condition of Mr.– At the end, a heart which is normal apparently failing him, so that he would have fallen had he not been caught. For all the world as though– But I must pull myself together. The letter from Salem was not authentic; why should I believe this?

Evanston, Illinois
August 12, 19–

Dear Madam:

I have read with great interest your account of the strange occurrence at the lighthouse at Robinson's Point, and would like to tell you of something which occurred here that same night and, allowing for the difference in time, at about the same hour.

I am not a spiritualist, but following a small dinner here, it was suggested that we try table levitation, and against my husband's protests, this was arranged for.

My husband, I may say, is not psychic in any way, and was greatly bored with the proceeding. We were not surprised, therefore, when after sitting in darkness for ten minutes or so, he fell asleep and began to breathe heavily.

I tried to rouse him but was unable to, when the opinion was given that he was in a trance state. As none of us were familiar with that condition, and as he began to groan heavily, I was greatly alarmed. There was a doctor in the party, however, and on his saying that his pulse was all right, we sat quiet and waited.

*He then said, "*Jane, Jane*" in an agonized voice, and as my name is not* Jane *there was some amusement, especially when he added, "She is asleep. I cannot rouse her." Almost immediately after that, however, he said, "Robinson's Point," and something about a boat there. (We think now that the allusion may have been to the lighthouse you mention.) After that he was quiet for a time, and I begged to be allowed to waken him, but just as we had turned on the lights again he got up, with his eyes still closed, and leaning over the table, seemed to be staring at the gentleman across from him. (Mr. Lewis, a very nice man, with whom my husband plays golf a great deal.)*

"I have not changed my attitude," he said, in a really terrible voice. "I repudiate you and all your works. I am not afraid of you. The thing is monstrous, and society should be warned against you."

I have forgotten to say that he had kept his right hand closed, as though he had something in it. He made a gesture as though he threw this something away, and then looked at Mr. Lewis again and said, "I have warned you; I shall tell the police."

He seemed to be in a state of great excitement, and hardly able to breathe. He fell back into the chair, and our doctor friend reached over and felt his pulse. He says now that, although his heart is perfectly sound, it had almost stopped. Indeed, he would have fallen had the doctor not caught him. In a short time he came around and seemed to think he had been asleep. He felt, however, very wretched the next day.

This may not interest you, but the mention of Robinson's Point in your article, and the similarity in time, has struck me as a strange coincidence. I am signing this in full, as an evidence of good faith, but I must ask you not to use it for publication.

(Note: I have since secured the writer's consent to the use of this letter, on condition that I withhold the signature.)

An element which works beyond our guess; Soul, the unsounded sea, says Browning. A poet's idea only, perhaps, but wasn't it Montaigne who said that all our philosophy is but sophisticated poetry?

What a joyous time little Pettingill would have with all this! Trotting about, a notebook in hand, adding up a glimpse here, a look there, until he had a complete panoramic view of all eternity. But the real question is, what would Cameron say? Not for him the amorous Hadly in the churchyard—a spot by the way, if our spiritists are right, not quite so exclusive as Hadly seems to have considered it—nor a teakettle moving about. His the coldly scientific method; the medium in a box, tied hand and foot; scales of weighing; cameras; notebooks; witnesses.

Not for him Pettingill's wide view into eternity, but a narrow slit, guarded by little bells on strings, through which the poor ghost must creep if he come at all.

I wonder what would happen, if I could induce him to come here?

August 17th.

ONE LIVES and learns.

Mr. Bethel last night lifted a small corner of the mystery and showed me a few of the wheels within. With the net result that we are where we were before.

He telephoned me at nine o'clock last night, the first time I have known him to use the telephone, and asked me to see him.

(Note: I have, I think, not mentioned in the journal that the three buildings, the Lodge, main house, and boathouse, are on one telephone. As this fact plays an important part later, it requires explanation.)

I found him alone in the library, but with certain changes from the last time I had seen him thus. The windows were closed and locked, and the heavy curtains drawn across them; both the rear and front doors in the hall were bolted, and when I was finally obliged to ring, I could hear the old man dragging himself slowly into the hall and there stopping.

"Who is it?" he called.

"Porter."

I was on the terrace, and he opened that door for me, working laboriously with his single useful hand. Once inside, he left me to close it for myself, and went back into the library. When I followed him it was to find him seated, with the revolver close at hand as before. He was a strange, half-sinister figure as he sat there, but when he spoke it was as the querulous invalid of our first meeting.

"I don't like your house, Mr. Porter," he barked at me, without preliminary.

"I don't like it myself," I admitted. "I am thinking of adding to the insurance and then setting a match to it. After you are out, of course," I added.

That brought a sort of dry chuckle from him, but the next moment he was back to the attack. He supposed he was responsible for the balance of the rent, but wasn't I morally responsible if he couldn't live there? I had known the stories about the house, and yet had let it to him. There was a question there.

"There is no question," I said. "I have no idea of holding you up for the balance of the rent."

It seemed to me, however, that he hardly heard me. He was listening again, as he had before, and when he spoke it was on a totally different matter.

"You find me rather on guard," he said. "I am alone in the house."

"Where's Gordon?"

"He went into the city this morning. He has not come back."

And there was something in the way he made the statement that caused me to look at him quickly.

"You mean that he has gone for good?"

"No. I wish to God he had."

There was fear in that, and I realized then that all the place showed fear, the locked and bolted house, the dim light—only one lamp going, and that on the desk—the revolver, and the old man's twisted body, crouched and watchful.

"I am afraid of him, Mr. Porter," he said. "I think he means to kill me."

"Nonsense!"

"I wish it were."

"Can't you get rid of him?"

"Don't you suppose I've tried?"

His story, if story it can be called, that rambling discourse broken into by his fits of listening, even once of sending me out to take a look around, is as follows:

He had picked the boy up in the city, knowing little or nothing about him, and from the time they arrived he had not quite trusted him. After a time, too, he began to suspect that he was getting out of the house at night, and possibly using the car.

"Not guilty in itself, perhaps," he said, "but it left me alone, for one thing. And it is not a house in which one cares to be alone." He glanced at me. "And for another—well, I needn't tell *you* what has been going on."

But he was not, at first, really suspicious of these night excursions, save for his resentment at being left there, alone and helpless, with a killer loose in the neighborhood. He kept a watch, therefore, not so much over the boy as over the house and himself in his absence.

"If he left a door or window open," he said, "I was at the mercy of anybody who chose to enter."

And this, he says, was the situation on the night of the 26th of July. He had gone to the boy's room and found it empty, and had after some debate decided to work his way downstairs and lock him out.

"And myself in," he said.

It took him a long time to do it; he says, too, that he was very nervous; there were sounds, especially in the dining-room. Nothing he could account for, but they upset him still further, and by the time he reached the kitchen he was in a bad way. He had to sit down there.

It was while he was sitting there that he heard sounds on the porch, and somebody at the doorknob. From then on he says he was beyond coherent thinking, but he had no doubt in the world, because of the stealthiness of the movement, that the thing he had feared was happening. It seems never to have occurred to him that it was Gordon.

He dragged himself to the stove, found the poker, and as the door opened struck with all his strength.

"It was only when he made a leap for the bell that I knew what I had done."

He was stricken. He felt the boy's pulse and knew he was not dead, but off somewhere near the sundial he heard someone moving, and that alarmed him still more.

"A man never knows his cowardice," he said wryly, "until he is put to the test. I have very little idea of what I did next; my only clear recollection is of finding myself in my room. I don't remember getting there."

But—and this is the point—the boy suspected him. He was sure of it. There had been a complete change in his attitude since that time. And watching that change, studying Gordon as he had felt obliged to, he had felt that something underlay all this. In other words, gradually he had begun to associate the boy with the other crimes.

"He is weak," he said, "weak and vicious. And there is that curious mental state called identification; the weak see the crimes committed by the strong, admire them, admire the criminal. Then they begin to ape them, as Gordon may have aped your sheep killer, finally even identifying himself with this unknown, adopting his symbol, or whatever one chooses to call it."

I listened carefully, trying to fit this new light on Gordon's injury with the evidence as I knew it. True, the weak link in our chain against him had been that he himself had been attacked. And this was now solved in a perfectly matter-of-fact manner. But there was some discrepancy there, something which eluded me until I had gone over in my mind the events of the night of the 26th in their sequence. Then I found it.

"But what about the man the boy saw enter by the gun-room window?"

"Pure invention, I feel certain. Had he accused me he knew the matter of his night excursions would come out. That was the last thing he wanted."

It was my next remark, however, which has left us, as I wrote at the beginning of this entry, just where we were before.

"You haven't said anything about the rope, Mr. Bethel. That was always—"

"Rope!" he said slowly. "What rope?"

"He was tied hand and foot when I found him."

He glanced at me, and then down at his helpless hand.

"It's a very long time since I have been able to tie a rope, Mr. Porter," he said quietly.

I remained with him until an hour or so after the last train from the city had arrived, but there was no sign of Gordon. I offered to remain for the night with him, but he declined. He would not go to bed, however, and I left him there at last, his revolver within reach.

Of that later talk there is one matter of real importance to record.

I have a strange picture in my mind, bearing on the relations of these two, the old man and the boy, and leading up to it; each watching the other, the old man terrified, the boy deadly. And on the surface, before Annie Cochran, all well enough between them; dictation taken, and the book growing. Small surface differences, perhaps, but underneath suspicion on one side and revenge and hatred on the other.

Then Gordon took to locking his room. It was Annie Cochran who told Bethel, and from that time on that locked room played its own part between them; the old man asking himself what was hidden in it, the secretary with his sneering smile quietly carrying the key. It grew, I gathered, to have a peculiar place in the old man's imagination; he wandered down the passage to it more than once; finally Annie Cochran caught him there, trying the knob, and he had made some excuse and gone away.

But the night young Gordon flung out of the house, the same night I saw the figure at the foot of the stairs, Annie Cochran had come to him before leaving, with a key in her hand.

"I thought you might like this, sir," she said. "I find it fits Mr. Gordon's door."

Then she had gone, and he went to the room and entered it. The knife and the rope were there, and *he took them.*

"What was I to say that night, when the constable came down and reported nothing there? In ten minutes, or an hour, you were going to leave me here with him. He was watching me; he knew."

And I dare say he was right. No matter what statement had been made relative to the rope and the knife, there was no reason for Gordon's arrest that night. In ten minutes, or an hour, they would have been left together, and who knows what might have happened?

August 18th.

GORDON CAME BACK early this morning. I invented an errand to the house soon after breakfast, but found that Mr. Bethel was still sleeping—as well he might—and that preparations for tomorrow's departure were well under way.

While Gordon was busy on the lower floor, Thomas and I made a tour of the house, with a view to closing it. I have instructed him to paint and put up the window boards which close the windows on the lower floor; I shall know no peace until the place is sealed, and left to its demons or its ghosts.

But I took advantage of my legitimate presence on the upper floor to examine the locked closet in which I had stored the red lamp. It is still there, and apparently has not been disturbed.

Halliday today advised for me a period of masterly inactivity. Not that he calls it so, but that is what he means.

"I have an idea, skipper," he said, "that this calling Greenough off the case was sheer bluff. Every move he made was being watched, and unless I miss my guess you'll find he's at Bass Cove, or some place near by, under another name. I thought I saw his Ford a night or so ago."

What I finally gathered is that Halliday wants to eliminate me from the case, for my own sake.

"Just now," he said, "you are sitting very pretty. But one more bit of bad luck and he's ready to jump."

Although he smiled, I have an idea that he is deadly serious; that he knows Greenough is not far away, and that for some unknown reason he expects another bit of bad luck. His face is thin and haggard these days, and from the fact that he sleeps a great deal in the daytime, I am inclined to think that he sleeps very little at night.

Between him and Edith, too, I surmise some sort of mysterious understanding. At the same time, there is a noticeable absence of those three-angled conferences in which, some little time ago, we were free to air our various theories.

Willy nilly, I am consigned to innocuous desuetude.

Hayward started yesterday on his vacation.

August 20th.

FOUR A.M. Mr. Bethel was murdered between eleven o'clock and midnight last night. Gordon has escaped.

7:00 a.m. Jane is at last asleep, and I have had some coffee. Perhaps if I record the events of the night it will quiet me. After all, one cannot forget such things; the only possible course is to bring them to the surface, to face them.

But I will not face that room.

Murder. The very word is evil. But no one has ever known how evil until he has seen it. Such things cannot be written; they should not be seen. They should not be.

We have had this murder. We have gone over, inch by inch, the scene of it. We have been spared no shock; the evidence of the struggle is on the walls, the floor, the furniture; we have the very knife with which it was committed. We have even gone further than that. We have followed it outside, along the drive to the garage, and from there by the car to the salt marsh beyond Robinson's Point.

And yet, according to Halliday, until we have gone still further, we have had no murder, according to the law.

Ever since daylight, I have been struggling to see the justice of a law where, when Gordon is found—and Greenough believes he will be found—we cannot convict him unless we also find that bit of old flesh and blood and bone which was once Simon Bethel.

Is it only necessary, to escape justice, that a criminal artfully dispose of his crime?

And by how narrow a margin he did escape it! A matter of minutes. Between my calling Halliday on the telephone and my meeting him at the terrace; perhaps even between that and our entrance into that wrecked room. A matter of minutes.

In one thing only did he make an error, and even that may not have been an error. He may coolly have abandoned his suitcase, packed and hidden in the shrubbery; may have stood there a second or so, considering it, and then decided to let it lie.

The most grievous thing to me is that I should have given him the warning. And the most terrible picture I have is that, when I called Halliday, he stood listening in at the telephone, craftily calculating, "Can I make it? Can I not?" With *that* behind him—

Crafty. As old in crime as crime is old, for all his youth. Out on the bay disposing of his horrible freight, and watching the lanterns as they searched for the boat; seeing them scatter, looking for other boats with which to follow him out onto the water, and then quietly heading back into the creek again, and escaping through the wood.

Crafty, beyond words.

August 21st.

THE EXCITEMENT is still intense. I have hardly seen Halliday since our trouble; he is working with the police, of which a number have come to assist Greenough. Curious crowds stand outside our gates, which we have been obliged to close and lock. A few of the more adventurous, gaining admission by the lane, are turned back there by guards who are on duty day and night.

Thomas, standing at the gate, has orders to admit only the detectives and duly accredited members of the press.

On the bay we have once more the familiar crowd of searching boats. Off the point dragging has been going on, but with no result. Owing to the fact that no guards were placed by the boat, a large portion of it has already been taken away by morbid individuals who will place their trophies, I dare say, on tables or mantelpieces, and thereafter gloat over them.

Truly, just as the lunatic always insists that he is sane, so do the sane often demonstrate that they are mad.

And so far, nothing.

Nothing, that is, which leads to Gordon's apprehension. From the time he turned back in the boat and, landing, made his escape into the woods above Robinson's Point, he disappeared entirely. Here and there a clue has turned up, to end in disappointment. Greenough believes that he will be found, that he cannot escape the police dragnet, but I am not so sure.

Although almost forty-eight hours have passed Jane has not yet opened up the subject of the telephone, and because of her morbid reserve on such matters, I have not told the police.

Asked how I had happened to be at the telephone and thus receive the alarm, I have replied that the bell rang, that I went to the instrument, and was immediately aware that one of the receivers was down, either at Halliday's or at the main house; that I heard a crash over the wire, followed by a second and a nearer one, and after that a silence; that following that I heard, near the receiver, the sobbing breath of exhaustion, and that immediately after that the receiver went up, and I called Halliday frantically; and that, on his replying, I told him my suspicion that something was wrong at the main house, and to meet me there at once.

But there is a discrepancy here which may cause me trouble if they come back to it. A telephone such as ours does not ring if one of the receivers is down. And the plain fact is that our telephone did not ring at all that night.

As I have not yet recorded the events of that tragic evening in their sequence, I shall do so now.

Halliday had dined with us, and had been more like himself than for some time past. The news that the house was to be given up had seemed to relieve him, for some strange reason. I remember he said something which puzzled me at the time.

"After all," he said, "we can't undo what has been done. And it may be the end."

After dinner he and Edith sat on the veranda, and going to lower a shade I saw that she was holding a match while he drew something on a bit of paper. But the match went out almost at once, and I would have thought no more of it, had I not heard Edith say, "And the cabinet was there?"

"In the corner," he replied.

I am no eavesdropper, so I drew the shade and turned away.

He left at something after ten, and Edith joined us. She was very quiet, and sat watching me play solitaire while Jane sewed industriously. At half past ten or thereabouts, Jane suddenly said, "The telephone is ringing."

Both Edith and I looked up in amazement; the instrument was in the small hall, not ten feet from where I sat; it would have been impossible for it to ring without our hearing it, and we had heard nothing.

"You've been asleep, Jane!" Edith accused her. But I glanced at her, and I remembered that she was oddly relaxed in her chair; her face looked white and her eyes were slightly fixed.

"It is ringing," she said thickly.

And that is how I happened to be at the telephone that night. And how, too, I gave the alarm which enabled the murderer to escape, by calling Halliday.

"Get your revolver and meet me at the main house," I said. "There's something wrong there."

I know that had I not rung the telephone, had I gone for Halliday instead, we would have caught the criminal. But to ring the one house was to ring the other; he may still have been standing there gasping. He had, for all he knew up to that time, the rest of the night in which to finish his deadly work; to dispose of the body, to gather up his suitcase, waiting outside, and get away.

But I called Halliday, and he listened. He knew then that instead of hours he had only minutes. He must have worked fast, in that ghastly shambles of a room; the car was probably already out, in the lane. He may even have stood there, at the corner of the lane, the engine turning over quietly, and watched Halliday running up toward the house. And perhaps he laughed, that secret laugh of his which had always rather chilled me.

Then—he simply got into the car and drove away. Cool and crafty to the last. No body, no murder. He made for the boat.

He left behind him only two real clues; the knife, which Annie Cochran identifies as one taken from the kitchen, and his packed suitcase. Not intentional, this last. He must have needed clean linen. And certainly that diary of his, in cipher—he would not want that in the hands of the police. But what would the diary matter, after all, if he himself escaped?

August 22nd.

As time goes on the case is complicated with the eagerness of all sorts of people to bring in extraneous circumstances which they consider important.

For instance, Livingstone's butler, the one who bought the knife in Oakville and caused so much excitement by so doing, has been over to get a description of Gordon, preserving an air of mystery which under other circumstances would be vastly entertaining.

Another story concerns a middle-aged man of highly respectable appearance and of a square and heavy build, who was seen walking uncertainly along the main road near the Livingstone place at 1:00 a.m. the night of the murder. A passing car, seeing his state, stopped and asked if he was in trouble.

He replied that he had been struck by a car an hour or so before, and had been lying by the road ever since. His condition bore this out, as he was stained with blood and dirt. He accepted the offer of a lift, and was left at the railroad station at Martin's Ferry to catch the express there for the city.

There have been many similar ones; an innumerable number of people are convinced that they have seen Gordon, and apparently almost any dapper youth of twenty or so, with what Edith calls patent-leather hair and an inveterate cigarette habit, is likely at any time to be tapped on the shoulder and taken to a police station.

Of clues of other and lesser sorts there has been almost an embarrassment. Both the library and that portion of the hall near the telephone have furnished fingerprints. But as Greenough says, "Fingerprints do not discover criminals; they identify them."

Nevertheless, great pains have been taken to preserve them. On the white marble mantel a very distinct imprint in blood was photographed without difficulty; others, less clear, were dusted with black powder before the camera was used. Detailed pictures were made of the library and hall, before any attempt to put them back to order was permitted, and these prints have been enlarged and carefully studied. One of them with a strange result.

Greenough, handing it to me today, said, "This print is defective. You can keep it, if you care to."

But I wonder if it *is* defective. There is what Greenough calls a light streak in the lower corner, but it requires very little imagination to give to this misty outline the semblance of a form, and to the lower portion of it the faint but recognizable appearance of brocade.

I have said nothing. What can I say?

One thing which puzzles the police is the violence of the battle; it seems incredible that Bethel could have made the fight for life which he evidently did. At the same time, they have two problems to solve which repeated searching of the house and wide publicity have not yet answered.

One is the disappearance of the manuscript on which Bethel had worked all summer. Annie Cochran has testified that this manuscript was kept locked in a drawer in the library desk; when Halliday and I entered the house this drawer was standing open and the manuscript was missing. It has not yet been located.

But perhaps the most surprising is the failure of any friend or relative of Simon Bethel to interest himself in the case. Cameron's note to Larkin before Bethel rented the house expressly disclaims any previous knowledge of him.

Here is a possible tenant for Mr. Porter's house, he wrote, *of which he spoke to me some time ago. I have no acquaintance with Mr. Bethel, save that he called on me a day or so ago, in reference to a statement in a book of mine. I imagine, however, that he would be a quiet and not troublesome tenant.*

Halliday brought up this curious situation yesterday, in one of the rare moments he has given us since the murder.

"Has it occurred to you, skipper," he said, "that it is strange that no one belonging to Mr. Bethel has turned up?"

"I dare say a man can outlive most of his contemporaries and most of his friends."

"He wasn't as old as all that." And he asked, apparently irrelevantly a moment later, "The two evenings you saw him and talked to him, how did he impress you? I mean, his state of mind?"

"The last time, of course, he was frankly frightened. He said as much."

"And before that?"

"He didn't say so, but he was more or less on guard. He had his revolver. Of course, those were rather parlous times."

As a matter of fact, the case is anything but a clear one against Gordon, as it develops. Greenough has been, all along, as convinced of Gordon's guilt as he had previously been of mine. But Benchley is more open to conviction, and a conversation between Halliday and him this morning, on the lawn near the terrace, is still running in my mind.

Halliday had been protesting against Greenough's method of "following a single idea until it went up a blind alley and died there."

"Of course," he said quietly, "you can make a case against Gordon; it's all here. But you'll have something left over that you won't know what to do with. We know that it was Mr. Bethel who hit Gordon and knocked him out some time ago, but who tied him? Where's the boy's own story about seeing a man at the gun-room window? Mr. Porter here later on finds that same window open, and sees a man in the lower hall. Who was that? The same hand tied the boy that tied Carroway, and Gordon hadn't even seen this place at that time. What are you going to do with that?"

"Then where's Gordon now?" Benchley asked, practically enough.

"I don't know. Dead, maybe."

Benchley stood thinking.

"I think I get the idea," he said. "The fight, you think, was between Mr. Bethel and this unknown of yours; the boy either saw it and got mixed up in it, or knew he'd be suspected and beat it. Is that it?"

"Well, I would say that a man about to commit such a crime doesn't pack his suitcase with the idea of escaping with it."

A thought which, I admit, had never occurred to me until that moment.

As a result of this conversation, Benchley has advanced a theory of his own which accounts at least for the failure of any relatives to make inquiry. This is that the old man was in hiding under an assumed name; hiding, in the most secluded spot he could find, from some implacable enemy who had finally caught up with him.

How he reconciles this with the Carroway murder and the disappearance of Maggie Morrison I do not know, but certain facts seem to bear out this idea. He was, in one sense, a man of mystery. His accounts were paid in cash; the automobile in which he arrived had been bought at second hand a few days before, by the secretary and in the same manner. And all identifying marks had been carefully removed from his clothing.

In addition to all this, there is the puzzling report on the knife itself. Examination under the microscope shows fibers of linen as well as fragments of cellular tissue. But it also reveals minute particles of tobacco leaf, showing it had gone through a pocket.

But Mr. Bethel was not a smoker.

At some one time, then, Bethel clearly secured the knife and wounded his assailant. Not seriously, evidently, since after that he was able to do what he did do, but sufficiently to turn the minds of the police toward the man who claimed to have been struck by an automobile.

This clue, however, has developed nothing. The night was dark, and his rescuers have no description of him, save of a heavy-set figure and a dazed manner of speech. They carried him to Martin's Ferry, but the conductor of the night express remembers carrying no such passenger.

Greenough today showed me Gordon's diary, rescued from the suitcase. It has at some time been dropped into water, and certain pages are not legible. If indeed that word may be used where nothing is legible; where each page presents such jumbles of large and small letters as the following sentence, which I have copied as a matter of interest:

Trn g.K. GTRgg UnMT aot LmGT MotrT.

The record is not a daily one, but apparently was used for jotting down odd thoughts or ideas. It continues, however, at intervals, for the entire period of his stay at Twin Hollows, the last entry having been made on August 17th.

Certain entries are neat and methodical. The one on July 27th, however, after his injury, is by hand, and shows certain erasures and changes. Once or twice in August the record is long, covering more than a page, while the July entries are all brief. On the last page, however, and without comment, he has drawn in, rather carefully, a small circle enclosing a triangle.

Greenough, while attaching a certain interest to it, has not yet sent it to be deciphered by the code experts of his department. As a matter of fact, I suspect him of holding it out, with the idea of being able to claim the reward if he finds Gordon.

Which reward, by the way, now stands at ten thousand dollars.

August 23rd.

HALLIDAY saw a red light in the house the night Bethel was killed. He has just told me.

He ran out, after I telephoned him, and from the foot of the lawn he saw it. It was gone almost at once.

He has asked me to experiment with him tonight, using the lamp from the attic closet. I have given him the keys. Apparently what he wishes to discover is the approximate location of such a light. I have no idea of his purpose.

I understand that the guards who have been watching the house at night have been withdrawn, and that hereafter only such watch will be kept as will suffice to keep away the curious crowds that still throng here in daylight hours.

Today Annie Cochran and Thomas have been putting the house in order, preparatory to its final closing. I shall never open it again. Thomas has already painted the window boards and put some of them in place. Let us pray that they keep inside what should be inside, and outside what should be out!

August 24th.

THE STRINGS *of small bells, fastened across the closed and shuttered windows, frequently vibrated as though a hand had been drawn across them.*

(From *Eugenia Riggs and Her Phenomena.*)

Any coherent record of our last night's experiment is difficult today; not only do last night's alarms always seem absurd in today's sunshine, but I am not at all certain now that I did not build up, out of my recent reading and what I knew about the house, a bugaboo of my own.

And yet—what a night!

A man is a fool who, preparing to spend a night in a haunted house, where a terrible crime has been recently committed, reads during the early evening the idiotic imaginings which other men have conjured out of their own disordered fancies. Or out of their disordered digestions, according to the newest theory.

Isn't it Wells who has the dyspeptic Mr. Polly sitting on a stile between two threadbare-looking fields, and hating the world in general and his own home in particular, after a meal of pork, suet pudding, treacle, cheese, beer, and pickles? And Fraser Harris who attributes "the transcendent nonsense of the post-impressionists" to the absinthe in their blood?

So, last night, I must needs poison my mental digestion, in advance; pick up a book which should be suppressed, or sold only to large ladies of a lymphatic type, to read with a box of caramels. And with it fill myself with elementals, hideous masses of matter given temporary life and strange forms; demons, summoned by the diabolical rites of the Black Mass; and ghosts of foul crimes, come to seek revenge on their slayers!

Even before I started, the untimely ringing of Clara's alarm clock, upstairs, set my nerves to jangling. And there was a certain psychological preparation for me in the very steps I was obliged to take in order to get out of the house. For a man of my age to put on his pajama coat, and retire into his bed otherwise fully dressed, was an act of deception nerve-racking enough in itself. But when Jane came in after I had retired, tardily remembering a missing button, and demanded the shirt I was still wearing, I broke into a cold sweat.

It was with difficulty that I got her away, shirtless, and settled down to wait until the house was quiet.

Halliday had opened the main house, and the red lamp was already in the den. Owing to the fact that the windows were boarded from the outside, we had no scruples about lighting it; but although it was better than complete darkness it added very little to the general gaiety. Halliday was quiet and somewhat strained, the house itself hot and airless and, with all outside sounds cut off, depressingly still. I lighted a match and glanced into the library; it was a ghost of a room, the floor bare, the furniture and pictures once more swathed in white.

Only the prisms of the glass chandelier reflected the light and seemed, as it flickered, to be quietly in motion.

Halliday had little to say.

"I would like," he explained, "to reproduce conditions as nearly as they were the night you saw the figure here." He smiled. "I don't suppose you really want to go and stand at the head of that staircase, skipper, but I'm going to ask you to, just the same."

I looked up the staircase nervously.

"If you are going to reproduce the previous conditions," I protested, "you may recall that I had a revolver at that time!"

"I also seem to remember that you fired it," he said, and grinned at me. "It will answer every purpose, and be considerably safer, if you will merely point your finger at me and say 'crash!' "

But no amount of lightness on his part or mine could do more than temporarily lift the gloom; the shadow of tragedy hung over everything at which we looked. Halliday felt it, and suggested that "we get to work and then get out."

The question in his mind, he said, was this: I had said that, a second or so after the shot and the disappearance of the figure, the red light had died out in the den. If, as he believed was possible, this glow came from the lamp upstairs, brought down for some reason, or from a similar lamp, this required that the man I saw had time to go into the den, extinguish the lamp and conceal it, (since it wasn't in evidence later on) get back to the library, and be ready to leave by the broken window before he, Halliday, had turned on the light.

"It's a matter of time," he said. "I was by the terrace when I heard the shot. I figure it took me ten seconds to pick up the chair, run to the window, and smash it."

It was nervous work going up the staircase, but I managed it and took up my position. He stood below.

I fired—theoretically—and he did what the figure had done; moved toward the door, still facing me, turned and went into the library. I heard him moving about and the light went out. Then in the darkness he ran into the library again, where he struck a match.

"Twenty seconds," he called.

His voice trailed off; his shadow extended through the den doorway into the hall, and as I watched it, it shows the condition of my nerves that it did not seem to be his shadow at all, but something quite different. For all the world like an old man in a dressing-gown. Then the match went out and I heard him coming out into the hall again.

"Did you move a minute ago?" he asked.

"Move!" I said. "I wouldn't move for a million dollars. Strike a light."

"Funny," he said. "I thought I heard something."

He groped his way back to the den, and the red lamp looked actually cheerful after the complete darkness. I heard him go into the library again and apparently stand there and listen, and very shortly after he reappeared and asked me to change places with him.

"See how you can make it, skipper," he said.

I came down rather more rapidly than I had gone up, and Halliday took my former position. I had never had any particular stomach for the business, and now my one idea was to get it over. I did as Halliday had done, moved to the library door, turned, and then, more or less holding my breath, dived into the library and through it to the den. I brought up there, close to the red lamp, caught my foot in the cord and jerked it from the socket. Instantly we were in darkness again, and in absolute silence. Halliday, I believe, was still leaning over the stair rail, waiting for me to complete the movement, and the sudden plunge into darkness had startled me more than I care to remember.

But I do remember that in a sort of panic I got down on my knees to feel for the connection, and that at that movement, whether due to overstrained nerves or not I cannot say, I distinctly heard a soft movement in the library. Trying to analyze that movement today I find it difficult. It was as though the linen coverings in the library had been set in motion, a soft and quiet motion, like that perhaps of a woman with a fan, and above that the faint click of the prisms on the chandelier, like the ringing of small bells. But whatever had caused it, it was dying away when I noticed it. As if somehow the extinction of the light had taken away its source of power.

(Note: It is to be observed that we secured this phenomenon later, during the seances. As no explanation of it has ever been given, it remains a portion of that unsolved factor in our equation to which I have referred previously.)

I kneeled there, my face covered with a cold sweat, staring in the direction of the library door. I felt that if I looked away, if I were to lower my guard for an instant, something would come through that door.

I was, in effect, holding it back with my eyes!

And Halliday had made no sound. He, too, I now know, was listening.

This, as accurately as I can record it, was the situation last night when the next move came. The house was absolutely silent again. Halliday was upstairs, and I was watching the door into the library, when the location of the sounds changed. Protected by my eyes, in front, I was attacked from the rear, so to speak. At the window above and behind me, something was trying to get in. I could hear its hands sliding slimily over the wood of the shutter, keeping on that blind and dreadful groping, until finally some sort of hold was secured and the shutter was shaken.

And with that every last ounce of my self-control left me, and I leaped into the hall as if I had been fired out of a gun.

"Halliday!" I shouted. "*Halliday!*"

He came downstairs; rather he leaped down the stairs. He says he found me in a corner, gibbering, and I dare say he did, but I must have told him my story with sufficient clearness, at that, for he left me alone again in that damnable place and ran outside. And as I had no intention whatever of being left alone again for the remainder of my life, I ran, also. There was nobody outside the window, but the fresh green paint was the thing that, according to Halliday, saved me from being sent today to some sanctuary for the mentally deranged.

It showed unmistakable signs of entirely human investigation. At least a hand with the usual equipment of thumb and fingers has left more than one impression on it.

Later: And now where are we? I am willing, even anxious, to accept Halliday's verdict, that the sounds we both heard in the library were due to an east wind blowing down the chimney, plus the settling and creaking of the old portion of the house.

But we have just returned from an inspection, in broad day, of the marks outside the boarded-up window of the den.

There is a complete imprint of the hand on it, and it shows a broad short thumb and a curved little finger. What is more, there is a complete absence of the usual whorls and ridges of the ordinary hand. One could take this imprint and put it side by side with the one in the bowl of putty. They are identical.

Halliday seems to have seen a great light from somewhere, but to me the situation is as absurd as it is maddening. It is as outrageous as that, out of some forgotten corner of my memory, I should have dug up a triangle within a circle, to find it cropping up soon after as the signature to a crime.

August 25th.

FIVE DAYS have passed since the murder, and we are apparently as far from its solution as ever.

What work is being done is now centering about the county detective bureau in the city. A deputy constable keeps up a more or less casual surveillance of the property during the day, but is careful to depart before twilight. The dragging of the bay has once more been stopped, and Benchley's idea of an unknown enemy of Bethel's has apparently been abandoned in favor of Gordon as the killer.

At the same time we are not without developments, of a sort.

Although he is reticent on the subject, Halliday seems to feel that the experiment the other night, incomplete as it was, negates the theory that the man I saw escaped by the broken window in the library.

"Then where did he go?" I asked.

"That's the point," he said. "Where did he go? When we've answered that we'll have answered a number of things."

But he tells me, surprisingly enough, that he has taken up a sort of temporary residence in the house.

"Whoever tried to get in the other night may come back again," he says. And assures me that the place isn't so bad "when one gets used to it."

"I read Kant," he says, as if that explains something.

I have offered to stay with him, but not, I dare say, with any enthusiasm. But he declines with a smile.

"You are too psychic, skipper!" he says.

But it is perfectly evident that he does not want me.

This morning, going unexpectedly into the boathouse, where this conversation took place, I found him sitting by his table, and spread out before him the bit of linen, the cipher, the broken lens, and the top of the ether can which constituted our various exhibits before I was gently eliminated from the case. But he also had a box of figs and a hand mirror before him, and when I entered unexpectedly he was studying himself in the glass.

As he immediately asked me if I cared to go fishing, which I did not, I saw that he was not prepared to make any explanation.

The other development, although it does not solve the crime, or touch on it, came to me through Lear today, and throws a new and interesting light on poor old Bethel himself.

Lear did not like his errand; he prefers a presumptuous skepticism to an irrational credulity, and knows no middle ground. Those things which lie beyond his understanding he refers to as "poppycock," a favorite word of his. And today he prefaced his business with a small lecture to me, taking me into the drive to deliver it.

"You don't look like a man who has been on a vacation," he began, surveying me. "I know you've had a bad time, but, after all, it's no possible responsibility of yours."

"I rented him the house. And I knew I had no business to rent it to anybody."

"Poppycock!" he said, and cleared his throat.

He had fallen into step with me, but at that he stopped and faced me.

"Now see here, Porter," he said, "there's a good bit of talk going around. Some of your friends are saying that you and Jane are laying the blame on some damn-fool nonsense about the house itself. That's poor hearing, and it's ridiculous into the bargain. The Morrison girl was not killed in the house."

"I'm not so sure she wasn't. At any rate, *he* was. And I believe the same hand killed them both."

"But a human hand, of course? You're not going to say—"

"Oh, I admit that," I said. "But there are a lot of curious things. If you think the house is normal, spend a night there and see."

"Normal!" he snapped. "Of course the house is normal. It's the people in it who aren't." And warming to his subject: "You and Cameron should be locked up together. And Pettingill," he added.

Which brought him to Cameron, and his errand.

Immediately on Cameron's return from the Adirondacks he had gone to bed with an infected hand, which had been torn by a fishhook, and had been too ill to look at the accumulation of mail. But the day before, although still very weak, he had gone through his letters, and there found one from Mr. Bethel, dated late in July.

In this letter Bethel recited various "abnormal conditions" in the Twin Hollows house, and asked Cameron, at the earliest possible moment, to go out and investigate them.

"And he wants to come?" I asked Lear.

"I tell you he's been sick," Lear said impatiently. "He wants to know about showing it to the police. He doesn't want to be dragged in, if he can help it."

"You've seen it?"

"Yes. There's nothing in it except what I've told you."

"He doesn't describe these abnormal conditions?"

"No. But he said he had made some experiments of his own, and was anxious to have his results verified."

"Experiments? Using a red light?"

"He didn't say," Lear said, with some asperity. "A red light! What in heaven's name has a red light to do with the immortal soul?"

He enlarged on that, savagely. Helena, he said, had been off in a corner saying, "Om, om," to herself half the summer, and when she dozed off in so doing, would waken to claim that her astral body had been off on some excursion or other.

"I can't appeal to her reason," he said, with a shrug of his thin shoulders, "but I have appealed to her decency. I've asked her if it is fair to intrude on the privacy every human individual is entitled to at times. But it's no good. She keeps a record, and I'm convinced it would jail her."

The only advice I could send Cameron was to use his own judgment concerning the letter. Personally, I do not see what value it has, save to corroborate my own ideas concerning the house. But it has suggested to me the advisability of asking Cameron to come here quietly and look the place over. I rather think he wants to do so.

August 26th.

ALL ALONG, I have been impressed by the attitude of at least the summer public to our tragedies; as each one came it brought with it its temporary thrill; for a moment, one might say, the dancing stopped and a bit of drama was enacted on the stage. Then the curtain fell, the band struck up, and the whirl began again, with some inconsiderable of the dancers missing.

Poor Carroway's widow is working at one of the shore hotels. And a small boy with adenoids delivers our milk and chickens; I caught him this morning chalking up a triangle within a circle on one of the pillars of the gate.

The main house shut and empty, a new assistant keeper at the lighthouse, and perhaps a closed room and grief at the Morrison farmhouse—these are the only apparent scars left, to mark our summer's wounding.

I saw Larkin this morning. He believes that we may be able to sell the property as a hotel site; as this would ensure destroying the house, it seems the best thing.

But one other change I have not recorded.

Watching Halliday as I do, affectionately and not too openly, I can see a very considerable change in him. He is like a man lit from within by some flame, of vengeance perhaps, of resolution certainly. And he is moody at times; his old gaiety is gone. He has put me out of his confidence, not because he does not trust me, but because for some reason he is afraid for me. And the same, I think, is largely true of Edith in the last day or two.

It is as though he said, in effect, "Keep out. It is dangerous. I am willing to take a chance, but I want to know that the rest of you are safe."

Now and then, however, I gather something. Thus yesterday he said, "You have to remember this; we are not dealing with a criminal, but with an idea."

Again, he has asked me for Uncle Horace's letter, and has been apparently making a study of it.

Only along the lines of what I call the supernormal phenomena of the summer does he show his old openness, and there he is frankly puzzled. My decision not to call in Cameron has, I think, disappointed him. But my reasons are sound. Cameron's coming might result in unpleasant press publicity for us, and more than that, puts me where I do not intend to be placed, among the believers in spiritism.

He accepted that decision today, however, without comment. But shortly after he asked Edith for the letter from Evanston, and sat thinking over it for some time.

"Of course, with a little imagination," he said, "you might figure that these people were somehow let in on what happened here last year. But why Evanston?" And after a pause, following a train of thought: "Of course I suppose, if you grant a spirit world, you have to grant that where time and space do not exist and only vibration counts—whatever that may mean—you could tune in Evanston as well as—well, as easily as you can on the radio."

But he got up soon after, saying that we were all crazy and he himself was the maddest of the lot, and went away.

August 27th.

LIVINGSTONE IS a curious chap; dapper, fastidious, and taciturn. He is almost too much of a gentleman; I have had the feeling, and I think Jane has also, that a part of his reticence is caution, that he is always watchful, subconsciously at least, lest the veneer crack, and something secretly vulgar be exposed.

I am still wondering why he came to see me today; he was sitting, gloved and spatted, in our small living-room when Clara brought his card to me in the garage and I hurried in. Sitting, too, staring at our ridiculous parlor organ, with an odd look on his face.

"Haven't seen one for years," he said, in his clipped and yet deliberate manner. "Where'd you happen on that one?"

"It was here when we came," I explained.

He gave it another glance before we sat down, and then apparently dismissed it. But not entirely. Now and then he looked toward it, and once I thought I saw a slight smile, as though back in his mind was some equally faint humorous memory. But he came to the point with a certain directness.

"You're a man of sense," he said. "I came because you've got a head on you."

"I used to have," I admitted modestly. "Lately, of course—"

He bent forward.

"Use it," he said. "Don't let this spirit bunk get you. Easiest stuff in the world to fake."

"I don't intend to let it get me."

He brushed that aside, and glanced once more at the organ.

"You take a thing like that," he said, "and start it in the dark. It gets you creepy in no time. They all use it; it used to be organs like that; now it's phonographs. They say it starts the vibrations! Well, I'll tell you what it does; it gets you worked up. Sometimes it covers something the medium wants to do."

"So I imagine," I agreed.

His volubility suddenly left him then, and he seemed rather at a loss. "Let it alone," he said. "Let well enough alone." After a pause: "There may be something, but let it alone."

And that, so far as I can make out, was the purpose of his visit. He showed a certain relief, as if he had got rid of something momentous to him, and soon after he took an abrupt departure. Being careful to remove his glove, which he had absently put on again, before shaking hands!

Thomas tells me that another attempt was made to get into the house last night. He had left his pruning-ladder outside under a tree, and found it upright against Gordon's window this morning.

Later: Halliday corroborates Thomas's story, with further details. He was on the lower floor, reading, when he was disturbed by the crash of a pane of glass above. He ran upstairs, but was evidently heard. There was no one on the ladder when he got there, and a thorough search showed no one in the house.

The window was the one through which we had watched Gordon leave the house by the rope.

August 28th.

IT IS IMPOSSIBLE for me tonight to draw any conclusion from last evening's discovery; I have not my old faith in circumstantial evidence. I can only ask myself if an innocent man hides in his own house.

Jane had one of her bad headaches last night, and at eleven o'clock I took the car and went into the village pharmacy. It was closed, however, and I was at a loss to know what to do. In the emergency I thought of Hayward's office; like most country doctors he keeps a medicine cabinet and fills many of his own prescriptions. I went there, therefore, and rang the bell.

It took some time and several rings to rouse the housekeeper, an elderly and taciturn woman, and when she finally opened the door it was to say that the doctor was away, and to attempt to close it again. I prevented this, however, and managed to get past her and into the hall.

"I only want to get some medicine," I explained. "The cabinet is in the back office, isn't it?"

"I'm not allowed to let anybody into the office."

"Nonsense!" I said sharply. "Anyhow, you are not allowing me. I'm going."

She seemed completely at a loss, and I thought, too, that she was listening. With my hand on the knob of the waiting-room door, I caught the attentive look on her face, and found myself listening, also. It seemed to me that there was somebody moving in the back office, and immediately after I caught the stealthy closing of a door somewhere. With that she appeared to relax.

"You are sure you know what you want?" she asked.

"Quite sure," I said, and went through the waiting-room to the consulting-office. She followed me and turned on the light, and stood there watching me intently.

The room was filled with tobacco smoke, and she saw that I noticed it, for she said, "My husband was sitting in here. I'd be glad if you don't say anything about it."

I am not suspicious, and the confession satisfied my faint feeling that something was not quite right in the house. I got the tablets from the cabinet, and being nervous about unlabeled bottles went to the desk; there, neatly piled up, were the month's bills for Hayward's professional services, written in his own untidy hand, and one not finished on the pad.

The woman was still watching me, and I managed to write my label, glue it to the bottle, and make my departure without, I think, showing that I had made any discovery whatever.

But nothing can alter my conviction that Hayward is hiding in his own house, and that he was in that back room when I rang the doorbell at something before midnight. Not even Halliday's opinion that, since Hayward is officially at home today, he had the right to be "not at home" last night.

"After all," he said, "give the poor devil his due, skipper. He works hard, and why shouldn't he get back a day earlier than he is expected and steal a few hours to get out his bills? He has to live."

But he seems to me to be a trifle too casual about it. I admit that he puzzles me, these days.

August 31st.

AFTER ALL, one can find the mysterious where it does not exist, I may not yet know why Halliday considers it necessary to watch the main house at night. But I do know the reason for Livingstone's extraordinary visit.

Mrs. Livingstone, sitting with Jane during her convalescence, read the letter from Evanston, and is eager to form a similar circle, to sit in the house itself. And poor Livingstone is opposing it and is making, for some reason or other, quite a business of it.

"After all, why not?" she urged today. "It can be quite secret."

She was supported in this by Edith, and even, halfheartedly, by Jane herself. A change of front which astonishes me. Mrs. Livingstone has apparently some absurd idea that we may receive "a clue, or something," as she vaguely puts it; and on my firm refusal departed, indignantly convinced that I have lost a great opportunity to solve our mystery.

Later: Halliday wants the seance! Nothing has so surprised me in years as his willingness to join the table tippers. But I suspected in him some purpose not far removed from Mrs. Livingstone's, although just what he hopes to discover baffles me entirely.

"Why not?" he said, when I told him. "After all, we have to keep an open mind on this thing, and we've had enough already to make something of a case for the other side."

"The other side of what?"

"The other side of the veil," he explained gravely, and then, seeing my face, was obliged to laugh.

"'There is a pleasure in being mad, which none but madmen know,'" he quoted at me. "I've heard you say that Descartes advises us to seek for truth, freed from all preconceived ideas. Who are we to stand in the way of truth?"

"And we are to search for it, sitting around a table in the dark?"

"Precisely that, skipper," he said, with sudden gravity, and has left me to make what I can of it.

Twelve days have now elapsed since the murder here, and the police know no more than they did on the morning of the 20th.

Now and then a car stops outside the gate, but our curious crowds are gone. Save that some nocturnal relic hunter has chipped a corner off the sundial, the place is much as it was before. All this water over the dam, and it has brought us nothing.

September 1st.

I DARE SAY there is no type of investigation in which the grave—no pun here—is so mixed with the gay, as in this particularly psychic search on which we are at present engaged. For, let Halliday use it for such purposes as he will, to Jane, Edith, and Mrs. Livingstone it is a deadly serious matter.

Their reactions are peculiar. Jane accepts it stoically and without surprise; it is almost as though, from the beginning, she has known that it was to happen. But she is nervous; she has eaten almost nothing all day.

Edith shows a peculiar and rather set-faced intensity. Whether she knows that something quite different lies behind it, or only suspects it, I do not know.

Halliday, also, is grave and quiet. He is less interested, however, in the manner of the sitting than in its *dramatis personae*. The list he has made out for himself; Hayward, the two Livingstones, Jane, Edith, and himself. On my pointing out a slight omission, namely, myself, he told me cheerfully that I belonged among the Scribes and Pharisees.

"The Scribes, anyhow," he said. "You are to sit by the red lamp and make notes. I am particularly anxious to have notes," he added.

On the other hand, Mrs. Livingstone has entered into it with extraordinary zest. She appeared this afternoon, slightly wheezy with the heat, carrying a black curtain of some heavy material and demanding a hammer and assistance before she was fairly out of her car. As it was apparently up to me to furnish both, I did so, but anything less conducive to a spiritual state of mind than the preparations which followed at the main house it would be hard to find.

To stand on a ladder in the heat and darkness of the den, and to nail up that curtain across a corner with no more ritual than if I had been hanging a picture; to place inside it a small table and a bell on it, while beside it leaned an old guitar, resurrected from the attic and minus two strings, struck me as poor psychological preparation for confronting the unknown.

But we are curious creatures. The sun was low before we had finished, and as we sat resting from our labors dusk began to creep into the house. And with it came—self-created, of course—a sort of awe of that cabinet I had myself just made; it took on mystery, behind its heavy folds almost anything might happen. It brooded over the room, tall and menacing, with folds that seemed to sway with some unseen life behind them.

I left Mrs. Livingstone placing chairs about a small table and went out into the air!

The arrangements are now complete. Mrs. Livingstone has brought over a phonograph, with a collection of what appear to be most lugubrious records; she also promises Livingstone, alive or dead.

"I left him sulking," she said. "But he will feel better after he's had his dinner."

And to this frivolous measure we start the night's proceedings.

Notes Made During First Seance

Sept. 1st; 11:15 p.m. Present: Jane, Edith, Hayward, the two Livingstones, Halliday, and myself. Livingstone and Edith examining house. All outside doors locked and windows boarded. The red lamp on small stand in corner diagonally opposite cabinet and my chair beside it.

11:30 p.m. All is ready. Mrs. Livingstone at end of table, next to cabinet. On her left, Jane, Hayward, and Mr. Livingstone. On her right, Halliday and Edith. A red silk handkerchief over lamp makes light very faint. I have started the phonograph, according to instructions. I was right about it; it is playing "Shall We Gather at the River?"

11:45. Small raps on the table, and one strong one, like the blow of a doubled fist.

11:47. The table is moving, twisting about. It ceases and the knocks come again.

11:50. The curtain of the cabinet seems to be moving. No one else has apparently noticed it. I have stopped the phonograph.

11:55. The curtain has blown out as far as Mrs. Livingstone's shoulder. All see it. Edith says something has touched her on the right arm. To my inquiry if anyone has relaxed his grasp of the hand he is holding, no one has done so.

12:00. The bell inside the cabinet has been knocked from the table, with such violence that it rolls out into the room.

12:10. Nothing since the bell fell. Livingstone has asked if less light is required, and by knocks the reply is yes. I have put out lamp.

(The following notes were made in the dark and are not very distinct. I have supplemented them from memory.)

All quiet since the last entry. There is a mouse apparently playing about in the library. Edith says that Jane seems to be in a sort of trance. She is breathing heavily. More raps, apparently on doorframe into library. I am cold, but probably nerves.

There is a sense of soft movement in the library; the covers are rustling; the prisms of the chandelier can be heard.

Edith says her chair is being slowly lifted. It has crashed to the floor. A hand has apparently run over the guitar strings. All complain of cold. I am alarmed about Jane.

I notice the herbal odor again; no one else has, apparently.

(Note: At this point, Jane's breathing continuing labored, and my apprehension growing, I insisted on terminating the seance.)

September 2nd.

JANE SHOWS no ill effect from last night, and indeed appears to have no knowledge of the later phenomena.

"I think I must have fallen asleep," she said this morning. "How silly of me!"

She has no idea of her entranced condition and I have not told her.

She accepts the idea of a second sitting tonight, without enthusiasm, but apparently with the fatalistic idea that what must be must be. She took a little tea and toast this morning.

As to what Halliday had hoped to discover, I am as completely in the dark as ever. On my decision to end the seance, and on turning on the lights as I did without warning, the group was seen to be as it had been at the beginning, except that Mrs. Livingstone's chair appeared to have been pushed back, and was somewhat nearer the cabinet than before.

Hayward, so far as I can tell, had not changed his position. His attitude throughout seemed to me to be one of polite but rather uneasy skepticism. Livingstone, on the other hand, showed strong, nervous excitement from first to last, but certainly never left the table.

He is ill today, which is not surprising, but I understand the intention is to carry on the experiment without him tonight.

Regarding the phenomena themselves, what can I do but accept them? Certainly they showed no connection with what Mrs. Livingstone likes to call the spirit world; on the other hand, either they were genuine, or they showed an experience in trickery utterly beyond any member of our small group.

And who would trick us? And why?

Livingstone was right, however, as to the psychological effect of the preliminaries; in spite of myself they influenced me. The music, the low light followed by darkness, the strange and fearful expectancy of something beyond our ken, all added to the history of the house itself and its recent tragedy, had prepared us for anything.

The billowing of the cabinet curtain was particularly terrible. Skeptic as I am, I had the feeling of some dreadful *thing* behind it; something one should not see, and yet somehow might see—

Both Crawford and Cameron believe that certain individuals have the ability to project from their bodies rodlike structures of energy, invisible to the naked eye but capable of producing levitations, raps, and other phenomena. They believe that these structures are utilized by outside spirits, or "controls." My own conviction is that if such powers exist, they are not directed from outside, but by the medium's subconscious mind. In that case, of course, it is possible that Jane was the innocent author of last night's entertainment.

Mrs. Livingstone suggests that if we secure anything of interest tonight, I consult Cameron with a view to his joining us later on.

Notes of Seance Held on Evening of

Sept. 2nd; 1:00 a.m. Largely from memory, since all the later part was held without light, but made immediately following seance. Present: Jane, Edith, Hayward, Halliday, Mrs. Livingstone, and myself. Livingstone absent.

I have moved lamp out from corner, and am now near door into hall. Doors from den and library into hall closed. Door into library open.

11:10. Table moves almost immediately. Edith says is rising from floor. It has risen, but one leg remains on floor.

11:15. All remove hands, and table settles down.

11:20. Loud raps on table. Construed as demand for less light. Handkerchief thrown over lamp. Curtain of cabinet billows into room. Guitar overturned inside cabinet. All quiet now.

No phenomena whatever for about ten minutes. Jane very quiet. Hayward feels her pulse; is fast but strong. Mrs. Livingstone asks if too much light, and rap replies yes. I have put out the lamp.

(Note: From here on I was able only to jot down a word or two in long hand, the previous night's experiment of making stenographic notes in darkness having shown its practical impossibility. The following record I have since elaborated from memory.)

The bell in cabinet rings violently and is flung across room, striking door into hall.

A small light, bluish-white, about a foot above Jane's head. It shines for a moment and then disappears.

It has flashed again, near the fireplace.

A fine but steady tattoo is being beaten, apparently outside of the door to hall. A tap or two on metal, possibly the fender. Silence.

Jane apparently in trance.

The sounds extend into the library, and there is movement there. The covers seem to be in motion as before. The prisms of chandelier tinkle like small bells. From where I sit I can see a small light over bookcase in library. It is gone.

The herbal odor again.

Jane is groaning and moving in her chair. Mrs. Livingstone and Hayward having trouble holding her hands. She calls, "Here! Here!" sharply.

Hayward says something has touched him on the shoulder. "Something floated by me just now," he says, "on the left. It touched my shoulder."

A crash on the table. I notice the herbal odor once more. Silence again.

Something is in the hall. It is groping its way along. It is at the door beside me–

My notes end here. I had reached the limit of my endurance and, as the switch was beside me, I turned on the lights. As before, Mrs. Livingstone's chair seemed somewhat nearer the cabinet; no other changes in position, except that Halliday had gone out to search hall and lower floor. The bell was on floor near door into hall, and lying on table, *Smyth's Everyday Essays.*

To the best of my knowledge this book was in the library at the beginning of the seance.

No signs of disturbance in library or hall, to account for sounds I heard. But an unfortunate situation has arisen, owing to Mrs. Livingstone's failure to lock door from hall to drive. She had pushed the bolt, but as the door was not entirely closed, it had not engaged. We found this door standing open.

This, however, although Hayward seems uneasy, hardly invalidates the extraordinary phenomena secured tonight.

Jane exhausted, and Edith with her.

September 3rd.

I HAVE SEEN Cameron, and he will come out. He has evidently been seriously ill, but it shows the dominance of the mental over the physical that he brushed aside my apologies and went directly to the matter in hand.

But it is a curious thing to reflect that, a short time ago, it would have been I who was the skeptic and Cameron who would have been ranged on the other side. Today it was I who was excited. And Cameron who was to be convinced!

"This Edith, of whom you speak," he said, "how old is she?"

"Twenty."

"A nervous type?"

"Yes, and no. Not hysterical, if that's what you mean."

Certain of the phenomena, too, seem to puzzle him. The table levitation, the lights, and other manifestations were not unusual, he said, with a strong physical medium present, and this he imagined Jane to be. The book, however, particularly attracted his interest. Over my notes on that he sat thinking for some time.

"You say it crashed onto the table?"

"At the last, yes. But Doctor Hayward, who was nearest the library door, says that after my wife called, 'Here!' he felt something pass his shoulder. Float past, is the way he puts it. He thinks it was the book, and that it dropped onto the table after that."

"About what you heard in the hall; was this hall dark?"

"Yes. There were no lights anywhere in the house."

"You heard footsteps?"

"No. It was like something feeling its way along. You know what I mean."

Toward the end of the conference he leaned back and studied me through his glasses.

"What started you on this, Porter?" he said.

He did not remind me, although he might well have done so, that my previous attitude, to him and his kind, had been one of a sort of indifferent contempt; that, during his entire time at the University, I had never so much as set foot in his rooms, nor asked him into my house; that on the two or three times only when we had met, I had taken no pains to hide my rejection of him and all that he stood for.

But it was implied in his question, and I dare say I colored. I told him, however, as best I could, and he smiled.

"I rather imagine," he said, "that when we pass over, our interest in this plane of existence is impersonal; we may hope to educate it as to what is beyond. But we hardly carry out desires for revenge with us."

Of all that I had told him, however, the Evanston matter interested him most. Over the letter he sat for a long time, his heavy, almost hairless head sunk forward as he read and reread it.

"Curious," he said. "What do you make out of it?"

"A great deal," I told him, and detailed my discovery of the letter behind the drawer of the desk, and my theory as to old Horace Porter's death. I had brought that letter, also, and he studied it as carefully as he had the other.

"'The enormity of the idea,'" he repeated. "That's a strong phrase. And he threatens to call in the police! Have you any notion as to what this idea may have been?"

"Not the slightest," I said frankly.

"I would like to keep this for a while, if you don't mind," he said at last. "I have a medium here in town—but I forget. You don't believe in such things!"

"I don't know what I believe. But you are welcome to it, of course."

It was only after this matter of the letter that he finally agreed to come out the day after tomorrow.

September 4th.

The words "making trouble," lightly underscored on page 24 of *Smyth's Everyday Essays*, are the key to Gordon's cipher. The entire sentence is: *It is often the ingenuous rather than the malicious who go about the world making trouble.*

In a few hours, then, we shall have solved our mystery, or at least such portion of it as it locked in the diary. Read with this key we have already translated the sentence I recorded here on the 22nd of August. Although we cannot interpret it without the context, it becomes: *The G. P. stuff went big last night.*

In the same way the scrap of paper found in my garage is now discovered to read: *Smyth, P. 24.* Edith's single error lying in the number, which she had remembered as 28.

Halliday suggests that the G.P. above may refer to George Pierce, but makes no attempt to explain the reference.

Halliday's story of his discovery is interesting; certain portions of the two seances he apparently accepts without comment save: "It was the usual stuff," and lets it go at that. Although *usual* is hardly the word I should myself use in that connection. But the book was, as I gather it, not the usual stuff.

"There was something about the way it came, that night of the seance," he says, and makes a gesture. "Mrs. Porter called it, and it came. Like a dog," he says, and watches me to be sure I am not laughing at him.

However that may be, the book and the strange manner of its arrival in our midst had interested him, and he had spent some time over it. Thus, he found where it belonged in the library, and tried to discover some significance in that. But there was none.

"I drew a blank there," he says. "I examined the wall behind, but there was nothing. You see, it couldn't have been *thrown* in; it wasn't possible. And when Hayward said it touched him, both his hands were being held. In other words, he didn't put it there."

All the time, I gather, he was feeling extremely foolish. He would pause now and then, in order to assure me that he felt "a bit silly." He didn't believe in such things; when there was a natural phenomenon there was a natural law to account for it. Maybe telekinesis, or whatever they called it.

"But there had to be some *reason* for that book," he says. "I just sat down and went through it."

He has taken the key words to the city, and has just telephoned (2 p.m.) that the detective bureau has put a staff to work on it.

"It will be several hours," he said. "It's slow work. But I'll be out with the sheets as soon as they've finished."

September 5th.

Too much exhausted today to make any coherent record. The four hours last night in the district attorney's office have worn me out. I have called off Cameron tonight, for the same reason.

The mystery seems to be increased, rather than solved, by the diary. By such portions, at least, as were read to me. And I do not understand the conditions under which I was questioned, nor the questions themselves. Good God, are they suspecting me again? Halliday is still in town.

Later: Edith has removed my anxiety as to Halliday's return. He has telephoned, and she has just brought me the message.

"He says you are not to worry," she reports. "He is working with them on the case. And you will not be disturbed again."

She looks pale, does Edith, and Jane is not much better. I have told Jane the whole matter; my absence last night had possibly prepared her, but the very confession that I had been subjected to what amounted to the third degree has roused her to a fury of indignation.

"How can they dare such a thing?" she said. "How can they even think it?"

"It's their business to believe a man guilty until he proves his innocence," I reminded her. "And Gordon thought it; you must remember that."

For nothing is more clear to me today than that this diary of Gordon's, which Halliday himself carried to the police, has somehow incriminated me.

September 6th.

HALLIDAY is still in town. I can do nothing but wait here, eating my heart out with anxiety, and allowing my imagination to run away with me in a thousand ways.

My womenfolk support me according to their kind. Jane serves me sweetbreads for luncheon, and Edith sits by, giving me an occasional almost furtive caress as an evidence of her faith in me.

But Edith is curiously lifeless; that small but burning flame in her which we call optimism, for want of a better word, seems definitely quenched. She is silent and apathetic, and has been so since yesterday.

She seems to resent our having sent in the key to the diary.

"If only you hadn't done that," she said today.

"What else could we do? We have to get at the bottom of this thing."

"I don't see that it has got you anywhere. It has only mussed things up."

What she has in her mind I do not know, unless, poor child, she has been building a future on Halliday's solving the crime, and that now that prospect is gone. She tells me that Starr has been on guard at the main house, quietly, for the two nights Halliday has been in town. But if she knows any explanation of his presence she does not give it.

"He's afraid to go inside," she said scornfully. "He just sits out on the terrace and smokes. If anybody said boo behind him he'd jump into the bay and drown himself."

She has apparently implicit faith in Halliday's ability to keep me from further indignity. But I am not so certain. The sound of a car on the highway sets my pulse to beating like a riveting machine; at the arrival of the Morrison truck a few minutes ago with some belated buttermilk I got up and buttoned my coat.

My place in my little world behind the drain pipe is neither large nor important, but it is difficult for me to imagine it without me.

"Suppose the worst to happen," said Matthew Arnold to the portly jeweler from Cheapside; "suppose even yourself to be the victim; *il n'y a pas d'homme nécessaire. . . .* The great mundane movement would still go on, the gravel walks of your villa would still be rolled, dividends would still be paid at the bank, omnibuses would still run, there would be the same old crush at the corner of Fenchurch Street."

This is the sixth. It was on the fourth, then, a few hours after Halliday had gone to the city, that a taxi stopped here, and Greenough got out. There seemed to me to be a trifle more than his usual ponderousness in his manner, and a distinct concentration in the way he looked at me as I came down the staircase. At the same time, he was civility itself, and he stated his errand matter-of-factly. They had a staff working on the diary, and he knew I would like to be present when it was finished.

"It's a long job," he said. "But we've split it into a half-dozen parts, and it ought to be ready by eight, or half past."

It was six then, and as our early dinner was almost ready, I asked him to stay. We ate cheerfully enough, took the seven-fifteen express from Oakville, and were in town and at the county building at something before ten. I was surprised but not startled to find Benchley, the sheriff, there, and three or four other men, including Hemingway, the district attorney. Hemingway held some typed sheets in his hand when we entered, and was reading them carefully. Halliday was standing by a window staring out into the square, and the first indication I had that anything was wrong was the expression on his face as he turned and saw me.

The second was a polite invitation to Halliday to leave the room, and his manner of receiving it.

"I'm staying," he said flatly. "If there's any objection to that, I shall advise Mr. Porter to make no statement and to answer no questions, until he can be properly protected."

"Protected?" I asked. "Protected from what?"

"From this strong-arm outfit," said Halliday, and surveyed the room with his jaw thrust forward.

"I am under arrest?"

Hemingway put down the papers and took off his glasses.

"Certainly not," he said. "Your young friend is being slightly dramatic. I know that you want this mystery solved as much as we do; more, since it directly concerns you. This is not a trap, Mr. Porter; we shall ask you some questions, and I hope you will answer them. That is all."

"I reserve the right to interfere in case of any trick," Halliday put in.

"We have framed no trick questions," Hemingway said quietly. "We want the facts, that's all."

He rang a bell, and a secretary came in. My mouth was dry and someone placed a glass of water before me. From that on, for four hours, I answered questions; at the end of that time I walked out, still free although slightly dizzy.

(Note: Halliday has recently secured a copy of the stenographic notes of that night. As they would make a small volume in themselves, I give here only such portions as seem to forward the narrative.)

Q. Your name, please.

A. William Allen Porter.

Q. Age?

A. Forty-six.

Q. Your profession is?

A. I am a professor of English literature at the University.

Q. You own the property at Oakville, known as Twin Hollows?

A. I do. I inherited it something more than a year ago, on the death of my uncle, Horace Porter.

Q. Had you known that this property was to come to you on your uncle's death?

A. It was always understood between us. He had no other heirs.

Q. Had you any previous acquaintance with Mr. Bethel? I mean, before he took your house?

A. None whatever. I never saw him until he came out to take possession. His secretary inspected the house, and negotiations were carried on through my attorney.

Q. In any of your talks with Mr. Bethel, did you gather that he had known Mr. Horace Porter, previous to his death?

A. Never.

Q. When you rented the house, did you retain any keys to it?

A. I have a full set in my possession.

Q. You had access to the house, then?

A. I never used my keys, if that's what you mean.

Q. On the night of the 26th of July, Mr. Bethel's secretary was attacked outside the kitchen door of the house, and managed to ring the bell there before he fell unconscious. Just where were you, Mr. Porter, when that bell rang?

A. The police have my statement as to that. By the sundial.

Q. Doctor Hayward was on the road in his car; you were by the sundial, close to the house. Yet when he reached you, you had apparently only found this boy. Is that correct?

A. It seems to me that the question there might be, was Hayward on the main road that night, as he says, or nearer to the house than he admits.

Q. You own a boat, I believe?

A. I inherited one with the property. A sloop.

Q. Do you sail the boat yourself?

A. I don't know one end of it from the other.

Q. In your various conversations with Mr. Bethel, did he ever mention the character of the house? By that, I mean any curious quality in the house itself?

A. He recognized such a quality. Yes.

Q. Did he ever mention a letter written by him to a Mr. Cameron, here in the city? A member of the Society for Psychical Research? Relative to the house?

A. Never. But I know of the letter. Cameron sent me word of it a day or so ago.

Q. Are you a believer in spiritualism?

A. I never have been. Recently, however, I—

(Note: Here I caught a warning glance from Halliday and changed what I had intended to say.)

Recently I have been trying to preserve an open mind on the subject.

Q. Why recently?

A. For one thing, Mr. Bethel had found the house queer; so had the secretary.

Q. On the day you asked the secretary to luncheon, the intention was to allow Mr. Bethel to go through his room?

A. Bethel? Certainly not.

Q. I shall read you this entry from Gordon's diary. (reads) "Porter asked me to lunch today, so B. could go through my room. They left the knife, but at least they know I have it."

A. That's a lie! I asked him to luncheon so Halliday could search his room. It was Halliday who found the knife. You can ask him.

Q. We'll let that go, just now, and come to the night you were found in the house, Mr. Porter, by Mr. Halliday.

A. I wasn't found in the house by Mr. Halliday. We had started for it together. The maid, Annie Cochran, had reported a quarrel between Mr. Bethel and Gordon, and that Gordon had gone away. You must remember that we suspected the boy of being the killer. I was anxious, and went for Halliday.

Q. What time did the maid tell you this?

A. About seven-thirty, possibly eight o'clock.

Q. And when did you go for Mr. Halliday?

A. It was about eleven, I imagine.

Q. What did you do in the interval?

A. She was nervous, and I took her home. After that we had callers.

Q. Did you see Mr. Bethel, in that interval?

A. No.

Q. Had it occurred to you that Gordon might be going to see the police?

A. I never thought of it. Why should he be going to the police?

Q. Did Mr. Bethel think of it?

A. I've told you; I didn't see him.

Q. On the night of the murder in the house at Twin Hollows, what led you to your discovery of the crime?

A. My wife heard the telephone ring, and I went to it. All three buildings are on one line, and the receiver at the main house was down. I heard a crash, and heavy breathing near the telephone.

Q. That made you suspicious?

A. I had been expecting trouble between Mr. Bethel and Gordon.

Q. Why did you expect trouble?

A. I knew they had quarreled. Mr. Bethel had told me that it was he who had struck Gordon, mistaking him for a burglar, and that Gordon suspected it.

Q. When did he tell you that?

A. I don't know exactly. About three days before the murder, I think.

Q. Can you remember the burden of that conversation?

A. Very well. He said that he was suspicious of the boy; that he was weak and vicious, and possibly criminal. He knew he was going out at night. On the night of the 26th of July Gordon was out, and he dragged himself downstairs. When he heard him at the kitchen door he struck him. But he maintained that he had not tied him. I believe that, personally. He had one useless hand.

Q. Did you ever have any reason to believe that Mr. Bethel exaggerated his infirmity?

A. Exaggerated it? What do you mean?

Q. You believe he was as helpless as he appeared?

A. I can't imagine a man assuming such a thing.

Q. Now, Mr. Porter, you have said that the telephone receiver at the main house was down, and you heard over it enough to alarm you?

A. Yes.

Q. It rang, and you went to it?

A. Yes.

Q. How could it ring, if the other receiver was down?

A. As a matter of fact, I didn't hear it. My wife said it had rung, and to satisfy her I went to it.

Q. Did the secretary, Gordon, ever approach you on a matter of money?

A. Money? I don't understand the question.

Q. Did he ever ask you for money? Or intimate that he needed it?

A. Never. He said something once about giving up his position.

Q. Where was he, the night you held the conversation with Mr. Bethel, relative to him?

A. Here in the city, I believe.

Q. And Mr. Bethel thought he might have gone to the police?

A. That's the second time you have intimated that Gordon had something to tell the police. I can't talk in the dark like this. If anybody wanted to avoid the police, it was this boy.

Q. I am going back to the night Mr. Halliday found you in the house—

A. He didn't *find* me. We had started there together.

Q. You say you saw a figure at the foot of the stairs, and fired at it?

A. I didn't intend to fire.

Q. You didn't recognize this figure?

A. No.

Q. It was not Mr. Bethel?

A. Bethel? No. He was locked in his room.

Q. You say you are not a spiritualist?

A. Certainly not.

Q. You have never made any experiments in spiritualism?

A. I have been present at one or two seances.

Q. When? Recently?

A. We have held two sittings in the main house within the last few days.

Q. When did you first hear of the symbol of a triangle inside a circle?

A. If you mean in connection with the crimes—

Q. Before that. You told Mr. Greenough, some time ago, that you had heard of it in some other connection.

A. I told him I had happened on it in an old book on Black Magic, and told a group of women about it. It was a purely facetious remark.

Q. Can you account for its use in connection with these crimes?

A. I have no official knowledge that it was used in connection with the crimes. Only with the sheep-killing.

Q. But you know it *was* so used?

A. I know that it was used once when Mr. Greenough did not find it.

Q. Where was that?

A. On a tree near where the Morrison truck was discovered. I have heard it was on Carroway's boat, but I don't know that. I know it was deliberately put on my car, after Mr. Halliday was hurt.

Q. You say, put on the car? Do you mean by that Mr. Bethel did it?

A. Bethel? How could he? We have thought lately that Gordon was responsible. We found a piece of his cipher near by.

Q. You have felt all along that Gordon was guilty?

A. I won't say that. I would say that the burden of the evidence indicated that he was guilty. Mr. Halliday has had considerable doubt of his guilt.

Q. Have you ever considered that it might be Bethel who killed Gordon?

A. Never. He couldn't have done it.

Q. But if he had had assistance?

A. Are you telling me that Bethel *did* kill Gordon?

Q. I am telling you that somebody killed Gordon, Mr. Porter. His body was washed ashore at Bass Cove this morning.

September 7th.

HALLIDAY HAS SAVED ME from arrest by giving to the police the information which he has been gathering on the case all summer. Has made a quiet gesture, which is like him, and given me back to life, liberty, and the pursuit of literature.

He came out late last night, and I understand is still asleep. He has had very little sleep, poor lad, for a long time.

I myself collapsed this morning, and Hayward has put me back to bed. Edith, spreading my coverings neatly before Greenough came up, says I am now so thin that:

"You really make a hollow, William. If it were not for your feet, nobody would know you are there!"

It is impossible to record in detail my conversation this afternoon with Greenough, covering as it did more than an hour. He came in, I thought, slightly uncomfortable and perhaps a little crestfallen, and I motioned him to a chair. He sat down and mopped his face with his handkerchief, and after that stooped and rather deliberately wiped his shoes with it. Then he straightened and looked at me.

"Well, professor," he said, "it's a darned queer world, there's no denying it."

"The world's all right. It's the people in it who mess things up."

"Like fleas on a dog," was his rather abstracted comment. He felt in his pocket, with much the same gesture as on that earlier visit of his when he had drawn the triangle within the circle on the back of an old envelope. Whether the movement was reminiscent to him, as it was to me, I cannot say. But he glanced at me quickly and then smiled.

"Sort of had me going, you did, there for a while!" he said. "But I was getting pretty close to the facts before this diary came along. Of course, it helped."

He had Gordon's diary in his hand.

"Naturally," he said, fingering the book, "your young friend's information was valuable; I'm not discounting that. The handprint on the window board, for instance. I'd have found it sooner or later, but it saved time. And the young lady, too. She's done her bit, all right. I've been handicapped by being too well known around here. And Starr's a fool."

He snapped out this last statement, and I gathered that he was still smarting under the knowledge that, without Halliday and Edith, he would still be nowhere. It was, more or less, his defense.

"Of course," he said, "ever since we got hold of this diary of Gordon's, one thing's been pretty clear. Bethel wasn't working alone. According to what I saw of him it wasn't possible. He couldn't even have made a getaway without help. The only question was, who'd helped him."

"So you picked on me?"

"Well," he said wryly, "you'll have to admit that you've seemed to go out of your way all summer to get into trouble! As a matter of fact, *I* didn't pick on you; it was Gordon." He looked at my clock.

"I've only got an hour," he said. "Your niece is sitting on the stairs now, holding a stop watch on me. I can't read you this thing, but I can tell you what's in it. And believe me, that's plenty."

Briefly, then, the deciphering of the diary had left me in a very bad position. When they had finished it, it was Benchley's idea to arrest me at once. They had the boy's body, a fact they had kept to themselves, and I was within an ace of a charge of murder.

But Halliday had stayed.

"He seemed to feel there was trouble coming," Greenough said. "He hung around and drove us all crazy. He insisted, as he'd brought the key, on his right to read the stuff as it came through; and as it went on, he didn't know exactly what to do.

"Finally, seeing what was in the air, he made a trade with us. He was willing to have you brought in and interrogated, but on condition that if you weren't held he'd come over with something of his own. You get the point, of course. There's a reward involved, and he'd been holding out on us a bit." He waved his hand. "That's natural. We don't hold it against him. But the point is, he made his trade."

Coming to my examination, my answers had apparently impressed Hemingway satisfactorily. On the other hand, added to the diary's constant suspicion of me, was Greenough's own case against me. He passed over that rather airily.

"I wasn't trying to make out a case against you," he said. "As a matter of fact, you couldn't have been the man who attacked Halliday. You weren't here."

"Naturally," I agreed, gravely, "I wasn't here. Of course, if I *had* been here–"

He glanced at me quickly, but went back to the night of the inquiry.

"The question was, whether to hold you or not. You may remember Hemingway going out, when it was over, and talking to Halliday outside? Well, it was then he made the trade."

Apparently the fact that Gordon had been the victim had not been the surprise to the police that it had been to me. For one thing, the microscope had shown one detail which the detective had not mentioned to me at the time. Caught between the handle of the knife and the blade had been a short piece of hair. The microscope showed this hair not only young, a matter readily determined, and the approximate color of Gordon's; it also showed it liberally coated with pomade. Poor Gordon's glistening, varnished hair!

But Greenough had been inclined at first to think that there had been two victims, instead of one.

"Dying and passing on," he says, "is not like taking your thumb out of a bowl of soup. It's bound to leave some sort of a hole."

And there had been no hole. If Bethel had died and passed on, no one apparently missed him. As time went on and no queries were received, the thing began to look ominous; as though Bethel himself had been hiding away, under an assumed name.

The idea that Bethel had had an enemy from whom he was hiding, and who had found him, began to intrude itself.

"But," he said, with engaging frankness, "that eliminated you. And you wouldn't be eliminated. You were like some people you've seen, when there's a cameraman about; always getting in front of the machine and into the picture."

"'And the king will not be able to whip a cat, but I shall be at the tayle of it,'" I quoted. He looked rather bewildered.

Then came the diary, and Gordon brought me in unmistakably, and in a way they had not thought of. Not an enemy, but an accomplice; Bethel hiding there, with my connivance, and the two of us, he the brains presumably and I the hands, working out between us some sinister design which even the boy could not understand.

Whatever it is, Gordon had written, shortly after the Morrison girl's disappearance, *he's got outside help*. And he wonders if I am guilty. But he is not sure of that; he even suspects Bethel, in one entry, of being less helpless than he appeared, and possibly of *working on his own*. He abandoned that idea, however, and there was a time when he suspected Thomas; even a time when he thought of bringing his suspicions to me.

But Bethel was beginning to be afraid of him. He thinks Bethel knows he has discovered the boat. He grows alarmed, and buys a knife; he records that "he can take care of himself." But there is bravado in it. Later on, he finds that he is occasionally stealthily locked in at night, for three or four hours, and he buys a rope and hides it in his room. After that matters moved rapidly.

He found the gun-room window unlocked on certain nights, and set a watch on it. And on one such night Bethel tried to kill him.

He tried to kill me last night, he writes on the 27th of July, and goes on to say that Bethel couldn't have tied him, and that *maybe it was Porter.* From that time on he suspected me.

And Bethel was watching him. Nothing is so dramatic in all the diary as the situation unconsciously revealed between the paralytic and the boy; each watching the other; the guard up between them, while the servant is in the room, and then down again. The boy recklessly mocking, the old man grim and waiting.

And nothing said. The boy goes to the city and tries to buy a revolver, but there is a law about that, and he fails. He has the knife, and has to trust to that. He thinks of going to the police while he is in the city; the reward would be a big thing. He says: *I could go around the world on ten thousand.* But his case isn't complete; he needs the outside man. He suspects me, but he "hasn't the goods" on me.

And there are times when he admits the possibility that I may not be the outside man. One night he hears the unknown in the house. There is a reddish glare and he sees a figure steal into the den. But it "did not look like Porter." And he is more puzzled than ever, for Bethel is in his room, asleep, and although the boy camps on the stairs until daylight, he does not see the figure again.

At daylight examined den and library. All windows closed and locked. It beats me.

It is about this time, too, that he begins to believe that Bethel is not only watching him, but that he is expecting trouble from some other source. He tells Bethel he has seen a figure go into the den at night, and Bethel shows alarm.

He and the other one have quarreled, he says. *And B.'s afraid of him.*

But on the night when he came home, to find Starr, Halliday, and myself in the house, his suspicions of me returned in full force. He decides that Bethel and I have had a quarrel, and that one of us has tried to shoot the other! But his knife has been taken; he steals one from the kitchen and carefully sharpens it; but he is not so frightened as he has been. Bethel and I have quarreled, and he "can handle the old man."

But matters were rapidly approaching a climax. Bethel was going to give up the house and let him go. He seems to have dared Bethel to discharge him, and to have more than hinted at what he suspects.

I can talk for ten thousand, he writes, *or keep quiet for twenty. He can take his choice.*

He has the upper hand now. The other man is no longer in evidence; they have apparently quarreled, and Bethel is left to bear the situation alone.

The boy lays various traps, but no one enters the house. "The murder pact" is broken, and the old man sits in his chair and broods.

"Blackmail is an ugly word," he says once.

"Not half so ugly as murder," retorts Gordon, and notes it with satisfaction in his diary.

Murder was the last word he wrote there.

But, for all his apparent frankness, Greenough's errand was clearly only to relieve my anxieties concerning myself. He refused all further information.

"We have a suspect, all right," he said. "I don't mind saying that. But we haven't a case yet, and it's touch and go whether we get one. Until we do, we're not talking."

September 8th.

HALLIDAY'S ATTITUDE is very curious. He is taciturn in the extreme; he avoids any confidential talks with me, and Jane commented on it this morning.

"He worries me," she said, "and he is worrying Edith. If you go out now and look, you'll see him pacing the boathouse veranda, and he has been doing it for the last hour."

I admit that he puzzles me. It was Greenough's errand, so far as I can make out, to relieve my mind as to myself, but to treat Halliday's case, as given to the police, as entirely confidential.

"It's the outside man we are after," he said; "and the outside man we are going to get."

But on my mentioning my right to know who was under suspicion, he only repeated what the detective had said.

"You understand," he said, "there's no case in law yet. Knowing who did a thing, and proving who did it, are different things entirely."

But they would prove it, he was confident. So confident, indeed, that before he left he inquired the make and cost of my car. Evidently he has already mentally banked the reward.

On the other hand, certain things seem to me still to be far from clear. Halliday, I understand, passed over to the police the following facts:

(a) A copy of the unfinished letter from Horace Porter to some unknown.

(b) A description of the print of a hand, left on the window board.

(c) A small illustration from the book *Eugenia Riggs and Her Phenomena*, and showing the same handprint.

(d) A sworn statement of the Livingstones' butler, the nature of which I do not know.

(e) An analysis of his own theory of the experiments referred to in the diary.

(f) And a letter to Edith from an anonymous correspondent. (To be referred to later.)

(g) The possibility that the two attempts to enter the main house are due to the fact that, in the haste of the escape, something was left there which is both identifying and incriminating.

But so far as I can discover, he has not told them that, from the time the guards were taken away from the house at night, he was on watch there.

In other words, from shortly after the murder he must have known that something incriminating had been left there, when Bethel and his accomplice, Gordon's "outside man," made their escape the night the secretary was murdered. He may even know what it is, and where. But he has not told Greenough.

Again, there is the fact that a statement by the Livingstones' butler was a portion of the evidence he submitted. Surely they are not endeavoring to incriminate Livingstone!

September 9th.

IT IS HALLIDAY'S IDEA to hold another seance, using Cameron's coming as the excuse for it. I gather that he believes that, under cover of the seance, another attempt may be made to secure the incriminating evidence left in the house. Not that he says so, but his questions concerning the sounds I heard in the hall during the second seance point in that direction.

"This herbal odor you speak of, skipper," he asked, "was that before you heard the movement outside?"

"Some time before. Yes. But the odor seemed to be *in* the room; the sounds were beyond the door."

"You don't connect them, then?"

"I hadn't thought about it, but I don't believe I do."

"Did you hear any footsteps?"

I had to consider that. "Not footsteps; there was a sort of scraping along the floor."

"And the moment you spoke this noise ceased?"

"Yes."

The whole situation is baffling in the extreme. I cannot ignore the fact that the seances were proposed by Mrs. Livingstone, that it was she who left the hall door unbolted at the second sitting, or that Livingstone himself was absent that second night, presumably ill. At the same time, it was Livingstone who indirectly advised me against the business.

"Let it alone," he warned me. "Let well enough alone."

So far as Halliday is concerned, it is clear that he does not like the idea of another seance, but feels that it is necessary. He assures me the police will be on hand, inside and outside the house, but he does not minimize the fact that there will be a certain risk, and that he dreads taking Jane and Edith into it.

"It's like this," he said today, feeling painfully the words. "In a sense, you and I are at the parting of the ways in this thing. We can let it go, and turn loose on the world a cruel and deadly idea which may go on claiming victims indefinitely." He made a small gesture. "Or—we put into the other side of the scale all we have in the world, and then—" He pulled himself up. "There's only possible danger," he said. "Unless things slip, there should be very little."

The same list of those present as before. There is an unconscious emphasis placed by Halliday on Hayward and Livingstone, but perhaps I am over-watchful.

I dare say, thus placed between my duty and my fears, I shall do my duty. I perceive that either Hayward or Livingstone is once more to be allowed access to the house, and under conditions more or less favorable to what is to be done. But which one?

Later: I have done my duty. I have telephoned Cameron, and he will come out tomorrow night.

September 10th.

HALLIDAY HAS TAKEN every possible precaution as to tonight. As it has been our custom to go over the house before each seance, and as Cameron may do this with unusual thoroughness, it has been decided not to place Greenough and his officers until after the sitting begins. Halliday has therefore today connected the bell from that room, which rings in the kitchen, to a temporary extension in the garage, with a buzzer. When the lights are lowered, he will touch the bell, and Greenough is then to smuggle his men in through the kitchen.

While no one can say what changes Cameron may suggest in our previous methods, Halliday imagines he will ask us at first to proceed as usual. In any event, I am to sit as near to the switch as possible, and when Halliday calls for lights, am to be ready to turn them on.

8:30. Everything is ready. But I am concerned about Halliday. Has he some apprehension about his own safety tonight?

He came an hour or so too early to start with the car for Cameron, and borrowing pen and paper, wrote a long communication to Hemingway. What is in it I do not know, but he took it with him, to mail on his way to the station.

(*End of Mr. Porter's Journal*)

Conclusion

CHAPTER I

THE JOURNAL takes us up to the evening of September 10th. It was to the fourth and last tragedy of that summer, which filled the next day's papers, that little Pettingill referred, in the conversation recorded in the introduction of this journal.

It was with this tragedy that, as Pettingill said aggrievedly, the story "quit" on them. And quit it did. We felt then that the best thing to do, under the circumstances, was to let it rest. Once more, *de mortuis nil nisi bonum.*

There was nothing to be gained by giving the story to the public, and much to be lost. The very nature of the experiment which had been tried was of the sort to seize on the neurotic imagination, and set it aflame. It was not considered advisable to allow it publicity.

Now, of course, things are different. The search goes on, and perhaps some day, not by this method but by some legitimate and scientific one, survival may be proved. I do not know; I do not greatly care. After all, I am a Christian, and my faith is built on a life after death. But I accept that; I do not require proof of it.

Picture us, then, that evening of September 10th, when the journal ends, waiting for we knew not what; Jane picking up her tapestry and putting it down again; Edith powdering her nose with hands that shook in spite of her best efforts; Halliday at the railroad station with the car to meet Cameron; and off in the woodland, where the red lamp of the lighthouse flashed its danger signal every ten seconds from the end of Robinson's Point, Greenough and a half-dozen officers.

Picture us, too, when we had all gathered; Cameron, with his hand still bandaged, presented to the *dramatis personae* of the play and eyeing each one in turn shrewdly; Mrs. Livingstone garrulous and uneasy; and Livingstone a sort of waxy white and with a nervous trembling I had never observed before. Of us all, only Halliday seemed natural. And Hayward, natural because he was never at ease.

What Cameron made of it I do not know. Very probably he saw in us only a group of sensation seekers, excited by some small contact with a world beyond our knowledge, and if he felt surprise at all, it was that I had joined the ranks.

He himself did not appear to take the matter seriously. He made it plain that he had come in this manner at my request; that his own methods would be entirely different. When Edith, I think it was, asked him if he made any preparation for such affairs, he laughed and shook his head.

"Except that I sometimes take a cup of coffee to keep me awake!" he said.

On the way up the drive I walked with Livingstone. Why, I hardly know, except that he seemed to drift toward me. He never spoke but once, and it seemed to me that he was surveying the shrubbery and trees, like a man who suspected a trap. Once—he was on my left—I was aware that he had put his hand to his hip pocket, and I was so startled that I stumbled and almost fell. I knew, as confidently as I have ever known anything, that he had a revolver there.

"Careful, man," he said.

Those were his only words during our slow progress toward the main house, and so tense were his nerves that they sounded like a curse.

Cameron and Edith were leading, and I could hear her talking, carrying on valiantly, although as it turned out she knew better than any of us, except Halliday, the terrible possibilities ahead. Hayward walked alone and behind us, his rubber-soled shoes making no sound on the drive. It made me uneasy, somehow; that silent progress of his; it was stealthy and disconcerting. And I think Livingstone felt it so, too, for he stopped once and turned around.

Yet, at the time, as between the two men, my suspicion that evening certainly pointed to Livingstone. Not to go into the cruelty of my ignorance, a cruelty which I now understand but then bitterly resented, I had had both men under close observation during the time we waited for Cameron. And it had seemed to me that Livingstone was the more uneasy of the two. Another thing which I regarded as highly significant was his asking for water just before we left the Lodge, and holding the glass with a trembling hand.

And, as it happens, it was that very glass of water which crystallized my suspicions. The glass and the hand which held it. For the hand was a small and wide one, with a short thumb and a bent little finger!

From that time on, my mind was focused on Livingstone. It milled about, seeking some explanation. I could see Livingstone in the case plainly enough; I could see him, pursuing with old Bethel the "sinister design" to which Gordon had referred, but to which I had no key. I could see him, with his knowledge of the country, using that knowledge in furtherance of that idea which my Uncle Horace had termed a menace to society in general. With the swiftness with which thought creates visions, I could even see him hailing poor Maggie Morrison in the storm, and her stopping her truck when she recognized him.

But I could not see him in connection with Eugenia Riggs and her bowl of putty. Strange that I did not; that it required Jane's smelling salts for me to find that connection. A small green glass bottle, in Edith's room, used as a temporary paperweight on her desk.

As I say, my suspicions were of Livingstone, during that strange walk up the drive. But I had by no means eliminated Hayward.

He was there, behind me, walking with a curious stealth, and with an uneasiness that somehow, without words, communicated itself to me.

All emotions are waves, I dare say. I caught the contagion of fear from him; desperate, deadly fear.

And once in the house, my suspicions of him increased rather than diminished. For one thing, he offered to take Cameron through the house, and on Halliday's ignoring that, and going off with Cameron himself, was distinctly surly. He remained in the hall at the foot of the stairs, apparently listening to their progress and gnawing at his fingers.

Watching him from the den, I saw him make a move to go up the stairs, but he caught my eye and abandoned the idea.

It was then that Jane felt faint, and I went back to the Lodge for her smelling salts.

The letter, undoubtedly the letter which Halliday had shown to the police, was lying open on Edith's desk, under the green bottle, and as I lifted the salts it blew to the floor. I glanced at it as I picked it up.

CHAPTER II

In recording the events leading up to the amazing denouement that night—the details of the seance—I am under certain difficulties.

Thus: I kept no notes. For the first time I found myself a part of the circle, sitting between Livingstone and Jane, and with Cameron near the lamp, prepared to make the notes of what should occur.

"Of course," he said, as we took our places, "we are not observing the usual precautions of what I would call a test seance. All we are attempting to do is to reproduce, as nearly as possible, the conditions existing at the other two sittings. And"—he glanced at me and smiled—"if Mr. Porter's admission to the circle proves to be disturbing, we can eliminate him."

He asked us to remain quiet, no matter what happened, and to be certain that no hand was freed without an immediate statement to that effect.

"Not that I expect fraud, of course," he added. "But it is customary, under the circumstances."

I am quite certain that nobody, except myself, saw Halliday touch the bell as the light was reduced to the faint glow of the red lamp.

It was not surprising, I dare say, that beyond certain movements of the table and fine raps on its surface, we got nothing at first! In fact, that we got anything at all was probably due solely to Jane's ignorance of the underlying situation. Livingstone, next to me, was so nervous that his hands twitched on the table; across, Halliday was beside Hayward, and as my eyes grew accustomed to the semidarkness, I could see him, forbidden recourse to his fingers, jerking his head savagely.

And, for the life of me, I could not see where all this was leading us. A breaking of the circle was, by Cameron's order, immediately to be announced. Even in complete darkness, when that came—as I felt it would—what was it that Halliday expected to happen?

But the table continued to move. It began to slide along the carpet; my grasp on Livingstone's hand was relaxed, and indeed, later, as it began to rock violently, it was all I could do to retain contact with the table at all. I began to see possibilities in this, but when it had quieted the circle remained as before.

Very soon after that came the signal for darkness, and Cameron extinguished the lamp. Soon Edith, near the cabinet, said the curtain had come out into the room, and was touching her. The next moment, as before, the bell fell from the stand inside the cabinet, and the guitar strings were lightly touched.

Without warning Cameron turned on the lamp; the curtain subsided and all sounds ceased. He was apparently satisfied, and after a few moments of experiment with the lamp on, resulting only in a creaking and knocking on the table, again extinguished it. On a repetition of the blowing out of the curtain, however, he left his chair for the first time, and with a pocket flash examined the cabinet thoroughly, even the wall coming in for close inspection.

When he had finished with that, however, I sensed a change in him. I believe now that he suspected fraud, but I am not certain. He said rather sharply that he was there in good faith and not to provide an evening's amusement, and that he hoped any suspicious movement would be reported.

"This is not a game," he said shortly.

Jane was very quiet, and now I heard again the heavy breathing which I knew preceded the trance condition, or that autohypnotism which we know as trance.

"Who is that?" Cameron asked in a low tone.

"Mrs. Porter," Halliday said. "Quiet, everybody!"

The room was completely dark, and save for Jane's heavy breathing, entirely quiet. Strangely enough, for the moment I forgot our purpose there; forgot Greenough and his men, scattered through the house; I had a premonition, if I may call it that, that we were on the verge of some tremendous psychic experience. I cannot explain it; I do not know now what unseen forces were gathered there together. I even admit that probably I, too, like Jane, had hypnotized myself.

And then two things were happening, and at the same time.

There was something moving in the library, a soft footfall with, it seemed to me, an irregularity. For all the world like the dragging of a partially useless foot, and—Livingstone was quietly releasing his grip of my hand.

I made a clutch at him, and he whispered savagely, "Let go, you fool."

The next moment he had drawn his revolver, and was stealthily getting to his feet.

The dragging foot moved out into the hall. Livingstone, revolver in hand, was standing beside me, and there was a quiet movement across the table. Cameron was apparently listening, also; he made no comment, however, and in the darkness and the silence the footsteps went into the hall, and there ceased.

I had no idea of the passage of time; ten seconds or an hour, and then Greenough's voice at the top of the staircase.

"All right. Careful below."

Livingstone moved then. He made a wild dash for the red lamp and turned it on. Hayward was not to be seen, and Halliday, revolver in hand, was starting for the cabinet.

"More light," he called. "Light! Quick!"

I had a confused impression of Halliday, jerking the curtains of the cabinet aside; of somebody else there with him, both on guard, as it were, at the wall; of some sort of rapid movement upstairs; of the door from the den into the hall being open where it had been closed before, and of a crash somewhere not far away, as of a falling body, followed by a sort of dreadful pause.

And all this is in the time it took me to get around the chairs and to the wall switch near the door. And it was then, in the shocked silence which followed the sound of that fall, in the instant between my finding the switch and turning it on, that I will swear that I saw once more by the glow of the red lamp the figure at the foot of the stairs, looking up.

Saw it and recognized it. Watched it turn toward me with fixed and staring eyes, felt the cold wind which suddenly eddied about me, and frantically turning on the light, saw it fade like smoke into the empty air.

Behind the curtains of the cabinet somebody was working at the wall. Edith, very pale, was supporting Jane, who still remained in her strange auto-hypnotic condition. Livingstone's arm was about his wife.

And this was the picture when Greenough came running triumphantly down the stairs, the reward apparently in his pocket, and saw us there. He paid no attention to the rest of us, but stared at Livingstone with eyes which could not believe what they saw.

"Good God!" he said. "Then who is in there?"

He pointed to the wall behind the cabinet.

CHAPTER III

THE STEPS by which Halliday solved the murder at the main house, and with it the mystery which had preceded it, constitute an interesting story in themselves. So certain was he that, by the time we were ready for the third seance, his material was already in the hands of the district attorney. And it was not the material he had given to Greenough.

For the solution of a portion of the mystery, then, one must go back to the main house, and consider the older part of it. It is well known that many houses of that period were provided with hidden passages, by which the owners hoped to escape the Excise. Such an attempt, many years ago, had cost George Pierce his life.

But the passage leading from the old kitchen, now the den, to a closet in the room above it, had been blocked up for many years. The builder was dead; by all the laws of chance time might have gone on and the passage remained undiscovered.

But then the medium, Eugenia Riggs, bought the property, and in making repairs the old passage was discovered. Although she denies using it for fraudulent purposes, neither Halliday nor I doubt that she did so. She points to the plastered wall as her defense, but Halliday assures me that a portion of the baseboard, hinged to swing out, but locked from within, would have allowed easy access to the cabinet.

But Halliday had at the beginning no knowledge of this passage, with its ladder to the upper floor. He reached it by pure deduction.

"It had to be there," he says modestly. "And it was."

Up to the time young Gordon was attacked at the kitchen door, however, Halliday was frankly at sea. That is, he had certain suspicions, but that was all. He had discovered, for instance, that the cipher found in my garage was written on the same sort of bond paper as that used by Gordon, by the simple expedient of having Annie Cochran get him a sheet of it, on some excuse or other.

But his actual case began, I believe, with that attack on Gordon. At least he began at that time definitely to associate the criminal with the house.

"There was something fishy about it," is the way he puts it.

And with Bethel's story to me, forced by his fear that the boy knew it was he who had attacked him, the belief that it was "fishy" gained ground.

"Gordon was knocked out," he says. "And that ought to have been enough. But it was not. He was tied, too, tied while he was still unconscious. Somebody wasn't taking a chance that he'd get back into the house very soon."

It was that "play for time," as he terms it, that made him suspicious.

All this time, of course, he was ignorant of any underlying motive; he makes it clear that he simply began, first to associate the crimes with the house, and then with Bethel. He kept going back to his copy of the unfinished letter, but: "It didn't help much," he says quietly. "Only, there was murder indicated in it. And we were having murder."

He had three clues, two of them certain, one doubtful. The certain ones were the linen from the oarlock of the boat, torn from a sheet belonging to the main house, and the small portion of the cipher. The one he was not certain about was the lens from an eyeglass, outside the culvert.

He began to watch the house; he "didn't get" Gordon in the situation at all; there was no situation there, really; nothing, that is, that he could lay his hand on. But on the night I called him and he started toward Robinson's Point, as he came back toward the house he saw the figure of a man, certainly not Gordon, enter the house by the gun-room window. When he got there the window was closed and locked.

He was puzzled. He looked around for me, but I was not in sight. Still searching for me, he made a round of the house, and so was on the terrace when I fired the shot. From that time on he saw Bethel somehow connected with the mystery, but only as the brains.

"There was some devil's work afoot," he said. "But always I came up against that paralysis of his. He had to have outside help."

On the night in question, then, he was certain that this accomplice was still in the house through all that followed; through Hayward's arrival and Starr's. He was so certain by that time of Gordon's innocence that he very nearly took him into his confidence the next day. But he was afraid of the boy; he was not dependable; Halliday had an idea that "he was playing his own game."

But if this man was in the house that night, where was he?

He grew suspicious of the den, after that, and he found out through Starr the name of the builder who had put in the paneling in the den, for Uncle Horace. It was a long story, but in the end he learned something.

Tearing the old baseboard prior to putting up the panels, the builder had happened on the old passage to the room overhead, and he had called Horace Porter's attention to it. It seems to have appealed to the poor old chap; it belonged, somehow, to the room, with the antique stuff he was putting into it. He built in a sliding panel; it was not a particularly skillful piece of work, but it answered. And he kept his secret, at least from me.

I doubt if he ever used it except, though no drinker himself, he put there a small and choice supply of liquors, some of which we found later on. And one bottle of which placed Halliday in peril of his life, a day or so after the night I had fired the shot into the hall.

He had borrowed Annie Cochran's key to the kitchen door, and after midnight entered the house and went to the den. Although he is reticent about this portion of it, I gather that the house was not all it should be that night.

"You know the sort of thing," he says.

But, pressed as to that, he admits that he was hearing small and inexplicable sounds from the library. Chairs seemed to move, and once he was certain that the curtain in the doorway behind him blew out into the room. When he looked back over his shoulder, however, it was hanging as before.

He had no trouble in finding the panel, and as carefully as he could he stepped inside. But he had touched one of the bottles, and it fell over.

"It didn't make much noise," he says, "but it was enough. He was awake, and paralysis or no paralysis, I hadn't time to move before he was in the closet overhead, and opening the trap in the floor."

He had not had time to move, and even if he had, there were the infernal bottles all around him. So he stood without breathing, waiting for he knew not what.

"Things looked pretty poor," he says. "I didn't know when he'd strike a match and see me. And it was good night if he did!"

But Bethel had no match, evidently. He stood listening intently, and in the darkness below Halliday held his breath and waited. Then Bethel moved. He left the trap door above open and went for a light, and Halliday crawled out and closed the panel quietly.

From that time on, however, he knew Bethel was no more helpless than he was. He abandoned the idea of an accomplice, and concentrated on the man himself.

Annie Cochran was working with him; that is, she did what he asked her, although she seems not to have known at any time the direction in which he was working. Her own mind was already made up; she believed Gordon to be guilty. She made no protest, however, when he asked her to break Mr. Bethel's spectacles one morning, and give him the fragments. But she did it, pretending afterward that she had thrown the pieces into the stove.

Bethel was watchful and suspicious by that time, and she had a bad time of it, but what is important here is that Halliday took the fragments into the city, and established beyond a doubt that they and the piece of a lens found near the culvert were made from the same prescription.

And he had no more than made this discovery, when Gordon, attempting at last the blackmail which he had been threatening, was put out of the way as quickly and ruthlessly as had been poor Peter Carroway.

"Twenty-four hours," Halliday says bitterly, "and we would have saved him."

But twenty-four hours later Bethel had made good his escape, and everything was apparently over.

But from that time Bethel as Bethel, ceased to exist for Halliday.

He was not working alone, however. Very early, he had realized that he needed assistance, real assistance. Annie Cochran's help was always of the below-stairs order. And he found the help he wanted after the night Gordon was attacked, in Hayward. As a matter of fact, it was Hayward who went to him.

"He was worried about you, skipper," Halliday says, with a grin. "He considered it quite possible that the attempt to wrangle English literature into too many brain corrals might have driven you slightly mad."

And breaks off to wonder, "by Jove," if that's where the English get their collegiate term of wrangler!

On the night, then, when Gordon was hurt, the doctor was impulsively on his way to Halliday and the boathouse.

"He came within an inch of having you locked up that night," says Halliday.

Later on, he did go to Halliday, and Halliday then and there enlisted him in his service. He was not shrewd, but he was willing and earnest, and from that time on he was useful. He had started, presumably, on his vacation but actually on a very different errand, when the murder at the main house occurred, and Halliday recalled him by wire.

But when he returned, it was, at Halliday's request, to hide in the Livingstone house. It was from there that he came, at night, to assist Halliday in guarding the main house. And to provide, by the way, that sworn statement of the Livingstones' butler, that after the murder they had concealed someone in the house, which threw Greenough so completely off the track.

One perceives, of course, that the Livingstones had been brought into the case. Dragged in, is the way Halliday puts it. But after the first conference between the doctor and himself they were in it, willy nilly.

"Who," Halliday asked Hayward, referring to his copy of my Uncle Horace's letter, "were likely to have access to Horace Porter at night?"

"No one, so far as I know. The Livingstones, possibly."

"Then the man who came in while he was writing this letter might have been Livingstone?"

"He was ill that night. I was with him."

"Then Livingstone's out," said Halliday, and turned in a new direction. "Some theory, some wickedness, was put up to him. And it horrified and alarmed him. A man doesn't present such a theory without leading up to it. Let's try this: What subject was most interesting Horace Porter during the last years, or months, of his life?"

"Spiritism, I imagine. I know he was working on it."

"Alone? A man doesn't work that sort of thing alone, as a rule."

"I'll ask Mrs. Livingstone, if you like. She may know."

And ask the Livingstones he did, with the result that Halliday got his first real clue, and elaborated the daring theory which culminated in that fatal fall from the ladder, in the secret passage on the tragic night of the 10th of September.

All this time, of course, it remained only a theory. Hayward scouted it at first, but came to it later on; the Livingstones offered a more difficult problem.

"They didn't want to be involved," Halliday says. "But after Edith's letter came I more or less had them. And, of course, after he'd tried to get into the house, and left the print of his hand on the window board, they had to come in. They'd denied any knowledge of the passage before that. But he knew it as well as I did, or better, and that there was a chance old Bethel knew it, too, and had used it."

This letter of Edith's, to which I have already referred, runs as follows:

Dear Madam:

I have read your article with great interest, and would like to suggest that a good medium might be very useful under the circumstances.

You have one of the best in the country in your vicinity. She has retired, and is now living under another name somewhere in the vicinity of Oakville. I understand her husband has made considerable money, but she may be willing to help in spite of that.

When I knew her she was known as Eugenia Riggs, but this was her maiden name, which she had retained. Her husband's name is Livingstone; I do not know his initials.

She has abandoned the profession in which she made so great a success, but I understand is still keenly interested.

The letter is not signed.

Halliday did not require that knowledge; he had suspected it before. But it gave him a lever. One attempt had already been made by Bethel to get back into the house. Time was getting short; before long we would have to go back to the city, and although he knew by that time who and what Bethel was, he could prove nothing. To go was to abandon the case.

He could not secure the arrest of a man because his lens prescription was the same as the murderer's. Or on the strength of an unsigned book manuscript left behind the wall of the den. He could not prove that Maggie

Morrison had died in the process of the experiment Gordon had puzzled over, because the mud on the truck wheels corresponded with the red iron clay of the lane into the main house. He could not prove his own interpretation of the abbreviations S. and G. T. so liberally scattered through the diary. And he could not prove that it was Bethel who, looking for the broken lens in or near the culvert, had found my fountain pen there. A fact which Gordon had noted in the journal as follows: *I have them now, sure. W. P. was here last night and left his fountain pen.*

But he could, through the Livingstones, take a chance on proving all these things. And, against Livingstone's protests and fears, prove it he did.

"As a matter of fact," he says, "they were in a bad position themselves, and they knew it. They had to come over again!"

Things were, indeed, rather parlous for the Livingstones. The butler's story had turned the suspicions of the police toward them. And on the night of my threatened arrest Halliday deliberately used them to avert that catastrophe.

"As a matter of fact," he says cheerfully, "I gave the police a very pretty case against them. It was all there, according to Greenough. Even to the handprint!"

But he held them off. He had done what he wanted, turned the police along a false trail and was free once more to travel along the true one. And in this he says, and I believe, that his purpose was not mercenary.

"The situation was peculiar," he says. "The slightest slip, the faintest suspicion, and he was off."

And he goes back again to the subtlety and wariness of the criminal himself; so watchful, so wary, that throughout it had even been necessary to keep me in ignorance.

"You had to carry on, skipper," he says. "In a way, the whole thing hung on you. Even then, you nearly wrecked us once."

Which was, he tells me the night of the second seance, when the criminal actually fell into the trap and entered the house. Livingstone was on guard upstairs that night, and everything would have ended then probably.

"But you spilled the beans!" he accuses me.

From the first the seances were devised for a purpose, and I gather that some of the phenomena were deliberately faked, in pursuit of that purpose. On the other hand, Mrs. Livingstone has always been firm in her statement that "things happened" which she cannot explain. The sounds in the library, the lights, and the arrival of the book on the table are among them.

But, trickery or genuine psychic manifestations, in the end they served their purpose. I called the third seance, and the mystery was solved.

It is not surprising that my memory of those last few moments is a clouded one; I was, of all those present except the police, the only one in complete ignorance of the meaning of what was going on about me. Edith knew, and was bravely taking her risk with the others; even my dear Jane knew a little; no wonder she required her smelling salts.

Actually, out of the confusion, only two pictures remain in my mind.

One was of Greenough staring at Livingstone, and then jerking aside the curtains of the cabinet, where Halliday and Hayward had opened the panel and after turning on the red globe hanging there, were stooping over a body at the bottom of the ladder.

The other is of that figure at the foot of the stairs.

I know now that it could not have been there; that it was lying, dead of a broken neck, at the foot of the ladder. I have heard all the theories, but I cannot reconcile them with the fact. How could I have imagined it? I did not know then who was inside the wall.

I am not a spiritist, but once in every man's life comes to him the one experience which he can explain by no law of nature as he understands them.

To every man his ghost, and to me, mine.

In the dim light of the red lamp, dead though he was behind the panel, I will swear that I saw Cameron, alias Simon Bethel, standing at the foot of the stairs and looking up.

CHAPTER IV

WHO ARE WE to judge him? If a man sincerely believes that there is no death, the taking of life to prove it must seem a trivial thing.

He may feel, and from his book manuscript hastily hidden behind the wall of the den we gather he did feel, that the security of the individual counted as nothing against the proof of survival to the human race.

But that he was entirely sane, in those last months, none of us can believe. Cruelty is a symptom of the borderland between sanity and madness; so, too, is the weakening of what we call the herd instinct. It is well known at the University that for the year previous to his death he had been distinctly antisocial.

Certainly, too, he fulfilled the axiom that insanity is the exaggeration of one particular mental activity. And that he combined this single exaggeration with a high grade of intelligence only proves the close relation between madness and genius—Kant, unable to work unless gazing at a ruined tower; Hawthorne, cutting up his bits of paper; Wagner's periodical violences.

The very audacity of his disguise, the consistency with which he lived the part he was playing, points to what I believe is called dissociation; toward the last there seems to have been a genuine duality of personality. During the day old Simon Bethel, dragging his helpless foot and without effort holding his withered hand to its spastic contraction; at night, the active Cameron, making his exits on his nocturnal adventures by the gun-room window; wandering afoot incredible distances; watching the door of Gordon's room and locking him in; learning from me of Halliday's interest in the case, and trying to burn him out; very early realizing the embarrassment of my own presence at the Lodge, and warning me away by that letter from Salem, Ohio.

It seems clear that he had not expected me at the Lodge; Larkin apparently told Gordon, but Gordon neglected to inform him. Just what he felt, what terror and anger, when I greeted him at the house on his arrival will never be known. I remember now how he watched me, peering up at me through his disguising spectacles, with the beef cube in his hand, and waiting. Waiting.

But the disguise held. My own very slight acquaintance with him, my near-sightedness, my total lack of suspicion, all were in his favor. And of the perfection of the disguise itself, it is enough to say that Gordon apparently never suspected it. He did suspect the paralysis.

He moved his arm today, he wrote once, in the diary. *He knows I saw it, and he has watched me ever since.*

"It takes very little to change an appearance beyond casual recognition," Halliday tells me. "The idea is to take a few important points and substitute their opposites. Take a man with partial paralysis; one side of his face drops, you see. Well, he can't imitate that, but he can put a fig in the other cheek and raise it. Put hair on a bald-headed man, and watch the change. And there are other things; eyebrows, now—"

Only once did I come anywhere near the truth, and then it slipped past me, and I did not catch it. That was on the night he sent for me, after he had struck Gordon down. He was frightened that night, we know now. Gordon was suspicious; might even have gone to the police.

And that night he tested his disguise and me.

I have recorded the revolt I felt after his attack on the Christian faith. And that I had the feeling of having heard almost the same thing, eons ago. I *had* heard the same thing, from Cameron, on the first occasion of my meeting him.

Much of the explanation of that tragic summer becomes mere surmise, naturally. There is no surmise, however, necessary as regards Cameron's coming to the third seance, at my invitation. So far as he knew, we still believed that Simon Bethel was dead. That our circle, so innocent in appearance, so naïve, was a cleverly devised trap seems not to have occurred to him. My frankness, the product of my ignorance, would probably have reassured a man less driven by necessity than he was.

But even had he suspected something, I believe he would have come. His other attempts to enter the house and secure the manuscript had failed. And any day some bit of mischance, a mouse behind a panel, a casual repair, and this book of his, with its characteristic phrasing, its references to his earlier works, would be in the hands of the police.

With what secret eagerness he accepted the invitation we can only guess. Halliday, carefully plotting, had already discounted his acceptance in advance.

"I knew he would come, of course," he says. "He wanted to get in. We offered him not only that, but darkness to cover any move he wanted to make. It had to work out."

And here he explains the necessity of having the criminal caught *flagrante delicto*. It had to be shown, he says, not only that Cameron had written the manuscript, but that it was he who had hidden it where it lay.

"The case against him stood or fell by that," he says.

But aside from this, much of the explanation of that tragic summer, becomes pure guesswork. We have, however, elaborated the following as fulfilling our requirements as to the situation:

We know for instance that on old Horace Porter's developing interest in spiritism, Mrs. Livingstone referred him to Cameron. But we do not know why that interest developed.

Is it too much, I wonder, to say that the house itself led him to it? In this I know I am on dangerous ground, and it becomes still more dangerous if one grants that Mrs. Livingstone's gift of a red lamp led him to experimenting with it.

We do know, however, that after he had had this lamp for three months or so, he got in touch with Cameron, and it seems probable that such experiments as were made there at night with this lamp roused Cameron to fever heat.

Mrs. Livingstone believes there was a pact between them, the usual one of the first to "pass over" to come back if possible. We do not know that, but it seems plausible. Neither Halliday nor I believe, however, as she does, that Cameron killed the older man, in a fit of rage over the rejection of his proposal to carry their investigations to the criminal point.

What seems more probable is that Cameron had very early recognized the advantages of the house for the psychic and scientific experiments he had in mind, and that he finally submitted the idea to old Horace. With what growing horror and indignation they were received we know from his letter.

They turned a possible ally into an angry and dangerous enemy; the rejection of the proposition, with the threat which accompanied it, left Cameron stripped before the world as an enemy to society. He went home and brooded over it.

"But he couldn't let it rest at that," Halliday says. "He went back. And the old man was at his desk. There was danger in Cameron that night, and the poor old chap was frightened. We'll say he crumpled his letter up in his hand, and Cameron didn't see it. Maybe there was an argument, and Cameron knocked him down. But he got up again, and he managed to drop the letter into an open drawer; after that, his heart failed, and he fell for good."

We acquit him of that. Of the others?

We are, with regard to the underlying motive, the so-called experiments, again obliged to resort to surmise. We know, for instance, of Cameron's early experiments in weighing the body before and immediately after death. He has himself recorded them. But in the manuscript of his book he distinctly states his belief that the vital principle, whatever that may be, is weakened by long illness, and his belief that those who "pass over" suddenly out of full health, are more able to manifest themselves.

He quotes numerous instances of murdered men, whom tradition believes to have returned for motives of vengeance. But he himself believes that this ability to return is due to the strength of the unweakened vital principle.

The *whole* spirit, he calls it. And although his manuscript in itself does not deal with any discoveries he may have made during the summer, there are accompanying it certain pages of figures which seem to prove that he made more than one experiment along those lines during his occupancy of the house.

What waifs and strays he picked up on those night journeys of his we do not know; poor wanderers, probably, with no place in the world from which they could be missed.

At the same time, Halliday feels that the experiments were not necessarily to be with life and death; he suggests that they were to lie, rather, in deep narcosis, pushed to the danger point, and that it was under this narcosis that Maggie Morrison, for one, succumbed.

Among Cameron's papers, later on, we found a curious document entitled: *The reality of the Soul through a study of the effects of Chloroform and Curari on the Animal Economy*, with this note in Cameron's hand:

The soul and the body are separated by the agency of anesthesia. The soul is not a breath, but an entity.

Of the nature of the further tests made we have no idea. Halliday believes that, shown the space behind the wall by Horace Porter, he later utilized it to conceal such apparatus as he used in his experiments.

"It seemed to be full of stuff," he says, "the night I found it."

But later on, as the chase narrowed, he got rid of it bit by bit at night, probably throwing it into the bay. This is borne out by the fact that, late that following autumn, going back to Twin Hollows to look over the property with a real estate dealer, I found washed up on the beach the battered fragments of a camera.

Only a portion of the lens remained in the frame, but this lens had been of quartz. As nearly as I can discover, the theory of quartz used in such a manner is to photograph the ultra-violet. In other words, I dare say, to make visible that strange world which may lie beyond the spectrum and our normal vision.

Did he obtain anything? We shall never know.

But sometimes I wonder. Suppose a man to have done what he had done to prove the immortality of the soul; to have taken lives and have risked his own, to give to the world the survival after death it so pathetically craves. And he fails; there is nothing. His own conviction has not weakened, but his proofs are not there.

Then, in the twinkling of an eye, he himself breaks through the veil. With that idea dominant, he passes over to the other side, perhaps to the long sleep, perhaps not. But in that instant between waking and sleeping, to prove his point! To make good his contention! To justify his course!

I wonder.

And I wonder, too, if at that moment of realization the supreme irony of the situation could have occurred to him? That the wounded hand, the one injury poor Gordon had managed to inflict on him, was the factor which had shot him, head foremost, into eternity?

Was Cameron our sheep killer? We believe so, with certain reservations. We know he was at Bass Cove, under an assumed name, at the time, probably looking over the ground.

At the same time, it seems unlikely that he killed the first lot of Nylie's sheep; that, we believe, was an act of revenge on the part of a man Nylie had recently discharged.

But that the idea seized on his imagination seems probable. He was planning that mad campaign of his, and it fell in well with what was to come. It prepared the neighborhood, in a sense, but it set them looking for a maniac with a religious mania. And it was an effective alibi for him, occurring before his arrival at the house.

Jane had always believed that he added the symbol in chalk deliberately to incriminate me. I do not. He added it, after Helena Lear had told him of it, as he had added the stone altar, a madman's conception of a madman's act.

Carroway's murder was incidental to that preparation of his, but in view of all we know, we can reconstruct it fairly well.

Thus we have the boy, tiring of carrying his rifle, putting it away in the darkness and possibly dozing. We have the appearance of the killer, and Carroway unable to locate his rifle quickly, following him to the water front and reaching it too late.

Underneath our float the killer should have found his knife, but as we know, Halliday had taken it away. They were two unarmed men, then, who met that night on the quiet surface of the bay. And one of them, although nobody knew it, was not sane.

Unarmed only in one sense, however, for Cameron had an oar. And used it.

When it was over, he apparently rowed back quietly to the creek beyond Robinson's Point, left his boat there, and walked to Bass Cove.

The proprietor of the small hotel there seems never to have known that he was out at night.

"He was a very quiet gentleman," he says, "and always went to bed early."

One thing which had puzzled us, in the Morrison case, was that the girl had stopped her truck, at a time when the nerves of the countryside were on edge. It seems probable, therefore, that on some nights, at least, it was not the square and muscular Cameron who went forth, but an old and crippled man.

Shown to her by the lightning flashes that night, age and infirmity by the roadside and a storm going, what wonder that she stopped? The only marvel is that, this bait having proven successful, it does not appear to have been used again–

And now, postpone it as I may, I have come to that portion of our summer to which I have earlier referred as the X in our equation. We have solved our problem. We may say quite properly, *Quod erat demonstrandum.* But there remains still the unsolved factor.

Much that impressed me strongly at the time has lost its impression now.

It is a curious fact that a man may see a ghost—and many believe that they have done so—without any lasting belief in so-called survival after death. And so it is with me.

On editing my journal, however, I find myself confronting the same questions which confronted me during that terrible summer.

Have I a body, or is my body all there is of me? In other words, am I an intelligence served by certain physical organs? Or am I certain physical organs, actuated by an intelligence as temporary as they?

Frankly, I do not know.

But any careful analysis of the extranormal phenomena of the summer seems to show, every so often, some other-world intelligence, struggling to get through to us. As though—

We have never had, as I have said, any explanation of the coming of the book during the second seance, nor of the sounds from the library. While much of the physical phenomena of the first two seances was deliberately engineered by Mrs. Livingstone, in pursuance of Halliday's plan to get Cameron into the house, these two things remain without explanation.

The same thing is true of my finding of the letter, of the lighthouse apparition, of the sitting at Evanston, and of Jane's clairvoyant visions. None of which, by the way, she has had since. And yet all of which had their part, large or small, in our solving and understanding of the crimes.

Peter Geiss, and the figure in the forerigging of the sloop, my own vision of Cameron at the foot of the stairs, when he lay dead behind the panel, what am I to say of these?

Am I to accept them as I do Jane's "vision without eyes," as no more extraordinary than the feats of somnambulists, who go through their curious nightly progress with closed eyelids?

Am I to accept them, refute them, or evade them?

There are, however, certain incidents which, puzzling as they were at the time, lend themselves to very simple explanation. Among these are the cough I heard more than once, and Hadly's story of the materialization in the Oakville cemetery.

Throughout Gordon's diary, here and there, were the letters S. and G. T. There was also, in one place, a sentence which translated, became *The G. P. stuff went great last night.*

Halliday believes that Gordon was what we know as a medium, and that it was in that capacity primarily that Cameron took him to the country. The S. he therefore translates as "sitting," and the G. T. as "genuine trance." After the G. T. there almost invariably follows the rather pathetic entry: *Feel rotten today*, or *All in.*

Hadly's ghost, then, in all probability was the secretary, securing data for the "sittings" which he so carefully differentiates from the nights when he went into genuine trance. Being honest with himself, poor boy, and honest nowhere else. And the same was no doubt true as to the dry cough which he practiced on me, the night I was in the garage, almost to my undoing.

It was during those "sittings," too, almost certainly, that under pretended control from beyond he began to ferret out, with the cunning of his kind, the story underneath; to bring back Horace Porter, and watch the reaction; to mention the boat he had discovered, and see the man across from him, in the dim-red light, twitch and tremble.

To play him, to fool him, and at the last to threaten and blackmail him. And, in the end, to die.

But there remain these things I cannot explain. One of the most curious is the herbal odor; that this was not a purely subjective impression is shown by the fact that both Hayward and Edith noticed it during the second seance. The scent of flowers is, I believe, not unusual during certain psychic experiments; Warren speaks of the impression of tuberoses being waved before him in the dark by some ghostly hand.

Of this, as of the other inexplicable phenomena, I can only say that at the time I did not doubt them; living them again, as I prepare this manuscript, I accept them once more. But I do not explain them.

"You wish," said Cicero, "to have the explanation of these things? Very well . . . I might tell you that the magnet is a body which attracts iron and attaches itself to it; but because I could not give you the explanation of it, would you deny it?"

In closing this record, I cannot do better than copy the following extract from my journal, made the following June.

June 1, 19—

Our little Edith was married today. Heigh-ho. And again, heigh-ho.

I have done the proper thing; led her up the aisle to Halliday (and would as lief have knocked him down as not) stepped back out of the picture and her life, and feeling for my handkerchief, like the besotted old fool I am, pulled out a washcloth instead.

Fortunate, perhaps, as I was on the verge of loud and broken sobs!

How we begrudge the happiness of others when it is at our expense! How I hated Halliday when, once in the house, he put his arms around her and held her close. How I resented that calm air of possession with which he took his place in the line beside her, and shook hands smilingly with the hysterical crowd that kissed and blessed them, on the way to the dining-room and food.

And yet—how happy they are, and how safe she is.

"My *wife,*" he said. "Forever and ever. Amen."

Old glass and new glass; china, silver, and linen; the Lears' candlesticks; every corner of the house filled with guests and gifts—and Jock. And for the two of them nothing and nobody; just a space filled with shadows which smiled and passed; themselves the only reality.

And perhaps they are. Love at least is real; the one reality perhaps. "Love, thou art absolute; sole Lord of life and death."

So they have gone, and tonight Jane and I are alone. Safe and quiet—and alone, alas, behind the drain pipe.

Heigh-ho!